The GUARDIANS

Witch Child

Book One

Louise Saville

Dreamweaver Press

ISBN: 978-0-6453602-0-2 (ebook)

ISBN: 978-0-6453602-1-9 (Paperback)

The Guardians: Witch Child. Book 1 of the Child Series

Louise Saville, Dreamweaver Press

tellavare@gmail.com

About the Author

Thank you for taking the time to read this.

Welcome to this debut novel.

The Guardians has been in the works for the last decade. It's been workshopped, rewritten, reworked, edited, reread, countless times, even put into the drawer to be forgotten (not as many times). Finally it has arrived and is available for public consumption. Needless to say it is an epic tale that has taken an epically long time to construct. Also, it is only the first book. There is much more to come. The story, the characters, the world, will span decades and Ages, and even generations. The Guardians is character-driven, yet the lore of the world is equally important. It is epic and high fantasy, yet with contemporary characters and dialogue. Despite its intricate lore, I believe I've crafted it in such a way as to be accessible and easy to read.

I have written for years, attempting to grow as a writer and refine my craft on writing workshop sites and read/reviews. The majority of my writing is fanfiction, and sadly there is no way to publish those stories. I have also written short stories, and I enjoy writing poetry, and personal quotes which are throughout this story. Most of all I like to have fun with my writing. I have not written an appendix for this, but I have included a brief history of the world and its people at the end of the story. If you feel you need a better understanding of the backstory, read that first. Although you don't need to, to follow the story.

For those who need to know -- I've used Australian spelling and single quotes. The majority of the Italics used is to represent telepathic conversations.

There's more to know about me of course, but only if you are interested enough.

tellavare@gmail.com

It is my hope that you will enjoy this story. If you read and you do like it, please take the time to leave a review. That would be lovely.

Thanking you again.

Louise

Contents

PART III 388

PART IV 577

MAP of New Empire –

Mid Region (Ryne & Coltrene on a split map)

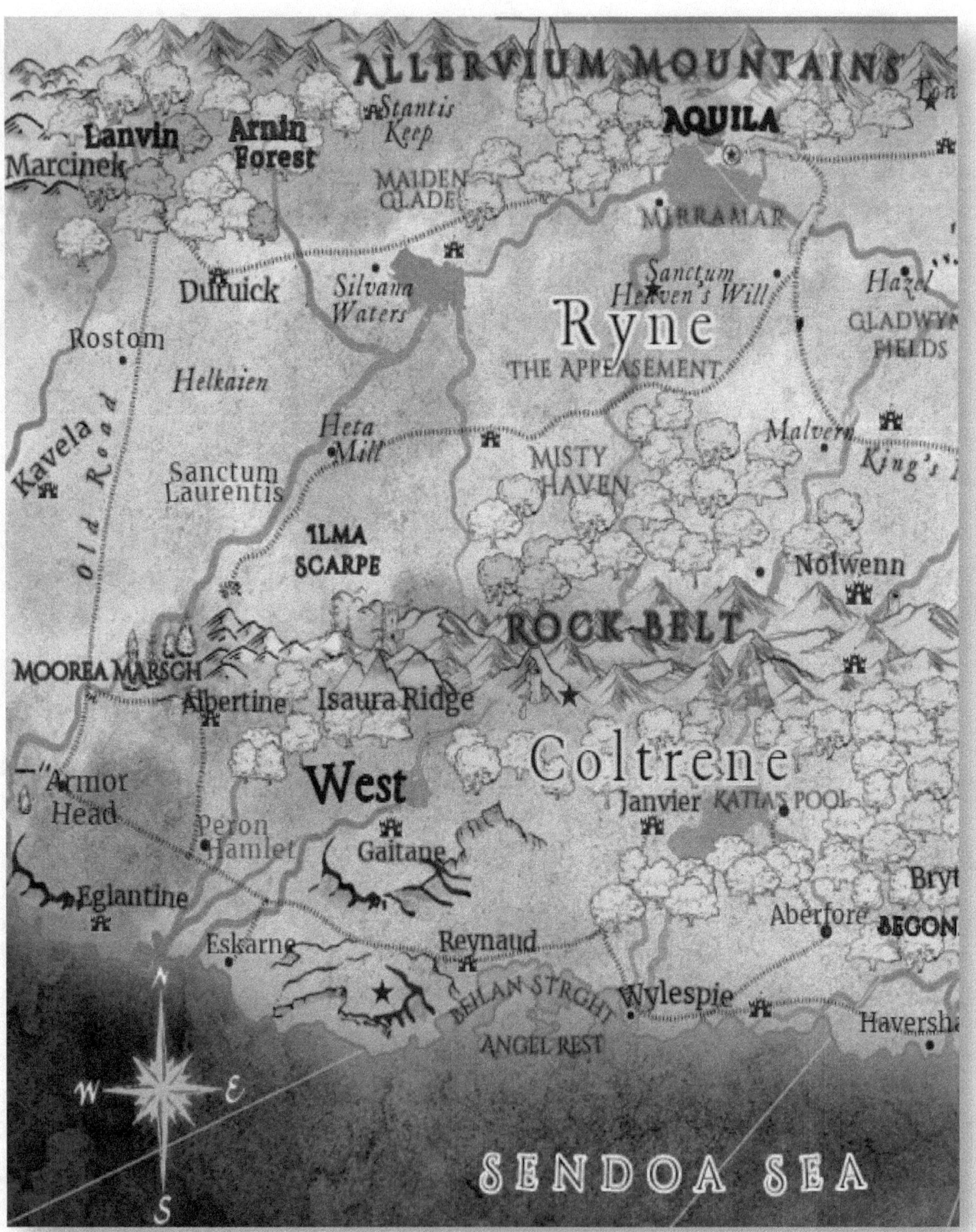

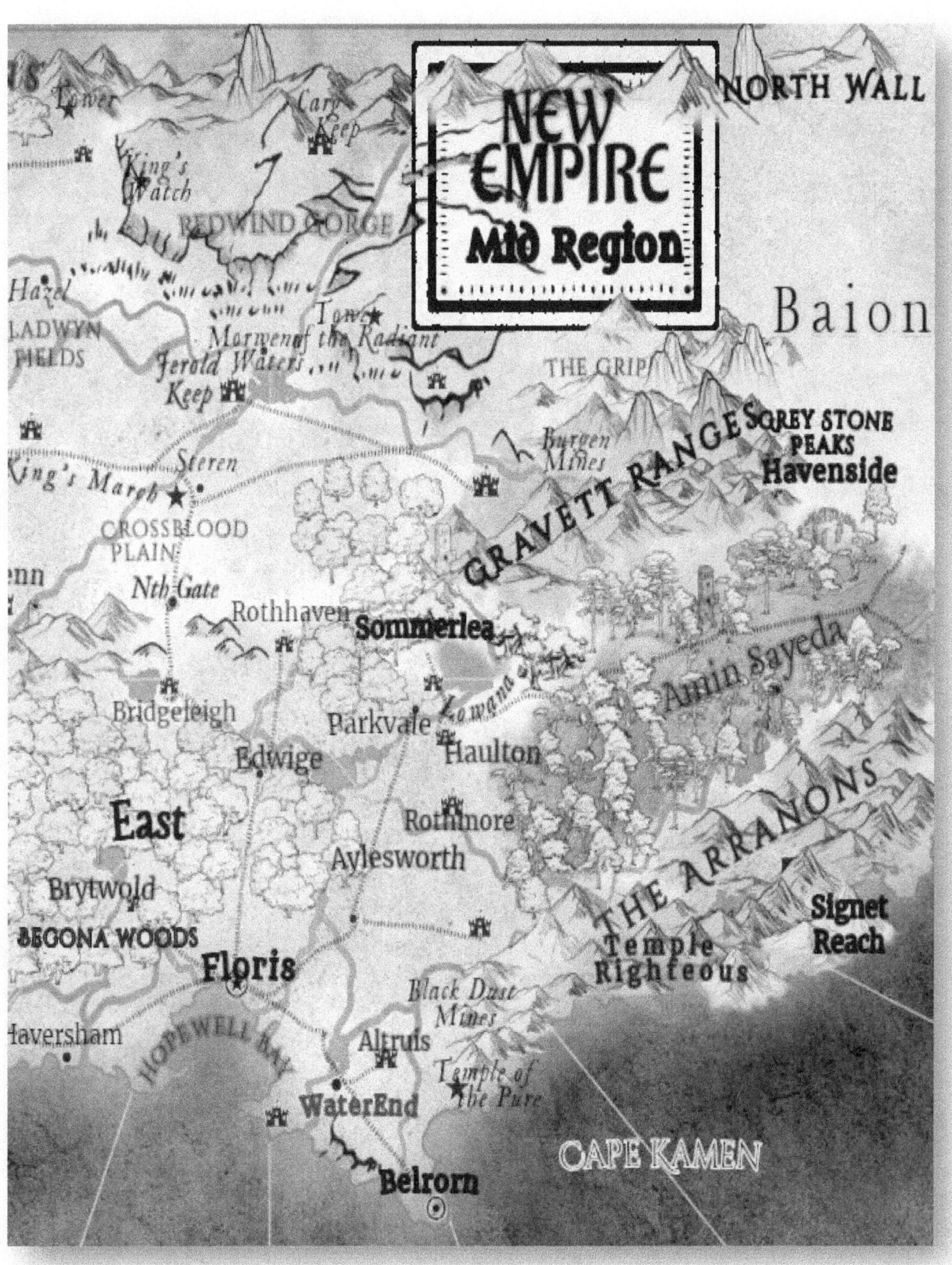

NORTH WALL
NEW EMPIRE
Mid Region
Baion
Tower
Cary Keep
King's Watch
REDWIND GORGE
Hazel
LADWYN FIELDS
Tower
Morwen of the Radiant
Jerold Waters
Keep
THE GRIP
Burgen Mines
GRAVETT RANGE
GREY STONE PEAKS
Havenside
Steren
King's March
CROSSBLOOD PLAIN
Nth Gate
Rothhaven
Sommerlea
Lowana
Amin Sayeda
Bridgeleigh
Parkvale
Haulton
Edwige
East
Rothmore
Aylesworth
THE ARRANONS
Brytwold
BEGONA WOODS
Temple Righteous
Signet Reach
Floris
Black Dust Mines
Haversham
HOPEWELL BAY
Altruis
Temple of The Pure
WaterEnd
CAPE KAMEN
Belrorn

A Fallen Land

What is the enemy of Light?
Is it Darkness, or the obstructions that produce the shadows?

Light has no enemies.
It only has those who turn away from its brightness.
They create their own shadows by obstructing the truth.

Harbinger of Night, Ei'myn Valáverïnn-shem script

Primeval darkness spiraled down and collided with her cocoon of light. Its iniquitous mass enveloped her glow of purity, seeking a way in. This was unfamiliar; the spiritual taint was always remote, never coming close to her rim of peace. The gloom of impiety swathed her thoughts. Her mind ached from the force of the foul entity. She conjured tranquility, yet the darkness was intent on entering her peace. Faces, distorted by evil, flashed in her mind's eye. People she knew and loved. Her shock fed the darkness. Dire moments passed as she struggled with the ethereal form of evil. An amber glow, bounding her meditation, provided the only protection.

Time has come to start your new life.

The authority of the voice cut through the chaos as if it were the master of light and dark. This battle had overtaken her thought life and was seeking to manifest on the earth.

Outside the ethereal, she heard footsteps running up the stone steps, permeating the quiet of the room. A gust of air caused the sheer curtains to flutter over her physical prostrate body. The back of her outstretched hands rested on flat gems, representing light and dark, and under her feet a ruby and an emerald - pain and healing.

Someone paused outside the door and was breathing hard.

'Enter.' Her voice, carrying her customary sternness, cut through the room's serenity, while her stomach tensed with an earthly anxiety.

A girl pushed the door in. Breathless and glistening with sweat, she stopped, suddenly embarrassed. 'High Priestess...' Clothed in the fashion of the temple, she wore a simple white frock belted with cord, and no jewelry, signifying the lowest rank. The High Priestess rose to her feet and the girl dropped to her knees before her, either from deference, or possibly exhaustion.

The High Priestess stood tall, her tan hands smoothed down her jewel-encrusted belt that went the length of her white linen dress. A similar piece of jewelry decorated her neck. Her fingers, covered with bright rings, waved the girl's humility aside. 'I know why you have come.'

The girl lifted her face, eyes widening under the High Priestess' commanding stare, and said between gasps, 'Priest Tarvis... has sent me. It is the queen... he has foreseen a tremor above the Chanin-Quyllar.'

'Where is he?' She turned her gaze to the open window. Flat white building tops shone between majestic pines against the verdant valley of Ami-Sayen. Her people were peaceful; their land rich in resources after centuries of nurturing. Not a cloud in sight; serene skies stretched as far as she could see, to the mountains in the south.

'On his way to the Agamon.'

Except there. Dark clouds would be forming over the temple ziggurat. Their unseen enemy had finally struck. The shift of authority over Ami-Sayen would soon incite hostility in the citizens of Cardmus, the location of the Agamon temple. The High Priestess raised a hand to her lips and kissed her fingers, and lifted them to the valley. 'I have loved you well, now I must love you to the last.' Tears wet her eyes, but she refused to let them fall. No time for the burden of sorrow. She turned to face the girl. 'What is your name?'

'Deri-yen-Shosharnius.'

Wind on the plains. 'Priest Tarvis was wise in choosing you. You must go to the Orders with great speed, conveying this message.'

Deri jumped to her feet.

'A Forbidden Gate is opening and the Lord of Darkness seeks to enter. The Amyntah must be summoned to aid us.'

The girl's face paled with apprehension.

'Yes,' the High Priestess continued, 'the queen has revealed her plans. A Gate opens in our home. How long can we bar hell's entry?'

Deri turned to leave and the High Priestess placed a hand on her shoulder in comfort. 'Daughter, make great haste.' She could not conceal the quiver in her voice.

Nodding, the girl dashed away.

She frowned at the closed door. 'However, will the power to prevent such a terrible deed be given into my hand?'

~ * ~

The people of Amin-Sayeda lined the paved streets and crowded into the squares. They parted before the racing chariot, and their cheers disappeared on sight of the High Priestess and her staff, rarely seen outside the Temple of Life. Driven by her attendant, her white horses drew her chariot through the throng. Her fine gown whipped behind her, and her black hair flowed in the breeze, increasing in momentum.

Scented trees bordered parks and opulent sanctuaries, and arches and pillars, embedded with gold and gems, graced the streets lined with luxurious houses. Clean walls and unique edifices were decorated with green and flowering colour and pleasant murals. Bright faces watched, innocently. Each one wearing clothes lavished with artistry and jewel adornments. They existed in a bastion of serenity, unaware of the malevolence striking and upturning the lands outside their valley. The strength required to keep such a peace was provided by the Chanin-Quyllar, the Eye of Heaven.

People on the street looked upward. Grey clouds billowed from the direction she traveled, east. Darkness was already brewing. Some in the crowd would have already let the deceptive evil nest in their thoughts. Pride and self-importance birthed a great evil. Even now, the poor souls did not comprehend the vast power their thoughts had over their land. The orb shielded them from the wars outside their home, but now their desire for perfection brought into their lands the corruption of the world outside.

Her male servant spurred the horses; the chariot sped at a greater pace. Onward to the heart of the land, the place they should protect at whatever cost. 'What are your instructions?' asked her attendant.

The pavement stretched out and the magnificence of the Agamon emerged over the waiting assembly. Citizens were everywhere. Giant colonnades surrounding the pyramid had them observing from their three tier arches. The steps of the ziggurat and the pergola on the top platform were the only place free of people. She replied, 'The time has come when you need not take instructions from me.'

She paid no mind to the people pushing and shoving to get a better view, and alighted from her chariot. The sight of the queen overwhelmed her with remorse. A woman stood at the top of the ziggurat beneath the open portico. Hands outstretched and staff aloft, her face held a commanding thrall over the people. Knee length hair, normally elaborately plaited, blew around her waist, and her red dress blustered in the strong wind. Their glorious queen, once possessing a gentle heart, now descended into a treacherous arrogance and slavery to the devil of her worship, Kerebus, the false prophet of Hell's army.

Brilliant white light emanated from the Chanin-Quyllar floating in front of the queen's chest. Embedded in this ivory globe was the Essenya, the Eye-key. Without this magikal emblem, the spiritual power streaming across Amin-Sayeda would lose its significance. In the shape of an eye, a powerful white glittering gem was at its center. Long ago, an enlightened race, the Fáerinn, gave the Sayeda the orb. In addition to the staffs and other gifts, it was to safeguard Amin-Sayeda from the coming wars foreseen to take place outside their cocoon of peace. Now, at the last, it appeared the plan would fail and by the ones who swore to watch over it.

The High Priestess raised her ivory staff and the crowd moved aside. People grumbled with confusion and anger. She arrived at the wide steps where a woman with short hair blocked her passage.

Shocked at the presence of her old friend, the High Priestess' voice trembled. 'Priestess Yestel?'

Yestel's eyes held an unexpected resentment. 'Nya.'

The High Priestess creased her brow, her sea-green eyes revealed discernment. 'You have fallen.'

'This is the way of excellence. You have been complacent too long and not worthy of the power you have been granted.'

'You cannot see. You are blind.' Breath fluttered in her chest, making her faint, but she continued, 'You have created a world of detestation from which you will spend an eternity.'

'It is you who are blinded - by light,' Yestel said, 'There are shadows in the light for which you cannot see.'

Nya realized the truth of it, she indeed had been blind. Now those shadows loomed across the land. How many others had fallen to the lies? Could they not see, their craving for perfection irreversibly led them to this state of abhorrence? Their quest for transcendence led them down to darkness, so encompassing it had become flawless. 'You are misguided. Light reveals, darkness conceals.'

The Chanin-Quyllar crackled above them. The sudden expanding light from the orb consumed her attention. 'The queen chanted into the darkening sky and the tip of the Staff of Majesty blazed a fiery red.

'This is the way of ultimate power and fulfillment. You cannot stop her.' Yestel's eyes flashed with building anger. 'She has become the Queen-Mage.'

A man spoke behind Nya. 'We have come.'

The comforting sound of Priest Tarvis' voice nearly overwhelmed her. She said to Yestel, 'We shall see.' Nya looked to the faithful priests and priestesses, barely a handful in number, but who had kept themselves pure and humble. Their attendants cleared a space in the crowd as best they could, and the priests and priestesses took positions to complete the summons for the Amyntah. With sadness, Nya watched Yestel climb the steps to join her queen.

An undercurrent of anger emerged in the mass of citizens. The queen's chant pervaded peoples' thoughts, polluting their minds with despair. The eyes of the unsullied held fear, yet those predisposed to the evil, reflected fury and violence.

Nya cried, 'We must begin.'

Amid panic and abrupt terror, clouds blotted out the sky. Shadows descended across the city. The anarchy from the world outside was starting to overtake the land. Apart from the various staffs, the shining orb provided the only light. Screams, pitiful and frightening, pierced the fierce wind. Waves of aggression moved the people, brawling and assaults were all around them. Screaming and wailing erupted as apparitions began appearing amongst the people. Alongside the evil from a fallen world, Hell's minions would march forth from the Gate that was opening on the pavement.

The queen lifted her hand and staff high, placating the clouds to defile the Chanin-Quyllar's purpose of creating light, peace, and healing. An impossible act or so Nya thought, but now she better understood how the queen came to wield such power. Someone granted her the rank of Queen-Mage, giving her access to forbidden magik. Who had given her the authority? Was Nya so neglectful of the queen's activities, or did the queen become so distorted as to deceive her High Priestess?

The priests and priestesses' collapsed from spiritual fatigue. The summoning spell required a tremendous amount of living energy. Strange figures emerged through the crowd, their faces hidden by black helms. Identical to the last detail, the seven-foot warriors were clad in shining black armor, each one bearing a sword and shield, with black and gold axes at their backs. The silent knights positioned themselves around the priests and priestesses in a wall of offense.

'Even if you kill me, the Eye of Heaven will still be mine.' A tremor of fear shook the queen's voice. 'It is now dedicated to my mandate forever.'

Nya could do nothing to prevent the decree of evil, except call forth aid to circumvent the queen's directives. She cast her mind beyond the present madness, envisioning the infernal presence of the orb upon the Earth and its consequences on future generations. Her opposing chant cut the air.

The queen wasted no time in opposing her declarations. A battle of prophetic spell casting ensued. For each prediction of the queen's, Nya produced a counterbalance stretching into times to come.

'I summon vessels for the service of darkness and it's expansion,' the queen's voice descended into a thick coarse speech, 'to carry out my bidding on this Earth. I command out of the void of unborn souls, my chosen ones to claim and bring forth the true world.' Her chant correlated with the fierceness of the swirling black clouds above.

'I rebuke you,' Nya's voice rumbled into an intricate crescendo of prophetic forecasting. Yet with each victory, the queen formed a counter-attack. At the last, Nya intoned, '…I proclaim freedom of choice, and proffer the gift of the will to those under the control of this Gate…'

'My followers shall rule under me. Evil will be written into their flesh, any other choice will be bound with pain and ignorance, and end in despair…' The queen's voice ascended into the thickening shadows, as did the heat of her terrible anger.

The women's powerful voices clashed against each other in a battle more profound than the contrast of sound; the height of light and the depth of darkness circled with the wind sweeping through the courtyard.

Distracted by shrill screaming, Nya glimpsed the Amyntah fling a hideous being from the holy men and women, and it crashed into the crowd. Violence surrounded the knights. They stood as menacing sentries, not allowing any to pass them. The priests' incantations gave Nya the strength she needed.

Ceasing her mantra, the queen laughed into the whirling wind. Her mouth curled in a mocking sneer and she directed her conceited gaze at Nya.

Missing the significant utterance, Nya recoiled with sudden fear.

'Your foretelling means nothing!' The queen's staff remained fixed on Nya, her harsh voice reverberating over the cacophony. 'The ritual is complete. I have full dominion, now and in the after-life. The Gate of Kerebus will open.'

Hell had been summoned. The Chanin-Quyllar's taint clung to Nya's spirit. She felt the ruinous stab, cutting into her heart and splitting her soul. Her prophecies would have no standing if the orb was not rendered ineffective. The time had indeed come. Clenching the Staff of Peace, she raised it resolutely. The radiance of its diamond head penetrated the bleak shadows. 'There is something you do not know about the authority of light…' Her voice lifted in a melodic chant of delightful words.

The queen's body shuddered with shock and she shook her staff at Nya in fury.

Nya's song rose from deep in her belly; its commanding lilt halted the bedlam on the pavement. Pure luminous light formed in the clouds above. It immersed her and streamed from her staff into the throbbing and expanding orb. 'It is birthed from above and has the power to vanquish the dark.'

Another Gate opened, this one from the sky. Sharp incandescent rays shot down, uniting with Nya's staff. Electric charges fired through the wood and into her body. With the power given her, she fired it into the orb. Sparking with arching static bursts, it exploded, amidst the horrible cries of the outraged queen. A dazzling radiance of white fire flared over the top of the Agamon, swallowing up the impenetrable black. It was finished. Both Gates closed. She watched the black clouds dissipate, and fresh air stirred on her face. She lay, empty handed, on the cruel stones with the Amyntah surrounding her and her faithful ones not far. The taint was gone, but her beautiful land would never be as it once was and she would never see it again.

PART I

Dawn

Secrets in the Shade

2100 years later
Fifth Epoch, Age of Reformation

1 - Breaking In

I do not suffer as one; we combat pain together to form a protective fortress
I do not grow as a single stalk; we combine our knowledge to create a plentiful harvest
I do not act on my own; we cast our strength as one mighty sword to swing
I do not endure alone; we sacrifice our needs to become a powerful army
I do not walk my own way; we march as one down the road set for us from the first day

Kin Pledge

Gold seraphim wings spread towards the center of the door's mantle. Encrusted in the gold, clusters of rubies, diamonds, and opals, shimmering in silvery light, formed a tapestry of exquisite colour and design. The giant Empyrean creatures rested on pillars in glorious splendour overseeing the underground chamber. Veins of rich crimson and glistening moonstone wound up the fluting of the gold pillars on each side of the fifteen-foot wide double doors the angelic beings guarded.

Jett admired the dazzling display without need of light. He could see in the dark; a side-effect that came with the Charer Gift. The door, well over twenty-feet high, was made of a black metal called malreus. Unlike any other known metal, it could not be damaged by Jett's Gift or any Gift possessed by his race.

He touched an etching on the smooth plate, of an immense angel illuminated from within with a silver hue. The ancient title, *Ushriya Ari'Shelomyth* was written in gold below the wings. 'Peace for the Dead,' he whispered. A shame no one could admire the beauty of the excellent workmanship. Eternity would come with it remaining in the dank dusty space.

Shadows stretched to life on the walls behind him. Dim light bounced on the stairs from a lantern being swung in a hurry. 'Jett?' A voice bounded off the stone walls in annoyance. 'Where have you gone?'

The lantern came to hover near Jett's shoulder, affecting his vision. He stepped away from the one holding it, his friend and one of his Kin, Marcus. Shorter than Jett, Marcus had muscles upon muscles and wide shoulders to support them, and under the stretching light, his normally rugged face looked like a boy's, and his brown hair was as untidy as it always was. Unlike Marcus, Jett was pale, and he imagined with his clear skin and black hair, he looked ghostly in the faint glow, and not at all boyish.

Marcus flexed a brawny arm, holding the light high to view the embellished doorframe. 'Tell me we're not going in there.'

Two openings gaped on each side of the chamber. Left, a ramp sloped downward. Jett walked to the opposite opening, towards a short set of steps and away from the ancient tomb. 'We're not.'

Marcus gazed at the doorway with the ramp. 'My guess, you didn't expect that.'

He was correct; the unexpected second entrance was a hindrance. The map was vague enough aside from extra doorways. He sent a simple sentence into Marcus' thoughts, delivered with a stab of irritation; *I'm not sure what's down here.* The direct telepathic statement was received by the member of his Kin as easily as words spoken.

'You're telling me now?' Marcus spurted in answer to his remark.

Jett grinned. 'Let's get this over with.'

Marcus followed after, grumbling, 'And what makes you think this is the right way?'

'The stairs look worn.' That was all he had to go on. He hadn't been able to find any clear directions on this underground section of the fortress.

In the new chamber, Jett sensed the change in pressure. Breathing deep of the less stale air, he came out from the slight overhang of rock and stood on a stone slab platform. He gasped at the size of the cavernous chamber opening up on his right. The highest point of the jagged rock ceiling was eighty feet and the rest of the cavern twisted away from his vision. Straight ahead there seemed to be another path. With his lantern shedding meagre light on his surroundings, Marcus walked forward, ignorant to the grandeur of the chamber. Jett yanked Marcus' arm and he stumbled backwards, sending a shower of grit cascading to the rocks below.

'What'd you do that for?' Marcus cried, brushing the dust from his pants.

'Can't you see that?' Jett leaned over the path's edge. A five-foot gap between where they stood and the other ledge would have dropped him to a painful death.

Marcus leaned over with his lantern dangling. 'Flamin' arse!'

Jett pointed to the other side where the flat appeared to slope down. 'It's a fake path. An illusion.' He looked towards the bottom of the chamber. Under the walkway and between the columns of walls, the rocks were covered with a dense mass of black; opaque layers of something that appeared organic. As his eyes focused on the strange sight, he saw more of it everywhere underneath them. Deep holes in the rock were coated in the blackness. He got off his hands and knees, having seen enough. 'We must be careful.'

Sharp to their left, Jett turned to a narrow pathway of black stone slabs, close to the wall on one side, but open to the cavern on the other.

Marcus followed and stood, half hanging over the un-walled side, looking down through the four-foot gap between the path and the limestone wall across from them. 'I see what you mean.'

'Stay away from the edges,' Jett flared with growing anxiety, 'and whatever you do, be quiet.' Along the wall of the path, was a carved mural of robed men carrying crowns, scepters and other treasures. The ancient carvings were cracked and eroded, but at least Jett got the sense they were headed in the right direction. The walkway turned a straight right. The gap between the path and the opposite wall fell back to near twenty feet, and a smaller space of three feet was now on their left. The path was now free standing, supported somehow from beneath. Smooth limestone blocks were fashioned into arches, creating alcoves holding empty fire brackets.

'Stay in the middle of the path,' Jett ordered.

'Gladly.'

Eventually the path curved and met with the high wall on the right. Jett had seen the decoration of the massive door glistening as he approached. He wished he could see it in its natural brilliance without the flickering of the patchy glow. In the same design as the previous door, the difference was the gemstones and the entities adorning the golden pillars. Lush sapphires and shades of emeralds and topaz' enhanced the dragons' mighty wings extended over the door's crest. The noble beasts' scales twinkled in a beautiful menagerie of glittering affect. Wrought into the pillars, as if it naturally occurred, iridescent veins of lapis-lazuli sparkled with vivid opulence. *Zohar Ari'Chanah* was written above the door. In awe, he swept his hand over the strong black door. Fingering the fine etching, he traced over the roaring dragon's haunches. Such a commanding creature had not been seen on Earth for more than two ages.

'Royal Treasures,' he said, 'this is it.'

In the middle of each door was a circle with layers of grooves carved into the malreus. The intricate channels around the curved edge needed a similar patterned disc to slot into it. He placed his palm in one of the deep impressions. 'The key hole.'

'It's malreus.' Frowning, Marcus placed his lantern on the ground.

'It will be stone underneath,' Jett said.

You hope. Marcus cast him a dark look and shouldered him out the way. *Should have known.* He pressed his palm into the indented circle. Jett waited while Marcus sent his Ethos past the Malreus and into the stone mechanism within the door. Similar to Jett being able to burn with his eyes, Marcus had the Gift of breaking solid objects with the touch of his hands. Everything that is, except the black rock, malreus.

After moments of Marcus feeling the polished metal and the intricate lock beyond, rocks split within the door, followed by a metallic crunch. He shoved on it with his side. A crumbling rattle followed, but the black plate remained in place. The door rolled in, and rubble from in between the plate fell to the dusty floor at the opening. The door stood ajar enough for Jett to walk through. Marcus stopped to eye his handiwork, scooping out broken granite from a chest high hole between the malreus panel.

Jett sucked in his breath at the stagnation in the chamber. Dust clouds made the space hazy. Healthy air was absent and he breathed in the musky choking stink. The end of the room was not visible, so crowded was it with archaic furniture and countless rows of decrepit shelving, and piles of wall hangings and rugs, turned to grey coated lumps of dowdy material. Wooden crates and chests, occupying every available space, were stacked with no order. Neglected armor stands tilted against trunks and shelves, or had fallen down altogether. The large amount of books and scrolls in the room startled Jett more than all the other items. Amongst the discarded objects, not a flicker of gold reflected back at them, only a grey gloom of abandoned possessions.

'Devil's bloody arse!' Marcus held his light aloft. 'It's all... junk.'

A grin spread across Jett's face. 'Did you expect them to keep anything of great worth in here?'

'Where do we start?'

Jett assumed what he searched for would be some of the last items thrown in. He went to the first of the arches along one side. Shabby chests, stacked on each other were beside a stand holding brass incense burners. Behind them stood an exotic gong, a mixture of staves and peculiar contraptions made of copper. Scrolls and a great number of leather books, once piled high, now spread across the floor and coated in grime. Marcus placed the lantern by his feet and stared down at the books. 'Must be quite an author to get put down here.'

Jett lifted a dust coated book from the pile and waved it at Marcus. 'Zaki'is Fur'Mole.'

'You found it already?'

'No, but these are his books.' Jett's knowledge of the man was limited. Fur'Mole proclaimed to be many things; inventor, explorer, philosopher, and historian to add to the list, yet it seemed no one took him seriously or made his titles official, hence his work was stored away. He was not a man of great repute.

'Wasn't that man insane?'

'So they say.' Jett lugged a chest across the floor, sending black dust flying. Musky air hit his nostrils when he opened it, making him cough.

Marcus opened the second chest. He tossed scrolls onto the floor, scattering them in a mess of pages. 'What's the name of this book again?'

'"Hot Springs in the Land of Tremors."'

Marcus pulled out a pile of books from the chest. '"A Wider Horizon" – "What to do with Leeches" – "Battles and other Oddities."' Shaking his head at the book, he chuckled. '"All Things Green" – "The Higher Intelligence of Insects." No wonder they thought he was mad.' He threw each book to the floor after speaking its title. '"You can Never be too Humble." Earona needs this one.'

Jett pulled out a plain brown book. He flipped through it and stopped to study a map of a country called Trevally, otherwise known as the Land of Tremors, in the far west. Moments passed as he read. Finally, he said, 'Found it.'

'Good. Let's get out of here.'

'Wait,' Jett said, 'I promised something for Shiarn for helping me, and Ethan.' He swiveled to view the room. Nothing valuable or attractive that he could see, at least nothing that would appeal to a woman.

From under piles of books in the chest, Marcus yanked up a sack. After sticking his hand in, he pulled out a sheathed sword. He whistled at the black blade. 'You can have your books, I'll have this.' He admired its curving hilt, shaped in a pattern representing wind.

Jett picked up a book from the bag. '"From Glory to Ruin, Amin-Sayeda."' He leafed through the pages. A sketch of a ziggurat caught his attention, and he stared for moments, transfixed by a white coloured orb at its top. As if recalling a dream, he knew he had seen the thing before. 'What did you say?'

'Ah… nothing.'

Jett could have sworn he heard someone speak his name. He closed the book and brushed the dust from its cover. 'Must be some echo.'

'Just you and me here.' Marcus shook his head at him.

'Fine. What shall we bring Shiarn?'

Marcus took a pendant from the same sack and swung it before Jett's face. 'This?' Circular in shape, its center was a white opal gem, in the shape of an almond eye.

Jett touched the gem. A jumble of incomprehensible words shot into his mind, and with sudden breathlessness, he snatched back his hand. 'I…'

'Ethan might like this.' Marcus tossed him a medallion, also from the box. Two malreus circles were joined together to form an eight.

Jett creased his brow as he studied it. At least it didn't invoke any strange visions. 'Doesn't matter. We have to go.' He opened the sack and Marcus gently placed the sword back inside, while the other items were thrown in.

'You don't sense anything?' Jett watched with surprise.

'Um, I sense the bag might be heavy with all these books.' Marcus chuckled at one he put in with the others. '"Philosophy for Those Who Know Everything." Keanan would appreciate it.'

Jett shook his head. He hoped Keanan would not find out what they were doing, and he didn't think he should have evidence to show for it. Keanan would be horrified by their misdemeanour. He put what books they didn't take, back into the chest. In case someone did come down, they would suspect nothing.

'I've got some for the others too.'

Jett sighed at Marcus' brazen theft. He hadn't told the rest of the Kin what they were doing, and now they were bringing them souvenirs of their crimes. 'Throw this one in too.' He tossed him the one on Amin-Sayeda plus the journal on the Land of Tremors.

Marcus lost his balance catching the books and tipped the incense stand. Lurching forward, he grabbed the falling dishes and they tinkled together.

'Marcus!' Jett hissed.

'Don't panic.' He stood and righted the stand.

On the way out, Jett kicked the rubble of the broken lock into the treasure room and pulled the door shut.

'That wasn't too hard.' Marcus started up the passage.

Faint clicking from an indefinable source echoed around them. A springing, ticking movement vibrated the walkway. Looking down at the stone beneath his feet, Jett halted. *Stop!* He looked to the limestone walls on his left, too far away for anyone to see even with a light. Countless holes were drilled into the rock. 'Down,' he shouted, diving onto Marcus, knocking him flat.

Whizzing above them, javelins flew, slamming into the wall on their right.

'Flamin' hell,' Marcus heaved, 'Traps!'

Beside Marcus, Jett laid on his back, watching the thin black spears thud into the limestone along the walkway, the lowest ones not more than half an arm above them. The fierce twang of the weapons rang out for moments after they hit. Silence descended after the last spear made contact.

Marcus crawled under the shafts, dragging the lantern, while Jett took the sack. 'You never said anything about traps.'

'I didn't think there would be.' Jett was just as surprised and now concerned. 'There was nothing here to guard.'

Marcus arrived first to the corner of the passage.

A monstrous ringing filled the chamber, booming and shaking the rock walls.

Jett looked down at the slab and cursed. A mighty bell clanged again. A pause and then it rang without ceasing. Screeching from the pits of the enormous cavern grew with volatile force. An entanglement of skittering and shrieking reverberated against the rocks, seeming to merge into the cry of one ferocious beast, filling the chamber with dread.

'Oh, hell,' Marcus cried. The bells had woken the arpers; vicious flying cave vermin. The only thing to intimidate them was Marcus' lone lantern. Not only did the chimes wake the creatures, it sounded an alarm. 'How long we got?'

'As long as we get to Shiarn.' She was Jett's insurance for the items in the bag. They could find him, but not the book.

A dense shadow swarmed towards them. The cave creatures batted against each other and the rocks, as they swooped and dived at the men's bodies. Marcus swung his light in an arc over Jett and himself, warding off the flying black monsters. It kept most at bay, except those daring enough to fly into the light. The arpers swiped at their faces, pecking and ripping with their needle sharp claws and protruding fangs. The size of a hand, one alone would not do any real harm, but there seemed to be hundreds all wanting to scratch at their flesh.

Jett pulled the blade from the bag, and cut into the glut of them, not knowing if he did any damage. In the midst of the swarm, Jett grabbed Marcus' arm, preventing him moving forward. 'Wait.'

'We can't wait here.'

Jett stood inches from Marcus' back, now grateful for the lantern's presence and stared at the twenty foot walkway. The traps were active that was clear. They had to be more than careful, they had to not get killed. He should have noticed it before, but now he saw it. 'Pressure plates are along here.' He looked at the wall on the right side. Erosion had exposed minute holes drilled randomly into the sculpture. 'If you run, you will die.'

'What then?'

Jett studied the flat black slabs. 'We have to set them off.'

Marcus groaned. 'How?'

Jett put his back to Marcus' and swung the blade at the creatures blocking his path. 'Come.' They moved quickly back to the spears with Marcus whirling the lantern at the frenzying creatures. He handed the blade to Marcus and grasped the nearest spear, wrenching it with both hands. Arpers slashed at his face and neck, their harsh bristles rubbed on his face, while they clamped onto his exposed skin. Jett's shouted curses ricocheted through the chamber and he bore with the pain. Ignoring the fangs biting through his clothes, he held the spear and connected with his Ethos to ignite his vision. He heated the rock enough to wriggle the spear free. With the spear, he hit the creatures hanging off his limbs, and squashed them under his boot with angry curses.

Back at the pathway, Jett reached out and pounded the stone with the spear's tip. Clusters of long needles whizzed past so quickly it was difficult to see. Crouching low and shielding his head and face just in case, he hit all the steps he could reach before he and Marcus moved on. Thin sharp points shot out at four different levels, piercing the flying pests. Though one shot might not kill a man, all of them together would eventually. They reached the last strip of steps.

Marcus leapt towards the stairs leading out and used the wall to steady his propulsion. Jett stepped more cautiously onto the black slab. The stone platform moved under his feet and he slid as the stone tilted down from his weight, sending the spear clattering to the rocks below.

Flinging the lantern into the adjoining chamber, Marcus stamped his foot down on the opposite end, halting the platform's sway. In the same moment, he flicked his sword away to safety and grabbed Jett's hand, preventing him from slipping down. Jett clenched hard to Marcus' grip, the only thing keeping him from falling through the crack. He scrabbled up the stone that wanted to swing and topple him down. Marcus pulled all of Jett's weight until Jett got a handhold of the stone's edge near the stair. Once Jett landed on the stair, Marcus removed his foot. The great black slab, grinding against the rock, continued swiveling after its restraint.

'Holy Kahm!' Marcus shouted, 'We're alive!'

Jett patted his shoulder, still recovering from his near fatal fall to the rocks below. 'Only just.'

Marcus grinned like an overgrown boy. 'Lucky I'm here to save your skin.'

Jett smiled back. He was not going to mention how he had saved Marcus' life moments before, because that's what Jett was there for.

Not having any time to spare, they ran into the first chamber. The ringing shook the air and pounded in Jett's ears. Forsaking the light of the lantern, Jett ran ahead up the staircase, slashing at more arpers that still seemed determined to flap around his head and fly into his body. A chasm lay to the left of the stairs, and Jett kept close to the wall on the right, not knowing what might happen next.

The creatures lessened as he neared the landing yet the chamber still resounded with the gongs. He breathed hard as he came to another door; plain and wooden, leading up to the fortress. *Shiarn?*

Marcus halted beside him and Jett pushed through the door to another stair made from cut stone. He bounded up the stairs two at a time. 'Shiarn!' He could see nothing, but that didn't mean she wasn't there.

A woman with red spiraling hair and bright eyes peering into darkness appeared suddenly. Her voice, normally deep and melodious was cross, 'Jett?! You've made a horrendous racket down there.'

Marcus ran up to them, bringing the only light.

She ran a hand over Jett's torn sleeves. 'What happened to you? Look's like you shoved your head into a meat grinder.'

'No time to explain.' Jett pushed the sack into her hands. 'Here.'

Lifting it, she squawked, 'Ow!'

'The sword's mine,' Marcus said.

'You can have your sword.' She rummaged through the bag. 'What have you got for me?'

Jett cried, 'We don't have time for this!'

'When did you two take up reading?' she lifted out a tattered dusty book.

'For the others,' Marcus said. 'There's jewelry for you.'

'Kahm above, don't tell me it's this.' She held the malreus shape and eyed it with disdain.

Beyond the door were footsteps and angry shouts.

'Shiarn, just take it.' Jett shoved it all back in the bag and hung it over her shoulder. 'And disappear.'

In an instant, she disappeared from sight with her words ringing in their minds, *I'll meet you later.*

The door flung open. Jett and Marcus stood staring at crossbows crowded into the lit corridor. Jett recognized every one of the men holding them. Leading the pack, a solidly built man with a hardened face and crooked nose, stepped forward. The Master Avare said, 'More of the rats coming up from the hole.'

Pushed through the men, was a tall young man with thick shoulders and a dense chest. His tangle of brown hair flopped over his eyes, and he looked down sheepishly. Ethan, one of Jett's Kin, should have been keeping a look out. *They came out of nowhere, sorry,* Ethan's thoughts were clear to Jett and Marcus.

Don't worry, I've got what I came for. Jett's hands clenched at his sides, surprised at the sight of the man before him. 'Rambaras.' *Why is he here? And why so many sentries on patrol?*

'That's Master Avare to you,' Rambaras growled. 'Kushar and Myrell, stop that cursed ringing and see what they have done down there. Errol, check them.' Two men pushed past Jett and ran down the stairs. Errol, a thin man, with a short neat beard, felt their bodies with a hard press of his palms. It was obvious they carried nothing except the lantern.

'What were you doing down there?' The Master Avare's stalwart voice boomed down the corridor.

'Nothing.' Jett's black eyes pierced the Master Avare's hard stare.

Rambaras' face reddened. His long dark hair swayed as he dashed forward, and unsheathing a black sword, he pointed it at Jett's throat. 'Get down!'

Under compulsion to obey, Jett knelt before his superior.

Rambaras moved the sword tip inches from Jett's neck. 'Now answer the question.'

Marcus said, 'We were explor—'

Rambaras directed the sword at Marcus, sending him to his knees as well. Ethan followed the two. 'Do you realize how much strife you are in?' Rambaras' heavy brows, knotting together, shaded his mean eyes. 'You've broken the door to the fortress and this one. God knows what you have done below.'

'We haven't taken anything.' Jett eyed the narrow corridor, gauging the space, hoping there was enough for an invisible girl to sneak through.

Marcus said under his breath, 'There was nothing to steal.'

The ringing from below ceased and Rambaras stared towards the door. After some moments, he let loose a chain of curses. 'You've broken into the Zohar and set off the traps.' His rage increased when he saw Jett watching with his dark eyes. His left arm lashed out, hitting Jett across the face, smearing the blood from his cuts over his mouth and enflaming them all. Before Jett could turn his face, Rambaras pushed his sword edge into Jett's already bloodied neck. Jett's eyes burned; his only thought was how he would kill Rambaras before the man had a chance to kill him.

Rambaras bent down inches from Jett's face and spoke, his voice as sharp as the blade. 'Why shouldn't I kill you right now?'

Jett didn't doubt he could do it right there and then. From the corner of his eye he scanned the men behind Rambaras. They included a few members of three Kins. The Master Avare's Kin, Blessed Hand, were stern looking men and they probably shared Rambaras' sentiment. The Golden Hound Kin were members of the Border Sentries and might be unbiased towards him. Also present were two members of a young Kin, like Jett's, the Crimson Hunters. Tarn and Brunel were both loose with their tongues and not enough intelligence between them to do anything productive. Besides that, Jett couldn't stand them.

'Because it would be murder.' Marcus spoke up.

Jett took his eyes off the men watching and stared at Rambaras' cruel face, daring him to act.

Marcus went on, 'There'll need to be a trial. Besides, we haven't even taken anything.'

'Shut your mouth, boy,' Rambaras barked, and his voice echoed down the passage.

'Why were those traps working?' Jett cut in.

'That's no concern of yours.' Rambaras withdrew his sword. 'Pity they didn't kill you.'

Jett glowered.

The men came dashing up the stair, breathing heavily. One of the Master Avare's men, Kushar said, 'There's some disturbance within the Zohar but we can't see if anything of value was taken.'

Myrell, a member of the Golden Hound, added, 'There's nothing there to take.' He looked with surprise towards Jett and Marcus. 'But the damage is great.'

Rambaras backed away and slid his sword back into his scabbard, a broad grin spread on his face. 'You have gotten you and yours into a mountain of trouble and you have nothing to show for it.' He chuckled softly. 'Your chances of leaving Tellávare are slipping through your fingers. I'd say this just about seals your fate.' He turned his back to the three and said to the men, 'Take them to the Sentry Pit until we get word up to the Eighfest.'

Jett scowled at Rambaras' back, but held his tongue.

Tarn and Myrell marched them off at the end of the procession, through the hall of the empty ancient fortress, The Seat of Halcyon. Jett walked behind Ethan and Marcus with Tarn bringing up the rear. Tarn muttered, 'You and your dogs will be stuck here. Scum under the nails of those more worthy than you.'

'One day, Tarn, I'm going to shut you up,' Jett snarled, 'for good.'

Tarn chortled behind him.

Far from hearing, Jett was already making plans. There was no way any man, or Prophet, or high and mighty Avare, would stop him from leaving Tellávare. Not even the Judge himself would be able to hold him back.

2 - Summoned

Dawn brings enlightenment.

Pale creeping light stretches through the trees, painting the silent landscape in a new radiance. Mountain shadows, a reminder light has not finalized its illumination of the earth, continue as a warning that darkness will always have a place. Slowly breathing in the unsullied air, souls are awakened by the fresh wind, hinting at goodness the day will bring. Seasons flow into a passage of life and death. Endless stars fade in and out in an undying frame, reflecting the permanence of existence. The spectacular has become hidden in the everyday and the miracles have receded into the legends of a forgotten season.

Across the earth, the sun's glory descends once more. Valleys disappear into dark depressions, leaving shrouds of fear unfolding over the last shards of salient light. Souls lost in ignorance, turn from the sun's fading strength and carelessly they forget what lies behind.

Dawn is not the beginning.

Night was always first. Night has been the master.

Dusk signals the approaching dark.

Ei'myn Geí-Serenmãh

Rhythmic pounding was the only sound in the oppressive tunnel. Iron rock cracked under a sharp pick, revealing its multi-layered ochre center. Another blow caused the slate to explode into jagged flecks. Cold air on Jett's bare back made his skin tingle. He flicked damp hair from his eyes and repositioned his calloused hand further up the shaft for a weightier blow, and slammed into another wall. Years of familiar hammering at the stone meant his mind could wander while he worked.

Nearly a month had passed since his punishment was decided. The worst sort of sentence and one he was well acquainted with; curfew and loss of privileges. No sparring, no weapons training, no taverns, and extra work time. He would have preferred being locked up. Humiliation was the true chastisement and one the Eldery were experts at dispensing. At least to him anyway. Marcus and Ethan suffered the same bans, but they didn't complain as much as him. The rest of the Kin were spared, although their reactions differed. Earona swore she would never speak to him again while Hellier said the same, except for a different reason. She was angry at being left out of the underground raid.

Keanan wanted to punch him. Of course, he was all talk. The morally conscious Keanan was too pretentious to do such an uncouth deed as hit someone.

Jett cut into the rock, his muscles swelling from the strike. A slight fissure appeared in the brown-grey texture. Hard hits usually fractured the rock too severely. Most times, all the stone needed was a focused tap in the right spot to make it split perfectly. But today he wasn't interested in mining for metals; he was hammering to kill the throbbing in his thoughts.

In a few days his Kin will reach their Sh'har, better known as their Coming of Age ceremony. At the auspicious occasion it would be announced whether the Kin would remain in Tellávare or venture out in search of the Aelyons, the sacred relics lost to the Fáerinn before the Age of Chaos. Most young Kin aspired to be selected to leave Tellávare, and it was always Jett's hope as well. Twenty years ago he was marked by the Prophets to be the Avare Initiate of a new Kin. At the time his Kin numbered five, including himself, with three more to join later. The youngest, Seth, five at the time, was chosen when Jett was thirteen. Jett wondered how much the Eldery regretted their decision to make him an Avare now.

The Sh'har was not only an important crossroad in the life of a Kin, it followed Jett's Echwud, when he would ascend the role of Full Avare. But now even that seemed unlikely after his recent run in with the Master Avare. To make it worse, one of the Eldery informed him his Kin wouldn't be permitted to leave Tellávare. This time he feared he had pushed Rambaras and the Eldery Circle too far.

He flung his tool across the tunnel. It clunked against the grey rock and fell with a dead thump. His skin dripped with sweat and he slumped to the hard earth, his arms and back aching from the relentless pounding. At least he had the map from the treasure house. *The Land of Tremors.* The name had stuck in his mind since childhood as the last known place his father had traveled. He searched for its location in the Da'thân, House of Knowledge. There was little on it except it bordered the west of Skarhane, and a reference connecting it to the writings of Fur'Mole. He was determined to one day trace his father's steps and find out what no one else had before him; what no one cared to find out. He would do it on his own if he had to.

A glowing lantern appeared at the end of the tunnel. Next to its dim rays a man peered into the vacuous space. His hand grasped the rock wall and the other hand extended the light. He called down the passage, 'You down there, slacker?'

Jett shifted towards the wall, hoping the man and his light would disappear.

'You s'posed to be working down there.' He squinted. 'What-cha doing?'

Jett reached for a stone and hurled it against the wall. 'Thinking.'

'Is that what you call having a wank now?' The walls muffled the man's hoarse chuckle.

'Hey, Cam?'

'Yeah...'

'Piss off!' Jett's harsh voice cut the stiff air.

'I'll cop you one when I get to you.' His mocking tone turned sombre. 'But it'll have to wait. You got to come up top. Judge wants to see ya.'

Jett froze with unexpected wariness.

'That's right, you been summoned.' The man and his light turned away, grumbling as he left, '...bloody arrogant arse...'

Jett sat waiting for the light to disappear. The day had finally arrived. He would find out what was to be his fate. After a moment his sharp curse broke the silence.

~ * ~

3.4 Mist 2120 AG5

I sense a change on the horizon of our peaceful existence. Although I assumed it would be as the sun sets or as the rain falls or as natural as the direction of the wind, and not destructive, as the pick breaks rock or the axe splits wood or as deadly as the flying arrow. Hence, I carry out my decisions with uncertainty, for if there was certainty would it truly be termed change? Through the doubts that assail me and frustration from weakened principles, I see a glimmer of what the future may bring. Descent into trials and hardship is the only way we shall rise to herald in the approaching closure of this age. Yet, they fail to comprehend you cannot be lifted up if you do not first fall. Nevertheless, my words are stronger than my heart, and my emotions weaker than all. Am I guided by what will lead us to triumph or am I adding a weft that will one day weave a hostile tapestry on the history of our people?

Judge Haldus Sage'Moon put down his quill and leaned back from his desk. He gazed at his study, his eyes trailing along the neat rows of books and artifacts, collected from his travels across the Earth, until his sight fixed on the austere sky outside his high windows. Weeks now, he had spent laboring over a decision that left him mentally weary. The discord over one particular Kin was present for years, and brewing in the minds of some in authority. He had avoided action, presuming the enmity would fade over time, but he was a fool to think so. For all his Prophetic Gifting, he should have been wiser. Now he had a semblance of peace and not so much with the solution, as ridding himself of the consuming thoughts. It was done. Nothing like this had occurred in the history of the current age.

He pushed back his chair; his indigo robes were warm against his skin as he walked to the windows, hoping to gain insight from the white city below. Through the arched windows of the highest level of the Eighfest, a citadel built into the side of Mount Ryzín, was the valley of Tellávare, which on a clear day would be a splendid spread of greens. Today, mist hovered above Melchior City, and gentle rain tapped on the white stone buildings and tile rooftops. Between cottages huddled in the rock, the cobbled streets zigzagged up towards the Eighfest. Light reflected off the whitewashed walls of the domed Sanctuary of Kahm, on the west ranges, its diameter so massive it was visible across the valley. Beside it, the Ei'tel Hákoreí Tower, that guarded the Ei'myn Geí-Serenmãh, reached to a great height, and disappeared into the brume.

In the east, the Emorim Ranges, and the Seat of Halcyon, the ages-old imposing fortress carved into the mountain. The stronghold stood as a poignant reminder from ages past when kings ruled the Fáerinn. Stone turrets, vacant of life, rose from the rocky crags as sentries, no longer needed, but dutifully standing guard down the ages. Black walls, once a walkway for the Mahar, the king's royal guard, reflected not the magnificence of court but the faceless mounts, the hollow remains of a glorious era brought to its slow bloody end by the curse of division and selfish pride. Also, of late, the scene for a couple of mischief-makers, intent on their own amusement in spite of the cost and consequences to those deserving more respect.

Haldus answered a knock on the door. A man, a few years younger, entered, wearing the blue robes and gold chains of an Elder. His heavy cheeks were red, and a knotted belt restrained his bulging girth. 'Sergus.'

'Judge Haldus.' Sergus' bulgy face was grave and his smile awkward. The two men faced each other in a tense expectancy.

'Well, speak up.' Haldus was surprised by the impatience in his voice. After all, he knew why the Elder had come.

'I heard a rumor you are permitting the departure of the Iron-Wolf Kin...' Sergus started with indifference, his contemptuous tone soon revealed his true sentiments. 'I presume you have not yet arrived at a decision.'

Haldus wished he could dismiss the stuffy man and turn back to the window. 'I have. It is true.' But politics was never that luxurious.

Sergus' fat jowls shook with shock. 'The prophecies forbid it!'

Haldus' blue eyes lit with the confrontation. 'No. The Circle's interpretation does.'

'You twist the words—'

'I make the decisions.' Haldus raised his voice.

Sergus stepped back, his face remaining a patchy red. 'You are willing to send a Kin to their death?'

That was far from Sergus' concern in the past. It was just another wile used to create uncertainty. Haldus' sigh was genuine and his gaze lingered over the clouds outside. His fine white hair wisped across his cheek from the damp breeze. One window remained open to the chill. Immediately his prophetic heart spoke to him, and he pondered the significance of the sign. An opening to the winter of the world outside. He stirred himself to answer. 'Not all darkness leads to death. Nor does despair denote defeat.' Doubt drifted in like the freezing air despite his declaration.

'You don't deny they are present.'

Haldus recalled a portion of the foreboding word the Seer Circle proclaimed over the Iron-Wolf Kin.

A door opens on a convergence of ancient evil and an innocent soul.
Corruption enters through a broken seal and a deceiving encounter.
Pathways of adversity are the only directions.
Malevolent darkness abides the hearts of the Gifted.
Lives collide, scatter, and fall to potential ruin.
History manifests as a recurring affliction.
Those governed by prophecy are commanded to subjugation.
The decisive key is a life sacrificed.

Haldus had pondered the prediction and there seemed to be an utterances missing. 'I believe it is as yet incomplete.'

'You go above the decree of the Eldery,' Sergus stated with bold conceit.

'This Kin will leave.' *Whether we wish it or not.* Regardless of the consequences to come from the Circle, he was compelled to follow his visions. The final pronouncement was the Judge's alone. He gauged whether Sergus would impose the Circle's will instantly and what he would be forced to do if he should.

'You have made your decision.'

'I am not the only one who thinks this is the correct course,' Haldus said in warning. It was known who those members were, although the minority.

'He will bring evil into our land.'

Haldus' face darkened and he brooded in silence. His sombre blue eyes searched out the sky through the arched windows once more. It was a touchy topic and he had wrestled with the same frame of thought. Over the years, he sensed an ominous hatred in the heart of the one they discussed, yet balancing that weight was a devotion to his Kin. 'The vision is unclear. The Seal has held and I believe it should continue to, and even more so after its renewal.'

A groan erupted from Sergus' overweight middle. 'Should? It's too risky. The very fact that he has such a seal should be reason enough to be cautious. Moreover the prophecies around this man speak nothing but misfortune and - rebellion. He is cursed, and always will be—'

A distant bang reverberated through the room, interrupting him.

'I believe the one you speak of approaches.' Judge Haldus could not dispute Sergus' words. The young man's recent actions piled more grievances on top of an already acrimonious relationship with those in authority over him. His lack of self-control was destroying any good reputation he had left, as well as opportunities. But the curse was a different matter, and rooted in past prophetic failings.

A shrewd smirk darkened Sergus' face.

The heavy door to the study swung wide, hitting the wall with force. Jett surveyed the room with an unhappy expression. His fair skinned, sharply etched face made him a handsome man. Raven black hair framed his clean-shaven face and his dark eyes peered scrupulously from below his damp fringe. Haldus knew Jett never cared about his good looks, nor did Jett see any benefit in them, and a cheerful smile rarely shaped his broad mouth.

Judge Haldus, his robes gliding around his feet, moved to meet him. 'Jett Storm'Heart, welcome.' He approached with open arms, unperturbed by Sergus' unwelcoming stance or Jett's hasty entrance. 'Come in.' Jett's hand was rough and firm in Haldus' smooth palm as they greeted each other. 'You are very prompt.'

Jett's normally steady voice belied an anxious strain. 'I came as quickly as I could, no point waiting.'

Judge Haldus turned to Sergus, who stood with a disapproving glare. 'We have finished.'

Sergus left the room and closed the doors behind him with a sudden slam.

Jett ignored the Elder's departure and stared into Judge Haldus' eyes.

Haldus avoided his direct gaze. 'I sense you are too restless to sit.' He motioned for Jett to walk by the windows. 'Come, let us talk. Have you learned a lesson from your punishment?'

Jett fell in with the elderly man. 'It's the same old lesson.'

Haldus nodded. 'A lesson you need to learn.'

'It is not what I wish to study.'

Haldus controlled his anger over Jett's obstinacy. Calm settled once again in his thoughts. 'One day you might wish you had studied harder.'

Jett folded his arms and turned his face to view the eastern Emorim range and the Seat of Halcyon.

'You have not yet told me what you were doing down there?'

Jett shrugged with indifference.

'I went down there myself.' Haldus paused to observe Jett's impassive face. 'I know where you were looking. That man had several worthy essays, however, most remain unverified.'

'We can't say what is true or not.'

'Indeed. Nevertheless, we have to retain some standard. A great quantity of his work is anecdotal ramblings. Despite that, I had his books moved to the Da'thân, where someone can ascertain their worth.' More importantly, he wanted to determine what might be missing.

Jett shrugged. 'I see...'

'I can make an assumption about your intentions, but that is not what I desire to speak of with you.'

Jett's back stiffened, and he halted. 'Yes...'

'Your Echwud approaches.'

Jett nodded.

'And will take place.'

Jett swiveled to face Haldus, bewilderment easy to read. 'Rambaras will conduct it for me?'

The Master Avare was the only one who could lead the Rite of the Avare Accession. Not even the Judge could affirm Jett's role as an Avare. Haldus had been in long hours of negotiation with Rambaras to sway him. 'He has changed his mind.'

'Why?'

'It is enough he will do it.' Haldus paused to look out the window, sadness dulling his eyes. The tension between the young man and the Master Avare was long-standing. There seemed to be no resolution between them over Jett's past transgressions, one of which was Jett running away from Tellávare when he was younger. Now there was this current misbehavior, and the destruction of property to add to his troubles. The conflict seemed to go deeper than simply a difference of opinion between two men, or even Jett's insubordinate attitude.

'That bastard!'

'You must show respect! Remember he has the authority to decline. Yes, a compromise has been reached and he has agreed.' Judge Haldus sighed and steeled himself to inform the young man an agreement had been struck with the Master Avare.

Jett arrived at the one open window and hung his head. 'What does it matter anyway if we aren't going anywhere?' His dark locks covered his sombre black eyes and he looked down on the city below.

Concern surfaced in Haldus' voice. 'That has been told to you?'

'Is it true?'

'You will be leaving,' Haldus stressed, almost defiantly.

Jett's brow lined with suspicion. 'I'm sure that is not the wish of the Eldery.' His hands gripped the smooth rock of the ledge and he stared straight at the clouded view of Tellávare. Drab grey clouds burdened the sky and rain fell in sheets over the foothills.

Haldus sighed with resignation. 'It is complicated.'

'It's me.' Jett's anger was swept up by the cold breeze.

'It is the prophecies.'

Jett shook his head with scorn.

With Jett, it was always the same; however, this time Haldus feared he might be correct. He stood erect with conviction. 'You know how the prophecies work. Some twist and tumble like the wind, while others are steadfast like the mountains. We protect the dynamics of our society by following the words and the prophecies. They are the underlying foundation of our customs, guiding us into understanding the direction of our life and the world around us. The very world we live in, from day to day, will speak to us, if we will listen.'

Jett turned a bored face from Haldus when he started his lecture and stared at the incoming storm with tight lips. 'I've never cared for words.'

Haldus felt all his two hundred years compound his body with weariness. Jett's arrogance tested even his patience. 'To your detriment.'

Jett grumbled, 'You'd think they'd be happy to see my back.'

Haldus was not about to mislead him now. Jett was too sly to be mollycoddled. 'The prophecies speak of danger to you—'

'To hell with the prophecies!'

'And danger to your Kin.' The only thing Jett cared for; the young men and women of his Kin, the only people he would do anything for, the only ones with any influence over him.

Jett creased his brow with new concern.

'Should I agree with the Eldery?' Haldus rested his hand on Jett's arm, almost in supplication. From the folds of his robe, he brought out a piece of rolled paper, and offered it to Jett. 'Perhaps it's best if you read it yourself.'

Jett took it, and opened it reluctantly. His features remained taut and expressionless, and beyond Haldus' insight to interpret.

Finally with a heavy sigh, Jett responded, 'It doesn't matter, I won't stay here.'

Haldus nodded. Jett would run again and not be found. In all probability, his Kin would follow him. This was the deciding factor of his decision. He would not be responsible for a rogue Kin roaming the Earth. At least this way he had control, even if it was from a distance. Why couldn't the Eldery Circle understand? The prophecy will be fulfilled no matter what restrictions they attempted to put in place. However, it was more than the prophecies creating this discontent, and was most likely the Seal over Jett's soul.

Jett passed the paper back to him, but Haldus pushed it into his hands. 'It is your right to have it, regardless of what you do with it. Once you leave here, your life and the lives of your Kin will be in your hands.'

Clenching the paper, Jett's eyes darkened, but he nodded his acceptance. 'I know.' He creased the parchment and stuffed it in his pocket.

Thankful he wasn't going to discard it right there and then, Haldus took a breath and went on, 'You will receive orders, and I shall inform you now. It has been decided your direct charge is to reside under the counsel of the Argent Archer Kin—'

'Devil's bloody arse!' Jett's face reddened with anger. 'We don't need a flamin' shite nurse-maid!'

'Quiet!' Haldus' anger flared. 'That mining talk won't help you. Try to use this time you have been given, wisely. Take this opportunity to prove yourself capable of staying out of trouble.' Perhaps time would pass and Jett and his Kin would be forgotten by the Eldery Circle. Haldus nearly cast a smile. Perhaps that was only wishful thinking. He observed Jett's profile that stayed defiantly turned from him. 'And you are not permitted to search for the Aelyons at any time.' To be denied the great honour and privilege of partaking in the search for the lost relics of their ancient race was a cruel order for any Fáerinn. This was one of Rambaras' compromises. The Master Avare knew exactly where and how to hit Jett with the most effective blow. Nevertheless, Haldus came to the decision Jett's Avare ownership was more important. He hoped Jett would also see this.

Jett remained still, his anger darkening his eyes, and his fists clenched on the stonework. 'I see now. Cuckolded to the last and no true purpose to speak of.'

Profound disappointment in the young man's voice was startling even to the Judge who knew him well. 'Be grateful you are leaving at all and that your Echwud will take place.'

Jett stonewalled his statement and growled, 'Where are we going?'

'Hakan-Kara. To dwell under the guidance of Avare Eagle'Song of the Argent Archer Kin.'

'The South lands.' Jett scoffed, 'As far away as possible. Under the guidance, my arse. More like watchful eye.' His voice was like gravel.

'Your Sh'har will be a private affair.' Sadly, the Eldery were reluctant to give their full blessing.

After some moments, Jett spoke. 'That's that then. We leave under the cover of gloom.'

What comfort could the Judge offer him when his own people scorned him? The time for comfort was over; it was time for counsel. 'You must travel down the Old Road to Floris, and take ship to Hakan-Kara and the city of Lakhish. There is dissension in Ryne so it is imperative you not stray towards the east. It is crucial you not overstep Fáerinn law in this matter, and you must especially not bring attention to yourself by using your Gifts.' He paused. 'You must not reveal your identities or get into any sort of trouble. Do not assume there won't be people observing what you do.'

Jett faced him head on. His dark penetrating stare revealed his contempt for the Eldery's control over his life. 'Why would I expect it to be any different?' After a brooding pause, he asked, 'Why do you care so much, Judge?'

Judge Haldus' opinion of the young man was concealed amidst the strange signs he had received over the years, concerning this particular unconventional Kin. The cold and distant air of the rebellious man was, to him, a definite sign of the very nature of the Fáerinn race. Whether he approved of his obnoxious attitude or not, he could not disengage from the tug of his prophetic heart that spoke to him more frequently than ever. Comparable to the window left open, this man, for good or ill, had to be released into the world. For some mysterious reason, he was yet to fathom why he was unable to speak to Jett of his visions. As usual, Haldus disregarded Jett's customary disrespectful tone and clapped him on his damp cloak covered back. 'Words have many meanings. They must be read with great consideration.'

Jett stared from under his brow, creasing in suspicion. 'But you don't trust me.'

'On the contrary. I do trust you, and moreover, I trust those appointed to your Kin. I shall give you a Word, heed it well, - Your Kin will guide your decisions. Do everything you can to protect them, and I believe you will make the right decisions at the right time.' Haldus' finished with a proud smile. 'And give me no reason to doubt.'

Jett looked across the valley and strained to see the distant Emorim Mountains in the south, and his shoulders sagged. 'I heed you.'

3 - Farewell

If we do not expand our knowledge, we remain as children
If we do not grow, we will not reach maturity
If we do not become wise, we will not know our true purpose

Ei'myn Yamshôan-shem script

Music and laughter spilled from the tavern and out onto the darkened street. Inside, musicians played to a robust crowd that seemed to be increasing by the hour. Small children, overexcited and confined to being indoors, ran under tables and scrambled through skirts of dancing women. A fire kept the air warm, and the smell of roasted meat made the room stuffy. Meals did not come out fast, but full mugs were aplenty.

Earlier in the day, Jett put up with proud fathers boasting, and mothers crying over their grown children, the members of his Kin. Now he sat in a back corner away from the rush of revelers and hoping to remain that way. The Sh'har was over and done. Without the usual pomp and long-winded speeches it was short. Jett decided he liked it that way. The ritual, conducted by Judge Haldus, was attended by a handful of witnesses, and Jett was glad Rambaras wasn't among them. The Kin had mixed reactions to the lack of members from the Eldery Circle. Jett, having no patience to speak of anyone in authority, sidestepped their questions, or just ignored them altogether.

He stretched his weary legs onto the table and crossing his ankles, his leather boots sprinkled clumps of wet soil. He was untroubled by the mess. His aching body was still recovering from the Echwud of the previous day. He had no idea it would be such a mental *and* physical trial. He wondered if Rambaras made it painful on purpose. Among all the symbols within the sophisticated pattern of lights, there was one near the center that was different in colour, it wasn't lit like the others, but was black. He also did not recognize is symbolism. A snake biting its own tail in the shape of an eight seemed a peculiar representation of him or anyone in his Kin. It wasn't the picture so much, as its significant position in the diagram that gave him alarm. He had no way of knowing what it meant, for Rambaras said nothing of it. He could talk to no one of it either. It was forbidden to disclose anything that went on in the Chamber of Transformation and he was under oath to never reveal the process that made him a Full Avare. Not only was the ritual physically grueling, no healing was permitted, and he rubbed the marked skin on his chest, still raw and sore, in memory. The body was required to remember the travail as strongly as the mind because the symbols would not be seen by the naked eye. There was no way he thought he could ever forget it.

In the middle of the tavern, three men forced a space amid the people to watch the entertainment. They were not regulars and their disheveled appearance and worn clothing contrasted with those dressed in their best attire. One of the men bellowed to a blonde haired dancer, twirling an older woman with a plump middle and long red hair. 'Fancy pants, that's not how you dance with a woman!' The dancer, dressed in an intense emerald coat, spared him a derisive glance and sped his steps up. The man continued, 'I'll show you how it's done.'

'You better mind who you talk to,' Jett said in a voice deep and severe, as he leaned his chair back against the wall.

The man aimed his gaze at Jett's raven black hair and dark eyes staring at him. His smirk altered his unkind demeanor, 'Jett, me lad.' He approached Jett's table, metal pitcher in hand.

The corner of Jett's mouth turned up. 'Sledge.' The men made a great noise pulling up chairs at Jett's table, and he said, 'what are you bastards doing down here?'

Sledge was past middle-age, and a long nose was the focal point of his pale and hardy face, and his thick hair had a fine dust near his scalp. His light eyes flashed with pretend disparagement and he turned to the other equally pale men. 'Has to ask us. We come to see you off. You think we want to drink here?' The three men laughed raucously.

The barkeep, a fat-bellied man with bright red hair, came through the crowd as if preempting some misbehavior, and with a grumpy look, barked, 'Jett, get your feet off my table. You know the rules.'

Jett gave Rusco an apologetic smirk, and removed his damp boots from the bench. The barkeep just as quickly disappeared through the space of people.

'See what I mean.' Sledge stood and from underneath his hide and woolen cloak he unbuckled a belt with a sheathed sword. He held the simple scabbard out with a jovial smile and flushed cheeks and handed it to Jett.

Jett stared at them before the sword consumed his sight. The hilt was visible and he could see it was made from a glimmering black metal.

Sledge pushed it towards him. 'Go on, take it.'

Jett took it roughly, but withdrew it with deliberate smoothness. The whole blade, hilt included, was crafted in malreus. The unique metal had the capability of channeling power and in the same instance be unaffected by it. Fáerinn alchemists had studied the mysterious components of the metal, yet its ability to be both a repellent and a conduit could not be solved conclusively. The only explanation suiting everyone to some satisfaction was it contained a spiritual element that united with the wielder of the weapon. Jett admired its length. A tentative press on the precise edge drew a touch of blood from his finger.

'Before you go saying you don't need it, I want to say, that's our malreus.' Sammy, similar in age and appearance to Sledge yet minus the heaviness, was not a man of many words yet even he could not contain his pride.

'Jasper did a good job, eh?' said Hammer, a short man also stout of face.

Jett, unable to hide his smile, agreed. Rounded mounds formed the hilt, making it comfortable despite its being made of metal. In the shape of a single flame, malreus formed the pommel and it matched the guard, crafted in a similar design.

'It's like your other blade, 'cept its malreus,' Hammer informed him, 'You got your two swords now so all that practicing ain't for nothing.'

'It'll match that ring of yours,' Sledge added with a pat on Jett's back.

Jett cast a fond glimpse to the ring of malreus on his third finger. A small horizontal flame appeared to blow towards the right, covering the black ring. An heirloom from his father via his mother. Whether she was aware of it or not, he could not say. It was obvious the men knew how much it meant to Jett they had made the match. 'I don't know what to say…' his words trailed off and he stood to feel the weight of the sword, its balance superb, '…but, thank you.' He sat and unable to keep the sword from his sight, it remained the center-piece of the table.

'The Ceremony is done, is it?' said Sledge, 'Quietest Sh'har in Fáerinn history, I reckon. I'm bloody glad to see you survived your Echwud.' He gave a loud chuckle.

Jett felt the same, because at the time he wondered if he would. He resisted the urge to run his fingers along the new invisible scars on his chest, and neither did he want his mind to be full of the images once more, even though he desired to reflect on all its hidden symbolism. That would have to be for a quieter time.

As if aware of his thoughts on it, Sledge changed the subject and squinted a shrewd eye. 'You seen your ma yet?'

'Yeah.' She had stared out the window as she usually did while he did the talking. Not that he did much of that. He was virtually invisible to her now. At least it was better than being abused. Her calmer demeanor probably had something to do with the Healer who now cared for her. His mother's rages overcame her, making her a danger to herself as well as others. For years the people on the plateau avoided her; known as the madwoman of Moorameer, and other names just as humiliating.

'We'll keep hoping. Your father had great respect up there.'

Anytime respect and his father were mentioned Jett assumed it was a reference to his lack of either and the later in both senses of the word. 'Maybe.' Jett gave him a cynical grin. 'But none is given to my mother.' He spent his childhood in various homes, existing as a lonely outsider to the normal folk of Tellávare, enduring the contentious gossip and the name calling, till it was a part of his lifestyle. Shame, on the other hand, was a difficult sentiment to settle.

'I've told you before, it ain't you,' Sledge said

Having heard this remark numerous times, Jett was as unconvinced as ever. The reality of her hatred of him broke through the stone wall of his thoughts. His vulnerability flared and his shoulders sagged. Sledge rumpled Jett's mop of unruly hair, the only one Jett knew who could do so and get away with it. Sledge and the men were the closest thing he had to family. They were miners like him and had been his father's friends, long before Jett was born. 'Don't you worry 'bout nothing. We'll be here for you. Those braggart bastards wouldn't know if someone had a hold of their dicks they're so daft, but we know how smart you can be, don't we boys?'

Hammer confirmed, 'You got to write your own prophecies.'

'They get so wrapped up in their useless twaddle, whether they should shit in this hole or what flamin' drawers they should be wearing,' Sledge ranted. The men chuckled at his crude humor. 'I don't half reckon the pisspoor buggers need some seer to tell them who to fuck. It's amazing this place runs at all.' Sledge went on, 'And don't you mind that arse, Rambaras. Everyone up top the plateau knows what face he's turning.'

Jett gave them an affectionate half smile, but they were unable to pull him out of his sombre mood. 'Those *arses* run the place and tell people like me what to do.'

'Yeah, but soon you'll be free of 'em.' Hammer lowered his voice and cast a squinting eye over the tavern patrons.

Jett also gazed over the guests, for the most part familiar. 'I'm not convinced of that.' He imagined them hounding him for the rest of his days.

'Your daddy would be proud.' Sledge shot in with the surprise comment. The men agreed loudly on his remark and banged their tankards together in a noisy clamor.

Jett shrugged and hid behind his mug, fighting not to show any emotion to men who knew him well. The yearning to retrace his father's last steps was always a light but persistent tap on the door of his mind. Now that the opportunity loomed, it was a resolute hammering in his thoughts. He turned an impassive face to the people in the tavern.

Sledge spoke in calm warning, 'Lad, you know I don't often agree with our rules, but I also know, going off the road will see you in worse trouble.'

Jett glared past him, aware of what he referred to.

'Your time will come. Don't foul it up for yourself by going west too soon. Think of them.' Sledge nodded his stubbled chin towards the guests.

Jett continued scowling. He had considered his Kin; they were the ones who prevented him from any impulsive actions, it had nothing to do with the stringent rules of the Eldery Circle. 'Have you been pulling much stone lately?'

Sledge took a large swig of ale and wiped his chin. 'Cut down past the Wellard shaft.' He watched him from the corner of his eye. 'Looks good so far, seen some diamonds, could be good malreus there.' He said, 'We miss having you down there, you know. Miss your happy chatter.'

Jett went on undaunted, knowing Sledge was trying to divert him from the awkward topic, 'that old tunnel?! That's as sturdy as old Merriman's heart.'

Sledge scowled. 'Listen to the kid who runs traps, telling us old hacks what's safe.'

A finely dressed man with neat auburn hair stopped at their table. An obvious contrast to Jett and the men, in his well-tailored olive shirt and tweed vest. Elegant pleats fluttered over his ringed fingers as he gracefully pulled out a chair. The men stood and Sledge bellowed, 'Mount'Wise, ain't it? Best to you!' He patted the newcomer's back, sending him forward. Sledge directed to Jett, 'We'll toss a few back later.'

Jett drank his ale without a word to Keanan. Keanan was almost as tall as Ethan, yet he lacked the intimidating fierceness that came with such a height. It was his intelligence that provoked the most trepidation.

Keanan spoke. 'Are you going to tell me what is going on?'

Jett had seen this coming. Keanan was too clever for subterfuge and he was never afraid of being frank. 'You want to know?'

'It is the prophecy?'

'In a way.' Jett avoided his searching stare that always felt as if it bored into his soul. Of course, he didn't have to say a word aloud, he only need let his thoughts rest on the surface of his mind and Keanan would hear them if he chose to.

Keanan went on, 'Indeed, the prophecy is far from inspiring.'

You know about it? His thoughts rippled with fear, enough to catch Keanan's attention.

Keanan stated without surprise, 'In a way.'

It was a precarious matter to discuss with Keanan. He was not enthusiastic about leaving Tellávare, nor did he share Jett's views on the strict rules they had to abide. Keanan glorified the Fáerinn's doctrines and was always praising their merits. If Keanan knew of the prophecy, the Eldery may have tried to persuade him to stay, thereby splitting the group. It would be disastrous. 'And you?' Jett swirled his ale, transfixed by it sloshing around the side.

'This is not how I wanted to leave.' *If you didn't get into trouble so readily, we would be treated with more grace.*

Keanan's frustration burned into Jett's thoughts, and went further back than he cared to search for and there was more. Keanan already knew of the Eldery's opinion of the prophecy. Maybe he had his own secrets. Jett said, 'Are *you* afraid of the prophecy?'

'You think *I* would prevent us from leaving because of the underlining interpretation of chaos?' Shock was in his voice.

A few years ago Jett would have thought so. Now he was not certain. 'Does it really sound like that?'

'Despite what you may think of my character, the truth is, I have gained all the knowledge I can from Tellávare. Now I crave wisdom beyond what the teachers here can give me. Even with these dark words, I must go forward.'

Jett understood this desire. He also needed something Tellávare couldn't give him; answers; to the fall of his family, but also a destination that was his alone. He wasn't sure where it was in New Earth either, but he was driven to search for it, despite his imposed boundaries.

'Prophecies are never clearly defined, however those in authority must act cautiously and examine the words on a magnified scale. In this case the words are not especially encouraging. In fact, they are quite mysterious on the whole,' Keanan went on after his prolonged thoughtful silence. 'I am far wiser than you give me credit for.'

It was his shrewd insight Jett was worried about. He attempted to let his breath out slowly. 'You won't tell the others.' *About the Circle's opinion.*

Keanan shook his head. 'I suspect it is your own shame that asks that.'

'I don't want them to share in it.' He lowered his voice.

'As usual, I am the bearer of bad news. It is too late to worry about that. We are fated to it and always have been.' Keanan's blunt reply was customary.

'Hell, you know how to ease my heart.'

'You realize that once we leave they will be the only ones who do not know.'

The rumors would circulate around Tellávare fast enough, Jett was aware of that. 'You won't tell them?'

'They will be livid.'

'At me.'

'Sacred Kahm! You just want to leave and damn everyone else! And what about Seth?'

'What about me?' A garish combination of emerald and purple swallowed Jett's vision. A young man, his wild blond hair caught up at the back of his head, fell into the chair by Jett.

Jett glanced at Seth's blissful face and eyes, currently green, and for the first time examined his extravagant suit closely. Underneath his green and purple coat, he wore a sky-blue shirt, hastily tucked in. The abnormal choice of colours did nothing to enhance the mix of browns in his rough woolen trousers. On Seth, it was not an unusual sight and remarking adversely on it was a waste of breath, besides, Jett was more than accustomed to seeing him in strange finery, he expected it.

Keanan replied, 'You are fresh out of school.'

Seth completed his schooling a couple of months ago yet he was still to learn the complexities of his Naturist Gift. Jett avoided Seth's probing thoughts and tried his best not to think about his own less than considerate desires. Drinking from his tankard, Jett stared at Seth's purple lapel and wondered how he made it so vivid.

Seth glanced at their blank expressions before a deep frown formed. 'You're worried I'm too young to go on this journey?'

Jett said, 'I didn't say that.'

From behind, Marcus slapped Seth's back. 'If there's danger, I'll be there, Sprout.'

'Danger? I highly doubt there will be,' Keanan said, and with an arrogant smile to Marcus, he added, 'No matter how much you wish for it.'

'Heavens, there better not be,' said a petite girl, dressed in a white gown under a matching kirtle, her curving hips accentuated with a silver ringed belt.

Jett looked up at Earona. Small white flowers held her flowing black hair from her face, and tedious blue embroidery across her neckline highlighted her brilliant blue-violet eyes. She was attractive this evening, but there was no way he was going to tell her. 'The only danger will be Marcus and Ethan starting a brawl in some wayside inn.'

Earona said, 'I agree with Jett.'

'Always a first time...' Jett muttered behind his tankard.

Marcus joined them, his warm eyes glowing with cheer. 'One day you'll have to admit that's what this Kin is about.' He teased, 'We boys know how to fight. That's what we do.'

Keanan said, 'There are more constructive and worthy pursuits other than those where you think force is required.'

Jett threw Keanan an irritated frown. Keanan had more destructive power in his hands than all of them. 'I'm sure we will be quite safe under the watchful eye of another Kin.'

'That is comforting.' Despite her slight stature, Earona stood proudly, overseeing the table. 'But it's quite unusual, and all the way to Hakan-Kara? It's so far.' She sniffed. 'And hot.'

'They probably picked it to irritate you,' said Jett.

Earona's dazzling eyes pierced his extremely dark ones. 'The Circle do not *pick* destinies. They are God ordained. Although this has been the most peculiar Sh'har I've ever heard of.'

'Because we are peculiar?' said Seth.

Earona continued, 'I sense there's something going on. I'm disappointed I did not receive a blessing from Elder Nissa and I know Keanan is too and even Seth has expressed sadness.' Her eyes narrowed at Jett. 'Have you got something to do with this?'

Seth ducked his eyes at the honest statement, and Keanan nodded.

Jett's face heated and his anger hid his guilt. 'Why are you so concerned? You don't want to stay, do you? I hope you won't be complaining for the whole time.'

Marcus looked at Earona with teasing wit. 'I'll Bless you, Earona.'

You can dream! Her cheeks turned pink and she scowled at him, yet ended with her pointed finger stabbing the air at Jett in warning. 'Things won't be so easy on the road like they are here. The words of the Circle could be invaluable to us.'

Jett returned her glare. 'We don't need their blessing or their words.'

Keanan stood from the table and placed a gentle hand on Earona's wrist to stop the tirade about to spew forth. 'Let us use this time well. Shall we dance?' His offer was received with pursed lips, but she stepped away from the table without a word.

Jett's chest remained tense and his anger would not go away. Not even members of the Circle could goad him as well as Earona.

Shiarn, a striking redhead, came to stand behind Seth and with her, wafted a fragrant musk scent. Resting her hands on his shoulders, her numerous gold bangles clanged together and she bent forward, exposing her cleavage above her green velvet bodice. 'Are my boys having a good time?' She breathed out with a natural seduction. It was obvious she had been enjoying a drink or three.

Jett gave a sharp wink at Marcus and Seth. 'So far.'

Marcus grinned and lifted his tankard. 'You look as if you're having a splendid time.'

Her thin eyebrows lifted at his mischievous smile. 'I have to make the most of this, who knows when we'll be here again. In any case, you don't look happy, you look bored.'

Seth swiveled to observe Shiarn and a piece of jewelry hitting him lightly on the back of his head. 'The prized treasure from your secret adventure.'

In the smoky light, she lifted the gold medallion, shaped like a white eye and viewed it with satisfaction. 'I've become quite attached to it.' She made a sweet smile.

Seth admired it. 'It's quite magnificent.'

Despite the diffused light, its shimmering brightness was captivating. Jett said, 'It truly is an unusual stone.' Every detail was embedded in his mind as if the thing forced itself into his memory forever. 'I suppose it's some type of white opal.' He wondered if it was wise for Shiarn to wear it, but like Marcus, it didn't seem to affect her at all.

'You, my dear,' her voice flowed like warm honey, 'can examine it later.' She winked and a charming smile followed. 'If you like.'

Jett didn't want to go anywhere near the thing.

Seth put his hand over hers and met her lively eyes. 'Are you up for a song or two?'

Her fingers ran across his gathered hair and lowering her head, she kissed his soft cheek. 'Anything for you, my sweet.' An attractive dark haired man grabbed her from behind. She twirled sharply, tittering, 'Raius.'

The man's hands remained on her waist. 'How 'bout a last jig?' Shiarn and her beau were swept up by the congestion of people.

Marcus watched the dance floor. 'Does she actually like being with that brown-noser?'

'I hope she does.' Jett also watched the man touch her with too much familiarity.

Seth slowly raised himself. 'I'm off to mingle.'

Jett watched Ethan and a couple of pretty girls at another table. Amid unruly giggling, the girls ran their hands over the back of Ethan's shoulders and through his tussled hair, before grabbing his hand and pulling him away.

'Good on him.' Marcus downed the last of his tankard. 'Where's Hellier?'

'With her brothers,' Jett said. Hellier had finally started talking to him again, but he guessed that was because of her excitement at leaving Tellávare. A girl with blond hair in numerous braids trailing down her back, chatted with two males, the splitting image of her. Unlike a woman's usual attire, Hellier wore hide trousers and a man's linen shirt under a leather jerkin. Her clear blue eyes, in an attractive tanned face, darted with awe between the two men. Jett said, 'She doesn't want to waste time with us on her last night.'

'Have we got a mission?' Marcus blurted.

Unprepared for the question, a blunt *No,* popped into Jett's thoughts without any control.

'And we're not going to have one?'

Jett sighed. *No mission, no purpose.* Only a future lived out under the command of another Kin. It was not a topic he wished to dwell on and he didn't have the heart to speak on it with Marcus. They would be cornered just like they were in Tellávare only on a smaller scale. Marcus knew better than to probe where he would get no satisfaction and only aggravation. Jett was thankful he left the subject.

Marcus admired the sword on the table without out touching. 'Yours?'

Jett nodded with an escaped smile. Ever since Marcus had claimed the sword from the treasure vault, Jett was envious. Now he had his own malreus sword to play with. Marcus unsheathed it and examined the workmanship. He swung it swiftly in a circle, much to the horror of Rusco, watching from the counter. Marcus just as quickly sheathed it with a warning scowl from the barkeep.

Jett said, 'It's a nice going away gift. Now we just have to go away.'

4 - New Empire

Our character determines the direction of our lives.
Happiness or sorrow, satisfaction or grievance, according to the outflow of our disposition
Whether we succeed or fail depends on the strength of our will.

Olvarus Claw'Blade, Reader's Wisdom

Jett and his Kin traveled three days through the wastelands of the Rim, the majority of that they skirted the Allervium Mountains, bordering the north of New Empire. The Rim, an uncharted mass of uninhabitable land, encompassed rocky scarps and drab shrubbery. Sandy piles of limestone and subtle tracks through broken blocks bore witness to by-gone civilizations. The crumbling hills were hazardous, made more so by winter ice turning the ground to a clumping mud. Despite the lack of human citizens the land was well populated with nocturnal beasts. The moon brought them howling over the vegetation in search of prey. Frost covered the ground during the night, and during the day a biting wind did not cease. Adding to the Kin's burgeoning difficulties, they suffered drizzling showers.

The westernmost point of the ranges offered the only accessible path through the Allervium. Although it made the journey longer it assured them of a reliable passage across the mountains. Higher up, the peaks were still dense with winter frost, but on the lower pass the snow had begun to thaw. It made pulling a wagon a slippery venture and precarious. Despite the difficulties, the Kin were more than grateful for its usefulness.

Jett rode his black horse, Thunder, alongside the wagon. Years earlier, and after much saving of gold he bought his horse. With the assistance of a Communicator, Jett chose and named Thunder from all the horses brought from the northern countries that day. More to the point, Thunder choose him. The Communicator also pointed out a smaller black, was Thunder's off-spring, and Lightning became Marcus' horse.

They came out from the hidden bend in the mountain pass and stopped to admire their first sight of the northernmost corner of Ryne, the largest of the Kingdoms of New Empire. The Allervium reached into the distant east on their left and in the west the mountains condensed into rocky outcrops. Down below and surrounding the valley road was a dark olive carpet, the expanse of the Arnin Forest. The sun broke the darkened grey in places, leaving a trail of glistening light across the rolling greenery. A welcomed sight. At least the weather would warm up as they moved south. Nearer to them it was not so cheery. Rain headed their way and to announce its arrival a blistering wind cut through their cloaks.

From inside the wagon, Seth, Shiarn, and Earona, peeked out past Ethan, guiding the horses.

Jett looked downwards, hiding his face from the wind, 'Lanvin.' Towards the south and joining with the faintly visible Old Road, a large stretch of buildings formed a brown patch against the green. To the right, were tiny flat squares of tawny yellow. 'Where we shall spend the night.' He stayed his horse while the wagon trundled by. Lifting his gaze, he stared west, into what he could see of the rocky highlands through the watery mist, and far beyond them, Skarhane, the lands of the Skar.

Keanan halted as the wagon passed and called back to Jett, 'We must get out from under this weather.' They made their descent into the foothills of the forest. As they arrived at the bottom, a cold wind struck their faces. They made swift movements, pulling their cloaks tighter around their cold bodies.

'Riding in the rain has fast worn out its appeal.' Marcus grumbled not for the first time.

Keanan's reply was just as annoyed, 'I would have thought those from the plateau would be accustomed to such miserable weather.'

'I'd prefer rogues to rain,' Marcus retorted.

Hellier stared into the shadows of the forest. 'I wonder if we shall see any of those.'

As far as Jett knew there would be nothing to upset their journey. The Circle would have taken every measure to choose the path of least potential trouble. He gave her a teasing smile. 'I hope we can get to Lakhish without incident.'

'She's already bored and itching for a fight.' Marcus gave her a broad grin. 'I know how you feel.'

Her voice rose. 'And what of this other Kin? Surely, we can look after ourselves.'

Jett remained silent; his sentiments matched hers.

Keanan answered, noting Jett's reluctance, 'We must come under the authority of an older Kin. It is the way of it.'

'And whether I like it or not,' said Jett with resignation, 'Keanan is right…'

A sweet singing voice from the wagon broke the gloomy air, and was followed by a languid tune on a flute.

'Listen to them.' Marcus laughed. 'Sound's like they're enjoying themselves.'

Ethan struggled with his cloak. No matter how much he tugged, it never seemed to cover all of him. 'And we're out here getting wet.'

Shiarn's voice increased in merriment while the flute challenged her tempo.

'What are you doing in there, drinking wine?' Ethan asked over his shoulder. 'If so, you need to pass it out here.'

Earona pushed the wagon canvas aside and sat on the bench. 'They don't need wine'. She snuggled up to Ethan and rubbed her hands together under her cloak. The trees grew close to the firmly packed road, and thick leafy branches, heavy with water, extended out towards their wagon. Not unlike the forest back home except for an assortment of unrecognizable trees.

Ethan glanced at her cheerful face and cheeks, made bright by the cold air, but through their mind-link came contrasting emotions. 'Missing home today?'

She frowned and an exasperated sigh followed. 'A little.'

'You will be fine once we are settled under the Argent Archer Kin.' Keenan rode alongside them. 'Whom I might add, have a rather prestigious estate in Lakhish. So I've been told.'

Hellier said, 'With our luck we'll be getting dirty doing their chores. Not fun,' she said, 'I'm not going to like being someone's servant girl or farm maid.'

Across the wagon horses Marcus responded with mock seriousness, 'We wouldn't like it either.'

Hellier turned a threatening stare his way. 'Laugh all you want, stable boy, but I don't want to spend my time cleaning pots. I've got things to do.'

Earona covered a giggling squeal with her hand. 'First I've heard of it.'

'Aren't we supposed to do everything together?' Ethan asked with playful surprise, 'What have we planned, Hel?'

Mystery hid behind her tight smile and her sky-blue eyes gave an excited flash. 'Nothing dull that's for certain. Some adventure, see the world, that type of thing.' She screwed up her face with abrupt horror. 'Who says we have to always be together anyway? Flamin' arse, I couldn't stand it!'

Marcus said in shocked amusement, 'You don't want to be with us for all time?'

'I'd rather die a slow death!'

A taunting sparkle in Jett's eyes was followed by a knowing grin. 'The truth is she can't live without us.'

She returned a mocking sneer, but did not rebuke his statement.

'I think you've all had enough adventure,' Earona retorted, 'Robbing the vault! I still can't believe you actually did it.' Her brows lowered with disdain at Jett.

Jett kept quiet, knowing what was coming next. He would prefer the subject be forgotten altogether.

'And without me!' Hellier glared, her eyes smoldering into flicks of orange. 'It still makes me boil. Why did I have to be left out?'

'Hel,' Marcus said, 'its best you keep out of the Master Avare's bad books. As it is—'

'It turned out to be dangerous.' Jett looked straight ahead, sensing her grueling gaze on him. With a third person it might have been fatal.

'And what was all that stuff you stole?' Earona's recriminating glance went from Jett to Ethan.

Ethan replied, 'Books, mainly.'

'A sword.' Marcus displayed a wide grin and reaching behind him he patted the black hilt of the new sword at his back. 'And that necklace and Jett found the journal.'

'That journal?' Hellier asked Jett.

'What journal?' Earona cried.

For some moments there was silence as they trotted along. Finally Jett had to reply. 'Something I was looking for.'

Earona screwed up her lips in contemplation. 'I see. Well, now you're considered thieves back home. It's most likely why our ceremony was so… underwhelming. And you found that gold pendant? It looks quite valuable.'

Jett didn't want to consider it might be significant, maybe even a sentient object. It was the last thing he needed. 'I don't want to talk about it and not out here.'

'And you've just taken it and that sword right out of the Royal vault and from home.' Earona spoke over the top of him.

He held his temper, but it was slowly building, and with gritted teeth, he replied, 'Nothing in there was important.'

'Look ahead!' called Marcus. At a distance along the fairly straight road a smudge of bright colour raced towards them.

Jett pulled his horse up abruptly. 'I don't want any more talk on it.'

'Typical!' Earona said.

Ethan pulled the horses to the side, giving the other driver the full benefit of the narrow road. Eventually a man could be seen driving a box style wagon. Not unlike their own, but instead of plain wood panels, the wagon's sides were a vibrant jumble of pinks and purples on a background of turquoise, and what could be seen of the top was a glorious yellow. Jett cringed at the unpleasant intensity of colour.

Marcus exhaled slowly. 'That's a gaudy sight if ever I've seen one.' He called, 'Sprout, stick your head out and see this.'

Seth popped his head out beside Ethan, and with a delighted grin, said, 'Fabulous piece of artwork.'

'Kahm above,' said Hellier, 'what sort of person rides in that?'

Keanan hushed them as the wagon approached. Hellier was about to have her question answered.

The man, dressed in a similar colour to the wagon, was driving at an unpredictable speed. On his approach they noticed the wagon was not simply a random mix of colours, but a skillfully drawn mural. On one side, a pink octopus was pestered by numerous fish, and the other, red sea creatures danced over coral. Enhancing it all from the top was a giant sun, its sprawling rays showering the aquatic life in a translucent radiance. Pulling the eccentric wagon were two white steeds with reins of silver. The sight of the noble beasts was strangely incompatible with the load they hauled. The man heading the van was dark skinned and wore a shimmering blue silk shirt and red pants tucked into knee high boots. A gold sash held his large belly in place and his neck held a hand-span of gold chains, and around his head a matching gold clothe was wrapped. A skinny boy peered out from behind him. He shared the same skin colouring, and his eyes, overly wide, stared at the Kin. The man shooed him back inside, and being intent on driving onward, he didn't spare the Kin a glance.

He was the first Nayinn, a non-Fáerinn, they had encountered on the road. The garishly attired man appeared as if he belonged in an opulent palace in Lakhish, not in the forest heading towards the northern reaches.

Jett rode out to the middle of the road. A groan arose from behind him, which he ignored.

The driver halted his wagon at a dangerous slant and his horses gave an indignant stamp on the road. Jett spent years perfecting the common language of New Empire, as well as the northern language of Varais. Like all Fáerinn he had an aptitude for languages, and along with a desire to live outside Tellávare, he reached high levels of expertise. In the tongue of New Empire, Jett said, 'Good day to you, fellow traveler.'

The man's small brown eyes squinted at Jett, and they were not conducive to a kind greeting. 'And to you.'

'Any news of the road ahead?'

The traveler settled back into his seat, the casual question appearing to ease him. 'If you insist, then I will advise you not to take this road to Lanvin.' His voice had a remnant of a deep accent and the blend of sounds was most likely infused with several dialects. 'It has been struck with disease and is not long for this world.'

Jett stared at him agape. 'You were going to ride on without a word of it?'

The man shrugged his indifference. 'None of my concern. I have no time to waste and left as quickly as I could. If you must know, you should pass it by.' Clutching the reins, the man called to his horses to start.

From the safety of the wagon seat, Earona called, 'Aren't you worried?'

He turned to her with a scathing glare. 'My matters lie elsewhere. Now, I go. Farewell.' He steered his horses away from Jett and started his team off. They started their fast pace on the road leading through the mountain.

Keanan, trotting his horse to the center of the road, watched the peculiar stranger race off. 'What an unusual man.' The Kin, bored watching the wagon ride away, started off again.

'I hope Nayinn are not all like him,' said Marcus. 'I wonder where he's going in such a hurry. There's nothing out there.'

'Devil's arse,' grumbled Hellier, 'there goes the thought of having a dry bed.'

'What are you so worried about him for?' cried Earona, 'Didn't you hear what he said? Lanvin has a plague. People are dying.'

Keanan rode his horse around to face her. 'It seems we can't visit the town as we had planned. If anything, we might carry it with us.'

Suddenly aware of her thoughts on the matter, Jett warned, 'Hold on, Earona!'

She jumped down from the wagon and landed unsteadily. Folding her arms in a huff, a burning pain was conveyed through her thoughts. 'Are you forgetting that I'm a Healer?'

His own temper rising, Jett glowered at the petite girl standing by his horse, piercing his stare with smoldering violet eyes, demanding his attention. 'There's no need to make us boil in your fervour. We shall make camp and discuss your cares.'

A wide grin emerged on her face. *You know I won't be happy with just talking…*

5 - A Dying Town

Do not withhold good from those who need it,
When it is in your power to act.

Servatus Gold'Wind, Age of the First Born

'Looking is not going to hurt.' Earona stood, hands on hips, her voice shattering the tranquil clearing.

'I know you,' snapped Jett, 'you always have to have your say.' They stopped on the outskirts of Lanvin, at an orchard beside the road. On investigating the farmhouse, it appeared to be empty of people. They decided it best to move away from the cottage and make their camp under the trees on the further side. Since then, Jett had debated with Earona whether to go into the town.

Earona tossed her curvy black hair over her shoulder. 'Surely you don't expect to ride on and do nothing?'

Annoyed at her haughtiness, he growled, 'If we have to we shall.'

Her mouth dropped into a well-practiced pout. 'In that case I shall go by myself.' Her upraised face taunted him. '*I* am not afraid.' She turned on her heel.

The Kin, erecting the pavilion behind them, shared amused grins at her posturing.

Jett stepped after her. 'You will do no such thing.' His hand circled her upper arm in a powerful grip and he spun her to face him. 'What do you think the Eldery would say if they knew you went off half-cocked into a plague infested village?'

She staggered in the soggy earth, and attempted to unlatch his hand. Narrowing her eyes, she huffed in defiance. 'That's poor coming from you!'

'What's that supposed to mean?' He shook her arm.

'You *know*.' She unclamped his fingers. *You don't care about their opinion, but you expect me to?*

His eyes flashed with anger at her blunt overconfidence. *That may be so,* 'but I'll be the one in trouble.'

'So damn arrogant! You're only worried about yourself, and not those Nayinn.'

'Don't be a self-righteous bi—' his eyes darkened. He would only be apologizing later '—bother.'

Her eyes made a blue squinting line, and her lips scrunched together in simmering wrath, daring him to speak.

He continued, the anger not abating from his tone, 'That's how it always is.' *And you're right. I don't give a flamin' shite about them, or the Nayinn.*

Her face reddened and she shouted with indignation, 'I don't believe it! And don't be such an arse! You do it on purpose.'

'No, *you* push me to the edge.' *And it is true, you and everyone here are more important than Nayinn.* His fists retreated to his side, 'But,' he let loose a resigned sigh, 'if it means that much to you.'

'It does.' She turned with her face lifting in victory. 'Besides, the Circle don't need to ever know, I can pretend to heal with my herbal salves.'

He shook his head, his anger lingering beneath his decision. 'That doesn't give me any comfort.' *They'll be looking for anything they can use against me.*

'And whose fault is that?'

Her words cut through his dignity, and clenching his teeth, his hands tensed and he wished he could smash them into something, anything that might alleviate the frustration. He rumbled under his breath, 'You're a pain in the arse.' He could not see her smug smile, but knew it was there. 'We need to be careful, and look first.' His words went unheeded, as he knew they would be.

Over her shoulder, she called, 'Hurry up.'

Jett followed after, and with a hurried call to Marcus to accompany them, the three set off to town.

The road took them past more fruit trees and minor fields. Sheep grazed in the distance, and as they neared a cottage, chickens squawked. The streets of Lanvin peeked out between stocky cottages, decorated with carvings and bright window frames. In the roadway a cow rummaged through a cart of abandoned cabbages. Wind suddenly swooped against Jett's face and whistled through the planking of a nearby house.

Earona dashed forward, spreading her arms wide. 'Where are the people?'

Marcus knocked on a door. It jutted open. He shrugged and entered.

Jett waited, listening to his querying calls of hello and his noisy footsteps on the stairs within. His steps were less hurried on his descent and he appeared at the doorway. 'No one home,' seriousness crossed his face, '...anymore.'

Earona stared at his back. 'There's a dead man, isn't there?'

'Yes.'

'Are you certain?' She shuffled closer to the door.

He cried with irritation, 'Course I'm flamin' certain.'

'You're not going in there.' Jett stepped in front of her, preventing her from running inside.

She fidgeted with the edge of her cloak. 'Should we bury him?'

There's a child... Marcus thought.

'A child!' She covered her mouth.

Jett shook his head. 'We are not burying people—'

'We could be burying the whole town.' Marcus kept walking and Jett followed.

After a moment of staring at the open door, Earona came behind with reluctance.

Overgrown weeds had taken over what was probably a lovely park near the center of town. Several fruitless quince trees bordered the space, and a few sheep tended the long lawn. A figure shifted behind the trees, moving too fast to be distinguished.

'That wasn't a sheep,' Marcus stated.

A loud crack of a cottage door, swinging open, startled them. Marcus walked in without a care. This time, returning at a faster pace. 'No one in there dead or alive.'

'Perhaps no one is left,' said Jett.

Marcus inclined his head down the street and Jett followed his gaze. A thin boy with shoulder length hair and vacant eyes, watched from the shadows.

Earona stepped forward in a rush. 'Hello, child.' Her words tumbled out in a jumble of anxiety, 'What is your name? Are there others here?'

His hands hung motionless by his side, his mouth gaped in silence.

Jett approached him. 'Where are your people?'

The boy looked behind him and pointed. At the end of the street was a large structure partly obscured by trees. Broad steps led up to a covered terrace. The child gave them one last astonished stare and sprinted towards the building.

The three followed him to the end of the street. Carvings of mythical beasts covered the roof's front and high pillars lining the terrace. Earona halted by the abandoned carts under the trees and stared up at the closed doors of the hall.

Marcus wrenched his hood over his head at the light rain suddenly falling. 'What is it now?'

Jett said, 'Changed your mind?'

'Diseases can be trying on your senses.' Earona cleared air away from her nose. 'So I've heard.'

A faint foul odour was in the air.

Marcus remarked, 'I'll wait out here in the rain, if it's all the same to you.'

'I can't believe you're so queasy.' She ignored his grunt of denial. *If I'm going in, we all go in.* 'Besides, you are lucky I am such an organized person.' She fumbled in her bulky leather bag, containing creams and medicines, none of which she needed to heal. She pulled out a wrinkled cloth and handed it to him. 'Tie this around your neck.' She demonstrated its use, and pushed his hand down as he attempted to place it over his mouth. 'Not yet. We don't want to scare them.'

'Would they even notice?'

She searched through her bag again. 'I'm sorry, Jett. I have none for you.'

He waved her words away and gave her a dreary look. 'I'll be fine.'

Marcus lifted the cloth. The strong scent filled the immediate air about them, and his nose scrunched in response. *Smells.*

'Lavender.' She smiled and started up the steps.

Girls and their stuff, came his vexed reply.

'I am listening.' She sang without turning her head.

Jett followed behind her as she neared the top. The door swung open and a gaunt faced, middle-aged man, wearing untidy yet elegant robes, barred the entry. Beyond him drifted the stench of vomit mixed with the sweat of fevers. Jett could not determine from the man's expression whether they were welcome or an interference, indeed his face showed little emotion at all.

His grim gaze studied each of them. 'I gather you are unaware this town is devastated by disease. We cannot accommodate you. You should move on while you can.' He dismissed them by entering the building.

Jett started to turn away.

Earona pushed past him. 'No. We have come to see what help we can provide.'

'Is that so?' The man's stare became incredulous. 'We have a herbman, Cerelic, who came to us a few weeks prior to this. Sadly, he discovered nothing can be done for those dying. What help can you possibly bring?'

'Maybe I can make a difference…' said Earona.

His shoulders sagged with a heavy weight. 'I would not wish to see you lying here like these others.' He waved through the door of the foyer. 'Those of us still moving are probably infected.'

Jett inhaled deeply and regretted it instantly; the smell was repugnant. 'You're right, we should move on—'

'No.' she gave him a look of ice, and said, 'I can offer assistance.'

The man flushed and his disposition became less curt. 'If you must persist.' His sigh was melancholy. 'Maybe you will change your minds when you see the disease close up. But I shall introduce myself, I am Barrard, Mayor of this town.'

Suddenly resigned to going forward, despite his ill-feelings about the venture, Jett sighed. 'What has the lord of these lands said about this?'

'He is not present at his abode,' Barrard replied with disdain, 'Apparently he is traveling to Aquila. The servants at his fortress came to town, but have since holed themselves up at the keep and we hear nothing from them.' Inside the hall, a man's cry interrupted their conversation. After a moment, a man came out, carrying a woman's body wrapped in a blanket.

Earona stared at the lifeless body and the man coming towards her. Jett tugged her from the man's path. At the bottom of the steps, the man placed the body on the cart and pushed it out of view.

Uncomfortable witnessing the mournful act, Jett turned with reluctance to view the hall.

Barrard, his face impassive, considered the three of them. 'Besides these here, others are still in their homes.'

Earona left the men and walked into the hall. A bleak chill was in the windowless high beamed room, and a stifling smell was overbearing. Benches were stacked against the wall and numerous bedrolls were set in rows with a man or woman on top. Those tending the ill did not look much better than their patients except they were free to move.

A lanky man, dressed in shabby brown trousers and stained shirt, rose from a patient and approached them. 'There is nothing that can be done for these people.' He spoke through a stringy beard and cracked lips. Without waiting for a reply, he whirled away in a huff and knelt by a feverish man, dampening his forehead with a cloth.

'That is Cerelic, our Healer.' Barrard spoke with quiet respect. 'Perhaps it distresses more those who should supposedly have cures for such things.' He shrugged. 'You are welcome here and any help you may bring.'

Earona loosened her cloak and let it rest to the side. 'I shall need water and medicinal plants.'

Barrard nodded. 'We had trouble with our well, but now draw water from the stream. The plants you request…?'

She knelt on the floor. 'Lavender.'

Cerelic lifted his head with a bemused gaze. 'Lavender. I've never heard it to be used for such things.'

Barrard's mouth curved down in puzzlement. 'I'm sure we can find that about.'

Earona smiled to herself. Aside from its pleasant aroma, it was easy to find. She mixed her powders into paste and was ready to find the sickest patients.

The boy they spied earlier squatted in the furthermost corner of the hall over a motionless woman. Earona approached in apprehension, fearful she had already passed.

'Hold on, Ma.' The boy sobbed, clutching her limp hand. 'They've come, just like I prayed.'

Earona settled by the woman, and asked the boy, 'What is your name?'

He peered through his shaggy brown fringe. 'Mal.'

From her bag, she brought out a bottle. She dribbled the ointment onto the woman's exposed chest. Placing healing hands on top, she rubbed the oiled skin.

He gave a shy nod and fixed his gaze on his lifeless mother. 'Is she going to… get well?'

'She will. Tell me her name.'

'Malona.'

'Here, help me.' She placed his cold hand on Malona's, if possible, colder one. Earona didn't need the assistance of the boy nor did she need the potions. With a simple thought, her Ethos immersed her body and streamed through her hands into the woman, charging to the organs with the greatest need. The Fáerinn's Ethos is the divine life force within them, where their Gifts manifest in a powerful form. So damaged by the illness, the boy's mother would have died in a few moments of waiting. A little while would pass before Malona could move sufficiently to walk. Earona could manage no more at that point, having accomplished all she could for the woman without tiring herself too much.

Mal called his mother's name until she responded.

Earona eased to her feet and moved to another woman.

~ * ~

The stink of the room was unbearable. Marcus pulled the cloth over his nose and mouth and breathed the sickly sweet scent; it was remotely better. After a time he hoped to be accustomed to the smell of the hall. Right then he had no wish to vomit, which he thought he might do at any moment. Others were already doing that. His stomach turned upward as he moved his vision from the direct sight of an ill man. He made a resolute decision to never get sick in his life.

He crouched behind Earona, his voice muffled by the cloth. 'If there's anything I can do, just ask.'

Sighing, she rubbed ointment onto another woman. 'You could clean up all those disgusting pails.' *If you are able to stomach it.* 'And ask Jett to help.' She gave the hall a studious inspection. Rows of ill people were spread across the room, and she hadn't touched half of them. 'It's going to be a hard task *and* we might get sick.' Jett, staring with a stern expression, pierced her benevolent convictions. Turning a blank stare, she decided to ignore him.

Did you have to tell me that?! Marcus responded with a horrified expression. 'If it's so hard, let some remain ill. Doesn't matter if you lose some here or there.'

She snapped under her breath, 'How can you say that? I must heal them all.'

He jerked up. 'Don't complain then.' He spun on his heel and said over his shoulder, 'I'll go and clean up. Not much else I can do.'

Earona glided past the people, unable to decide who to touch. The hem of her blue dress fluttered over ashen faces, and feverish eyes, dry and insipid, looked up at her. She could not heal everyone at the same time, and time would not permit everyone to be saved. Some would surely be lost. Marcus would be ingenuously correct. *Curse him,* she thought glumly.

As the afternoon progressed, more patients were cured, and Marcus crouched beside her. 'You really know how to bring life back to someone.' He handed her a flask of water with a daring chuckle. 'Looks like you've been training with me.'

She couldn't imagine anything worse than combat. 'Never.' She had to admit, she felt wretched. Exhausted and wet with perspiration, her lovely silk dress was damp under her arms, and her long hair, which she neglected to tie back, was soggy around her neck. She gulped down the water he offered and glanced at the large number of people still sick. If only Bajun, the legendary healer, were here, he could probably heal them all from the center of the room with a wave of his arms. Yet even that was an exaggeration. On hindsight, she should have listened to Keanan in the first place. She scrunched up her face irritably, or even Jett. *I made the decision, now I've got to follow it through.*

'Blue, if you can heal all these people, I'll be amazed.'

He wasn't one to use her childhood nickname, in reference to her blue-violet eyes, unless he was attempting a genuine compliment. But it still irked her. She leaned close to whisper, 'It takes too long to heal one person.' *This way is so tedious.*

'Maybe Jett knew what he was talking about.'

Too tired to dispute his remark, she passed to the next patient. The rest of the day, she spent kneeling over sick bodies and infusing lavender heads and using the last of her ointment. By the end, more people came to the hall begging for her touch. A number of them had already been healed earlier. By evening she was ready to collapse from exhaustion. She would be facing another draining day, and she speculated as to what possible end it would have, if any.

6 - Night-Time Discussions

*Watch out for the demon that inhabits a man. Its foul spirit deceives and subverts the
natural order, it eats the essence of the soul and poisons the flesh.*

Harbinger of Night, Ei'myn Valavérinn-shem script

Within the pavilion, Jett sat, propped up against baggage. Next to him, Seth lay on
his mat still awake. Coals, smoldering under an iron grate, held Jett in a hypnotic thrall,
and he stared, lost in his thoughts. About them, the others slept amidst gear they
haphazardly threw in earlier. Earona was supported back to camp exhausted. It was a
laborious day for the Healer and more difficult than she anticipated.

'She will keep going?' Seth's quiet voice broke through Jett's daze.

A sharp chill swirled with the warm air and Jett pulled his cloak to cover his front.
Tired and attempting to unwind, he stirred himself to answer. 'She says so.' He nudged
the lumpy sack with his back and closed his eyes. His sigh was a guttural hum. 'I could
throw her over my shoulder and carry her off. She'd cry for weeks and hate me for years.
Besides, it's partly my own cursed fault we are here.'

Seth stretched under his blanket. 'Are they suspicious?'

After a long pause, Jett opened his eyes. 'Most of the villagers don't give a rat's arse
how she does it, but the herbman… he's studying her and her methods.' The kindling in
the shallow dug-out crumbled and he was lulled by the soothing glow. 'And she says she
must collect more plants before she can do more.'

Seth gave the embers a languid poke with a charred stick.

'As you know, some villagers are sick again. This, so she tells me, shouldn't happen.'
Jett's gaping yawn revealed his fatigue. His customary misgivings over his ability to lead
the Kin, battled with his conscience. He had gone over it throughout the day and the
thoughts were old, but still potent.

There's something more here than just an illness…

Picking up on the uncertainty in Seth's thoughts, Jett ordered, 'Tell me.'

Seth studied the blackened iron over the coals. His face reflected a red tint, and he
shifted the burning charcoal. The more he wavered, the grumpier Jett became at his
evasion. He dared a peek at Jett. 'Have you considered it might be coming from an
unnatural source?'

Jett narrowed his eyes and sat up, his back as stiff as a board. 'Is that possible?'

'I've been pondering a presence I've heard the trees speak of...' Seth rested on his elbow and his stick wielding hand waved in a circle, indicating the woods outside. 'Something is polluting the woods. I've wondered if it could be related to this.'

Exasperation made Jett's words bristle. 'What are you saying, some type of..... tainted... substance?' Mentally exhausted, his mind was left open, *why the devil did I even stop at this cursed place?* 'I can't believe I'm fool enough to have led you all into this disease ridden town, and possibly something worse.' *And Earona is working her guts out trying to heal these godforsaken people, and you tell me this, now. I'll be paying the cost if anything happens to even one of you...* 'Why couldn't you have told me earlier?'

'I wasn't sure it was anything.' Seth rolled onto his blanket and covered his body. 'It's probably nothing to worry over.'

'Not even two weeks from home and this,' he growled. 'Tomorrow we find out what it is. Maybe it will explain this plague.' He stretched himself out on his mattress. Anger quickly sent him into a foul mood and it was best to shut everything out. He decided to apologize to Seth in the morning, if he remembered.

~ * ~

The wind gushed against the darkened treetops, yet below, the leaves rested in the quiet moon filled night. The man, struggling past tree branches and scratching shrubs, was annoyed. If he had his way he would have stayed in the comfort of his cottage. As it was, he did not have a choice. The man who requested the midnight meeting was a villager previously known as Walston. Although Walston no longer went by that name anymore, referring to himself as Rafah instead. Walston, or Rafah, or whoever the man was now, had observed him sneaking in the woods the previous day, carrying a dead body. No way out of it, he had to negotiate a beneficial deal with Rafah and discover what else the man knew of his actions.

A light stroke dragged along his neck. He tripped and fell forward. After righting himself, he dashed under branches, while groping at his neck, making certain nothing was there. He yanked his hood over for protection and walked as fast as he could, cowering under the trees cloaked in the night. His eyes darted in calculated panic, watching for a thousand eyes he imagined were there. Guided by the dazzling moon and the pale glow from the white bark of the winter-wood tree, he eventually broke through into a space, dominated by hefty rocks and a dead tree. He spotted the silhouette of an overweight figure slouching by a stone.

Rafah, his smooth head gleaming, growled a greeting. 'Finally. I thought I might need to be more forceful.'

'If you chose a more suitable meeting place I might have been quicker.'

Only a week ago Rafah was a reclusive farmer. 'This place is perfect.' His distorted sneer showed his rotten teeth. In no way was he that simple man any longer. 'My faceless ones can watch you better.'

The newcomer cast a deliberate eye about the woods. After a prolonged moment of staring, he saw a shadow pressed against the white of a tree. As he watched, it shifted.

His eyes bulged at the fearful sight. Now there were more creatures he had to watch out for. 'Who are you? And what do you want?'

Rafah's menacing grin was a glint in the shadows. 'We have discussed who I am, but not what I want and that is a good place to start. Don't think about running, Cerelic.' He scowled and stepped closer. 'I'll be honest, I like what you did to this village.'

Cerelic responded with a frown of denial, but a smug smile surfaced. He was, after all, meeting with an aberrant character in the dead of night; it shouldn't be a surprise he knew of his secrets.

'I like the evil pest you summoned and how it has procreated already, ingenious *but…*' Rafah's voice changed and a cutting spite emerged. '…you have chosen the wrong village.'

'Why should a man like you care?'

'I don't care about them.' His spittle flew onto Cerelic's beard. 'But I am concerned about one particular soul.' He held up a plump finger in front of Cerelic's eyes. 'As far as you are concerned, you should be too.' His finger turned on Cerelic in a pointed stab.

A familiar foreboding churned in the pit of Cerelic's stomach. 'Who?'

Rafah's anger increased. 'A girl. My Master's servant is coming for her. If he finds her dead, he won't be pleased.'

Cerelic's pasty face drooped and he racked his mind, picturing the girls he had encountered. Several had already died.

'I'm trying to scout her out. It seems she has disappeared, but she hasn't passed over. She might be ill.'

'Maybe the healer will save her.' Cerelic's voice lightened with hope.

Rafah grunted at the mention of the healer. 'She's no normal healer.' The overweight man sprang at Cerelic and grabbed him around the throat. 'Redeem yourself by finding this girl-child and healing her before those people get to her, and before she dies.' Again, saliva went flying, this time landing on Cerelic's cheek.

Cerelic wiped the drops of spit, caring less for his neck than the gelling moisture.

'You must have an antidote for yourself. Use it on her. You can tell me where she is when you find her.' With one hand Rafah shook him. 'If she dies, my Master might have use of your services in compensation.'

'Yo…your…' Cerelic gulped and gasped for air, 'mas…ter?'

The man's chubby face conveyed a wicked smirk. 'If you are obedient, the Master may keep you on forever. If he is feeling kind, he might kill you quickly.' He chortled and threw Cerelic down to the wet earth.

Cerelic scrambled to his feet and rubbed his neck. He knew where he stood for the time being, at least until he could figure out how to get himself out of the mess he was in.

'Remember my faceless ones are watching, so you better not go squealing to anyone and you better hope she is not dead.' Rafah waddled into the night, leaving Cerelic to stumble from the clearing.

How was Cerelic to know his summoning spell would incur such a drama and maybe at the cost of his own life? It was a complicated spell to cast, taking days and rare ingredients, and he still had to hike through the forest in search of the creatures, bottling up the poison; always anticipating a bite on the neck. At first there was only one and almost overnight more of the evil beings appeared, and he had no control of them, which was a pity. Now the whole fearful enterprise would be for naught.

He faltered through the shadows, his frustration building by the moment. Cerelic knew something was wrong about the healer, all those ridiculous plants and the speed which she healed the villagers. It was unnatural. Even without Rafah's demands, his plans would have been foiled by the interfering woman. He had to leave soon; the villagers would discover their missing valuables and sooner or later the entities in the forest would spread. He looked around at the night forest, seeing none of Rafah's faceless ones. But he knew they were there. He could feel their beastly eyes, watching. Fear chased him and he quickened his pace, not knowing what to be more afraid of, Rafah's creatures or his own.

On the journey home, he ran through his options. He wondered if he could tell the outsiders about Rafah. Maybe they could protect him. They might even pay highly for his knowledge. But what if they discovered how he involved himself in the first place? And what people could possibly protect themselves from Rafah and the depressing darkness surrounding him. Evil had unlimited power, that was a well-known fact.

There was always the girl child Rafah spoke of. Perhaps he could discover why he wanted her so terribly. Information, after all, was power, and second to riches, was what he craved. Rafah was correct about the antidote, he did have a vial, but he had no wish to waste it on some girl.

Last option, running away. He realized it wasn't an option, but the finale to the debacle he had caused by his supernatural interference. Leaving the town would need to happen and soon.

~ * ~

The girl fought against an encumbering sleep to open her eyes. The luminous full moon swamped her vision and made her eyes hurt with its brightness. She lay in a sleepy confusion, attempting to understand why she was outside in the forest that was unnaturally silent. The stink of incense smothered her breathing, and cool dewy air aroused her naked skin. She tried to cover her nakedness, but discovered her arms were restrained. Her legs were also bound. She pulled and writhed under the rope. It only chaffed her skin and made her more irate.

Someone chanting registered in her hearing. That could only mean some sort of Ward was set up, and she was in it. Three hooded figures stood around her, and an altar with candles and other ritual objects was nearby. Under the trees, she spied a cow, and she scowled with annoyance.

One of the hooded figures wore a carved mask of a cat's face. The other, the one chanting, wore a face of an owl. The third person wore no mask, and her eyes glimmered in a pale wrinkled face within the hood's shade.

Rage burned inside the girl at her predicament. When her mother sent her to the pitiful back-water village, she never mentioned this level of ritual taking place. 'What are you bitches doing?'

'Quiet, child!' The woman's voice was elderly and harsh.

The girl cried, 'Wendessa?! Why the hell are you performing a ritual on me?' This was the one appointed by her mother back in Aquila, to take charge of her. Someone she should be able to trust.

'It is necessary.'

They could try all they want, the girl wasn't completely powerless. '—' her own incantation fell dead on her tongue. With alarm, she spat out, 'you put a seal on my mouth?!'

'You are surprised?' The old woman nodded towards the cat-face witch. 'Let the Infilling begin.'

'Does my mother know of this?' The girl was no stranger to blood rituals. She had witnessed enough of them in her short life, even partaking, but for this she was not prepared.

While the Owl-face witch continued her somber indistinguishable chant, she brushed damp ash over the girl's arms and legs and across her body. The Cat-witch heated a bone needle over a candle. The altar was laid with an open book and an onyx dish, and a collection of bottles of mystical ingredients. A satchel lay open revealing black and bone blades and needles, and other painful looking instruments.

Wendessa's tone was menacing for an old woman. 'She will not know.'

The Cat-witch approached with the twig-shaped bone blade.

The girl yelled, 'Who are these low-life witches who dare do this to me? I want to know who they are!'

Wendessa ignored her and stared at the super moon. 'We call on the Spirit Messengers, Azamor, Belmoth, Spirits of Rebellion and Allurement. The Vessel is that which was created in Darkness. The child is that which was suckled by the foster-mother of the Underworld. In the tomb where the unliving dwell. The tarnished that which abides in ruin. The treachery that lies with sight-less eyes. Is now offered to the Ones fated to the authority of all decisions. Change what is into what will be into what was.'

At the last word, the Cat-witch slit the flesh of the girl's chest with the fine hot tip of the needle-blade.

The sudden pain caused the girl to shriek, but the words of the unknown incantation frightened her more. 'I'm going to kill you! All of you!' She tried to leverage her body off the table, but her arms were held firm. 'You're all going to suffer pain and wrath for this.'

The blade was dragged through her flesh. Blood streamed between her breasts and down around her raised stomach.

'Think of the life within you and look into the moon.' The cat-witch continued carving her skin.

'No! I'm going to kill you! All of you.' She cried with pain at the tip tearing through her flesh. 'As soon as I get out of here.' Her howls escalated into curses for the three, and despite her words, the glowing moon transcended the sight of the witches. 'You'll be sorry you ever touched me.'

'That which is bound by the death of curse – we capture moon light, we capture free blood, we capture earth dawn.' Wendessa cut her own palm and placed it over the bloody circle on the girl's chest, letting her own blood mingle with the girl's.

The woman with the cat mask spoke, and her voice sounded as old as Wendessa's. 'Work swiftly, the Ward of Silence is—'

'I know, she is strong.' Wendessa turned to work at the altar. She came back holding a vial gleaming with silvery light.

The girl wiggled and struggled in vain. Her voice trembled with foreboding. 'What is that?' The pure light seemed to burn her vision.

Cat-witch replied, 'It's for your own good.'

'Leave me alone.' She pulled against the ties. 'I don't want it.'

'Stop this imbecilic tantrum!' Wendessa held the girl's throat, restraining her, and muttered, 'you only make it more difficult for yourself.'

'What…' the girl wheezed, 'is this scar-mark for?'

An enigmatic smile appeared on her gaunt mouth. 'You will find out.'

'Perhaps it's best to think of it, as protection for that life inside you,' the cat witch said.

'Why should I care about something so insignificant?!'

Wendessa poured the contents of the bottle over the blood drenched scar-mark. 'Now rebuke curses, now estrange darkness. Ydob eht nopu ezies tsohg. Nam eht hteduorhsne kaolc a ekil nomed live. Tieced si eugnot esohw tpurroc si ydob esohw eslaf si ecaf esohw nam live.' Shimmering white trickled out of the glass along with the deep red of Wendessa's blood. 'Reviver of purity, Guardian of graves, Destroyer of temples – here chain, Starlight Seeing Water, Queen of Night, Ash of Ivory, Pearl of Midnight Summer, Solstice Moonlit Rain. Be now imprisoned by silver radiance of Nevereve, and confined at moon's tide end to never lessen in strength despite fate or evil might.'

The girl sensed all her energy drain away and her body became a dead weight. She stared at the moon and it came alive with dancing and shifting forms all clothed in dazzling white.

'By the Heavens, by the earth, by secret realms, by the Underworld, by living and by the dead, and by those not known. It is to be.'

An unfamiliar and peculiar feeling settled within. She had never felt this way in her life, and she questioned what strange magik they had performed on her. The cow gave a last wretched bellow and the girl slipped off to sleep.

''tis a grave risk,' the Owl-face witch said, 'will she accept it?'

Wendessa began wiping down the girl. 'Her mother is powerful, but it will help that she is far from her. I can only guide her till she is stronger, but I fear…'

The witch nodded. 'To get stronger she will need an infilling over some days. This is only the start.'

The Cat-witch turned to Wendessa. 'You must leave before the dark servant comes. Then all might be for naught. And her mother will surely become aware.'

'I know this,' Wendessa grumbled. 'I will tend her while we are on the road.' Then she would have to hope that the girl would choose the path to freedom.

7 - Life Returns

Wisdom through Humility

~ MOUNT CLAN ~

Earona woke to stiff muscles and a stuffy head. Never before experiencing such aches and pains, she curled up on her blanket and groaned. Eventually she pulled herself up and poked her head through the tent flap.

'Morning,' Shiarn sang as Earona dragged her heavy feet across the grass. 'How are you feeling?' Shiarn's face and brushed hair minus any grime was neat.

Earona, fiddling with a lock of her thickening hair, admired her with envy, and she mumbled a greeting.

'Not good it seems.' Shiarn handed Earona a chunk of camp bread. 'There were eggs, but, I'm sorry… the boys ate them.'

Earona was starving and she would take whatever she could get. The mention of an egg raised her morale. But, to eat them all, couldn't they have saved her one? 'What a selfish lot.' Shiarn's full lips, smiling in a condescending manner, aggravated Earona and she turned from her to view the camp.

Past the fruit trees towards the track leading to town, a small group of townsfolk convened. They waved at her while giving furtive glances around the clearing. Creasing her brow, she stared at them in a daze. Sitting on the cut log, she gobbled the bread down, surprisingly tasty that morning, but she was hungry.

As the food filled her body, she went over the work she faced that day. It was best to head into town as soon as possible, yet it was so hard to move. Shiarn joined her on the log. Together they watched Marcus through the gap of lemon trees. He stood alert, propelling his muscular arms in a swift circle. Usually Earona teased him over his obsessive need to exercise, but her heavy thoughts occupied her.

Shiarn opened a cloth wrapped parcel to let Earona inspect its contents. A collection of plant stems were in an organized pile. 'Seth picked them this morning. He also mixed paste and the bowls are in town.'

Aromatic scents filled Earona's nostrils and she breathed in the invigorating smells. She handled the cloth and her eyes scanned the collection. Feverfew stems, foxglove leaves, even goat's rue, and none of them flowering, but this would hardly be a concern.

'This morning…' It would have taken him a good deal of time to gather so many. 'What time is it now?'

Shiarn looked skyward, 'Nearly noon.'

'Heaven's Peace!' She spluttered. 'I've slept too long.'

Shiarn moved back to the fire and shifted patties on the griddle. 'You needed it, deary'

Through the trees, Keanan came towards them. He glanced at the townsfolk and waved, and he handed Earona a small apple, accompanied with a cheery greeting.

The apple was a welcomed delight after making short work of the bread. This time she chewed at her leisure, conserving her energy. '…I must be off.'

Keanan looked at the patient villagers. 'They are back I see. They have been waiting for you.'

'You should have woken me.'

He took a seat beside her. 'Jett said we were not to. You were too tired.' He studied her deep set eyes and the darkness underneath. 'And still are, I gather.'

She recognized the waiting people. They must have friends and family in need.

'They were here at dawn. Perhaps earlier.' He watched them pace restlessly. 'Jett shooed them away—'

'He didn't!?' she cried, her mouth bulging with apple chunks. *His heartless attitude is appalling.*

'He wanted you to rest as long as you needed to. He told them not to bother you until you were ready.'

'Codswallop!' She chewed and did not mind speaking as well. 'He's just… trying… to get at me…'

Keanan rolled his eyes. 'We shall go shortly but, I would like to know how you are?'

She would have lied yet it would achieve nothing. 'I'm good enough.' Her fingertips touched her throbbing head. 'Feel's like I've been running for miles without a rest.'

'Do you realize how long it could take you to recover?'

Earona sighed and slumped on the log. *I could be killing myself.*

'Possibly,' he replied to her thoughts. 'Do you have any idea how they are falling ill?'

'You sound surprised I don't know.'

'What have they been teaching you all these past years?'

'Mind your tongue!' she retorted.

'In any case, and regardless of your methods, we shall surely leave rumours behind us. We will have to hope they don't reach home.'

'Right now, I'm not worried about them back home or even what the people here think. More may have fallen ill or worse, died.' She stood and took a shaky step. Dizziness swept over her, and Keanan offered his forearm in support, saving her from falling into the mud.

He gripped her arm and sat her down again. From inside his cloak, he pulled out a silver flask. 'Before we go anywhere, I want you to take a sip of this.'

Earona recognised the worn flask with its fine scratches over the polished surface. The flask, a family treasure passed down through the eldest of the Mount Clan, had seen many generations and was precious to him. The content of the flask was also of priceless value.

'It will give you a surge, so to speak.'

She gingerly took the heirloom from his hand. 'Your quartza.' A secret concoction formulated by the alchemists of Tellávare and an expensive brew only afforded by those with monetary prestige. The ingredients were unknown, and rumours had it, there was something to do with melting diamonds and a purification process taking several years.

'You only need a sip and you will have strength to start your day and continue it.'

'I should not be drinking this.' Despite her reluctance, she took it. Her finger pressed on the engraved owl while she read the flowing script etched above it.

Keanan had only drunk from it twice and even that sparingly, and he looked unconcerned. 'It was given to me for such a purpose as this.'

Realizing he was not going to accept no as an answer, she took the stopper off and took an elegant sip. Silver liquid ran smoothly down her throat. The overly sweet drink warmed her like wine only it was stronger. She licked her lips, *lovely, wish I could drink the whole thing.*

'You would not be able to control the energy.'

'Will you stop doing that?' Earona pushed it into his chest and jumped off the log. 'Now, come on, I have people to heal.'

Keanan's warm eyes flashed with pleasant delight.

She abhorred physical labour, avoiding it as much as she was allowed and that was not much considering she lived on a farm. If not for her mother, who believed children should share in farm duties, she would have spent years in contented lazy bliss. As it was, the secret potion produced an excess of adrenalin, firing up her muscles and shooting through her blood stream, making it impossible to stand still. It was like nothing she had ever felt before and she bounced from one foot to the other.

Keanan called to Marcus to catch them up and they jogged to keep up with her. Behind her, Marcus laughed once Keanan told him what she drunk.

She doubled her pace and couldn't wipe the grin from her face. A girl waiting with the group, latched onto Earona's arm. Accompanying the girl was her mother and two men, and they all rushed to keep up. Earona marched down the road with focused purpose. As they walked, they conveyed who was sick and she nodded prudently. Keanan and Marcus trailed after, not able to get any closer.

At the edge of town more people waited. They tramped along with the gathering procession. A crowd assembled outside the temple, becoming excited at her appearance. Faces beamed and tears flowed down bright cheeks. Arms reached and waved; hot bodies pressed against her, preventing her from leaving their overpowering embrace. A woman cried, 'I beg you bless my child.' Her sobs wrenched at Earona's heart. A man clutched her arm, his eyes probing into hers, and he exclaimed, 'Thanks be to Manmagma. He has saved us.' A name circulated amidst their praise and the people shouted, 'Ineena'.

Blushing, Earona decided the only way through was with force. Keanan and Marcus had so far not served well as guards and they stood back, as bewildered as she.

'A goddess walks among us.' Another woman cried for permission to touch the servant of her god.

The talk of foreign gods and being likened to them was disturbing. Earona had no wish to be associated with these deities. Marcus pushed through them, creating a path to the door. Earona and Keanan walked in and he shut it with the people still declaring their adoration outside.

Inside the hall, Barrard clasped her hand and his tight grip surprised her. Energy coursed from her hand into his warm palm. His eyes lightened at the thrill of having heightened senses. 'Ineena! You have saved us. How can we repay you for what you have done?' He bent in a solemn bow.

Ethos surged through her body. Willing herself to slow and catch her breath, she pulled her hand from his grasp. 'It is payment enough to see you live.' She could not determine whether the elation came from her Ethos or from the quartza driving her to new heights of power she had never experienced.

The people clapped at the sight of her. Their loud praises added to the celebratory atmosphere. Marcus and Keanan watched in amazement at the fuss made over her. Remembering that some in the hall were still ill, Earona addressed them all. 'Thank you, but I must get back to work.' They crowded around her and she turned to Keanan and Marcus, and whispered, 'They put so much faith in my abilities when I haven't truly stopped it.'

Keanan's hand rested on her back. 'It is not whether you can heal or not that is of concern, but that you cared enough to stop and consider their plight.'

Nodding in agreement, she steeled her resolve, and knelt by a woman in the midst of a fever. She shuffled through her bag while Keanan brought her bowls of tepid water and new cloths.

Nearby, an old woman hunched against the wall. Neck bent forward, her cloak shaded her face. Her knotted knuckles held what appeared to be a chunky tree branch. A light in her eyes revealed she watched Earona work.

Aware of her company, Earona asked, 'Have any passed?'

A hoarse voice came from within the hood. 'They wait for you.' She pointed her stick at a woman. 'She is the worst.'

Potent Ethos poured out of Earona's hands and into the dying woman without hope of restraint. Natural pallor appeared on the woman's face instantly.

The old woman watched the recovery take place before hobbling to the other side of the room. With the support of her staff, she squatted by the wall.

Marcus stood behind Earona with a cheeky grin. 'What does Ineena mean?'

His flippant question irritated her. *I've no idea.*

Keanan answered on her behalf. 'Rynian religion states Ineena was a handmaiden to Ershar, Goddess of the Stars and daughter to Manmagna. Ineena is a light from the sky. The stars are like divine beings to Rynians. It's only folklore, but they believe it here.'

Marcus looked at Earona with unguarded affection and whispered, 'A star, eh?'

Keanan cast a sideways glance at him, followed by a deepening frown, but said nothing.

~ * ~

Earona could barely control or even contain her Ethos; the quartza caused her to heal faster than she thought possible. Life was returning. Waves of joy spread through the hall as people woke from their feverish sleep. Soon enough the murmuring became talking and the people rose from their beds. Men slapped each other's backs and children ran outside to proclaim they were better.

In a far corner, Earona sat observing the scene, and wondered if they would start returning sick again. Time would eventually move on, months would pass, then years, only the graves would symbolize what happened in the town. How did they adapt to death so easily? The reality was startling; these people had no other option, no one to heal them, no one to make their bodies whole.

A shadow obstructed her view of the cheerful commotion. Suddenly separated from the noise of the room, she shivered. The old woman squatted and her brown skirts fell across Earona's feet, and using the thick branch as support, she leaned towards her.

Earona stared at the unusual staff. Exquisite carvings of miniature trees and rocks curled around the top knot of the sturdy branch. Fascinated with the art, she focused on the small forest scene and glimpsed tiny wooden gnomes peeking over rocks and hiding in the folds of the wood. Never in her life had she seen anything similar. The little men shifted their position. Their tall hats flopped and fat noses twitched. She attempted to fix her gaze on a particular one. It did nothing but frustrate her. She discovered in looking away, she could see a good deal more than when staring straight at one.

The old woman watched the interplay with exasperation, showing no regard for what Earona stared at and in fact, it appeared to be more a nuisance to her than anything interesting. She interrupted Earona's thoughts by shoving an item into her hand and closing her fingers over it. 'Give this to Evenhand. Keep it safe till then.'

'What?' A silver amulet the size of her palm lay in Earona's hand, and she squeaked, '...*Who?*'

'You will know who to give it to by this sign. Evenhand will know of the devil's mask and what covers the earth.'

Looking at the amulet, Earona noted the half-moon and sun were separated by clouds in the center, and surrounding all was a tarnished silver ring. She screwed up her face and shook her head. Obviously the old lady had mistaken her for someone who might possibly know what she was talking about. 'You must be wrong. I don't know any Evenhands.' Her flabbergasted words tumbled out in a mess. 'Who are you?'

Her hood fell, revealing wrinkled skin resembling bark much like her own staff. Shadowed by broad brows, her eyes searched Earona's face. Earona resisted probing into her eyes, forming suspicions as to the woman's nature. Myths regarding a witch's eyes were fraught with bad memories from childhood stories. She was wise enough to know it probably took more than a look, but she didn't want to find out the truth of that right then.

'I do not know who Evenhand is.' Every word from the old woman was drawn out and delivered with care. 'That is the message I was given. You are the Healer. Here is the amulet.'

Earona stared at the strange symbol, her fingers curling around the warm metal. 'I don't understand.' After some moments, she looked up and the woman was gone. She jerked her head back and bumped it on the brick wall.

Marcus crouched where the old woman should have been and was moments ago. 'I am not that frightful, am I?'

She jumped up and scanned the room. 'Where is she?' The trinket dangled in her hand and she rubbed the back of her head. At least she knew a woman spoke to her, she had evidence. 'Did you see that woman? Old, hooded, carrying a long staff, looked like a tree branch, the staff that is.' She pleaded, 'Tell me you saw her pass you?'

'Calm yourself.' He took hold of her arm, preventing her from dashing across the hall. 'You look as if you have seen the dead.'

'She spoke to me.' Holding the amulet loosely, she swung it before his eyes. 'Look, she gave me this and said I must give it to someone. Walking dead don't give you objects, do they?' *I've never even heard of Evenhand and what's a devil's mask supposed to mean?* 'What am I expected to do, gallivant over the country looking for the owner of this piece of rubbish?'

He took it from her and bounced the light-weight metal in his hand. The edges were faded, revealing copper underneath the silver plate. 'The woman was old and bent and leaning on a staff? If so, she was here earlier and she spoke with you briefly.'

She slowly shook her head and moaned. 'But you didn't see her just now?'

'I shall take this.'

'*I* will take it.' She snatched it from him and tucked it into the pocket of her skirt. 'If there is some curse I would only be passing it on.'

'Look's like junk.' His face creased with anxiety. 'We could leave it somewhere.'

Her bright blue eyes stared at him with astonishment. 'We can't do that. What if it's an important treasure to someone of life changing potential? Besides, if it is cursed it is irresponsible to leave it about where anyone can find it.'

'It's only a suggestion,' he grunted, his face reddening. *I could shatter—*

'You're not going to destroy it.'

His glare did nothing to deter her. *I'll tell—*

'You're not going to tell Jett. I will tell him.'

He folded his arms and attempted a fierce stare. 'Well, Miss I-have-an-answer-for-everything, Barrard says there are people ill in the town and can you see them?' He paused and relaxed his glare. 'One of them, an elderly man known as Stony. An old man hanging on to life… you performed miracles, bringing back the dead,' he said, 'well, almost.'

'Can't you be serious ever?' She scowled at him. 'One of these days you are going to show some compassion.'

'But…' his rugged face looked hurt and he proclaimed in good humour, 'Not good for my image, you know. What will people think?'

As much as she wanted to swat him she laughed, unable to restrain herself from sharing in his merriment, after all, it was turning into a joyous day. If only she could get the old woman's eyes from out of her mind and discover the cause of the disease. 'Really, you shouldn't have to question the old man's survival. I'm sure there's a reason he's called Stony.'

8 - Mara

Every man will be a slave to something
However, are you free to choose what will be your Master?

Heavenly Ascension

Mara bolted out of the cottage, sending the door slamming against the wall. She raced through the garden and into the forest. She didn't see Wendessa inside and she didn't know if she wanted to, or ever again after what happened last night. Yet despite the bloody ritual, she woke in her bed, clean and dressed, her wound covered with bandages. Her sleep strangely solid without any of the usual dark images.

Once on the forest track, she slowed, and fingered the new charm hanging so low it went past her breasts. A straw mouse, so tiny, the size of her fingernail. Contemplating throwing it away, she gripped it in her palm. It must be from Wendessa. But, why... and why did she feel this —difference. Something had changed inside her.

Wet leaves underfoot crunched out an organic scent, and ferns crossed her path. She ran her hand over the damp fronds, feeling the water arouse her skin. Walking through a forest was an unfamiliar experience. She felt... that was it. She felt. Like she had never felt before.

She let her hood slip back, and her fiery-blonde hair was exposed to the winter air. For the first time in her life, anger was not dictating her actions, even her words seemed to have disappeared. A new type of sense was surfacing in her mind – but what was it? It was almost a child-like disposition, but, wasn't she still like a child herself. Was it gentleness... but how could that be – she didn't even know what that was?

Trees guided her path, their black skeletal arms waved against the deepening grey. Intimidated by their majestic presence, she imagined herself as a rough stone of contained bedlam leaving a dirty stain over the serene embodiment of something eternal, something with purpose. She did not belong. Somehow the woods knew that too.

Her stomach peeked out through her cloak to remind her even though she felt these new sensations, she was not innocent. Tears burned her eyes. 'This...' she placed her hand on it, almost as if for the first time. 'What has happened to me?' But she remembered it was all lies and scheming. Planned and manipulated by her mother in Aquila. Mother. All Mara's life her mother had stood over her, with rules, never to be disobeyed on pain of torture. Cruel acts of punishment Mara accepted as her role as child.

Not a single word or action of tenderness did her mother share with her. All those around her mother were the same, even Wendessa. Everyone that is, except him, and in the end, even Mara had used him.

She grasped with sudden realization at the knowledge, and then came fear. Why could she see this now? A wall had collapsed in her mind and light streamed through but not yet lighting the whole room. Just her own face. It was ugly with threats of her own towards others. Terrible deeds she had done. Her open palms stretched before her, she gazed at them with horror. She had beaten, even… no, she wouldn't recall other terrible deeds right then. *Let this strange light only warm my skin. Until I understand. Until I can accept it.* She was not only the perpetrator, others had abused her as well, like a cycle of pain, suffering and blood. So much blood. Always covered with it.

Birds chirped across the way and watched her from their secure perches. Was she frightening to them? Or did they think themselves safe from the foreign entity walking their home. A sea of feathery foliage covered the ground, and moss spotted the winter trees. Drenched bushes with purple flowers let off a refreshing fragrance infused with pungent nettles, and her nose twitched.

Her skirt caught against shrubs and swept up the bracken. Her fingers touched dangling leaves and grabbed the wood, as if showing the trees she had some authority. But she was the interloper in this world of tranquil slumber. Here, under mighty beings, she existed as if she were a new creation. She stepped hard on sharp rocks half buried in the soil and forced another branch aside, its dry appendage scratched her forearm. She shook her locks free in the chill air. An unfamiliar peace was attempting to overtake her. Some part of her wanted the new sensation, but to let it into her soul was dangerous, it would only hurt her more when it was taken from her. Her mother would never allow this weakness.

Her mother sent her to Lanvin to meet someone, an acquaintance. One of mother's mysterious associates. Mara wasn't told directly, but she discovered her mother was planning on opening a Gate to the Underworld, and she was searching for a "Key" and somehow Mara was to aid in this. It was all scheming and collaborating with those in her mother's clandestine world. Mara obeyed every command, without question. But now - she feared everything her mother had told her.

The bubbling brook broke her sullen trance. Under the bending trees, the stream flowed towards the town. She walked the slope to reach it. Water burst on the rocks, and foam rushed along the dips. She breathed the wet grass and scrambled up on a flat rock by the water's edge. Moss under her stomach made a spongy cushion. Crawling further along, her hand hung in the water and she swirled it. Her chest tightened and she shifted her stomach into a comfortable position. Cupping a handful of water, she drank.

At a distance, gobs of slime clotted together, forming a coverlet on the surface. She frowned at it floating away into the foam. Another gush of thick lime followed after. It was not unusual, it appeared days ago, but this was denser and flowing at a greater speed. She withdrew her hand and contemplated the vista up the stream. The trees grew in an interlocking fashion above the water, framing the stream in tangles of grey and brown.

Laying on her side, she stared at the bulge of her stomach and brooded over the life within; still so hard to believe. Usually she ignored it, but now there was movement. She recalled her mother saying, the infant would be significant in her plans. At the time Mara didn't care at all, but now, something had shifted inside her soul that she couldn't fully grasp. She needed to get back and speak with Wendessa, there were too many unanswered questions.

Wendessa was waiting outside the cottage. She held the door open for Mara and they both walked through in silence.

Once inside Mara stared into Wendessa's dark stormy eyes. 'I need to know.'

Wendessa closed the door. 'I will speak as much as I am able.' She gave a resolute nod. 'It was the only chance we had of performing the ritual.'

Mara's amber gold eyes flared with indignation. 'What have you done to me?' Her hands flew to her chest. 'Why do I... feel like this?' She couldn't even explain the unfamiliar thoughts ravaging everything she had previously known and taken for granted. 'Different.' She pulled out the small mouse charm. 'And what does this do?'

'I'm glad you still have it, never take it off.' The old woman pursed her lips and gave a measured stare. 'There is much to tell you and I will over time. But that charm, will keep you hidden from the scrying eyes of your mother.'

Mara gripped the charm in her fist, attempting to comprehend why Wendessa would want this. 'Tell me now!' Her patience burst. 'You did a Moon-tide Blood ritual on me, and you left a curse seal. You expect me to accept that?'

'It was necessary, and you'll understand more once we leave.'

'Leave?' Mara barked, 'I'll tell mother.'

'If you wish to be free, you will think again.' Wendessa's eyes turned to steel.

'Free?' Mara rolled the curious word on her tongue. Its comprehension was beyond her. 'What does it even mean?'

'A life making your own decisions.' Wendessa nodded at Mara's confusion. 'Your mother would never allow it.'

Mara's hand dropped and she stared through the old woman, dazed. Did that mean no more beatings, no more wicked deeds... no more of her mother? She muttered, 'decide my own fate...?'

'Don't be foolish. No-one decides their own fate.' Wendessa's face lightened. 'But we can choose the path.' She gripped Mara's shoulders. 'For the first time your thoughts are clear, you can think for yourself. Don't you feel it?'

Mara glanced at Wendessa's hands holding her. Peculiar warmth came from her, she had never felt such a comforting sensation. 'For myself...' And that was it, she could have an opinion. 'But it's not only that?'

'Yes, there is more.' Wendessa lowered her voice. 'We must not be here when the Dark One arrives tonight. The Seal is too fresh for you to withstand him. We will search for the "Key" without your mother, or anyone else.'

'We're going to open a Gate, on our own?' Mara asked with suspicion.

'No, we're going to stop her from opening it.' Wendessa continued, 'You are the only one who can complete it. You will make the final choice.'

'I really don't get...' Mara suddenly held her stomach, as a wave of nausea hit her.

'But we will need to find the "Wolf". I'll explain on the way.'

That's right, someone was coming to take her away. And now, Mara had no desire to go with this stranger. She wanted to taste what this freedom was like. She doubled over, and within moments, she passed out and lay on the floor.

~ * ~

Cerelic arrived at the cottage on the edge of town. Painted carvings of symmetrical patterns edged the eaves, and petite flowers grew in window balconies. He cared nothing for the appearance of the cottage; he only cared it was on the outskirts of town. It gave him time to make his enquiries without pesky townsfolk chasing him down.

An old woman and girl were staying at the cottage, and they were newcomers to town. No-one knew anything about them, and his interest was roused. Due to his own less than reputable ways he could smell a falsehood a mile off. He was not about to let a secret pass by, especially if he could gain information to keep Rafah off his back.

He knocked on the door and changed his sour look to concern.

A lean woman opened the door, her thick grey plait lay over her blue checked dress, and she eyed him with a steely gaze. She was elderly, but her face was alert. He noted vague recognition in her eyes and he received a firsthand appreciation of what the townsfolk were saying of her. Despite looking like a grandmother, her demeanor was unwelcoming. But as long as he could get to the girl, he could find out what he wished to know. 'Good day.' His smile was a fake twist on his mouth. 'You are the resident of the house?'

She nodded. 'And you are the doctor.' She made no motion for him to enter.

He would have to go beyond his usual parody of kindness. 'Sadly, the illness is rife. Is there a chance you could depart?'

'Perhaps.' Her face remained fixed like a stone mask. 'But currently, my granddaughter is already in a fever.'

'I see.' Genuine worry paled his face. 'There might be one in the town who can heal her. I shall see the girl and give what aid I can while you seek out the healer. It takes them very quickly and it is best to take every precaution.' He pushed his thin brown hair from his eyes and straightened his stained clothes in an agitated fidget.

At last she responded, 'Someone can heal this sickness?'

'It is true.' Insufferably true. His plans were progressing faultlessly until the healer ruined everything by bringing back all those people from certain death. 'I have come to bring what comfort I can and keep alive those who are ill.'

'In that case,' she glanced upstairs, and turned back to him. 'I shall take you to her, and I shall find the healer.'

Upstairs in a small room, Mara lay in a narrow bed. Wendessa stood at rigid attention and said with sudden force, 'If anything happens to her, I will come looking for you.'

His brows stood high with indignation. 'I assure you I shall keep her alive until your return, nevertheless you must be quick.'

She backed out of the room. He paid her no mind and seated himself at the squat stool by the girl's bed. Blankets were pulled up to her chin in protection against the cold.

Perspiration wet her face and her red-gold hair covered the pillow. She moaned, and mumbled words he could barely hear.

Once he heard the front door close, he snapped to attention. The child was older than he was led to believe and he questioned whether he had the right girl at all. Rafah made no mention of her being an adolescent.

No time to spare, he got to work. In a rush, he reached inside his bag and pulled out a folded green leaf. Wrapped inside was a greenish mixture still fresh. He studied at the Aquila Academy of Medicine, but he never completed his schooling. The discipline was more challenging than he had the temperament for. The experience still provided him with useful knowledge which over the years proved invaluable. The leaf from the Astle flower was a most wondrous relaxant, but it could also be used as a truth inducing drug.

He opened the girl's mouth and placed a dab of paste on her tongue and made her swallow as best as possible. 'Now my dear, I wish to know who you are.'

'Mara.'

'That won't get me anywhere.' Cerelic scratched his chin with surprise. 'How about where you are from?'

'Aquila.'

The drug was good, but directing people's answers was more difficult. 'Why are you here?'

'I'm…' the girl appeared to struggle to speak. '… meeting someone.'

Cerelic clenched his fist and grumbled, 'Who?'

'I… someone who wants the "Key"'

He rubbed his forehead in frustration. 'A key? To what?'

'It opens a Gate.'

He couldn't keep the shock from his voice. 'Is this why Rafah wants you?'

Her eyes opened to slits and she muttered, 'My mother wants it.'

'Hold on, are you that *Mara*?' His voice lifted with sudden revelation. 'Your mother, Yavinia?'

'The Summoner of Souls is supposed to wake the demon nation.' She lifted her head off the bed. 'And you will join them.'

'I'm afraid I won't be staying around to see it.'

Downstairs, the front door opened and closed.

From a tiny vial, he dribbled a little sleep potion onto her lips, and she fell back into a deeper sleep.

The door opened and the old woman approached the bed. 'The healer is coming.'

'Good. I have given her relief.' He stood from his stool and hurried past her. 'My talents will be needed elsewhere. Good day, my kind woman.' He found his own way out of the cottage and walked briskly up the road considering the ominous information. The more he mused over the girl's remark about a Gate and demons, the more answers went unfilled. Now he had more, but knew less. What was the Key and the Summoner of Souls, and who was the one she was to meet?

Cerelic's time in the town had run out. The reasons for him staying were nearly depleted. They were poor people, nonetheless their valuables would fund him till he purchased more herbs and then onto another town, preferably a smaller one. It would take a few days for them to realize things were missing even so they would probably blame each other for looting or better yet, the meddling newcomers.

9 - Discoveries

"If you seek, then surely you will find," so a famous Seeress once said. I've searched many a decade, but I am yet to discover the reason for the Maze of Doors. They exist, as we know, as a space in the fabric of our knowledge. An empty stark space. A number of witless folk have fallen through—'

'Like holes,' interrupted my apprentice.

'Of a form, yes. Not to fear, my son. Those who enter the Senyu Menhrs go forth to other lands with some chance of returning home. In time.'

'Not like the Gates?'

'No, not like the Gates from which there is no return. They are of a spiritual nature and a matter entirely forbidden to us.' It was best to warn the boy; my tone turned to a simmering wrath. 'The Gates are closed to us. No man can enter nor should. Only evil can come from it.'

Tiverbius Salt'Brew, Bard of Bards

Jett and Hellier pressed aside branches and stamped over the wet carpet of underbrush as they made a path into the woods outside Lanvin. Through the muddied bracken, Seth stepped carefully ahead of them. Rain fell in annoying smatterings. Small birds swooped from low branches of the covering dense pines. Ferns shimmered with raindrops as the three brushed past them. Branches blocked the view of the clouds, and in the distant mountain range, thunder boomed. Jett was not pleased another dreary day was upon them and would have preferred to see the woodland under a clear sky and in dry clothes.

Seth ambled between low branches and decaying logs. Soon he was out of sight, except for his blonde head bobbing up and down; he tilted precariously as if losing his footing only to swiftly move upright upon finding it.

Jett watched him with furrowed brows as they walked up slippery embankments and dodged springy undergrowth. They meandered on a confusing zigzag trail with no apparent reason for being so. Entanglements of thorny shrubs created an unsteady path. In fact, Seth appeared to be missing visible tracks in favour of ones extra demanding to navigate. Jett shouted his annoyance, 'Why are we going on this winding route? It's a cursed nuisance.'

Seth continued on his way without a word.

Jett was amazed by the usefulness of Seth's Naturist Gift. He didn't understand how Seth did what he did, but he trusted Seth knew what he was doing and that was good enough for him. He was also good at what he did even though his training was cut short. Given the option of staying to finalise his study, Seth decided to depart, knowing if he stayed the whole Kin would remain in Tellávare. Jett was selfishly thankful he chose to delay his studies even though he sensed the niggling doubt in Seth. Jett never mentioned it, stubbornly convincing himself it was for the good of all.

Seth halted and stared at an overhanging tree. Drenched leaves dripped onto their cloaks. Hellier and Jett placed themselves in the clear while Seth stood indifferent to the water trickling down his fair-skinned face. If his hair were not caught up near the top of his head it would be soaked. The sound of dripping water was peaceful, and the clearing was an oasis of calm.

Jett said, 'Have you found anything?'

'Madness.' Hellier's irritation broke the pleasant moment. 'We're lost! Nothing but mud and wet trees and more trees.'

Seth gazed at a far off cluster of bushes. His wet cheeks flushed with pleasure.

'Seth?!' Jett grabbed his elbow and shook it, his volume increasing with each word. 'Can you hear me?'

Seth's eyes shone a sparkling green. 'Seems to be a number of unwelcome guests in this forest.' *I do hope it's not us.* Finally, he gave the two his attention. 'I have to hope we are being led to what we are seeking.' His changing eyes suddenly reflected the grey of the wintry air as he looked heavenward with a sly grin. 'Glorious weather, don't you think?'

The Allervium rumbled with thunder, set to let loose a formidable downpour. Hellier voiced her response to the weather with a frustrated grunt.

'I could take off my clothes and wash.' He bent forward and stared at Hellier, hiding under her hood, glaring. 'I would say you could do with one yourself.'

Jett's impatience echoed off the trees, 'Spare us the shock and reassure me we are not lost.'

'Flamin' hells!' Hellier retorted. 'I'm up to my nose in water. I want nothing more than to be dry. And now we are lost in this.' She sent her arms out wide.

Looking up, Seth scanned the trees. 'I might not know where we are, but... we aren't lost...'

'Oh, that's reassuring,' Hellier said.

Jett asked, 'And why are we going back and forth?'

'We were? Must be the leading of the winter-wood.' Seth pointed down to his feet. Flat near the earth were dainty blue flowers that would go unheeded if you didn't know they were there. 'The hyglis is special here. We must be careful not to step on it.' He gave Hellier a warning frown.

Jett sighed at his own foolishness for asking.

Hellier said, 'What does it matter?'

Seth replied with a sniff, 'The woodland protects itself. We are the trespassers here.' He wheeled from them and started on his way again.

'Just hurry up and get on with it.' Jett started after him.

Seth responded to a question not verbally asked. 'That's right, I wonder that myself. How do I manage these humans?' He moved ahead with his eyes on the higher branches.

The winter-wood became more prolific as they went. The tree's white sheen amongst the lush green lined the track they were forcing.

After a time, Seth quickened his pace and spread the distance between him and the two following. Eventually he called through the space of trees, 'I am onto something. But, what exactly am I onto?' Not long after, he exclaimed in an elevated voice, 'Aha! I've found something.' As Jett made the dash over the underbrush in the direction of his voice, several hyglis were trampled much to the silent dismay of the winter-wood.

Jett and Hellier came upon Seth, leaning his hand against a granite stone, taller than himself and double his width. Across from it, two others were of identical size. All three stone pillars stood, their ends buried in the earth and forming a triangular shape. The immediate flora, circling the stones, appeared reluctant to grow within. It was an outlandish sight as the wild groundcover had no quandary growing over everything else it could reach; the space looked to be cut back and tended with precise detail.

Peering into the triangle and keeping his head from passing the stones, Seth studied an inscription etched in the granite on the opposite side. 'Very interesting, but this is not what we are searching for. This is ancient and permanent.'

Hellier looked up and down at the barren space. 'Is it what I think it is?'

'A Senyu Menhrs.' Jett placed his hand on the stone and stared with astonishment at the nothingness. 'Better known as an empty hole.'

Seth walked to the second pillar and examined the symbolic carvings. 'And a well-marked one at that.'

Hellier replied with surprise, 'Some aren't…'

'I expect time has destroyed many signposts of these doors.' Jett crouched down to observe the empty space of dirt devoid of stones and any living matter. 'Even if you put a hand in you would not be able to pull it back, you would be stuck. The only way to escape would be through it, come what may.'

'I've always wanted to see one.' She searched for a stone and threw it between the stone pillars. It disappeared before hitting the ground.

A Senyu Menhrs was a three-sided door leading to other Senyus around the lands. No entryway led back to where you came from. You could go in and out searching for your homeland indefinitely. Rumour of a map of the various paths had circulated for ages. As yet no one had seen evidence of this and no one was willing to actually take on the task of charting it themselves.

'The inscription is too old to read.' Seth let the invading vine hang again by the outside stone face.

Hellier breathed out slowly. 'How exciting it would be—'

'Don't even think it.' Jett watched her captivation and said with reproach, 'Landscapes have changed. In some cases been decimated. Do you know how perilous these things can be?'

She met his dark look with glowing eyes. 'But think of the adventure.'

He gave her a half smile, appreciating her need for stimulation. 'Others have made the same assumption, but no one has seen the length of the Maze of Doors and spoke of it. Many theories abound, recorded maps and a grand room where hundreds of doors open up to the Senyus of the world—'

'That's a fantastic image,' Seth interrupted, 'although I do think there is some method to it.'

With a hand on her sword hilt at her back, Hellier nodded at the door with self-confidence. 'Surely it wouldn't be that difficult to map, you just continue going in and out.'

'I'm sure if there was a way, you would find it.' Jett gave her a stern look. 'But that will have to wait. This one is almost in good repair.' His hand smoothed the damp pillar with consideration. 'You wonder if it is used.'

'Maybe,' Seth said, 'but, there are no obvious tracks.' He glanced upon a path under the trees and he gave a sheepish grin. 'I do believe our camp is not as far as we have walked.'

Jett's eyes searched through the groupings of trees, and he recognized a boulder they had passed. He decided nothing useful could be said about it and replied, 'Remember, if you see a space of earth devoid of life it's possibly an empty hole.'

'I know that,' she stated bluntly. 'What if it's on stone?'

'It's too late and you're in trouble,' Jett replied, equally brisk. 'Sprout, this is not what we were searching for?'

'No, this is an added find.' He set out again without being told. 'Let's keep moving.'

The three explorers made off again in rain, lightly falling, and through woodland heavy with water. Seth led them on a new trail through broad intertwining branches and thick undergrowth. Now there was no way they could avoid stomping on the coarse ground cover. Seth eventually came out beside a quickly flowing brook, which was more or less where he wanted to be, so he said.

The edges of the stream were overcrowded with scrawny twisted trees vying for a view of the water. Seth's balanced footsteps held him firm on the wet wild grass as he gripped the trees and pulled himself along the water's edge.

Jett and Hellier followed with more caution. They had traveled a long way and Jett still wasn't certain they were not lost. There was nothing he could do, but trust Seth could lead them back to camp.

At least the rain had eased, but the sky still foretold of more to come. The lean trees, reaching across the water, came together in a tangled mess of knotted foliage above. Growing between the wily trees were spindly water grass and knee high spongy undergrowth. Breathing in the scent of rain, Jett was lulled by the bubbling stream. He could almost forgive Seth for his precarious trail and his enigmatic explanations.

Over the time they walked the water's edge, Jett noticed a green build up around the rocks. He called to Seth, 'It's thick up here.'

Up front, Seth halted. He took a careful step inward and compressed his slender frame in between close growing trees, and bowed his head in meditation.

Jett stopped and Hellier came up behind him, grumbling, 'Apart from the dirty water, there doesn't seem to be anything wrong—' an oversized wet droplet landed on her forehead. Her hand touched the substance and her fingers trickled with green ooze. 'What is *this*?' She tilted her face upward. Spiraling down at an unsteady speed was an iridescent green spider the size of her head. She shouted in surprise as it landed on her. With a spontaneous swoop of her hand, she flicked it from her face. The creature's lean legs latched onto her wrist. As much as she vigorously shook her hand, it held on all the tighter. 'Bugger!'

Jett connected with his Ethos and his eyes glowed a tinge of red. The spider fell in pain. He brought his foot down on its squirming body. A clot of innards poured out and was lost in the similar coloured grass. No sooner did he do this, another spun down at his head. He swept it aside and another bulbous body came aiming for his face. Stepping backwards, he withdrew his blade from his back and swatted at its belly.

More spiders jumped across branches that previously camouflaged their movement. Hellier drew her malreus sword and held it up, daring the others to coil down.

Seth pointed to the center of the stream. 'Look above!'

Jett stared into the trees' leafy cover. Partly obscured by the interlocking branches was a cocoon held together by thick greyish webbing, and protruding from it was a decaying arm. Through the hanging flesh, bone was visible, and a globulus green substance seeped from the tree and into the stream.

'Devil's arse!' shouted Hellier. 'That's not a pretty sight.'

Another spider crept over the cocoon and Seth called out a warning, 'It's not the only one.'

Cramped in the twisted tree branches was another cocoon. A human skull had broken through the wrappings, and other body parts were cruelly exposed. Spiders rushed over the concealed corpse with alarm and numerous black eyes observed the intruders with watchfulness. 'There's more through the trees along the stream.' Seth climbed up the low branches to gain a better view.

'Don't climb up there!' Jett yelled.

Seth froze in mid-movement near the curving branches that pulled towards the middle of the stream. His urgent thoughts came to Jett. *I think I found the mother.*

Across the water, the thin branches shuddered. From its hiding place among the leaves a long spindly leg emerged, followed by another. The spider, like the smaller ones, was a vivid green, yet its body was the length of half a man. The creature's legs held its body high off the tree branches and its weightless movements continued uninterrupted. Its fat abdomen lowered over the cocooned corpse among the trees where Seth perched.

Before Seth could move from its path, the spider suddenly leapt with alarming speed and purpose. The soft haired legs of the creature latched onto Seth's upper arms in a suction grip, and its double mouth snapped at his turned away face.

The spider struggled and writhed with discomfit even as Seth did the same. However, the spider's pain came from a searing heat from Jett's burning vision as he bore into the spider's overweight mass. One of its mouths squeaked and its eyes focused on Jett below. From its second mouth, green ooze spewed forth.

Jett avoided its descent and prepared for the second spurt. It came fast, landing on his cloak. He dodged the spider's direct range and stepped into the semi protection of the tangle of branches.

Seth reached for the long knife at his belt and slashed at the spiders legs. The thing let him fall through the spaces of the thin trunks. The unnatural creature gave a high pitch squeal, letting the forest know its unhappiness. Its body thrashed from side to side above the branches, uncertain which way to run as Jett continued burning its body.

Jett caught Seth's blade as it clattered through the trees. He climbed up the gaps, maintaining as much of his vision on the bulk of the spider as he could.

With unusual slowness, Hellier attempted to swing her body up into the trees. A shallow splash came from below where she fell into the foam. The wounded spider backed away from Jett, its mouth still spewing out the thick substance.

Jett had no way of moving safely towards it, but he couldn't let it escape or worse, let it attack Seth while he pulled Hellier from the water. Along with speed and some skill, he hurled the knife at the spider's retreating form. It cut through the air and embedded in its abdomen. Thrown off balance, legs flailed in the air while one of its mouths let out a wailing screech. Its body quivering, it withdrew into the leaves where its legs curled towards its heaving body. Jett let his body half fall through the branches and leapt to the edge of the stream.

Tears wetting his eyes, Seth supported the unconscious Hellier in his arms. 'She must have been bitten.'

Jett flicked her wrist over and studied the swollen puncture marks. He took her from Seth's arms. 'She's breathing.' He settled her in his arms and spoke gruffly. 'You worry about getting us back. And Seth, make it quick.'

10 - Unwelcome Visitors

Life is the sum of a man's reflective thoughts, the propulsion of his emotions, and the vitality of his memories – without these, man becomes a creature, an empty shell of animated flesh.

Ei'myn Yamshôan-shem script

Earona shivered from the chill whistling through the cracks in the small room. She was led upstairs by an elderly lady while Marcus waited downstairs. The woman had eyed Marcus' double sheath of swords with distrust, making it clear she did not want a man so armed in her granddaughter's bedchamber.

The woman left to fetch hot water on Earona's request. Rubbing her upper arms for warmth, Earona approached the narrow cot where the girl lay. Pale and motionless, she appeared dead. Earona pulled a squat stool close, and once settled she discovered it was not made for comfort. Regardless, here in the empty room she was free to be herself and she placed her bag by her feet, having no need of it.

White skin enhanced the beauty of the girl's slender nose and pale lips, and her shuttered eyes were huge in her shrunken face. Despite the illness the girl had a delicate beauty. Earona folded back the blanket and placing her hand on the girl's chest, cold skin alarmed her. The girl was near death.

Earona found the effect of the disease. But she also discovered abrasions and fracture scars, evidently healed, and a strange murkiness permeating the girl's organs. Some of the injuries were extreme, but all were too old to be healed. The gloomy din of the girl's body repulsed her. A malignant tendril extended towards Earona's Ethos as if seeking a new direction. After a great deal of effort and more than was normally needed, she finished healing the girl's body.

Earona sat resting, desiring a few peaceful moments to cleanse away the effect of the tainted thoughts she encountered. Power dissipated from her hands and she felt drained by the healing. Yawning, she wondered if the quartza was wearing off. A bitter scent touched her nose and she scrunched her face at its sharpness. A folded leaf on the sill caught her eye. She picked it up and gave the paste a sniff. Puzzled, she questioned whether the herbman left it earlier, and she popped the packet into her bag.

'Who are you?' The girl snatched her hand away and her amber eyes blinked in confusion.

'I'm Earona.' She responded with as much cheer as she could considering what she had felt in the girl's body. 'You were ill.'

Her eyes darkened with mistrust and she looked away.

'You're better now.'

The girl's sigh was a fast rush of air and she kept her face to the wall.

'You are with child?' The tiny life spirit had swirled under her spiritual touch with sudden joy at being restored to health.

'It's none of your business.' Her sharp words hit the wall.

Her anguish bubbled to the surface. Earona would have examined the girl's spirit if she had the ability, but spiritual healing was a lost Gift. 'You are barely a woman.'

'It happens to some.' An angry scowl soured her face.

Earona leant forward to whisper, 'Has someone hurt you?'

'That's nothing to do with you.' Against the pillow, her fiery hair spread in damp creases.

'You won't be the first to be abused in such a way. Men are horrible brutes when they want their desires fulfilled. Nothing stands in their way.' Not that Earona knew anyone who had suffered any sort of indecency, nor had she experienced any uncomfortable situations with the opposite sex. The only uncomfortable relationship she had was being in love with Keanan for years and him never returning her affections. All her knowledge about the brutishness of men came from Shiarn. Shiarn was a walking compendium on the matters of love and men. From her she had learnt a great deal, much of it not by choice.

'I would be better off if I had no child.' Scrunching up her brow, she fixed her eyes on Earona for the first time.

Earona blinked at her in wide-eyed astonishment. She would never do such a terrible deed as destroy a life spirit. Nayinn could procreate at will without thought and they did most of the time. Whereas the womb of a Fáerinn woman was dissimilar; in her lifetime she might have one child or she could have a dozen. With no way of knowing how many she would be granted, each child was a precious and divine Blessing. 'When your baby comes your heart will change,' she said. 'You have family here to help you?'

'I'm from Aquila, and it's just me and my grandma here. It doesn't matter either way.' Her face reddened with an increasing vehemence. 'If you have finished, you can leave.'

Earona ignored her abruptness and continued, 'I know you don't know me, but I care about your situation.'

She gave a cynical chuckle. 'You don't know me.'

Before Earona could ask what she meant, a mighty boom sent vibrations up the wall by the bed. The sound of clumping and crashing downstairs followed. Guttural howls startled Earona more than toppling furniture.

Mara lifted the bed-covers and her feet touched the floor. 'Oh no, I think…' she muttered, '…they're here…'

Earona peered out the half open door with a puzzled look. 'Who?'

'Someone… bad.' Mara stood behind her, fear paling her face.

It sounded like a team of men trashing the place and all of them had brought their dogs. She couldn't hear Marcus and she hoped he wasn't hurt in some way. But then again, his aloofness added to his egocentric warrior image. 'You could be right.'

Mara hissed, 'I've got to get out of here.'

Earona lifted her palm and hushed her. Extending her thoughts in search of the link she shared with Marcus, her harried thoughts met his calm ones. *Marc, what are you doing?* There was nothing from him.

Earona's blood was chilled by the growls. It wouldn't surprise her if she fainted from terror. 'Get your cloak.' She took in Mara's appearance, her eyes stopped on her feet. 'And shoes.'

Frowning with irritation, Mara snatched her cloak and crammed her feet into leather shoes.

A tremendous tearing noise and a loud crash shook the cottage. A tremor ran through the floorboards. The furniture jolted and the bed slipped towards the opening hole. Earona cringed and wondered what Marcus was doing. A treacherous sway in the floor and walls made her afraid of being upstairs. Except for an abrupt crash from an object tittering on some mini precipice, semi peacefulness ensued. 'You will have to come with me.'

Mara responded with a suspicious frown.

Earona said with more force, 'You cannot stay up here.'

Mara followed Earona down the short passage. The balustrade swung by lengths of fragmented wood. Earona stepped hesitantly down the frail stairs and Mara trailed after, attempting to follow in Earona's steps. Once reaching the bottom, the stair collapsed. Cracking shards of wood flew off in all directions. The girls stood immobile, sheltering themselves from the flying debris with their slight arms.

Earona took a few moments to recover from the shock of the room's devastation. Besides the state of the stairs, the front door was torn off. Strewn about the room was pottery in shattered fragments. Exploded and shredded cushions fluttered over the broken items and even the curtains were gone. These things were hardly noticeable next to the massive hairy beasts, dead, about the room. The creatures' foul black blood gushed from the bodies, polluting the floorboards. The cottage had holes and caved in sections of walls where the beasts had thrashed, and the middle beam of the room was fractured and rickety. The front window had jagged remains still attached and outside was another ugly mass of fur.

A group of spectators surrounded the beast outside. The townsfolk, even in their weakened state, came running. On seeing the destruction, they hung back. At the center of the wreckage, Marcus prodded one of the creatures with his boot, admiring his handiwork.

Earona's incredulous gaze settled on Marcus with horror. 'Oh, by sacred Kahm! What a massacre!' Finally he could make use of what he learned in the Combat Academy, but she had to question whether it was necessary to demolish the cottage.

Marcus wiped his sword on the dead monster. The bulk of its body was up to his knee. Contorted around his leg were hairy limbs that would allow the creature to walk on four paws or two. Its black claws still had a deadly edge. Its head resembled a wolf, although a wolf's head was smaller, and rows of sharp teeth were a dull yellow.

Lifting up her blue skirt, Earona stepped over dark blood to reach his side. Despite his swaggering, his fearful thoughts were tangible. *Lucky I could take them down, imagine if I wasn't here.* His taut face was damp with perspiration and his muscles flexed under his freed shirt. *I don't want to think about it.*

Her apprehensive thoughts bombarded his mind. 'Are you hurt?'

'Few scratches.' Blood soaked through his shirt on his upper arm from an open gash and she grasped his arm, careful to avoid the blood. He dared a roguish grin in front of her. 'Don't mind that, but you could help with that woman.' He looked around the room. 'Where did she go?'

'Heaven's peace, you have made a terrible mess of their home.' She stepped over the broken table and attempted righting a chair.

Towards the back of the house, the old woman crawled through the kitchen doorway, leaving a pool of blood behind her. She fell back against the doorframe.

'Wendessa!' Mara ran to her and knelt, her mouth agape with shock. Seeing the extremity of the cut across her chest and legs, she let out a sob. 'You can't... not now...no.'

'Earona!' Marcus called as he raced to the woman.

Wendessa's mouth moved and she took a sharp breath. '...yes...I knew there would be a blood price...but,' her navy eyes grew weak, but she fixed them on Mara. 'They have come. You must go with them.'

'Eh?' Marcus quizzed the overheard dialogue with a raised brow.

'No,' Mara wailed. 'I won't.'

'Don't be stubborn,' she wheezed. 'I didn't tell you, but... I've also got a scar-mark, for years now – from the same ritual...she never knew it,' she reached for Mara's cheek, 'Take my charm. Be strong, it's you or her ruling over you. Find the one who can control the key. It's the only way...'

Earona crouched by her and touched the woman's fatal injury.

'Take her...' She took a last gasp and her head rolled to the side in death.

'You're free now.' Earona bowed her head. After a moment she looked to Mara. 'I'm sorry, she's gone.'

Mara wiped her eyes and moved Wendessa's grey plait from her bloodied chest. From around the woman's wrist, she pulled off a leather band with symbols engraved on it, and put it on. 'You were the only thing I had.' She lowered her face to the dead woman and mumbled, 'And now I have nothing...'

Earona stood with a heaving sigh. *I was too late...*

Head down, Mara muttered to herself, 'Now what am I supposed to do...' she glanced around the room. 'These creatures...?'

'Baskharef,' Marcus replied.

She frowned with some recognition and stared at the other beasts.

His face reddened. 'Ah, witless things, but dangerous all the same. '

Earona stared at him with an annoyed frown. *Did she really need to know that?*

'Earona,' *you know these are Skar pets, don't you?* 'We must get back to camp. The others should know of this.'

Earona glanced at the dead woman, the girl's grandmother, and pondered her last words. Their cottage was turned into a shambling mass of broken furniture and stinking carcasses. No longer fit to live in, and more suitable for burning. 'We can't leave her here.' She nodded to Mara, standing over her grandmother's body. 'You have family in Aquila?'

Mara's petite body shuddered and she clutched her arms. 'I'm not going there.' Voices from the crowd outside grew frantic with fear and bewilderment. The crowd increased, with those newly recovered joining them.

Marcus watched the growing number of spectators. 'Time to leave.'

Earona turned her back on the watchers outside and lowered her voice. 'Why were those things here?'

'Someone came demanding to see the girl. She—' he hesitated and glanced at the body, 'wouldn't let them in. Soon after, the beasts came...'

Mara's head jerked up and her mouth pressed together.

Earona said, 'She should come with us where she will be safe.'

'Take her back to camp?!' He barked, ignoring the wide-eyed look Mara gave them. 'Devil's hellfire, we can't! Think what Jett would say?!'

'You saw what these creatures did. There might be more about.'

He glowered at her, his skin flushing with anger.

Mara shivered and her arms went stiff at her sides. 'But, no, I'm not.' She looked at each of them in turn with an irate frown and her hands turned to fists.

Marcus threw up his hands at Earona's arrogant pretensions. 'You have no *real* idea what you are asking.'

'If those Baskharef came for her it's a good enough reason for her to come with us.'

Good enough reason for her to stay. Underneath his breath, Marcus growled, 'I wish I hadn't said anything.'

Keanan ran through the open doorway and stopped suddenly at the black beast. 'Hell and dread!' Behind him came Stony, the elderly man Earona healed earlier and with him, spectators peered over his shoulder or stared with morbid alarm through the smashed front window. While Keanan attempted to kick the creature to the side and stepped wide to span its length, he was assailed with Earona and Marcus' account of the trouble.

After moments of listening to two people talk at once, he responded, 'This news bodes ill, I fear. Jett found something in the forest and Hellier had an accident. You must come quickly.'

'But.' Earona cast a glimpse at Mara, looking annoyed at the two of them. 'We can't leave her here.'

'Getting back to camp is more important than having a kid trail after us,' said Marcus.

Keanan entreated them with raised palms. 'Heavens, let the poor girl speak for herself. You would think you were talking about your pet hound. The girl has a mouth, has she not?'

Marcus smirked at Earona while she frowned with consternation.

Mara looked up to the tall red-headed man. 'I'm not about to leave with you.' She asserted herself with a harsh rebuke. 'How do I know you are not part of—' A heavy sigh became a soft moan.

Keanan collected her limp body as she passed out.

Combined with smugness of being right, Earona was earnestly fearful of the girl's health. Moments ago she was healed, now she was ill again. 'She is not well, we must take her.'

'Perhaps you are right. She would seem incapable of looking after herself right now.' Keanan settled the girl in his arms. 'We can discuss her options back at the camp.'

'Discussions. Anyone would think that was all we ever do.' Marcus' pride was dented. Soon enough, a grin emerged on his face as he stared at the dead Baskharef.

Keanan carried Mara as they left the cottage. Stony, a thick-chested man with long graying hair, approached the Kin. 'I've seen these beasts before. They're demons.' His statement prompted panic from the crowd. 'A strange turn of events.'

Keanan gave him a brief nod. 'If there are more creatures like this they might follow us and leave you in peace.'

'We can hope,' said Stony.

Behind Stony, the people banded together with unchecked foreboding.

Earona recognized them all. She sweated over their bodies, poured her heart into their dying flesh. She attempted eye contact, but none of them were willing to acknowledge her. Opening her mouth to speak, there was nothing she could say; all her words would be coated with her own damaged pride.

The old man was the only one to look her in the eye. 'Maybe there's a price for the lives we stole from the gods.'

'There's also the body of an innocent woman inside,' Keanan said. 'Will you see to her?'

The three left the village with no one asking any questions about the unconscious girl, showing how little regard she had in the town. On the way to camp, Earona voiced her disappointment and growing rancour at the hypocritical nature of Nayinn. One day praising your godlike abilities, the next, presuming you wanted their unhappiness. 'It's madness! Are we to expect this attitude from all Nayinn, everywhere we go?' Her shoulders slumped at the miserable notion. 'If so, I think it's intolerable.'

'It is the way of the world,' Keanan responded. 'It justifies the reason why we are to blend in with society and kept our Gifts secret. Besides, some things you do not learn from books or school, you learn from living. The school of life. It may be an old truism, nevertheless, it is wiser to see through your own heart than view it through another's. We must respect the laws of our Elders. Needless to say, it is best not to have the opinion you are a divine giver of life. A mistake the ancient Guardians made.'

Earona pondered his words, knowing they were aimed at her, yet not totally agreeing with them. Mentioning the name Guardians outside of Tellávare was strictly forbidden. Keanan was not one to break the rules and she marveled he said it. She remained stubbornly quiet, no longer complaining about the fickleness of people, she mused over other mistakes the Fáerinn of old had made.

'I believe you must know yourself well,' Keanan continued, 'and more importantly, accept who you are, then it doesn't matter what people say or think because you know the truth about yourself.'

Deep in thought, she questioned how their ancestors survived their existence outside of Tellávare. Of course, everything was different back then.

'We shall speak of it no more,' Keanan said, making it clear he was aware of her ruminations.

'Master Konral says,' Marcus spoke regarding his old combat instructor, '"Knowing yourself is the first lesson, yet always it is the last you must pass."' *I don't care about the customs of the old Fáerinn, all I know is they failed.*

'Codswallop!' Earona cried, 'I think I know myself well. Well enough to know those people are ungrateful and bigoted.' She stamped along the dirt track and considered her own hypocrisy, was it truly contagious?

Keanan and Earona received visions of Marcus reminiscing over his last session with Konral. *The best fight I've ever had, because I beat him.* He laughed loudly. *A rare and unique moment in history.*

Earona shook her head and walked ahead while Keanan was preoccupied with his own thoughts and the girl asleep in his arms.

11 - Forced Departures

There is a deceiving fog. It exists in the wasteland of our minds.

The Sleeping Sword

From the wagon seat, Cerelic peered down the darkened street, hoping not to spy anyone hiding in the shadows. Earlier, a nasty commotion was at the cottage he visited. Townsfolk rushed by his door while he hid inside knowing it probably had something to do with Rafah. Maybe Rafah got what he wanted. Cerelic's plan to depart seemed easier than he imagined. Almost as easy as stealing the townsfolks' possessions. Their meagre wealth would at least fund his next exploit.

Drizzling rain coated the road, causing the wheel to veer into the dirt. Swearing, Cerelic pulled on the horses and stepped down. He attempted side-stepping the slippery earth to examine the wheel. After he cleared a stone from its path, he shook the trail of mud from his shoe and looked above. Clouds concealed the moon. No light tonight.

He scanned the street for the umpteenth time. Still deserted. He stood alert, doubting. He could have sworn he heard something.

'Leaving?' A voice wheezed from the shadows between two cottages. 'So soon?'

Cerelic had been caught red-handed before and he always wheedled his way out of it. But this was different. For some reason, meeting Rafah produced in him an irrational panic. He sensed he was encountering a nightmare he would never be free of. He squinted through the overhanging dark in tense apprehension.

'It's no surprise,' Rafah breathed through his toothless mouth, 'you didn't heal the girl.'

Cerelic's mouth sealed tight and his hand clutched the side of the wagon, steadying himself from the fear making him tremble.

Rafah stepped closer, his foul breath touched Cerelic's face and rage darkened his eyes. 'If you had done what I asked, she wouldn't have got away.' His spittle landed on Cerelic's chin. 'You've angered me.' Grabbing Cerelic's throat, his fingers pushed into tender flesh.

The obese man was intent on killing him. Being found dead on the street where the townsfolk would find his body and his secrets was not acceptable. An eruption of anger coursed into Cerelic's limbs. He kicked at the overweight man, his knee hitting the solid mass. The peculiar man must have feeling *there,* under the bulk of all that weight. Again he kicked, this time putting determined force behind it.

Groaning, Rafah loosened his hand from Cerelic's neck.

Cerelic freed himself and moved to the wagon. Rafah came at him with an overextended lurch and latched onto his shoulder. Cerelic swiveled in time to face him. Exposed between the partings of his cloak, a flash of silver.

Rafah stiffened. 'You're going to kill me?'

Proud he had the upper hand, Cerelic swirled the knife in front of Rafah's face. 'I'm leaving and you will not be following me.'

Rafah clutched Cerelic's swaying hand and they struggled for dominance over the weapon. Whilst Cerelic had control, he thrust the blade into Rafah's chest. It ripped through his thick flesh.

His contempt veiling any pain, Rafah stepped away.

Knuckles white and rigid, Cerelic still clutched the blade, covered with blood up to his hand.

'You think I care about this body?' Rafah's face paled. 'I care about this body as much as I care about yours.'

Smirking, Cerelic stepped back from the dying man. Perhaps Rafah was not the fearful demon he supposed him to be. Blood gushed over Rafah's shirt and soaked his pants. Despite the lack of pain on his face, he swayed to and fro. Cerelic said, 'You asked for that.'

'You're a fool,' Rafah said, 'you've… achieved nothing…' He swerved and his voice wavered, '…they know… where she is.'

'And,' Cerelic pulled himself tall and pointed the knife, 'I know about the Summoner of Souls, and about the Eye.'

Rafah's eyes flashed with fury. He fell to the ground and took his last breath.

Cerelic prodded Rafah's prone body, making certain he was dead. He laid the knife aside and held the dead man's wrists and pulled his great weight. A time wasting exercise, but he thought it best to make an attempt. Too heavy. He would have to leave it lying on the street. The townsfolk would have to think what they liked, it was time for him to leave.

~ * ~

Thunder boomed overhead and the whole tent swayed in the answering wind. Yellow light flickered upwards and shadows loomed the length of the roof. Outside, the storm continued, but the Kin hardly noticed inside the warmth of their pavilion as they focused on a building debate.

Earona queried, 'You suppose someone put that creature in the forest on purpose? Who would do such a thing?'

'We cannot say,' Keanan responded, 'from what Seth said it seems an extremely unnatural occurrence. Whether it is of malicious intent, we cannot say with any certainty—'

'I've seen it and I'm sure.' Jett's tone was stern. 'Barrard knows of it now and he will send word to the nearby duke and that's enough for us. Hellier is healed and the creature dealt with. The worry is the smaller ones and if they are somehow connected with what happened today.'

'At least the mayor has been warned,' Keanan agreed. 'And they can take precautions with their water.'

And this girl has no one to look after her—

'Earona,' Jett's voice cut through the silence that had descended, 'she cannot stay with us.'

'She has no family here and it's not her home town,' Earona replied. 'Where is she supposed to go?'

'Back to wherever she came from.'

Earona's voice grew loud with offence. 'You can't expect her to travel back to Aquila alone? In her condition?!'

'Her condition?' Jett's umbrage matched hers. 'What are you talking about?'

She's expecting.

'Devil's bloody arse!' Jett shouted. 'She can stay here at the town.'

'Shush,' lowering her voice, she said, 'She shouldn't be the way she is.' *I healed her and she keeps fainting. She's done it more than once since being here.* 'It's not right.' She considered Mara, laying still, her face hidden under the blanket. 'Besides that, her grandmother asked me. It was her parting wish.'

'Flamin' arse – I don't care if it was the king himself!' Jett cried. 'Some old woman—'

'There's a reason.' Earona bristled with exasperation. 'She's not safe. Ask Marcus what hap—'

'I have.' Jett stared her down, and a cynical edge gave bite to his words. 'If it does have something to do with her, those things will come after us.' He became more irate, 'What, by the pit's fury, do you think… we are going to trot over to the capital of Ryne and take her home?'

Keanan offered, 'Certainly, she cannot travel on her own.'

'Thanks, Keanan,' Earona said.

Jett cast a cold eye on Marcus. 'Did that visitor know the girl?'

Marcus was quick to reply, 'He just wanted the girl of the house. The old woman didn't seem to know him. She told him to leave and shut the door on him. Then the Baskharef appeared.'

'Someone in the village knows the girl or of her,' said Jett.

'Someone not very nice,' Earona sat back with her arms folded, 'otherwise he would have been let in.'

'She is here with us now,' Keanan said, 'In the morning we shall speak with Barrard and find this man Marcus speaks of.'

Marcus turned to Earona, 'the old gal wasn't clear about "taking her". It was more like, take her… somewhere, but she died before she could say it.'

Earona glared at him. 'That is speculation.'

'I don't care either way,' Jett rubbed his temple in irritation, 'I'm not taking anyone anywhere.'

Feigning sleep, Mara listened to the strangers' intense discussion, and grew more uncomfortable at every word. She could make a guess about the strange beasts that had something to do with who she was supposed to be meeting. But, what was certain, she had no intention of returning to Aquila. Cramped and uncomfortable, she shifted. Thunder shook the earth beneath her and the fire-light reflected the stormy expressions of the people around her. Not wanting to see their stares, she lay on her back and squinted at the swaying tent roof.

'You're awake.' Earona knelt beside her and a sweet scent followed, and was overpowered by wet wool. 'You must be hungry, with all the sleeping you have done.' She handed her a platter of cold meat and bread. 'Hopefully you won't faint again.'

Not looking forward to the discussion, she sat with reluctance.

Earona moved Mara's wavy fringe and placed a cool hand on her forehead. 'I don't understand why you are so weak.'

Mara jerked her face away from the unexpected caress and gobbled down the dry meat. Earona was right though, she felt weak, and there was an underlying vulnerability to her emotions. She was on edge, ready to explode with rage or start crying at these interfering strangers. Despite Mara's animosity, she craved the sensitive touch. It disturbed her, yet when she felt the warmth it seemed to calm her for some reason, but she was unable to admit it. Amid mouthfuls, she retorted, 'Some illnesses… have no… cure.' While she ate, she recalled what took place earlier; and most significantly, her new found release from the commandeering hold of her mother, and sadly, Wendessa dying. She didn't feel very hungry anymore.

Earona spoke over the top of her. 'And we can look after you… for a time.'

Everyone's gaze turned to Mara with blatant probing.

Unable to contain her annoyance any longer, she stood. 'I can't stay here. I've got to put my grandma to rest!'

'That's not so easy,' Keanan said. 'It's late for a start, and there's a storm. In the morning you will be free to do that.'

With a sudden arching pain, Mara grasped her head. It was the same pain she had been feeling since Wendessa died. She could only assume it came from the blood ritual and the scar-mark. 'I… can't stay…'

Earona turned scolding eyes on the dark-haired one who led the argument. 'That's all your talk about leaving her here.'

Mara reddened at the inference.

Jett sprang to attention and his arm flung wide. 'That's a flamin' cock-arsed statement if ever I've heard one. I don't care where she stays, but we aren't taking her anywhere.'

Keanan stood beside Mara. 'Indeed.' He eyed Jett's disapproving glare with misgiving. 'We take responsibility on ourselves your grandmother is dead.'

Much to her shock, Mara found her eyes riming with unshed tears at the candid confession.

'Tomorrow we shall enquire whether anyone could take you in, but,' Keanan said, 'is it possible someone wants to harm you?'

She feigned innocence. 'What? … Who? You mean trying to kill me?' It was true in part, she had no idea who it was she was supposed to be meeting.

Keanan looked at Earona and shrugged, and turned back to Mara. 'Destinies begin in little feats. Even the great ones must be born and live under the rule of normality.' A teasing grin broadened his face.

Her hand went to her stomach. 'Are you talking about me?'

'Who can say? That is one of the reasons we discussed taking you back to Aquila where Earona says you come from.'

'That,' Jett added, 'is highly unlikely. The best option is taking her to the duke's nearby castle, and from there they could get her back home.' He eyed Earona and said, 'Push all you want, we are not going to Aquila. That's an order from on-high.'

Earona sat stiffly and her face dropped into a pout of annoyance.

Mara's heart sank. Traveling back to her mother after the ritual and not meeting her mysterious acquaintance would bring horrendous punishments. The Seal had opened a door in her soul, and her emotions were all over the place. She didn't know who to trust or even what she should do, or where she should go. She had to admit that Wendessa might be right, and she should go with these people. But they hardly seemed to want her. A prophecy Wendessa spoke, apparently regarding Mara, came to mind.

Out of Mist and from Iron
The Wolf converges with the Mouse
The Mouse desires the Eye
The Eye is the Key
Together they dominate them all

Now she was left to figure this out by herself. But first she would have to run away, because she would never be able to do anything if she was sent back to Aquila, and she wanted to explore this new freedom.

12 - Winning and Losing

Failure is often construed as weakness that leads to defeat.
Failure reveals the point of greatest deficiency.
That which can ultimately become the strongest attribute.

Empirical Warfare Command

Hellier walked across the damp clearing. The Kin were asleep, and after the intense discussion, it was peaceful. Not being able to sleep, she volunteered to keep watch. She stared into the shadows under the line of trees, hoping to see something, anything. If only she could do something useful. Paralyzed *and* having to be healed without doing anything in her own defence, embarrassed her. Her failure subdued her usual confidence. She had listened to Marcus, boasting his Baskharef kills, with envy. Even though she suspected he exaggerated the fight, she wanted to know every detail. He was fighting demon beasts while she was incapacitated, helpless as a babe from a creature no bigger than her head. Embarrassed was not the word, more like humiliated.

Clouds blanketed the sky, but she stared on. The debate over the girl irritated her. Earona and Jett were always arguing, no matter how trivial the problem. But if those creatures were really after the girl, they could come again.

Seth approached from behind. 'It's quiet.'

'It's night.'

He rolled his eyes under the shadow of his hood.

Her braids were a pale reflection trailing over her blade at her back. She needed no cloak, she did not feel the cold air. Although weary of being wet, she hated the weight of extra clothing more. She shrugged off his stare. 'Shouldn't you be asleep?'

'Couldn't.' He stepped under the cover of the branches.

Seth was right though. The forest was unusually sombre. 'What is it?'

'I'm... not sure.' Enveloped in his green woolen and hide cloak, he disappeared into the gloom of the shadows.

'Sprout?'

I'm going to see what I can see.

What are you going to do, fall on it from a branch? Be careful, you silly dolt.

Charming as always, he replied.

Despite the Kin sleeping a few feet away, she felt a peculiar remoteness. Crouching, she placed her palm on the wet earth, and to break the silence unnerving her, she muttered, 'something's out there...' *Seth, don't do anything dangerous. I'll get in trouble.*

Moments passed and Seth's thoughts finally touched hers in a weak impression. *Someone's here. Can you come? Oh, there's another one...*

What are you doing? Hellier shouted in his mind. She waited a moment for a reply that never came. 'Flamin' arse. I knew it!' Hoping he was not wounded or worse, she wondered if she should alert the others when she realized she had to do something straight away.

She slipped her sword out and up as she ran through the rows of fruit trees and into the woodland. Once entering under the tall slender trees, she swore. With storm clouds above, it was dark. Warily, she stepped further in. Unable to avoid the bracken, her boots crunched and she halted. *Seth?* She walked another ten feet, seeing no sign of him.

Maybe about fifteen feet to your right. If that's you.

I hope it's me. Rain dampened her skin, but she continued towards his thoughts. A muffled scraping came from behind. Swiveling in time, she blocked the blade coming down at her face. Stepping back, she regained her balance before he swung at her again. Their swords hit in a noisy grind, but it was too dark to be effective with her blows and she could only defend. Sounds of clanging blades were not far. A guttural voice shouted. A grim warning more intruders were in the forest.

Her attacker's cowl fell back, revealing veiny ashen skin on a hairless head and face. She gasped at the sight of his lipless mouth and pointed teeth, and his lack of ears. Despite her shock, she did not let down her guard against his fierce attacks. Towering over her, he hammered down on her with brute strength. Her Ethos seared her flesh. Fire erupted from her skin along her sword arm, burning her sleeve to ash. It rushed down to her hand and into her sword, transforming it to flames that lit the clearing. Now she could see — but, she was disappointed she had to resort to her Gift so quickly. His life or hers, and she would do everything to win. 'Bet you weren't expecting that!' Her cry was fueled by excitement.

Green-yellow eyes glowered at her fire. With a throaty cry, he raged with more force. Attacking with blade and knife, he cut into her shoulder. Flinching at the pain, she pulled her fire-blade across his leather vest, setting it on fire and enflaming his skin. His sharp swallow teeth emerged in a grimace and he aimed for her neck. Her quick step and burning sword appeared to hinder him, and she kept up her defence.

Anger and adrenaline rushed through her body, and she burst out with a ferocious shout of challenge. Her strength matched her rage, and without thinking, she dodged his strikes and advanced on him. Swiping at his face, she burnt his grey skin. He growled out a response she had no hope of understanding, and she gave a hate-filled snarl of her own.

Rancorous growls came through the woods. With a distracting fear for Seth, wherever he was, she determined to finish this. Defeat was not an option, not twice in one day.

~ * ~

Mara sat erect, her breath catching in her throat. She had slept too hard and too long, and she needed to get away that night, before anyone woke. Amongst the unfamiliar slumbering bodies, she looked for the one who called her. No one was awake. Anxiety churned in her stomach, but it was nothing compared to her anger at her captive situation. Shaking her head, her body heated with chaotic aggression. She feared the lack of control, similar to the other time when she killed… back home.

Outside, the voice called again. It evoked strange yearnings, and whispered to her soul of some inner fulfillment that she wasn't even aware of. As if in a waking dream, she stepped out into the night air, not caring her light dress offered scant protection from the chill.

A figure, attired in black, his head covered with cloth, with only the glint of his eyes visible, waited. Hand outstretched, he beckoned her to join him. A sleek voice filled her mind, crooning her name, settling her unease.

The more she craved the voice, a stronger sense of wickedness invaded her thinking. But she couldn't stop desiring it. She would go to the figure and he would offer her release. 'I am here.' An intense need to meet with the stranger burned inside, and she felt power surging through her at his nearness. It was a tumultuous force that could destroy, even herself. Unseen spikes scraped her flesh, paining her. Fire burned her body within. She walked on into a cavern of darkness.

'Go no further!'

The command shot into her mind, disturbing her thoughts like a tangible weapon cutting her mind. His abrupt grip on her arm caused her to falter. With bewilderment, she glanced up at the one who spoke. Dark eyes looked down at her with clarity, and his rage was striking.

The two of them became the only solid objects in a world spinning around them in a mesmerizing kaleidoscope of colour and sound. Indefinable scenes moved at the speed of thought. Visions of malicious apparitions, eyes flaming like demons, flew at them. A power was in her hand controlling the fate of thousands. A bright globe and a woman in red, hands lifted to swirling storm clouds overhead, blurred to a swirling dark hole. A vision of Mara kneeling in a pool of blood while a beautiful woman poised to touch her. Layers of voices spoke, like an indiscernible roar in her mind, yanking from her soul the wrath currently contained. The dark eyed one stood above her in the vision, his hand on her chest pushing her down with submission. The terrible evil twisting around him made her afraid. Behind him was a black throne of bones and dead flesh, and they were surrounded by the abyss. From below, the sound of a million voices yelling for blood repulsed her. An uncontrollable force rushed through her, swelling into a frenzied need to vent her hatred. She recognized a staff, it was as big as herself and covered with all types of charms and fetishes, and she saw herself reaching for it. Something she would never dare to do. Her head hurt and she gasped for air. Beside her, his eyes flicked over the stupefying scenes.

The night sky returned. Energy drained from her limbs. Empty and suddenly faint, she curled her hands up to her chest as if to calm her racing heart.

Jett looked at the girl with confusion. Clutching the sword at his back, he turned his piercing glare on the mysterious foe.

The figure's hand dropped to his sword at the appearance of Jett. 'You are here.'

'Why do you want the girl?' Jett drew his malreus blade and kept a firm hold on her.

'It is her rightful place.' His voice was a confident utterance behind the cloth. 'She will come to me willingly.'

Pale, Mara's face was a twist of pain and shock, her mouth open to speak, she said nothing.

Whether she wanted to go with the stranger or not, Jett would not have it. He heard a voice in his thoughts. It evoked an unreasonable rage in him, a type he fought to control over the years. He couldn't imagine such a man would consider the girl's welfare. 'I don't know who you are, or her, but she's not going with you.'

The man's eyes burned red and he slid out his sword. 'I shall take her.'

Shouting and the sound of fighting came from beyond the trees.

Marcus ran out of the tent with both his swords already out.

Don't worry about me, find Seth and Hellier. Jett tried not to show annoyance, but his anger at the threatening situation thrust on his Kin was mounting. He pulled Mara back and ordered, 'Go into the tent. Stay there.'

Wide golden eyes stared with shock and she nodded. With faltering steps, she ran under the flap.

'She does not belong to you.' His blade came down on Jett, and would have sliced into his neck had he not blocked in time.

Dismissing the vain remark, Jett drew his second blade at his belt. The clang of swords intensified, and more intruders entered the camp. Keanan and Ethan already dashed past, but he was unsure where they had gone.

'We shall burn her out.' A flaming arrow ignited the tent roof and began to spread.

'To hell with you!' Jett's sight remained on his opponent's body in an effort to sear through his clothing. All the while, he felt the same sting of the man's burning gaze. He had no time to be shocked. His opponent's swing came quickly. Jett parried in moments of its nearly hitting him. He knew how to fight against his own Gift, having spent hours in two weapon training with an instructor who drilled his body into movement with the burning vision of his eyes. Speed and unpredictability were the keys. The stranger fought in a similar pattern, meeting him blow for blow. They seemed to be so similarly matched the fight continued without either landing a hit, and their weapons collided without wavering. Jett could not afford to hesitate. His focused offence countered the man's precise strokes.

Distracted by the flames, Jett paused and the enemy slashed his wrist, causing him to drop a sword. On the back foot, Jett was unable to recoup his weapon, and he dodged, defending with his first sword.

The veiled man cut in and towards Jett, his strikes becoming more determined. The combat went on for intense moments until Jett fell back under his pressured attack. Maintaining his defence, he guarded against a hit coming for his neck. The enemy poised, sword midway through the air with a black blade piercing his chest from behind.

Marcus withdrew his weapon. 'You let your guard down.'

'You will see me again.' The stranger's body transformed into black smoke and dissipated into air. His clothes fell to the ground, empty of its occupant, even the weapon was gone.

Stunned by the supernatural disappearance, Jett leaned his hands on his knees and breathed hard.

'Balaam's bloody bollocks! What in hell's name just happened?' Marcus padded the pile of robes, needlessly. Nothing was left of their attacker. He nudged the remaining metal headpiece within the folds of material. 'Malreus.'

Hellier ran to them, breathing heavily and holding her bloodied shoulder. 'They were Skar.'

Marcus gave her a half-cocked grin. 'I noticed.'

Jett stared agape at the empty clothing before a grim frown settled on his face. *But this one was different. Could it be…?* He gazed at the clearing. The only evidence of the skirmish was the Skar transformed into mounds of molten ash, and the blazing tent. The intermittent sprinkle of rain did nothing to dampen it. Their horses neighed with fear at the close proximity of the flames. Jett had an anxious moment, considering the journal, before remembering it was in his saddle bag. He couldn't restrain his worry. 'Where's Seth?'

Grimacing, Hellier pressed on her wound. 'Up a tree.'

'Safest place for him to be,' Marcus said.

'Except they had arrows.' Jett released an irritated sigh and watched the burning tent. He had to trust no one was inside it.

She stared at a pile of crusted black sand, a deceased Skar. 'Holy Kahm! Why those devils?'

'The Baskharef must have been theirs.' Marcus bent down to examine the tunic beneath the robe, but found nothing noteworthy. 'Is Ethan with Keanan?'

Still coming to terms with the bewildering vision, and his mysterious opponent and the reason he had attacked them, Jett was drained of energy. 'Not sure. I have to look for the girls.' Raising himself with the support of his sword, he watched Keanan enter the clearing and attempt saving some possessions from the edge of the fire.

'Why would Skar be here?' Hellier stared at the space where a man should have been. 'And this one…'

Jett studied the clearing. The worst of the view, the flaming tent and their things burning in a grand spectacle. 'I'm not certain…' *No, I just don't like to say.*

'Skar are to the west. It's unusual for them to venture this far and attack humans, although not unheard of.' Keanan stopped by Jett and his voice held disbelief. 'But this,' he indicated the empty clothing, 'It couldn't be… not only Skar, but a Narahk?'

Jett shrugged with weariness and remained fixated on their temporary home going up in smoke. Light rain was not doing a good job on it, but it was certainly affecting them. He noted they failed to care about that. 'There's been no sightings…' *Could it really be a Narahk?* There had been no reports of them since the Age of Anarchy. They were entities created by the powers who manipulated darkness, and possessing similar gifts to the Fáerinn, it made them a formidable enemy over the ages. *It was presumed they were all dealt with.* 'That we know of…'

'He could be a real one?' Marcus asked.

Suddenly heavy with foreboding, Jett had an overwhelming need to find the girl, and see that Earona and Shiarn were safe. 'Whoever or whatever it was, my guess is they weren't expecting to find us or a confrontation.'

'Perhaps so, but they got one,' Marcus stated.

'Why are they here, is what we should be asking?' Keanan replied. 'Let's hope that was the end of it, but indeed, it's quite ominous.'

Jett nodded, feeling too exhausted to respond. Although he could surmise it had something to do with the vision he shared with the girl. It wouldn't be a strange thing, Skar and a Narahk uniting, but there would have to be some purpose. *It's the girl...*

'I see, so she is important to someone.' Keanan continued, 'In ages past Narahk were elite servants among those who commanded the elements of Dark-magik.'

Jett nodded. 'Whoever sent him, will most likely be aware he is deceased.'

Barging through the trees, Seth ran to them, 'Jett!' He clutched Jett's arm hard. 'They're gone! I can't find them around the camp, nor have I felt any sign from the forest.' He inhaled deeply, trying to catch his breath.

Jett's brows lifted in astonishment. 'Earona and Shiarn?! And the young one?'

Seth lowered his fair head. 'Neither could I sense Ethan.'

'Have you searched?' Marcus demanded.

Seth's face was a mask of fear.

'He's right,' Keanan said, 'I can't feel any connection nearby.'

Jett reached out with his thoughts for the familiar sense of Shiarn and Earona's' Ethos, including Ethan's. Nothing. Clenching his fists, Jett lashed out with frustration, 'Arse of the devil, those cursed bloody demons!' To sate his fury, he kicked the nearest mound of hardened ash, sending the grit into the air. It seemed their enemy had fulfilled its purpose, and gained what they had come for. There was never a time when the idea of leading them through trials was not present in his thoughts, and at the first chance he had, he failed. He had failed them.

13 - Disappearances

The most powerful forces on Earth cannot be seen, yet despite this obvious fact, common fallacy dictates, 'I cannot see it therefore it cannot be real.'
Our reality is not limited by tangible matter; it is a weakness to think such. It is influenced by spiritual powers beyond our sight, yet present in everything we do.

Olvarus Claw'Blade, Reader's Wisdom

Mara stumbled into the tent, her mind a knot of foreboding. The sharp clash of metal merged in a frightening discordance outside. Because of her. The only protection from the uproar outside was the canvas wall, and the one fighting the malevolent stranger. A stranger who called her name.

Shiarn paced the tent. A knife flashed in her hand.

Earona's eyes flicked from Shiarn to Mara. 'Who is out there?'

Mara shook her head. Recalling the vision and the voice in her mind, she cringed and bile hit her mouth.

Earona cried, 'Let me help you.'

'No!' Mara's hands clasped her head in an attempt to steady it. 'I don't want your help!' Her throat was dry and her voice cracked. 'Don't you see… it must be me.'

Shiarn threw her hand in the air. 'Why is that?'

Mara was a bundle of chaos inside, wanting to run away, yet staying only because the dark-eyed one commanded her to. 'I…'

Earona's violet-blue eyes shone in the shadows and she rested her hand on Mara's arm.

Pulling away from her, Mara looked to the ceiling. Earona and Shiarn followed her gaze. Flames shot along the roof and extended to the walls on the far side.

'We've got to get out of here.' Shiarn raced to the back of the tent and stabbed her knife into the canvas. She ripped downward, creating a hole and she pushed Mara through the flap and Earona followed. The cool air was revitalizing even mingled with the smoke fumes.

'My bag!' Earona shouted, 'I must get it.'

Shiarn rebuked her, 'Don't be a ninny.'

'I must—'

'I'll go. You move from here.' Shiarn darted in through the smoke.

Earona and Mara dashed into the shadows of the trees and watched the flames begin their destruction of the tent.

Shiarn returned and threw the satchel at Earona. 'Lucky it's so big and ugly, I never would have found it. Now, let's get away from this.'

The girls walked further into the forest and away from the din of fighting. Not a great distance from them came the breaking of branches and a snapping growl.

'Run,' Shiarn ordered.

Mara ran, trying to avoid anything she could see. With a rasping bark, the creature sprinted on all fours, spreading and destroying the underbrush as it came behind her. Swiping at her leg, it slashed into her flesh and tripped her up. She cried at the sudden pain and rolled onto her stomach. The gruesome thing stood over her, its acrid breath hit her hair. Cringing, she shut her eyes; too afraid to see her own death.

The creature paused. Amidst dirty tangled fur, its shining yellow eyes stared down at her.

Sudden anger erupted within Mara, and she growled with surprising vehemence, 'Get away from me!'

The monster was motionless, breathing down into her face, baring its teeth, but not coming any closer.

Her leg surged with burning pain, yet she scrambled up and sped away at a limping pace, thinking for certain it would permanently maim her.

The creature growled and sniffed the earth, searching for them once more. It would see them soon enough, Mara's blood would lead it to her. From out of nowhere her hand was grabbed and held tight. She could see no one. To her astonishment she could no longer see herself. Giddiness overtook her, and she felt sick.

Earona's voice sobbed. 'I'm so glad you weren't—'

'Hush!' Shiarn tugged on Mara's hand to shift her. 'Don't panic or cry out and don't let go.'

Mara wanted to know if she could throw-up. Her stomach leapt in resistance and emptied. It fell to the ground, and she had no way of seeing if any of it was on her dress. Touching her face and stomach, she closed her eyes, imagining her body parts still there.

'Disorientation will pass,' said Shiarn.

The beast howled as it tracked Mara's blood.

'We have to move. Quickly.' Shiarn pulled them along, one on each hand. 'It can smell us.'

Mara leaned into Shiarn, not able to walk the fast pace.

Shiarn said with irritation, 'You wait here and heal her.'

Exhausted, Mara appeared and fell into Earona's arms.

The Baskharef howled and thrashed against the trees in a terrifying display of anger and destruction. Mara came in and out of consciousness until she could stand once more. Somehow her wound was healed enough for her to walk, but not enough to diminish the pain.

After some moments, Shiarn took her hand and they became unseen again. Mara prepared herself for the disappearance, even so the initial shock sent her head spinning. She wondered how she did it, make a person vanish.

'Holy Kahm, that was disgusting.' Shiarn rushed them on with great speed, with the beast continuing its search.

'You didn't kill it?' Earona asked.

'No,' Shiarn retorted, 'I had to move quick, I saw a Skar nearby. They're on to us now. Curses, I lost my knife too.' They struggled through the trees, eventually discovering what might be a track. Shiarn finally said, 'That blade was Gran Hesta's.'

The evil creature growled on its pursuit of their scent.

Earona tripped and fumbled in a waist high bush. '...sorry.'

'We can shake this beast if we are fast,' Shiarn said through gritted teeth.

They trotted at a speed suiting all three with Shiarn supporting Mara as best she could.

Earona halted, forcing the other two to stop, and gave an alarmed shout. 'I've lost my amulet. It must have fallen from my pocket. Curse it.'

'We can't look now.' Shiarn puffed and pulled Earona forward. 'When it's light.'

Gradually, the sound of the beast disappeared altogether. The peace of the forest was welcomed, and the three became visible again.

Earona's skirt caught on a low branch. She yanked on it, ripping the pale blue material, and she grumbled, 'Where are we?'

'In a forest,' Shiarn replied just as cross and she gathered as much of her skirt up as she could.

'Do you think the others are still...?' Earona whispered, 'in danger?'

Shiarn replied, 'We are some way from them.'

A couple of large boulders dominated the space between the trees and a low log.

'Help me, Shiarn,' Earona cried.

Shiarn and Earona supported Mara to a fallen trunk. They sat with her between them. A white-stone pendant around the neck of the red-headed woman caught Mara's attention. It filled her mind till she thought of nothing else. She wanted it, as if her life depended on it.

Shiarn removed Mara's fingers from the glimmering pendant. 'No time to look at jewelry.'

Mara's face remained blank, not comprehending her irrational desire for the object. She shook her head, shaking away the ludicrous notion. 'There's...' Her fingers pointed at the woods and a figure dashing between the trees.

A man charged towards them with a knife. Mara squawked and rolled off the log onto the wet bracken, losing her other shoe.

Ignoring Earona and Mara, he came after Shiarn. Shiarn stopped the knife and the two fell to the ground, wrestling each other for dominance. Mara could only watch the attack with shock. The man wore no shoes and seemed to be dressed for bed.

Earona picked up a rock with two hands and stood over them as they scrambled together. She lifted it in an attempt to aim at the man as he fought Shiarn. The two suddenly disappeared and Mara caught a glimpse of a glinting object on a figure crouched by a tree. The small figure bolted through the trees.

Earona dropped the rock and chased after the child, calling his name. Torn between desiring the pendant, and not wanting to be left with a knife-wielding attacker, Mara decided to get away while she could and limped after Earona.

Shiarn grasped the man's wrist preventing his intended strike. Instincts took over, making her aware of the value of fighting exercises. Fortunately, his frame was slight, but his determination to slash at her was baffling. The two wrestled together, tumbling onto moist shrubbery. Shiarn forced back his dagger from her neck, but his strength was unyielding. Proving the weaker of the two, her only option was to create a change by turning invisible. His disorientation might offer a chance of escape, but only if he let go of her. Yet anything looked better than being knifed.

The man's bewilderment at the invisibility was not to last and his ferocity increased. Her body was trapped under his weight and he held fast to her upper arm. Considering the pointlessness of being unseen, she became visible once more. The use of her Gift incited more anger, and his eyes flicked an eerie white as he cursed her.

'Earona!' Shiarn screamed, beginning to panic at her predicament. *I'm going to kill her,* she thought once she realized she was gone. She summoned all her strength to keep the dagger from being imbedded in her face, although the tip remained inches from her eyes. Hindered by her own cloak, she would not have minded being soaked to the skin if it meant she could move and maybe preserve her life. The man did not have to worry about such cumbersome clothing, dressed only in light woolen under-drawers. She grunted, 'why are you doing this?'

Through clenched teeth, he answered, 'I want the Eye-key.'

She could only assume madness had overtaken him. 'I don't know what that is.'

'You know it,' the man hissed. 'And I will have it.' The knife sliced across the top of her shoulder and she bellowed from the sudden pain.

Unprepared for the axe, swiftly swiping at his neck, he toppled to the side, dead.

Shiarn shoved the body away with revulsion, trying hard to avoid the blood gushing from the wound. All the same, his head came to a stop beside her.

'Not a chance of that, you miserable creature,' Ethan remarked to the body. 'That wasn't a normal villager, was it?'

She shook her head unsure of the answer and she winced from the cut near her neck. 'A nasty piece of work, whatever he was. God above, I don't think I've ever been happier to see you in my life.' Promptly remembering her fury, she stared around the cramped woods. 'Where is she? I'm going to have words with her.' She sprinted in the direction she thought Earona had taken with Ethan following after.

They did not go far when they came across Mara. In an instant of viewing the girl, she disappeared into thin air or so it seemed. Shiarn's warning shouts went unheeded and the two could do nothing, but watch her enter the senyu Menhrs.

'I can't believe it.' Shiarn's chest heaved from the short run. 'You think Earona went through too?'

Ethan approached the senyu and studied the tracks leading up to it. The ground cover was nearly stomped flat. 'I think she did, the ground has been trampled. Of course, it might have been Jett and the others earlier. Could she be that foolish to go through one of these things?'

'Mara probably doesn't know any better, but Earona should.' Her red hair frizzled up, creating a messy frame around her face which flushed with exertion. Her lovely linen dress was splattered with mud.

'That girl….'

'Yes, probably the reason we're out here in the first place.' Shiarn tried to peer through the trees.

Ethan called for Earona and no answer was returned, and she did not appear to be hiding in the nearby shrubbery.

'Doesn't she realize what she has done?' Shiarn moaned. 'She must have more sense than that.'

'Maybe she didn't know this was here. She's been busy healing.'

She shook her head in amazement. 'What is Jett going to say? Nothing good, I'm sure.'

'By the might of Kahm! Why are you worried about him? Think where those girls are now, alone, with nothing on them to sustain them,' he said with grim resolution, 'they are who you should be worried about.' He sighed. 'We must enter and find them.'

'You're daft!' She looked at him as if he had gone mad. 'How can we walk through willy-nilly into God knows what and expect Jett to be happy about it?'

'When you think about it, you know it's the right thing to do. The more we stand here discussing it, the more danger they may be in,' he reasoned, 'No time to go back. At least we can be with them, to protect them. The Kin is split up now as it is and we will all have to eventually go through. Why shouldn't we go through now and make it even.'

He was right in a roundabout way. However, it did not sit comfortably with her, because she liked having Jett onside. She retorted, 'You talk too much. Have it your way. Heavens, let's just go through and be done with it.'

'Wait.' *We could leave something…* He pointed to Shiarn's pendant, hanging out from her cloak.

'Now you want my favourite piece of jewelry. I've lost my dagger, now I lose my white stone.' She handed him the pendant. 'I better get this back or it's on your head.'

'All the better then. They will know we willingly left this as a sign and if they have any brains between them they will know we entered here.' He ignored her sour look and rested the pendant on top of one of the granite stones, letting the shining gem be visible.

'I'm sure they will think we are capable of such an insane act.' She sulked. 'Jett will anyway.' She clasped her cloak around her in an effort to shut out Ethan's sensitive gaze. 'Anyway, my shoulder is aching and dripping blood all over. Remember, your idea. He can bite your head off.'

'You are exaggerating.' His large hand swallowed her dainty one in a secure hold. 'Sometimes you deserve his scolding with all your eavesdropping. Let's go, we are wasting time.'

She remained coldly quiet, too insulted to answer.

They walked into the empty hole with a steady step. Ethan's axe was ready in chance any hostiles were there to greet them.

With an overwhelming sense of dread, Shiarn yelled, 'Wait!'

14 - Shortcut

'It wasn't that I was lost—' what would those skulking gephyrophobiacs know? *'—it was simply a case of not knowing where I was going.'*

Notes of a Roving Savant. Zaki'is Fur'Mole

'We should not be so quick to assume the unthinkable,' Keanan said, breaking the mournful silence that had descended over the Kin. 'We must search further out.'

'I fear the worst has happened,' Hellier replied, 'I sense it in my bones. I feel it in this bleeding shoulder.'

'That's thinking positive,' Marcus added, dryly.

Jett stepped away from them and looked past the floating ash remnants of their tent. *Where are you all?*

Keanan added, 'Ethan must be with them.'

'We can hope,' Marcus said.

With his back to them, Jett stared into the shadowed tree line. If they face what he just did, he dreaded to imagine what was possible. 'We will search. Now. We'll never get any sleep anyway.' He called to Seth, standing under the trees at a distance, 'How does the forest look?'

Seth shook and appeared to break from his daydreaming. 'Currently the trees are not happy… they are quiet.'

Hellier rolled her eyes to the night sky.

Seth responded with impatience, 'They do not like fire, nor evil things trampling over their own. At this moment they are not helpful.'

'The trees can go to h—' Jett held his thoughts, remembering a time when he was young and not so prudent.

Seth replied, 'I'm hoping your reputation with flora has not traveled this far. Besides, I have a thought they were invisible.'

'They should have been,' Jett said without a hint of shame at Seth's mentioning of his past indiscretions.

Hellier asked him, 'Do trees see invisible things?'

'The Concealment Gift applies to all life forms,' Seth said, 'I'm not sure about the spirit world though.'

Hellier grimaced, 'Flamin' hell, that's not what I asked.'

Jett said, 'I will be the one searching.' After asking Keanan and Seth to follow him, he instructed Hellier and Marcus to stay with the horses and gather what belongings remained and wait. Jett inspected the area where the girls exited the tent while he waited for Seth to wrap Hellier's wound, before his own injury was tended. Seth had to scavenge what cloth he could from the wagon and pad their cuts as best he could.

Searching the wet earth, Jett examined a subtle trail the girls would have made. His Charer Gift gave him the natural trait of seeing in darkness. Everything in his night-time world gave off an inner illumination. The sky became a pale grey as if a muted sun was in the distant background and his environment was clear as an overcast day. A useful Gift, even though the only time he had rest from the light of the world was with closed eyes.

Even though Jett was able to see in the darkness, the random spattering of rain made the ground messy. He studied the disturbed earth and turned his attention to the sky. 'Curse this rain.' They traveled further in and Jett peered at the ground at various spots. Kneeling closer, he scrutinized a patch of shrubs. 'Blood is here.' He continued poring over the area, taking as much time as his tolerance would allow. 'Something large passed… I suspect a Baskharef.' He stepped nimbly over the sopping undergrowth, not wanting to miss any signs. Abruptly crouching, he picked up an object and waved it over his shoulder. 'Someone's shoe.'

'I don't recognize it.' Keanan squinted at it with puzzlement. Jett threw it to him, and catching it, Keanan remarked, 'It doesn't bode well.'

Jett continued studying the turned over and damaged undergrowth. 'Blood trail.'

'Someone is injured?' suggested Keanan.

Eventually they came across piles of ash and a dead Baskharef. All three noticed it, but it was not on the trail Jett was following. 'Deep gouges. Most likely Ethan.' Bending down, he slid out a dagger and held it up for them to see. 'In its eye.' He hooked it onto his belt. It gave him no assurance of the girls' safety, Shiarn was now weaponless. Plus, Skar must have been in the area, and perhaps still were. 'We need to be careful.'

'Someone was sick!' Seth called to them.

Jett nodded and came to stand beside him. From there he followed what appeared to be a semblance of a track left by people. They could all see the material stretched across the bark of a tree. Earona's clothing gave Jett encouragement, at least they were moving in the right direction. It became more apparent when Jett noticed the area of black ash, otherwise near invisible to Seth and Keanan. *We're heading in the right direction.*

They arrived at a space between the trees. A dead tree lay under the lofty branches, and not far from it was the headless body of a half-dressed villager. Jett scanned the space and saw no ash mounds. 'This is a peculiar sight.' He walked to the log and placed a finger on a line of moisture.

'There was a fight,' Keanan said. 'This man must have been using that dagger. His head was lobbed off. Why would Ethan do that?'

'If Ethan did it,' Jett speculated. 'There's blood on the knife.'

Keanan bobbed down near the log and rose with another matching shoe. 'Wherever she is, she's barefoot.'

Seth stared up at the trees in silent meditation. 'They were here.' Finally he said, 'The senyu is not far off.'

Jett turned to search it out. Seth and Keanan ran after him. On finding it, Jett stared transfixed at the white and gold pendant. His hand hovered by it, but he did not bring it down, fearing any strange visions it might invoke.

Seth took it and rubbed it with his thumb.

Jett knelt to view the broken vines. 'They've been trampled.' He rose with a dejected sigh. 'That might explain it.'

'It's true,' Seth said, 'but why?'

Jett contemplated a handful of reasons, but it was still baffling. 'We can only guess for now.'

'Maybe chased through…' Keanan offered, 'Apprehended?'

Seth considered the necklace. 'She wouldn't willingly hang it here like this without good reason.' He put her pendant around his own neck.

'Yes, well, whatever the reason.' Now Jett was simply annoyed. The urgency of their disappearance was not so dire, yet they had to leave as soon as they could manage it. 'We know where we have to go.' He started walking back the way they came.

Seth looked at the empty space with a glint in his eyes. *I could follow through right now.*

'Don't you dare!' Jett commanded. 'We go together.' He marched into the forest. Over his shoulder, he snapped, 'Look's like Hellier will get her wish.'

Seth grinned at the stones and turned to follow him.

It was arduous guiding the horses through the forest. After a lot of coaxing and profanity, more than was necessary, they arrived at the clearing near the senyu.

Jett walked through first, leading Thunder. He appeared in a grove, and worked fast to guide his horse aside from the doorway. The night sky was still present but clear, and neat piles of stones signified the existence of the supernatural doorway.

The Kin came through and they moved the horses from the entry as much as they had space. The horses stamped and pulled, thoroughly unsettled against the close growing trees. The last thing Jett needed was a horse vanishing back into the empty space.

Hellier, hands on hips and her horse's rein firmly in place, gave the clearing a scan. 'They aren't here, are they?'

Marcus, holding his stamping horse steady, said, 'Excellent observation.'

'And our horses are stomping on any tracks.' Keanan had a tight grip on Forest and also Sunny's rein, one of the wagon horses.

Jett said, 'Surely, they did not enter again into the senyu.' A sombre quiet descended as he considered the likelihood of that happening.

'I don't believe,' Keanan finally remarked, 'that all of them would be so daft, possibly one might do such a foolhardy act.'

Nodding in agreement, Jett stared into the space and out into the forest. No one interrupted his train of thought as he contemplated the fate of the missing ones. 'I can't feel them nearby. Curse it. Would they wander off by themselves?'

Marcus said in a short yet affable manner, 'mad buggers.'

Seth left his horse tethered to a tree near the edge of the clearing and disappeared into the dark.

'Don't wander far, Sprout.' Jett walked into the trees in the opposite direction.

Keanan called to Jett, 'Any sign?'

'People have been walking here.'

Seth broke through the branches of a soft pine to meet Jett as he crouched. 'Numerous people have been through this space. A while ago now.'

Jett and Seth followed a trail of broken bushes and undergrowth that no longer cared to grow. They came out onto smooth stones of a wide road. Appearing to be the only option, they started bringing the horses via the same pathway.

The sun was visible for a short time when they were all settled on their horses on the road. A direction could not be determined before knowing their location. Seth bowed his head by a tree. He scurried up it and scouted up and down the road, shading his eyes from the half hidden sun in the east. He waved a carefree hand down the road running south. 'Forest down there.' He looked in the opposite direction. 'More forest that way.'

Marcus scowled with annoyance. 'That's helpful.'

'Which way then?' Hellier grumbled.

'The trees aren't clear, but there was a lot of traffic here last night. Numerous wagons and people.'

Jett shaded his eyes and looked down the road. 'Whoever they were must have taken them.'

Seth climbed down. 'Probably. I get the sense they were moving south. We could ask the wagon coming this way what is ahead.'

Soon enough what he spoke of peeked over the short rise. As well as the wagon, a few riders traveled alongside. The small band slowed on their approach and the driver sang out a friendly greeting, and the Kin droned out theirs.

'Are you off to the city?' The man, his wagon full of produce, appeared to be a farmer, dressed in worn homespun trousers and comfy shirt, on his head a floppy straw hat.

Jett replied, 'We might be at that.' The Kin's lack of provisions and damp clothing was an unusual sight, and yet, despite their lack of travel gear they were all sufficiently armed. The driver and the riders studied them with sudden mistrust. Given the odd condition they presented, Jett was as civil as possible. 'Would you tell me where this road heads?'

The farmer's brow lifted at the strange question and despite his clear misgivings, pointed down the south bound road. 'Floris up ahead and back north leads to Edwige, and eventually Ryne.'

Jett gave a curt nod. 'My thanks.'

'We'll be off then,' he answered, unable to wipe the suspicion from his face. The wagon set off and the Kin were obliged to move aside. As it trundled past, the riders placed numerous glances over their shoulders at the Kin.

Jett stated with relief, 'At least we are in Coltrene.'

'It's convenient we are so near the port,' said Keanan, 'a shame it isn't Hakan-Kara.'

'But what has happened to them and how do we know which way they went?' Marcus freely voiced his irritation.

Jett pondered the wagon in the distance, speeding down the road surrounded by dense woods on either side.

'We can assume they have been taken against their will,' Keanan said.

'Yes, otherwise they would be here,' Marcus added with dreary sarcasm.

Hellier shed a thought to them. *I think I see something, stay here.* She galloped up the road in the direction of the city. Taking no heed of her, they trotted after. She walked River into the border of the outlying trees and grabbed a scrap of material and waved it at them.

Keanan examined the crumpled strip and gave her an approving look. 'Good work, girl!'

Seth stared into the bushes. 'You think they left it for us?'

'Possibly, but even so, it tells us they travelled this way,' Jett concluded. 'It's one of Earona's.'

Marcus took the rag and put it near his nose. 'Yep, it smells.'

'Off to Floris,' said Seth, 'and that's about a fortnight quicker than planned.'

After riding for some time they crested a hill. The dense woods transformed into farming fields and scattered cottages. Miles to the east, the wall of Floris was like a giant grey line. Buildings and farm lots spread out from it, as if the city could no longer house its residents. Within the city, the palace prevailed as a majestic tower overlooking the sea and forest. A mix of architectural styles appeared to have been rebuilt over the centuries, creating a flawless abode fit for royalty. Beyond this spectacular sight was a line of grey.

Seth commented, 'Rather impressive.'

'Flamin' huge,' Hellier added.

Marcus questioned, 'I wonder how we will find them in that.'

A sudden fatigue descended, and a mental exhaustion dominated Jett's reasoning. 'We need to rest first.'

'Dry out, and heal…' Hellier slumped in her saddle, her damp cloak lay across her horse's rump.

Jett shook his head to wakefulness. 'And work out how to find them.'

15 - Ride to Floris

Rage is like strong liquor,
You regret both in the morning.

Or, it is similar to a snake in the grass.
You never know when it will rear its venomous head.

The Sleeping Sword

Mara appeared and Earona heaved a choking sob. She gazed through the empty space at tall pines and the same night sky although less sullen. A couple of decaying trees, lying crosswise, were nearby, and flat stones marked the corners of the senyu. Mara glanced at the new scene with speechless astonishment.

After some time, Ethan and Shiarn appeared. 'No need to cry. We're here now.' Ethan held his axe mid-way up the shaft. Its glinting edge was a menacing sight.

Earona wiped her cheek and said with irritation, 'What would you know?'

'That's the thank you,' Shiarn directed at Ethan, and turning her back to Earona, she peered into the shadows.

Earona pointed to the space devoid of life. 'Mal went through.'

Shiarn replied, 'Mal?'

'A boy,' Mara said.

Shiarn shrugged. 'Nothing we can do about it. He was bound to especially if you don't know how these portals work.'

Earona crossed her arms and lifted her chin. 'You're all heart.'

Ethan slid his axe into his back sheath and put a consoling hand on Earona's shoulder. 'Sorry, maybe when the others get here we can go after him.'

That was unlikely and another sob escaped her.

Shiarn said, 'Now we're stuck in another cursed forest.'

'We'll wait till they come.' Shivering, Earona rubbed her freezing arms.

Shiarn wrapped her arms around her chest under her cloak and her voice was stiff like her body. 'It's going to be cold and boring till they do, if they even know where we are.'

'You think this is my fault,' Earona responded, gruffly.

'You're the one who ran off.' Shiarn's hands went to her hips in defiance. *For another kid.*

Earona cast a glance at Mara, staring in shock, and back to Shiarn. 'You really are heartless.'

'There's no need for arguing—' Ethan attempted calm.

'*I'm* heartless?!' Shiarn snapped, 'You left me. I was nearly killed!'

'You're here now.' Earona's face grew hot at the truth of Shiarn's statement, but she folded her arms and glared. 'Sometimes you have to put others above yourself.'

Shiarn pushed Ethan aside, and her tone was like acid. 'You are truly a vision of perfect virtue. When are you going to think about something or someone other than your adoring vision of yourself? Why don't you put some thought into what you do?'

'You think I'm the '*vision*'?!' She shouted and gestured at her. 'Coming from you! That's truly the farce of the age. Prancing around, posing, "how lovely do I look?"'

Shiarn raised her arms in fury, her emerald eyes pierced the tension and she shouted, 'you puerile half-wit! You have the intelligence of – a lazy – slug.'

Ethan spread his arms between them in an attempt to stop them hitting each other. 'Will you both be quiet?'

'That's just like you to make it personal,' Earona shouted, 'because you lack any sort of decency—' *and dignity.*

'What horse-shit!' Shiarn's voice rose with indignation and she pointed a finger at Earona's chest. 'The only reason we were stuck at that place was because of *you*. Yes, queen of petty. You really don't give a brass about this Kin.'

'How dare you say that!' Mouth agape, Earona's eyes became slits and her shrill voice cut through the night. 'Everyone knows *I'm* the caring person in this Kin.'

Ethan gave a futile shake of his head at Mara, sitting, her mouth agape, watching the pair argue.

Despite stepping closer, Shiarn did not lower her voice, and her finger stabbed the air in front of Earona's face. 'You're a little do-gooder pest. But all you do is make trouble—'

'What a self-righteous bully you are,' Earona yelled, 'if we are going to start mud-slinging, you know what you are—'

'You haven't got the wits!' Baiting for an answer, Shiarn lifted her chin, and her red-hair bounced over her shoulder.

'You're too cocky,' her words shot out with brazen meanness, 'you harlot—'

With abrupt sharpness, a man's voice broke their argument. 'Lay down your weapons.'

Earona's hand fluttered to her open mouth, and her body stiffened with fear.

Soldiers armed with crossbows, moved from the darkness to surround them. The same man demanded, 'What is your business here?'

The girls, suddenly quiet, stared at the cocked weapons with alarm.

'I'd like to think our business is our own.' Ethan pulled out his axe and laid it on the ground. 'We are waiting for friends.'

A man stepped up to Ethan and jabbed him hard in the back, pushing him towards the speaker.

Earona gasped at the harshness of it.

The soldier barked out his question, 'Where are you from?'

Earona was sure they were still in New Empire due to the common language. But, to their current location, there was no way of telling.

Ethan replied, 'Past the mountains of Allervium.'

'You went through Ryne?'

Ethan smiled. 'In a roundabout way. Perhaps you can tell us where we are?'

'Coltrene, East Province.' The man addressed his troop, 'Take them back to the carriage!'

Shiarn cried, 'What for?'

'You have stolen significant information regarding the security of this kingdom. We had word you were last seen in Rothhaven.'

Ethan sighed. 'That's absurd.'

'It's not us!' said Shiarn.

'You are waiting here under incriminating circumstances for your friends.' The soldier spoke as their wrists were tied and they were marched off with crossbows at their backs. 'No more talking.'

They were led through the forest with no one speaking a word. The woods were tranquil except for the many feet clumping through the bushes, and a fervent load of thoughts shooting from one mind to the next. Their only guide was the soldier in front, as he led them over shrubs on a straight track.

After walking some time, they emerged on a hard road. Lamp light reflected on a line of carriages. Three, lavishly extravagant, and the others were covered in thick canvas. Marched to the second carriage, they stood as more soldiers gathered to stare at their captivity.

A man, waiting by the step, watched them line up with a puzzled frown. 'This is *them*?' His robes were velvet blue, and over his slick black hair he wore a silver cap. 'I suppose this female could resemble the description. The infamous "Raven" of the Mouratairs.' He stopped at Earona and studied her appearance, 'Although she appears quite insipid.'

Earona scrunched her brow and her bottom lip turned to a pout, her fear forgotten momentarily.

'Sir,' Ethan started, 'You're mistaken. We are not the ones you want. We—'

With a nod from the man in the robe, a soldier pushed Ethan in the back, forcing him to his knees.

'You think I would believe anything you have to say? No, it does not work that way.' His skin was like marble in the yellow light and his beard was a neat triangle. 'How convenient that would be for you, and how unlikely. You have also stolen a particular item—'

'You can't arrest us without some evidence.'

He walked to Shiarn and stood a hands-breadth away from her face. 'We shall see.' He lifted a strand of her tangled hair, and ran his fingers along her chin. She jerked her face away. 'Take them away. But not this one. Untie her.'

~ * ~

Marched to the back of one of the covered wagons, Earona, Mara, and Ethan were ordered to climb in. Amongst the clutter of luggage, Ethan sat on a box by the side overlooking the backend. Earona and Mara attempted to find a space on the floor. Earona's bag was thrown in. It landed on her lap with the contents spilling about her. She was amazed she received it back, but she could tell they had already gone through it. At least there was nothing of any real value in it. The only other thing she had of importance was the amulet, but it was gone along with the poor child who found it. Confounding her misery, the back flap of the wagon remained open, letting in the freezing night air. Without her cloak, Earona shivered and huddled closer to the luggage. Mara lay half slumped over a chest, the mud and blood hardening on her dress front.

Outside, the guards talked in anxious tones regarding one of their own who disappeared in the forest. Apparently the soldiers searched for their missing comrade but found no trace of him, which gave the soldiers more to speculate over the prisoners.

Earona shook her head with sadness. 'That poor man.'

'What a mess we are in,' said Ethan, 'if it weren't for you two—'

'Don't.' Earona's grief threatened to overwhelm her. *I'm already guilt ridden.*

'How you say the things you do to each other… I'll never know.'

Earona shuddered.

Ethan sat, hunched over. The cramped space provided limited arm movement, and the position of the girls hampered any leg room he might have had.

Earona examined the contents of her bag. 'Ethan…' An idea took shape in her mind. 'Can you…' *Move something with your hands tied?*

'It may be difficult.'

This cloth to the trees outside?

'I'll try.'

Two soldiers mounted their horses behind the wagon and started their slow procession into the night.

Distraction, Ethan suggested.

'Hello…' Earona lifted herself forward and waved her bound wrists. 'Hello there.'

Ethan's bound hands reached forward. The cloth glided across a bulging sack and came to the low door of the wagon. It fluttered to the edge and fell to the ground. The slight breeze tossed it into a shrub on the side of the road.

The guard scowled at Earona. 'What do you want?'

Earona enquired, 'I would like to know where exactly we are going?'

'To the palace,' he growled. The riders passed the white scrap. Ethan maintained his vision and palm in view of the waving material. It floated upward, out of sight of the guards. 'You. Get back in there,' the other guard yelled, 'Don't try anything.'

Ethan settled back into his hunched position.

'Whose palace is that?' asked Earona.

'The Royal family of Coltrene. No more questions.'

Earona sat back, doubtful they would actually see the king at the palace. Mara watched the floating cloth with wonder in her eyes.

Ethan said, 'I'm not sure anyone will see it.'

Earona said with hope, 'At least it's something.'

Mara whispered, 'What do you think will happen to us?'

'I don't know.' Cramped in the tight position, Earona was able to rest her head on Ethan's knee. *There's nothing we can do... Who is this Raven they think I am?*

Who knows? He pressed his fingers on her forehead. 'If only I could help you.'

She looked into his concerned eyes. 'We're together, that's enough.'

'I'm worried about you. And Shiarn.'

'I'm sure everything will be smoothed out when we get there.' She twisted her head to see Mara with her eyes closed.

Ethan nodded. 'I wonder what they are doing.'

'Looking for us. Getting angry...' She tried a small smile. *I wonder if they will even see that rag, if they don't...* Closing her eyes, she yawned with weariness, and relaxed against his leg. 'I'm glad you are here.'

'Me too,' he said, 'because I have a feeling we won't be getting to Hakan-Kara anytime soon after this.'

~ * ~

The others were led away, leaving Shiarn alone, shivering and rubbing her freed wrists. The man in blue opened the carriage door and indicated for her to come. Entering the warm interior, she stepped into a sweet aroma. A man sat against plush red cushions, watching her. Having no choice but to sit, she lowered herself onto the softness. Dirt covered her shoes and shins, and her ripped dress hung against the compartment, and she dreaded the frizzing volume of her red curling locks. Velvet upholstery was a welcomed comfort. She wished she could curl up and sleep.

The man stopped on the step and said to the one inside. 'This is she.'

He replied, 'You were correct after all.'

Shiarn had never seen a man so extravagantly dressed as the one who spoke. White frills filled the opening of his cream shimmering coat that had matching pants. Countless silver buttons adorned the front. They appeared to have no purpose, except add to the frivolous attire. His face was almost as pale as his shirt, but his hair, most likely a wig, was a glorious gold and tied at the nape of his neck, with a single ringlet bedecking his shoulders. His eyes seemed to watch her every move, yet his face revealed nothing regarding his thoughts. She squirmed under his direct gaze.

'Of course, sire.' He stepped into the carriage.

'Morgal, ride with Gaspar.'

Morgal glanced at Shiarn and a note of arrogance was in his voice. 'You should not travel alone.'

'She is not going to harm me.' He lifted a dainty hand to his nose in a flurry, 'Except, perhaps, maim my senses with that appalling stink.'

'Excuse me!' Shiarn finally found her voice and retorted, 'I didn't ask to be here.'

'I wish to be alone with her. Now, go.'

Morgal was waved from the doorway and he closed the door behind him, leaving Shiarn alone with the pompous looking man. She clenched her fist and pounded the cushion out of frustration. 'How do you know I won't hurt you?'

His eyes were like small lights, alive in the shadows and they stared at her soiled hair down to her soggy shoes. 'I did not say you did not want to hurt me. I said you would not. You know we have your... accomplices. What is your name?'

'Shiarn.'

'Refreshingly foreign.'

'We aren't thieves or whatever you think we are.'

He relaxed onto the cushion and looked out the window at the passing darkness. 'It really is irrelevant what you did or did not do.'

'You can't just arrest people. There are laws.'

'Indeed!' He directed a scornful gaze at her. 'Do you know what the punishment is for espionage?'

She could imagine any number of consequences, none of them pleasant.

He replied with satisfaction, 'That is correct.'

'What do you want with me?' Her voice trembled as she realized the position she was in.

He covered his yawn with a gloved hand. 'In short, you are going to be my favoured guest. For a time.'

She could hardly believe it would be that simple. 'Why?'

'It is my desire, and that is all you need to know at this time.'

'And my friends?'

'They will be executed—'

Shiarn gasped and sprang forward.

He raised a hand. 'If you do not adhere to the ways of your new home in a congenial fashion.'

'You mean prison.' She fell against the seat. If she weren't so weary she would shout with offense.

'It is best not to view it in such a brutal manner, if you are wise.'

The swaying wagon was a lovely prelude to sleep and Shiarn dared to close her eyes.

'I deplore being so straight forward. It is such a bore.'

She slit her eyes to study him. He almost sounded like a reasonable man. 'Who are you?'

'Many things. Your lord, protector, beneficiary, advocate—'

'Abductor.'

'Well, then, I am your keeper.'

She grunted, not having the energy to give a rebuke.

'Perhaps... companion.'

Not when her friends were being used as blackmail. That was pushing it. Through the window only the inky blackness of night could be seen. She stared regardless as if there was something interesting to keep her attention, so she didn't have to think on Ethan and Earona and her cruel parting remark. Even though Earona was tied up somewhere, Shiarn still felt angry. If only she got in the last word.

Startled from a light sleep, Shiarn stared at the predawn light across the countryside.

'You shall soon see the fields that surround most of the expanse about the city.'

What he described came into view and in the distance the magnificent walls of Floris, and the Royal Palace beyond.

PART II

Day

Harbour in the Storm

16 - Arrival

...self-indulgent city, sprawled like a wanton princess on the compromising slope of a rocky rise, seducing and accepting every ship from Hale Island to yonder into her massive port, the honeypot of Floris, centered between two mile long outcroppings going out to the bay of Hopewell. And what an apt name it is.

The palace is cleverly situated at the top of the rise with all the other affluent Florisians, for which there seems a fortunate few living in luxurious villas away from the sea stink that permeates every household around the docks. Did I write of the gambling dens? In a day, one could be a man of wealth, the next, seeking an instant loan from an irrefutable shylock, for which there is an abundance.

The most marvellous of cities for which I have a great fondness...

White Lady on a Rocky Hill, Zaki'is Fur'Mole

Four Square was so named due to the four avenues surrounding the commons. Old trees spread their branches over the lawn, and inns and stores shaded the streets bordering the park. Dario Rionauldi stood under a tree, playing his pipe for those walking the main thoroughfare into Floris. The mood of the crowd was becoming as dismal as his day. So far his morning had been shockingly eventful and most unpleasant, and it was not even midday. His childhood friend, Vivella, had been recruited by another sham cult. If that wasn't frightening enough, she revealed dark arts were in operation at the palace where she lived, and she was going to attempt unearthing the perpetrator. He had ordered her not to get involved with such dangerous activities. Now, she refused to talk to him. Not long after their argument, and by a stroke of predictable misfortune, he was sacked from his apprenticeship at the Potter's Shop by his own uncle, and was currently unemployed.

Miserable over the state of his life, he accidentally roamed down the lane of an old herbalist known for her natural, yet bizarre, remedies and whimsical eccentricities. He suspected there wasn't anything 'natural' about her concoctions, and until that morning he never wanted to find out. But, he was desperate. He needed help, even if it was a potentially poison potion. The crone of a woman turned out to be as crazy as he imagined she'd be. At the interesting and somewhat humiliating interview, he was informed he was cursed and under a prophecy from years ago, as well, he would have to make a decision over two women. Either choice could potentially lead to his death - apparently. He came out worse than when he went in, although now possessing a miracle cure in a small vial.

Due to his pouch being lighter, he decided busking was the only way he would get anything to eat. Usually he enjoyed the music, but his lacklustre playing was boring even him. He hooked his pipe in his belt and pulled the vial up to his eyes. Swirling the silver liquid, he tried to recall the old woman's instructions. *Drink it all, or was that just a sip?* He uncorked it and whiffed a metallic scent. He downed the thing in one fel gulp. Sweet and syrupy; it soaked his throat like fine wine. An impressive drink with a taste surprisingly delicious and nothing like he expected. He drank every last drop and licked his lips longing for more.

The unnatural substance didn't take long to start working. His body jolted with chaotic energy. The throbbing under his skin shot up his legs. Pounding sensations made him tremble. For some tense moments he thought his heart would stop, or fly out his chest and through his mouth. He wanted to run, dance, and sing, all at once. Charged with potent energy, he jumped repeatedly on the spot, feeling the existence of every hair follicle he had. Aflame with the new power, his internal emotions flared out of normal proportions, he needed to embrace... anything. He only hoped his body could contain the force of it. Rational thought became irrelevant. He tried to recall the conversation with the old herbalist, but even her face faded from memory.

Enthralled by walkers on the street, the wild scent of the trees, and sounds filling his ears, his senses sprang to life in a new type of ecstasy. A spontaneous tune sounded on his pipe, lively and intricate. Music, he never dreamt possible, came from his awakened heart. People stopped to listen.

Glancing across the street, the sight of a girl mesmerised him. For the first time in his life his heart beat with desire. Graceful and slender, she had bright blonde hair dangling in braids to her waist. Unusual yet not unattractive. Her leather pants and a man's shirt was an uncommon sight on a woman, but it made her more appealing. In a sweep of seductive movements, she alighted from her horse and scanned the street with a flick of her head. His eyes connected with a pair of perfectly shaped ones in a beautiful tanned face. Could this woman be the one the old lady spoke of? He decided he would have to find out.

~ * ~

Shiarn's companion sat in silence, giving short glances to the window. Too tired to try conversation again, she looked out on the streets of Floris with indifference. Eventually, they entered a stone wall enclosure where more people rushed about.

'Our humble garrison.'

'It's clean,' she muttered, 'at least.'

'I wish the same could be said about the rest of the city.'

The carriage rolled along until it arrived at another gateway, again opening before them. Passing another tunnel, they came to a larger courtyard. The horses' hooves echoed on the paving stones in an enclosed space. Finally they stopped at steps leading to a single open door. A servant dressed in grey opened the carriage door. She stepped out after her companion, hoping she wasn't going to tumble onto the cobbled walkway. With a startled flick of his eyes, the servant reached for her hand. She noticed the storage wagons had gone, leaving only the finely decorated carriages in the courtyard.

Shiarn stood before the servants staring at her with fascination. She glared back, dreading to think how awful she looked.

'Servants standing about,' her companion remarked, 'Of course, there couldn't be anything productive for them to do.' He looked them over as they bowed and curtsied. 'Ducell, send for Regina. See to it she looks after this woman.' He fluttered his hand at Shiarn and started up the steps. 'Be certain to get that dreadful smell removed, and get those new clothes up to her room as soon as possible.' Without a glance in her direction, he disappeared through the backdoor of the palace.

Shiarn gaped in embarrassment unable to say a word.

Ducell instructed a maid to take Shiarn to the Lady's Suite, and he hurried them past him. Shiarn had the impression he did not wish to soil his hands further by touching her himself. She was lead up stairways and through narrow corridors. Through arched doorways she caught glimpses of elaborate halls. They came to a corridor with a couple of chairs and old portraits, and arrived at a door near the end. The maid bade Shiarn enter. Then she left without a word, locking the door behind her.

Red and fuchsia cushions embellished the sumptuous upholstered furnishings. Matching the décor, the floor was spread with rugs in the same reds. Emblazoned on the main rug were two deer. Portraits of naked ladies and couples kissing adorned the walls. Two walls were taken up with murals. One, a group of picnickers danced, ate, and embraced. The second was similar except they frolicked naked. It provided a good indication of what the room might be used for; love or lust, depending on your penchant for sexual relations.

On the alcove seat, she knelt on the burgundy cushions and opened the window. The exhilarating sea air hit her face. Down below, drab stone buildings and marching soldiers. Cliffs were to the southwest, and towards the north the city walls and the palace courtyards. She had only seen the ocean in books, and now she was denied a real view.

The door rattled and flew open. A portly woman in a tight fitting red and white gown, rushed in. Her bosom bulged from her bodice, and her brunette hair was bundled at the top of her head. 'Good morning.' She attempted to catch her breath.

Shiarn nodded curtly.

'I am Regina, your attendant.'

'Tell me why I am here?' Shiarn demanded, 'Am I to be some type of whore?'

She smiled. 'Would you like it in those terms?'

'I do not like it in any terms!'

Regina said with glee, 'It's in the way you wish to look at it then.'

'I'd like to see someone in charge.'

'Oh, you will.' She frowned at Shiarn's ripped and soiled dress and the dirty prints on the rug left from her shoes. 'It's fortunate he was able to see you through that grime, but I knew he'd find you in the end.'

'This is outrageous!'

'You will like it here once you get to know how things work. We all get used to working here.' Regina's smile was out of place on her hard face and it gave Shiarn a disturbing sensation. 'But now, you are tired. You must rest.' Maids entered, bringing between them a giant iron tub, and another arrived with a cart of jugs of hot water. 'Be patient while your bath is prepared.'

Shiarn paced like a caged animal.

'You are weary.' Regina gestured toward a maid carrying a tray. 'Here is warm nutmeg milk.'

The woman's cheerfulness annoyed her, but the thought of a drink and hot bath was tempting. She gazed at the desirable liquid accompanied by a moist cake. A long time had passed between warmth and food. *Curse this woman.*

'Do you like your bath hot or warm?'

'Hot.' She would have the bath then think about what to do next.

Regina continued with the same frivolous grin.

After her bath, Shiarn satisfied herself with food and drink. She lay on the grand bed, her body clean and comforted by luxurious pillows. Exhaustion took over and she collapsed into a deep sleep.

~ * ~

Mara tried to doze. Sleep was impossible due to her cramped position, not that she really wanted to drift off, she only wanted a rest from thinking. On entering into the chatter of voices and animal sounds she sat straight as much as she could. They passed cottages, busy farmers, and women carrying baskets. In the distance, she viewed farmlands sprawled up to the forest. They trundled through a gateway and caught a glimpse of the high wall of Floris.

Ethan said, 'Look's like we have arrived.'

'Who could imagine we would enter Floris like this?' Earona whispered.

Mara stretched her neck and peered out at the city. She had never been to Floris, but she had heard plenty about it. Not so much its citizens, but its aristocracy. An arrogant class of people she had no wish to see again.

Alongside the road, people stood to attention, stopping their business to stare. The avenues were lined with buildings and trees, and the people looked warm in their woollen dresses and caps, and everyone, she noted enviously, had a cloak on. A strange odour was a mystifying thing. She realized they were breathing in the ocean air.

They passed another gateway and entered an enclosed courtyard. A couple of servants took a second odd glance at them in the back of the wagon before another gateway was upon them. More soldiers stood about idly watching. The wagon continued before stopping at a two story building where soldiers came to and fro.

Mara remained on edge at every glance. The closer they got to the palace, the more panic rose within her. Lanvin was miles away, but she didn't care about that. It was leaving Wendessa without saying a proper goodbye, and more than that, it was all the unanswered questions she had regarding her new state of mind. The sadness she felt over Wendessa's death was a strange sensation. She bit her lip and rubbed her arms, wondering how she had gotten into this predicament. But if it weren't for the dark haired man who knows where she would have ended up, probably in a lot worse of a situation. She had gone towards to the stranger in the night far too easily and more readily than she thought possible. It was even beyond her control or comprehension. Once more she replayed the vision in her mind, wondering how it fit in with the stranger and her mother, but it left her bewildered.

Ethan's deep brown eyes looked them both over, and as if he read her mind, he said, 'It will work out. Somehow.'

The wagon came to a full stop. Not far off, men shouted commands, and the sound of marching soldiers echoed around the courtyard. The soldiers dismounted and ordered them out.

Unable to get down on her own, Mara lifted her tied wrists and her voice rumbled with arrogance. 'I can't do it like this.'

Surprise flashed on the guard's face as he lifted her to the ground. Earona gave him a biting remark and he was obliged to lift her down also.

Barred windows were along the bottom of the stone building. Another prison. This one obvious. They were led inside and down a narrow passage. They continued in single-file down a circle of stairs and arrived below ground level. Desks, covered with papers, and rows of drawers, were at the end of the room and more cells were through another door. An official guard rose from his chair and took a package and papers from the man who brought them down. Earona's bag was torn from her shoulder and flung by his desk, and the guard waited as the man read the papers.

The official looked up at them, but Mara hung her head, avoiding eye-contact and hoping she would not be singled out. He yelled at his men, 'Why are we bringing young girls in like this?'

'Captain Morran.' The first guard stepped forward. 'Orders of the Crown Prince.'

'I know. I can read.' The captain waved his hand, impatiently. 'Can't you see this girl is with child?'

The guard remained silent and the captain said, 'Take the girls down to the end,' he ordered, 'put him in the first cell.'

Earona's voice warbled as she shot her words out. 'Sir, we've done nothing wrong. You can't lock us up.'

'We can and we are.' The captain looked down at her with indifference. 'A patrol from Rothhaven has been searching for you, so called Raven—'

'But that's not me!' Earona cried.

His palm opened and he revealed a sachet of paste. 'We also found this in your possessions. A truth inducing drug.'

Earona's eyes widened with fear-filled shock. 'But, no, that wasn't mine at all. I found it. I had no idea it was something like that.'

'That's your excuse? Nevertheless, it gives us enough reason to take you in.'

Her eyes welled with tears and she whispered with confusion, 'Everything is wrong.'

His eyes narrowed, and he said, gruffly, 'We shall get to the bottom of this.' He flashed the scrawled piece of parchment in her face. 'We have every authority to arrest you.' He sat with a heavy sigh. 'Take them away.'

Guards took the girls, with Earona declaring their innocence and accusing them of cruelty. They arrived at an open cell and the guards untied their ropes. Mara walked in without needing to be told while Earona resisted and continued pleading their virtue. Pushed inside, Earona stumbled and the door was slammed behind her. The resounding bang travelled up the corridor. Through the small barred window Earona watched the guards walk away.

Mara stretched out on the straw bedding. The cell was cold and in places worn weave matting covered the floor. Near the low ceiling was a window, and in the corner, a bucket. A thin blanket added to the cell's penury.

Earona planted herself on the mattress, laid her head in her hands and sobbed.

~ * ~

The Kin did not ride far from the city gate before Jett stopped outside an inn across from the grassed park. He looked at the swinging picture. 'White Horse.' The three-story inn, founded on stone, had a terrace around its front and side. Jett dismounted and told Hellier and Marcus to stay with the horses while he went in with Keanan and Seth.

The two, left outside, loosely tied the horses. Marcus reclined on the terrace, gazing at the passing people, and grumbled, 'Why is it always us?'

Ignoring him, Hellier, on the bottom step, taped her foot to the musician's song across the street. A growing crowd were tossing coins into a hat near his feet. He did not appear wealthy, but had a clean shirt, brown pants and long leather boots, and a broad hat flopped over his shoulder length blond hair. He was too thin, but regardless of his odd face and appearance, Hellier thought his music was excellent. His eyes met hers through the huddles of moving people and she smiled.

He scooped up his hat and money, and scattering the crowd, he crossed the street. She waited in amazed silence as he advanced on her. With a broad grin and a passionate glint in his eyes, he clutched his hat near his heart. 'Glorious hue of divine beauty, today my eyes are eternally blessed to be consumed by such an enchantment. Descend goddess, oh, radiant sun, into my drab morning.'

'Uhm...'

Stifling a chuckle, Marcus leaned over the railing.

Dario dropped to one knee on the damp hardened earth. 'Transparent loveliness, swathed in gracious air.' His voice rose in enthusiasm, and an open twitter came from two passing ladies. 'You are a magnanimous victress.'

'A what?'

He swept his arms wide, his brown hat scrunched tightly in one hand. 'Muse of striking themes, vivacity and adventure. May I enter your surreal space of favour?'

She backed away with wide-eyed indignation. 'Back away!'

'If I appear forward it is only the sight of your splendour creating a frenzy in my pulsing heart,' he gushed, 'I am in love.'

Marcus guffawed, loudly.

She put her hand up against the strange Nayinn. 'You must be insane.'

He stood and reached for her arm. 'Don't go!'

Gripping his wrist, she twisted it behind his back, and hissed in his ear, 'Don't ever grab me.'

'Your body so close, your breath on my skin…'

She shoved him away and he stumbled onto his rear. He gave her a queer uncomprehending stare from under the fringe of his tussled hair.

Curse it. It wasn't her style to beat up weaklings. 'I don't like strangers touching me.' She reached for his hand.

He grasped hold of her. After righting himself, he placed his hat on his head. 'I shall introduce myself. My name is Dario Rionauldi and I am at your service, my lady.' He bowed while clutching onto her hand and raised it to his lips for a kiss.

'I'm Hellier.' She prised his hand off hers. 'You shouldn't be saying those things, you don't know me.'

'The words explode from my mouth at the sight of you.'

Keanan emerged from the inn and told them to bring the horses around back to the stables. He and Marcus began untying them.

'I have to go.'

'I must see you again.' His eyes lit up with joy.

'Dario—' she yawned. 'I'll be staying here…' She wondered the wisdom of informing him where she was staying, too late.

'Splendid news, Hellier.' Her name rolled over his tongue as if they had been friends for years. It only added to the creepy sensations he was giving her.

She followed the other two down the side alley, leaving Dario staring at her retreating back. 'Flames below!' she muttered, 'Something's wrong with him.'

Marcus mimicked the eccentric Nayinn, 'Radiant sun, muse of, what was that—' She punched his upper arm and he yowled. 'That's it, striking theme! Did he say surreal? I've been in your surreal space. I'll gladly tell him, it ain't favourable.'

She blushed, 'Shut up or I'll do worse!' But still, the truth was no one had ever spoken to her in such a charming manner. It felt curious and not all together bad.

17- Prisoners

To one, a diamond is a jewel. To another, it is a sharp rock.

Prophetess, Janna Meadow'Fox 4th Seat Elder

Shiarn woke to a noise from the wardrobe. She opened her eyes to a girl hanging garments. Her dreams were spoilt by a recollection of the morning's events. Before getting cross, she decided the girl really had nothing to do with it. 'Hello.'

Curly blonde hair was covered by a white cap, and kind blue eyes peeked from underneath. The girl, not more than fifteen, curtsied in such a rush she almost tripped over her feet.

'God above, don't curtsey.' Shiarn swung her legs from the bed and stretched fiercely.

'Yes, milady.'

Shiarn cocked her head at the dresses spilling out from the chests. 'What's all this?'

'Your garments.' The girl busied herself putting the gowns away again.

'Those other chests?'

'Your accessories.'

'How ludicrous!' Clothes and jewellery were a joy of Shiarn's, but how long did they think she was staying here?

'Milady?'

Shiarn drifted over to one of the other chests and flung the lid back. She pulled out a green velvet hat covered with tiny glass beads.

'I know just the thing for that.' She struggled with a garment in the wardrobe and drew out a dress in the same material. The low cut bodice appeared too small, but perhaps it was the fashion. Delicate beads over the full skirt caught the afternoon sun in a lovely shimmer, and the short sleeves were transparent and gentle. 'Isn't it lovely?'

'Extremely.' Shiarn was not happy admitting how close it was to her own taste. 'Where did all this come from?' She pushed the many gowns aside, noting with surprise all the dresses would probably fit her.

'The king's tailor, I suppose.'

An object amongst the various hats caught her eye; a wooden chest. Despite its plain appearance, the contents were far from average. Pearls, diamonds, rubies, set in gold chains, rings or brooches, were neatly ordered inside. A necklace of emeralds came with matching earrings. The girl knelt on the rug, mouth hanging open at the treasure box, her earlier politeness discarded. Shiarn thought of her own necklace hanging on the stone of the senyu and hoped the others had found it. She swung a blue opal pendant the size of a long nail before her eyes. 'Now, this is a gem.'

The girl pointed at a gold ring. 'That's pretty.'

Shiarn laughed at the girl's timidity. 'Have a look at it.'

'I... I don't know...'

'Go on, who is going to know?'

The girl picked up the ring hesitantly and slipped it on her finger. She admired the pink diamond.

'What's your name?' Shiarn saw a potential friend in the girl.

'Sasheya.'

'I am Shiarn. Most likely you know that already.'

Sasheya nodded. 'I'm fortunate to serve you. My mother passed away and I was given her duties.' She smiled. 'You are so lucky. It's like a dream come true.'

'I'm sorry about your mother.' Shiarn exhaled a grumbling breath. 'Lucky, eh? Being a prisoner.' She rummaged in the jewel box. 'No, thank you.'

'A prisoner? You are the favoured lady from a far off land.'

Shiarn snorted in an unlady-like manner, but she glimpsed the dreamy stare of the impressionable girl. 'Whatever they tell you, it's a lie.'

'You don't like the palace?'

'I don't like not being able to leave.' Shiarn threw the jewels back in the box, suddenly not able to appreciate their beauty.

'I... didn't know.' Sasheya took the ring off and laid it in the box.

'Can you do something for me? Is there some way you can find out about the people that came with me?'

'Not those people who were arrested?' Sasheya's face paled and her lips tightened in fear.

Shiarn jumped to her feet. 'But they haven't done anything. I don't want you to get into trouble, but, if you could find out if they are well and nothing more.'

Sasheya's bright innocent face looked up at her for a moment. 'I might be able to find out something, I suppose.'

The door to the suite opened. Regina marched into the bedroom, and Sasheya bolted from her fierce glare. Regina watched her leave and turned to Shiarn with an overly sweet smile. 'You have rested well.'

'As well as can be expected.'

'Good.'

Shiarn stood to meet her. 'I demand to be freed from this prison.'

'I see.' Regina's stupid old-maid expression infuriated her.

'You are holding me against my will—'

'I'm tired of this discussion. It is the way of it and you will soon adjust,' she lectured, 'You have been shown mercy by being brought here.'

'And what of my friends?'

'That is not for me to decide. If you don't make a fuss, perhaps they will be assigned to menial labour.'

Shiarn considered Earona scrubbing pots or feeding pigs. She would have laughed if the situation wasn't so dire. Recalling their argument, remorse churned in her stomach.

Regina pulled open the wardrobe and threw a blue dress with pretty flowered adornments onto the bed. 'You may dress now.' Without waiting for any acknowledgment she left the room.

Shiarn was left staring at the door wondering what to do. It was best she not be there when anyone came to see her. Several times she gazed at the dress on the bed. The cool air made her skin creep under the sheerness of her nightdress; the finest cloth she had ever felt, in fact all the garments were of the highest quality. She changed into the blue dress.

She did not know exactly what her plan was. The only concern was how far they would go with their threats; most likely there would be no hesitation in doing the worst to Ethan and Earona, and the poor girl with them.

Assuming the door would be locked, she turned it indifferently. It opened and she laughed with surprise. Covering herself with her Ethos, she became Unseen to the temporal world. At the threshold of the door her foot kicked something hard and she yelped at the pain. Her hands rested on a solid surface. In a panic, she skirted the doorway edge with her fingers. A solid wall, yet nothing was visible except the empty corridor. A personal ward? What could they want with her to form such an elemental corruption?

Shiarn backed away from the magikal barrier and slumped on her window seat. For the first time since being captured, she was truly afraid.

The sun descended and Shiarn hadn't moved when Regina returned to her rooms. 'Are the rooms more agreeable?'

'They are not.'

'The door was open,' Regina said, 'I'm glad you are dressed.'

Shiarn frowned with puzzlement at the woman's incongruent remarks. 'Something on the door prevents me leaving.'

'That certainly is convenient.'

Shiarn growled, 'What is going on?'

Ignoring her demand, Regina carried on, 'Tomorrow we will run through palace etiquette procedures. An upcoming banquet will be attended by a number of important people, and you are invited. I hope you don't make a fool of yourself in front of them. You would not wish to embarrass yourself.'

Shiarn threw her arms in the air. She might as well talk to her bed or the wall, or anything else for that matter. 'Is that all?'

'For now.' Regina left the room.

Shiarn slouched with resignation. All she could do was wait for her keeper to come.

~ * ~

Jett sat with Keanan, Marcus, and Seth in a booth near the back of the nearly full tavern. A long counter lined the right side, and along with the tables, several booths made up the seating. Dim smouldering from the fireplace warmed the room. On a platform by the front doors, a slender man with messy blond hair and dowdy attire provided entertainment on his pipe. The stables were clean and spacious enough, and Jett had already checked their horses. Their inn room was surprisingly comfortable, although they had to rent two. Fortunately they were connected by an internal door. But Jett hoped they weren't staying long enough to get that comfortable.

Finishing the last of his stew, he listened to Keanan discuss their finances.

'...we were going to sell the wagon to fund our voyage over to Hakan-Kara.' Keanan leaned back stiffly in his chair.

Seth asked, 'We won't have enough?'

'Not if we keep eating and drinking,' said Keanan.

'It doesn't matter either way. Until we find them we aren't going anywhere,' said Marcus.

Jett nodded; they would never be able to afford the travel costs, not when they had to rent a room. 'When the time comes we might have to sell a couple of horses.' The Kin gave him sad and grim stares, aware he referred to Rose and Sunny; the horses who hauled their wagon for the short term of their journey.

Hellier came to the table and nudged Marcus across, pushing Jett nearer the wall. Seating herself beside Marcus, she said, 'What were you talking about?'

'Selling you off.' Marcus pointed at the stage. 'Look who's here.'

She growled, 'I noticed.'

'Maybe there's a chance of lov—'

'If hell empties its pits,' she muttered, '...he looks like a reject from man school.'

Marcus responded with hearty laughter.

Jett creased his brows at the odd looking man bouncing to his music. 'Who is he?'

'Hellier's new fr—Oohf—' Marcus ended with Hellier punching his thigh.

Hellier said, 'Just someone I met earlier.'

A man, with a dirty apron covering his round middle, approached their table and put a bowl of food in front of Hellier. 'Your friends ordered it for you.'

Hellier took it and looked up at him with a grateful smile. He had a full head of grey and looked as if he had made the most of his sixty odd years. Under his grey moustache, a stubbled chin protruded. His eyes showed no emotion, yet he smiled in a cordial way. 'Hope it's to your liking, missy.'

She pulled the spoon up short and directed it at him. 'My name's Hellier. And what shall I call you?'

'Call me Burgman, Guz Burgman. When you need something, give a holla'.' He turned to the others. 'You lads need something?'

'Another round?' Marcus held up his empty tankard.

Keanan glared at him, but said nothing.

'I'll fetch it for you.' Burgman went back to serving behind the counter.

Jett said, 'I've been thinking—' He stopped at the sight of Dario pushing a path through the crowd towards them.

Hellier muttered, 'Oh, hell.'

Dario arrived with a blissful grin. Clutching his hat, he bowed with a grand flourish. 'Good evening, merry patrons.'

Seth said, 'Great tune.'

'My humble thanks. I created it this morning along with a couple of others.' Dario's eyes gleamed and his cheeks flushed. 'I haven't long, the crowd have become demanding.' He placed his hat upon his head and raised his brows at Hellier.

'Fine. Dario, this is Marcus, Seth, Keanan,' she said in a rush, 'And Jett.' They gave him pleasant greetings, except Jett, who stared with a dark frown.

Dario directed to them all, 'Do you play?'

'We do, but we haven't instruments right now, we lost them all' Hellier replied, 'I play the fiddle.'

Dario's eyes lit up. 'I could take you to a place that sells them,' he said to her, 'Tomorrow you and I could go out.'

'Umm...' She mumbled.

Jett raised his eyes at Dario's presumptuous request. He was disliking him by the minute.

Marcus asked, 'How much you making, Dario?'

'Started out at two silver.' He looked at the new customers filing into the room. 'But if this crowd increases I could get two gold. A wonderful bonus, I get a free meal and a room.'

'A room, eh?' Marcus smiled. 'That's not bad coin.'

'I must get back to it. My audience is waiting. Perhaps I shall see you later.' He gave a gracious nod and proceeded to the stage.

'Strange fellow,' Keanan said.

Jett eyed him across the room, and noticed the stares he was receiving from women.

'I've been thinking...' Hellier said between mouthfuls, 'We could make money by playing too.'

'Fantastic, 'cept,' Marcus said, 'we don't have instruments.'

Keanan said, 'It was something we would have been able to do, but now—'

'We have Ethan's drum,' Hellier said.

'And Earona's harp. How ironic,' said Seth, 'The only ones who left them in the wagon.' *Still can't believe I lost my beautiful flute...*

'I haven't even thought on the loss.' Jett didn't have any instruments of his own, but he knew how much the Kin were attached to theirs. The loss of his Kin was far more grievous.

She replied, 'Can't we work on getting more.'

'I'm afraid we could not afford the outlay,' Keanan told her. 'Nor do I think we could make enough coin for a trip by sea.'

'Enough talk about leaving,' Marcus huffed, 'what are we going to do about them?'

Jett pushed his back against the chair and exhaled a tense breath. 'Sailing to Hakan-Kara is by the by. We must find them before we consider anything.'

'Are you suggesting we search for them—' Keanan started.

'You know that.' Suddenly understanding Keanan's thoughts, Jett butted in, 'Don't even think it.'

'You have to admit a Tracker would be more than useful in this situation.' Keanan's hazel eyes turned to steel.

'We are not going back to Tellávare.' Jett delivered his words with equal determination. 'You included.'

'They might be in serious danger,' Keanan said. 'On top of that, home should be informed of the Skar attack. As well, the identity of that entity should be investigated.' *And don't forget we need to be mindful of the prophecy.*

'We don't really know anything about that attacker, and we'll look like cowards.' *I agree about the prophecy to some degree, but I won't be led like that.*

'You are over-confident,' Keanan growled, *this could be the very outworking of the words.* 'And what about our appointed arrival date?' *You really don't care what I think.*

'I do, but this is more important than...' *the thing is, we can handle this.* It wasn't only his missing Kin to consider. The girl was wanted by a Narahk, and she was now alone with his Kin, and they would have no idea. She was important to someone, whether good or bad, he couldn't determine. He doubted whether the Eldery would see it in the same way. 'We've saved a week getting here.' Jett knew the consequences of not turning up in Hakan-Kara, or at least for him anyway, but there was no turning back, and no one else taking responsibility. 'We search fast.'

Keanan's voice was lined with angry frustration. 'If it comes down to it, one of us travels to Lakhish.'

'I don't like it and I'm not going to think about it till I need to,' Jett said to Keanan, knowing he suggested it because he was the one wanting to go. The Circle's condemnation would hang over Keanan's head like a lead cloud.

Seth looked between them with curiosity. 'What prophecy?'

Averting his gaze, Keanan remained silent.

'You don't need to be concerned about it.' Jett's temper flared in his tone. He didn't want to lose it at Seth, but the prophecy was the last thing he wanted to discuss.

Marcus said, 'If you've finished arguing, can you tell us how we're going to find them?'

Keanan tilted his head at Jett with a smug grin. 'Yes, I'd like to know.'

'We search in as many ways as possible,' Jett said, 'Keanan, you go and enquire at the gate. We had to register, so must others. We can find out who or what came through at — dawn?'

Keanan said, 'Taking everything into account, Ethan was last seen before midnight, we finish up with those things after midnight, in the interim they go missing. They are on the other side waiting, they have been taken and that seems to be obvious, question; why are they not concealed?' He paused. 'Perhaps two reasons. I assume Shiarn is tired. She would not easily have been able to make four people disappear and the other reason, simply, they were caught by surprise.' He stopped and took a sip from his tankard.

'And?' Hellier asked, 'Was it dawn?'

'We came through about dawn, they were long gone. It took us more than a couple of hours to get to Floris by horse. So supposing they were taken near midnight they may arrive an hour before dawn by horse, by wagon at dawn or maybe slightly after. Mind you, that's all speculation; if they came into Floris at all.'

Jett said, 'whoever took them would surely stopover in the city. I don't think those gates open before dawn. Keanan, start there tomorrow.'

'If that's the decision you have made,' Keanan said. *I just hope it is right.*

'You know what I'm worried about?' Jett asked, even though the answer dominated his thoughts.

'Slavery?!' cried Hellier.

'How on earth are you going to find out about that?' said Seth.

Keanan added, 'It's difficult to imagine.'

Jett heard rumours back home of slavery in New Empire. He assumed it was alive and working. 'There must be a way of finding out what goes on here.' To envision the rest of the Kin separated and sold as slaves, maybe never seen again, he couldn't contemplate.

'Dario's a local.' Hellier shrugged. 'He might be able to help with news around here.'

Jett nodded his agreement. 'Marcus and Seth, you get to know the city.'

Seth said, 'I would love to see the sea.'

'It's not a sightseeing trip.' Marcus smiled at Seth's dreamy gaze. 'But that's where we will go.'

'And I will make some enquiries of my own,' Jett informed them. 'Watch yourself with this local, Hellier, we don't know him. Be careful what you say to him.'

'I will,' she assured him. 'I don't know what he's talking about, but he seems nice enough.'

~ * ~

Shiarn ate alone in the spacious fire warmed room. The food was good, but given how hungry she was, she would have eaten cabbage. Not long after came a knock. The door opened before she had a chance to answer, much to her growing annoyance.

The extravagantly dressed man from the carriage sashayed in with pompous self-assurance. His eyes settled on her with a pensive stare.

Shiarn had no idea who he was, yet she instinctively sensed her curtsy was lacking. Watchful of his every move, she took the opportunity to admire his elegant attire. Dressed in the same fashion as earlier, a navy vest was over a cream shirt and without a wig, his honey-coloured hair was tied at his neck.

'This room has improved tenfold.' He studied a painting of a naked woman lying on a couch. 'Previously it was rather shabby. Now it is fit for a princess.'

She shrugged with indifference.

'I would appreciate it if you would relax. I will not bite.' He flourished his hand, and his rings glinted in the light.

'You have not yet told me your name.' Shiarn folded her arms and remained stiff.

'Oh my, dear, you are right.' His hand fluttered to his forehead in reproach. 'How remiss of me. It explains why you would be so aloof. I am Prince Bastion Maustaton.' He bowed. 'But you may call me Bastion when we are alone.' He reclined on the red velvet lounge. 'Is there anything to drink here?'

Creasing her brow, she observed him afresh. What would the future King of Coltrene want with her, an unknown woman from a foreign land? She poured drinks from a carafe on the sideboard. Shoving the goblet at him, she said, 'Well then, Prince Bastion, I would like to know your intentions towards me.' She might as well find out sooner rather than wait hours.

'Orianna's fate! To be so forthwith must be exhausting.' He politely took the cup despite her abrasive manner. 'There's no need to be like that.' He leaned forward and pulled the armchair to face him. 'Come, sit here.'

At his compelling command she sat.

'I see you are quite spirited under that furrowed brow.'

In defiance she kept her steely glare on him.

His gaze flowed over her face while he took a steady sip from his goblet. 'Quite simply, I wish for us to be friends. Nothing more, nothing less.'

Her scowling face transformed into one of confusion.

'I will look after your friends if you abide by what I ask.'

'What is that exactly?'

His smile was enigmatic, but not unkind. 'We shall get to know each other, you and I.'

'And?'

'You must heed me and stay here.'

She mused over his innocent request and weighed his proposition. It seemed like air she couldn't catch hold of. 'I really don't understand at all.'

'You do not need to.' His light voice turned stern.

His glib persuasion irritated her just as much and she mumbled, 'If that's the way it is—'

'It is. Otherwise I am not sure what will happen to those you came with.'

She rolled her lips attempting to decipher any hidden purpose.

He appeared bored with the discussion and flipped his head with self-confidence. 'You are far too beautiful to let sourness dictate your face.' Leaning closer, his allure was undeniable and his voice was smooth as silk. 'Your hair is a magnificent colour, like a flame at sunset. Take it down so I may see it free.'

She stared into his eyes, sparking a deep ocean-blue. Her heart burst in a flurry of anticipation and she granted his request. Wisps of gold tumbled on to the deeper red in large curls that fell around her shoulders. He continued on in his captivating manner, 'Your eyes?' He lifted her chin.

How could she refuse his request given in such an endearing way? She gazed into his eyes and found intelligence; he knew more than he was sharing with her. It surprised her. But, after all, she was trapped by a supernatural ward this man must surely know of.

'Perfect. Hair of fire, eyes like gems, and flawless skin. Lovely,' he said, 'you must have the personality to match.'

'My personality far outweighs my looks.' She flirted, as if somehow she had to secure his affections.

A smile played on his face and he raised his cup. 'Well, what do you think?'

She took a gulp from her petite goblet. The dark amber liquid warmed her from her toes up.

Watching her, he sipped his. 'This is good, not like some of the watered down cordial we have around here.'

She copied his relaxed disposition and settled into the armchair. 'I can't say I have experienced any of it.'

'I hear the weather here has been atrocious, nonetheless, we shall get out as soon as it's clear.' He informed her, 'There are some events coming up which you shall attend.'

'I expect I have to.'

'You have not spoken about your new gowns.'

'They are exquisite and will probably all fit.'

'That pleases me.'

'How did you do it so soon?'

A smug smile came over the prince's face, making him look whimsical. 'I had a little insight on your arrival.' He lifted his chin and stared at the oversized mural. 'I shall dine with you nearly every evening. I hope I will not bore you too much.'

She did not want to think about coming nights, how long was she supposed to stay here anyway, forever? But the thought of company lifted her morale, and she couldn't help but tease. 'I'm sure you will be interesting enough.'

They chatted for a time, and he suggested they play a game of King's Square, which she discovered she knew as King's Men from Tellávare. Over the game they talked about court life, gossip, and events of the next few days in a strange detached conversation. He informed her they would visit the gardens soon, and she made no more mention of Earona and Ethan. After a surprisingly challenging game, Shiarn won.

Bastion responded with a warm chuckle. 'Next time you will not be so lucky.'

'It has nothing to do with luck.' Shiarn cocked her head with a delighted grin.

They wished each other a goodnight and he left, locking the door behind him.

Shiarn collapsed into her bed. The heady drink and pleasant game caused her to forget her troubles even if it was for an evening. On one hand it felt normal speaking with the prince, yet if she considered it, it was the most peculiar encounter. He was not as bad as she originally supposed. He was charming and had not made any advances on her at all. It made her wonder what his plan really was.

~ * ~

Once evening came, the cell reflected an insipid glow from the damp stones. Mara shivered under her blankets and Earona did the same next to her. Earlier, a guard threw in extra blankets. 'Captain's orders,' he said sheepishly, as if he needed orders to do a good deed. The girls had also been given a bowl of soup each and bread to share.

'Just you and me.' Earona's eyes were dull lights in the darkness and she pushed into the mattress, attempting to get comfortable.

Mara contemplated her bulge. '...and this.'

Earona gave her a tight smile. 'What do you think it is?'

'Don't really care.'

Earona's smile dropped away. 'May I?'

'I guess.' Mara lifted a brow in suspicion.

Earona put her hand on Mara's stomach.

The baby swished to and fro. Mara gasped at the tiny limb pushing at her flesh.

'Well, I think it's a he and he seems happy enough,' Earona said, 'How about you?'

Mara slumped forward. 'I've lost the only person who probably cared about me... and now this.'

Earona withdrew her hand, and tears shimmered in her eyes. 'I'm sorry for this, and your grandmother. Now you have no home.'

'My home...'

'But what about parents? Your mother?'

Mara stared at the ceiling. 'I'll be happy if I never see her again if you must know.'

Earona stared with blatant curiosity. 'Is she truly that awful?'

'Do we have to talk about this?' Bitterness spiked Mara's words as the familiar hatred billowed to the surface.

'When you want too I'll be happy to listen.'

Mara remained in her wrathful silence. Earona's clingy kindness annoyed her. Mara was always on edge, split between venting her rage, or cogitating on the unusual sensation of considering about others. She could only assume it came about from the blood ritual which must have loosened her emotions in ways she couldn't understand or even control. With Wendessa gone, she had to figure out what to do with these new thoughts on her own.

18 - A New Skill

'Wild as the roaring sea is she
Her presence as the storm drove night
Her kiss sharp as the strongest steel
My lady, bright, and bound for my bower, the fairest of sights...'

Song of Evelonne Bloodflower

Sleepy eyed and yawning, Hellier left the room she shared with Keanan to face the morning. She had a restless night, waking often with her lost Kin weighing on her mind.

Dario slouched against the opposite wall, and he sang a merry greeting. 'Fairest of beauties, I hope your sleep was pleasant.'

Confronted with his cheerfulness, she wanted to shut the door again. Socializing was far from what she wanted to do. 'I slept.'

'I know what you desire, my lovely. Your bath awaits.' His thin torso bent forward in a farcical bow. 'Come this way.'

Her face softened with a smile at the mention of bath.

Downstairs at the back of the inn was a wash room. A blackened grill lay across a stone trench. Buckets of water on top were steaming from the smouldering coals. A rusting iron tub was to the side, and shirts and pants hung on lines opposite. Without a thought Hellier started pulling up her shirt. Noticing Dario staring, she glared, hoping he would get the hint.

'You don't seem to have much in the way of clothes so here's a shirt.' A folded taupe shirt was on the bench. 'I'm sorry I couldn't manage the pants. I can wash that shirt.'

Did he mean wash it while she bathed? 'I can wash my own shirt.' She pushed him towards the door. 'I'm grateful for the bath, but I want to take it alone.' She shut the door and locked it.

'I'll just wait out here?'

She hung her shirt on the door handle. 'You do that.' The key hole was small, yet large enough for a strange man to peek through. Despite his forwardness she was more than happy he had gone to so much trouble. She relaxed in the warm water. Her sore shoulder also appreciated the soak. After she finished eradicating week old dirt from her skin, Hellier decided to let Dario show her the city.

~ * ~

'I have a friend who sells instruments,' Dario said as they walked the street.

Intrigued by the overt stares of the passing people, Hellier stared back in the same inquisitive manner.

Dario said, 'If only I could emulate your wild, organic look.'

People's opinions had no effect on her and she had no need of his patronizing attitude. 'I shall send you to the woods where you shall get the look you desire.'

'The sojourn would be paradise if you were to accompany me.'

She shook her head in mock scorn. No man ever dared to flirt with her in such a blatant manner, but neither was Dario the type she would regard. Most likely he would fall down with a slight hit to the chest. In spite of his less than perfect appearance, she was enjoying the attention. 'Have you always lived here?'

'My childhood was spent at Bridgeleigh Manor,' he replied with some reticence.

'And what is your friend like?'

'My friend?'

'With the instruments.'

'Oh, Boral. Like an old musician, artist, inventor, craftsman, all rolled into one. I have known him for years. Vivella introduced us.'

'Vivella?'

Melancholy came over his fair features. 'An old friend.'

A teasing smile played on her lips. 'Old girlfriend?'

'Not at all,' he said. 'We had a disagreement...'

She sensed the potential gossip. 'About?'

He stared in puzzlement. 'Nothing, really.'

'You should make up if it's not that important,' she said.

He smiled with ease. 'You're right.'

'Is this store near the sea?'

'Everything here is near the sea. You will see it eventually, whether you want to or not.' The streets they walked sloped upwards. Some of the houses had courtyards and gardens, and pruned trees lined the lanes. In spaces between buildings, Dario pointed out the grey sea where it met blue sky.

"Music Nest," read the sign on the cottage they stopped at. A quaint path led past shrubs to the door. Inside, shelves held several varieties of instruments, and a pigeon-hole shelf, contained scrolls. At the back of the store an elderly man shuffled past the counter. After a careful look he called, 'Dario.'

'Greetings, Boral.'

Boral observed Hellier just as meticulously and she stared back. His mass of white hair was going everywhere and his face was a wrinkled cream complexion. 'I don't know you, do I?' he asked almost apologetically. 'I am certain I would remember.' Stooping, he supported himself on a walking stick.

'I'm Hellier,' she said, 'we have never met.'

'Boral, we have come to peruse your instruments.'

Hellier investigated the shelves. Seth would be impressed by the well-made flutes and Keanan would love the string instruments. 'No fiddles.'

Boral responded with understated excitement at her whispered remark, 'The old violin.' He shuffled back to his workroom.

She ran her fingers across the strings of a lute. 'These instruments are too much.'

'I never paid any mind to the prices. V always paid.' He looked at a small plaque and whistled with surprise.

She picked up a flute and felt the weight in her hand; light and well crafted. 'Beautifully made.'

'He makes them himself.' He came up next to her. 'You are right about the price.'

Hellier shrugged and replaced the instrument.

Boral came back, violin in hand and offered it to her.

Placing it under her chin, the wood was smooth against her skin and fit perfectly in her gentle grasp. She pulled the bow across absent strings and smiled.

Dario returned her smile. 'I wish I could buy it for you.'

She handed it back with reluctance. 'I can't—'

'Not yet anyway,' Dario said. 'Can you keep it for us? We shall be back.'

'I still have to finish it, but I can keep it aside. As long as it's not weeks.' Boral offered Hellier a knowing smile. 'I see you have a passion for it.'

~ * ~

They walked away from the store and Dario put his arm around her shoulders. 'I'll take you somewhere special.'

Climbing more slanted streets, they came to a high cliff. Few houses were along the crest except a tall tower with a blazing beacon at the top. They took shelter from the wind under the eaves of the cottage attached to the tower. Hellier lost interest in the tower once she saw the ocean. The harbour stretched for miles it seemed and the sea beyond spread as far as she could see. She sat on the damp gravel under the shelter, and Dario joined her.

The docks crawled with activity. Four jetties took up the centre of the harbour and numerous smaller ones were on either side. The rocky point on the opposite side also blazed with a great fire. The tower on that side had more structures and appeared less accessible. Rocky cliffs on both sides of the harbour reached out to sea. A ship was setting off. Sailors unfurled the sails while smaller fishing vessels drifted in and out.

Behind them, the city was like a mismatched quilt thrown over the soft slope. Even in the grey light of a rainy day it was an intriguing spectacle. Its design was not unlike Melchior except the city of the Fáerinn lacked the density of people and buildings. The streets glistened in the moist air. People moved on the various stairs and ramps going up between houses on uneven levels. Giant sea pines stuck out in random clumps. Hidden lanes and obscure houses crammed in tight next to larger structures. Gulls circled on the air or carpeted the higher roofs also observing the citizens of Floris.

Dario pointed out where they were staying on the flat near the walls at the top end of the city. And to the left of Four Square the royal palace was a sprawling mass of spires and balconies all enclosed by a high wall.

'Amazing!' she proclaimed at last.

'It truly is. I don't think I've ever really looked at it,' he said with surprise.

'All that water,' she exclaimed, 'Reaching as far as I can see.'

Dario pointed out to sea. 'This is Hopewell Bay. The Meidiva Archipelago is that way,' he indicated the southeast, 'and straight ahead is the Seven Realms of Anahara. Not that I've ever been there, I've just met enough people to make me feel as if I have.'

'That's where we are going.' She hadn't thought about her lost Kin for the last couple of hours, but now, their fate rolled into her thoughts, blackening her mood again. How could they ever get to Hakan-Kara without them?

'You're going there?' he asked with shock.

'I'm not going until we find our missing friends.'

'That's serious. What do they look like?'

'Ethan is tall like Keanan and broad shouldered and lots of dark brown hair. Shiarn is beautiful, curly red hair, and,' her hands shadowed her chest, mimicking larger breasts, 'if you know what I mean...' she said and he nodded at her implication. 'Earona is the same height as Marcus with long black hair and lovely blue eyes. Very sweet. Much like a girl should be.'

He raised a puzzled eyebrow. 'You are inferring something?'

She shrugged, realizing what she revealed. 'It's nothing.'

'You don't want to be like that....'

'I...' A hard laugh bubbled up unexpectedly. 'No, I don't!'

'I like the way you are.' He faced her and a solemn look came over him. 'I mean it when I said I have feelings for you.'

'You mustn't.'

'I want to.' He stared intently at her face. 'A deep fire comes forth from your eyes. Something in you is drawing me. I can't get enough of seeing you or being with you.' He caressed her cheek. 'Or touching you.'

Her skin sprang to attention at the carefulness of his touch. He directed her chin close and a shiver ran down her neck. Feeling caught in his gentle hand, she whispered a hesitant, 'No.'

He responded with hurt, 'Why?'

'It's not...'

'How can a shivering man say to the roaring fire, 'Shed not your heat on me, I do not desire it?''

'That's nice, but...' She turned her face to the harbour. 'Do you know if people have slaves here?'

Dario drew back with a puzzled stare. 'I'm sure they do.'

Hellier gave him a serious stare. 'How do you buy them?'

He scratched his chin in contemplation. 'I've never considered it, I mean, who are these people?'

'Those people might be my friends.' Her body tensed with pent-up sadness.

'You think that's what happened?'

She rested her chin on her raised knee. 'That's what we believe.'

'Come to think of it, I've heard it talked about at the table.'

'What's that?' She gave him a quizzical glance.

He tapped his head. 'I have an idea – just now. Maybe we could "play two fiddles with one stick."'

'How?'

He said, 'Have you played Double-up or One-eyed Jack?'

Her eyes lit up. 'Card games?'

'We can play for money for instruments and maybe meet some shady fellows while we're at it.' He winked at her.

She nodded. 'Play alongside criminals?'

'Not all of them are.' He blushed. 'I'm not bad at playing, and I don't consider myself a criminal. Well, mostly. Not.'

Hellier chuckled. 'It would be fun at least. We could win money and find out about slaves.'

He tugged a pack of cards from his pouch. 'You'll pick it up fast enough.' As he shuffled she recognised pictures of fancy kings, queens, princes, and the four elements. They spent time in the slight shelter protected from drizzling rain, playing. The games were not too different from what she knew. What was more important was how to bet and win.

'We will go shortly, but first, we must always pretend not to know each other.' He explained the ins and outs of how to conduct herself in the gambling room, the signs he would use to reveal his cards, and who was cheating. She had to act as tough as she could; roughnecks were known to push women about. 'I know a few tricks myself.'

Hellier was not surprised. 'You mean you cheat.'

'Well, of a sort. You can't do it all the time,' Dario said, 'What we will do is play the table. In essence, I will forfeit some of my good hand allowing you to win. You won't be able to do this, you lack the experience. The Gamblers Guild get annoyed about cheating.'

'Gamblers Guild? So it's legal?'

'Not exactly. It depends on the governor of the district you are gambling in. Racen Square is low risk for getting caught, but it makes for small winnings. The trouble with gambling is if the officials don't get their tax. The worry isn't whether it's legal or not, it's the guild that can be the problem, more than that, the gamblers themselves.' He stood and offered her his hand. 'Not to worry, we shall be fine.'

She stood with him and they started off down the hill. 'What were those signs again?'

~ * ~

The "Rosy Parrott" was a rundown tavern in Racen Square. Situated in a type of gully, the district had practically no sea views, and the shadow from the rocky overhang was always on it.

Hellier watched Dario enter. After waiting some time, she followed into the smoky haze and headed to the bar. The men inside kept their eyes fixed on her. The only other female was the waitress, and she gave Hellier a toothless grin. A middle-aged scruffy man held out his wooden mug in offering. 'Eh, missy, come drink with a sailor.'

A man sauntered over in bright red pants, knee high boots and stained shirt. 'You don't belong here!'

Without a thought, Hellier said, 'I go wherever I want.' She spared the old drunks a pitying glance.

The same man followed her. 'I don't want you here.'

She swivelled to face him. He eyed the black hilt of her sword extending from the sheath at her back. They stood eye to eye and she wondered if he knew how to use the sabre at his side. She said, 'You afraid of a woman?'

His face lit up with rage and he pulled his sword half way out of its scabbard. An older man stopped him with a weathered hand on his arm.

Hellier turned away and said to the barkeep, 'I want to go downstairs.'

The barman nodded. 'Who sent ya?'

'Silmon,' she repeated the password Dario had given her.

The barman gave a nod towards the counter. Hellier threw down a couple of coppers, and the barman pointed to a door. The man with the red pants cursed her loud enough for all to hear.

Ignoring the threats, she made her way down a narrow stair, lit with oil lamps. Quiet talking came from below. Two armed men, sitting on a couch, met her with bored expressions. Three tables were in the compact room, and a plank laid across piles of crates formed a bar.

Dario showed no recognition as she sat across from him. The overweight man on her left gave a nod, introducing himself as Big Pat. On her right sat a well-dressed man wearing bright rings and a felt hat with a tall white feather. The third man seemed like an old pirate with his long unbrushed hair and gold rings in his ears. She received dubious stares and inquisitive smiles, but the game started and they were all business and only interested in her coin.

Once the flow of cards was in motion and hands dealt, Hellier relaxed. Keanan gave her a little coin, not that he knew what she was doing with it, and Dario lent her a couple of gold. Hardly any conversation passed unless it had to do with a rule. She doubled her pile and tried her hardest to remain cool over her winnings.

Dario scratched behind his left ear. A cheater at the table. Over the next couple of games she watched the big man on her left with careful sideways glances. A sly flick with his fingers and a card disappeared into his long sleeve. Dario never really said what to do if someone was cheating, so she left it to her instincts. She leaned down, reaching for the knife in her boot. Positioning her hand on the man's thigh, she rested the blade tip on his testicles. 'You're cheating.'

'What?!' His eyes bulged at the steel pressing into his flesh.

'Your game is up!'

Sweat darkened Big Pat's shirt and he sucked his breath in sharply. 'I never—'

'They're up your sleeve.'

'I ain't done any cheating. See, I'll lay me cards down.' He threw his cards in haste and one slipped from his sleeve in confirmation. Big Pat whined. 'Who put that there?'

The foreign man drawled in his thick southern accent, 'Always a cheater.'

One of the armed men ordered Big Pat to leave and a black mark was rumoured against his name. On his way out, he gave Hellier a murderous glare which did nothing to make her regret catching him.

They continued playing with new players arriving to take up places at the other tables. Hellier had no idea what time it was in the windowless room. Soon enough, a hungry moan from her stomach informed her it must be getting on to evening. After thanking all for the game, she rose to leave.

Cautiously, she emerged from the doorway and walked up a narrow flight of steps leading to the street. A quick peek revealed no one waiting for her. No matter how tough she thought she was, she had no wish to confront Big Pat, or the man from the tavern she encountered earlier. The more she thought on her day in the gambling room, including the men she offended, the more she realized it was best she said nothing of her activities to Jett.

Twilight tinged the sky a stormy grey, making her anxious to return to the inn. Behind, Dario ran to catch up. She said, 'I gained coin,' and flashed the gold in her palm.

'Not bad. I'm probably on even. Together we have done quite well, but still a way to go,' he said, 'From today you might get a reputation as a hard opponent.' He added, 'A good thing by the way.'

'They didn't talk about slaves at all.' She jiggled her money with a wistful sigh. 'We'll come again tomorrow?'

He grinned. 'We can play again, but not the same place. We go to different places. We have a bit more to play with. You have to have the gold to win the gold and you have to be prepared to lose some of it as well. We may have to mention we are interested in the slave trade.' He looked himself over. 'Although, I might not pass as that sort of person.'

'We will keep trying. You won't mention it to the others.'

'Will do, I mean, I won't do.'

'It's better we don't return there. I met an obnoxious man inside.' She described the man with the rude mouth.

'Not him!' He moaned. 'He's a notorious pirate *and* insane. He's a sailor on the Shining Moon. They're smugglers.'

'I don't think he likes women.'

'He doesn't like anyone.' He rubbed his head as if it suddenly pained him. 'And that's the very people who would know about slavery. We don't need to get on their bad side. They would sell you off, rather than kill you.' He sighed glumly. 'We have to be careful!'

She could almost hear Jett repeating the exact thing. It was uncanny.

19 -Opening Up

'Not all gems are to be found in gold and silver

Book of Humility, Amos the Pure

Startled from her doze, Mara sat up on the mattress. The light of morning tinged their cell. A voice was calling her, similar to the previous time. Fearing loss of control again, she considered it better to be locked up than free on the streets. At least here she couldn't be led away by some stranger, or be seen by anyone. She slouched against the wall, where she spent most of the time, and in a "morose silence", as Earona called it. She liked to think she was reflective, except she didn't want to think on anything in particular. Earona was already pacing the cell, every once in a while letting loose a miserable outburst.

A guard brought a tray of cold food and a new bucket, much to Earona's embarrassment, but she thanked him anyway. Upturning the bucket, Earona stood on it and peered out the window. 'Everything is so gloomy.' She sat on the bedding with a weighty thump.

Mara took her turn at the window. She stood on tiptoes to see the drab courtyard.

Earona said, 'So who is the father of your baby?'

'Why?' Mara screwed her face up at the intrusive question.

'Well, it must be someone.'

Mara clenched the stonework, her body stiffening with irritation. 'He's…' Anger got the better of her and she spun around to glare. 'It's nothing to do with you.'

Earona gasped, her eyelids flicked up and down in disbelief. 'Good Heavens, does it really matter if I know or not?!' After some moments of silence, she sighed. 'Alright, I'm sorry.'

'Anyway, I really thought it was…' No, she never thought it was love, but what was it? In a way she had some fondness for him, but nowhere near what he probably had towards her. Mara jumped down, her hands making fists at her hips.

'He was a young man who didn't know better I expect.'

'He wasn't young.' Mara shut her mouth, realizing she said too much. A man in love with an adolescent was not a normal situation, or even right to some. But she was not normal, nor was she even right.

Earona's intense blue eyes studied her. 'I see. And your mother probably disapproves? That might explain why you were at Lanvin.'

Mara wavered over her astute observation. But it was only half the reason she had to leave. 'Maybe.'

'Does he know you were there?'

Mara spoke with cold defiance. 'I don't want to talk about it.' The truth was she had no idea, and if her mother had her way, he would never know or find out.

Earona scrunched her face up in curiosity. 'It makes some sort of sense. Your mother found out, she was livid at him. You have to run away to save your baby and the family from any shame or future harm from a lecherous male...' She stopped and looked away.

Through gritted teeth, Mara lashed with fury, 'Will you shut-up?!' She didn't care if he knew or not, she hardly cared about the baby herself, how could she expect he would? Her mother, that was different, she knew and cared, but not in a motherly sense.

Earona took a long breath. 'What I wouldn't give to play my harp right now.'

Moments passed before Mara was calm enough to speak, although her anger and the troublesome memories from home remained under the surface. 'I've never played an instrument.'

'I would have been four when I first touched one.' Earona smiled at some distant memory.

Sorrow came over Mara's face. 'I don't remember being that age.'

'Oh... I'm sorry.'

'Why are you always sorry?!' Mara flashed another wrathful scowl. 'We can't all have perfect lives like you! Your arrogance is incredible.'

Earona's eyes shot open and she opened her mouth only to shut it again.

'Self-righteous people make me fume.' Mara's voice grated with restrained rage. 'You don't know anything about me.'

'My life is not perfect and I never said it was.' Earona's face reddened. 'And right now it's gone off into a ditch. I did save your life remember. You were the one who was angry.' She grumbled, 'You didn't even want your baby...'

Mara sighed with sudden despondence, losing the motivation to argue or even talk.

Earona slumped against the wall, similar to Mara earlier. 'The reason we are here is because of me.' A tear fell from her face followed by a stream.

Mara sat beside her, suddenly drained of anger. It seemed easier back then, to be done with it. What would be the baby's future if she were on the run with creatures and her mother chasing her? 'I can't trust people.'

'I gathered that.' Earona wiped her tears away and reached for the small straw animal dangling near Mara's stomach, she fondled the plaque with tiny symbols. 'Pretty.'

Mara pulled the long cord away from her and held the charm up to her chin. She rolled it in her fingers, surprised the straw mouse had gotten free from the security of her dress. 'Yes...'

'Lucky they didn't take it.' Earona sighed. 'They certainly seemed thorough.'

Creasing her brow, she nodded and buried it down her front again. The guards would never have seen it due to its magik. But how it escaped Mara's concealment, she didn't know. Did the charm wish to be seen? She considered Earona, not for the first time in vexation. The healer woman didn't seem interested in knowing about it though. 'It's... ma—' she stopped herself. 'Probably because it looks so... insignificant.' She fiddled with the leather wristband, gaining some comfort in the mystical possession.

Earona stared at the band. 'That's interesting...'

'It was my gran's. The only thing left of her.' And that was the truth. She didn't have much, but everything she did own was in the cottage.

Earona's blue eyes darkened. 'It's a terrible tragedy.'

Mara crunched forward, and holding her knees tight, she dropped her face onto her skirt, thankful Earona wasn't going to apologize again. Her eyes were dry, even though she was remembering Wendessa. Wendessa taught her not to cry and it had its benefits, but now... the tears refused to come. She couldn't recall her early years, but she knew somehow Wendessa was there, and as she considered it, Wendessa had always been there. Mara had taken her for granted not realizing the old woman must have known so much about her mother. After some moments of sitting in a tense silence, the events of the last couple of days gnawed at her thoughts. Without lifting her face, Mara finally mumbled, 'What is his name?'

'Who? Ethan?'

Mara turned her face, yet avoided her puzzled gaze. She shook her head. 'The dark haired, angry man back at Lanvin.'

Earona stared for moments, bewilderment rife on her face, before light dawned in her eyes. 'Oh, you mean Jett?'

Mara recognized the name spoken in her vision. She let it rest in a brooding pause as she remembered his wrath in the tent. What did she do to deserve that anyway? Earona was the one who brought her to the arrogant man. She had already decided she didn't like him, but she wanted to know... 'Who is he?'

Earona swivelled her torso to face her with wary curiosity. 'Jett is our...' she paused, 'leader and friend. At times he is overbearing and strict, as you may have seen. For instance, he didn't want to take you home—'

'I didn't want to go!' Mara would have run away again given half the chance.

'Ha! He still would have dropped you off to the nearest lord without a backward glance.' She folded her arms in a huff.

From his furious reaction to Mara's presence it would have been no surprise if he dumped her on the side of the road. In hindsight, it might have been the better option. But, that was before they shared the vision. Would his mind have changed? Then again, she recalled the malice surrounding him in the vision, and terrible wickedness emanating from his presence. Perhaps it was best he was not around. She let loose a great sigh and leaned her weight against the wall. 'And now here we are. Doesn't matter anymore.'

Earona made a fist, she clenched with her free hand. 'Yes, and Jett is probably really livid and annoyed.'

Mara stifled a giggle. 'It's not your fault.' Earona's timid disposition seemed abnormal for the pushy woman.

'You don't know him like I know him.' She gave a short nod and peered at her from under her dark fringe.

The distant sound of painful yelling echoed from some distant passage below them. They jumped to their feet and Earona was first to the door. It continued as a faint noise against the walls, but it was distinctly male. Silence, then shouting and a wail came down the corridor.

Earona let out a sudden sob. Clutching the bars, her knuckles turned white. 'Leave him alone! He's done nothing wrong!'

Mara said, 'Torture shouldn't kill him. He looked strong.'

Through her tears, Earona cried, 'It's me who's not.' She wailed, 'It's my fault.' Her hands covered her face and she sniffled.

'It's just the way things happened. You wanted to save that boy...' she stopped, remembering the lost child.

'And look what happened to *him*.'

Mara attempted consolation. 'Can't be helped now.'

Earona dropped back down onto the mattress and lay in an unforgiving state of mind. Mara sat beside her in silence. Outside it started raining and the cell darkened to a chilly cave. Mara pulled the blankets up to her chin, making sure to cover Earona and they tried to warm themselves.

~ * ~

Near closing time, the tavern was almost empty and quiet without the music. Jett sat drinking at the bar after his Kin went upstairs for the night. He spent the day walking the city, knowing his Kin were sequestered somewhere and he could do nothing to find them. It was a waste of time and now he was tired. The only information of any significance they got from the Registry at the gate; an entourage of royal carriages came into the city at dawn yesterday and no one else for a couple of hours after. Jett was left to question whether someone from the palace had taken them. He wondered how he could follow that up without asking an official.

As the city produced no leads, Jett began doubting his decision to stay. It didn't help Keanan mentioned travelling home, again. Angry at his own stubbornness, he clenched his mug and took a long swig. He was still torn between grief and rage at his Kin for getting lost in the first place. He couldn't let anyone else find them, he had to do it. He grumbled under his breath, 'Cursed pit of a city...'

'That'll be your last.' Burgman stopped on the other side of the counter.

'What?' Jett lifted his head ready to rebuke him.

'Your friend said you weren't to have any more.' Burgman nodded at his tankard with a wry smirk.

Jett tightened his fist on the smooth wood. Damn Keanan and his arrogant presumptions. 'I'll decide that.' He slammed the mug back down.

Burgman chuckled. 'He probably wants to save some coin.'

Jett snorted. No, he didn't want him drunk.

A man approached the counter and said, 'Burgman, I'll have two Rubies.' His arm collided with Jett's tankard, spilling what ale was left over the bench.

Jett tipped and stared into his empty mug with a sour look. Burgman made a great rush to wipe up the liquid dripping over the side.

'My apologizes,' the man said, 'I'll order you another.' He held three fingers up to Burgman. 'A Ruby.'

'No, I'm fine.' Jett was just glad he didn't end up wearing it. He gazed at the man, clothed in a forest green cloak, his hood was back, revealing an intelligent face and a closely shaved beard and short hair. 'Besides, the drink isn't helping any.' He had to admit, it made him more irritated.

'The drink is a fair-weather friend.' He leaned his elbow on the bar and looked at Jett in contemplation. 'I see you are a man under a cloud.'

'I've good reason.' Jett felt his back stiffen in defence.

'Ahh, the fair city of exotic loves and flash wealth has disillusioned another aspiring soul—' he gave him a bemused smile.

'Floris can go to hell and everyone in it for what it has taken from me. Those dearest to me…' Jett was in two minds whether he should walk away before the drink made him start something he would regret, but he was compelled to voice his troubles.

The man's eyes narrowed with some concern. 'How unfortunate.'

Burgman brought Jett a goblet.

'I'll find them and the bastards who took them.' Jett turned back to face the counter and despite not wanting it, sipped the dark red wine. 'Even if it's the flamin' king himself.' He ended with a wrathful mutter, 'I'll kill him.'

The man took his drink from Burgman and left coin on the counter. He gazed at Jett while taking a sip. 'If you're serious—'

'Never been more serious.' The wine loosened his tongue and fired up his heart.

'I'll give you a name.'

Jett cocked his head to see how genuine he was.

His lip turned up in a half smile. 'Captain Shark is the one to speak to about getting in on the "Trade." He touched his nose and nodded at Jett. 'Ask for him down at the Rosy Parrott. Tell him, Fern sent you. He should be obliging. At the least he will talk to you.'

'The "Trade", so that's how it is…' Jett lowered his brow, wondering who the man really was before him.

'Let's just say, Captain Tonius Shark knows about *missing people*. He's sly, so mind what you tell him, but he does enjoy negotiating – it's like a game. Maybe you know what I mean.' He cast a glance around the tavern. 'Get in on the trade and you might come across your people.' He broke out in a wide smile. 'You have to start somewhere.'

'Fern, is it? Thanks.'

Fern bowed his head. 'Good luck.' He took the two goblets and headed to his table near the back. A cloaked figure, with the hood pulled right over the person's head, waited for him. The person was so well-concealed Jett could not see their face, but he guessed it was probably a woman.

'It's best not to be too curious.' Burgman leaned on the counter and cast a quick glimpse over his shoulder at their table.

Jett drank from his goblet and diverted his gaze. 'There really is a Captain?'

Burgman's stubbled face screwed up in thought. 'Yer, probably is. He never talks to no-one like that.'

'Who are they?'

'They come in late sometimes, sometimes he's alone, but always when the crowd dies down.' Burgman shrugged. 'Never asked them their business. They aren't the type that you ask questions.'

Jett gulped the smooth liqueur down, enjoying the warmth of the expensive drink. He headed upstairs light-hearted from the quality wine, but also from gaining a semblance of a plan.

20 - Jett Investigates

*Do not needlessly awake the bear in his lair
Neither should you enter empty handed.*

Empirical Warfare Command

After checking over his horse, Jett headed out into the busy street. Once he found a course through the laneways, he arrived at Wardock Street and The Rosy Parrott. Apparently it was one of the seediest bars in Floris, so Burgman said. The dark, dingy tavern wasn't small, but unsurprisingly, it was dirty. Bone scraps were pushed to the side of the grimy floor and the patrons were not better off. Every one of the crude looking men wore a weapon of some type, and a few stared, defiantly. Most gave him no regard at all. Jett decided against the stool and leant on the uneven counter.

The barkeep asked in a lazy manner, 'What will you 'av?'

'I'm looking for someone,' Jett said, 'Captain Shark.'

The barkeep was a thin man with a neat beard and his voice was rough. 'Is that right.' He studied Jett with a steady gaze. 'In that case, you need to speak to Waylan Corps.'

Frustration surfaced in Jett's voice. 'Where can I find him?'

He nodded to a table where a lone man sat.

Jett crooked his head.

A man with a blue scarf over his forehead, glared back at him. His red pants and frilled shirt had seen better days.

Jett approached Waylan's table and pulled out a chair. 'Can I sit?'

Waylan narrowed his eyes and stared into Jett's dark ones. 'Are you asking or telling?'

'Guess I'm telling.'

Waylan's eyes sparked with awe at the sword at Jett's belt. He dragged his eyes from it and stared at Jett's ring. 'You have the privilege of knowing my name, now I must know yours.'

'Jett.'

'Where did you come across that blade?'

Jett fingered his lone sword. Normally his second would be at his back, but he had thought better of walking the streets armed in such a manner. 'What is your interest in it?'

Waylan leaned towards him. 'Black-gold is rare and valuable, sought after by many with the coin to buy such things.' He stared at him with puzzlement. 'To have a blade is a great find.'

'This was not a find,' Jett said and Waylan gave him a yellow-toothed grin. 'I want to speak with the Captain.'

Waylan grumbled, 'And how do you know about him?'

'Fern sent me here, looking for him.'

'You one of his?' He lost the smile and studied him with a roving eye. 'Where are you from? Ryne?'

'From all over.' Jett replied as vaguely as he could get away with. 'I have trade to bring you.'

'You have something to trade, weapons like that? Or where I might find them?'

'I can get you this type of weapon, plus people.'

'There's a demand for women. Young ones.' Waylan stroked his chin. 'You see the Captain first. He will be interested in your black-gold if you have any like you say. If you are lying he will deal with you.' He flicked a knife from his belt and flashed it before Jett's face. His voice rose to an irrational ferocity. 'If you cheat me, I will cut your throat.'

He replied, 'Where can I find the *Captain*?'

Waylan's voice returned to an even tone. 'Naragie's Rug Shop in Cordinne Street. Ask for him there.'

Jett stood to leave.

Waylan's demeanour changed again and he snapped, 'You better not come back here, bilge-scum, with all your cursing.'

Jett left the tavern with concerns over the man's sanity and whether he was actually being sent on a futile chase over the district.

After searching the street signs and enquiring from a passing local, Jett came across Cordinne Street. He noted a pile of rugs toppled over on the path and a placard, "Naragie's Rug Shop" in flowing script. He walked past rows of rugs and came to a dark skinned man at the back of the store. The man, he assumed was Naragie, had a long moustache and bright orange turban. Jett said, 'I'm looking for the Captain.'

'Always looking for him, never buying my beautiful rugs.' His accent was strong, similar to Waylan Corps. 'And who is it who sent you to my humble store?'

'Waylan Corps.' So far Jett had nearly walked all over the district with nothing worthwhile to show for his half day of travel. His patience was on a fine edge.

Naragie heaved a standing pile of rugs aside, revealing a narrow door. He knocked a quick three times.

A brawny man with wide shoulders came out and stood over Jett. His pants were baggy and a blue shirt was under a worn leather vest. He spoke with a chesty grunt. 'Who are you?'

Jett noted his thick appearance was more fat then real muscle, and his face lacked any intelligence. 'Waylan Corps said I would be able to speak to Captain Shark here. If you don't mind, I'd like to do that.'

'I'm him,' the man folded his arms, 'Speak to me.'

'I find it hard to believe you are the one I seek.' This time Jett studied him with annoyance. 'I have important matters to discuss with him.'

His coarse voice rang out in the shop. 'Discuss with me.'

'Surely the Captain would not have me deal with someone like you,' Jett replied. 'You don't look able to tie a lace let alone have a conversation.' He shifted his cloak aside to expose his malreus blade, boasting a new appreciation of its worth. He gave the wall a sideways glance and discovered a painted portrait of a wealthy noble from Anahara. It would take no trouble at all to disguise peep holes in the picture.

Without warning, the oaf landed a punch to Jett's chin. While they scuffled, Naragie cowered behind his counter, not uttering a word of complaint. Before the man could get in another hit, Jett reached for the knife at his belt and held it at the man's throat. Jett yelled towards the door. 'I have business to discuss with you, Captain.' He gripped the man's arm and pushed his blade tip into his neck. 'I don't want to waste time with useless men like this.' It drew blood and the man remained still, also looking at the door. 'Fern is the one who sent me.'

A small man, who could easily pass for a boy, poked his head out from the door. 'Capt'n says come in.' His manner was cheerful and he gave an order to the brute, 'Mac, go see what the Corps has done now.'

Jett let Mac go and walked past the slight man. 'That's more like it.' He entered a long corridor lit by torches. At the end, the wall was rock, and stairs led downwards into what he assumed was the rock cliff. The guide opened a door on the left and waved Jett through. Oil lamps cast a lush glow on shelves lined with indistinguishable artefacts and books. A brocade set of lounges was on an intricate woven rug. On the opposite side, a burgundy curtain covered the entire wall. A desk was on top of an animal hide of what once had been a great spotted creature.

With a sweeping glance at the opulence, Jett gave his attention to the man at the desk and a hefty woman standing behind him. She watched with crossed arms and a stern face, and could easily be mistaken for a man in the dead of night, or through a drunken haze. Dangling at her side was a curved sword.

Captain Shark stood as Jett approached. Dressed in a green velvet jacket, it complimented his red hair and beard. He was far from what Jett expected a smuggler to look like. Maps and scrolls covered the desk and over them was a wide brimmed hat with a red feather. Jett cut his grin off before he chuckled. The Captain indicated for him to sit. Reluctantly, he took one of the seats in front of the desk. Stifled in the formal setting, he attempted to relax, but it was impossible with the thin man-boy seated behind him, out of his direct vision.

Tonius Shark gestured at a decanter, half-full of a dark honey liquid. 'Would you like a drink?'

Jett tossed his head. 'I'd rather not. But thank you all the same.'

'This must be serious business.' Tonius laughed, sharply. 'You've been speaking to Fern. I'm surprised he's back in the city. Is Raven with him this time?"

'I'm not sure,' Jett bluffed as he wondered if the woman with Fern was this Raven.

The Captain creased his eyes at Jett's remark. 'He's a hard man to catch, and you have seen him and spoken. You certainly have the appearance of being one of his. So who do I have the pleasure of meeting?'

'Jett.'

Tonius stared into his eyes without a glimmer of curiosity. 'Of course you are.' He glanced over Jett's shoulder before turning his eyes back on Jett. 'Don't worry about him. I am interested in what sort of deal you are looking for. Despite what you may have heard from Fern, I'm not unreasonable. Now, tell me what business you would like to discuss?' He asked, as if Jett might be open to any form of money-making scheme.

'Simple enough, I need to do some trading.'

Tonius' thin lips turned into an amiable smile. 'You, on behalf of Fern? Buying or selling?'

'Both.'

Tonius leaned forward, his elbows rested on his desk and he scrutinized Jett with shrewd eyes. 'You aren't from around here?'

Jett's features remained diffident. 'No.'

'You look young for this type of business.'

Jett sensed there was more in what he was not saying in the subtle statement. 'You must have been young once…'

Tonius was at least middle age himself. 'You won't get by on nerve alone.' He crossed his arms under Jett's forthright gaze. 'I am a good reader of people and you aren't a true smuggler.' His eyes glanced over the exposed black hilt of Jett's blade. 'Did you get that blade where you came from?'

'I did.'

'And what have you to trade?'

'People.' Jett fingered the malreus flame on his sword pommel. 'Weapons…'

'Weapons, made from black-gold?'

'I have a source.'

'May I?' Palm up, Tonius stretched his hand across the desk.

Jett tapped his fingers on the hilt. He stood and withdrew his blade. Instead of passing it to Shark, he held the sword horizontal for the man to view. The woman shifted uneasily and Shark took a nervous breath. An unnatural silence fell for several moments. Tense, Jett remained motionless aware of the precarious situation of baring a blade neck high at the purported smuggler lord. But, there was no way he was going to hand over his finest possession to the unknown man who most likely was corrupt to the core of his character. He held the sword steady and the light glinted on the sharp black edge.

A bead of sweat appeared on the Captain's forehead. If he felt any apprehension, he concealed it with slick finesse and took his time over the blade. Appearing satisfied, his eyes lit up, if only briefly, and he breathed deep. 'Fine piece of work.'

Jett sheathed his sword and sat down more on edge than ever.

The Captain narrowed his calculating eyes. 'Black-gold demands a high price and a blade like that is a rare sight. I've only seen one other and you say you have more?' Eagerness entered Shark's eyes, but he paused and studied Jett. 'But one does not trade such a weapon. What is your true game here?'

Jett had to let some of the truth out if he was going to get anywhere with him. 'I am looking for some people.'

'That's a coincidence, so am I.' Suspicion crossed Tonius' eyes and his thin lips tightened. 'Perhaps we can help each other. Who are these people?'

Jett remarked with open condescension. 'I'd rather not say at this point.' Tonius Shark might be an uncompassionate cold smuggler, but he was smart. Jett would credit him that much.

'You make it difficult for me to help you,' he replied.

Jett kept his face clear of surprise. 'I'm looking for two women and a man.'

'I see. I'm looking for a girl. One worth the price of that blade.'

Jett attempted to disguise his disgust. Did he expect him to find a girl for him? 'I assume it's not any girl?'

'No. This adolescent is special. Her distinguishing features are her auburn-blonde hair,' he drew his words out with care, 'and she's Rynian.'

Jett's throat clenched at the description, but his voice remained calm. 'That's really not so special. Why do you want her?'

'No, that's not what makes her special. Someone quite important is willing to pay a great deal for her. And apparently she's here in the city, somewhere.' His saccharine grin masked any truth Jett might have seen on his face. 'If you or Fern discover such a one and bring her to me, I will pay well.'

Jett lifted his chin and studied him anew, wondering who it was who really wanted her. 'I'll keep an eye out for her.'

'Perhaps we are searching for the same person?'

Narrowing his eyes with distrust, Jett snapped, 'If I find this girl, I'll let you know.'

'Now, down to business.' Tonius regarded him with a blank stare. 'How many weapons do you have?'

Jett said with brazen self-confidence, 'I can get at least four more weapons.' He could not help but notice Tonius' startled reaction.

'I wish to see them.'

Jett touched his hilt. 'You've seen this.' He dug around in his pouch and held up between his fingers a black stone smoothed to perfection. 'And this.'

The Captain nodded, a satisfied grin on his face. 'You would trade a black-gold blade for these people? Their value must be high?'

'Yes.'

Tonius eyed him shrewdly. 'What do you think you would do on seeing them?'

Jett attempted to answer as equally as astute. 'Negotiate and deal in the appropriate currency.'

Nodding his understanding, Tonius remarked, 'That leaves a lot to personal interpretation. If you make any sort of trouble your life will not be worth living. I say that on behalf of all participants of the trade. It's a privileged business and some of the clientele are the finest of Florisian aristocracy. They may not like new business brought in. But wares are wares and a sell just a sell if you have enough coin.'

Jett's face remained stony and unreceptive. 'I'm not here to make trouble.' He was doubting whether he would get anywhere with the man.

'New blood is always good. Besides, if Fern sent you, he knows what he's doing. So, agreed, you can attend the next Meet.'

Jett nodded. 'And that is where?'

'First there is a fee to get in, as there is a fee for everything in this town.' Tonius' eyes flicked, deviously. 'Our city of self-indulgence.'

'How much?'

'You can pay a debt I owe.' A note of cheer was in his voice. 'It helps him out and it certainly helps me and ultimately you.'

Jett's mouth gaped. 'Pay your debt?'

'In exchange he will give you details of the Meet. Where, when...'

Jett's eyes darkened, having reached the end of his tolerance.

Tonius became less courteous at Jett's change of mood. 'If you think about using force the door to the trade will be closed to you. And don't think about beating this man up, he is my tailor.'

Jett's decision had already been made. An open door to the people trade was more important than his personal umbrage at that moment. 'Who and where?'

'Pioter Derygen on Albury Road in Sybil's Rise.'

He stood to leave before Tonius added any additional tasks.

'Don't forget the one I'm seeking. She will be found eventually. I know this city inside out.' An arrogant smile was on his sleek pale face. 'But the more looking, the better.'

Jett didn't doubt it. If a Narahk was after her, he wouldn't be surprised who else was seeking her out. But it did bring him a margin of comfort that she wasn't in this smugglers hands, which meant it was possible the others were also not held by him.

The small man held the door open for him. As Jett passed, he had an instinctual sense he would run into him again.

Back on the street, Jett cut a sombre path through the rain, dodging puddles and walking close to the buildings. Harassed with new thoughts, he needed time to let them unfurl. If it was the same girl from Lanvin it opened up a range of possibilities. He had to find them before the Captain or they might be in more danger. But what was really troubling, how in hell's name did they know she was in the city?

He couldn't head back to the White Horse for fear of being followed. Instead he entered another inn, "Sleepy Dog." Wet and bedraggled customers filled the tavern. Men created space for him at the counter where he asked for a cheap room for a few nights.

Upstairs in the sparsely furnished room at the back of the inn, he locked the door. He pushed open the only window, the rotting wood shutters still serving their purpose. A narrow laneway separated the inn from another building. Perfect for what he planned later.

He closed the shutters and sat on the bed, unhooking the pouch on his belt. With all the talk of coin, he realized he would need a jeweller and a good one. He emptied the contents into his palm and examined the precious gemstones along with a nugget of malreus he carved from the plateau. At the time he did not think he would be using them this soon.

Downstairs, he enquired of the barkeep of any reputable jewellers in the district. After gaining information about a man called Rufus, he was on his way again.

Rufus turned out to be a quiet non-descript man with a guarded booth on the busiest side of the dock markets. Jett bypassed the stall's hired guard and Rufus stared warily at his approach. But Jett showed him a gemstone and Rufus soon changed his disposition.

After some moments of pressured debate, Jett left with a smug grin and satisfied with the weight of coinage in his pouch. Rufus was good and shrewd, an accepted prerequisite of the trade. Fortunately Jett knew his merchandise and the cost of making fine jewellery. His pre-cut blemish-free gem was especially expensive. There was no way he could be swindled, instead he received more than what he hoped for. Rufus, so impressed by the cut of his ruby, requested he bring further gems to him. Jett said he would keep him in mind if any such jewels passed his hand again, as he thought of the ones already in his pouch.

Lifting the hood over his head, he let his cloak fall around him. He waited under the protection of eaves and observed people walking. So far he noticed no one following and he started off to the tailors.

Finally finding it, he opened the door to a silent shop. No one came to greet him so he inspected the clothing. Shirts hung on hangers while others were folded on the bench top. Patterned embroidery was on some collars and sleeves. Drawn to one group of garments, he ran his hand over crimsons, yellows, and blues, lavished with fine needlework. He would never wear such extravagant clothes, but Seth would be delighted. The quality would even meet Keanan's standards. Something on the shelf caught his eye, small enough he could slide it into his leather pouch.

At the back of the shop, a door opened. Despite his middle years, the tailor stooped like an old man. Sewing tools adorned his apron; shears, leads, pins, and measuring tools, even an eyepiece stuck out from his shirtfront. 'Can I help you?'

Jett lifted a black linen shirt. Similar coloured embroidery was over the soft wide collar, and gentle pleats lined the cuffs. Neat leather lacing was on the front. 'How much?'

'Black is more.' He admired it up against Jett's trim torso. 'It would fit.' He stated in a friendly manner, 'Five gold.'

Pleased with his new wealth, Jett handed him the coin and he looped the shirt over his belt.

The tailor watched, his eyes blinking in shock. 'That is a good shirt,' he cautioned with a wagging finger, 'Look after it.'

'Now, I wish to speak with you regarding other matters.'

He creased his brow in suspicious expectation.

'Apparently Captain Shark has a debt with you?'

Pioter stepped away with sudden apprehension. 'I make him nice clothes and that Tonius cheats me,' he declared with anger, 'No more clothes until he gives me what he owes.'

'How much?'

'Ten gold,' Pioter cried with exasperation. 'Maybe it doesn't seem a lot, but I'm trying to run my business.'

'I've come to pay it,' Jett informed him, 'on one condition.'

Pioter sighed. 'What is it?'

'Where and when is the next trade meet?'

'You in the people trade?' Pioter looked him over with consideration. 'I should have known.'

Jett contemplated his unflattering words. At least he looked the part of a smuggler, whatever that was.

'I tell you the night it's on and on that day you come back and I tell you where.'

Jett's eyes darkened with frustration.

'That's how it is. Same for everyone. They don't want any trouble with the guards and the guards don't want trouble. They get enough trouble with the racketeers. As long as they don't take Florisians off the streets.' He added, 'No point looking like that. I don't know where it's going to be anyway, it's decided on that day.'

'If that's the way of it. I give you five gold now and on that day I give you the rest,' Jett said, 'Do you think that's fair?'

Pioter shrugged. 'It's a cutthroat business. I'm not even a dealer, yet I get roped into being a middleman. What do I care, I just want my money.'

Jett could sympathize, he just wanted his Kin.

Pioter creased his brow in heavy thought. 'Come back here in seven days and I'll tell you where it will be, on that day.'

Jett handed him half the gold. 'I'll be back then. Maybe I will buy more clothes.'

'You do that.' Pioter gave a faltering laugh.

Jett gave him a questioning look.

'Tonius was waiting to purchase that shirt. I said he couldn't till he paid me.' Pioter shook his head, his merriment fleeting. 'I'll say someone bought it because he took too long, that'll show him.' He looked troubled despite his cynicism.

Jett smirked at the image of the disgruntled Captain. 'If he gets mad it should be at me. Good day.'

The rain had eased, but everything outside was wet. He stepped over a dirty puddle and stood under an awning to watch the street. The thin man from the Captain's peered out from a cramped laneway. What could Jett expect from people who made a living from abducting people?

Jett made his way up the opposite side. Swivelling, he spied the slight man dash back into the lane, and he smiled. It was turning into a productive day, if not expensive and it was far from over.

Inside the Sleepy Dog, he pushed his way through the crowd to the bar and ordered a meal. He ate and listened to the conversations around him. Sunlight was fast fading. He wondered how much the others were worried about him. Even so there was no need to give them extra anxiety.

Up in his room, he pulled off his tan shirt and replaced it with his new one. The warm linen fit loosely, just how he liked it. He pulled out the black powder dye he swiped from the tailor's. He felt remorse at not paying, but he had no wish for anyone to be the wiser it was in his possession. The one following him would speak to the tailor sooner or later.

The powder used by the miners back home, gave him an idea. Of course, that powder was created by the Alchemists and glowed a startling blue once dusted through the caverns to safe guard miners travels. This dye would mark any movement in his room. He sprinkled a line next to the door and on the handle, and also by the window. It was visible if he looked hard, but otherwise it was obscured by the dark wood flooring. Lastly, he disturbed the bed covers.

He opened the window and shutters, and peered down the lane, penetrating the shadows with his night vision. He was a suspicious soul and untrusting at best, but still it was imperative he not be followed. Otherwise they might all suffer the consequences; their possessions stolen and worse, a slit throat in the night.

No movement could be seen in the lane. With his old shirt tucked under his belt, he stepped over the black powder by the window and half hung on the ledge. Observing the alley repeatedly, he stood on the outside awning. Once assured he had no watchers, he pushed the shutters closed and jumped the five feet to the other side. A tile rattled. He froze, anticipating its fall. None came and he breathed a grateful sigh. The shadows were motionless down the alley even so he stared for several moments to be convinced. He eased over to a window slightly ajar. Discovering it stuck in that position, he breathed a frustrated curse and generated a small amount of Ethos through his eyes. He burnt a splinter of wood and the window opened enough for him to wedge it further.

He climbed through into a bedroom. Quiet, he opened the door and spied stairs down the corridor. Trusting he could sneak out a back exit, he crept forward. Once near the bottom, he halted at the chatter of two women and peered around the corner. A short space led to what might be the kitchen and supposedly a back doorway. From his concealed position he saw a young woman with a dark tan dress and wild long hair, speaking to an elderly lady similar in appearance. The young woman moved to confront him.

Jett placed his hand over her mouth and twirled her around till her back fronted his chest. 'Don't shout, I'm not going to hurt you.' He added, 'I'm being chased. It's the racket that trade in pe—' A heavy object came down on the side of his head. He stumbled with a sudden churning of the stomach. The elderly lady stood, a rolling pin hanging from both hands. Fortunately she could barely lift it, aside from swing it.

The younger woman took advantage of Jett's weakened grip to shove his hand away while giving the other woman a reproachful stare. 'Mama!' she cried, 'You could have killed him.'

The old lady rolled out words in a foreign tongue Jett was too dizzy to understand.

The lady pushed him into a chair. 'Sit down.'

He sat heavily and breathed deep. His shaking hand went to his throbbing head. The young lady spoke to the old one who shuffled off to the kitchen and turned to Jett. 'You run from the traders?' The younger woman asked, 'You're not Coltrenian? I can tell.'

'I am...' he said in a daze, 'I'm not from here.'

'They go after foreigners. I should know.' She informed him with pride, 'My husband is an Officer in the Watch.' She spoke with an accent Jett could not discern, and she said with genuine worry, 'You have escaped?'

At the mention of the Officer, fear tightened his throat. 'They have not caught me.'

She nodded and smiled. 'Good and they will not. Have you seen a man called Vlaus Dabrowski?' She continued, 'He is my brother. He was coming here to live, to start a new life.' She looked towards her mother with melancholy. 'I miss him and fear he is now in their hands. If you know anything about him...'

The old lady pushed a cup into his face. Without thinking he drank it. It made him less nauseous, but tasted sour. He rubbed the back of his head, checking for blood. 'What does he look like?'

'Tall.' Her hand reached high above her head. 'Very skinny, like a stick, his hair is mousey. He has hazel eyes and sunken cheeks.' She sucked in her own cheeks comically. 'He is from Selon like me and mama.'

'Selon...'

'My name is Vanya and mama is Vida.'

Jett grimaced at the old lady and she responded in her own tongue.

Vanya said, 'Mama say she is sorry.'

'Thank you for the drink,' he said, 'I have to go.'

'Have you a safe place to stay?' Vanya asked, and the old lady continued smiling inanely.

'I do. If I hear anything about your brother I will tell you.' He concluded that selling people was indeed a nasty business.

'My husband tries to fight these people, but they are sneaky, always changing the rules. If you get into trouble, you come here and we try to help you.'

'I will keep you in mind.' Jett stood and tested his balance. After a moment the room settled and he could walk. 'Tell your mama she is courageous, but foolhardy. If she takes on the wrong people, she'll be in trouble.' He pressed a coin into her palm. 'For your kindness.'

Vanya said nothing, but smiled gratefully.

He left through the back door and came out to the night sky. He went past the outhouse and entered the laneway beyond. The Kin might start roaming the streets in search of him if he didn't return quickly. He snuck down the alleys behind buildings, avoiding the streets as much as was possible, all the while, checking over his shoulder for anyone following.

21- The Fights On

There are two things a woman should never learn, brawling and sword fighting, and as sure as I'm built like a mountain, she should never be taught the one if she knows the other. Women fight in their own manner, something outright different. Always seems to be personal and about some flamin' lover. Scratching, biting, the gouging, the hair pulling and groin ramming, all add up to one hell of an excruciating mess. And if you want to keep your manhood intact, by hell's fury, don't give her a sword...'

Life of a Champion, Zab Thunder'Fist

Jett entered the White Horse from the back. Inside the noisy tavern, the air was stifled by smoke. On glimpsing Keanan's red-hair above the crowd, Jett pushed his way through to him. Keanan and Seth stood by the bar, looking relieved at the sight of him.

'Well, well,' Seth said, 'you decided to return.'

Jett patted him on the back. 'Were you worried?'

'Indeed,' Keanan replied.

Seth pinched the sleeve of Jett's black shirt, admiring the pattern with an envious pout. 'This is new.' His eyes travelled to Jett's face and he turned his cheek, examining the bruise by his eye. 'This, also new. How did that happen?'

'A brash idiot and bad luck. You should see the lump on my head.' Jett's hand went to it and he grimaced.

Through the crowd, Hellier appeared next to him. 'Good to see you're back.' She frowned at his facial bruising and like Seth she pouted. 'What on earth have you been doing?' *Without us.*

'Something I had to do alone,' said Jett, 'but don't worry, you'll be a big help in a few days.'

Keanan remarked, 'We should talk upstairs—' His speech was broken by a burly man shoving him out of his path to get to the bar. He leaned on the counter along with his friend, and caught Burgman's attention with a flick of his hand.

'By the devil's whiskers!' Burgman rumbled, 'What do you want now?'

One of the men, his scruffy hair tied at his back, replied, 'More people here, more coin.' A distinct smell of spirits rode on his breath at each word.

Jett eyed the men, wearing hide jackets over their broad torsos, and one had a white scarf tied in the fashion he had noticed on the streets. He wondered if they were in the Captain's employ.

'More?!' Burgman was irate at the notion. 'I've had it with you thugs coming in—'

He was stopped by the man's pointed finger. 'You pay or you know what happens.'

'Get out,' Burgman yelled, 'Now!'

The one with the dirty white scarf snarled, 'You'll see us again.'

Keanan stepped forward, blocking their path. 'The wisest thing you can do is leave and never return—' The thug turned and punched Keanan in the face. Keanan swung into Jett who stopped him from toppling to the floor.

Hellier growled, 'Why don't you pick on someone who can fight?' She lifted her knee to meet with the man's testicles. He stooped in pain and she uppercut his chin. Cheers and excited cries came from the patrons and they clamoured to get a glimpse of the girl punching the thug.

Amidst the uproar, Burgman shouted, 'Not in me pub!'

Marcus emerged through the crowd and barred the second man from throttling Hellier, by grabbing him in a headlock and dragging him outside. Grinning, Hellier joined him with the other, his arm twisted behind his back. The people emptied onto the terrace. Dario climbed out through the window and continued playing outside, his music adding to the spectacle.

Keanan wiped the blood from his lip and said to Jett, 'I'll watch them.' He followed the commotion outside.

Too tired to deal with more activity, Jett took a stool along the abandoned counter. Seth sat alongside him.

Burgman asked, 'Aren't you worried about your girl?'

'Yes.' Jett grimaced in frustration. 'Because of her, we'll probably be seen by all the low-life numbskulls from all the wrong districts. What's the story with those men?'

'It's the rackets 'round here,' Burgman said.

'Go on.'

'They've been coming last couple of weeks. Beat me up the first time. They're a few planks short of a bench. Soon, I'll have to get me some protection.' Burgman sighed at the jeers of drunken people and Dario's song lifting to a frantic melody.

'Can't you tell someone in authority?' asked Seth.

'The Watch said they know about it and they're onto it, but they need to be here to catch 'em and so forth.' He paused, as if considering the guards' story. 'Too busy 'round Racen Square and the Docks... not enough guards. Blow me to Belrorn, where are they now?' He nodded his head in the direction of the street outside.

'We should have held onto those men for you,' stated Jett.

An almighty cheer was followed by clapping and disjointed chatter. The fight must have finished, even Dario stopped playing.

Seth mused. 'Wonder if there are casualties?'

'They've run off.' Burgman strained to see out the window. 'Ah, see why. Guards coming 'round the park now.'

Jett grunted. 'So much for not being noticed.'

Amidst the patrons, the three came up to the bar. Marcus and Hellier received pats on the back and a free round of drinks with congratulations all round. Hellier said with reproach, 'You missed it, Jett.'

'Was there anything to see? Those men were drunk,' he said. 'It would have been smarter hanging onto them and handing them over to the guards.'

She sat down next to him, puffing hard. 'You're right.' She felt her red and bloodied fist. 'But it was fun.'

'Agreed,' said Marcus. 'How's your face, Keanan?'

Keanan's nose was red and his lip was no longer bleeding. He replied with a nasally sound, 'It's not broken. That bastard gave me a nasty welt.'

'Thanks for helping me with those rogues,' Burgman said. 'Maybe we can work something out.'

'We weren't able to hold onto them. With the guards coming up they bolted, and we didn't want to get caught fighting either.' Hellier flexed the shoulder she had previously wounded. 'Do you think they will come back?'

Jett scowled at her words. 'You pissed them off. I'd be back.'

Seth asked, 'Does anyone sleep in the stables?'

'Only Bertie, my stable hand,' Burgman replied, 'He ain't as good as you.'

'Someone will have to stay down there,' said Seth. 'If something happens to the horses—'

Hellier offered, 'I'll sleep there.'

'You're not,' said Jett.

'I'll be there too,' Keanan said.

Marcus guffawed. 'What can you do?'

'You would rather?' said Keanan.

'We can't have someone sleeping in the stables every night nor have a brawl every evening.' Jett sighed. 'Maybe we can find out who's behind this.'

'I think we need to go upstairs and talk about matters,' said Keanan.

They left the tavern and went to their room to discuss the events of the day. Jett stretched out on his bed while the Kin sat on their beds and chairs.

Keanan said, 'I put in a report at the public bureau—'

'I didn't want you do to that.' Jett sighed with fatigue.

Keanan's tone turned cross. 'No need for concern. I got the impression it's purely superfluous paperwork with no follow up.'

'We can hope.' Jett lowered his head back on the bed board and considered the girl again. 'I don't want anyone linking them back to us.'

'Even if it's helpful?' Keanan retorted.

Jett pressed his lips together and his remark was snide. 'I'm fairly certain we won't be getting them back through the justice system.'

'We're doing it illegally?' Marcus gave him a mischievous smirk.

'Probably.' Jett relaxed his body into the mattress.

Keanan threw his hand in the air. 'What a surprise!'

'Whatever it takes.' Hellier sat at the chair, arms folded and nodding her consent.

'And what did you do today?' Seth directed to Jett.

Jett stared up at the ceiling, speculating on how productive his day was if at all. 'Bribed some information out of a madman, got beaten up by a mindless lackey, did some trade, bought a shirt, met a pirate captain, rented a room, got hit on the head with a rolling pin.' Again he cringed on recollection. 'Spent a lot of gold, and the highlight of my day, I have potentially sold two of you as slaves, and possibly all your weapons.'

Marcus chuckled. 'All in a day.'

Hellier said, 'And who gets to be slaves?'

'Clothing, how fortunate you are.' Seth admired Jett's new shirt once more.

'You definitely get to be a slave.' Jett pointed at Hellier. 'And Seth, and I can't decide between Marcus and Keanan, but that's a week away when I find out where the blasted thing is.' He looked to Seth. 'I'll talk to you about the shirt tomorrow.'

'Hold on,' Marcus lifted his hands, 'Our weapons?!'

'I offered them in trade.' Jett chuckled at Marcus' angst.

Seth gave a nervous laugh. 'Thank Kahm, I don't have any.'

'Don't worry about it now.' Jett returned to the current issue. 'Currently, we might have a problem with these idiots coming back.'

'Someone should be on guard in the stables, in case,' Keanan said with exasperation, 'they looked the type who would burn a building down for the hell of it, or at least steal our steads. Hellier and I will not feel the cold.'

'If they come back don't let them get away this time,' Jett instructed him. 'We'll hand them over to the guards.'

Keanan and Hellier gathered some of their gear and left the room.

Marcus lay on his bed, his hand under his head. 'Ethan would have enjoyed tonight.'

Seth said, 'He certainly likes a good punch up.'

'I miss Shiarn,' Marcus paused, 'and Earona…'

A melancholy tone in Marcus' voice caused Jett to crook his head in contemplation. An underlying connection was present, he was not aware of previously. 'We'll get them back even if we have to sell everything we own,' he said, 'even if we have to sell ourselves and I mean that.' Jett knew how Marcus was feeling, because he was feeling it too - a despairing doubt; maybe they would never see the missing three again.

~ * ~

Bertie, the stable hand, had responded with confusion when Hellier and Keanan made themselves at home in his stable. They sent him back to his room where a small stove warmed the air.

By the first horse's stall, Hellier sat watching Keanan lay their blankets on the cosy nests he made in the hay. Enough light came from the one small window to see by, but they would be asleep soon enough. Through a parting made from a loose slat, one of the horses nudged her. 'Sunny, I'll find you a treat tomorrow.' Before she went off with Dario, gambling again. Her pouch had grown heavier over the last couple of days along with her conscience.

Keanan lay on the hay. His face hit the blanket and he recoiled. 'I had forgotten how dreadful the smell of hay and horse is so close up.'

Hellier lifted the blanket, disturbing Keanan's neat folds and splayed it out on the hay, waving more of the repugnant smell over him. 'Hope you don't snore tonight.'

'What are you talking about, girl,' he said, 'I'm not the only one who snores in this room.'

Like Keanan, she had no need of any covering for warmth. She nestled into the single blanket. 'As long as I don't hear it when I'm asleep, I don't care.' She shut her eyes.

Over the dripping rain, Keanan muttered, 'It seems daft being here.'

Her voice was a faint hush. ''Cos we let those mongrels get away.' She opened an eye to see him staring at the ceiling. 'Can't sleep?'

'No. I mean, why are we here?' he speculated, 'It's as if we have been thrown into the wind with no time for conjecture, no way of being assured where we will be in one week's time or if we shall even be together. Consider where we were a week ago.'

Hellier closed her eyes again. 'I suppose.'

'I speculate, why we have been separated in this fashion? Our traditions and lineage proclaim purpose and destiny for our people. So what is the purpose in all this?'

'You mean right now?'

'Leaves scatter, collide, and fall,' he said under his breath, 'Strength of the branch cannot prevent their descent. Malevolent wind inflicts torturous scar. It does not relent until flesh and bone is stripped... ' He paused, 'It's possible it speaks of our current situation.'

Hellier mumbled an agreeing observation.

'Fate has doors and windows in many shapes and irregular forms, some small, others enormous,' he went on in a retrospective state, 'We walk through a door to squeeze through a window only to be dumped through a hatch.'

'I've fallen in the hay. Sleep is my purpose.' Hellier drifted off to sleep, leaving Keanan to work out his thoughts.

Later on she woke to a noise outside and lay listening. The rain had stopped. Over the slow dripping of eaves, she heard scratching and a soft knock. After a moment, came a scuffle of feet outside. She shook Keanan awake. *I hear movement.*

This time we get them. Keanan rose from the hay and stood alert near the door.

Hellier peered through a crack and passed her thoughts to Keanan. *Wait, they're coming in.* She unsheathed her sword.

Is a sword necessary?

One of the stable doors opened. A man looked surprised to see Keanan waiting. Keanan grabbed him by the shoulders and kneed him in the face. While he was stunned, he swung him into the post of the stall. The second man rushed at him.

Hellier jumped out to confront his back. 'Come back for more?'

The man she brawled with earlier swivelled in alarm and stepped back, fumbling with his sword while she slashed at him. He blocked her swipe and swung at her leg with his blade. Shifting in time, she continued with her strikes. Their swordplay became intense, yet all the while her concern was Keanan being struck by the first man. Not the best at hand to hand, Keanan was cornered and doubled over from punches to the stomach. Distracted by the assault on him, she thrust her sword on an upward angle, driving it into her opponent's chest. A crunch followed. He fell backwards, her sword remaining between his ribs. He stared, stunned, his eyes freezing into lifelessness. She slid the sword free and grabbed the other bulkier man kicking Keanan. Yanking his long hair in a powerful grip, her sword cut into his skin. 'You move an inch, you're over.'

Keanan recovered enough to disarm him. He tied the man's wrists behind him, and his ankles were also bound, as well as having a rag stuffed in his mouth. They dragged him twisting and writhing to an empty stall at the back.

Hellier said, 'He won't get free?'

'Those knots are good,' Keanan stated breathlessly, clutching at his stomach.

She noticed the blood around his mouth and the bruising on his head. 'Are you hurt?' *You could have been killed.*

'I would have burnt the bastards.'

'You would have burnt the place down.'

They chuckled together and Hellier indicated the other man, lying in the blood stained hay. 'What about him?'

'He's dead, nothing we can do.'

'Be serious. What am *I* going to do?' she asked with growing apprehension over what she had done.

He spent a moment considering the body sprawled across the entrance of the stables. 'I think we should wake our un-esteemed leader and confer with him.'

'God, do we have to?'

'I'll wake him while you watch the prisoner.'

'Gladly.' No way did she want to be the one waking Jett up.

After Keanan left, Bertie stuck his head out to see if the noise had finished. Hellier ordered him back to bed which he did without argument. She dragged the body from the path of the door and propped him up against the wall behind it. She closed his eyelids. The feel of his skin was a shock to her touch. She looked at the man, who was no longer angry or had cruel intentions, or anything. He was a dead man, she had killed.

~ * ~

Jett was in a deep sleep when Keanan poked his bare arm. He rolled on his back to see Keanan hovering over him, whispering, 'We got them.'

He mumbled a curse and replied, 'Tie 'em up. We'll talk to 'em.' He added, 'in the morning.'

'There's a problem with that, that's why I'm waking you.'

With one open eye, Jett paid him more attention.

'One of them is dead and we were unsure what to do with the body.' Keanan paused and watched him process the information in his waking state.

Jett slowly rose from his bed. Wearing only under-drawers, he shivered. The room's fire had died down to embers, but it would still be warmer inside than out. 'I'll dress and come down.'

~ * ~

Jett followed Keanan through the door. Jett stared at the body. His torn shirt was soaked with dark blood from a hole in the centre of his chest, while his scarf-wrapped head flopped unnaturally onto his chin. 'You did a good job on him.'

Hellier creased her brow with annoyance. *What is that supposed to mean?*

Keanan asked Jett, 'Do you think we should tell Burgman?'

'Not right now, that's for sure.' Jett lowered his voice to a whisper, 'This complicates things. We can't be involved in this sort of… assault. There are laws here. I don't want us to be up at the guardhouse, or wherever, explaining this and having them scrutinize us. I don't think we could put it on Burgman either. Curse it.' His last words came out in a growl. The last thing he wanted was to be seen with any guard, in case he was being watched. It was bad enough Vanya knew his name and Keanan had registered his missing Kin. He finally said, 'It would be ideal if we could get him out of the city…'

'Dump him in the sea,' Hellier suggested.

'How can we move his body without detection,' Jett remarked. 'I suppose we could leave him on the street somewhere.'

'But his partner is still alive, and talkative,' Keanan said. 'Maybe he can tell us who sent him.'

If the man had connections to the Captain or anyone to do with the trade, it could be dangerous. Jett strode past the stalls to the other man, tied up to a post, and kicked him awake. 'I want to know who you are working for. Maybe we can negotiate something.'

'You's are murderers,' he bellowed, 'you killed me mate.'

'You are thieves and cutthroats and the destroyers of proper—' Keanan stopped at Jett's upraised hand.

Jett went on, 'You haven't answered the question. We killed him, so killing you won't make a difference.'

The man spat in Jett's face.

Jett pressed his lips together. Scowling, he wiped the spittle with the edge of his cloak. Then he punched the thug in the face, knocking his head sideways. 'I've been woken up because of you - I'm not in a good mood.'

Blood came rushing out of the man's nose, his voice rasped as he spoke, 'I don't give a rat's turd. He's called the Collector, some fancy pants big wig… goes to some room above a hat shop in Salisbury.'

Jett demanded, his voice cracking like ice, 'Name?'

'What?' The man asked slowly as if lacking any wits, 'Whose name?'

Jett clenched his fist to hit him again.

Keanan said, 'The hat shop.'

Bubbles of blood came from his nose and he strained, 'Margo's Hats.'

Jett rolled his eyes at the man's stupidity and rose from his crouched position.

The man rambled, 'He said I get payment depending how much money I bring in from the rounds, is all.'

Jett stared at Keanan with a thoughtful expression, ignoring the man's pleas.

He continued, 'you're not gonna kill me, are ya? I told you, I did.'

Keanan responded with a questioning shrug to Jett and he placed the gag over the man's mouth and they left him to squirm.

Meanwhile, Hellier had placed a couple of empty sacks over the man's head and body. 'I didn't want to look at him.'

'What are we going to do with that one?' Keanan thumbed to the live man.

'Hand him over. He's probably just a numbskull who's made bad choices. We can't kill him.' *As much as what I don't care about him, it would create more problems. Like another dead body.*

'He will fabricate his own story,' said Keanan, 'make things worse.'

Casting a glance over his shoulder to the back of the stable, Jett lowered his voice. 'Yes, like tell the guards we killed his friend.'

Hellier said, 'It really was an accident.'

'It wasn't the smartest thing to do. But, it is what it is and we'll survive it.' Jett somehow could not be totally mad at her. After all, if it had not been for her, Keanan might have been in serious trouble, as it was, she saved him from being beaten, possibly killed.

In a quiet excited voice Keanan suggested, 'How about a beer barrel?'

'What?!' Hellier whispered with wonder, 'Put his body inside?'

'They are large.' Jett tossed it about in a whisper, 'We could roll it somewhere.'

'Not roll it,' whispered Keanan, 'we get a hand cart and push it.'

Hellier made a sour face. 'Won't that be disgusting?'

They both turned to stare at her with bewilderment. Keanan shook his head. 'Too late for that.'

'I think it best if we get rid of the body altogether,' Jett said, 'then no trouble for us or Burgman. And Burgman can take that man in to the guards. At least there won't be any evidence to speak of.' He whispered, 'Just a *missing person.*' Considering the possibilities, it could actually work. 'We could use the barrel and take it out through the gates and bury it or dump it somewhere, maybe Burgman needs a delivery done, and we can get a wagon. It'll be morbid business.' He muttered, 'We'll talk to him first thing tomorrow.'

Hellier grinned. 'Great idea.'

'I'll take credit for that,' Keanan said.

'Someone round here has to have them,' Jett winked at Keanan, 'at least some of the time.'

22 - Last Touch

A prudent man sees trouble far off
However a foolish man walks blindly

Empyrean Ascension

Earona's heartache over Ethan and her lost Kin overwhelmed her, and she shuddered with grief in the chill morning air. Her head ached from trying to reach his thoughts. Sensing his misery was more than she could bear, besides, she had the impression he didn't want her to read his thoughts. The smallest thing irritated her; the cold, lack of food, even the need for a bath. Mara was unsympathetic. In fact she was downright rude. The girl seemed happy in the cell, even content, while Earona exploded with worry or sobbed like a child.

During the morning, a guard opened their cell. Captain Morran walked in and his words boomed off the stone. 'Good day, ladies.'

Unsure how to respond to his civility, Earona blinked in shock.

'I've come to inform you we shall be considering better accommodation for you.'

'What about Ethan?' Earona's voice cracked with emotion. 'How is he?'

'He has been charged with some serious offences, one of which is abduction—'

'You tortured him,' she cried, 'Of course he would tell you anything. Anyway we weren't abducted.'

'I would be quiet if I were you.' He creased his eyes with suspicion. 'You are not the ones who were abducted. He has confessed to coercing you girls into aiding him in his crimes.' He glanced over his shoulder at the two guards. 'Take them upstairs.'

'What's going to happen to him?' Earona asked with trepidation, fearing it would be a death penalty.

'Most likely he will be sent to the Rocks.' With no further information, the captain left the cell.

She yelled after him, 'More questions? Haven't you done enough?' She turned on the waiting guard. 'What are the Rocks?'

He retorted, 'A hive of criminals.'

Her eyes glowered with wrath.

The guard herded them from the cell. 'Take your blankets.'

Mara picked them up and jostled Earona out before the guard had to do it. They walked down the hallway with a guard in front and behind.

Ethan's hands stuck out of his cell window. Her Ethos coursed through her. She clasped him and would not let go until she restored something within his body. His warm eyes misted with sorrow and she reflected back the same helplessness. The guard wrenched her hands from him and hauled her away from his reach.

It was the only way. His tranquil thoughts pacified her.

She hid her distress, having no wish to add to his sadness. The guards dragged her along the hall and upstairs to another corridor. All the while her thoughts were consumed by Ethan and when she would see him again. As long as she *did* see him again.

The guard pushed her into the new cell. It was drier and the bed was off the ground. Glass was on the window, but so were the iron bars. Earona did not want any special favours; she would have preferred a miserable cell nearer to Ethan. Swamped by depression, she sat on the bed.

Mara sat and bounced on the mattress. 'Different cell, same prison. I wonder if this is what he meant by better accommodation.'

Indifferent to her chitchat, Earona tried to imagine what the Kin could possibly do to save them.

~ * ~

Jett sat in the tavern the next morning, waiting for Keanan and Hellier. The room was empty and this suited him fine. When the two finally entered, he said, 'How's our friend doing?'

Hellier sat by him. 'He's moaning and groaning, but still tied up.'

'Good, now we wait for Burgman. Did you sleep well?' Jett's eyes rested on Hellier.

'Didn't sleep.' Her eyes skimmed the counter, avoiding his piercing gaze.

Burgman walked into the bar. Taking a second look, he stared at the three with surprise. 'You's up early.' He yawned and rubbed an eye. 'Wassup?'

Keanan said, 'Good morning, Burgman.'

Burgman grunted. 'It ain't good 'till after me brew.' They waited while he poured himself a dark steaming drink from a pitcher warming on a grate in the kitchen. He took an untidy slurp as he walked back to them.

Jett started, 'We had an incident last night in your stables—'

'Is Bertie still alive?' He retrieved his stool. 'Maybe I should sit down for this...'

'Bertie's fine,' Jett assured him.

'Those thieves came back?' Burgman asked.

'They did and one of them won't be bothering you ever again,' Jett said, 'the other is out there, bound.'

Burgman cried in shock, 'You killed him, didn't you, in me stables!'

Jet cut him off, 'In self-defence.'

'Maybe so. But you'll be dragged to the judges! Also depends what the other man says about it and how important he is to someone. The guards don't like foreigners doing whatever they please.'

Jett nodded. He got the talk from the official when they registered at the gate. Weapons were tolerated as an accessory, but they were not to be used.

'Depends what the guards think of you too. You got a bad name with the Watch?'

Having a bad reputation with the guards was the least of it. Jett didn't want to be known by them at all; especially not for murdering someone. 'I have an idea, but I need your help. We want to dispose of this person.'

Burgman stared at him blankly.

'How do you transport your ale?' Jett said.

'I use my wagon,' Burgman explained, 'When me barrels are empty I go to the village front, to Oaty's and he fills us up.'

'That might work,' Jett said.

Burgman's criticizing gaze fell on Jett. 'Why did you have to go kill someone?' He bemoaned, 'It's so easy, ain't it, but then there are consequences, ain't there, and you don't think about these,' he ranted while Hellier looked dejected at each accusing word. 'If I cop anything from this, from the guards... and what about retaliation from whoever knows this other man... you can get hung for this, you know...' After a bated pause, he eyed Jett shrewdly. 'Do you think he'd fit in a barrel?'

'We'll make him,' Jett said. 'Once we get rid of the one, we can hand the other over.'

'You better hope whoever he works for don't come looking for him and asking at the guardhouse.'

'I'm hoping he is just a hired thug,' Jett said. 'It sounded like he was working for someone in the Salisbury district.'

'If you're lucky, that person won't want to know him,' Burgman said, ''long as there's no trace of a body in me stables,' he warned, 'at all, I'll be happy.' A smile broke out on his old stubbled face. 'My wagon's out the side. Trouble is, I'm going to have only two other barrels to fill instead of the six, which might look strange.' He pondered the problem a moment. 'Bad batch maybe. I'll send you out with six, including three real ones. They have to come back though.'

'Would they taste them?' said Jett.

'Maybe. How 'bout a delivery to my friend Wenger Naras? He's in the village front as well, not far from the forest.' Burgman indicated to Keanan. 'You can go as the driver, you look more respectable, and Jett goes as the help. I'll send my niece Crissy along. You've seen her around. She gets on famously with the guards.' He asked Keanan, 'Can you read?'

Keanan's face dropped with astonishment. 'Of course! Several different languages.'

'I'll write down the address so the guards can see it if they like.' He grew more excited as the plan progressed. 'We'll fill the dead barrel with some ale just in case. That'll be the bad batch.'

Jett chuckled at the devious old man. 'Burgman, you are surprising.'

'Haven't always done bar work. Only inherited this place from an old friend. I'm from Ryne, but that's another story and a long one. Now, don't want you to go, missy, you're far too noticeable.'

Hellier offered no argument and even smiled at the mention of 'missy'.

'Don't just stand there, get going. I'll send word to my niece,' he instructed them, 'you better send Bertie to me.'

~ * ~

Keanan and Jett moved the restrained and gagged man to Bertie's room and tied him to his bed. He fought them all the way, but Jett didn't want him to know what they were doing with his friend in the other room. They soon discovered that shoving a body into a barrel was a macabre affair. After pouring jugs of ale and water half way up the barrel, they finally got the lid on tight. They pushed it outside, and together lifted the other barrels onto the cart that had Burgman's horses fastened.

Burgman introduced them to his niece Crissy who Jett assumed was just a serving girl in the tavern. Not one to be shy, she made a point of telling them how lucky she was, riding with two handsome men. On more than one occasion, Keanan and Jett shared an exasperated look over her flirtations.

As it was, the guards were more interested in Crissy's half exposed chest than the delivery. They took the empty barrels to Oaty on the outskirts of the village front of Floris. Jett and Keanan left Crissy there, and for reasons, which they justified as private errands, rode away with the full barrels.

The wagon trundled up the road about half a mile through the forest before Jett called a halt. They lugged the heavy barrel through the scrub under the cover of the forest shade. Heaving and puffing, Jett half pushed, half rolled the unbalanced container, while Keanan carried the shovels. Their voices seemed unnatural amid the tranquillity of the woods as did their brutish ripping of the innocent shrubbery.

Keanan scouted around for a suitable site. 'It isn't going to bury well.'

'We'll find a way,' Jett breathed hard. Once finding a natural dip in the ground, he cleared away the lush undergrowth. 'Glad Seth's not here to see this.'

Keanan started digging through bush roots and thick soil. After many gruelling moments of breaking roots and shovelling through dirt, he commented, 'I find it extremely perplexing we are out here perspiring over a certain girl's handiwork.'

Jett allowed himself a short chuckle despite his annoyance over the gruesome business. Hellier dashed out of the inn with Dario in tow without any explanation as to where she was going or any inclination to help them load the barrels. 'She'd be no good at hoeing the earth anyway. See what happens when you give a girl a sword. What can we expect?'

'She's going to do damage?'

'Ain't that the truth and it isn't a nice sight.' They created a deep hole, and rolled the barrel over the undergrowth. Jett burnt off the labelling and the barrel's numbers with his eyes, and finally they were finished with the grisly job.

Once they were trotting down the road again, Jett spoke in an offhanded manner. 'Am I being polite to Crissy?'

Keanan laughed gratuitously. 'I don't think you've said more than three words to her. But, you haven't snapped at her and that's remarkable.'

Jett nodded in agreement. 'I swear, if she comes on any stronger, I'm not going to be able to hold my tongue.'

'She could be quite charming if she didn't talk so much,' Keanan commented thoughtfully, 'Perhaps she thinks you are shy and underneath you like her.'

'What?!' he spurted. 'I've got an idea, tell her Hellier and I are, you know, together, give me some breathing room.'

'Even better, I could say Marcus fancies her.'

At the thought of Marcus and a girl an image of Earona popped into Jett's mind. *Marcus...and Earona...?*

'Yes, tell her that,' Jett continued, 'Hellier's been spending every day with that fellow Dario.'

Keanan remained in a meditative silence. *So that's how it is...*

'I'm not even trying to think about what you're thinking about.' Jett knew Keanan was going to tell him anyway. He had that look he was working himself up to complain.

Keanan scowled with offence. 'It's just, you obviously know something and I'm left getting the dregs from your thoughts.'

Jett sighed with regret. 'You know how it is. You pick up thoughts here and there and sometimes it's not really meant for you. The truth is I don't know anything. I've picked up some thoughts coming from someone else, but I can't interfere. We have to be able to have some privacy, if we don't have that I think we'd all be insane.'

'I wonder if she will ever love me as she used to...'

'That's not for me to answer,' said Jett, 'I have no idea what her thoughts on it are.' It was difficult having any sympathy. Earona spent years in love with Keanan while he fell in love with someone else who eventually ended the romance. 'You care for her that much?'

Keanan shrugged half-heartedly. 'I do... look, we have arrived.' He smiled at the waiting Crissy, and Jett groaned.

23 - The Furnace

'Two types of men fight. One hits with his fists, the other, hits with his brain. Who do you think will win? The one with the brains? Should do. The first one will crack you over the head before you can put a h- to your -it. What you got to do? You got to think faster...'

Life of a Champion, Zab Thunder'Fist

Marcus spent the previous day with Seth, roaming the city, visiting the docks and admiring the ocean. But, for Marcus, they should be doing more important things. As he gave it consideration, he realized not enough was being done by him. Each day he was more downhearted over their disappearance. Even more so over Earona, and that worried him as much as her disappearance. He had always liked her, but never voiced a tinge of affection. Her feelings for Keanan justified his silence. But lately he wondered if that had changed.

Burgman watched Marcus swirl his porridge round his bowl. 'Is it to your liking?'

'It's fine.'

'You had a smile on your face last night,' he commented, 'I can tell where your talents lie.'

Marcus stared down into lumpy oats.

'Been down to see the fights?'

This perked Marcus' interest. 'No, what's that?'

'Place called the Furnace. Men fight in the rings. If you win you get money and prestige.' He stared at the muscles under Marcus' shirt. 'You have to be good though.'

'Hand to hand?'

'Yep, no weapons allowed. You should go see if it's your type of game. At least it's something to do around here.'

'There's a champion?' Marcus said.

Burgman chuckled. 'Cougar Reilly's on top. He's fit, older than you, no hair, taller too.' He creased his brow at Marcus in consideration. 'But I get the feeling size doesn't matter to you.'

'Not to me.' Marcus grinned. 'He been champion long?'

'Couple of weeks, they come and go,' he replied, 'but it's usually the same ones circling the top.'

After a brief chat about the Furnace, Marcus said with renewed enthusiasm, 'It sounds worthy of a visit.'

Seth took a seat beside him and said with cheer, 'Morning all. What was all the commotion this morning?'

'You don't want to know,' said Marcus.

'And I'm not the one to be telling you,' said Burgman. 'Want some porridge?'

Seth frowned with puzzlement at Burgman's back. 'Why does Burgman know and I don't?'

Marcus laughed at his genuine grievance. 'I wouldn't have known if I didn't catch what they were doing.'

Burgman came back and pushed a bowl of lukewarm porridge before Seth.

'Eat up,' Marcus said, 'I'll explain on the way.'

'On the way?' queried Seth. 'We have some place to go?'

'We do.'

Marcus pulled his cloak closer to his body as he walked and finished explaining the activities of the previous night. '...they are dumping the body somewhere as we speak.'

'Hellier killed someone...' Seth said, 'I wonder how she feels...'

Marcus reprimanded himself at not staying in the stables in place of Keanan who didn't know how to fight. 'Bound to happen.'

'I had no idea that girl was Burgman's niece.' Seth joked, 'I had a thought she fancied you.'

Marcus was not in the mood to talk about girls as the two did on occasion. 'I'm sure she'd much prefer Jett.' Unable to manipulate his thoughts, an image of Earona burned into their minds.

'The more you try to restrain it, the more likely it will become stronger and invasive,' remarked Seth.

Marcus groaned. 'But I don't know what to do about it.'

'Admit it, at least to yourself,' he advised, 'so you can deal with it appropriately.'

'I'm afraid of that.'

'You, afraid?' *That's hard to believe...*

'Anyway, it's not just that,' replied Marcus, 'she might not feel the same way given the way she felt about Keanan.' His insecurities over the issue were tangible.

'I don't know about that,' Seth rambled, 'Just think, you wouldn't even have to say anything. You could think lovely thoughts to her.'

'Lovely, eh, that makes me feel better. I'll probably think something daft about being naked and everyone will hear it.'

'Knowing you I'd say that's tame.' Seth blushed scarlet, and went on with amusement, 'You would need to be alone a lot.'

'Hell, what are we talking about?! We don't even know where she is. I wish I could say something to her, *anything* would be fine right now.' Under his breath, he said, 'Even making an arse of myself.' They walked in silence with Marcus sulking and Seth watching the passing citizens of Floris.

Finally Seth spoke. 'What is this place about? The Furnace?'

'Fighting hall.'

It was all Marcus needed to say to bring a horrified look to Seth's bright grey eyes. 'You are going to fight? Do you think that wise?'

A glint of humour was in Marcus' eyes. 'Probably not, but it would be worth getting out the tensions I'm feeling and besides, it would be fun.'

'For you maybe. A lot of ranting men, yelling for blood,' Seth's face paled. 'Pushing and heaving and more yelling *and* you might get hurt.'

'Nah, apparently it's controlled,' Marcus assured him, 'Death only happens by accident.'

'And that's so comforting... why? So, death does happen? And that's aside from broken bones.' He sighed. 'I'm assuming you told no one about it.'

'Burgman knows...' Marcus brooded over Seth's accurate judgments. 'We can check it out. If it's mean fighting we'll go.'

Seth's reply was dismal, 'Fine then.'

Situated in a converted warehouse, the Furnace, was on a street back from the harbour. Men were everywhere, coming and going through the double doors, talking and smoking pipes, under the shaded front terrace, and watching the crowds roam in.

Inside, the spectators ranged from bare-armed wharfies to scrupulous looking foreigners, and well-dressed nobles in strange wigs, huddling with their own kind. Women with low cut bodices and skirts higher than the average woman would wear, draped themselves over men and leaned against walls. People yelled and hollered. Cheers rose up in different places and men shoved their way through to the money-handlers, standing on crates, shouting the odds. Next to them stood a type of guard, watching the crowds. Small windows lined one side of the room and the whole place was smoky grey. In the middle and raised up above the other two rings was a roped off platform, the centre ring. Humidity from damp sweating bodies, sunk the air, making it pungent. Marcus sensed the adrenalin in the room, the blood in his own veins rushed through his body. *Just like you said.*

Didn't think it would be this loud. Seth didn't even try speaking above the din as he followed Marcus intent on getting closer to the first platform.

'That one in the middle must be the top ring,' Marcus remarked as if Seth were interested, and he turned his attention to the fight nearest them. A young blond-haired fighter punched a wily, deeply tanned man. The blond was taller and doing a fine job at hitting him. The wily man was also skilled yet seemed to lack strength in his strikes. The younger one eventually downed the other. They watched as he stood up, bloodied, but walking. Marcus grinned from ear to ear. 'Wasn't so bad, was it?'

Seth shook his fine-haired head. 'Somehow I knew you were going to say that. You can take the boy out of the fight, but you can't take the fight out of the boy.'

'Come on.' Marcus took him by the arm, ignoring his comment completely. 'I've got to see where I can join in.'

They stood behind men waiting at a desk where a man was taking down names. Marcus' turn came and he was asked a bunch of questions; name, how many top ring challenges, if any, and did he know the rules. The man explained the rules; you fight three times in a row, if you win at least two you get a red chip, if there is no one to fight during your three fights you might be lucky enough to get a rest. With a red chip you can fight in the top ring anytime. If you lose in the top ring you lose your red chip, if you win you get a blue chip and go directly to the top ring any time, providing the Furnace is open to fight. He took Marcus' silver coins and gave him a white chip, informing him he was in ring two. The man turned to Seth with a bored voice. 'Name please?'

Seth gave an exaggerated laugh. 'You are joking?' And he tagged along after Marcus.

Stopping at ring two, Marcus took his cloak, sword belt plus harness, and shirt, off, and handed them all, in a dishevelled heap to Seth. Seth strapped Marcus' belt around his own waist and the second sword hung over his shoulder. Unaccustomed to weapons, they flapped uncomfortably at his side. He folded the shirt trimly, and the cloak he arranged across his arm and shoulder. 'I hope you know what you are doing, I don't want to carry you back as well as this gear.'

'Don't worry, Sprout.' Marcus turned to watch the current fight. A man younger than Marcus faced off against an older man with flabby arms and a thick middle.

'You know, you don't have to prove anything...' Seth spoke to the air.

Marcus was too preoccupied stretching his arms and legs, and doing unusual movements with his hands and feet.

Sensing the inquisitive stares, Seth was the one embarrassed while Marcus seemed oblivious.

At last, the older man thumped the younger one hard and he was down for the count. He got up again much to Seth's relief. Marcus' turn came to enter the ring and Seth said, 'Good luck.'

It won't be luck.

Marcus jumped onto the platform with a serious expression. The bigger man, Torel, had the disadvantage of being tired as opposed to Marcus, fresh and ready to go. Marcus bounced as they hedged around each other. Torel lashed out with a curved punch. Marcus clamped down on his arm and punched him in the stomach, doubling him over. An uppercut to the underside of his face toppled Torel back onto the rope. Shaking his head, he cursed Marcus and rushed him. Marcus stood square until he closed in and he stepped aside, striking him on the side of the head.

Something cracked. Seth hoped it was a nose and not a skull. Torel lay inert for several moments. The official nudged him with his foot and he rolled over to the side and off the platform. Seth caught a glimpse of the man's purple, bruised face. He wondered how Marcus was able to find bashing a man senseless, fun.

Marcus stretched his limbs and jogged on the spot. He grinned at the blond-haired man stepping up to the platform. The man from the first fight they viewed.

Soon their strikes became fierce and fast. Marcus received a hit to the head. His opponent stepped in and both men grabbed each other around the middle. After realizing the futility of it, they unanimously broke apart. The man tried another punch, but Marcus moved too fast for it to connect. The crowd cheered and bellowed, their excitement grew at each winning hit. Seth only felt the crush.

Gripping his opponent's arm, Marcus head-butted him, momentarily stunning him. Two fast punches to his chest and face followed, downing the younger man. Glowing with sweat, Marcus seemed unmindful to his body's exertion. Seth, however, was tense and exhausted. Watching him fight was a hard feat to stomach. Marcus grinned like a devil, enjoying himself. Seth smiled back weakly, thinking at least Marcus was having a good time.

His next opponent was fresh, but Marcus still looked confident. The man, introduced as Mac was big and heavily built with solid arms. He had the audacity to laugh at Marcus' size. Seth thought with chagrin, it would cause him unnecessary pain. Mac took a boxing stance and did a couple of fake blows as they circled each other. Reaching out with unpredictable speed, he hit Marcus' face. Again Mac tried the same move, but Marcus dodged and caught his wrist. His foot came up high and kicked Mac in the side. Clutching himself, Mac cried out. Marcus twisted Mac's loose arm behind him, it would break with a firm push.

Delighted with the brutality, the crowd yelled for him to break it. Mac wrestled to twist free, but his struggle only made it worse. Marcus shoved him to the ground. Sitting on his back, he hooked his arm around Mac's neck, pulling the thrashing man's head up, pinning him. The crowd screamed obscenities with abandonment, or so it sounded to Seth. He was the only one not raising his voice. With dismay it dawned on him, he had not placed a bet.

Marcus grabbed the man's hair and slammed his head into the floor three times. Such a violent act caused Seth to wonder how Marcus could perform such deeds. *Thank Kahm, the man is still alive.* Marcus left the platform grinning from ear to ear like an overgrown boy. Drenched with sweat, he met Seth, and the raucous sound of cheers and congratulations.

'Flamin' hell, that's fun.' Marcus, breathing heavily, flicked his head, sending sweat flying. 'Had to take the first one quick so not to tire. Their plan is to wear you out.'

'Is that it?' Seth had no care for strategies and he was more concerned with the people tugging and pressing in on him.

An adjudicator handed Marcus a red chip, accompanied with his congratulations. 'Not done yet,' Marcus said, 'Come on. To the top ring.' He walked off while Seth trailed after like an obedient packhorse.

They stood at the back of the throng of people watching the current fight in the top ring. Seth watched Marcus stretching his arms and his thoughts wandered to him. *To match you, a man would have to be highly competent. Your proficiency is honed to perfection.*

Marcus tapped a finger to his head. 'The mind is faster than the body. It's a case of the two coming together in unison, although I'm far from perfect.' He turned to view the current fight. 'Those two know how to fight well.'

One was muscular with cropped brown hair. The other, bald with a long beard, was smaller with a dense middle. They attacked each other with an equal fury. 'That man is fast,' Marcus commented about the muscle bound man. 'The other hits hard. Guess it's better to not get hit.'

'That would be an excellent idea.'

The shorthaired man eventually knocked the other down and the fight finished. The two men left the platform and a man hung off the ropes calling for participants with the red chip to come up.

'Aren't you nervous?' Seth's own stomach churned, 'God above, I am.'

Marcus patted him on the back. 'I divert the nervous energy. This is good practice and I need it.'

Seth stared at him wide-eyed in total disbelief.

Marcus approached the platform holding up his red chip. He observed his partner, named Tychus, come to join what he called the dance; powerful strikes flowing together in an effective sequence of moves. A fraction taller, he was also muscular, but unlike Marcus, Tychus had seen more years.

They skirted each other's space, and the restless crowd shouted at the two, driving the adrenalin to greater levels. Tychus struck first. Marcus' head flung sideways and he showed no reaction to the sudden ache. Fast on his feet, Tychus tried the same manoeuvre. Marcus, now aware of his moves, crouched low and punched his stomach. Quick, he rose and planted a neat hit. Tychus stumbled back, smearing the blood from his lips.

Marcus paid no mind to the blood on his own face. Anticipating Tychus' approach, Marcus stepped clear, preferring his position of leading the dance to following. A thought surged into his head and niggled at his thoughts. He pushed away the distraction.

Tychus came again with focused speed. Marcus sacrificed his chin to the hit and caught hold of Tychus' arm. With Tychus' arm caught, Marcus punched him in the side, doubling him over, and kicked his knee into his head. As the man fell, Marcus elbowed him in the ribs. Tychus lay motionless long enough for Marcus to be handed a blue card.

Marcus looked for Seth; he was nowhere to be seen. He sprung off the platform amid backslaps and congratulations to where Seth had been. Panic seized him like no fight could ever do. He searched for Seth's thoughts.

Outside... Seth's faint response travelled back.

Marcus shoved men from his path as he raced to a back door. In the alley, Seth slumped against the wall, blood trickling from his nose, and his tied-up hair was half pulled out. Puffing hard, Seth pointed up the lane. 'He took your sword belt and Shiarn's necklace.'

A green-cloaked man walked without a care.

Marcus ran after him. The man cast a glance behind him and turned into another alley. Marcus rounded the corner and was met with a stinging pain in his shoulder. Disregarding the stab wound, Marcus grabbed the man's knife arm and head-butted him. The thief fell against the wall and the cord of the pendant could be seen in his shirt pocket.

'Give me my swords and the necklace.'

The thief swung in a daze, but dug out the pendant, and Marcus' sword belt and other stolen items fell to the ground.

Marcus punched the thief in the stomach while holding his knife arm. 'Drop your knife.' He twisted the thief's wrist and the blade clattered to the ground. 'You're coming back with me.'

The thief's face twisted in fear and he kneed Marcus in the groin.

Marcus groaned.

The thief slid from his grasp and ran down the alley. Cursing him, Marcus pressed down on his shoulder wound and the blood seeped through his fingers. He picked up all the items and rushed back to Seth. He found him inside, speaking with a Furnace guard. Marcus buckled his sword around his waist and good shoulder and handed Seth the necklace. He thought better of putting his shirt over his bleeding skin, instead he draped his cloak over his shoulders.

Seth looped the cord over his neck. 'Thanks Marc, this is important to Shiarn.'

'He got away,' he said in surprised anger, 'the bastard stabbed me.'

'What's he look like?' asked the guard.

Marcus gave him the description.

'Probably just a thief,' the guard said, 'you should get that wound looked at though.'

Stunned by the cut, Marcus pressed with increased force on his bleeding shoulder.

Seth neatened his hair up. 'We better go and clean up.'

Thoroughly disturbed by the assault, Marcus asked, 'Are you hurt?'

Seth's hands went over his bruised body parts. 'Stomach is sore, nose is hurting, less.' His fingers gently rubbed his slender nose. 'Everything feels in place. He was bent on getting the jewellery. I hardly knew what he was asking, the key of the eye... something like that. He dragged me out here and demanded it from me. I could do nothing about it.'

Marcus stared at him incredulously. 'Did you call me?'

'I did...' Seth watched his face droop with disappointment. 'You were in one of those moods.'

Marcus responded wretchedly, 'Devil's flamin' arse.' He recalled a word in his thoughts, yet nothing definite. 'I have to be more tuned in to you, to everyone.'

'Don't be hard on yourself, you are good at what you do,' Seth encouraged, and they started walking back to the place they called home. 'By the way, you dropped this.' He passed him the blue painted chip. 'Seems you won. Sorry I didn't see it.'

Fighting was the last thing Marcus wanted to think about. He grumbled with remorse, 'Don't even know what it's for.'

'You can fight in the top ring straight up anytime. If you lose you forfeit your card. If you win a second time you keep your blue card and you win good coin.'

Marcus smiled at him; he had assumed he had not paid attention.

'I asked the guard.'

'I wonder what Jett will say.' Considering Jett's reaction brought a new dread. Jett trusted him to look after Seth, and he took him to a potential abode of criminals and cutthroats, where he got beat up and nearly killed. On top of that, Marcus had a knife wound. He was not proud of his actions. 'Let's not tell him about the champion fight, save a lot of anguish, or better still, don't tell him about any of the fights...'

Seth smiled with satisfaction. 'Agreed.'

It continued to bother Marcus, Seth's call for aid went unheard by him. If Seth were in serious trouble or anyone in the Kin, he would be of no help. The thought gave him terrible unrest. As they walked, he rubbed his aching shoulder that grew to a throbbing pain. He half collapsed into Seth's arms.

As if from a great distance, Seth called, 'You're not well.'

Supporting him as best he could, Seth grabbed a lady passing on the street, and pleaded, 'Can you tell me where I'll find a healer or whatever type of medicine men you have here?'

'He's quite sick.' She stared into Marcus' greying face. 'There's a woman down near the docks, Annabella. It takes them quick, doesn't it?'

24 - Place to Heal

Peaceful earth
Paradise, home of love
No violence to mar perfect splendour
Who is the one to destroy innocence?
Father?
Husband?
Where is the gate of comfort?
Behind the nurturing spirit, gentle hands of mother and wife no more.
Fading heart, do not waste away.
Who will love the children?
Who will protect the daughters?

Lament for Niesta, Birth Mother

Jett drove the wagon into the inn's yard. Keanan jumped off and held out his hand for Crissy. She gripped it and his arm, taking her time stepping down. She lingered by his side, a lock of brunette hair curled in her fingers and a teasing smile on her face.

Burgman appeared and gave her a sharp order. 'Crissy, I've got ale to be drawn.' Her flirtatious gaze remained on Keanan as she strolled inside.

Burgman helped Jett and Keanan roll the barrels from the cart while giving them an excited run down of earlier events, '...I told the guard, Bertie and me took him by surprise. I said we beat him on the head and roped him up. Told him it was only one even though he swore black and blue his mate was there. 'Course, we said not to listen to him he's a liar. He'll be locked up a while. Apparently they know him up there.' Burgman cackled. 'Everything went smoothly?'

'Like a baby's bottom,' Keanan said, 'Though come to think of it, that has its unpleasantness.'

'That's right. This whole thing has a lot of stench about it. All's well and good.' Burgman started for indoors with Jett and Keanan following, and said over his shoulder, 'Think I'll get more visitors?'

Jett said, 'There's a place in the Salisbury District we can go to check out this Collector.'

'Wouldn't be surprised if he's some sort of official.' Burgman went to the other side of the counter while the two men sat on stools. 'There's crooks that do it legally, you know.' He handed them each a plate of food. 'For your troubles. Then there's those who get greedy. You reckon they make enough already, but no, they have to have more.'

'They think they are above the law,' responded Keanan.

'Exactly right!' said Burgman, 'And you know what makes me boil, *they are.*'

Jett mumbled between mouthfuls. 'We're thinking about visiting this person.'

'You be careful, he might have friends. I don't want anyone lying around in my stables again.' Burgman pointed a warning finger at Jett.

'Neither do we,' said Jett.

Afterwards, Keanan decided to have a wash, as he was feeling the grime from the gruesome morning. Jett headed out the door, and Burgman called, 'You going down to see the fights?'

Jett stopped to give him a puzzled frown. 'What's that?'

'Told Marcus to go see 'em. He looked game for it.' Burgman chuckled. 'He took the lad too.'

Jett promptly gave him his attention, knowing Marcus would be more than game for it. 'Where is it?' He fumed, wondering how he had ever expected they could pull off being unknown slaves. Marcus was probably flaunting himself in front of the entire underground world and with Seth along to watch.

~ * ~

Before heading off to the Furnace, Jett had his own interests to see to. He scanned the street of the Sleepy Dog Tavern. The man following him from the previous day could not be seen, but he was probably lurking around somewhere. He entered the Sleepy Dog and went upstairs. He opened the door to his room and stepped over the faint line of powder. The dust at the window was also untouched and everything was as he left it. At least it was possible to assume they thought he was staying there.

Back downstairs he spoke to the innkeeper about his room, and he was ready to leave. Once out on the street, Jett spotted his 'tail' crouched by a wall.

At the Furnace, rough looking men congregated outside. If he were to see Marcus and Seth it would be problematic. Jett would have to see them before they saw him. Men pushed and yelled, and on the rings they fought hard and dirty. No sign of Marcus or Seth, but out of the corner of his eye he glimpsed the weedy man following him. Discovering a door near the back, Jett snuck out into an alley. He walked along to another laneway and waited.

The man rounded the corner. He startled at the sight of Jett who gripped his neck with his arm and landed a rigid punch to his stomach. Jett growled, 'I'm fed up seeing you.'

The slight man wheezed.

'Stop following me.'

He gasped, 'Capt'n won't be happy.'

Jett clenched his neck tighter. 'Right now, I don't give a demon's arse what he thinks,' he snarled, 'I'm sure your boss doesn't tail everyone he does business with, or does he?'

He panted, attempting to breathe. 'No...'

Jett barked into his ear. 'Not me anymore. If he pushes it, so will I.'

'I'll tell him,' the man choked out.

Jett released him and elbowed him hard. He fell to the ground and lay in a puddle, groaning. Jett left, hoping he had scared him enough without endangering his chances of getting to the Meet, but there was no way he could risk being followed anymore. Jett entered back through the Furnace.

A guard gave him a grim stare. 'Watch yourself out there.' He nodded in the direction of the door. 'Been trouble in the lane and we don't want anymore.'

Not one to pass up information freely given, Jett asked, 'What trouble?'

'A thief beat up one man and the other tried to catch him. Hard to catch them. They'll do anything to stay out of the Rocks.'

Anxiety crept into Jett's heart. 'What did they look like?'

'A skinny blond lad, and a tough looking fella,' the guard chatted, seeming to enjoy the conversation.

'When?'

'Couple of hours maybe, maybe longer,' he mused it over, clearly having no idea, 'Not really sure now.'

Sounds like them, but surely they would have been back at the inn by now. Jett decided it best if he went back to find out and he disappeared into the crowd.

~ * ~

Seth half-lugged, half-carried Marcus to the street the woman described. Part way down, between narrow houses was the shop. He pushed the door and a tinkling bell rattled the silence. 'Hello,' Seth called with flustered fear. 'Anyone?' Marcus' head lolled to the side and he was almost a dead weight in Seth's arms.

A yelping dog jumped at Seth, but left Marcus alone. An old lady followed after, white hair piled on top of her head, and by her feet, a more placid dog. Soon enough both animals scurried around her and Seth. She gave Marcus one look and said, 'Bring him through.' They went out to a cosy backroom with a kitchen, workbench, and chairs. She tied back a yellow curtain, revealing a single bed in a quaint room. She pulled back the colourful quilt and Seth laid him on the bed.

'Can you help him?' Seth asked.

'Maybe.' Gently, she separated the bloody, purple skin around Marcus' wound. 'What's his name?'

'Marcus, I'm Seth.'

At her workbench, she pulled out bottles and a bowl from the rows of shelves. 'What's the wound from?'

'A knife.'

With a pestle she pulverized ingredients. 'You got it?'

'I don't think...wait...' He reached into Marcus' boot and handed her the knife.

She touched the hilt and held the blade close to her eye. 'I ain't an alchemist, but I reckon it's poison,' she said, 'I might be able to use this.' She dropped the blade into a jar of clear dense solution. A stout green separated from the blood and snaked upwards. 'A good sign.'

'It's not… fatal, is it?'

'Poison can be,' she said, 'but also, unpredictable. What are your friend's strong points?' She continued mixing and pounding what smelt like oats and old cheese before reaching for another bowl in which she poured a glutinous liquid.

Such an odd question Seth had to calm himself to consider it. He slumped in the only chair and said, loud enough she could hear in her work area, 'He's focused, dedicated and tough.' He paused. 'He enjoys a good joke and doesn't like losing. He's quite resilient and doesn't like looking foolish. But that's not really a strong point, maybe a flaw.'

She raised a brow and came to stand beside Marcus. 'Can't say I've met many men who *like* looking the fool.' She sprinkled white powder onto the wound. Marcus groaned and she told him, 'It hurts, but it stops the blood.' To Seth, she said, 'Even though his body is incapacitated his soul is not and these traits are still part of your friend. They're good ones to have.' Onto his shoulder, she slapped a floury dough substance, much like bread before baking, and wrapped it with linen.

Suddenly weary, Seth still felt compelled to enquire, 'Can I do something?'

She gave Marcus a grim frown. 'You wait… you pray.'

~ * ~

Later that day, Earona and Mara's cell opened and Captain Morran marched in. 'Today you are leaving.' A pleased looked came over Earona's face, and he said, 'and going to the Temple of Niesta where you will be indentured for several years of service.'

Mara stared with a blank expression. Several years of service couldn't be that bad, could it?

'You can't mean it?!' Earona cried, 'That's slavery!'

'Indeed. Do not forget you are a prisoner,' the captain said as a guard tied her wrists.

They were lead outside into the speckled light of the afternoon sun. Mara squinted at the rays shining between the dark clouds. After climbing into the wagon, she crammed between men in red uniforms, with weapons resting at their sides. Earona frowned at each of them. Mara nearly giggled at the sight and wondered if Earona would vent her anger on them, she half wished she would. But the older girl remained in a frigid silence.

The wagon rolled through the city. Mara watched the citizens going about whatever it was they had to do and that was whatever they liked because they were free.

Eventually they moved into a quiet place and stopped. A clattering bang and voices speaking outside was followed by a gate creaking. The wagon door was lowered. Refusing the guard's aid, Earona jumped down, and Mara came behind. She was untied; this time he handled her wrists with care. Another soldier handed papers to a blue robed woman with long plaited hair, and she also took charge of Earona's bag.

The man said, 'The two from the captain.'

With a stern gaze, the woman looked the girls over. Earona's light blue dress was ripped and muddied, and a brush had not been through her tangled wavy hair in days. Mara was no different, except more blood covered her dress and she was barefoot.

'This girl is pregnant!' The woman exclaimed, 'What have you done to them?' Her critical reproach left the guard speechless. The woman pointed at the men in recrimination. 'You tell the captain, he should take better care of his prisoners, especially one so young.'

The lieutenant smiled. 'Yes, counsellor.'

She read over the papers.

'Is it in order?'

'It's never in order, but you are free to go.' The woman hurried the girls through the gate and locked it with a jingling bunch of keys. 'Before you meet Mother, you will wash. Follow me.' She started at a brisk pace and with just as much speed, twirled back to them. 'My name is Counsellor Elata.'

They walked through a large, pleasant yard. A storehouse was at the back of the compound, and a vegetable garden occupied the majority of the yard. White-clad women and a few dressed in plain clothes, tended the grounds. As the girls passed, they received curious stares. Satisfied with staring, the workers returned to their tasks. From under a wide terrace, chatter and laughter came from women sewing.

Once indoors, they were led past the open kitchen door. Loud talking and the clash of utensils was heard, and a counter repetitively thumped by a firm object. Pleasant smells wafted through the doorway. Mara was instantly famished.

In the washroom, two girls heated buckets of water over a long fire pit. Iron tubs in the centre of the room were half full. One of the girls said, 'You girls look a mess. We're nearly done and we'll be out of your way.'

The second girl was thin and her hair was in an unruly plait. She lifted the bucket. 'I used to work the docks. What are you in for?'

Her mouth agape, Earona stared at the adolescent.

Mara's lip formed a cruel line and her eye twitched. 'Murder.'

Earona stared at Mara much the same way the other two girls were doing. In horror. 'That's not true.'

The first girl looked between them, her expression a mix of terror and disbelief. 'What…well, whatever…'

Mara chuckled and started wriggling out of her plain dress. No longer fit for wearing, she threw it far from her. She ran her hands over her belly and viewed it with indifference.

The other two girls finished up quickly and nearly ran out of the room.

Earona turned her back on Mara, but her voice held no inhibition. 'You really shouldn't be saying that. It will only make it worse for us.'

'In a place like this, you need to make them fear you.' Mara touched her charm, making sure it was still there and she sank into the warm water with a contented moan. 'You're lucky I didn't mention the spying, or your true name.' Her laughter reverberated against the stone bricks. 'Raven.'

Earona peeled off her dress and covered her exposed breasts as she stepped into the tub. 'Not funny. Who knows what crimes that person has done?'

Mara started scrubbing at every part of her body. 'I almost feel normal again.'

'Perhaps that explains your frivolity.'

Mara frowned. How far from the truth that was.

'What is that mark above your heart?' Earona tilted her head with a curious gaze.

Suddenly defensive, Mara covered the newly made curse seal. 'Just a scar.'

'It's a snake biting its own tail in a figure eight within a circle.' Earona went back to scrubbing her legs. 'That's hardly a scar and it's fresh. Who gave you such a… ugly thing?'

Mara rubbed her hand over the mark that was more like a wound. 'Hell you're nosey.' She still didn't know what it meant or what it was supposed to do, but she realized that it had changed something in her that she couldn't put her finger on exactly.

Earona exhaled a frustrated breath and sank under the water.

After they washed and the water was cold, they dressed. An annoying under-dress prevented the wool of the white gown chaffing Mara's skin, but at least she felt clean. She tied the white cord under her stomach, and was ready to leave the washroom.

Not sure where they were supposed to go, they walked down the initial hallway, and spying a door, Earona opened it to a great hall. Rows of tables had flat planks as benches. On one side was a fireplace. At the far end was a stairwell and another door. Along the length of the right side, gardens were visible through the tall windows.

At one of the benches, Counsellor Elata waited. Her face brightened as they came through the doorway. 'Now you look like young ladies. Come, I will show you to Mother.' The counsellor walked across the hall and past the stairs, and down a corridor without a backwards glance at the girls following her. She halted, causing them to pull up and bump into each other. She rapped on the door and a voice within answered, and she stuck her head in. 'The girls from the captain.'

A firm voice called, 'Come in.'

Counsellor Elata opened the door for them to enter, and she left, closing it behind her.

Mother was seated behind a neat desk in a sunlit room. Behind her was a window with a view of the workers in the garden. Bookcases lined one wall and an airy shelf containing rolled up parchments was against another. Mother, an elderly lady with plaited grey hair and wearing a navy gown, indicated for them to sit. 'Captain Morran said one of you is possibly the one known as Raven?'

'That's a mistake.' Earona blushed and her hand fluttered over her chest. 'I'm not Raven, my name is Earona.'

'I see, it's an alias then?'

'Not at all. It's mistaken identity.' Earona's tone boiled with annoyance. 'There was never a trial.'

'Regardless if you are or not, we don't use alias' here, you will be known as Earona.'

'Thank Heavens.' Earona eased back in the chair with a relieved sigh.

'And you are?' She looked to Mara.

'We're sisters.' Mara avoided Earona's drilling glare. 'I'm Maree.'

Earona frowned, her lips pressing together.

'She's your sister?' The Mother leaned forward, observing Earona.

Earona turned to her with a confident smile. 'Of course.'

Mother glanced down at the papers from the prison. 'There's no family name.'

'It's Dawn'Weaver,' Earona replied.

Mother studied the girls one at a time. 'Now that I see you, these papers make more sense and especially from the description of the state you arrived in.'

'I can explain,' Earona burst out, 'They are wrong. We are innocent of any crimes.'

Mother's smile was condescending. 'If I listened to every girl who said, "I'm innocent", there'd be no one in here. You should be thankful you are here. Many others would love the opportunity as there are worse things.' She put her hand up, stopping Earona from speaking. 'I've heard it all before. Now you are indentured, you will be working with us for seven years.'

Mara remained indifferent to the news while Earona's mouth fell open in shock.

'The indent girls wear white robes and are assigned duties within the compound. Free women wear what they like and come and go, however, after a week they are required to seek employment and bring in their earnings, but you don't have to worry about that.' She paused. 'As indent girls you work for the house, you don't leave the compound!' She stressed this rule in a severe tone. 'If you do, chances are your contract is extended or you go back to the jail. Continuous bad behaviour could see you sent to the Rocks.'

Earona replied, 'I've heard of that place.'

'Not a nice place. There are women in the Rocks, however, they aren't like normal women anymore.' She grilled them with an insightful stare. 'We don't allow men in here. Men are allowed to visit free women in the courtyard next to the temple, but you don't go there. When you have your baby you will be moved to the nursery for a time. It's attached next door.'

Mara stared wide-eyed, and her hand grazed over her stomach as if remembering she had a baby inside.

'How old are you?' The woman's wrinkled eyes were devoid of compassion, but watched Mara with an alertness that bothered her.

Mara mumbled, 'Fifteen...'

'Really? You seem younger.' Her tone became grim. 'We watch girls like you closely. You have your babies then you are ready to have fun with the boys again. I won't stand for that. No man for seven years. Will you manage that?'

Mara had to wonder how she would even be able to meet a man anyway.

'I'm sure we will,' Earona assured her.

'I shall get one of the counsellors to explain the rules. They will inform you of worship procedures. Niesta, Goddess of Womanhood is the Head of our Order and through prayer we seek her wisdom and guidance. She is our inspiration and protector in a male dominated city. We encourage worship of Niesta in the temple and that's where you will attend your reformation sessions.'

'Reformation?' Earona squealed.

'You will need lessons in how to conduct your life in a more positive and beneficial manner.'

Mara snorted and covered her laughter.

She received a reprimanding glance from Mother. 'Here are your things.' She lifted Earona's bag and passed it across the desk. 'The counsellor will show you the dormitory and give you your duties.' She glanced out at the stretching shadows across the lawn. 'Tomorrow you can begin a routine.' She opened the door and the girls stood to follow.

Back in the main hall, Counsellor Elata took the girls upstairs to an enormous dorm on the second floor. Rows of bunk beds with white sheets had warm looking covers. The counsellor showed them their beds and informed them the evening meal would soon be called, and she left.

Mara stretched out on the bed. Sighing with delight, she nestled her head into the soft pillow.

Earona pulled back the blanket and touched the clean linen. 'I have to admit, it will be nice to sleep in a bed.'

Mara lay staring at the bottom of the bed above her for some time. She wasn't sure if she were happy about the new situation, yet for some reason she felt safe. 'Dawn'Weaver is so pretentious. Did you just make that up?'

'No!' Earona cried, 'It's my name.'

'You told them your real name?!' Mara sputtered with disbelief. 'That was daft.'

Earona creased her eyes with irritation. 'I...' Her cheeks tinged pink and she grumbled, 'Surely it won't matter...'

Mara shook her head at her ignorance.

'Is that why you lied? And about your age?'

Under her breath, she said, 'It's easier that way.'

'Should I assume Mara is not your name?' Earona narrowed her eyes.

'Of course it is.' Mara sighed, wishing she hadn't told her in the first place. Earona continued staring, her eyes becoming vivid orbs of suspicion. Mara sat up and leaned across the space. 'Look, it's not that I normally lie.' Even that was a lie. 'It's better they don't know who I am or where I come from.'

After a moment of studying her deadpan expression, Earona sighed. 'For once, I understand what you mean.'

25 - A Message

Wind is the power of air - enraged.
Its direction unknown to all but itself as it seeks Matter that will stop its propulsion, and bring calm to its chaos.

Valfaèr, Elements of Arcane Power

Marcus' flesh was dead white and wet with perspiration. Once more the herbwoman peeled the poultice from his shoulder. The gooey substance came off as a dirty muck that she crumbled into a bucket by the side of the bed. Another thick dough went back on. He lay in a bitter fever, unresponsive to Seth or Annabella's handling of his body, and appeared to grow weaker despite the poison being drawn out.

Seth watched her remove the treatment twice already. 'Is it doing anything?' He sat on the edge of the chair, not knowing what to do, but sensing he should try to do something useful.

'We wait, we watch,' she said, 'the poison has him.'

Marcus' thrashed and mumbled some unintelligible words, but Earona's name was one of them. Jett had to be informed, but Marcus couldn't be left in case the worst happened, besides that, Seth was not allowed to wander the streets alone. He jumped up with a sudden idea; a possible, yet untried way to get a message to the Kin. He went to the stair and stood, looking upwards. 'What's upstairs?'

Annabella eyed him with suspicion. 'Ms Macready is on the top and we share the middle floor.'

'Can I go up?' He was ready to bolt up the steps even without her permission.

Caution left her eyes and she said, 'Ms Macready is out right now. Do what you have to, but don't touch her things.' She turned her concentration back to Marcus. 'I'll call if I need to.'

Seth raced up, calling his thanks. He dashed up to Ms Macready's rooms. A pleasant sitting area opened onto floor length doors, revealing a walkout balcony. The view was partly of the sea and rocky cliffs to the east of the harbour. He was hoping for a view of the city, but this would have to do. Not that he was certain it would even work wherever he was. He stood on the balcony, and generating his Ethos, he imbued his thoughts with the surrounding nature. There wasn't a great deal to speak with; a few trees and potted plants. What he sought was the wind that dominated the city.

He briefly studied Wind Talking at the academy, but nothing in practice. It was a dangerous element of his Gift. Unlike trees and other flora, wind was highly temperamental. Depending on the degree of its power, it had the potential to engulf one's mind and sweep parts of your thoughts away with its impetus.

That day's wind, driven in from the sea was soft with a hint of restrained power. Fresh salt spray brought a refreshing cleanness to his senses. Wind filled the streets with its cacophony of a multitude of words from across the ocean. He shut out its overriding speech, clamouring for his attention with stories it wanted to share yet he couldn't hope to decipher. Right now, he wished to impart his words, or at least one word. It would be all he could manage, if at all. The task was not easy and took Naturists years to become proficient in the art of Wind Talking. Necessity would have to be the best step to advancing his Gift.

Seductive currents of air drowned his thoughts. He breathed the exhilarating scent deep into the core of his being. Beginning as a gentle caress, it swelled in force as he summoned more of it to himself. Tendrils of wind enticed him to beckon more of it and then more. He raised his hands, sensing the energy held back by the wind's master stream. More of it flowed towards him in anticipation of some direction. His thought melded with it in the secret place where his Ethos dwells. The air became his thought and he became as air. The wind took his word again and again until he felt exhausted. It swirled around him and was carried away.

~ * ~

Ethan's cell had transformed into a gloomy pit, reflecting a dank grey from the moist walls. Shivering from the cold, he couldn't move for aching muscles. Not that he wanted to move. On the mattress of stuffing, he lay on his stomach. His tan woollen shirt was by his head and near what appeared to be brown broth. He had to move, he had to eat.

He imagined the wounds, crisscrossing the length of his back. Earona's healing brought some relief, but not enough to mend his flesh completely. He hadn't been able to see what they used on him; although he could guess. Strung up by his wrists, his legs were also restrained with metal cuffs. His chest drove into the freezing wall in an attempt to escape the agony. The iron bands, he still wore, rubbed on his wrists. A hot rod was laid across his back and pushed into his skin, followed by what must have been a short whip with heated ends. By that time he was beyond awareness, yet the painful memory increased the current ache of his tendons.

One man tortured him, another did the questioning. First they asked him about a rare jewel he had supposedly stolen, which was connected somehow with the black token they had taken from him. How they would even know about that, he couldn't guess. He confessed a pendant was left in Lanvin. That wasn't good enough for them. The questions became so ludicrous to be beyond understanding. He was accused of working for someone by the name of Lucien of the Mouratairs, and how was Ethan connected to Raven? From what Ethan could gather they were a bunch of criminals, yet none of it made sense and he knew nothing. The only thing Ethan was adamant over was that Earona was not Raven. Gradually he came to realize they would continue their interrogation as long as they wanted, something had to give. He would confess, and clear any speculation over Earona and Maras' involvement as he could. His driving focus, to save the girls going through what he was enduring.

Ethan no longer sensed Earona's Ethos. Her persistent probing had been in his mind, but he could do nothing for his own safety let alone hers. Her distress caused him to feel more helpless. Hopefully she could get free and find the Kin. Regarding his own fate he was uncertain.

Never experiencing this level of pain before, he groaned shamelessly as he sat up. When he was younger he broke his arm, even so his Healer mother tended him as she did with all his scrapes. Indulging in thoughts of his parents, he wished one of them could be there. The more he considered it, the more he dismissed the idea. It would mean them knowing what was happening and it would give him more stress. He never liked his parents to be worried about him and so often they were, and frequently with good reason.

A tap came from the door. 'Ethan?'

Another servant girl wanting his attention, but this one spoke his name. He stretched his limbs, making every effort to rise.

Golden ringlets bounced around a prim hat. Her flawless skin and blue eyes were a dazzling contrast to the grey walls. She frowned as he neared. 'They hurt you?'

'How do you know my name?' He clutched the bars, bringing him closer to her face. This girl was prettier than all the others.

'I know your friend Shiarn.'

'Shiarn!' Ethan's voice lowered. 'Where is she?'

'At the palace.'

'Palace?'

She ducked from his sight and pushed a round loaf through the flap. 'I've bought you food.' The fresh fragrance was a heady scent, but he didn't want to remove his eyes from her kind face, no matter how much he craved something to eat.

'I've no time to explain. She wanted to know how you are faring.' She looked him over. 'Not good I expect.'

'If I could get out I'd be happier.'

She shook her head.

Ethan gripped the bars harder. 'Can you tell me if you have seen two girls in here?'

'I haven't seen any.'

Ethan nodded with relief.

'I don't have much time,' she said.

He cringed and swayed, wanting to sit, yet needing the human contact.

She gasped. 'The guards are brutes.'

'Tell Shiarn I miss her and I...' his words tumbled out, 'tell her... just tell her I'll take the blame.'

She covered his hand and his heart was warmed by the sensitive caress. 'I will and good luck to you.' Heavy footfalls were coming along the passage. 'I must go...'

A guard arrived. 'Get moving!'

She ran down the corridor.

Ethan sat with the bread, and breaking it, he felt a remnant of warmth at its centre. Shiarn was in the palace, what did that mean? Hopefully, Earona and Mara were free and he could breathe easier over them. Then he realized he forgot to ask the girl her name.

~ * ~

On his way to the White Horse, Jett walked the back lanes. He cast glances over his shoulder unable to shake the apprehension someone was following him. If it wasn't the man he beat up than someone else. No one was lurking in the gaps. Head down, eyes averted, he passed other walkers, like breathing shadows, as if obeying an unwritten rule of silent passage. This style of transit suited him. Lost in his thoughts, he came through an open crossway of lanes shaded in the fast approaching dusk.

A gust of salt drenched wind swirled close, sending his cloak flying. The force of it nearly toppled him sideways. He stopped, suddenly motionless with an imprint of Seth floating past his mind's eye. The invading wind cried a name over and over into his thoughts. He raised his face to the grey clouds between the building tops and questioned aloud, as if the wind also carried an answer, 'Annabella? What in Balaam's cursed name does that mean?'

He walked out to the tapering lane to a wider street. Catching hold of the first man he saw, Jett asked if he knew anyone called Annabella. Jett received an odd look and no satisfaction. Another man was asked, and Jett received a similar reaction. Quiet curses flew Seth's way as Jett wondered if he was to ask everyone in the city if they knew someone by that name.

A large woman carrying a basket of fish stopped when Jett approached. She dropped her load and wiped her forehead. Two children at her side promptly ran off down the street.

He began, 'Excuse me, Ma'am—'

'Ma'am, eh?' Her overpowering voice halted his speech. 'Don't hear that often.'

'I was wondering if you could tel—'

'You're visiting Floris, ain't ya, that's why you're so polite. My name's Jenna Crustybelle, pleased to meet you.' She waited expectantly for him to respond.

'I wanted to kn—'

'Good to meet visitors and try to, you know, make them feel welcome. Hope you're enjoying your stay in fair Floris. Can I help you with anything?'

He fired out, 'Have you heard of someone called Annabella?' Attempting to smile, he ended up wincing in frustration.

'Annabella... yes,' the woman replied with thoughtful laziness, 'isn't that an odd thing, yes... I've heard of an Annabella, in fact I know an Annabella quite well.'

He breathed out hard. 'Good.'

'Don't know if it's the one you want,' she looked him over with a shrewd eye, 'she's an herbalist, of a type. If you need that kind of help.'

'How do I find her?'

With extraordinary detail, she informed him where Annabella lived. He gave a rushed thank you, and dashed down the road leaving the woman shaking her head after him.

Jett heard her hollering for her children, her voice fading as he ran. Cutting a corner, he crossed a couple of streets and arrived at a slender lane. Half way down he found the shop 'The Food of Seeing and Drink of Knowing.' As he opened the door, a bell tinkled. From a back room a dog yapped incessantly and an elderly woman ordered the animal to be quiet. She walked through, followed by two small dogs. The animals kept away from Jett and stuck close to the woman. The woman, in a purple dress with yellow shawl around her waist, raised her brows with concern. 'You come to see your friend?'

He gazed at her with bewilderment. 'I'm not sure...'

'Come.'

He followed her through to the backroom.

Seth emerged on the stairs, rubbing the back of his head. 'You're here!' He gave a smug grin. 'It worked.'

'Whatever you did, it worked,' he responded. 'Where's Marcus?'

'Here.' Annabella waved Jett into her side bedroom. 'He's mighty sick.'

Marcus lay still, his pale skin had a deathly tinge.

Annabella said, 'It's poison.'

'Tea for all.' A humped old lady shuffled into the backroom with a tray, supporting a pink dotted teapot and odd cups. 'Oh, another boy.' Her thin brows wrinkled as she viewed Jett. 'Fancy that.'

'This is Ms Macready.' Annabella cocked her head to the elderly lady. 'She's my... neighbour.'

Turning on Seth, Ms Macready narrowed small creased eyes. 'You finished messing 'round on my balcony?' She went on, 'First, he's waving his hands in the air and swinging,' she swayed with her frail arms waving, 'like this. Then later found him all crumpled over. You'll get a nasty pain in your head if you do that too often.' She headed back upstairs. 'I'll get another cup.'

Seth sheepishly rubbed his head again.

'You did well.' *Despite it being a grave risk.* Jett turned back to Marcus and ran his fingers over his cheek. His skin was like cold stone. He touched the wrapped wound and turned to Seth. *How did this happen?*

Annabella blurted, 'You them special people, aren't ya?'

Jett and Seth shared an anxious stare, and Jett turned a questioning look her way. 'I'm not sure I know what you mean.'

'You know stuff, 'bout the world, 'bout history. You can do things others can't.' Her gaze went back and forth between their unchanging expressions. 'They taught me stuff up in Baion.'

'At this point it's not important,' Jett replied, 'Marcus must recover...'

They shared a hot brew and Seth informed Jett what happened while Annabella reapplied the poultice. Marcus' lifeless body, normally strong and virile was a hard blow, and bore down on Jett's soul, making it difficult to breathe. His inner forebodings would be obvious to Seth, as if painted across the wall.

'One lousy thief...' Seth said again, his voice brimming with sorrow.

'Can't believe he was there... and with you...' Struggling with his conflicting emotions, Jett finally said, 'I need to get back.'

Seth's red rimmed eyes glowed in the dimming room. 'I'll stay here with him.'

Jett stood and lowered his face by Marcus' forehead. *Keep fighting, my friend.* He gave Seth a commanding stare. 'If you need to send word I shall keep my window open and an ear to the wind.' He approached Annabella with a grim expression. 'Thank you for this.

'Don't thank me yet, thank me when he gets better,' she said. 'You going?'

'We have other friends unaware of where I am.' He sighed with weariness. 'And I must tell them.'

26 - Lost in Sadness

The trials of hardship and suffering are but a test
We only need persevere and we have passed

Heavenly Ascension

A clanging bell echoed through the dormitory. Mara and Earona joined the women going downstairs to what Mara hoped was dinner. The hall was warmed by the wide fireplace, and tables were covered with white cloth. A buffet was set with stews and baskets of bread. Pleasing aromas filled Mara's senses, and her stomach ached for wholesome food.

Once she topped her bowl, she and Earona sat at a table for indentured girls. Chatter and laughter bounced off the walls, but Mara didn't want anything to do with the cheerful atmosphere.

A girl, her white-blonde hair shading her large eyes, looked down at Mara. 'Can I sit here?' Pushing her way in between Mara and Earona, her protruding belly brushed against Earona's shoulder. 'My name's Sandi.'

'I'm Maree.' Mara cast a sideways glance at Earona, making sure she heard.

Sandi straddled the bench and breathed heavily as she twisted into a comfortable position. 'When are you due?'

'Don't know.'

'Mine's coming any day, so they say.' She plonked her bowl down, and putting her back to Earona, spoke to Mara. 'How old are you?'

Her cheeks flushed, Mara finished her mouthful. 'Fourteen.'

At Mara's statement, Earona coughed and nearly choked on her food.

'We're the same age.' Pouting like a child, Sandi glanced down at her bulge crinkling the cloth on the table's edge. 'I'm hoping for a girl, how 'bout you?'

'I don't care.'

'I don't want a boy. It'll remind me of his father. I used to work with a wharfie gang.' She nodded towards her stomach, appearing to have no care in divulging the mistakes of her recent misspent youth.

Mara said, 'Are you scared?'

'Hell, yes.' Sandi shrugged, nonchalantly. 'But nothing I can do.'

'It's going to come out whether you want it to or not.'

'Blazes, that's true! But… my ma died when I was born.' Sandi spoke with a mouthful of soggy bread. 'I don't have a father, I was raised by my step-mother and she was a bitch.'

'I can understand that.' Half listening to the girl's prattle, Mara observed the hall. Mother and the counsellors sat at their own table at the front of the hall. The majority of women were dressed in white robes, and a small group, the free women, a motley bunch; bedraggled and unsmiling, were in civilian dress. Nearly all of them looked as if they had lived a hard life.

One woman, past middle-age with decrepit yellow hair in a scraggly heap at the top of her head, caught Mara's eye. Despite her wrinkled face, her eyes did not look aged and they gazed back at Mara in recognition. Mara gasped - why she thought she would be safe in the temple, she didn't know.

Sandi chatted, '... who really wants to be a counsellor anyway? You have to swear, no more sex...'

Her remark pulled Mara from her staring match with the old woman. 'Gods, for the rest of your life?'

Sandi nodded repeatedly.

Earona blushed red and cried, 'What on earth do you girls know of such things?'

Mara chuckled and pushed her stomach higher.

Sandi ignored Earona, and said, 'The Head Counsellor left a few months ago, apparently for a man, and they all moved up to fill the spots. You worshiped at the temple yet?'

'No!' Earona snapped.

'It's the best.' Sandi piled more stew on her spoon. 'I get a break from chores. Sometimes they let us sit on the terrace.'

Mara's eyes brightened. 'You go out?'

'On the terrace at the front of the temple.'

Earona said, 'How do you get to worship?'

Sandi laughed at her. 'You have to worship. Your counsellor will arrange it.'

Mara's eyes went back to the old hag to find she was gone. She wasn't among the crowd, and no empty spot was at the table where she sat. 'Crud!'

~ * ~

Another day came and went with Shiarn still stuck in her room. Prince Bastion was her only visitor apart from Regina and Sasheya, who brought her meals. He was polite and surprisingly entertaining, and against her building ire, his charm was disconcerting. But, despite his pleasant company she longed for activity outside her 'cage.' She was delighted when he informed her of the banquet that evening. Finally she would get out, although she wondered how much of a lease she would be on.

Shiarn chose a powder blue evening dress with crinkled sleeves and sapphire jewellery to match. She admired herself in the glass. Once she was ready, she and Regina left the room together. Shiarn stared at the doorframe in wonder she could leave at all.

Harp music filled the corridor before they entered the dining hall. The dreamy sound relaxed her, and brought unexpected memories of Earona. Wide tables adorned with gold cloth and silver dinnerware shimmered under the glow of tall candles. The room cascaded with golden light from lamps along the walls, illuminating paintings of people feasting. Guests gathered together, their chatter hesitant and subdued.

An uncustomary shyness came over her in the presence of Coltrene's aristocracy. With a smile plastered on her face, she endured the introductions, the rampant curtsying, the hand kissing, the 'yes, my ladys,' the 'yes, my lords.' On top of the forced pleasantries, she had to tolerate the stares. People wanted to stare and they suffered no embarrassment in doing so. She wanted to explode with indignation and wished she could tell them to put their eyes back in their heads. Remaining calm, she could be as charming as any high-class lady and talk the same slow, finely pronounced dialogue.

King Basylus arrived, followed by the prince and their officials. He sat with pompous ceremony at the curved table at the front of the hall. Beside him sat his son. Another table on the left had more disinterested looking guests. The king, although elderly, did not appear unfit. He wore a wig of perfect ringlets, and his short beard was a similar white. Dressed in a royal-blue velvet coat with high ruffles around his neck, he watched his subjects with an obvious dispassion. Bastion, dressed similarly to his father only more extravagantly, had a similar detached look.

Bastion glanced her way and Shiarn covered a yawn. He turned to speak to the lady next to him, Duchess Vonzella. Also on the same table, a short underweight man introduced as the prince's chamberlain, Gaspar, and the man who met them on the forest road, the king's advisor, Morgal. His cruel mouth curved down at her. Unlike the other men, he wore his real hair slicked back under a navy cap. His cold eyes, often on her, repulsed her for some reason, and she kept her gaze from him.

She admired the musicians at the back of the hall. A minstrel sang in a dialect she couldn't understand and she gave a loud despondent sigh.

'Lady Shiarn, are you enjoying the entertainment?'

On her left, the wealthy, according to Regina, Lord Belleguarde attempted to evoke conversation, again. At least twice her age, he was dressed in a mauve ensemble with bright white frills down the front, lined with gold buttons. 'The music is pleasant.' Staring at the lord's profile, she noticed he was not as dour as she perceived. His distinct features sharp yet not hard.

He placed his fork on the plate, his rings clinking on the silver. 'I presume from your accent you are not from Coltrene. Perhaps Rynian?'

Previously she wasn't in a good temper to discuss anything to do with her. As the night progressed, the strawberry liqueur induced a lazy tongue. 'Not Rynian, past the Allervium Ranges.'

He leaned back and considered her with interest. 'Oh, yes?'

She flicked a stray strand over her shoulder. 'A lot farther.'

Lord Belleguarde creased his brow and stated with a bored flourish, 'Rather a long way from home?'

'Indeed.' She spooned a sauce-covered cheese ball into her mouth. 'This is divine.'

'Truly?' His meal was barely touched. 'They are serving their less esteemed dishes this evening.'

His pompous words made her feel she came from a backwater town. Which was more or less correct.

As if deducing her thoughts, he asked in a boorish off-handed manner, 'It would seem you have not been here long, my dear?'

'Not at all,' she replied, growing tired of his falseness, 'I'm here for the prince.'

He raised his eyebrows. 'Perhaps from a very small village then. I should think you might need lessons in etiquette much like the serving girls when they arrive.'

Shiarn's neck heated with a building indignation, and grimacing, she attempted holding her tongue.

Belleguarde leaned back to speak with Regina on Shiarn's right. 'Lady Regina, you will need to show the lady here, the comportment life in this court requires. I fear she may accidentally overstep the mark with some proud lord.'

Unable to restrain herself, Shiarn fumed, 'I assure you, I neither need nor want lessons in how to be a pompous trite.'

Regina gasped in terror as did several others in earshot, although they were less horrified and more incensed. The newcomer was unashamedly exhibiting her foreign ignorance; she could read from their disdainful stares. Lord Belleguarde's lips pursed, but his eyes suddenly glowed. 'Without question you shall provide the prince with much stimulation. He is indeed fortunate.'

She gasped, nearly coughing her mouthful over the table.

'You are correct. You do not need the lesson. You are more adept than I realized.'

Her fingers fluttered over her neck and she took a great gulp of wine.

'Clandestine love affairs are quite common, a mistress here, a lover there, and with women of more import than your ladyship.' He rested his palm on her hand, assuring her all was as it should be.

She snatched her hand from under his, wishing she could kick him under the table or stab his fingers with her fork. Regina went back to smiling sweetly, suddenly not caring in the least. Shiarn longed to speak to any of her friends or anyone sane for that matter.

Belleguarde went on to inform her of an upcoming picnic. '... will you delight us with your presence?'

'It's not up to me.' Although she hoped to be there; opportunity for escape might be broader. Out of curiosity, she looked at Bastion and wondered if she would speak with him that night. She had to admit, she missed his company.

'I am sure he could be persuaded to invite you.'

'I'll try my best.' With a smug smile, she lifted her goblet to him and took a drink.

Lord Belleguarde remarked with a disdainful toss of dark brown curls, 'Similar to dinner, this is not their best wine.'

'Your standards must be commendably high.'

'Indeed.' Lord Belleguarde's face creased with conceit. 'For such an occasion, one of distinction expects quality refreshments.'

Shiarn sighed. 'One would expect grace be a worthy enough merit for a lord?'

'Is this something you are acquainted with?'

His remark cut into her mellowing thoughts. 'I know when I see it.'

'Your rural humour is a surprise and a distracting pleasure.'

'The pleasure is all mine.' Shiarn lifted her goblet in mock honour. 'You have intrigued me with your upper-class droll. It is a fine art for which I am no expert. Aristocratic wit is beyond me, although I have discovered it is an expedience for those who lack anything else to say.'

'Ah, as sharp as a hacksaw in a buttery.'

Shiarn spent the remainder of the evening avoiding eye contact with the arrogant lord and for much of that, her face was flushed. Whether it was his derogatory words or the wine, she could not say. In her attempt to ignore him, she ended up anguishing over her deteriorating situation. Hard to believe only days ago she was safe with her Kin. Now she was sipping wine at a banquet hosted by the King of Coltrene. It appeared everyone knew why she was present even though she was not certain of it herself. Everything around her invisible prison seemed set as if prearranged for her capture. She had no idea what had become of Earona, Ethan, and the girl caught up with them. On top of it all, and irrationally, she dreaded Jett's reaction to their disappearance. Yet even so, she didn't care what he said, she longed to hear his voice, even if it had to be stern.

Finally the king left his table and the guests were free to leave. Shiarn was only too thankful. The whole experience was a drain. Having to sit straight in an absurdly tight dress, not dance, not mingle at will was boring and completely out of line with her personality.

Regina stood and took hold of Shiarn's elbow, and said to those around them, 'We shall say good evening to all, Lady Shiarn.'

Shiarn stood and turned to the expectant lord. 'Good evening. Your idle chatter has lessened the burden of this evening.'

He also stood. Taller than her, he was not unattractive for an older man despite his fastidious air. 'Good evening.' He bowed. 'It has been an amusing exchange. I hope to see you in the following days. The prince is a highly favoured man.'

Pink tinged her cheeks, and she murmured, 'We shall see about that.'

~ * ~

Back in her suite, a fire took the chill from the air, and Shiarn curled up on a lounge and dozed. She woke with no idea how much time had passed. The fire was low, yet the warmth remained. She decided to change into her nightdress. Not long after pulling the covers down on her bed, she heard the door to her rooms open. She came out to reprimand Bastion on his lateness.

The king's advisor stood in her suite, his gaze taking in her sheer gown. His lips formed a maniacal smirk and her skin prickled with alarm. 'Why are you here?'

Morgal strolled towards the sideboard and poured an amber drink into two small cups. 'He is not here I see.' His eyes lingered on the explicit paintings on the walls. The firelight could not dull the lewdness.

In the presence of the uninvited stranger, the copulating lovers sickened her.

He glided closer to the lounge. 'Shall we have a drink and make this an easy state of affairs for both of us.'

She crossed her arms and ignored his proffered cup. 'I'm not interested in having a drink.'

He narrowed his eyes and his temper changed, becoming less charming and more loutish. 'I had a feeling it would be this way. In answer to your question, I want something from you. It is one of the reasons for your presence here.' After a drink of the liqueur, he placed it on the table.

'One of the reasons?' She eyed him suspiciously.

'I want the Essenya. A gold and ivory-opal medallion in the shape of an eye. Most likely it was in the same place you found this.' He held up a black trinket in the shape of an eight.

Recognition flickered across her face at the sight of Ethan's pendant. 'I don't have it.'

His lips tightened with irritation. 'Perhaps your counterparts will know more of it.'

She wanted to touch her neck in memory of her necklace, but kept her arms clenched by her body. 'Obviously you searched them already. They don't know anything about it.'

Abrupt rage enflamed his face. 'You know what I'm asking for. Where is it?' He fixed a depraved stare on her body, a naked silhouette beneath the flimsy gown.

She backed away, sensing her vulnerability in the proximity of the stranger. 'I don't have it anymore. It's gone.'

He rushed at her and slapped her across the face, spinning her sideways. 'Then *you* will tell me where.' He gripped her arm and threw her down onto the table.

The solid shove against the wood, pushed the breath out of her, and she gasped. 'I left it in Lanvin.'

His hand squeezed her neck in a strangling hold, thrusting her bruised cheek against the table; his other hand, heavy on her back, pushed her stomach into the wood. 'You can't lie to me. I know it's in Floris.'

'Then find it yourself,' Shiarn forced out the words. Her chest ached under the weight of his body. But at least she knew Jett and the Kin must be in the city.

'Where?'

'Don't...' she rasped, '...know.'

He leaned down to speak near her ear. 'I shall enjoy getting the information from you. However, I hoped it would be easier.' His sour breath touched her ear.

Wincing, she strained trying to wrestle away from him. From his merciless and aggressive handling of her body, it was clear he was no stranger to abusing women. 'You devil!'

He squeezed harder. 'Who has it?'

'How do I know?'

He hiked up her nightdress and after parting his robe, he forced himself into her. Held in the clamp like grip, her cheek stung from the pressure. Her struggle turned inward as the pain raged inside. Shiarn looked away, her hatred for him burning deep and fast within her shaking body. Her abdomen hurt from the fierce jolts impelling her into the lurching table. She avoided even a remote glimpse of the murals, subliminally mocking her honour. Flicking her eyes across the sofa, she glimpsed the disturbing shadows of their callous joining. After moments of thrusting against her and further groaning, he was relieved of his lust. He was slow to release her, and once more, his hot words seared her face. 'I will find it, with or without you.'

While he adjusted his robe, she whirled to slap his face. 'Get out!'

He caught her wrist and held it high while reaching for her other. His hair fell on his forehead from his vigorous tussle, and he frowned. 'You better think about where it is.' He shoved her onto the floor. 'And maybe I will be less severe next time.' He left the room.

Shiarn rushed to the door and pulled on the handle, locked. In a shocked daze, she wandered to the bedroom, realizing how much she wanted to wash and rid herself of the whole experience.

Full of churning emotions, she ripped off her nightdress and threw it across the room. But neither could she bear to be naked and she put her evening dress back on. Not knowing what to do, she paced. She sat, rubbing her bruised neck, and crying in desperate smatterings.

What was so important about that pendant that two men in the space of a few days wanted it from her? How could she willingly tell him that one of her friends had it? Then the awful realization hit her. Would she have to face him every night?

She retrieved the stoker and lay on her bed. After some moments, she opened the window and stared at grey storm clouds and she shut it again. Afraid and hurt, she sensed deep inside she was not the person she was a couple of hours ago. Adding to her anguish, was the horrid sensation she could still feel. Him.

Hard to believe it had happened to her, harder still she could not stop it. Did not. It was as disheartening as the horrendous act itself. She was desperate to come out with something positive. However, it looked bleak, she could find nothing redeeming in any of it, least of all in herself. She crawled under the covers and pulled them over her head. In the soft darkness, she sobbed.

~ * ~

Jett headed out from Annabella's into the cold dismal night. Consumed by anxious dread, he walked with lead feet, wondering if he would drop under the weight of his burdens. If the Eldery knew of his predicament, the Circle's disapproving opinions and scepticism would be validated. Those who said he would not be a worthy Avare would gloat relentlessly. The extent of his failure crashed into his spirit. How did fate conspire to make everything go so terribly amiss? His mood was as miserable as the cloud tossed sky as he approached the White Horse. Through the back door, faint laughter drifted over the vigorous music.

He entered the stables and went to Thunder's stall. Leaning over his horse, he couldn't stop the hurt pouring out in wracking sobs. Music from the tavern faded to an annoying noise till all he heard was a raging flood. Thunder nudged his shoulder, but his attentions went ignored. Hearing someone push open the door, he wiped his face.

'Jett?' Keanan walked through the dark and stopped opposite Jett with the black horse between them.

Jett kept his face lowered. 'How did you know I was here?' His voice caught in his raw throat.

'Bertie said someone was out here.' Keanan gave a small laugh. 'I came out and felt your Ethos like a brick thrown at my head.'

Jett's miserable emotions were strong enough to touch Keanan, but he wanted nothing more than to lose himself in his desolation.

'What has happened?' Keanan stood tall, eyeing Jett over the horse. 'Where are Marcus and Seth?'

Jett's wall of darkness remained impenetrable. 'Marcus is deathly ill, from poison. Seth is with him. A woman is caring for him. I came back to tell you.' *Despite not being able to speak a word.*

Keanan stared, his eyes misting with confusion. 'How is he?'

'I'll check first thing tomorrow.'

'And you?'

'Not sure...' Jett shrugged. 'I... I can't explain... you wouldn't understand.' *I'm not making sense.* He expired a pent up breath and rested his head on Thunder's side. 'Avares have hidden responsibilities,' he muttered into his horse. He wished he was free to speak about his intricate link to the Kin's life and function; requiring a life long commitment and indefinite debts of the soul that he was feeling right then. 'I'm responsible.'

'That's typical of you, but we all have responsibilities to ourselves and to the Kin,' Keanan intoned, his irritation making his words brittle, 'You can't make choices for us. We all have to be captains of our own lives. You can't wipe our arses all the time... maybe sometimes you have to wipe some people's arses, but truly...'

Jett remained rigid. Keanan would never understand the significance of the Avare, he was never meant to. 'It's not that simple...'

Perhaps the prophecy is now occurring—

'Don't you think I know that,' Jett cried. It was becoming more obvious every day they were separated.

Keanan grunted. 'Then you know why you were so stubborn despite it.'

'Damn you, why are you s—'

'Insightful?' Keanan's lip turned up in a half smirk.

'Such a pain in the arse,' Jett muttered, and he paused, considering Keanan's remark. 'No, you're right. I remember why.' He wanted to leave Tellávare and damn the consequences. Now he was paying for that decision.

Keanan nodded with gratification. 'Ah, and so, you should also know, we will help you carry your loads.'

'I suppose...' *but I can't do it if I'm not in control.*

Keanan replied to his thoughts, 'And that's always been your problem. But the truth is you can't do it all alone.'

Jett's smile came up from a tired body. 'I'm not convinced.'

You don't want to be, I expect. Keanan gave a weary sigh. 'In any case, are you going to come in and eat?'

'Not into that.' He indicated the hearty noise inside.

'Mm, agreed. How about we eat upstairs and talk about Marcus.'

'I'll meet you up there,' Jett said.

'Come up when you are ready.'

Jett's bleak mood was hard to budge. Keanan's remark about the prophecy aggravated the burden. The words of the Seers gained intensity in his mind since leaving Lanvin. Also, he was surprised at his concern over the girl. The tangible vision was a mess of terrifying scenes, and the attack of the Narahk would not be a passing thing. It was all significant, and somehow related to the girl, but how exactly he couldn't guess. And she was out there with his Kin. From that alone they could be in perilous danger. He knew they needed him, somewhere, somehow, but he was helpless. Their loneliness and afflictions affected him and he could do nothing to alleviate the throb in his chest. As he pondered the gloomy sensation, he realized the grief of the whole Kin was falling on him. A profound ache for them to be reunited besieged him.

Under his shirt, he traced the throbbing pattern on his skin from his Echwud. His flesh carried an individual symbol for each of his Kin, signifying their connection; a connection that would grow stronger over time. He wondered how he could bare any such separation after many years. The Kin were all part of the whole and the members would be striving to return to this state of unity. Whether they knew it or not, their spirits were compelled to come together again. He could read it in his Ethos as if it was written there in ink. His deliberations over the missing ones only served to make him feel worse. Yet even with the heartache, and the dismal prophecy, he determined to continue until they were united.

Later that evening, after Jett, Keanan, and Hellier had eaten, Jett stood on their balcony, viewing the sky. Distant clouds, billowing with ashen peaks, formed a ceiling of ominous shadows. A stormy night was ahead. He looked seaward in the direction of Annabella's and wondered how Marcus was. He had considered walking back, but the evening had been pleasant with Keanan and Hellier. Unable to shake his melancholy frame of mind, he voiced his sad thoughts.

Hellier had replied with comic disdain, 'Can you get any more depressing?'

He thought on her honest words, but it was hard to shake the notion they were dwindling. Some time passed before he lay on his bed, knowing sleep would be elusive. A scene from his childhood came to mind. The Kin were youngsters, playing in the meadow. Innocent and carefree and blissfully unaware of life's traumas and how quickly it changes into something less fun. He was teaching them a particular game and what everyone's roles would be.

In disagreement, a young Earona, hair pinned up neatly, piped up, 'You can't boss us around like we don't know anything. You're not smart at all.'

Jett was the Avare and he wished to assert his authority. He stood; his conceit in full flight. 'I'm the leader, you have to do what I say.'

'No I don't! Stop being a mean old bossy boots,' she reprimanded in her grown-up-girl voice, and chanted with a pointed finger. 'Bossy boots, bossy boots, nothing but a pig-head know-it-all!'

Marcus pounced on him, tackling him to the ground. 'I've pinned the Avare! Look who's the boss now.'

Ethan also enjoyed wrestling and he piled on. Not one to be left out, Hellier leaped onto the boys. They laughed at Jett struggling to free himself. In the end even he laughed. That was when being an Avare was a game, a bizarre concept; he had no real comprehension of its true meaning. After that time, he viewed himself as their equal, having to earn their respect. For many years that was what he endeavoured to do. An uneasy sleep overtook his weary body with dreams of death besetting him.

27 - Recover

Healing cannot always cure the pain
Rest does not always bring peace to the turmoil

Hope covers the ills
Companionship gives solace

Fellowship of Healers. Age of the First Born

Light was streaming through the gap of the curtains for some time as Shiarn lay staring at the ceiling. The previous evening flooded back as soon as she opened her eyes from a restless sleep. Emptiness stretched over her like a dark pit pulling her down.

Voices came from the adjoining room, and a knock on the door. 'It's Sasheya. Can I come in?'

'I suppose.'

Sasheya peeked in. 'You haven't eaten your breakfast.' She sat on the bed beside her. 'A bath will make you feel better. You can't always get one. It's hard work hauling the water up the pulleys.' Outside the room, another girl moved about with a trolley. Together they dragged a giant steel tub in. Water sloshed inside and they poured in more from a metal pitcher. Sasheya sprinkled fragrant oil over the water and the other girl left the room, closing the door behind her.

'I can't stay long,' Sasheya said. 'The dragon might catch me.'

'She's a horrid woman.'

'If she finds us talking, I will get into strife.' Sasheya pulled Shiarn's blanket back and her eyes widened. Shiarn's evening dress hung loose as she sat up. 'Your face?!'

Shiarn touched her sore cheek. The mark was overshadowed by other injuries less obvious yet hurt deeper down. 'It will heal.'

Sasheya looped her arm around Shiarn's shoulders. 'Was it...' She paused 'the prince?'

Shiarn broke away, shaking her head in response.

'Who?'

Touching her cheek, Shiarn slumped. 'The king's advisor.'

Sasheya sucked in her breath. 'Him!' She spat, 'He's a beast. There are stories about him.'

'I'm sure they are all true and probably worse.'

'Oh, it's awful...' Sasheya turned her face from her, allowing her to undress and step into the oily water.

Shiarn relaxed into the tub, the warmth softening her skin. 'This is sorely needed.'

'You will tell the prince?'

She scrubbed at her body, desiring to clean every part. 'I'm worried...' If Bastion was part of Morgal's plan he too might want the jewel.

'He won't like your swollen face? After all, he is the one spending his nights here with you doing...' She blushed. 'What men do?'

Shiarn chuckled.

Sasheya said, 'You laugh!'

'How do you know what men *do*?'

'I have heard the girls talk.' Sasheya jumped off the bed. 'That reminds me. I spoke to your friend Ethan.'

The news gave her a burst of happiness. 'Is he well? And Earona and Mara?'

'I saw no one else.' Sasheya continued blushing.

Shiarn's hair, in damp ringlets, dangled over the edge of the tub. 'What did he say?'

'He will take the blame.' She gave her a questioning glance. 'For what?'

'It's so typical of him,' she muttered, 'oh, Ethan - but what am I supposed to do?'

Sasheya's voice lifted with passion. 'The prince will help you.'

Shiarn lounged in the water and mumbled, 'Maybe you are right, I could try.'

~ * ~

Later that morning, Bastion sauntered in without knocking. Shiarn dragged herself from the book she was reading despite the text swimming before her eyes, to stare with dispassion. He looked handsome in clothes a little less flamboyant than usual.

'Dear gods! Your lovely face.' He rushed over and held her chin up. 'How did this happen?'

'Morgal...' Her wrathful reply startled her.

'No...' He said in disbelief, searching her eyes. 'It's true?'

'Indeed.' Recalling the vile act sent her back into a dismal mood. 'And there's more.'

'This is preposterous. Did he touch you?'

She took a breath and chose her words with care. 'He did, but apparently, he wants something he thought I had.'

Bastion frowned in puzzlement. 'What could you have that he would want?'

'A jewel.' She watched him, attentively. 'But I don't have anything.'

'Did you know what it is?' Bastion stroked her arm.

She pressed on his arm, stopping his caress. 'No. Did you know of this?'

He took her hand in his and his thumb rubbed her palms. 'Honestly, he did mention a precious heirloom was stolen from Rothhaven, and it was he who expected your presence that night.'

In shock, Shiarn started, 'He...?' Morgal was behind it from the beginning. If it hadn't been for Ethan she would have had that necklace and Morgal would have taken it. 'You knew I'd be there?!'

'He must have been wrong about the item.' Bastion cupped her chin, and his sky blue eyes probed hers. 'Yes, I knew to some degree. But not too worry now, you will be safe from him.'

Shiarn stared, transfixed by the depth of his mellow tone, and found she could not respond. How was he going to guarantee that?

His eyes penetrated her thoughts to distraction. 'This afternoon I thought you get out from here and we could picnic in the gardens.'

For some reason she could do nothing under the allure of his soothing gaze, but listen.

~ * ~

Bastion and Shiarn came out onto a raised courtyard with a view over the lawn spreading through the trees into landscaped scenes. A staircase down to the park separated into two pathways. In between was a large twenty-foot waterway structure. At the end was a merman statue, his beard swirling about his torso. His spear sprayed water into the air, and a shell was in his other hand. Bastion explained, Nesvar, God of the oceans, answers the cries of sailors, making him a favoured god in Floris.

To keep from the chill, Shiarn clutched a wrap, matching her chartreuse dress, tighter to her chest. A large brimmed hat with grey and silver needlework partially covered up her facial bruising. From under its shade she glanced above, observing the massive castle. On the other side were her rooms, facing the sea cliffs and a portion of the city's western wall.

Other strollers bowed and curtsied to the prince although he stopped for no one. Most likely Shiarn's face brought him some embarrassment and she pondered why he would bring her out at all. During their trivial conversation, they drifted over the lawn, and no matter how she squeezed it into their talk, he would not discuss her friends or situation. However, he chatted about his royal life with childlike merriment. He started, 'The ceremony last night was somewhat lacklustre. Did you enjoy yourself?'

'The food was delicious.' Was all she could say of the event.

'Who was that drearisome bard? Singing about a fat hound and a maudlin pesky princess, and some sort of bird-wolf creature, or something ridiculous. Verse after verse on a talking horse, or imagined, I am not sure. Did he mention it played a pipe... perhaps I dozed.'

A giggle escaped her. 'It's a folk tale, I presume.'

'I am pleased to hear you laughing, Shiarn, considering all things.' Her name rolled off his tongue, as if he savoured a fine wine. 'Your company was not too arduous I hope.'

'He was pleasantly distracting.'

'Lord Belleguarde is a haughty fool and extremely self-possessed.' He gave an enigmatic sigh. 'I haven't met a charmer with a glibber tongue. Ladies seek him out and he's had his fair share of them.'

His comment surprised her. 'He seemed far from charming.'

Pressing on her arm, Bastion leaned his head close and smiled. 'Perhaps you struck an unplayed chord. My guess, he is deciding to step carefully.'

'He's stepping on hot coals.'

'He was married once.' Bastion paused. 'She died. Then he found he liked women too much to marry again.'

She said, 'Besides him, the evening would have been a lot more enjoyable without Regina.'

'Oh, by Orianna!' He tilted his head back and laughed into the air. 'If she smiles at me with that uncanny grin one more time, I am going to have her imprisoned.' He said, 'But for now she is your attendant and we all must bear her, no matter how odd the sad woman is.'

She tightened her lips in vexation. Her predicament was too much for her to comprehend and instead of arguing, she would enjoy the gardens while she was outside. Content to stand under the wispy shade of a weeping tree, she admired the flowering bushes, and noticed flora she never knew existed, billowing down to a trickling stream. Bastion was thrilled to point out the unknowns to her.

They stepped over a modest bridge crossing the quaint stream to lawn chairs and a table with platters of food and drink. A few feet away was a tranquil pond with striking maroon lilies reflected in the water. Shiarn breathed deep in appreciation of the fragrant air. 'Bas, this is beautiful.'

'It is a mere reflection. I have seen the Sanctuary of Ludeisica.
"No other will satisfy the heart.
From her all gardens spring,
Growing dreams of wonder.
She will never decay,"' he sang, 'and the poem goes on. Our gardens are lovely, nonetheless, I have seen the gardens of the Ivory palace in Aquila.'

'How wonderful. You could be a bard.'

'I hardly think I would have the patience.'

Shiarn viewed the garden with a new perspective.

'I long to see it once more,' he mused. 'Although that opportunity is unlikely while this dissension with Ryne continues.'

Not in the mood for politics of New Empire, she let the statement fade, and escaped into the fantasy of beauty. 'It's best to enjoy what you do have.'

'Quite right, and today we shall indulge.' He took her hand and led her to the chair. 'On a following night I have organized entertainment from Belrorn.'

She laughed. 'At least you're not turning into some tyrant...'

'A tyrant? Never.' He leaned down and an earthy sweetness aroused her senses. He brought her chin up and kissed her. His closeness startled her and she gasped when he broke away.

Smiling at her surprise, he sat and poured her a wine. 'Let us relax for a time, because I can tell you, we both need it.'

~ * ~

An hour after dawn, Jett's entry into Annabella's shop nearly shook the bell off its hook. With a mighty swoop, he yanked her curtain back. 'How is he?'

'Good morning to you too.' Annabella wore the same purple dress from the day before, and her hair was now a lopsided lump. She looked up with welcomed cheer. 'Seth has gone upstairs for a lie down. He's been on that chair all night.' Finally, with grave weariness, she said, 'He's improved, but can't go anywhere yet.'

Jett noted her drawn out eyes. 'You have laboured during the night.'

'His ointment needed changing—' Yawning, she paused. 'It's the only way.'

Colour was on Marcus' skin and his breathing was noticeable. Jett took the seat beside him and called his name. His eyes were slits and he managed a weak smile.

Annabella came through with a tray and laid it on the sideboard. 'You have a rough night?' She poured a tea for herself and Jett.

'Considering everything, it wasn't unexpected.' Jett took the cup. 'I will pay you for what you have done.'

Her eyes shining, she leaned in to him. 'You are them special people, aren't ya?'

Too mentally exhausted to evade the question, Jett replied, 'Maybe, although I'm not sure we are talking about the same thing.'

'Tickle my big toe, I knew it!' she cried with triumph. 'It's a great thrill to help you. You people did good things for me.'

'Who were these *people*?'

'In Baion when I was young. One of their names was Maris and Jonral, there were others...' She fingered her chin, as if trying to recollect some past event.

'Can't say I've heard those names.'

'It's a long time ago now, wouldn't expect you to know them.'

He was not about to reveal the average Fáerinn lifespan was nearly three times more than that of a Nayinn. There was always the possibility these particular Fáerinn were still alive today.

'Have you come to help with the war that's brewing?'

'No,' Jett said, 'we are going to Lakhish.'

Her eyes downcast, she was silent for several moments. 'That's a shame. Baions being killed and the king and queen are no more. Many peoples' lives are in danger, and they'll take over the lands of Selon for sure now.' She carried on with a pointed finger and more conviction. 'And what about the royal children of Baion? No one knows what's happened to them.'

He could understand her frustration yet how could she expect he act on the behalf of the royal family of Baion? His Kin were not the saviours of the surrounding kingdoms of Ryne, it was ridiculous to think so. 'The King of Ryne is doing this?'

'That devil! Not just him, his queen too. She's the cause, but what do I know. I just know me homeland is being wrecked by Ryne.' Her face went a bright red. 'And what if they take Floris? Oh, well, you gotta do what you gotta do and all and I'm not the one to be stopping you.' Appearing to calm suddenly, she patted his knee in a patronizing manner. 'We just gotta hope we all get through it alive. You know you can give me all the money you want, but the true reward, and that's the payment I'd like, is you doing what you can to help the people who really need it.'

'It's not that easy.' Jett felt obliged to explain. 'Our duties are determined by others.' He had no idea why he was attempting to divulge Fáerinn practices to this pushy old woman, except perhaps she had done so much for them.

She nodded like a patient mother.

'We can't decide to do whatever we like after being instructed where we are destined to go.' To his own ears, he sounded as if he were justifying actions he had no desire to carry out.

'Is that right?'

'We have people expecting us in Lakhish.' His tone became harsh. 'Look, you've been more than kind to us, but I don't think I should be trying to explain these things to you.'

'Guess it's left up to fate what happens. Often it's that way and that's who really decides in the end.' A wise smile lightened her disposition. 'It's better that way, saves us messing it up.'

Why then did he feel he was messing things up, and that 'fate' appeared to be acting in a very cruel manner? 'Besides all that, I'm not going anywhere until I find my friends.'

'Seth told me of your friends.' Her face crinkled and a frown dominated her face. 'It's painful trying to get to where you need to be. But, if the destination is noble it's worth the travail. Think of it this way, if there's no trial you ain't going no-where.'

The fire of rebuke surged towards his tongue, but he held his antagonistic response fast. It was like speaking to Judge Haldus. 'If that's true, then right now, I wish I wasn't going anywhere.' What could be worth this heartache?

'See your friend there, he needs to rest and get his strength back.' She looked at Marcus and gave an enthusiastic nod. 'And he will.'

Jett's shoulders relaxed with relief. 'I'm glad of that.'

'You can come back later if you need to do something,' she said, 'He'll be fine and Seth is still here.'

He reached for Marcus' hand. 'I'll talk to you later.' To Annabella, he said, 'You should get some rest.'

'Don't you worry 'bout that.' She chuckled. 'You look after yourself, don't be getting into any more trouble.'

'That can't be guaranteed.'

They said goodbye and Jett departed feeling more hopeful.

28 - The Rocks

Integrity will give power to the weak and tenacity will aid the one pushed down.

Tome of the First Born Reign

Guards came to Ethan's cell and took him back to the dark torture room. The same mean-mouthed torturer awaited him with his gloating sneer and blood stained apron. Once more, Ethan was strung up by his chained wrists to the bolt in the wall. This time his scarred back pressed against the damp stones, leaving his chest exposed. The torturer readied his instruments of pain; iron rods lying across a pit of embers. From what Ethan dared to view, each point had a different shape. What more could they want from him? At the first press into his chest, he understood. Each mark was another agony to endure. After the symbols were scarred onto his skin he was numb and exhausted.

Back in the cell he slumped against the wall with his head in his hands. A dull awareness was in his mind, and his burning chest caused his body to ache in unison. Blood oozed from the branding that stated his bondage to Coltrene.

Later on, the door opened again and a guard ordered him up and out. Once outside, they pulled him up into a wagon, and he sat between guards. They started on their way through the gates. Engrossed by the sunlight and fresh air, he watched what he could see of Floris, fearing where he would end up next.

Finally the wagon trundled through another gate in a high wall. Onerous buildings loomed, casting shadows over the trail of the wagon. They stopped and he was ordered out. Guards appeared in the familiar black tunic, yet they had a mean look, as if Ethan had wronged them in a personal way.

Pushed through an undersized doorway, he stumbled over his own feet and nearly collided with a wide desk. A tall rotund man came from behind it, his eyes scanning Ethan, head to toe. The man's black bearded chin lifted and Ethan received a disdaining nod. 'I am Captain Talskin and I am in charge of this compound.' He walked around him, scrutinizing his appearance while the guards looked on with boredom. Talskin finally spoke. 'If you are well behaved you need not see me again.' He pulled down Ethan's soiled shirt front revealing the new markings on his skin. He returned to his desk, and with quill in hand wrote into a large open book. He ordered the guards, 'Take him to the mid cell.'

They took him through a door Ethan failed to notice upon entering. After going through a dim narrow corridor, they came to another door lined with several locks. After searching for the matching keys amongst their small horde, they opened the door.

Ethan ducked his head to pass through into a dark windowless passage lit by torches spaced along the grey walls. The group kept on down the corridor gradually turning to the left. The floor became hard packed earth and a damp draft blew on his face. The corridor sloped into a cavern twice his height and deeper than he could see. On either side, thick bars were embedded into the rock far above. Giant archways ran the length of the center of the cavern, a good distance between the two cells. Along the arches were brackets, holding bulky lanterns. Further down, more lamps lit up more cells.

He heard the raucous jeering and cursing before he saw the source responsible for such a racket. Through the dark, men in both cells became visible. He was unsure if the taunts and name calling were for him, except the hollering continued after he was pushed through the door. With lightning speed it was slammed shut behind him. The guards disappeared down the corridor.

The rocks reflected an eerie light, and men, standing and sitting, were all packed together. It appeared to be a small cell, but Ethan's eyes adjusted and he discerned openings set at intervals along the walls. A horrible mix of rank smells overpowered his senses.

A giant of a man shoved men away and stood face to face with Ethan. His eyes held a feral glare, and a mass of straggly hair fell around his face and past his shoulders, and a matching beard connected it all. A menacing voice burst up from the man's belly. 'New face.' He put his fists up to Ethan. 'Let's see if you're worth me talking to ya.'

Ethan frowned, shaking his head. 'What makes you think I want to talk to you?'

The man faked a punch. Ethan paced backwards, avoiding his reach.

'You want *me* to not kill ya?' He pushed his fist out again, this time with more direction. The strange discussion gathered its observers.

Ethan dodged back, raising his fists. 'I've got chains on, it's not really fair.'

'You yellow-bellied? Not as tough as you think, eh? You one of those spineless devils,' the man spat. 'I'll knock you flat.' His hand moved fast, hitting Ethan square on the chin.

Ethan shook his head and gave the wild-man a slanted stare. Suddenly feeling the urge to vent his frustrations on another human being, his fist landed on the side of the man's face. Rowdy laughter was the man's response and Ethan punched him in the stomach. Cheers and catcalls rose up for the new boy. The man appeared unmindful to Ethan's punches, but he felt the shock to his own body.

They circled each other like predators about to pounce. His partner's peculiar happy expression was unnerving, even so, Ethan was up for the fight. He caught up the chain and stepped behind the big man, dragging the links around his neck and pulling it tight. 'I told you it wouldn't be fair.'

The sight of the big man falling to his knees, trying to loosen the chain caused boisterous hollering from the spectators.

Ethan released him and pushed him to the ground. The man rubbed his throat and grunted. Maniacal laughter exploded from the giant. Ethan shook his head with contempt.

While clutching his reddened neck he stood, and wheezed, 'You can come and share my space.'

Ethan creased his brow with scorn. 'What does that mean?'

He clutched Ethan's upper arm, his laughter rumbled across the cell. 'New boy, me name's Maddog.' Ethan followed Maddog as he ducked through an opening in the rock wall to another chamber also crowded with more dirty, bedraggled men. Iron bars replaced a portion of the rock which brought light in from the lamps beyond it. Ethan spied more openings to other chambers in the jagged rocks. Men sat or lay on worn matting or the dirt floor. Maddog moved past one group and headed towards the back of the chamber where it was darker. Ethan could see the dull shine from men's eyes as they watched him.

'Newcomer, what time was it?' The one who spoke had a bushy beard and hair. Dark circular marks were over his right cheek and forehead, and a long plait hung down his tan shirt.

Ethan blatantly stared at the men, all of similar appearance. 'Midday...'

Maddog's voice echoed in the chamber. 'He's going to share our space.' He slapped Ethan hard on the back, causing him to wince.

The man shrugged. 'Do we have a choice?'

Maddog lowered himself onto the floor, stretching out on his elbow. He ordered Ethan to do the same. The man who asked about the time said, 'Might as well, nothing else to do.'

Leaning on the rock, Ethan sat cross-legged on the matting. The men around him had the same broad shoulders and square faces, ruled by the dark tattoos; some had more while others less. They had beards, yet everyone in the cell had facial hair.

'I'm Loc,' the first man introduced himself, 'and right here is Branan.' A young man by Loc's side glanced at Ethan without a word. 'And this is Grith and Gailtram.'

Grith's red hair was bright even in the shadows, and Gailtram's hair was a tangle of black and grey, and his facial markings covered nearly all his skin except one slender space on his right cheek. Curving around his outer eyes, the designs spiraled down, and Ethan supposed they went under his beard. 'I'm Ethan.'

Loc said, 'You come from the streets?'

Ethan's eyes wandered over the men in the cell in an attempt to comprehend what sort of place he was in. 'The jail.'

Abruptly, Loc yelled to a passing man also of the same short stocky frame and long plaited hair, 'Gart, it's day. You were right again.'

Gart chuckled and walked over to another group of the same men. Ethan observed the exchange with puzzlement.

Loc said, 'In here it's neither day nor night.'

'Or it's both,' Maddog said.

'You can't ask the guards?' asked Ethan.

Maddog jumped up with wild chuckling and went to the bars. He hollered down the passage.

'We lose track of time in here,' Branan said with irritation. Lacking a full beard, his face was not as square as the other men's and his tattoo was minor. Instead of the one plait he had two.

'He's insane,' Loc said to Ethan watching Maddog, 'he likes to separate the wheat from the chaff.'

'That's daft.' Ethan said, 'Holding up a fight doesn't guarantee you're a decent person.'

'Aye, we know that.' Loc shrugged indifferently. 'Like I said, he's insane.'

'Thank Targe, he is not one of us,' Branan said.

'People in here are different.' Gailtram's voice was deep and unfaltering. 'You be the same soon enough.'

Ethan shook his head and scowled at him. 'I don't think so.'

Maddog came back and plopped himself back on the floor. 'Stinkin' bastards can rot in hell.'

Branan retorted, 'What did you expect?'

'Do they feed you here?' Ethan asked.

Loc sighed. 'It might be called that.'

Branan added, 'They feed us any time and something that's supposed to be food.'

'My new friend's gonna need a bowl.' Maddog leaped up and disappeared into another chamber.

Loc tapped the silver bowl hooked onto his belt with a short leather cord. 'You need one of these.' He pointed to the end of the chamber. 'Through there is where you do your deeds. There's a hole.'

Ethan blinked with disbelief.

'We don't know where it goes.' Loc pointed in the same direction. 'Sea's out there.'

'Sea?'

Branan sneered, '...lots of water, waves....'

In a distracted manner Ethan commented, 'I've never seen it.'

'Where you been living, man?' Branan exclaimed.

'Up north.'

'Anyway,' Loc interrupted with disinterest, 'all these chambers lead down to it. Supposedly.'

Ethan raised his eyebrows. 'How long have you been here?'

From down the line of men sitting against the wall, Gart replied, 'We've had six meals here.'

Loc nodded his thanks to Gart.

Ethan was beginning to understand his predicament. 'What is this place?'

A deep rumbling voice, like rocks grating together, came from Grith. 'It's hell.'

Loc said, 'We're off the books, dead to this city and all that.' He raised his eyes to the ceiling, indicating the world above.

Maddog ambled back, and putting his hand on Ethan's shoulder threw a dented tin bowl into his lap.

Ethan said, 'Where did you get this?'

Maddog's grin spread with cheer. 'Some arse-ugly.'

Ethan held the bowl up to him. 'You stole it?'

'No. I took it,' Maddog roared, causing all to stare with a mix of casual interest and disgust.

'I don't want anyone taking stuff for me.' Ethan stood and shoved the bowl into Maddog's stomach. 'Take it back!'

Confusion clouded Maddog's eyes. 'What!?'

Loc chuckled at the two of them.

Branan gaped at Ethan in shock. 'You're mad!'

Ethan yelled, 'I'm not going to be the one who takes some poor soul's possessions. If I want something I'll get it myself. Take it back.'

Maddog growled and spat on the ground. The slag missed a man sitting by them, and he swiftly moved from the big man's radius. Maddog stood at the opening between the two large chambers and called to a man within. Having gained the owner of the bowl's attention, he threw it at him. Maddog made a great noise of sitting down. 'You gonna starve.'

Ethan sat with a heavy thump and hung his face between his raised knees. He lifted his head and scowled at Gart eyeing him.

Gart spoke. 'It is wise to hold onto your inner nature.'

Ethan shook his head and rubbed his forehead.

'You do well to listen to Gart,' said Loc.

Ethan let his head fall back onto the rock behind him. The heated throb of his back was consuming him. He had no inclination to enter into a debate about what he should or should not do, especially about his character. He knew he did not wish to be the bringer of more misery and suffering.

Maddog gave Ethan a firm punch on the arm. 'Gart's giving you a message boy, pay attention.'

Gart growled at Maddog, 'Shut up you son of a filthy slut.'

'Yar, yar, quit your whining,' he replied with glee and a note of affection.

Under his breath, Ethan mumbled, 'Is this forever?' Not wanting to face the sight of the dingy overcrowded cell, he closed his eyes. Any chance of his Kin finding him was remote and he questioned whether he would ever see them again.

Loc said, 'We do not know what our fate will be.'

After a moment, Ethan asked, 'Any chance of escape?'

'Aye, that's always a point of discussion,' Loc said. 'As yet we have not formed any plan.'

'No way out of hell,' Maddog stated, his eyes still closed, 'unlessen the devil opens the door.'

29 - Losing Control

Some are blind to their transgressions, those less simple, are fully aware of their crimes.

The Sleeping Sword

'I've washed hundreds of bowls all morning.' Earona studied her wrinkled fingers.

Mara walked beside her amongst the other women on their way to the temple. Accustomed to Earona's grumbling, Mara ignored her, it was the least she could do. But aside from her aggravating attitude she was useful at times, especially when it came to healing her back after a day of laundry.

'Finglestumps!' Earona peeled back a weakened nail too late to save. 'You wouldn't believe what I had to do. I cleaned the latrine!'

'Quiet at the back!' A counsellor called from ahead.

Earona continued with a moan, 'That's going to be a daily torment.'

Mara added her own complaint. 'I've got a damn headache after listening to kids shouting all day, and now I've got you—'

'Is there any chance I can work in the orphanage?'

'You want to?' Mara glanced down at her shrivelled hands, red and raw. 'But I did baskets full of washing.'

'But, still...' Earona twisted her lip in grievance.

'At least I'm not inside all the time.' She couldn't stand being couped up in the kitchen all day.

The group jammed through a single door and into a curtained off foyer. Cold brown walls suddenly amplified every sound, and plunged them into a daunting quiet. Every rustle of a garment and patter of shoes could be heard against the bare stones as the women gathered in the temple.

Mara breathed deep the heady spice aroma. Her eyes were drawn upwards to panels of glass lighting the enchanting scenery on the domed ceiling. It depicted a woman with white hair curling in the wind and surrounded by children. At a distance, a man stood, dressed in sable and iron. Light was on her while he stood in muted shadows. Shallow azure pools along the side of the walls shimmered with speckles of daylight from above. Statues of women in varying personas overlooked the pools. The stone figures included a pregnant woman, her hands out-stretched, and another woman held a sword. An archway at the end led to another foyer, and maybe the world outside, Mara mused.

Counsellor Adiana addressed the group while Mara walked to the water. A luminous turquoise glow captured her attention. Sapphire-coloured tiles were embedded into the pool's floor, and blue mosaic was around the edge.

The women knelt on padded cushions before the pools and bowed their heads. Adiana remained behind the marble altar, and spoke. 'Niesta, Mother of Mankind.' Her voice was boosted by the stone walls. 'We worship your nurturing heart and dedicate these women unto your service.'

Mara, reluctantly, lowered onto the cushion. The counsellor's words of worship and service grated in her mind and she restrained herself from lashing out in defiance.

'We pray for the strength to take on your labours and become lights, shining with virtue among the impure of this city, the enemy of all that is beautiful, nurturing, and righteous.' Adiana's voice softened into a mellow tone that built into a mesmerizing song of an unknown language.

Mara stared into the blue, folding against the mosaics, her mind crowded with rebellion. Against her stubborn desire, tranquillity washed over her till she could not recall what she was thinking.

'Cast your cares into the pool. Let Niesta hold you in her bosom, she will be your mother.' The song weaved through her introspection.

You are not a part of me. I cannot accept you.

Mara's eyes flicked open at a peculiar voice whispering in her ear.

Your servitude to another cannot be undone.

'What?!' She hissed.

I can offer no consolation. But hear my wisdom, you can choose the form your service will take.

I will serve no-one. Peace left her and rage surged up again. She glanced around, wondering if others could hear anything. Heads were bowed and the counsellor's chant continued. Beside her, Earona had her eyes closed. Mara turned back to the water, muttering, 'Who the hell am I supposed to be a servant to?'

You are a vassal of the Wrath.

Whatever that meant... 'Bloody bollocks.' The end of the song startled her. Gradually, she stood, noticing she was the last to do so.

Adiana and Earona waited for her. Earona's serene countenance repulsed her. Mara grilled her with an abrasive stare, sending her back a step. Adiana nodded at Mara, and her tone was impervious. 'You have heard the voice of your Mother.'

Mara's fist clenched into balls ready to slam into someone. 'She's not my mother.' Her face grim, she stamped out of the temple.

Frowning, Adiana watched her leave, but said to Earona, 'It's time to get back to your duties.'

Earona raced up to Mara. 'Did you hear something?'

Mara fumed at the invasive remarks. But should she really be surprised, she didn't belong there or even with normal people. 'I thought I liked it here... but—'

'Yes?'

Mara opened her mouth, but shut it in a cruel grimace.

Earona said, with sudden irritability, 'Tell me.'

'I... there's nothing to tell.' How could she explain she was damned by something she didn't understand? She pressed on her charm, safe under her robe, hoping there its purpose was true and it was working.

Earona sighed and latched onto her arm. 'When there is, I'll be waiting.'

Mara pulled her arm away and walked ahead.

~ * ~

Dario strolled the pavement, basking in the heady thrill of a gold filled pouch and the affections of a blonde-haired, blue-eyed beauty. Gambling was never this fun, and certainly it was not as dangerous with Vivella. He and Hellier had been at it for nearly three days straight, but still, there was no way it could last, they had to make the most of it. If they kept going the way they were, they would get caught. Eventually.

He was on his way to see Vivella while Hellier visited Marcus at a shop down by the docks. 'Annabella...' He remembered her shop and the woman like a blurred dream. The mention of her brought back an ill-feeling. Fiddling with the empty vial he still kept, he recalled she gave it to him, but with a disturbing realization he didn't know why she did...

He arrived at the servants' gate of the palace. Vivella rushed across the hectic courtyard, her loose brown hair flying behind her, to grab him in a tight embrace.

'You received my message.' He hugged her plump torso and held her away to appraise her appearance. In a flowing pastel green dress, her bosom bulged over the bodice, and her demure eyes shone with affection. 'You are an exquisite picture, like the sun shining on the high meadow. Delightful.'

'This is a wonderful change. You haven't taken a hit to your head?' She giggled and linking her arm through his, they strolled towards the servant entry.

'My heart compels me, and my mind agrees.'

'And I assume you have come to apologize?'

'Apologize?' He had trouble remembering what he did to offend her, however, he was not about to ask. 'Of course, my sweet rose, I apologize.' He crooked his head and kissed her cheek.

A faint pink touched her pale skin. 'Let us go up to my rooms.'

Vivella's suite was the size of a house. But, she was the king's niece, anything less would be shameful. Her rooms were lavished with white and gold furnishings, and miniature pieces of art that only seemed to need dusting. A servant brought in a tea tray and bite-size crab on tiny biscuits. The only reason Dario was permitted to enter the palace was Vivella allowed him. Her royal family humoured her. He was happy as long as he didn't have to speak to them, especially King Basylus.

They reclined on embroidered cushions on her enormous lounge and Dario relaxed amid her familiar chatter. Vivella began with haughty self-assurance, 'My mission for the Shrrozrak is coming along, even better than I expected.'

'Your mission?' The Shrrozrak were an illegal religious group known for beguiling the wealthy and naive. Not surprised by her admission, she was always being duped by some cult or organization.

'Exposing magik here in the palace.' She nudged him. 'Remember?'

Confused at why he had no recollection, he mumbled, 'Why is that?'

She sat forward on the seat and her hand fluttered with enthusiasm. 'I sense the pull of magik centering on some important event.'

The Shrrozrak were rumoured to use civilians to further their own plans. Why she would be involved with such people, he didn't know. A forgotten memory of them arguing and falling out on this issue alarmed him. 'It will be dangerous. You must keep away from such things.'

'You're worried about me. That's sweet. And I understand your concerns.' She waved her finger at him. 'But I'm not as weak as you might think.'

He gulped down his food with surprise. 'You know I don't like it. But — I'm not going to stop you.'

'You can't anyway.' Smiling, she shifted closer and placed a firm hand on his thigh. 'There's an event coming up in the gardens and I want you to attend. I have clothes you can wear.' She pressed on his leg and her breast touched his ribs.

Dario's body woke to the pleasurable touch of her hand sliding up his thigh in a slow caress. Gazing into her hungry eyes, he saw a wanton attractiveness there. She had flirted with him countless times, but this time her overt sensuality aroused him. Seizing her face in his hands, he kissed her, igniting a passion he never felt before. He wanted her as much as she wanted him and stopping it was impossible. Not understanding how she previously escaped his attention, he reacted with the same intense ardour he was receiving.

She whispered in his ear, 'you've changed, Dario, and for the better. Let us retreat to the bedroom where we can be less inhibited.'

'The bedroom?' Trembling hesitation assailed him. 'You mean, me and you…'

~ * ~

Hellier had visited every gambling room Dario knew of, and with every group of gamblers and every coin tossed in, the grief over the loss of her Kin was forgotten. As well, with each winning hand, adrenaline pulsed through her like wine, making her hungry for more. Only when she finished at a table did thoughts of Earona, Ethan, and Shiarn crash into her mind. The gambling created a greater need than just money. But underlying her dangerous activities was her fear of Jett finding out. It wasn't she didn't want to tell him, but the longer she left it, the harder it was to say anything.

Marcus' illness shook her out of her craving for the next win, and also compounded her need not to tell Jett what she was up to. It would add to his worries. She spent the morning with Marcus. Once assured of his recovery, she came back to the White Horse to wait for Dario.

Eventually he breezed in with a wide grin, and strolled over to her. 'I apologize for my tardiness.'

'I see you had a good time.'

'Very much so.' He flopped in the chair beside her. 'We drank tea, reminisced.'

She snapped, 'We are going to the Ruby Ring this afternoon?'

'Perhaps, my lovely one, we should expand our activities.' He winked at her and reached for her hand, caressing it softly.

She was itching to get out and play cards. 'Not right now.'

He stroked her cheek, bringing it close for a kiss. 'We could make sweet music together?'

Her lips pressed on his, but she pulled away fearful someone would see. 'I want to play a little more. I've almost got enough.'

Disappointment cleared from his face. 'Of course. Shall we be off?'

They had visited over a dozen taverns; Gull's Nest, Round Tower, Gold Leaf, were a few Hellier recalled with fondness, the ones she won the most coin. All of them turning out to be classier than the Rosy Parrot, but the Ruby Ring was the cream of the bunch - the gold mine, as Dario said. No dramas had befallen them and their underhanded schemes ran smoothly. The amount of money crossing her hands amazed her.

They arrived at the Ruby Ring with a few hours of daylight left. Situated in the Salisbury District, the tavern was one of the wealthiest in Floris. Hellier entered sometime after Dario. She walked into bright lighting from glass lanterns on the wall, and underfoot; luxurious red rugs ran the length of the whole room. Silver plates and matching utensils were on every table, as well as candles in red glass holders. Dario was not wrong about the opulence. Despite his assurance, 'disreputable looking characters frequent the back room,' she was anxious over her unconventional appearance. Now she longed to see someone who remotely resembled her.

Patrons, dressed in velvets and stiff lace, sat at round tables with red cushioned chairs. Their wigs were crimped to perfection, and the room was scented with perfumes mixed with spicy tobacco. She scanned the room, sensing eyes on her, but not wanting to look directly at anyone.

With a boastful swagger, she approached a neatly dressed man behind the counter, so wide she leaned over to whisper the password. He directed her to a door away from the diners. Once she entered the stale air of the back room, she sighed with relief. Similar in appearance to the room out front - thick carpet, chunky round tables - yet the people resembled those she was accustomed to seeing. She almost felt at home.

Thankfully, a chair was free at Dario's table. She was glad to see a number of scruffy, mean looking men amidst the better dressed ones. Just because someone wore decent clothes did not mean one was wealthy, so Dario told her. She was fast learning how the game 'worked', and she created her own deceptive mask.

The game started and it wasn't long before she realized how high the stakes were at this new venue. Now she better understood why Dario left this place till last. You needed the coin just to sit at the table. As the game progressed the bets got higher. Shiny gold coins made a messy pile in the centre of the table. She took her share, happy to see her heap grow. Soon enough the stakes increased, and small gems appeared amongst the coin. Hiding the trepidation in her eyes, she glimpsed Dario, staring deadpan at the gems. After a few more rounds, he threw down his cards in defeat and took his winnings. He left by a back exit.

She felt the second pouch under her belt; the one from the dead man. Her hand searched through it. She put one of the gems down, hoping it would keep her in for a few more games. Without Dario, she was at the disadvantage, but she wouldn't back out now.

Throughout the game, one man caught her attention. An older man with a wide face and auburn hair, slouched most of the time and spoke with a lazy drawl. Under his bushy brows one of his eyes glinted gold from its glass centre. His conversation lurched from cargo ships to underground trade, and her ears pricked up at every word almost too distraction. Even with all he said, it was never informative.

'...found us some missing people,' his lethargic voice pushed through everyone else's conversation, 'Cost me a fortune in food, but you got to feed 'em.' He chortled, staring at Hellier. She gazed back, making the most of the opportunity to look at his unmoving eye. He went on, still staring, 'Opened one of 'em like a book, left my mark.'

A man in frills and maroon velvet lifted his chin. 'It is not surprising to discover you deal in second rate merchandise.' His curly haired wig remained stiff against his collar as he turned his head.

A stretch of smoke coiled from the rolled tobacco of the glass-eye man. 'Got to test the goods.'

The well-dressed man sat up and snorted. 'I believe you mean, break the goods.'

The other man's loud belly laughter shook the table.

Hellier glared, daring him to speak to her.

'No matter what, they bring good coin.' His good eye traced a line down Hellier's torso.

If she didn't speak she would explode. Slapping down a card, and with a heated stare, she snapped, 'Who are these people?'

'Never asked their names. Why?'

'I'm interested.'

'I know outsiders are worth a heap.' He flicked his eye to her face, giving her a piercing glare. 'Women even more and blonde women are double their weight in Lakhish.'

Hellier glowered, 'You can't afford it.'

'Reckon you're right.' He eyed her seriously while tossing his cards face up on the table. He nodded towards the sword sheathed on her back on a slant. 'And that would be worth more than ten of you.'

Barely able to concentrate on her hand, she growled, 'I don't need you telling me how much I'm worth.'

The man sat back in his slouch and chuckled along with the other men at the table. 'You better watch yourself, or you'll be finding out more than what you'd like to know.'

Hellier held her tongue, and focused on her playing, suddenly feeling repulsed by the man's one eye watching her every move. Finally she took a full hand and reaped in some coins. She stood and left the table and the room through a back exit. Apart from a single torch in the alcove of the doorway, the lane was dark. Her mind raced with apprehension over the time. Now the game had finished, the guilt was heavy.

Dario moved towards her from the shadows of a side alley.

Another figure loomed ominously. 'I knew it! You're working together.' Fists up, Big Pat punched Dario, sending him reeling to the ground like a sack of oats. Big Pat kicked him in the ribs.

'Get their money and we'll be off.' Another man appeared behind Hellier with a knife to her throat. 'Hand over your sword and your coin and this will end nicely.'

She had not come this far to be robbed. Elbowing the man in the ribs, she startled him enough to grab and twist his wrist. Surprise in his eyes, he cried in pain. She snatched the knife and slashed upward, cutting his forearm.

'You wanna play like that.' Smirking, he stepped in, trying to catch her arm.

'Come on.' She taunted him to get closer.

He moved with brash arrogance, gripping her knife wielding arm. She threw the blade over him, and caught it with her other hand, and stabbed into his ribs. Their bodies touched and she stared at his astonished expression and into eyes, growing weak. He dropped to the ground, dead.

Big Pat witnessed the fall with wide-eyed shock and started running. His cumbersome weight made him slow, enough for Hellier's flying knife to land solidly in his retreating back. He tripped, falling hard with a great thump. Moaning, he crawled, attempting to escape.

'Blood 'n shite!' Hellier barked, dashing to the gibbering man. There was only one way she was going to free herself from the mess she unexpectedly produced, and she had to act fast, they had already lingered too long. Yanking the blade from Big Pat's back, she stood over his bulk. He squirmed in vain as she lifted his head, and turning her face away, she dragged the blade across his throat. She threw the knife down and wiped as much blood from her hands on his shirt as she could manage. She lifted Dario to his feet and supported his beaten body into the dark of the laneway.

~ * ~

Hellier supported Dario through the back door of the White Horse and placed him on his bed. She examined his bruised and swollen face. He groaned when she pressed on his ribs. Her apologizes flowed, as if somehow the whole evening's chaos was her fault. She did not want to reflect on the dead men. In the explosive attack she thought it was the right thing to do, but now… she didn't want to dwell on it.

'That was…' his smile was slow. '… fun.'

She flinched. 'That's not the word I would use.' Obviously he had not witnessed her drop the men like they were old pigs. She decided to wash up first and take some moments to calm herself. The thought of facing Jett unnerved her.

Hellier spoke to Burgman at the counter, explaining Dario's condition and could he check on him with a bowl of food. He hurried off to see how his prize entertainment was faring.

Jett and Keanan sat in a booth in the tavern devoid of music, although it appeared not to affect the intake of the inn. Approaching their table, she smiled while Jett stared darkly and Keanan looked perplexed. Covering her thoughts with the best superficial mask she could muster, she sat beside Jett and took a spoonful of stew. After swallowing, she muttered, 'How is Marcus?'

'He's better,' answered Keanan.

Jett's brooding stare was fixed on her. 'What happened?'

223

She sensed his penetrating judgments, but her thoughts were all over the place and she couldn't distinguish them herself. 'Nothing… really.'

'And where is Dario?' Keanan inquisitively lifted an eyebrow at the stage.

Avoiding eye contact, she attempted a half truth. 'He was beaten up. He's in his room now, recovering.'

Jett frowned with suspicion. 'And you were there?'

'Yes.' She paid special attention to her food. 'He won't be able to play tonight. I hope Burgman doesn't lose customers.'

His glare intensified. 'And where did this happen?'

'Umm, Salisbury District,' she mumbled, *we went to a tavern, the Ruby Ring. To eat.*

'You're eating now,' commented Jett, shrewdly looking at her dish.

She gulped her food down. 'It was too expensive so we walked around and this man wanted to rob us and he started laying into Dario.'

'Why didn't you tell me?' His tone was menacing though his eyes conveyed more hurt than anger.

She glanced at him with distrust in her sharp eyes, sensing his impending rage at her subtle deception. 'No need. Everything is fine now.' She ate as much as she had stomach for and stood from the table. 'I'm going to see him.'

Jett watched flabbergasted as she walked from the room. He shook his head in dismay at Keanan. *What is she up to?* 'It's time I had a talk with Dario.'

'Sounds like an idea.'

30 - Abrupt Meetings

The Heart can sustain a limited degree of pressure before it bleeds into the body in uncontrollable acts.
The Heart must learn wisdom in acknowledging its burdens.

Valfaèr, Elements of Arcane Power

The next morning, Hellier sat on her bed in the small room she shared with Keanan. Sinister apparitions paraded through her dreams, leaving a morbid mark on her wellbeing. The sensation of slitting soft flesh continued occurring in her memory, as well as his last words. They had played cards together, they talked, she knew his name. Now, forever in her mind, he was sprawled in an alley, blood spreading with the dirty infested puddles.

After washing again, she went to Dario in his room in an attempt to gain some solace.

His weak smile was almost obscured by his red, puffy face. 'How are you, my intrepid doveling?'

She sat beside him on his bed and studied the wounds on his twig-thin bare chest. 'I wasn't hurt. How are you?' She bound new dressing around his torso to hold his bones steady.

'As fragile as a dry leaf. However, I told Burgman I can still play.' He laughed and clenched his side, groaning. 'He was very understanding.'

'That's because you are very popular.'

'My apologizes for last night, I shouldn't have waited—'

'No, I'm sorry,' she interrupted. 'I shouldn't have played on. The wealth on the table was outrageous. What was I thinking?' Passion for the win stole her senses. Even now, she wanted to play to wipe the tainted thoughts away.

'You say you had gems? In hindsight, you probably didn't need to gamble at all.' He struggled to cough. 'I could have taken you to a good jeweler.'

She grinned, tapping on her bulging pouch. 'You still can.'

'How did you do?'

'Fabulously, I'll share with you later. Now, remember what to tell Jett when he asks.'

'You think he will?'

'I'm sure of—' She shut up at a sharp knock on the door.

Dario answered with a shaky, 'Come in.'

At the sight of Jett, Hellier sprang from the bed.

'morning.' Jett raised a wary eyebrow at the half-naked Dario. 'I've come to see how you are.'

Dario sat straighter. 'I'm much improved, thank you for asking.'

With mistrust in his eyes, Jett glanced at Hellier. 'Can you go upstairs while I have a word with Dario?'

Grimacing at him, she rose to her feet with reluctance. *Don't you hurt him!* She fired off as she passed him.

Jett scowled and shut the door behind her. He sat rigid on the only chair. 'I hear you got involved in a brawl last night.' Dario repeated the same story Hellier gave him, as he expected. Jett said, 'Can I have a look?'

Dario lifted his arm.

Jett prodded his ribs with a hard finger. 'You'll live,' he said, 'As you can understand I am very protective of Hellier.' He studied Dario's blank expression, waiting for his words to take hold. 'If your intentions towards her are anything but honourable you could find yourself in serious trouble.'

Dario's cheeks flushed a dull pink under the swelling.

'Hellier has taken a liking to you, but if you do anything to hurt her.' Jett pointed firmly into Dario's chest. 'Then you better hope I don't find you. Take this as advice as I hope we can still get on as friends.' He finished in a more or less cordial manner.

Dario nodded, coughing loudly, and rubbing the spot where Jett's finger had him. 'I care about Hellier. I would not do anything to hurt her.'

Jett patted him hard on the shoulder. 'Hope you get better soon.' He left the room and spied Hellier lingering near the stairs. They locked eyes in silence, her features showing a deep sadness while he looked intense and unyielding. She gave him an indignant cold shoulder before running upstairs. He watched her unrepentantly, feeling the burden of her mistrust.

~ * ~

Keanan waited on Forest in the walk-about area. Jett took Thunder's reigns from him and mounted in silence. They led Lightning and Rose out of the yard with Keanan making idle chatter, ranging from Marcus' health to Dario being brutalized. Jett's only response was agreeing grumbles or blatant reticence. Keanan finally let out a heavy sigh. 'Are you going to *say* what's wrong?'

Jett snapped, 'I don't want to talk about it.'

Keanan remained quiet throughout their ride to Annabella's, and Jett's bleak mood did not change by the time they arrived. Leaving Keanan with the horses, Jett pushed the door in a brusque manner, and called, 'Ready to go?'

Marcus and Seth sat at Annabella's cluttered table saying their farewells. Seth played with the dog, Sweetie while Konan ran around Marcus. Marcus slowly stood from the chair. 'We are.'

Annabella handed Seth a leather pouch of medicinal mixtures for Marcus' dressings. Marcus gave Annabella a stiff hug, and he and Seth did not miss out on a motherly embrace. The two men thanked her again as Jett held the door open for them to leave.

He turned to her and pressed a pouch into her hands. 'As you know Marcus is worth a lot more than this to us.'

Rolling the clinking pouch in her hand, she looked at him with surprise. 'You are generous. This will come back to you, you'll see, because *you* know what I want,' she said and waved at Keanan through the window and he kindly waved back. 'Take care of yourself and your friends. Whether you think so or not, they really do need you.'

Jett's eyes narrowed skeptically. 'You also take care.'

Annabella stood at her door, watching them leave her street.

~ * ~

On arrival back at the inn, they noticed Hellier was nowhere to be found. It only aggravated Jett's sullen mood. He planned to investigate what he could of the prison near the docks, but first he decided to visit Margo's Hat shop in the Salisbury District. In his current mood, he didn't think it wise to converse with guards and officials especially since he had no idea how he would be received. A situation of that magnitude would be best handled by someone with more diplomacy, someone like Keanan.

Colourful buildings and petite trees lined the cleaner streets in the Salisbury District. People sashayed past them in flashy attire. Jett observed an occasional man wearing the unfamiliar, yet seemingly fashionable wig. It was flagrantly apparent they had entered the better part of Floris.

As they walked, Keanan continued pushing Jett for conversation. 'If you don't want to talk about it at least stop thinking it.'

'You should have seen the way she looked at me.' Jett finally cracked under Keanan's prodding. 'She actually likes that weed of a man. And, I think she hates me.'

'She has been acting odd lately, but we have all been on edge. Hate is a touch extreme.'

Jett dug his hands in his pockets. 'I can't talk to her.'

'Regardless, you will have to eventually,' Keanan said. 'This is the place. Do you have the decorum for this?'

They stopped at a shop front with a red carved hat swaying above the wide window display. Hats and long curly wigs on head stands decorated the shelf inside. 'I'm in the mood,' Jett said, 'for this.'

A plump middle-aged woman in a lace-ruffled dress, watched with a puzzled frown as they entered. Her dark pink dress nearly tipped her bosom out as she leaned towards them. Suddenly her disposition changed from cool to loquacious, and she gushed, 'Good morning, young gentlemen. What a pleasure—'

Jett slammed his hand down on the counter. 'We want to see the Collector.'

Disappointment stole her cheerful smile. 'I see.'

Keanan stepped forward and eased Jett away. He said with genuine politeness, 'We haven't an appointment, but it's quite important.'

The woman gave Keanan her full attention, her pout turning to a coy smile. 'Have you come regarding the taxes?'

'We have indeed.' Keanan smiled, his eyes lighting up with realization.

The woman, assumedly Margo, informed them the Tax Collector was currently upstairs. 'First door on the left.'

They walked upstairs and Jett knocked at the door. A weak sounding voice bade them enter. He opened the door to a small yet lavishly decorated room. Broad legged chairs were in front of a scroll scattered desk, and seated behind, a man in a dark velvet suit, wearing the customary wig. Busy rifling through papers on his desk, he did not spare them a glance. 'I presume you are here for the tax jobs?'

Jett walked across the red rug and stood at the front of the desk.

Without waiting for a reply, the man lectured, 'It's strictly daylight hours. Night time collections are no longer viable at this time. If you have to use force more than three times you have to think of an alternate method, if you are able to give that some thought.' He chuckled, and dragging his attention from his papers, he glimpsed Jett's unfriendly expression and looked back down again. 'In your line of work it shouldn't be too difficult to think of something. You get a quarter each of the take, and only once a week—'

'We haven't come for a job,' Jett spat out.

The man looked up and responded with mild surprise, 'Oh?'

'We've come to tell you to stop harassing and robbing innocent hard workers,' Jett growled.

Dropping his papers, the Collector stood from his desk with sudden alarm. 'And who are you to make such a demand?'

Jett reached across the desk and took hold of the man's shirt front. He would have preferred his neck, but it was out of reach. 'Someone who doesn't like taxes.' He shook him, causing his face to turn crimson.

Keanan clasped Jett's hand, loosening his grip. After disentangling his fingers from the man's ruffles, Keanan said in a reasonable manner, 'We are looking out for the interests of the people. You don't look as if you need extra coin.' He paused, and the man's face continued to flame a bright red. 'We appeal to your sense of humanity and to the consideration we will go to the authorities with everything we know.'

The Collector adjusted his sliding wig, attempting to recover some dignity. Avoiding eye contact with Jett scowling with anger, he stated to Keanan, 'You have no idea what you are asking. I would like you to leave this instant.'

Keanan responded, 'Think wisely about this.'

Stepping out from Jett's reach, the Collector moved to the door and opened it for them. Jett glared at him all the way and Keanan followed. 'Thank you for your time.'

'Humph!'

Outside on the street, Keanan looked up at the window. The curtain was pulled back and the man's face watched them walk the street. 'I have no idea how that went.'

Jett remained sullen.

At last their pace eased although they still walked in silence. Keanan said, 'Do you think he'd have us followed?'

Jett finally answered, 'I don't think so. He was unprepared for that... Kean... I'm sorry about what happened back there.'

'You were bordering on *murderous*.'

Jett cringed. He was too bottled up with anxiety to act rationally.

'Let's hope he doesn't have the guards looking for us.' Keanan sighed grimly. 'Now where?'

After some moments of brooding, Jett said, 'We could go to a tavern.'

'A tavern?'

I know where it is, I asked Burgman. He headed towards it, with Keanan tagging behind, protesting.

Set a little way from the street, the Ruby Ring was an imposing red building. Vermillion flowers hung from delicate trees along the miniature walkway, and looking down on the quaint frontage was a wrought iron balcony. 'Oh, by Kahm, this is extravagant,' Keanan said.

Jett jumped up the short flight of steps and gazed at the carved tangle of roses on the mahogany double door. It was difficult to picture Hellier drinking in such an elegant establishment.

'At least there is a place by that name,' Keanan said.

'Jett. How fortunate to see you here.'

The Captain's voice sent a swift tremor of anxiety through Jett's gut and he turned to greet him with a congenial nod. 'Tonius Shark.'

'How have you been enjoying Floris?' Tonius Shark spoke in a friendly manner. However, Jett knew better.

'It's been interesting enough.'

Accompanying Tonius was a man wearing a curly wig matching his extravagant attire, and he stared at Jett with arrogant aloofness. The Captain went on, 'What brings you up to this more distinguished part of town?'

'I heard this is a good tavern, I decided to see for myself.'

'It is.' His cordial smile faded, replaced by a frown of distrust. 'Strange coincidence you are here after what happened last night.'

Knocked off guard, Jett replied with genuine surprise, 'I don't know what you mean.'

The Captain studied him diffidently. 'Aren't you inquisitive?'

'I don't want to pry,' Jett replied. *Keanan, don't speak a word!*

'I've an investment in this tavern, and I hope it doesn't lose its reputation over the double murder last night.' He stepped nearer, his eyes flicking with intensity over Jett's face. 'They were good workers.' He paused. 'Don't be concerned. I received your message from Sim.' Slight lines of care creased Tonius' forehead, and his eyes took in Keanan standing at Jett's side. 'You make me more curious when you wish to hide.'

'I value my privacy and that is all I meant by it. I'm sure you would understand how I might feel in regard to being watched.'

'Notice no one has been following you.' His disengaging tone left Jett more distrustful than ever. 'The trouble with this murder.' His voice rose with unexpected anger. 'They were killed in a despicable manner at the back of my premises and I have a problem with that.'

'A terrible misfortune,' Jett replied. 'Any idea who did it?'

'Not as yet. I'm going to question the staff to find out who it might be. There's some speculation the person came from the back room.'

'Back room?' Jett had no idea what he was referring to.

'Betting tables are out the back, although I don't make that public knowledge. I'm in quite a rush and must be off. No doubt we shall meet again.' The Captain stepped past Jett.

'I hope you find what you need to know.'

'I shall and I'll take care of whoever has done this to me. It's unthinkable,' he said with genuine fervour. He and his companion entered the Ruby Ring.

Jett exhaled slowly, and walked away without a word with Keanan trailing after.

With irritation, Keanan finally spoke. 'And that was?'

'My contact for the slave trade,' Jett said over his shoulder as he dodged people along the busy street. After several moments of intense brooding, Jett declared to Keanan who caught up to his fast strides, 'I bet he has men waiting outside the gambling room to rob those coming out.' His anger swelled, his thoughts becoming more enraged as he tossed it over in his mind. 'Or… they saw her sword. Curse it.' *I'm so flamin' furious, I'm going to kill someone.*

'At least we know what might have happened to her,' Keanan offered. 'Are you going to slow a moment and talk to me?'

Jett fired back, 'I don't know who to be more angry with, that fiend or Hellier.'

'I think it's time you had that talk with her.'

~ * ~

They walked back to the White Horse under a cloud of growing apprehension, and with Jett's fury increasing as his mind replayed Hellier's actions. Once back, Jett sat at the bar while Keanan went upstairs to see if she had returned. Under dark furrowed brows, he watched Dario sitting alone at a nearby table. Jett leaned over the counter. 'Burgman, can I ask a favour?'

His moustache bristled over a mischievous smile. 'Sure, long as it's legal.'

'If anyone asks, Hellier no longer lodges at this inn,' Jett whispered, 'she's gone missing and you haven't seen her. Don't say anything about us or our connection with her.'

Burgman frowned. 'Am I going to look like a liar?'

'No.'

'Am I going to get any more visitors?'

'I hope not.'

Burgman pressed his lips together. 'Good enough.'

Keanan stood at the doorway, shaking his head at Jett.

Jett pulled out a chair and dragged it to face Dario. He sat with a loud thump. A look of nervous alarm alighted Dario's face. Wound as tight as a spring, Jett leaned towards him. 'Hellier's not here, can you tell me where she would be?'

Creasing his brow, Dario sat upright to meet him. 'I don't know if it's for me—'

Jett pounded the table with his fist, bouncing the candle-holder and upturning mugs, and making Dario jump with fright. 'Wrong answer,' he growled. 'Those men who beat you up last night, who were they?'

Under Jett's severe glare Dario trembled. 'I… don't know.'

'Well, I do. They were men employed by the Captain.'

Dario's look of sudden terror was palpable.

'I'm guessing you've heard of him. Now, you and I know what happened to those men.'

Dario nodded, pressing his lips together.

Jett stated with measured deliberateness. 'Tell me where she is.'

31 - New Face – Old Race

Victory is in store for the upright and the course of the just is guarded

The Hidden Shield

Dinner was the same stew Mara had eaten for the last couple of nights. For once she agreed with Earona's complaints, she too would have liked an apple pie or roasted chicken. She attended worship in the temple that day, and it seemed a pointless exercise. Unlike the first time, she heard nothing in her thoughts, but a stone hard silence. As much as she tried to find peace in the song, it had become just noise to her. Initially she was happy, but now her resentment was growing.

'…dirty sudsy water.' Earona turned over her prune-like hands. 'How many dishes do they use here? I've never seen anything like it.'

Mara walked a few steps ahead with her bowl. 'I watched the children play again.' She mentioned it because she knew it irked Earona. For Mara it was a lot of noise and commotion that gave her a headache.

'Just your luck.'

'Most of them are orphans.' Mara put down her bread, and leaned close. 'One boy is blind.'

'Terrible.' Earona's gaze was on her stew, but her mind was elsewhere. 'I wonder…'

'You could heal him?'

'Shush!' Earona put a finger to her lips. 'I don't see how anyway.' Under her breath, she said, 'Besides I'd probably get into trouble.'

That night, across the space between their beds, Earona said, 'Did you hear a word today?'

'Why would I?' Mara punched the pillow down.

'Hmm.' Earona watched her with a furrowed brow. 'You're lucky. I'm hearing the weirdest thing.'

Mara closed her eyes, expressing as much disinterest as she could, despite wanting to know.

'Maybe it's not so strange,' Earona said, 'The voice said I have to watch out for you.'

Mara's eyes flicked open in sudden suspicion.

'Which I was quite glad to do anyway.' Earona lay down and added, 'But, it really does make me wonder…what could I do against anything that would come after you…'

Silence stretched between them. After the lights in the room were extinguished, Mara spoke in a trembling whisper, 'You mean something… like those things at Lanvin?'

'Do you think?' Earona was quiet for some moments. 'Those horrible beasts. That's why I wonder — does the voice mean watch over you or… does it mean something else?'

'Who cares? I'd prefer no one watching me at all!' Mara's heart sank at the notion. What would that arrogant voice know about her anyway?

~ * ~

Jett pulled his hood over, shutting out the people on the streets, and he wrapped his cloak tighter against the ever-present sea breeze. He was alone with his thoughts and it was not a pleasant place to dwell. Dario told him where Hellier might be and a lot more besides. Jett had dashed off in search of her. The chances of the Captain finding her were high. She stood out like a flag on a wall; brawling on the street and visiting taverns. To make it worse, she carried her malreus blade everywhere. Tonius was sure to hear about it. Another grumbling curse escaped him. Hellier and he were always close. He liked to think they still were, but right then he had his doubts. She had turned from him to a stranger. It did not sit well with his pride.

Inside the music shop, he spoke with the elderly man and money was exchanged. He left the store humbled, but no less worried about her whereabouts. It was an uneventful walk to the east of the city, with no guarantee she would be there. Finally, he trudged up the slope to the tower on the cliff. A great fire blazed on the tower top, illuminating the twilight sky. He walked around to the side facing the blustering wind, and a ledge, providing a splendid view of the port and ocean.

Concealed by her hood and cloak, Hellier sat motionless. Whether she knew Jett approached or not she made no sign to acknowledge his presence. A fierce wind blew, cutting through his clothing; his skin bristled underneath. He made a noisy display of clearing the gravel beside her and sat down.

'What are you doing here?' Her voice cracked with emotion and she kept her eyes on the ocean.

'I bought a peace offering.' He revealed the wooden box from the shop and handed it to her.

She took it onto her lap and unhooked the bronze latch. Drawing a tapered breath, she stroked the violin's fine wood. 'Oh…'

They shared a tense silence, until Jett was compelled to speak. 'We have a problem.'

'Really?' A bite was in her tone. 'I thought that obvious.'

Jett bristled with annoyance. 'Now we have more problems.'

She took a long loud breath. 'I know…'

'You have to learn control—'

'You don't understand.' Her words fired out with sudden angst. 'It started with that Skar in Lanvin, and then some men… and… I can't … it's like… I can't seem to deny my — nature. All my training… what is it for?' *It's too easy… to kill.* 'I feel… wrong.'

He listened in a grim quiet, her sadness weakening his fury. 'I do understand. Better than most.'

She scrunched up her lips and stiffened her shoulders.

'I know what it's like to bear the consequences of hard decisions.'

'No.' She shook her head free from her hood. 'You see, you don't understand.'

Rubbing his forehead, he took a resigned breath. 'Right. I get it.' He disliked talking about this particular issue, but in this case she needed to hear it. 'You think you need to take it as far as you can, to push it beyond what is expected.' He paused. 'As if you have to prove something.'

She glowered and lowered her chin onto her raised knees. *It's not fair—*

'You don't need to prove anything to us, and you should no longer need to prove it to yourself.' *Even I…*

'What about you?'

'How do you think I know what you are talking about?' He looked past her acrimonious gaze. 'It's true, sometimes I need to prove myself. But *you* have to exercise self-control. Don't react impulsively.'

It's not just me. 'Why not you—'

'Because it's you who is in serious trouble. And because of that, it's all of us.' He placed a hand on her shoulder and shivered in the freezing wind.

'It's cold up here?'

'Very.'

Hellier put her arm around his waist and held tight, giving him the supernatural warmth of her body. He turned his gaze to the sea in contemplation, and let his thoughts slip into her mind, *sorry I haven't been there for you, if you needed to talk about it.*

She nestled her head onto his shoulder, comfortable in his embrace. Both of them looked out at the ocean growing dark with the fading sunlight. Waves rolled in grand sweeping walls and crashed against the outlying rocks. In the far distance, a flash of lightning struck the sea, illuminating the horizon of mountainous clouds. She eventually broke the shared peace. 'You know what happened?'

Her words brought the situation crashing back into his thoughts. He stood, reluctantly, in the new night and offered her his hand. 'It's worse than you think,' he said with stern reproach, 'You pissed off the Captain.'

Staring wide-eyed, she took his hand and clutched the case close to her chest. 'The one you've been talking about?'

'The same.' He reported what transpired earlier, as they walked the incline. '—and you are carrying an expensive sought-after blade. He may trace us through that.' He finished with mock severity, 'And, we really should talk about your gambling problem.'

Hellier smiled. 'Really, Jett, it's no longer a problem. I have enough coin for everyone to get an instrument.'

'Why weren't you up there buying them?'

A tinge of pink highlighted the blue of her eyes. *I couldn't…*

He didn't push the issue. 'You won't be spending so much time with Dario either.'

'It's not his fault. I'm the one who dragged him into this mess.' *Got him beaten up.*

I doubt that. After this incident, he trusted Dario less and less. 'You like him?'

'It's surprising, I never thought I would.'

'That's a shock.' He held back his caustic reply and said, 'He's not really your type.'

'How would you know?'

It was no secret Hellier held a special fondness for Jett, but he persistently kept himself from caring about any girl. He shrugged, his expression blank. 'Maybe I was assuming too much, but I thought...' *someone more like me...*

She pouted. 'Don't joke with me.'

They walked in an awkward silence for several minutes. Hellier eventually grumbled, 'You can't have everything you know.'

After a moment, he said, 'I don't trust him.'

'What a surprise.'

'I can't explain why.' He sighed loudly. *Maybe it's not just that. Maybe it's...* something he was incapable of talking about with her.

'You're not jealous?'

He searched his thoughts for the answer. Once discovering it, he did not feel like being truthful about it.

'You are!'

I'm not going to talk about it now.

She shook her head in astonishment.

He said, 'Don't let your feelings for him deceive you.'

Hellier gave a throaty snort in return.

~ * ~

That night the Kin stayed in their rooms. The fire was a warm crackling, and Burgman gave them a bottle of mead to share. Hellier pulled out her new fiddle to show off to Burgman. He was cross he could not make use of her skill, she would have fetched a great crowd. After he left, she dumped her earnings, as she referred to them, on the middle bed for all to see.

Astonished by the pile, Seth gasped. 'And where has all this come from?'

She ran her fingers through the glaze of gold, silver, and bright gems. 'I don't know how much is there.'

Seth rolled his eyes. 'I didn't ask that.'

'Well,' she started dramatically, '...it's a long story...'

Jett jumped in with an irritated scowl. 'It's from card games.'

'You've been gambling?!' Seth's voice flowed with excitement. 'I would never have guessed.'

'Gambling, eh?' Marcus said, 'Dario's not the sop we thought he was.'

'He's not,' she snapped.

Marcus viewed the winnings. 'Can you teach me some plays?'

'Umm... love too.' She went to her things and pulled out a deck of cards, and sat at the table where Jett was already seated. Marcus and Seth joined them.

Keanan inspected the abundance of coins. 'Are you just going to leave this scattered about?'

'Can you take it?' Hellier sensed everyone's eyes boring into her. 'What? I don't want to hold onto it anymore.'

Keanan scooped up the small fortune and put it back into the pouch. 'We can really do with this.'

Smiling sweetly, she said, 'Let's play.' She shuffled the cards and glanced slyly about the table. 'Who's in?'

'Me,' said Marcus.

A playful sparkle was in Seth's eyes. 'Me too.'

She smiled at Jett with a glint in her eye. *Just tonight.*

Jett shook his head at her pretentious attitude. 'No more gambling rooms.'

'I'm good you know.' She narrowed her eyes and started dealing.

'You're not good at all,' Jett said, 'you're a hellcat.'

Ethan was roused from a light sleep by a rasping cough close by. Opening his eyes, he viewed scruffy undernourished men sitting and laying about. A constant flow of mutterings and movement made it impossible to sleep well. The air was colder now, but the light of the cavern was unchanging. He lay restlessly on the fraying mats and noticed the few men with blankets had the physical prowess to demand such luxuries. He had a thought it was night, yet he could not say how long he was asleep. He had only arrived that day and already time was lost to him.

He spent what seemed like hours talking to the stocky long haired men. They were Harn from Stonharn, islands in the eastern ocean. Their ship was overrun by pirates who killed their captain along with other crew. Most of them could speak the common language of New Empire while the others spoke together in their own tongue. Ethan did not feel obliged to talk about his own story, but as the candid conversation continued, he was more comfortable describing his experience in the jail. As well as mentioning his friends, he spoke of the senyu Menhrs that brought him to Floris. These structures were not unfamiliar to the Harn and were known as Veyers Stars. The Harn tossed around plans of escape. Over all it was fraught with difficulties. Ethan contemplated what his power could do to help him escape, but he said nothing of that to them.

He stood on shaky feet and stretched his rigid aching body, and stepped between the men's bodies crowded up against each other. Numerous haggard eyes reflected the helplessness of despairing men. The smell of the deep hole within the dark chamber hit his senses, and he spent a short time there. On the way back to his 'space', he brushed against a man as big as himself. With a bald head and messy beard, a mean glint was in his eye, and his voice cracked. 'Oi, you!'

Ethan turned, paying him polite attention.

'Don't touch me, boy.' The man had rotten teeth and old scarring along the side of his face.

Putting his cuffed wrists forward, Ethan shrugged with a sheepish grin. The man glanced at the chains and shoved him out the way. Ethan stepped on a man's leg and he groaned with pain.

Ethan plonked himself down and leant against the wall.

Men rose to their feet and hollered. Ethan did the same. Half a dozen guards, outfitted with short crossbows and long pole weapons, came up the chamber passage. They stepped aside for a muscle bound bald man wheeling a monstrous iron pot.

Loc came up beside him. 'Feeding time.'

Ethan wondered if it was foolish to give away the bowl. Pushing and jostling for the pouring ladle, men held their bowls out through the bars. His stomach screaming for food, Ethan stood behind a smaller man and looked with hope to the one pouring out a pale broth.

The one bearing the food frowned at Ethan, and unhooking a tarnished bowl from his belt, he filled it. 'You're lucky. Someone didn't need it no more.'

Ethan took it with grateful words and stepped away from the mob.

Loc said, 'Wait.'

After the pot was emptied, the man broke off chunks of bread from round loaves and threw them into the chamber. The men fell over themselves grabbing any scrap they could reach. Over their heads, Ethan caught a lump the size of a small hand. He went back to his space to devour it and his broth.

Loc noticed his eagerness. 'You got to savour it.'

The men from Stonharn sat against the wall, taking their time over the meagre meal as if it was a feast. Maddog sat beside him with his bread, and silence reigned as he ate. The broth had little flavour and did nothing to fill Ethan's stomach, but he made the most of it.

~ * ~

The Harn, Gart, sat cross-legged on the worn mats, clearing the loose dirt away. On the smoothed floor, he used a stiff flake to mark indiscriminate lines. Ethan watched his movements with concentrated interest, as did others around him. The slightest new activity occupied Ethan's attention and he studied every new man who entered, as if it would somehow be someone he knew. The boredom was excruciating and on the same level as the cold and hunger. Even the mix of rank smells he could overcome and the ocean smell was now a part of the air he breathed. The time of day or night was completely lost and he existed in this unchanging twilight in a half awake dozing state.

Fish, a lanky man with a black scraggly beard, sat across from Gart. He was not Harn, yet like Ethan, had attached himself to their group. Gart handed Fish a handful of rock splinters and he rolled the stones onto whatever Gart drew onto the floor's dusty surface. Gart bent his neck to examine the picture the stones and markings depicted. The two men spent time discussing it.

Ethan strained to hear, but could only pick up random words of encouragement. The stones were gathered and Gart turned to Ethan with a commanding wave to come. Motivated by a need to do something, he hurried over.

Gart redid his picture. There might have been a mountain, and wavy lines could be water, besides that, Ethan could make nothing of it. Placing all the pebbles in Ethan's hand, Gart closed his fingers over them. 'Let your fears and desires rest in your thoughts. When you feel ready, scatter them over the Auryn.'

'But what is this?'

From under his bushy brows, Gart stared in wonder. 'A reading.'

With some foreboding, Ethan threw the stones.

Gart studied the layout. 'You have a lot to do with water. It's coming through in two places. You don't like the water.'

'The sea?' As far as Ethan knew he didn't have a problem with water, but, the sea was an unknown element.

'Could be. It's big water.'

'And freedom?' asked Ethan hopefully.

'Always about freedom, but that's understandable. You have freedom from water.'

Ethan turned his lip at the unpromising remark.

Gart tapped a red rock splinter far below the mountain, and remained in silent contemplation.

'What does that one mean?' Ethan asked with gruff worry.

'Mmm, it's not good. But — other things are very hopeful.' He placed his finger on the stone below the mountain. 'When you're in this dark place remember more is to come.'

Ethan moaned. 'I'm not finding that encouraging.'

'I mean, it's not the end.' Gart pointed to a tiny chip on top of the mountain. 'When you get here, you will weaken,' he went on quickly, noting his heavy hearted expression, 'but you will get stronger. Very odd, there is forest around you, and terror—' Startled by a queer strangled cry, he looked up. The contorted voice echoed through the chamber.

'What is that?'

Gart looked at him darkly and gave warning, 'Don't you worry about it.'

Ignoring him, Ethan frowned with concern. 'He's in pain.' He moved to the rock archway separating the chambers.

Loc came up beside him and roughly grabbed his arm. 'Boy, don't get involved.'

'What is it?'

'You really don't know?'

Ethan shook his head with naïve puzzlement.

'Garutz and Zigor and their lot... they get their pleasure any way they can.' Loc gave him a pitying stare.

Ethan exclaimed with seething fury, 'That's sickening.' The restraining power of Loc's hand on his arm prevented him going to the next chamber. 'How can you let them do that?'

'Survival.' Loc's tattooed face was grim. 'It's best not to attract their attention, they already hate us.'

The man's tortured bleating grew weak and almost disappeared.

'Who is this Garutz?'

Loc gave him the description of the man Ethan bumped into earlier. 'It's disgusting.'

'Aye,' Loc eased his grip and said with understanding, 'but we are in a hideous place. Will the behaviour of its residents be any different?'

'Yours are,' Ethan replied stoically, 'and mine.'

A small smile flicked his whiskers. 'Aye, but this is not our home. We long for a better place and this hope and desire keeps us sane.'

It would take Ethan time to register his words, but Loc's understated way of associating him with the Harn had its effect.

32 - Unexpected Company

A foolish man thinks he needs nothing
An arrogant man refuses to ask
A wise man acknowledges his need

Ei'myn Geí-Serenmãh

Towards the end of the day, Sasheya came to assist Shiarn prepare for the prince's party. Fed up with being inside, Shiarn would give anything to go out even if she had to contend with supercilious aristocrats. Although the thought of seeing Morgal caused her anxiety.

If only her Kin could see her. In a deep mauve gown, her breasts were squeezed into the short bodice, and the skirt's plush folds and purple gossamer sleeves would bring an envious scowl to Earona's face. Sasheya pinned up Shiarn's hair, letting a few red locks float down beneath a snug cap. Once her matching pearl earrings were on she was ready to face the evening.

Regina arrived and gave Shiarn a nod of approval. However, Sasheya received a condescending glare and she dashed from the 'dragon' woman's disdain and out the door.

Shiarn and Regina left the suite and walked the hallways and stairs, their skirts flouncing as they swept past. The 'dragon's' expression remained stern and uncaring. Shiarn's stomach turned into a ball of agitation as she prepared to see Morgal.

Rapid tunes of a flute drifted down the hall. Laughter and chatter within the Music Room prepared her for people's merriment. Her eyes darted over the crowd, not resting on anyone long enough for them to pierce her gaze. The king was not amongst the revelers, and Morgal it seemed was absent. Her sigh was a loud gush of air.

Skirts shimmered, and rich velvet coats added warmth to the glitter of dazzling jewelry. It seemed the wealthiest citizens of Floris were gathered in the one room. She grabbed a goblet from a passing servant and took a long sip. Musicians played a fast and bustling beat. Overjoyed at the glorious mix of tunes, she tapped her foot, desiring to twirl and bounce. The dance was not unlike those at home, only the steps were extravagant and the hand movements over pronounced.

The crowd parted and the prince came to greet her. Clasping her hand, his pink tinged lips slid gracefully on the back of it. 'My dear, you look divine.'

Shiarn replied with a demure smile.

'This evening might brighten you up.'

Her smile remained a frozen line. 'Perhaps.'

'Indeed, we shall have a dance soon. First, I must introduce you to Floris' gentile.' Holding her hand like it were a feather, he walked her through the crowd. Now that she was accustomed to men in wigs, she had to admit, it had a form of seduction. Bastion was especially attractive. Gold ringlets were tied near his neck, and a white shirt peeked from under a cerise coat, accessorized with silver frills and buttons. The cuffs dangled past his coat sleeves and over his hands and bejeweled fingers. He was much like a strutting peacock awaiting its mate. The men were attired similarly to the prince and in mannerisms little difference. The women were dressed like her, yet unlike the men, they had no wish to speak with her. She would be content with a friendly serving girl than an arrogant wealthy lady.

Bastion demonstrated the dance steps and she caught on quickly. She swayed across the floor, her cloth shoes kicking out in perfect time. It was a challenging delight and a way for her to forget her troubles. For a night at least. They danced until he was breathless and beads of sweat dampened his forehead. His attention was called away and she stood alone.

'Good evening, lady Shiarn. I am enchanted by your presence once again.' From behind, a smooth toned voice greeted her with familiarity.

With a silent gulp of foreboding, she turned, preparing for derision. She cocked her head and responded, sweetly, 'Good evening, Lord... Belleguarde.' Even he seemed handsome this evening with a dark wig and plum jacket revealing a cream shirt with numerous ruffles. Not unlike Bastion's flamboyant style, Belleguarde wore long black boots instead of cloth shoes. She purposely stared past him. 'You are not with that woman?' Earlier he was gazing into the eyes, or perhaps half exposed chest of the stunning older woman.

He raised his brow with genuine offence. 'My dear lady, you speak of the Duchess Vonzella Hetsworth.' He bowed slightly and his mouth turned down. 'It would be terribly improper of me to disclose her diversions before one that may ignite her envy.'

'This is a surprise all the same.'

'A pleasant one I hope.' He almost sounded disappointed.

'You hope for pleasantries?'

'Your abrupt wit certainly keeps one awake in this uninspiring seat of languor.' His smile dropped, but she sensed he spoke in good humor.

'You don't find this grandeur inspiring?' Her arm stretched, taking in the colour and glamour of Floris' upper-class.

'This is mere every day.' He smiled with a wealth of charm. 'However, you are a different matter and have me at a disadvantage. I must fall back on a gentleman's fundamental attribute.' He took a large gulp from his goblet while frowning over the top.

'Pretentious pride will oblige you to disengage?'

'No, on the contrary.' He spoke seriously. 'I shall be forced to disarm you of your acerbic verbiage.' His eyes glinting, he said, '*Charm*, my dear. That it even needs mentioning is an affront to my dignity. Indeed, you certainly have an unprecedented way about you.' His voice returned to a louder tone, and he said before she could respond,

'Dancing may cause you to lighten and perhaps impart your favour. For selfish reasons, I do admit, because tonight I find you absolutely beautiful to gaze upon.'

'The gentleman's secret weapon. I see how well you play this.' She couldn't tell if it was his charming words or the wine, but she pouted with a puzzled frown. 'You are good at it and I'm out of my depth.'

'It is an art for those who play court, and my artistry is exemplary.'

Shiarn eyed him suspiciously, 'Mmm, I see. Truly, there's not much you can gain from me, and it's not really in my interest to tell you how handsome you look this evening, and I expect I won't enjoy the dance despite you appearing very skilled at it.'

'It has revealed itself, your silver bladed tongue.' His noble chin lifted and his back stiffened. 'Perhaps if my charm were sharpened I could possibly attract some young lady?'

She replied with mock seriousness, 'Considering the competition, you may have a good chance.'

'I win by default?' His expression transformed into a sad one. 'I am humbled by your honesty. In effect, I am too old and you are already taken.' The comment led them to notice the prince laughing and dancing with a young lady. Bastion appeared happy yet his eyes lacked a sincere sparkle of contentment. Belleguarde sipped wine from his goblet. 'He is in high spirits. Your robust company must provide him with great enjoyment.'

'Once again your flattery strikes.' Under her breath she muttered, 'but I find it hard to believe it is me.'

'My dear, flattery is such an unbecoming phrase and more suited to those who have need of some superfluous elevation. Honest admiration is a type of gift and can only be given by those with a capacity for genuine speech. Despite my frivolity, my words are true.'

She mulled over his words, struck by his openness. 'Without doubt you have skill with it and it certainly has the sense of the dramatic.' She turned to him with a bright smile. 'Nevertheless, I thank you for your gift.'

He bowed his head, and offered her his hand. 'I have had enough of speech. Shall we dance?' He took her arm in his and led her to the floor where they joined other couples. Lord Belleguarde was a fine dancer and she was surprised to find he was not as pompous as she first presumed.

The night progressed and she danced with Bastion again, and several men whose names she could not recall before stopping to catch her breath.

Lord Belleguarde's sudden approach caused her to take a fast breath. 'Lord Bell—'

'By all means, you must call me Jonas, none of this lord talk between us anymore.'

She gave a surprised nod, and wondered, if like her, he had too many wines. 'Jonas it is then.'

Discretely he leaned closer, his tone becoming more sincere. 'I have spent time with you this evening so I must not keep you further. Nonetheless I must enquire, how have you enjoyed your time in the palace thus far?'

Hesitant to respond to his unexpected question, she frowned with foreboding. 'It hasn't been much at all if you really wish to know. But I'm not sure you should know of it.' She kept a firm reign on her tears, concerned the drink would expose her grief.

Jonas narrowed his blue eyes, and they softened as he examined her face. 'That's truly a shame.' He paused. 'I am surprised the prince would make you feel this way.'

'It's not him.' With a tense longing for her Kin, she turned her gaze from his caring look. 'It's…Morgal…' she uttered his name with reluctance. 'He wants something he thinks I have.'

'That is an odd predicament,' he said. 'The king's Advisor is an unethical creature. Tell me, are you going to the picnic the king has organized?'

'Bas mentioned something of it.'

'Perhaps you can speak more on it then.' His eyes moved to the direction of Regina. 'I believe it is near time for you to depart.' His words were uncharacteristic of his flamboyant style. 'Good night, Shiarn.' He left her and was drawn into conversation with Duchess Vonzella.

Regina pressed through the crowd, and grabbing Shiarn's arm, she guided her away from the glut of people. Under her breath, she demanded, 'What were you and Lord Belleguarde discussing?'

Taken aback by her pushy attitude, Shiarn cried, 'What business is it of yours?'

'You are not to cavort in such a manner.'

Was the woman going to dislike everyone Shiarn spoke too? 'He's just an old flirt.'

'It is time we left. Come.'

Suddenly fearful Morgal would be waiting in her rooms, she stepped back. 'Shouldn't I say good night to the prince?'

'It is not necessary, he will understand.' Regina placed a steely grip on her arm, causing Shiarn to wince. 'I must take you back.'

Regina escorted her to her suite and left. Shiarn checked the rooms, praying the pleasant evening would not be spoilt by Morgal. Taking the stoker, she closed her door and placed a chair against it. Now she was making herself a prisoner — in a beautiful gilded cage. Reluctantly she undressed and slipped into bed, pulling the covers up to her chin.

Shiarn ran through darkened hallways, a penetrating chill seeping through her nightdress. Rattling on locked doors in desperation, she tried to find a safe place. She could no longer remember where that was. Hopelessness pervaded her determination to escape, and she realized the fear she ran from was inside her. The same corridors, the same doors kept appearing. Somehow she knew it was not real, but a dream. The trance-like sleep was strong, but her Ethos, fired up by panic, allowed her to open her eyes enough to squint into semi-consciousness.

A sweet acidic odor saturated the air, and shadows drifted towards her, and a figure — coming closer. A short beard on a pale face was distinct. Numbness overtook her and she fell back into dreams.

~ * ~

Through the blur of grey silhouettes, Mara entered the private chamber of her mother and stopped. She was summoned into her presence, and the further away she stayed from her physical reach, the better.

On a chair carved from black marble, Yavinia sat with a hateful expression. Her cheekbones looked more severe with her deep crimson hair pulled from her face into elaborate braids circling her head. Amber eyes, like Mara's, glared with malice.

Mara rubbed her arms in the freezing room and steeled herself for the tirade sure to come.

'I made arrangements for you to travel with my acquaintance. These plans have taken years to consolidate and the preparations have been costly. The ritual at the Sanctuary must take place at a specific time. However, you disobeyed me and ran away. My rage will only be sated on your return.'

'I don't want to go!' Mara's voice echoed in the frigid marble room.

Yavinia stood. Her magenta painted lips twitched into a snarl. 'You will do as I say, daughter, without any insolence.'

Despite her mother's abrupt rage, Mara crossed her arms in defiance. She knew my mother's acquaintances, arrogant self-serving magik-users, masquerading as priests, but the stranger on that night was a different breed of man, if he was even a man at all. 'Does your husband know of this?'

'Quiet!' Yavinia's hand flashed out at her, her long sleeve almost touched the floor as she pointed at Mara.

An invisible weight fell on her and she dropped to folded knees. Lowering her face, she could only listen.

'It is irrelevant. He will not be concerned with this or you, regardless of what you carry. Your task will benefit this kingdom. For that he should be grateful,' she snarled with vehemence. 'His line shall reign eternal.'

Not able to shift from her forced submission, Mara fingered the wristband from Wendessa. Realization hit her, she was not there. The object gave her strength to voice her own thoughts. 'It's not him who rules or even you…'

Yavinia stepped close, her green skirt sweeping over Mara's legs. She bent down and snatched Mara's chin in her fingers and jerked her face up to view her fear with a shrewd glare. 'What has that bitch done to you?! How dare she think she can turn you against me?' Her mother's eyes became flames, swirling into hypnotic vermillion. They pierced Mara with deadly fury. 'You can try to run.' She pinched her skin and yanking her face up, she growled, 'But I will find you and I will take you back to where you belong.'

Mara woke to a pain in her jaw and a hand covering her mouth, suffocating her. A hooded figure leaned above her. Biting at the hand, Mara struggled against the force attempting to subdue her. Still dazed from the Sleep spell she must have been under, she struggled to free her own hand from under the covers.

The figure spoke. 'Alqua-elzat-varan——'

Mara slapped the face hidden in the shadows of the hood, revealing straw-blonde hair and a crinkled face. The old hag held a black dagger at Mara's neck. 'You're coming with me.'

Mara bit on her bony finger, loosening the pressure. 'Get off me!' She rolled from the woman's reach and tumbled to the floor, half wrapped in her sheet.

'No you don't. Alqua-elzat—'

A pillow flying across the bed broke her speech, and Earona yelled, 'Leave her alone!'

The witch looked at Earona with shock and dashed from the room. Women in the dorm woke with lit candles and whispering voices. Earona helped Mara from her blankets and set her on the bed. Her voice shook with fear. 'Who was that?'

Mara stared bug-eyed. 'How… how did you…?' Strange enough Mara escaped the Sleep spell, but surely the witch would have taken every precaution?

'I…' Earona creased her face in thought. '…was woken by a baby screaming, and I saw the knife and the woman. If she can be called that.' She put her arm around Mara's shoulders. 'But you…you're shaking…'

Mara clutched her arms, too shocked to reply or push her away. 'It's…' She recalled the dream-vision of Yavinia, but surely she hadn't pierced through the charm's spell so quickly? If not, who was the witch? 'Damn her to hell.'

'Who was she?' Earona started straightening her sheets.

'She's…' Mara was reluctant to speak the hateful word aloud. '…probably from my mother.'

Earona fell back on the bed beside her. 'God above. She wants to kill you?'

Mara shook her head. 'She wants me to return.' The ritual at the Sanctuary was more important than Mara thought. But she was starting to enjoy this new freedom. Now more than ever, she must never go back.

Earona embraced her shoulders and held tight. 'I take back what I said about getting you home.'

Staring down at her hands, Mara could only nod her assent.

33 - Saved

Honour your God with the courage of your conviction, the efficacy of your duty, and your self-less mercy.

Tome of the First Born Reign

Prisoners waited at the bars, hollering for food. Those in the front pressed their limbs through, waving their bowls. Earlier, more men were jostled into the overcrowded prison and a thin reckless man shoved his way through the incoming prisoners and tried pushing through the gate. He was halted by a crossbow bolt, felling him in a crumpled heap. The guards kicked his feet in and slammed the door shut. Men gave the corpse a wide berth. The guards refused to remove the body despite the men's demands, and anger and dissent was building ever since.

With his bowl out, Ethan waited alongside Branan who cursed the guards much like all the men. One of the guards, a young man stepped closer and smirked at the men's degradation. Branan latched onto the arm of the fresh-faced guard. He hit Branan on the head with the shaft of his spear, but it only infuriated Branan. Ethan tried to wrench him from Branan's grip, fearing what may happen if Branan did not free him.

A crossbow was levelled three feet from Branan's face. It was miraculous he was not killed. 'Step back,' the holder of the weapon commanded, 'I'll use this.'

Ethan let go of Branan's wrist, but Branan was not so compliant.

'Branan!' Gart's stern voice belted over the heads of the men. 'Let him go.'

Branan glared at the one threatening him with the crossbow and removed his grip, causing the guard to stumble back.

'Move to the door,' the older guard ordered, 'Now!' Numerous weapons were directed at Branan and Ethan.

Branan stomped to the gate, his face wrathful.

The guard yelled at Ethan, 'You too.'

'Me?' Ethan cried, 'I didn't—'

'Move it scum!'

Ethan walked quickly, shaking his head. The inmates moved back from the bars to let them pass, not wanting to be caught in any crossfire. As the door opened, the men shouted for the body to be taken away, but the guards were too incensed to do anything the prisoners wanted. Ethan and Branan stepped over the prone body with a bolt sticking out of his chest.

Once outside, Branan's wrists were tied together while Ethan was left in his chains. They were marched past the cell. The Harn trailed them with mournful expressions and Maddog called out obscenities. With armed men between them, they walked single-file through narrow tunnels sloping down. An occasional torch lit their way in the dark passages. A chill draft touched Ethan's skin, but he was more shocked by the awful smell. A solid bolted door appeared through the dark. From a room not far off, a man with limp hair, and in a vest of black fur, came at a wearying pace towards them.

'How's the water, Saybar?' The guard teased with a smirk.

Saybar clinked a great chain around his neck, looking for a particular key hanging amongst the many. 'It'll be right for what you want.' He pounded the key in and after a few attempts of twisting it, he yanked the door open.

They stood on a wide ledge looking down at an immense chamber of silver grey rock surging with water. Ethan shielded his eyes from light glistening through an opening in the rocks at the far end. As he adjusted, he glimpsed grey outside and foam rushing in. A carved rock stair led down to the deep cavern basin already filling with water.

Saybar took more rope and looped it through Branan's tied wrists. He came to Ethan and after examining his chains, squinted up at him. Ethan stared back, not able to discern what the man was thinking. Saybar said, 'They're ready.'

They were pushed down into the basin and Saybar followed. Seawater lapped up to Ethan's thighs making him gasp at the freezing temperature. Even at that shallow depth, the waves pushed at his legs causing imbalance. He began to understand his predicament.

Saybar ran another rope under his chains and Branan's rope and strung it across the water, tying it to a heavy bolt at the side of the chamber. He moved back to the opposite side and started turning a large pulley which tightened and raised the rope high above them. The rope rose taking Ethan's cuffed chain with it. His wrists stung as his body lifted out of the water until he was suspended by the line.

'If you survive,' the guard yelled over the rush of waves, 'you go back to your cell. If you don't, then you don't.' He laughed at his own stupid joke. Saybar and the guards dashed back to the ledge, complaining of the cold water. The guards left, leaving Saybar with one guard, and the two sat on the stone.

Swirls of water flooded in. Ethan was unprepared for the mighty force of it dragging his body outward. For all his great height, he couldn't put his feet on the ground. His chains twisted together, causing his skin to tear, and his body whirled in the swell that seemed to be deepening as it churned around his chest. He had no ability to steady himself in the water's propulsion - his body swept forward only to be sucked out again. Added to the torrents, the freezing water numbed his limbs. If he couldn't regain some momentum of his own he would be in serious trouble if it went over his head. As it was, it broke around his neck, crushing his chest and splashing into his mouth. He gagged at its foul taste and tried his best to keep his mouth shut. His weight combined with the water thrust caused his wrists to bleed.

He pulled the chain together and scaled his hands up, slowly lifting his body from the wash. Clutching the rope above, he cursed as his hands slid along it. He gripped it tight and kept his head up from the battering of waves.

Branan, alot shorter than Ethan, stretched his face above the water and gasped for air. His bleeding wrists still locked together, he spun around, struggling to maintain balance. He maintained his angry glare; the one that got him into trouble in the first place.

Ethan nearly laughed before realizing he would drown if he couldn't lift himself up. He yelled over the choppy waves, 'I'm going to help you.'

Branan turned his head, giving Ethan a bemused stare.

Fighting to keep level in the impetus, Ethan let one hand free from the rope. His palm waved at Branan and he connected with his Ethos. With his Mover Gift shooting from his soul, he boosted Branan up.

Branan gripped the life-line and gave Ethan a questioning smile. 'Gods... it's cold...'

Ethan rolled his eyes and nodded his agreement. The water surged around his chest, yet the solid anchor from above meant he wasn't at the mercy of the waves. The two remained silent, conserving their energy against the onslaught of water. Amidst the roaring of the rising tide Ethan heard the faint sound of the men on the ledge, playing a game of dice, heedless to the trauma faced by the prisoners.

After some time, shaded light entered from outside and the force of water receded into the ocean. Under the dull glow of torches, Saybar took the exhausted men down. Ethan and Branan were half dragged and shoved back to the cell and thrust in.

The Harn supported Branan to their space in the prison. Ethan followed, his boots squelching and his clothes clinging to his sodden body. Shuddering, he rubbed his bloodless arms and lay on the dirt floor, cold and hungry with his teeth chattering.

'Wrap this round ya.' Maddog placed an old blanket over him and pulled him to his feet. 'You got to keep up and moving.'

Ethan grimaced and tried to make his numb lips move.

Maddog patted him on the shoulder. 'Knew you'd make it.'

'What's—' Ethan's mouth shivered with cold. '— wrong— with— you?'

'What?!' Maddog leaned closer and looked fierce. 'Can't I be worried?' He admonished for all to hear. 'You're a pisspoor bugger if ever I met one...'

Unsure if he actually insulted the man, Ethan gave a sheepish smile.

'I believed.' A laconic smirk broke out on the madman's face. 'That hell born lot left you for dead.' He nodded to the Harn.

He shook as he tried to move. 'I've seen the ocean,' he croaked while his teeth chattered, 'can't say I liked it...'

~ * ~

Mara woke to Earona shaking her shoulder. Groaning, she dragged herself from bed, realizing she only slept for a couple of hours.

Over breakfast she was too tired to think of the woman who sought to steal her away, and she didn't want to listen to Earona go on about it. Earona scanned the room,

248

determined to find the woman who attacked her. It was not a surprise the crone couldn't be seen.

Counsellor Elata came to inform them Mother requested their presence. The counsellor took them through to Mother's room and they sat in front of her desk once more.

'Apparently there was an incident last night.' Mother looked at Mara. 'You were accosted in your bed?'

'Ah...' Mara hesitated. How did she even know that so quickly? '...yes.'

'She was attacked,' Earona butted in, 'by an old hag.'

Mother frowned at Earona and said to Mara, 'This elderly woman threatened you in some way?'

'She had a knife!' Earona cried in disbelief.

'She...' Mara's voice dropped. '...was an old lady. Maybe she thought my bed was hers.'

Earona gasped and stared at Mara, her mouth hanging loose. 'She spoke in another tongue.' Her voice turned to ice. 'She was a witch, I'm certain of it.'

Mara remained quiet, staring down at her hands.

Mother's perturbed gaze went between them.

'You need to find this woman and she needs to be dealt with.' Earona sat forward in her chair, directing her austere gaze on Mother.

Mother pursed her lips together. 'You should not form any premature conclusions. There are foreign women here. I wouldn't want the girls to panic.' She stared at Mara fidgeting in her chair. 'You are not afraid someone wished to harm you?'

Earona turned to Mara, her eyes gleaming with smugness.

'Why would anyone want to harm me?' Mara muttered.

'Yes, why?' Earona sat back, folding her arms.

Mother raised a brow at Mara. 'Perhaps you are the only one who can answer that.'

Earona demanded, 'Will you look for this woman?'

'We shall.' Mother restrained a curt smile. 'And get to the truth of the matter.'

'Good,' Earona huffed.

Mara remained stiff in her chair, avoiding the eyes of both women. They could look as much as they liked, they would never find the old witch.

At the end of the day, Mara fell into bed. She spent the day washing, and out of sight of Earona. Over dinner Earona stared daggers at her. Mara didn't know her that well, but it was surprising all the same. She never saw her with nothing to say. But now they were alone and the dorm was quiet, she dreaded the lecture she was bound to get. Although she couldn't blame her, she really did lie this time.

Earona didn't say a word as Mara changed and climbed into bed. She couldn't take her brooding anymore. 'Are you going to say something?'

'You.' Earona's violet blue eyes glared icicles at her. 'Are infuriating!'

'Is that it?'

'Aren't you feeling guilty?' Earona's voice was coated with self-righteousness.

Mara was silent as she assessed what happened. *Curses.* Earona had after all saved her. 'It doesn't matter what Mother thinks or the counsellors. They can't do anything—'

'You don't know that.' Earona's tone was seething.

Mara leaned over the bed and matched her anger. 'I do. And I don't want them speculating about me.'

'What if she comes back?'

'I don't know...' This is what Mara didn't want to think about. And it wasn't "if", it was probably when.

Earona rubbed her head. 'If I'm supposed to be 'watching out' for you, you can at least let me help you.'

'I don't need your help!'

Earona threw herself back on the bed with a frustrated groan. 'Why so many secrets?'

Irritated at herself, Mara twisted a strand of her red-gold hair and considered her honest remark. 'Can you really talk about that?'

'What is that supposed to mean?' Earona turned on her suddenly.

'You have secrets of your own. Like, how do you heal?' She said with smug conceit, 'And how did your friend make us invisible?'

Earona leaned on her elbow. 'First tell me about yourself.'

'There's nothing much to tell,' Mara said with disinterest, 'I ran away from home and now my mother is after me.'

Earona cried with worry, 'What sort of woman is she?'

'She's got a black heart.'

'God...' Earona blinked in sudden apprehension.

As long as Mara wore the charm she would be safe, so Wendessa told her. But it would seem her mother had found her. 'What about you?' she asked with a hungry curiosity.

Earona frowned at her eagerness. 'It's difficult to explain.' Now she twirled her black hair with nervous fingers. 'It's a special ability.'

Mara recalled Earona touching the red-headed woman and the cut on her shoulder disappearing. 'Like magik?'

'Not really,' she whispered. 'It's a part of who I am.'

Inquisitiveness widened her eyes. 'And you all do something?'

'That's not for me to say. And truly it's best you never mention it to them.' Her tone was grim.

'Oh?' Maybe Wendessa was right after all. Mara's voice softened. Maybe these people were like her, using magik and controlling elements. 'But, I don't get how?'

Earona watched her with furrowed brows. 'It's complicated. It has to do with spiritual abilities...'

'It must be...' Mara looked up in thought. '...do you use blood?'

'Holy God, no!' Her face paled.

Mara's face fell with an unexpected disappointment. 'You can do it without rituals?'

'Of course, it's all natural.' Earona stressed her plea, 'You must not tell anyone of this.'

'Who would I tell?'

34 - Truth Comes Out

"Dawn to even-time
Wandering joy-less hills
She weeps her heartsong
Her soul is no man's
Save the one who breaks the childhood refuge"

Song of Evelonne Bloodflower

With disinterest, Shiarn glossed over the people mingling on the lawn. The grogginess she woke with had faded, but her nose twitched at the organic smell still in her nostrils. She stifled another vision of Morgal in her bedroom, sensing his presence over the last couple of nights went beyond dreams. Brisk air on her exposed neck and cleavage made her shiver. Overhead blue sky was emerging, but in her current mood rain clouds would be more fitting.

Regina, having no sense about her own appearance wore a gown so tight her plump sides bulged. 'Princess Byester arrived yesterday and we hope she shall attend today.'

'We? I don't think so.' Shiarn took the drink offered by a servant.

'Do not get drunk again.'

Shiarn had never drunk so much in her life as she had in the last few days. It dulled the emotions far too well, although, her clarity of thoughts had degenerated.

'Here they come.' Regina curtsied while tugging at Shiarn's dress to do likewise, as if she was still unaware of the procedure.

The king passed them, followed by the prince. Shiarn kept her head down, not wanting to meet Bastion's gaze or Morgal following behind them. He trailed after Bastion like a poisonous snake. His latent power over her made her vulnerable, and she had no wish to be in his presence.

After the entourage passed, Shiarn snapped, 'now what?'

'We socialize.'

'Just what I need.' She couldn't think of anything worse.

Low chairs and coloured rugs were under the trees circling the lawn. If her disposition was not so dismal it might have been fun.

Bastion walked towards her. She was oddly delighted to see Lord Belleguarde accompanying him, but less thrilled at the duchess, and in another fine red dress more appropriate to a grand feast. To her relief, Morgal remained with the king, but Gaspar followed Bastion like an impatient pet. Bastion was handsome in his pastel-green and cream suit, his frills were shorter and so was this day's wig. Minus any wig, Belleguarde wore a beige shirt, without a jacket, and long tanned boots gave him a rural appearance. Shiarn noticed the broadness of his shoulders, and in the natural light, it was difficult pinpointing an accurate age.

Her smile was genuine if not melancholy and she took Bastion's outstretched gloved hand.

'My lady.' His gaze appraised her sky-blue dress. 'How wonderful you look today, much better dressed than these ninnies.' He flashed his hand, indicating the heady mix of accessories and satin.

'Thank you, I guess.'

Jonas took Shiarn's hand and raised it for a kiss. 'My lady.'

She glanced into his eyes and received a perplexing look. He became more of an enigma each time she met him. Then, to her utter displeasure the duchess sashayed between them with a haughty nod to Shiarn.

Gaspar tottered forward. 'Highness, would it not be better to keep with the king in the main party?'

Bastion raised his brows. 'By Varg's flame, Gaspar! Stop making a fuss.'

Not far off, the king reclined on a chair among elaborately dressed men and women, including Morgal. Also in the party, a woman in a pink gown, her long hair sparkling with gold netting, and beside her, sprawled in his chair, a lanky blonde man. His awkward fidgeting made him look out of place.

Bastion remarked, 'Even my irksome cousin, Vivella, has turned out, and with her insipid pet. How drab. I have been trapped inside with that lot too long. I need a change of scenery, even if it is only a few hours.' Gaspar's 'buts' were waved aside. Shiarn's chortle increased the weedy man's indignation. Bastion continued, 'Shiarn and I shall partner, while you, Belleguarde, partner Vonzella, and we shall get this game underway.' He slid his gloves off, and holding Shiarn's hand, walked her to their starting position. Over his shoulder, he called, 'That leaves you with the Lady Regina, Gaspar, if you care to play at all!'

Gaspar remained in a defiant silence, his grumpy red face, evidence he was not happy with the suggestion.

Shiarn declared she had no idea how the game worked, and Bastion hurried to instruct her. After he struck the ball, he volunteered to assist her swing. Positioned behind her, he covered her hands as she held the long wooden mallet. The light touch of his body was enough to draw unpleasant sensations. She breathed the comforting aromatic scent from his skin to calm her mind.

His head came over her shoulder and he spoke in her ear. 'Hit the ball gently, but firm.'

She swung and the ball flew wide missing the loop. A watching servant ran off to retrieve the ball.

Bastion applauded with enthusiasm. 'A brilliant stroke. You shall get the gist of this in no time.'

She forced a smile, but could generate no cheer. 'Do you think?'

His eyes widened with exuberance. 'No need to look like that. It is a beautiful day.'

'The weather is the least of my concerns.'

On placement of the ball, he started his turn and said, as if discussing a fault with a servant, 'About that incident. It really was a terrible mistake. I have done all I could—'

'Mistake?!' Sputtering for a moment, Shiarn raised her voice in a tremulous cry. 'That's a lie.'

Bastion placed steady hands on her arms and whispered, 'He is a scoundrel. Nonetheless, I have done what is in my power to do.'

She released pent up air and fixed burning eyes on his uncomprehending ones. Amid miserable consideration, it dawned on her, how could she expect Bastion to aid her? She was the prisoner whereas Morgal was a significant man at court. Now she was angry for informing him. She shifted from his grip and stomped to their ball. Hands quivering, she attempted to hit it, but it rolled a great way off course. She restrained burning tears in a stony face while inside she fumed.

Bastion's face conveyed more conviction. 'No matter what he may say, I have asked him not to harass you further.'

She lacked the strength to contradict him, unsure of what additional trouble it might bring. For now she had a gnawing fear Morgal was in her room during the night, using magik to lull her senses. Bastion endeavoured cheering her up and he would be successful if the issue was not such a traumatic one.

After the game, Bastion and Jonas chatted and decided to play once more, this time swapping partners. 'Fabulous idea,' Bastion gushed.

Shiarn wondered if Bastion really desired a break from her sullen mood. Over the morning she observed Jonas and Vonzella flirting. For some reason it vexed her in a peculiar way. Now she was partnering with him, she was despondent to chitchat, and played in silence. Eventually he caught her attention. 'How has it been with the prince since the party?'

She pondered her thoughts and gave a weighted sigh. 'I'm not sure. He is quite charming and seems to have a lot to say, but I come away and I...'

'It is as if he has not actually said anything at all.'

'That's it. Mind you, I could say the same about you.'

Her frank remark brought laughter from him. 'You get so accustomed to it you do it with no thought at all.' He hit the ball through a wooden hoop sticking out from the ground and without looking up, said, 'Please excuse my candid request, but what is your opinion of the duchess?'

Surprised by his forwardness, she said with gall, 'You would heed my advice?'

'In such a crafty way you make my query truly redundant.' He cast an interested glance at the duchess warming up to the prince.

Shiarn watched her and Bastion flirting. 'She is an attractive older woman. I expect she is quite rich yet sickeningly superfluous.'

'What!?' he gave a dry chuckle, 'Unlike me?'

His frivolous question seemed beyond her current anguish and she had no desire to talk about his love life. 'I get the impression the illustrious Duchess Vonzella would not stop if I was dying in a ditch by the wayside.'

Jonas laughed, loudly.

She muttered, 'It would pain me if you were similar.'

'Indeed,' he said, 'I also would suffer.'

She had the impression he was not really concerned with her opinion at all. 'Unlike our previous meeting, your charm will not warm me today.'

'That saddens me,' he replied. 'Perhaps you are in need of an honest word, or I am not the man I believed myself to be.'

She gave a heartfelt laugh and shook her head disapprovingly. Despite him being at least twenty years her senior he was a handsome man. However, something deeper was being exchanged between them. She could not explain it nor could she brush it aside, neither did she want too. But what could she possibly be thinking by it? She was a prisoner and he a flirt and as rumour had it, a womanizer. 'You certainly have the skill, it's just... I'm not in the proper frame of mind.' After a pensive moment, she added, 'The duchess would be extremely lucky *if* she managed to tie you down.'

'Now, who has become the beguiler?' He pulled his shoulders back, and said, 'Duke of Hetsworth, Jonas Belleguarde. Doesn't sound too grandiose, do you suppose?'

'I am convinced that if you were given such a position you would go above and beyond in fulfilling its pretentious duties, whatever they may be,' she finished under her breath, and continued on with a firm hit to the ball, but she had given up being enthusiastic and Jonas was doing all the hard work.

Jonas rested on his mallet and watched her swing her bat. 'If you do not think it impertinent of me, what were you and the prince disputing?'

She studied his broad mouth, turning down with concern. Were she and Bastian really that obvious? 'I don't think I should say. It may cause more trouble...' she caught her breath, 'more hurt.'

Lifting his fine brows, he waited without a word.

Finally she felt compelled to speak. 'I'm afraid if I say...'

'Afraid,' he enquired with surprise, '...of hurting?' Stepping nearer, he paid her more consideration, and looked into her eyes with earnest. 'I will not hurt you.'

Amid all his arrogant mannerism, she sensed the truth in his voice, but he didn't know what was occurring behind closed doors.

'You spoke of your discontent previously. I assume it has something to do with your maudlin mood?' His eyes held astuteness she had not discerned previously.

Her eyes trailed after Bastion and Vonzella in a noncommittal silence.

Jonas bent down to finish their play to the last red flag. His gracious prompting to speak encouraged her, and she mumbled her dilemma for his ears only.

Inhaling sharply, Jonas knocked his ball off course, and cried, 'Blood 'n bollocks!'

After seeing the ball go awry, Bastion commented from a distance about his lack of focus and Vonzella scowled at the pair.

Jonas regained control of the emotions running across his face, yet his eyes remained troubled.

Shiarn watched his well-composed demeanour falter, and she questioned the damage she triggered by her confession. To her dismay, he was unable to look at her. She frowned grimly at Bastion when he suggested they retire for lunch. Bastion linked arms with Vonzella and they strolled to the chairs and rugs where servants placed platters of food.

Unable to speak to Jonas, Shiarn walked on with heavy steps.

Catching hold of her arm, he swung her about. With his free hand, he squeezed hers and his eyes were a storm of blue. 'What a horrendous shock.'

Instead of the half smile she attempted, she groaned. 'And so much more.'

'The prince knows?'

She shrugged, holding back a flow of tears. 'I fear he does not understand.'

'That you have been violated?' he exclaimed in astonishment.

'Bastion's interference might have made that devil more deceitful,' she whispered, 'I'm sure he came to my rooms again, but has dulled my senses.'

He continued looking dazed. 'His purpose?'

'He wants something he thought I had.' Was he hoping to drag the information out of her while she slept? She shivered at the possibility.

They approached the others. Jonas started a conversation about a man she didn't know as if they hadn't discussed her trauma at all. Bastion reclined on a squat chair next to Vonzella. Preferring the rug, Shiarn sat and kicked off her shoes. Her peace was not to be, as Regina joined her.

After they ate, Bastion started on a new topic. 'Confound this dreadful mess with Ryne. It is foolhardy and pathetic.'

Jonas lifted a golden pastry from the tray. 'I agree.'

Gaspar clamped his hands together and seemed to lighten up. 'It is not foolish. We have much they would like to possess.'

'Foolish on their part, it will yield nothing. And now, so we have heard, they have lost their darling princess. There are even whispers that we are blamed for this! Do they need some sort of excuse to make war?' Bastion said, 'Besides, what would we do with her?'

'Keep her as a leverage.' Gaspar smirked.

'If they cannot put effort into protecting their own, why should we believe they would care enough for any blackmail threats? If anyone has the child, it is one of their own nobility. I am certain there are enough who would like to see the girl gone,' Bastion went on, 'This is why Rikard wants to keep it secret. Thankfully we have ways of discovering these things—'

'Perhaps you should not speak of this,' Gaspar's head tilted at Shiarn, 'in front of the woman.'

Bastion sat up in his chair and stared his advisor down. 'The knowledge of a missing member of another court is of no great significance to us. Do you suppose this woman has taken her?'

Shiarn rolled her eyes at the remark. 'I know nothing of what you are talking about.'

'It is not in the knowing, but the revealing of certain things. It is wise to not belittle a potential war.' His presumptuous opinions voiced, Gaspar hesitated, his cheeks reddening. People around them witnessed the conversation and halted their own chatter to listen.

Jonas raised his eyebrows at the fumbling advisor in amazement, and Vonzella smiled wickedly.

'My attitude,' Bastion's eyes pierced Gaspar's weak stare, 'towards war is of no surrender. It is the best they will get and they and *you* should expect nothing less. Unless there is something I am grossly unaware of, that is also the view of my father, who, I might remind you, is still king of you, and me for that matter.' He delivered his cutting words with an adept calmness.

Gaspar bowed his head and his tone became humble. 'War would be a terrible foreclosure.'

Jonas added, 'Nevertheless, war may be imminent. Whether they find this girl or not.'

Vonzella clapped her hands and chimed with a gleeful smile, 'How exciting!'

Jonas gave humorous attention to the woman. 'The Rynians are far from lacking in military skill. The challenge would be great.'

'Gods, Belleguarde!' Bastion interjected, 'What he is trying to say, my dear, exciting is hardly the word you would use when describing warfare.'

Vonzella frowned at the prince. 'Men in polished suits, bright swords blazing and saving their homeland are exceedingly gallant and brave.'

Shiarn covered an unruly chuckle, making Belleguarde smile. Vonzella gave him a cold glare. Jonas replied, 'Perhaps, and provided they are not stamping through my estate.'

The discussion made Shiarn curious and she said, 'Ryne wishes war, because of this missing child?'

'No, nevertheless that may change,' Bastion replied, 'The Rynians have been hot under the lace a few years now. We had peace, but now he has withdrawn ambassadors and stopped royal trade.' He looked darkly at Gaspar, daring him to speak. 'We wonder what will be next.'

Jonas added, 'There are rumours they invaded Baion.'

Gaspar finally spoke, turning his gaunt face to Jonas. 'We are yet to hear anything substantial.'

'We must take seriously the King of Ryne's threats,' Jonas grew solemn, 'no matter who they are directed at.'

'The fundamental question,' said Bastion, 'shall we act now or wait till our border forts have them knocking on their walls?'

Shiarn gasped loudly. 'An awful predicament!'

'Politics - not a game for the compassionate,' remarked Jonas.

'There is much to say on it and tonight will be full of it, with my over-zealous sister here to harp on about her plans,' Bastion said. 'Gods forbid her entering into negotiations to trade land as we recently heard.'

'Hopefully it is only a rumour,' said Jonas.

'Enough of this talk. Such a dreary subject.' Bastion waved at a passing servant carrying a large pitcher. To Shiarn's delight it was Sasheya. She filled the prince's cup and moved to the others, filling Shiarn's last.

Sasheya smiled and contained a giggle. 'Having a good time, malady?'

'Nothing better to do.'

Regina said, 'That girl is trouble.'

Her remark sent Shiarn back into a grumpy mood, but decided a response would only cause more strife for Sasheya.

A woman dressed in billowing yellow skirts, and surrounded by a handful of gaudy looking people, appeared with the king's crowd. Bastion said, 'Here comes the Princess of Pomposity and her foppish husband. Come to start a fuss about her overrated opinions.'

'I shall keep my underrated opinion to myself,' Lord Belleguarde stated, 'She outranks my remarks considerably.'

Gaspar frowned at their brazen laughter. Shiarn looked on in wonder at the princess who had such little respect. The king's crowd separated, and Bastion's cousin, the over-weight woman in the pink gown walked towards them, followed by the tall man in green.

'So soon? Something must be stirring,' Bastion said, 'I believe I shall be summoned momentarily. What a bore.'

Vivella approached them and gave a sweeping gaze, leaving out Shiarn and ending on Bastion. 'Your father orders your company.'

'And a merry good day to you too, my favourite cousin.'

'Are you enjoying yourself, Bastion?' Vivella's smile was awkward on her freckled face.

'I was.' Bastion looked Vivella's companion over. His suit was sitting unevenly at his waist and his shirt hung loose. 'How did you enjoy the king's tone today, Dario? Did he wear a grim smile or was he pleasantly scowling?'

Dario stared blankly and Bastion's words fell flat and ignored. Vivella elbowed him in the ribs, wrenching his attention from Shiarn.

Bastion gave Shiarn a teasing smile. 'Perhaps the sights around the garden are more inspiring than my father's droll anecdotes.'

'Ah... your father is as sombre as he is grand,' Dario replied. 'The garden is teeming with delights, and new flowers I have never seen before.'

Vivella clutched Dario's arm and dragged him away and said to Bastion, 'You are required in the tower. Do not take your time.'

'How she tolerates that dolt, I shall never comprehend.' Bastion frowned. 'Did you see his face? Black and blue from God knows what — falling over himself more than likely.'

Shiarn remarked, 'The tower sounds dark and dismal.'

'It is as you say.' Bastion stood and straightened his clothing. 'You will be there, Belleguarde?' He asked the older man, although it was less of a question and more of a statement. 'Gaspar, go and freshen up.' His advisor's face crinkled with anxiety, and Bastion said, 'Do not worry, I will be there shortly.'

'Yes milord.' Gaspar dashed away at a dignified pace.

Bastion was suddenly distracted by Regina, looking pinched and pale. 'You look frightful. Are you ill?'

'I... I feel...' She swayed, appearing disorientated. '...quite unwell.'

Bastion caught her and held her arm while she recovered herself. 'Go and lie down. You look as if you need a rest.'

Without objection, she walked towards the palace, leaving Shiarn dumbfounded at her sudden departure. Bastion linked arms with her and began an unhurried walk up the same path. 'I shall escort you back. We cannot have you staying out here alone. Belleguarde, you and Vonzella go on ahead.' He waved them to pass, and said to Shiarn, 'Let us take a slow stroll so I can avoid those nobles and you, your room.'

'Yes, let's.'

'At least you seem a little happier,' he said. 'I'm working on something that might help you in some means.'

'Something to do with your father?'

He replied, 'I cannot really say at this point.'

'Do you and he get on?' She thought lovingly of her own father. Her bright red locks were from her mother but it was her father's fiery nature she had inherited.

'What an odd question.' He seemed to muse over her words. 'Indeed, he is a fearful man, but "get on"? I wonder. He's quite likeable as kings go.' He explained, 'He is an example of what I am to become.'

'And your mother died so young,' she murmured. Bastion had already spoken of his life, but his mother remained a mystery to her.

'Yes.' Sadness filled his eyes and he went on, 'She took her own life, you realize. I was too young to understand.'

Shiarn was breathless at the new insight. 'Understand why she did it?'

'No, whether it was true or not.'

'Oh?'

He sighed. 'Rumours do a terrible thing to a person. You forever question events and people's character.'

She stared with fascination at his wise perspective.

Bastion's voice became steady once more. 'My father's first wife was murdered. That is a fact.'

'Yes, you told me.'

'She is my sister's mother.' Disdain was evident in Bastion's simple statement. 'The rift between us is irreparable, she will always resent me.'

'Because she cannot rule?' Coltrene would only permit a female to be crowned if no males were in the direct line.

'It gnaws her to her bitter core.' He went on, 'I must ask you, you do not like Gaspar?'

'For some reason I think he is rushing off to whisper in Morgal's ear.' Or it could be because she despised both men.

'Perhaps that is true.' He muttered under his breath, 'I wonder what could be done?'

'About the imbecile you have as an attendant?'

'You sound concerned for me.' He chuckled. 'It's quite ironic, wouldn't you say?'

He was right, but she had to admit she didn't want anything happening to the only one who might be able to get her out of this situation.

The courtyard was vacant of people, except for a couple of ladies. All the men had retreated to discuss affairs of state. They entered the palace and walked to the grand staircase.

She embraced his arm closer to her side. Bastion leaned in with a wistful gaze. 'If it was another time and place, you and I might have become something more.'

For the first time, she felt she received a heartfelt statement, and she smiled. 'You might be right.'

'Thank you, my sweet lady, the day was an enchanting pleasure.' Bastion kissed her on the lips with warm affection.

Shiarn was breathless as he drew away.

'I must be off and see what father is planning. I trust you will not wander.' He smiled and gave her a small bow. 'For I shall look for you.'

She returned his smile. 'I know.'

He walked away, and standing on the landing, she watched him disappear down a hall on her right. The great hall had tiers of balcony passageways, with two massive staircases. Giant tapestries hung across white walls. Elaborate crystal candelabrums in extensive layers dangled from the top floor and the lower balconies. The ornate gem decorations reflected fractured rainbow light from windows in the seventy foot high domed ceiling. She gazed in awe at the polished décor, but she had little time to waste in admiring the architecture.

After making sure no one was present to see her, she ducked into a doorway. Ethos surged through her veins, permeating her skin and concealing her flesh with an unseen force. Now that she had some freedom, she was not certain how to use it. The only thing she was sure of was a need to find out about Ethan and Earona.

She dashed across the majestic hall. High archway corridors were to her left and right. Afternoon light filtered through the glass slits in a perfect position to illuminate the marble statues opposite. Without knowing where the jail was or even the exit from the palace, she moved quickly down the left, hoping it led somewhere helpful.

Whispers echoed down the hall from behind. Servants dawdled with trays and pitchers. A shadowy opening provided an escape from their path. The servants turned the corner and came at a faster rate, forcing her down the passage to a stairway. She ran up it and stopped at the small landing, catching her breath and deciding which direction to take. More stairs led up, and to her left, a corridor.

A figure came through the shadows, and Regina marched towards her. Shiarn had a pang of fear. But, the 'dragon' turned and carried on up the stairs. The woman's vacant eyes were incongruent with her determination to get some place fast. Shiarn hastened after her. Two servants, bearing refreshments, trailed behind them. Regina entered a doorway with a circular stone staircase. Ceremonial weapons and shields were dusty in the fading light coming through window slits along the wall.

Finally Regina arrived at an open door. Male voices spilled from the room. Shiarn glimpsed men seated around a grand table. She decided to invite herself into their assembly until Morgal emerged from within. He and Regina shared a bothered glance. The double doors shut behind him and with a flick of his hand, Regina followed him up another staircase. Shiarn chased after them, intrigued as to why they would be connected.

They entered a darkened room. Shiarn squeezed past, knocking Regina's leg. The woman did nothing to acknowledge the disturbance. She was relieved, yet it confirmed something was wrong with the woman. The door shut and a tingle of foreboding assailed her. Morgal spoke a command and the candles lit up one by one, making Shiarn more uncomfortable. The room was cluttered with bulky bookshelves and work benches. An imposing desk was littered with coloured bottles, miniature statues, and decorative dishes. On the right, heavy red drapes probably concealed a doorway. A smouldering pot hung from a brass stand in the corner, giving off an acidic scent reminding Shiarn of her night-time visions. Common sense shouted for her to flee. But some curious part of her argued, if she could discover who this man was, wouldn't she be better off?

Morgal retrieved a trinket hanging from a stand shaped like a tree, on his desk. He placed his hand on Regina's head and dangled a ruby before her eyes. He spoke in a foreign tongue then said, 'Your obedience is to your Master. Who is your Master?'

Her eyes stared through him. 'You are, Master.'

He finished with Regina and walked towards Shiarn, stopping a few feet away. Holding her breath, she trembled at his nearness. He poured a drink and tossed it down his throat. A peculiar bubbling came from a dish on the desk. He slammed his glass down and went to it. He drew his finger across the churning liquid, causing it to swirl red. The bubbling ceased, and he looked into its depth. 'Your majesty?'

'How are my devices proceeding?' A female voice flowed from the water, filling the room with a suffocating presence.

Despite her powers of invisibility, Shiarn sensed her vulnerability.

Morgal fingered a sapphire gem hanging on the stand. 'The king will soon be in my hand.'

'I do not care for your petty desires. I want my plan fulfilled.'

'I have your best interests in mind, my queen, as I always do.'

The dish gurgled and the voice lifted. 'My old subordinate is also searching for the Summoner. If he has discovered my plans I will be livid.'

A grim frown appeared on his face. 'Not the Arch-mage Varouse? He would not possess the power to stop you.'

The water gurgled. 'Do not underestimate him. He has been gathering dark arts for over an age. He must know about the Essenya-Key.'

'It is in the city.' Morgal smirked.

The woman shouted, 'Sooner or later the Summoner will meet with the Key.'

'My devices are searching for it,' he said, 'If we have the Key, we find the Summoner.'

'The Key will not be an easy thing to apprehend. It will be protected by its Master.'

Morgal's eyes reflected a hint of fear. 'It is said he is a savage fiend from hell, even an evil overlord. Would such a one walk the earth?'

'Not in a form you understand.' She added, 'However, I have summoned others of a similar evil to assist me.'

Morgal looked surprised. 'Not those foul women?'

'I don't care who they are. If you fail the ritual of resurrecting the Queen-mage you instigate your own destruction.' The water bubbled and the candles flicked from a gust of wind from no window. 'Look at that pitiful creature. What can they do for you except wet your own erotic desire?' There was silence and the voice stated, 'There are more effective ways to gain immortality than using *Teirarza-magi*.'

The hairs on Shiarn's neck prickled with alarm. Somehow the entity could see them. She was not safe in her Ethos protection.

His sly grin returned. 'Not at all, the spell of Life-Essence is perfect.'

'There is a presence you have not mentioned nor have I met. You are either hiding someone from me or you have an intruder.' The voice rumbled with anger. 'Truly, will you ever grow in knowledge? If it is a spy, find them. I shall trust you with this.'

Morgal started a chant and crafted a sign in the air.

Shiarn bolted for the door and swung it wide.

He shouted to Regina, 'Go — check the prisoner. Make sure she is where she should be.'

Shiarn had no desire to return to her room, but felt little option in the matter. She didn't stop till she reached the familiar corridor and slowed on approaching her room. Breathing hard, she entered her confinement, passing the ward without hindrance. She picked up a book and sat on her window seat.

Within moments, Regina flung the door open and marched through. She grabbed Shiarn's arm, wrenching her onto the floor. Yelping, Shiarn tried twisting out of the vice-like hold.

Regina yelled, 'Where have you been?'

'Here!' Struggling against Regina's uncanny strength, she cried, 'Let me go!'

Her grip loosened. 'If you try to escape you will be dealt with harshly.'

Shiarn rubbed her reddened arm. 'I will inform the prince of your brutality.'

A mean smirk made the woman ugly. 'He will understand and if he doesn't it will be made clear to him.'

Shiarn remained on the floor with legs splayed uncomfortably while Regina headed to the door. She shouted, 'What do you want from me?'

'You are yet to serve your purpose.' She left the room.

Shiarn shed a smattering of helpless tears as she slouched against the couch.

35 - In the Shadows

The Glorious Ones are driven by their need to uphold justice and the integrity of their name

The Day of Steadfast

At sundown, Dario arrived at the White Horse, puffing from his run through the streets. Disregarding Burgman's shouts, he ran up the stairs two at a time. He banged on the black chipped door until it squeaked open a finger width and a grey eye peered at him.

'I must talk to Hellier.'

Seth let him rush through and locked the door again.

Hellier sat with Marcus at the table where cards were spread. 'I'm fed up stuck in here.'

'You look splendid, Dario.' Seth admired his forest green pants and matching coat. Although, his attire could not counter the hat imprint on his damp blond locks, pressed to his forehead.

Dario held his lapel and pushed his chest forward. 'I don't often miss a chance to dress up.'

Hellier swung in her chair and looked him over, giving him an approving wink.

Marcus said, 'What have you been up to?'

His exuberance returned and he stuttered with excitement, 'I've been to the palace.'

'How grand,' Marcus drawled with no real enthusiasm, 'how did you get to go there?'

'My friend has rooms there.'

'Lucky you.' Hellier stared wide-eyed.

Seth nodded his approval. 'Very impressive.'

'I suppose it is. But that's not important.' Dario cried, 'I've seen her, your friend!'

'Who?' Marcus threw his cards down and stood to face him, knocking the chair backwards.

Seth asked, 'How do you know it's our friend?'

'Great news.' Hellier wore a proud smile.

Marcus demanded, 'Who is it?'

'The red-headed one,' Dario said, 'Shiarn, I believe.'

'No one else?' asked Marcus.

'No-one.'

Hellier hugged him and a grin spread on his face from the exchange.

'Why is she there? What shall we do?' Seth splayed his hands out in helplessness. 'Is she a prisoner?'

'Vivella says she's been in the palace a short while. Apparently as... umm, the prince's mistress.' Dario was suddenly mortified by his own words.

'Mistress?' Hellier breathed out slow. 'Blood 'n shite!'

Marcus' face reddened and Seth sat heavily on the bed, looking distraught.

Dario stared at them with remorse. 'My apologizes.' In an attempt to generate cheer, he said, 'I have a type of plan, if you are interested.'

A knock on the door broke the sullen air. Seth answered it to find Burgman. 'Ah, there's that scallywag. Dario, will you be coming down to play?'

'I will.' Dario looked at their gloomy faces and considered it a good time to depart.

Burgman left the doorway satisfied with his answer.

'I've got a servants dress you could wear.' Dario turned to Hellier. 'I've been invited to the royal ball in a couple of night's time. You could come.'

Hellier glanced down at the floor. 'I will need to talk with the others.'

Dario left, quietly closing the door behind him.

'Flamin' bastards!' Raw anger exploded from Marcus. 'I'll kill them!'

'But, why hasn't she escaped?' questioned Seth.

'At least we know where she is.' Hellier paced the room with restless energy. 'We should be taking up Dario's plan.'

Jett and Keanan walked through the door. On hearing Dario's name, Jett was instantly suspicious. 'And what would that be?'

They remained silent.

Jett tuned in to the sombre mood. 'This sure is a pit of misery.'

'It's Shiarn,' Marcus said.

Seth sat with his arms folded, staring at the floor.

Hellier received Jett's piercing stare, and said, 'Dario saw Shiarn at the palace.' She paused. 'With the prince. Apparently as his mistress.'

'God above,' muttered Keanan.

Jett's tone was sceptical. 'He knows this for a fact?'

'He knows what she looks like and he found out her name.'

Jett remained rigid unable to move his stunned body. He stared at their grief stricken expressions with a gaze suddenly stripped of outward emotion. The new information was bittersweet.

Keanan whispered, 'Dear Shiarn.'

'It is alarming to say the least.' Sensing their grief, Jett noted them watching him with expectation. 'Do you think I don't care?' He shook his head at them.

Hellier threw her hands in the air. 'But, how do we get her?'

'We will find a way,' Jett said, 'Shiarn is resourceful. Maybe she is using some guile while being captive.' He attempted reassuring himself as well as them. 'How did Dario find her?'

'His friend is in the palace.'

'The palace.' Jett brooded over this new knowledge that begrudgingly came from Dario.

Keanan remarked, 'So there was a connection to the palace after all.'

'It seems,' Jett said, 'And Dario can get in there? As much as I hate to say it, we could do with his help.'

Keanan said, 'Burgman's got Dario playing downstairs.'

'We will have to wait till tomorrow.' Jett slumped into a chair, in weary contemplation.

~ * ~

Shiarn woke from a groggy sleep. Through eyes partly opened, she observed moving shadows in her room, and once more an orangery smell irritated her nostrils. A constricting pain flared across her chest and she attempted shifting her body.

Like a nightmarish vision, Morgal approached the bed. He laughed. 'I told you I would get that information out of you, and there's nothing you can do.'

The paralyzing effect of the spell was strong, who knew what secrets he was dragging out of her. She closed her eyes, wishing she could close her mind off as well.

From out of nowhere a hard wallop caused her eyes to flash open in surprise. Giving a shocked cry, Morgal fell with a thump to the floor.

A faint whisper followed from someone else in the room. 'But maybe I can.'

Shiarn saw nothing. Whether the person was hidden in shadows she could not determine. But in the dim light the wrath on Morgal's face was clear as he tried to stand and write a sign in the air. Abruptly, his arms were folded up behind him without anyone there constraining him. A strange sight. Stranger still, Morgal was rammed into the wall, causing his forehead to bleed. His chant was halted by a dull thud, and he collapsed to the floor.

'You think—' Morgal wheezed, possibly due to a weight on his back, '—rope will hold me?'

'Yes,' the voice said, 'and this.'

His thrashing and muffled grunts were an odd sound in the dark empty room. Tottering sideways, he stood with a gag over his mouth. He was righted and shoved through the door and out of her rooms. Warmth soon circulated through her numbed muscles. She drifted into sleep, dreaming Morgal was finally done away with, but by whom, she could only wonder.

~ * ~

Jett resisted the pull of wakefulness, but a draft caressed him out of sleep. Was the balcony door ajar? Remembering he shut it before going to bed, he jerked his eyes open. A man was bent over the next bed. Within the shadows of the cloak was a thin bearded face, and he held a slender dagger at Seth's throat while fingering the white gem. Jett's hand crept under his pillow, searching for his knife. He cursed himself for leaving it in his boot. His Ethos flamed through his mind, and his vision bored into the man's hand.

The thief flinched and withdrew his arm.

Tossing the covers aside, Jett pounced on the intruder. Both of them hit the floorboards with a clumsy thump. Jett grasped the man's wrist, holding the weapon, and they wrestled. Due to his night vision, he assumed he had the advantage, but the assailant, fighting like a wild-man, deflected Jett's punches. Baring his teeth, he forced Jett on his back, and bit his neck. Jett punched his throat.

The man garbled from a pressed windpipe, 'I want the Eye-key.'

The heat of Jett's burning eyes didn't slow him, but his face contorted in pain from the ongoing fire on his skin. Control of the knife became a match of strength with neither of them being the victor. Marcus tossed in his bed, waking up, and the thief ran to the balcony with Jett chasing after.

The thief thrust the dagger at Jett. Jett dodged in time, having his suspicions of how deadly it was, and grabbed the man's wrist. Against the man's strength, he twisted his arm, driving the blade into the thief's flesh. With a yell, he kneed Jett in the groin and hurdled over the railing.

Groaning from the hit, Jett watched him land and roll, and run away into the shadows.

Marcus ran to him. 'Have you been hurt?'

Jett sat on his bed, wincing and clutching his groin. 'What does it flamin' look like?!'

'I mean.' Marcus shook his head at him. 'Have you been cut?'

'Not me.' Jett breathed deep and pressed hard on his stinging neck wound, hoping to stem the blood.

Seth lit a candle, and sitting up in his bed, he looked at the two, dumbfounded. 'What was that all about?'

Marcus came back from looking over the balcony. 'Another thief, Sprout. Maybe the same one.'

'Seth.' Jett held his palm out and ordered, 'Hand it over.'

Seth frowned with sleepy-eyed bewilderment. 'What?'

'That pendant,' Jett barked. 'That thing has nearly gotten Marcus and you killed. Twice now.'

Seth pulled it over his head and passed it to him.

Jett hesitated, recalling the first time he touched the stone. He closed his fingers over the jewel in a determined clench as if daring it to enter his mind. The jewel was an abnormal weight in his hand, like a sudden burden in his mind he really didn't want. Opening his hand, he studied the fine band of exquisite gold in an oval shape curved around a perfect white shimmering gem; a beautiful jewel that was somehow a key. 'I'll hang onto it now.' He tried to remember anything from the journal about the item, but could recall little. What was so important about this pendant? He had seen Keanan reading the book perhaps he could shed some light on it.

Keanan opened the door from the other side of the room. 'What's the noise about?'

Marcus chuckled. 'You missed the fun.'

'Tell you in the morning,' Jett said, 'go back to sleep.'

Keanan shut the door.

Marcus climbed into bed. 'You think he'll be back?'

'If he's got antidote for his poison blade…' Jett smiled at the thought of the man getting sick. 'He might be back.'

'Let's hope he doesn't,' said Marcus.

Jett put a chair in front of the closed balcony doors. He got into bed and closed his eyes.

Seth blew out the candle. In the quiet, he muttered, 'How did he walk away from falling that high?'

'He didn't fall, he jumped,' Jett mumbled, 'There's a difference. It would take some skill.'

Marcus added, 'He's a thief, don't they do that sort of thing?'

'How can I sleep now?' Seth whined, 'Burgman should put locks on these balcony doors if thieves break in so easily.'

'How did he know where you were?' Jett reflected with annoyance. 'He could have taken it while you were at Annabella's. Why did he wait till now?' The two could give no answer. He drifted back to sleep troubled over why the amulet was so important.

36 - Into... the Web

Love lost stains her jealous hands
She abides no lover to choose a separate way
My lady's craving is wrought in me
Her words are supreme, I must obey

Song of Evelonne Bloodflower

In the Kin's room, Jett dragged a chair from the table and pushed Dario onto it, and he paced before him. 'Where did you see her?'

'At the picnic—'

'You spoke to her?' Jett scrutinized him with an intimidating glare.

Under his fine fringe, Dario's eyebrows shot high with alarm. 'No, she was with the prince. Vivella and I saw her, but I... Vivella would not allow it...' Dario fidgeted with the rim of his hat, looking uncomfortable at the five pairs of eyes intent on him.

Jett raised a questioning brow in distrust. 'How did she look?'

Dario creased his brow in reflection. 'Her hair was held back and she wore a lovely blue dress—'

'Not her clothing,' Jett exclaimed with exasperation, 'I mean her face, her demeanor.'

Dario looked away with a thoughtful expression. 'She looked withdrawn and apart from the normal chitchat.'

Scowling, Jett stared into Dario's eyes, and Dario squirmed in his seat. Jett released him from his piercing gaze and looked at the others. 'I don't know why she is still there.'

Dario replied, 'The wing to those rooms could be locked.'

Jett ignored him and speculated. *She cannot leave of her own free will.*

'It is puzzling,' suggested Keanan.

'Perhaps.' Jett chewed it over aloud, 'But where would she go if she were able? There might be worse consequences if she were to attempt escape.'

'She would not know where we are.' Keanan added, 'It would be problematic.'

Jett spun back to Dario. 'What of Earona and Ethan?'

'No one else is with her.' Fright covered Dario's face at the question.

Jett studied Dario for several moments. 'You can get us in?'

Eager eyes sized Dario up, and he protested, 'I can't get all of you in. Only one.'

'You have a servant's dress?' Jett said.

Dario nodded. 'I'm attending the royal ball and Vivella has arranged a room for me. It seems your friend's room is below.'

Jett's eyes simmered at the mention of the room.

Dario added, 'I can go as a tailor or bard, and Hellier can accompany me.'

Jett locked eyes with Hellier, and said to Dario, 'You were expecting Hellier to stay in this room with you?'

'It can work.' Hellier put a hand on Jett's arm. 'Dario can get me in and I can get to her.' She cooed, 'Don't you want to know about Earona and Ethan?' *Now's not the time to get overprotective.*

She was right and besides, it was the best plan for the moment. 'You know what it is.' *You'll be with him and away from us.*

Whether I want to spend time with Dario or not, I make my own decisions.

Dario glanced from one to the other with bafflement. Realizing the others were listening to their thoughts, he looked at her blonde hair trailing down her back. 'You will need a wig.'

She touched her finely braided hair that was growing out.

'I know where to purchase a wig at a shop with older second hand wigs.' Dario reasoned, 'We couldn't really get a man's good wig.'

Jett directed to Dario, 'I assume it's best she not be seen with you or seen as little as possible.'

Dario avoided Jett's potent stare. 'I'll make sure she's safe, but she has to do what I say and not go wandering about the palace.'

Jett smiled smugly at her. 'I couldn't have said it better myself.'

Hellier scowled at him and Dario. Dario squirmed as much under her fiery gaze as Jett's.

'You must not endanger yourself, Hel,' ordered Jett, and to Dario he said, 'I'm trusting you. You don't know how hard that is for me to do.'

Dario scratched his head in thoughtful confusion. 'Thank you, I think.'

'Now, we must prepare and wait.'

~ * ~

Another meal came and went, and Ethan's hunger remained, as torturous as the cold and boredom. At one point he attempted counting those in the cell, such was the need for something to do. More than four hundred prisoners, and nearly fifty Harn were crowded into the confined area, and more men were being shoved in. From the adjoining cell, Maddog shouted at the new inmates. Meanwhile, men shuffled past, exercising their legs and casting shadows over those sleeping. Although Ethan knew how elusive sleep really was. He said to no-one in particular, 'How long has Maddog been here?'

Loc replied, 'He was here when we arrived.'

'He seems to know alot about this place,' said Ethan.

'Aye, but getting anything sensible out of him is like pulling teeth.' Loc paused. 'Fish said he's spent too much time in the hole.'

Ethan gave him a questioning glance.

Loc shrugged. 'Fish says not to ask him. I think he's had a nasty head injury.' He tapped his forehead.

Ethan leaned his head back and let the gnawing hunger wash over him; it now consumed every waking moment. 'Surely they can't keep pushing men in here.'

Gailtram muttered, 'The bastards.'

The first chamber filled with boisterous shouts and prisoners banging on the bars. Guards marched into the corridor with their crossbows and behind them they dragged a prisoner, screaming and crying.

Ethan jumped to his feet and raced to the bars to stare with awe. His ears did not deceive him; the guard was hauling a girl by her wrists towards the cells.

The men clamoured over each other with a deafening noise of excitement. She cried in distraught fits and attempted yanking the guard to a stop. Ethan clenched the bars, his knuckles whitening. She was wrenched along, shrieking, to the cell door. This new abominable act had no justifiable excuse and no human explanation. Without mercy she was shoved in and a guard slammed the gate behind her. She was lost in the midst of insane savages; her terrified wail ascended the animalistic uproar. This time there would be no convincing Ethan of the validity of his non-involvement. It was an intolerable act and more than he could bear.

Loc approached him as if reading his profound vexation.

Not so naive this time, Ethan knew what was occurring in the first cell. 'Don't tell me.' The muffled crying of the girl and men jeering, in front of the callous guards, watching with heartless smirks, offended Ethan more than anything so far. Breathing hard, he thumped his head on the bars.

Loc said, 'You can't help everyone.'

'Why, by the devil, shouldn't I try?'

''cos you'll get yourself into trouble.'

'I'm already in trouble.' With new determination, Ethan faced him. 'If I can't say or do something I'm going to *lose* myself.' He stepped past Loc watching him with dismay.

Pushing men out of the way, Ethan reached the group around the girl. Garutz stood, hauling up his pants. Beyond him the blond-haired girl was sprawled on the floor, her arms restrained, and her dress, already rags was torn down the front. Her fearful pleas went ignored by the surrounding men and her pitiful struggling did nothing to give them fear she would fight back.

Ethan stood over her legs, his deep voice boomed above the heads of the men. 'That's enough. You leave her alone.' He noticed Maddog leaning against the rocks, but he had no wish for him or the Harn to get involved. He didn't know how it would end, he only knew he had to do it for his own sanity.

A thickset young man, Horry, cried, 'He wants her for himself.'

Garutz looked shocked. 'No!' His gaze changed to one of condemnation, and he snarled, showing his yellow teeth, 'He wants to save her.'

Ethan appreciated the complexity of the situation. 'You won't touch her again.' He narrowed his eyes and stared at Garutz. The men's attention shifted to Ethan and Garutz. Even the guards, stepped closer to listen.

Garutz spat near Ethan's foot and sneered, 'Where's yer dog?'

'He does what he wants.' Before Ethan had a chance to prepare himself, Garutz' fist slammed into his chin. Ethan twisted to the side, but did not stumble. With the attack, he became aware how fatigued he was.

'He's a piss poor do-gooder,' Garutz announced to the gathering spectators.

Preparing for the inevitable, Ethan landed a hit on the side of his opponent's head. For good or bad, it was on. His fighting style was a combination of brute strength and swift fists. The chain was a hindrance, but necessity drove him to get accustomed to it. Stimulated beyond control, the inmates cheered and jeered. The question of who was winning was irrelevant, and if the men had coin they would be betting. Blood dripped into his mouth, but it wasn't the pain slowing him down, it was weariness. The sight of Garutz' fist swinging wide and hitting him in the stomach registered too late. Ethan doubled over, and through the mob of elated men, he saw the sly Zigor on top of the girl.

'Whore lover!' Garutz spat through his smirk and raised his fists. 'Not so tough.'

Pausing to catch his breath, Ethan gathered his strength, and rammed Garutz up against the bars behind him, knocking the breath out of him and shaking the whole frame. Ethan was now past caring about Garutz' life or the overexcited mob might tear him apart given half the chance. The fight could escalate into a heated brawl at any moment.

'He doesn't want to fuck her.' Garutz' foul breath polluted Ethan's nostrils. 'I know his type.' He threatened, 'I'm gonna kill you, son of a fraggin' whore-maker, if it's the last thing I do.'

Ethan forced Garutz' shoulders into the bars again, making them vibrate. So close he could see the unhealed scar on his cheek. A vicious growl came up from his belly, 'I'll kill you first.'

Unexpectedly a cry rang out in the cell followed by a cracking thud. A bolt flew over the men's heads and ploughed into the rock. Silence settled over the prisoners. 'Easy with that bow,' an older guard admonished the younger one. 'I said aim it, not shoot it.' He turned to the cell. 'That's enough from you, we haven't got all day and you two are wasting our time.'

Ethan blinked with speechless shock at the uncompassionate guard, yet less surprised at the crossbow pointed at his chest. Garutz shoved Ethan away.

'Get to the door,' the guard shouted, 'no scum in there dictates what's going to happen or not happen.'

Ethan proceeded to the door in mute disbelief while Garutz chuckled. How could Ethan expect anything else from the guards? Their wickedness rivalled that of the prisoners.

The guard snapped at Garutz, 'You too, wise arse.'

Now a couple of crossbows shifted to Garutz as he made an angry path to the cell door. The girl's fearful sobs rang in Ethan's ears. This was a new insight into the rocks lack of humanity, and another assault on his senses.

Garutz' red face was a vivid contrast to Ethan's pale miserable features. His shoulders slumped, Ethan walked from the cell, sparing a short glance at the girl partially covered from his view. Fortunately a guard was positioned between him and Garutz. He imagined

Garutz wanted to kill him there and then. They passed by the cell and Maddog shouted, 'You go down the hole, 'member it ain't caving in.'

The group of guards and prisoners separated. Ethan and his three escorts branched off to the left, and Garutz was taken to the sloping passageway. The crossbow poked into Ethan's back as he followed the first guard leading with his torch. The cramped underground passage was devoid of moving air or any chill draft. They stopped at an open door, and the guard said, 'Get in.'

Ethan peered into shadows. A round door was in the dirt floor. 'You can't be serious?'

The guard flicked his chin at the opening. 'You spend time in there till you figure out what it means to exist in the Rocks.' He was not an unattractive man, Ethan noted as he studied him intently, but his eyes were mean. As he watched, he noticed them flick to the guard behind.

'I'll be damn—' Ethan's world went black.

~ * ~

Darkness engulfed Mara in a familiar sweltering heat. In short stabbing gasps, she tried breathing. Paralysed with dread on a pillar of rock surrounded by a burning abyss, she waited. Hot wind whirled, blowing up her dress and hair, blurring her vision. Through the shades of black on another pillar, a woman in red emerged. The crimson was stark against the consuming emptiness. Magnified in Mara's vision, the woman beckoned to her. Her black tresses melded with the shadows, and her eyes transformed to black fire. This nameless woman haunted her dreams, promising fulfilment and purpose. Somehow, Mara knew what the price would be, pain and loss, even the death of her soul.

Still, she could not deny her innate call. If only she could cross the death-bringing chasm and speak with her. Countless times before she had stepped forward at the command of the mysterious woman. Stretching out her hand, she grabbed hold of an indefinable power she could not visibly see, but felt in the core of her soul.

As she had done before, she stepped, but — her foot slipped. Screaming with terror, she fell down into the pit of fire.

This time, and unlike every other time, a hand latched onto her arm, preventing her descent into nothingness. Pulling her up from the crack, he gripped her. His steady hold shook her to awareness. She looked up to see him; the dark haired one. He spoke and her heart raced with emotions she couldn't discern — and, as much as she tried, she could not bring his words to mind.

Her heart still pounding, Mara woke. The nightmare was the same as the other times, except, this time she was pulled up, and the one who saved her had a face, and a name.

She opened her eyes enough to see a woman leaning over her. Mara's limbs were heavy under the covers. Panic gripped her. Her angry complaint was a guttural mumble beneath the gag over her mouth. It was not the old hag, but a woman dressed in civilian clothes, and holding a scented cloth over Mara's face.

Mara attempted breathing shallow the acrid smell of some sort of potion, but it was too late. Light-headed, Mara muttered a curse as the woman pulled back the blankets. She lifted her from the bed and laid her on the floor. Dazed, Mara did nothing as the woman rolled her in a rug and picked her up. Mara cast a sideways glance to Earona, still asleep. No dream of a crying baby to wake her this time.

In and out of wakefulness, Mara sensed she was carried out into the cool night air. She could hardly breathe in the stifling space, but soon she was laid on the ground again.

A gate squeaked open and she heard the footsteps of another person.

'Got her,' the woman said to the newcomer.

Above Mara came a man's voice. 'Let's hope you got the right one. Is she Rynian?'

'I'm sure,' the woman said, 'but, she's pregnant.'

'Hmm?' A moment of silence followed. 'If that's the case, she could double her worth.'

The rug was pulled down, revealing Mara's face. In her sleepy state, she peeled an eye open. The man's fine hair fell around his hollow cheekbones and his neat goatee. He took a strand of her hair and ran it through his fingers. 'A pity I cannot keep you for myself.' He caressed her head. 'But you will fetch a high price. Possibly even more than I expect.'

Mara glared and mumbled a curse under the wrapping.

He pulled up the rug and stood. 'My thanks to you. As I am true to my word, here is the payment.'

The woman shook the pouch of coins. 'Anything for you, Lucien.'

'I shall be off with the package.' The man picked Mara up and she lay, wrapped in the rug, in his arms. 'Until next time.'

The door shut and Mara was carried off into the night by her silent captor.

37 - Waiting for Light

Do not consider you are safe
Alone in your mind there is no safety

Journal of Night

On the day of the ball, Hellier came out of her room wearing the grey servant's skirt and white blouse. Not allowed to wear her leather jerkin under her shirt, she wore a corset the boys bought her. Lace was on the cuffs and similar material hemmed the neckline. It was uncomfortable and she felt ridiculous. Marcus laughed outright at her and Seth, unable to restrain himself, also chuckled. Mortified, Hellier cried, 'I hate it!'

'It's not that bad,' Keanan said, 'We are not accustomed to seeing you in a dress.' He sounded confident, yet Hellier suspected he was trying to be nice.

Jett smiled with merriment. 'Are you wearing trousers under that dress?'

She lifted her skirt, showing off her close fitting pants.

'You will have to take those off,' Dario stated. Everyone's gaze turned to him. He blushed and added, 'It might be noticed.'

Jett said, 'Take them off and put your wig on.'

The pants were off, the wig and white cap went on. Her blue eyes appeared smaller under the dangling brunette curls. She swung her cloak over her shoulders and Dario picked up the bag they packed. She walked to the door with a self-assured swagger. 'I'll see you all as soon as I'm back.'

~ * ~

On the way, Dario laid down some rules, the most important, Hellier was not allowed to initiate conversation with anyone, including any arguments. His underlying apprehension was the probability of his lady friends meeting. 'What's going on with you and Jett?' Since noticing the tension between the two it was playing on his nerves. 'I don't wish to step on anyone's toes. Especially his.'

'Nothing's between us.' A fiery glare turned his way and she demanded, 'What did he say to you?'

'It's what he doesn't say.' He fiddled with the tailor tools at his belt and watched the people, suddenly preoccupied by their passing. 'I thought maybe he had feelings for you.'

Hellier linked her arm through his. 'Jett and I are good, old, friends, that's all.'

That only unsettled him further. He knew what could happen between good old friends.

'I used to have feelings for Jett, but he…' Her eyes lowered, the ground becoming more interesting.

Dario raised an eyebrow at her unpromising words. 'Use to?'

'No, not now.'

'You love him?'

'In a way.' Hellier let her breath out loudly.

Dario marveled at the revelation. 'He spurned you?'

Hellier cried, 'Not exactly.'

They arrived at the servant's gate and two guards watched them approach. Dario informed them he was a tailor whose services were required by various noble ladies, one of whom the Duchess Vivella. He added, 'Min is the extra help for the evening's festivities.' They studied Dario's attire while Hellier, as Min smiled shyly, and without any questions they were both waved in.

They moved through the servant's quarters first. Walking past dorms and guest rooms, Dario pointed out places he considered informative for a servant to know. Servants bristled and fluttered with whatever it was servants did. Hellier had no idea, but Dario instructed her to just 'look' busy. They walked up flights of stairs and Dario pointed down the corridor leading to Shiarn's room. Up another floor, they arrived at the vacant room. An old lounge suite and table with chairs were in the front room. The bedroom, darkened by heavy drapes, had a luxurious double bed. Hellier threw off the wig and plonked down on it. 'Dark and gloomy.'

Dario eyed the room, noticing the single oil lamp. 'I think it best we don't have a fire.'

'Won't you be staying here with me?'

'I will be here later. I have the party to attend.' Unsure how he would juggle the attentions of the two women, he pushed it from his thoughts and walked to the window of the room. He threw it open and pointed to a window on a diagonal from theirs, two floors down. 'That's her room.'

Dario sat on the bed and she joined him. Her expression softened at his careful attention of her face. A fragile look entered her eyes and she caressed his cheek. Moments of breathless anticipation followed as he enjoyed her fondling of his neck and hair. Pulling his head close, she kissed his lips. He responded to her warm mouth, and her eagerness turned to fiery passion. Under his shirt, her hands searched over his chest. Unable to stop the tide of desire, he fell hard into her needy embrace. The pain in his side did nothing to deter him, or the consideration Jett might discover their dalliance.

'We haven't much time,' she crooned in his mouth.

Shivers sped through his torso, igniting a yearning in his groin he didn't think he could control. 'Are you sure? Now?'

'No other time.' She nuzzled his neck with gentle bites.

Rational thought flew out the window. Love overtook him with an unstoppable flood of physical need. Her abandonment to him would not be refused. In his wildest dreams, and he had had a few, he did not imagine a lover could be so on fire. He pulled off her shirt and she did the same for him. He wanted to stare at her body, but the depth of her kisses consumed him. His hot hands massaged her supple mounds and she moaned under his mouth. His hand brushed a deep scar on her back, and he touched the outline with care.

She yanked his pants off, and after her skirt was dropped, her nakedness aroused him to a new level. Soon enough his lust escalated and her cries added fuel to his ecstasy. All his pent up passion exploded into one moment, overwhelming him with loving desire.

Afterward they lay on the tangled covers together. Hellier rolled onto her stomach, and placed a hand on his chest. Her bronzed slender body was flexible, and so dissimilar to Vivella. Above her buttocks was a tattoo of a flowing design, interlocking each line in a maze of spiraling shapes. He traced his finger over the flawless circular lines, and a type of script was at its center. In the relaxed quiet, Dario said, 'Now, I must go.' Despite his words, he had no desire to leave and he moved leisurely to the side of the bed. 'How did you get that scar?'

Her peaceful expression turned defensive. 'I was attacked.'

He glanced at her with uncertainty, recalling with disturbing clarity her skirmish with Big Pat and the other unfortunate soul in the alley. A tremor of fear traveled up his spine. 'By something big?'

'It was.'

After a moment of speechless surprise, and imagining Hellier doing away with people and creatures, Dario started with an awkward tone, 'I have to meet with Vivella and prepare for this Ball.'

She turned on the bed and her bright blue eyes gazed at him with longing.

Truly beautiful, she was worth waiting for, but now… he wasn't sure what he had committed himself to. Overcome with guilt, he was unexpectedly afraid.

She swung her legs over the side and watched him dress. 'That was my first time.'

Stunned to his bones, he stammered, 'you never sa— I mean— I didn't know…' If he had any inkling he would be better prepared, maybe he would have thought twice, maybe he would have—

'Does it matter?' Frowning, her features grew sombre.

'I…well… it does—' Dario gulped and caught his breath. 'I would have preferred knowing. I might have been more… sensitive. But you were exceptional.' What had he done? And more importantly what was he to do? Any option would certainly incur wrath from both women. Not for the first time, he contemplated running away, maybe taking a long trip to anywhere.

She narrowed her eyes and her fists clenched the bed sheet. 'You enjoyed it?'

That she would think to ask such a question made his head swim. 'Your heart is alive with a living fire, fervent and deadly. A man could asphyxiate in your amorous embrace through your passionate devotion.'

Bewilderment started to cloud her eyes.

'Yes, with all my body and soul.' He put his hands on her shoulders and looked into her trusting eyes. 'Now you must keep out of trouble tonight. The palace is dangerous for those unfamiliar to it. Sometimes servants get…abused.' In the fading light she looked like a goddess of the sun. He kissed her with extra tenderness. 'Good luck tonight.'

~ * ~

The door shut and Hellier fell back on the bed, staring at the ceiling. Dario was not reacting in the way she expected. He was gentle and she was physically excited by his body and the new sensation of having a man, but something was missing. His eyes were guarded and his voice not honest, and her heart did not leap at his careful stroking nor did he share any special thoughts with her. The truth was startling. She was not in love with him as she thought. But — she had finally been with a man and the act was not as fulfilling as she expected. Perhaps it got better the more you did. She wondered if there would be another chance. She sighed with melancholy at how difficult that would be.

Dressed again in the maid outfit, she added the wig. She hid her gear and left the room. In the halls, she spotted a noble here and there and servants hurrying about, lighting lamps. She hurried down two levels in the direction of Shiarn's room. The design of the floors appeared different to what she expected. The corridor ended and she doubled back. Following another, it led her through the center of the level and to the hall Dario pointed out. This one had numerous doors on either side, and came to an alcove and window. She peered down the narrow passage and a man appeared from the shadows.

He demanded, 'What are you doing here?'

Startled, Hellier curtsied. 'Sir, I'm looking for a room.'

He had a thin moustache and black hair flattened under a cap. His dark blue robes were like nothing she had seen in Floris. 'Whose room?'

'Lady Shiarn's.'

'Is that so?' He stepped closer, his face mere inches from hers. 'Who sent you there?'

'Netty, head of room cleanup.' Hellier repeated the name Dario mentioned earlier.

'No one goes to Shiarn's room except Regina.' His hand took hold of her cheek and he glided it down her neck. He whispered by her mouth, 'I've not seen you before. What is your name?'

'Dora.' Preparing to run, she added with restrained anger, 'Sir.'

'We need to discuss your service in private.' He locked tight to her neck.

She smacked his hand away and punched him in the stomach. Holding her wig tight, she sprinted down the hall without a backwards glance.

'I'll find you!' He shouted, 'Guards!'

Eventually, she found the stairs and ran, cursing herself all the way for her rash behaviour. She did not stop till she arrived at her room, and closing the door, she locked it. For several moments she caught her breath and kept watch through the key hole. The corridor remained empty, but it would be impossible for her to leave her rooms now. Surely the man would search for her, he probably went hunting for the miscreant servant straight away.

Her finger became a flame and she lit up the lamp in the room. She took the wig off and changed into her own clothes. After she ate the bread and sausage she packed, she unfolded the rope and noticed the two lengths already tied at one end. Yanking on them, she tested their combined strength. Evidently Keanan had not trusted her knot tying skill and did it himself. Sitting cross-legged on the bed, she tied more knots at intervals along the rope. It was laborious, but made scaling a smooth wall easier. No light was visible from Shiarn's room so she would have to wait. There was no way she would return with nothing to show for her visit.

~ * ~

It wasn't until breakfast Earona's worry over Mara reached its limit. The girl's empty bed gave her some concern, but she reasoned she might be on early duties somewhere and forgot to mention it. But when the women gathered in the hall, Mara was not amongst them.

Through the slow crowd of dispersing women, Earona pushed her way to Counsellor Elata. 'Counsellor, have you seen Mar...ee. I haven't seen her this morning.'

Elata gave her a curious glance. 'I haven't seen her myself. Perhaps she has duties at the orphanage. Don't fret—'

Earona grabbed her arm, refusing to be brushed aside. 'No. You must look for her. I fear something awful has happened.'

The counsellor's stare became cross. 'I'll see where she is.'

Earona worked in the garden, her anxiety growing worse as the morning progressed. She watched every girl walking the yard, looking for Mara's red-gold hair, but she did not appear.

Eventually, Counsellor Elata came back and stood over her with a stern expression. 'Mother has requested your presence.'

Wiping her hands on her skirt, Earona stood. 'Is it Maree? Have you found her?'

'Just come.'

At her desk, Mother shuffled through some papers while Earona entered.

Rigid, Earona sat, clenching her skirt. 'Well?' She leaned on the edge of her chair. 'Something's happened, hasn't it?'

'It's quite serious. We cannot locate your sister anywhere on the compound.'

Earona clutched her chest. 'Oh, my God! She's been kidnapped.'

'Perhaps.' Mother gave her an ambivalent stare. 'But we really cannot be sure at this point.'

'What do you mean?' Earona cried.

'The lock on one of the back doors of the yard has been forced,' Mother said. 'It's possible she might have escaped.'

'I don't believe that,' Earona stated. 'She was attacked the other night.'

'Yes, that's interesting.' Mother sighed and raised her hand to stop Earona's reply. 'How can you be certain she didn't run off?'

'I...' Earona looked past her in thought. *No. She wouldn't. Would she?* Despite wanting to believe the best in Mara, she could see her making such a decision, and leaving Earona behind. She suddenly felt a terrible sense of loneliness. She breathed, '...no...,' and went on with more conviction, 'she wouldn't leave me here.'

'Perhaps that's true.' Mother continued, 'Regardless, I've sent word to the Watch. When they find her, she can be dealt with.'

'Dealt with?' Earona shuddered at the ominous word.

'If she intentionally broke her contract, she will be sent to the Rocks. But if she's held by some abductor she will be apprehended and brought back here.'

Earona's eyes welled with genuine tears at the loss of her young companion and she whispered, 'I just hope to see her again.'

~ * ~

Ethan opened his eyes to complete darkness. He attempted moving from his cramped position and his head hit the ceiling. Reaching above in alarm, he scraped his hand on hard earth. After tracing the wall with his fingers, he discovered a circular door above him. Out of frustration, he punched the iron and hurt himself more. He ran his fingers over the grill in the door, thinking cynically how they wanted to keep him alive by giving him air to breathe. His yells echoed as a muted muffle. Hungry, sightless, and cramped, he questioned if it could get worse and he gave a facetious smile, thankful it was not wet.

The gloom was quiet, but his thoughts were thunderous. Recalling the girl in the cell, he questioned what she could have done to deserve such treatment. He could bear physical scars for the rest of his life, but that sort of torture was soul destroying. But, because of his views he was the one in this hole. Maybe Loc was right, he shouldn't act like a fool.

Sleep was the only thing to shut off his thoughts, but it was not lasting. Visions of his Kin tortured his senses with longing. He wondered what Jett would have done, or Marcus, but it was not them in a hole. At least Jett would see his cell and Marcus would have been out days ago. His maniacal laughter descended into loud crying.

He heard a dull ringing in the soundless space and wondered if he had gone mad. The compact space was stuffy and it seemed the ceiling pressed down on him. With his fist clenched, he hit the walls with fury. Fatigued from that small exertion, he took shallow breaths. The longer he was there, the more he breathed the dead air — and with no way of knowing how much time had passed. Time was irrelevant, all he knew was hunger and darkness, both never ending.

Death could take him and no one would know of his fate.

Waking brought more confusion and a profound loss of time. The oppressive weight of the rocks did not abate. Even the walls shrunk in on him, intent on crushing his breathing. Contemplating the time it would take for a man to suffocate, an image of his Kin flitted across his mind once more. Deep inside, he felt some part of him was dying.

38 - The Golden Net

There is a hope that sprouts at the sight of approaching love.

Prophetess Janna Meadow'Fox, 4th Seat Elder

Shiarn was startled from her doze by someone prodding her shoulder.

Sasheya sat beside her in the pre-dusk light. 'You wouldn't believe what I had to go through to serve you. But, if the *dragon* finds me here.' She drew her finger across her throat.

In earnest, Shiarn whispered, 'Don't jest like that.'

Sasheya began lighting candles about the room. 'You look more troubled than usual.'

'It's that obvious?' She replied. Morgal was dealt with, but somehow she sensed it wasn't the end of it.

'Tonight they will see you in your finest splendour.' Sasheya laid the midnight blue dress on the bed. 'Hurry, I must do your hair.'

Shiarn went behind her screen to dress and remarked with candid gravity, 'Sash, I have this awful feeling I'm being used, as if in some type of game.'

'Why on earth do you think that?'

'And,' Shiarn bemoaned, 'I think the prince might be used as well.'

Sasheya gasped. 'By who?'

Shiarn avoided her curious gaze, realizing how vulnerable the girl was. 'Morgal is... was involved.' She wriggled into her dress. 'Regina is not who she seems to be either.'

Sasheya pulled the lacing of her bodice. 'What are we to do?'

Shiarn held her breath as the corset was tightened around her chest. 'You are to do nothing.'

Sasheya completed the tying of the dress in silence. The midnight hue velvet transformed Shiarn into a royal beauty. Glittering gems bordered the bodice and sleeves, and delicate lace peeped out to enhance her bosom. The skirt flowed out from her faultless waist and swirled about her feet. Looking at her reflection, tears wet her eyes.

'Don't cry, you'll spoil yourself. Let me finish your hair.' Sasheya pulled Shiarn's hair till it rested at the top with elegant wisps dangling by her neck.

'How pretty.' Shiarn admired herself in the hand mirror. 'Wish you could always do my hair.'

Sasheya blushed with a smug smile.

Shiarn hopped up and dashed to her drawers. She tugged one open and took out a tiny pouch. 'I must give you something.'

'What is it?'

'Don't open it until you are safe in your room and no one is watching. It is a gift from me. Well, not from me, but it's all I have to give.' She took the girl in her arms for a warm embrace. 'To show my appreciation.'

'I haven't done so much, but thank you.' Sasheya peeked in the pouch and gaped at the pink tinged diamond ring. 'I really shouldn't…'

Shiarn pushed it into the safety of the girl's bodice. 'You will.' Her face turned grim. 'No one will know. But remember, you must be careful.'

'I'll… I'll try.'

~ * ~

Regina came to escort Shiarn from her rooms. Once she closed the door, Regina locked it and dropped the key into her purse, hanging amidst the folds of her emerald ball gown. They proceeded through semi-lit corridors, and past servants carrying candleholders to light the lamps. Other splendidly dressed people joined them as they neared the Grand Celeste Ballroom.

Two great halls were separated by open concertina doors. The ceiling was painted in sweeping skies and rolling fields dotted with a marching army. People in bright and stiff attire crowded into the vacuous space. At the end of both halls, double doors of decorative glass opened up onto the courtyard lit by the twilight sky. Cushions plumped up couches, and gold painted chairs framed the enormous breadth of the dancehall. Detailed tapestries, depicting great battles and famous monarchs, hung high on the cream walls. The royal seating faced long banquet tables in the dining hall. Marble surfaces glinted amid the silver embellished tableware under the hazy glow of lights set high in gold candelabras.

Regina had not spoken a word since retrieving her from her rooms, and Shiarn was not about to waste time conversing with her now. The less she said to the cruel woman, the less she would speak in return. Shiarn took a glass from a passing servant armed with a tray of refreshments.

The musicians stopped playing and the noise of the room ceased at the appearance of a herald in gold and red. In a booming voice, he announced the king's entry. The king, dressed in gold with an abundance of white ruffles spilling from the front of his suit, appeared on the stairs. Next to him, the prince, a younger version of the king, except his blonde curls were longer, and his clothing more extravagant. Princess Byester wore a stunning gown of similar gold fabric covered with sparkling glass beads. A diamond tiara shone against her black curls. Byester's husband, at least twenty years older than his wife, was not much to look at. Obviously, the princess was not married for aesthetic pleasure.

At the sight of Morgal, Shiarn gulped for air and cringed as his eyes darted over the people. She had hoped he was permanently removed from her life. It was in vain. The perplexing scuffle in her room had no lasting effect. Once again she questioned who the stranger was to have protected her yet still leave Morgal to torment her.

King Basylus strolled past bowed heads and curtsying women, and stopped at his table. He glanced at the hovering servants, and stepped onto the raised platform. Bastion sat on his right, and the princess on his left. Oddly enough, Morgal sat by Bastion, and the king's brother sat on Morgal's left. Shiarn noticed the peculiar discrepancy, and wondered if others would be aware. It wouldn't surprise her if Morgal was not popular among the king's people.

A servant led Shiarn and Regina to their seats. To her delight Lord Belleguarde arrived at the chair beside her. He bowed his head and she gave him a tentative smile. After the initial formalities they were permitted to be seated and Jonas took the opportunity of helping her settle in her chair. She said, 'I hope there is not much more of that.'

'How delightful to see you are chirpy this evening.'

'Sitting next to you will relieve my boredom,' she said. 'Did you plan this or was it Bastion?'

'Certainly it was our mutual friend,' he replied. 'I hope you don't mind, he is good at masterminding such things. He did it on our first meeting.'

She was taken aback that Bastion would consider coordinating people's seating arrangements.

'And to answer your previous question, yes, there will be a lot more of that,' he informed her. 'Positively monotonous and droll, nonetheless, you cannot possibly have these grand galas without all the pomp and ceremony.' He waved a graceful hand across the table.

Throughout the first course she focused on her food and listened to Jonas drone on about the lack of service in the palace. Previously, he was a fastidious boor, and on this occasion he was beyond his usual arrogance.

'You really ought to cheer up,' he mentioned flippantly. 'Why do you not get out more often?'

His patronizing conduct was disheartening and she replied with melancholy, 'You really think so?'

'Well, as I was saying, Gerty, my serving lass, fell into such a bother I had to give her a drink.' He laughed and other diners shared his mirth.

Shiarn's ears perked up with intrigue. 'What was that?'

He lifted his head and his eyes skimmed those seated across from him. 'She saw an apparition and it spooked the life out of her.'

'It would spook anyone.'

'Yes, undoubtedly, if one actually saw something. Truly, the poor girl said it was in the tower and dressed like a servant. At least it could have been an old king or queen.' He carried on, 'And the figure spoke.' He leaned over the table so those farther down were able to partake of his repartee. 'Gerty was far too afraid to even pay heed.' He laughed and others shared his merriment at the expense of the poor servant, most likely seeking aid from an ostensibly noble lord.

Sasheya passed through Shiarn's mind, and she said, 'Should the girl's fear be mocked?'

'Are you interested in the blubberings of a serving lass?' He raised an eyebrow at her. 'She probably fell down a stair and knocked her head. I mean really, who could believe it?'

She had no wish to argue with him and went back to eating her meal.

'I believe she ran off screaming. Good for her I say, at least she did not faint on the way.' He nodded at Lady Magda looking down her unattractive nose at him.

Shiarn switched off from listening to Lord Belleguarde and chanced a glance at the royal table. Morgal was staring at her with a strange calculating expression and it repulsed her. Her eyes flicked away and she pretended to listen to Jonas' inane account of an old friend of his.

Speeches and formalities interrupted the dinner at intervals before the delicate melody of the instruments swept over the noisy chatter. Bastion found her and after greeting Jonas, he led her into the flow of dancing couples. Holding her hand loosely, he folded her arm into his and said, 'I believe this might put you at ease and take away that dark look.' He rubbed her hand with genuine kindness. 'Tonight you look absolutely divine and without any question you are the most beautiful woman here.'

The touch of his hand was a strange sensation and she managed a smile, but even that weak token was only for him. 'Am I noticeably tense?'

'To me, yes.' Their conversation paused as the rhythm quickened. She spent the time losing herself in the movements, letting her thoughts meander over the people she linked hands with, not wanting to think of her own problems. The dance finished and Bastion left her, promising to come back soon.

She grabbed a goblet of wine and sat on a velvet couch. Jonas sat beside her. After a stylish sniff of his drink and a dainty sip, he commented on its vintage and faultless flavour. His voice carried, leaving those about him no choice but to take note of his declaration.

In earnest, Shiarn considered his handsome features that seemed to suit one of noble birth. His clean shaven face had chiseled lines that added to his appeal, and his blue eyes were dazzling and at that moment very attentive. 'I see you are not with the duchess tonight.' She spied Vonzella in another striking red gown.

Jonas replied with a flutter of his hand, not at all disturbed by her question, 'And she is such a charming woman.' He leaned close, his face inches away. 'However, far too ambitious for one such as myself.' A disappointed look crossed his face and he exclaimed in a whisper, 'Besides, I do believe she had plans for marriage.'

'Really, I thought you shared that desire?'

'True, I amused myself with visions of grandeur. However, I am unworthy of such an honourable position.' With a whimsical rise to his brows, he said, 'And I would never be able to talk to ladies such as yourself so freely.'

Her mouth twitched with a taunting smile. 'I'm sure you would find a way.'

'A way, indeed.' He whispered, 'For instance, I wouldn't be able to easily enquire how you are this day?'

She mulled over his query and thought better of revealing her mind. 'I thought I was better, but... I cannot speak of it here.'

'You are right. Such a conversation requires a private interlude.' Stroking his chin, he turned and in a pretentious manner commented about the musicians' outstanding play. An elderly man seated nearby agreed courteously. Jonas faced her again. 'Soon I shall speak more frankly. But now, let us dance.'

A slower tune began and they joined the other dancers. Shiarn could not take her bewildered eyes off him. 'Are you purposely trying to befuddle me?'

'Only because things are beginning to stir and shake.'

As they danced, she had the impression he spoke only when his back was facing the open side of the hall. Once discovering Morgal was watching her, Jonas' lack of chatter was understandable. She suddenly wondered who the man before her really was.

'I do nothing without a purpose. Nevertheless, at times I must deliberate on what action best suits the need,' he said, 'in the interim, prepare for every contingency that may be possible.'

She narrowed her eyes at his discerning remark. 'And how do I do that?'

Kindness softened his words. 'Have you played Kings Square?'

'Of course.'

'Ah, good to hear. I take it you understand what I am implying when I speak of that game.'

'Perhaps.' She tilted her head and smiled. 'I'm quite good at it.' There would not be one in her Kin who could beat her, except Keanan sometimes.

'Mayhap, we will play together one day.' He smiled and continued, 'Often it is convenient to be someone you are not. It covers all types of difficult situations. Not being present is also advantageous. Some advice, create your opportunity, and use whatever your environment offers.'

She stared at him with a frown, exasperated by his riddles.

'We shall speak later, if I am given the opportunity.' They broke apart after the dance ended and Jonas said, 'I must speak with Lady Penelope. I ought to apologize and make amends to the poor woman, calling her brother a blathering fool was most disrespectful of me, no matter how true that is.' He left her and trailed after another woman without giving Shiarn a backward glance.

Shiarn lingered without an escort as long as she could until Regina appeared at her side. 'What was Lord Belleguarde speaking to you about?'

Maintaining the façade, Shiarn laughed. 'An amusing story about Lady Penelope's brother.' She exaggerated a brief event Jonas described earlier.

Regina looked with suspicion at Lord Belleguarde prattling on to a dark-haired woman in a pink gown. 'He has many stories to tell.'

'But he does ramble on too much.'

A serving girl carrying a tray of cups walked past. Shiarn accidently jostled a gentleman in her path, tipping the tray down the front of Regina's dress. A dozen people witnessed the drama, a few women dared to snicker. Lacking any decorum, Regina cursed the girl. Her scarlet cheeks and foul language drew many an eyebrow up. Tears reddened the girl's eyes and the gentleman tried his best to calm Regina.

Shiarn slipped to a corner, lost in the cluster of spectators and watched the debacle from a safe distance. Bastion came and assisted Regina, ordering her upstairs to change, and he disappeared into the colourful crowd.

A man in a bright blue suit appeared and bowed to Shiarn with an eccentric flourish. 'Lady Shiarn, I did not think you could be any more beautiful after the day in the garden, however, I was woefully wrong.'

Recognizing him, Shiarn gave him a smarmy smile. 'That's very kind, but—'

He stepped closer and took her hand. 'I've been looking forward to meeting you.'

'Excuse me?' She leant back with unease, her hand still in his.

'I know your friends.' He grinned with excitement.

Startled by his remark, she took a moment to respond. 'Who?'

Bastion's cousin, in a flowing green dress and her hair elaborately braided around her head, came to stand beside him. She said to her companion, 'There you are, Dario! I was waiting to dance.' She yanked on his arm.

Dario stood his ground, but responded with a hearty smile. 'And we will, V, but Shiarn was talking with me.' He turned back to Shiarn and his eyes lit up.

Shiarn grabbed hold of his other arm, unwilling to let him go. 'Tell me, who do you know?'

Vivella glared and pulled Dario to her side. 'He is not going to keep company with one such as you. You harlot!' She spat out with unexpected vehemence, 'I forbid it.'

The insult pierced the wall of indifference she hid behind. Stunned, she stared with heartfelt pain washing over her.

Vivella dragged him away and he said over his shoulder, 'I know Hellier and Seth and the others—' He disappeared among the crowd.

Grim, she stared after him, holding back her tears. The one person she really wanted to talk to and he was gone.

Jonas appeared with two goblets. 'I believe you have need of this.' He handed her one and stated, 'Finally, I have you to myself. Now, we can escape the 'dragon', or perhaps there is more than one.' His eyes flicked to the direction of Vivella.

Startled by his use of the word dragon, she let it slip for now and took the wine. She let him guide her out to the courtyard and along the balcony, away from the noise flowing through the open doors. They stopped at the wall overlooking the garden; the trees cast giant shadows across the lawn, and not far was the bubbling fountain. A cool breeze made her catch her breath.

'Without doubt this is the best the king has to offer.' He sipped his wine.

'I love a good chat, but tonight… as you probably know, I've got things on my mind.' Now she had met someone who knew of her Kin and she couldn't speak to that person, made things worse. 'Although, I appreciate you inspiring me to be rid of Regina.'

'You are welcome, however, I did not think you would be so dramatic or so quick.'

'I don't do anything discretely.' She tasted the rich burgundy, and murmured, 'it seems.'

He was tall and he watched her over the rim of his goblet. 'See, did I not say it was exceptional.'

She narrowed her eyes and fixed a brazen gaze on him. 'You're a very enigmatic man and under more pleasant circumstances I should have liked to have gotten to know you better.' After another drink, she continued with more cynicism, 'But you speak as if you know more than you say. Now, I'll be frank. If you know why I'm here, you better tell me,' she became more cross as she went, 'And, before you say anything, I'm quite livid that evil man can walk around without any consequences to his actions.'

'I know.' He shook his head, his untied curly wig skipping over his shoulder. 'You are right, of course. This whole situation has become a horrendous state of affairs.'

Her mouth hung open and she stared in acute bewilderment.

His eyes darkened and he was furious when he spoke. 'Morgal is a blight in this palace, and like you say, an evil man.' He paused. 'In truth he should not be here anymore.'

She shook herself from her confused daze. 'I don't understand. He is still here.'

'I wonder if you have friends searching for you?'

At the mention of her friends again, her bafflement increased. 'They are locked up somewhere…'

'There are others?' Concern was suddenly revealed on his face.

'Others?'

His perceptive eyes probed hers.

She continued, guardedly, recalling Morgal also questioned her about someone else possessing the pendant. 'If I do, how would I find them?'

'A dilemma indeed.'

Shiarn narrowed her eyes. 'What do you know of this?'

Jonas exhaled a heavy breath. 'I shouldn't talk about such things here, but suffice to say, it is a job of mine… to unearth secrets.' He reached a hand to hers and gave it a comforting squeeze. She observed his smooth hands and glanced at the various rings on his fingers. A couple had gems; one was thick gold with a single letter. His warm hand caused her to realize the air was chilly. He led her with gentle force down the steps to a vacant bench along the garden path.

Her skin tingled from the intimate touch. 'People will talk.'

'People speculate on me all the time and truly, enticing a beautiful lady such as you, away, would not be a new piece of gossip.' He smiled and swept away debris from the seat. They sat on the wood bench in sight of the steps. 'My sweet lady, let us sit.' His charming tone brought confirmation of his seductive nature. Although, nothing she previously assumed about him could now be believed.

Away from the glare of the open doors, Jonas appeared more relaxed. 'It's simple, well, I should say that is how it started off. Presently it has transformed into a complicated debacle.'

Shiarn went stiff and turned to him with a perplexed stare. 'What are you talking about?'

'Why you are here.' He took a breath and continued, 'There's an underlining issue that began this. The prince made a decision to have a lover. It couldn't be any woman of this court or Coltrene. But who would this woman be? He wondered.' His eyes darted away and his hand tightened. 'Morgal gave him the "word" he would find this woman, and she would be the answer to his problems.'

'Me?' She tried to dig some sense out of the insanity. 'But, we were never lovers.'

'No.' Jonas paused with a sad gaze. 'And you probably never will be. That is because… his preference is not towards women.'

She gasped with realization. 'I think I understand.'

'In this family and kingdom it is seen as perverted behaviour and is not tolerated in one's public life. No one must know of this. But I fear the king has discovered it.' Jonas' tone became harsh, 'Bastion is too stubborn. He did not wish to marry and have his secret discovered, and live a false existence attempting to create an heir.'

'He wanted to create rumours about his manhood for a time.' Shiarn sighed at how well it worked. 'Who better than a foreigner with no idea about this court?'

'I was hoping he would discover and come to enjoy the company of a woman.' Jonas pursed his lips together. 'It was not to be, although he is fond of you, he would never be able to disclose himself to a woman.' Pain entered his eyes and it carried through onto her, startling her with its intensity. 'He remains wrapped up in his need to find approval from men.'

'Bas is an attractive man and under different circumstances, maybe…' Her cheeks tinged pink at the revelation. 'However, there is so much more going on aside from his reticence towards me.'

Absorbed by her heartfelt declaration, he lowered his eyes.

'I believe Morgal might have ensorcelled the king and Regina,' she blurted, suddenly not caring how much he knew.

'You may be right.' Anxiety, she had never seen on him before, troubled his face. 'And considering Regina's background, it is obvious, however, it baffles me why he would ensorcel her.'

She shook her head. 'Too allow Morgal to watch me? He despises me, because I did not have this jewel he wanted. The Essenya key.' Her head lowered and she stared into her fast disappearing wine.

Observing her bowed head, he said with concern, 'Interesting. I have never heard of it.'

She raised her eyes, creasing with suspicion. 'Why should you know any of this? And how did you already know about Regina?'

'The truth is, I know very little.' He considered her for several pensive moments. 'I am quite intimate to the happenings of the prince and I am here to aid you in a silly type of way, I have come to realize.'

Shiarn stared with astonishment, her heart plunging into disappointment. 'You are watching me like she is?'

He laid aside his cup and turned her rigid shoulders to face him. 'It is no longer like that.' He stared her full in the face and spoke in gentle reassurance. 'You have affected me more than I thought possible.' His voice became rough. 'I had no idea this trauma with Morgal would happen to you. At the beginning I set my hand to help, yet even that was done with selfishness at its heart.' He appeared to struggle with an inner conflict, and grief was obvious in his eyes. 'When I discovered others were with you and they were hastily and illegitimately apprehended, I was appalled. I had no idea how evilly wrought Morgal's scheme was until I saw it unfolding.'

Shiarn's eyes pierced his anguish. She glimpsed a real man beside her, not the pompous lord she had initially known. After a thoughtful pause, she said, 'Morgal's plan was to steal this pendant from me.'

In a distracted manner, Jonas said, 'An intriguing development. All along he has worked towards his own desires, knowing exactly what he wanted from you. Consequently, because of our own self-absorbed plans, we were used for his.' He gave a contemplative sigh and stared at the open doors into the hall. 'It seems all the players have their own agendas. The king does not trust his children. Most likely his son won't produce an heir, his daughter will not rule unless there are no males before her. He was in negotiations with his brother, but that was before—' He stopped and put his hand over hers in her lap. 'You will have to escape, however, do not be hasty and attempt it on your own. I shall help you.'

She covered his hand and nodded. They rose from the bench and with her hand held tight, he walked her to the steps. A look of dread came over her as she watched the small crowd congregate outside the doors.

Jonas remarked, 'I believe we have created enough rumours to last a fortnight, if lucky, maybe a month.'

'That's all I need.' Lacking the disposition for humour, she said with seriousness, 'Why are you helping me in this way?' She speculated aloud as they approached the courtyard and people milling in the sphere of light, and Regina waiting, an impatient scowl on her face.

Jonas patted Shiarn's hand and murmured in her ear, 'Because I'm Gifted, my sweet, just like you.' His breath, tickling her ear, and his profound proclamation, sent a shocking ripple down her spine.

He sauntered on to Regina. 'I discovered your charge roaming the gardens and I sought to apprehend her and deliver her back to you.' He gave her a charming chuckle and stepped towards the pouting Vonzella.

Shiarn stared on in speechless wonder he would mention he was Fáerinn at the end of their conversation. He dallied with an unhappy duchess and it dawned on her, by his beaming smile, he was aware of her astonishment. The revelation presented a clearer picture of what might have occurred in her rooms the night before.

'It is late.' Regina stood close and guided Shiarn's elbow. 'Let us leave.'

Shiarn expected as much and she followed her across the hall and upstairs to her suite. At least tonight she had some hope of resting easier.

39 - Through the Dark

Endure the darkness
And you will see the stars
Even the smallest light
Will show you the way

The Latent Path

A chill penetrated Shiarn's clothing, but she couldn't move her hands, or any part of her body to warm herself. She forced her eyes open. The sight of Morgal jolted her mind awake. She was not in her bed or even her room, but lay on a slab of stone like ice.

Candle lights flickered across the unfamiliar walls, and behind an altar Morgal read aloud from a scroll. A woman's voice, the one from Morgal's chamber, chanted along with him, reaching a passionate crescendo. On the right a girl lay motionless on another table. *Sasheya.*

Morgal's voice reverberated against the dank backdrop in an ancient tongue. Whatever he was doing, it wouldn't be good. Lifting his face, he watched another altar on the far side of Sasheya. Light exploded in a cinereous flash. A noisy hiss ensued and a red mist drifted up forming one mass. It travelled to a bottle in front of him and descended into it.

Heavy oppression darkened the room, and a silhouette of a figure appeared beside Morgal. Malicious laughter came from the female figure and she spoke. 'My awakening begins.'

Shiarn watched with trepidation, having no wish to be a part of their bizarre ritual.

Out of nowhere a female voice whispered in her ear, *'You can move.'*

No-one was there, nor could any presence be felt.

'I want to help. For Sasheya,' the voice said, *'When I say now, roll onto the ground.'*

Shiarn blinked her acknowledgement.

'The key is near the door.'

Morgal and his counterpart finished speaking and a flash on the second table enveloped the space. A loud hiss was followed by a fluid blue mist, snaking towards the bottle. It disappeared within. Sasheya was gone. The woman took on more colour, of a deepening red with sweeping black hair.

Shiarn would be next and she wondered irrationally what her colour would be.

At the end of their chant the voice whispered, *'Now!'*

Exerting her Ethos, she plunged to the floor with a bulky thump.

The altar flashed and Morgal shouted in alarm. A ghostly feminine figure, dressed in servant's attire, poised midway on the slab, smiling down at Shiarn. A greenish haze swirling with black floated into the bottle.

Morgal's face twisted with wrath. 'You conniving bitch!'

It would have been wise to leave the room right then, but Shiarn decided, stealing the bottle that captured her friend, was the least she could do. She crawled unseen along the floor, warming her arms to life.

Across the room, Morgal raged, cursing her and the spirit who sacrificed herself. A shudder ran through the air and the presence of the transparent woman filled the chamber. 'What have you done?' A flat dish containing a black glutinous liquid boiled over. 'You worthless servant!'

Ignoring the voice, Morgal yelled, 'Don't think you can trick me again.'

The black substance frothed onto the altar. 'It is too late. The transformation has failed,' the ghostly voice screeched. 'I have been disfigured.'

Shiarn clamoured up to the altar and clasped the coloured bottle, making it invisible.

Morgal chanted and crafted complicated signs in the air.

She hobbled to the door, and reaching the handle, she rattled it. Locked. Her outline became visible and she snatched up the key by her feet.

'My plans will not be stopped by you,' the female voice shrieked, 'I want that urn.'

He spoke to the air with scorn, 'I will get your urn.'

Turning the key in the door, it opened.

He swiped at her. 'I'll be glad to get my hands on you and be done with you finally.'

She pulled the door onto his hand. 'Can't stop to chat.'

'Morgal,' the voice growled, 'the soul urn?!'

He gazed down the winding staircase empty of movement.

Shiarn did not stop to listen, but ran down the stairs.

~ * ~

Hellier swung her legs over the bed in a rush to get moving. The room was near black except for the light of the night sky through the window. She put her hand out and felt the sprinkle of rain. No light from Shiarn's room, but that was irrelevant. She would get to her no matter how she did it.

The heavy foot of the bed held the rope tight and she knotted it and threw the length out the window. She flicked her cloak about her, hoping it would give some protection against the rain and prying eyes, and backed out the window. Fine rain dripped into her braids and ran into her eyes. She grumbled under her breath.

She landed on a wide ledge, parallel to Shiarn's window, about fifteen feet away. A greyish tint reflected on the walls, giving her enough light to see. Holding tight to the rope, fast becoming slippery, she stooped in the small space offered by the ledge. She stepped and swung out through the smattering of rain, and impacted the wall near Shiarn's window. Not near enough. Placating herself with the idea she was getting a feel for the distance, she held the rope and let it settle back to its natural position. Once again she leapt from the ledge and pounded into the wall. She restrained her cry of pain. Each time brought a better comprehension of the distance, but also sore ribs.

With her legs in a type of sitting position, she propelled herself until she hooked a foot into the window alcove. Grateful for long legs, she pulled herself onto the ledge of Shiarn's window. She tied the rope around her waist and pressed her face to the glass and peered into shadows. She tapped at the window. Nothing. She rapped louder. No answer. 'Bloody hellfire,' she cursed, 'she's not there.' In the corner of the alcove, and smoothing her back against the stone, she nestled in to wait. Determined to stay until she or someone arrived, she wondered how long she could endure the same position before falling asleep or getting bored.

Time passed slowly, with no idea how long she had waited. After some time of sitting in the wet air, Hellier was grateful she was immune to temperature. A noise came from inside. She knocked on the pane until the outline of Shiarn approached and the window opened.

Hellier toppled through and despite her restricted position, jumped to the floor and stood, her dripping cloak forming a puddle on the rug.

Shiarn stared in open mouth shock. 'Hellier?!' Her eyes flicked over Hellier and the darkness outside the window. 'How on earth did you get here?'

Hellier dropped her hood and shook her head. Water flew over the walls from her long braids. 'I'm glad to see you too.' She loosened the rope at her waist and tied it to the chair by the window.

Shiarn poked her head out the window. 'Have you been sitting out there?'

'I'm not sure how long, not hours, I'm sure.' Waiting outside was the least important thing. 'What has happened to you, and the others?'

Avoiding her gaze, Shiarn sat on the bed. 'I can't explain it all, but I'm a prisoner. Earona and Ethan were used as a type of coercion. I have no idea where they are.' She asked abruptly, 'How did you get in here?'

Not wishing to go into details about Dario, Hellier gazed at the large bed and ornate bureau. 'Help from a friend — ' *What luxury...*

'Oh that man in the blue suit, I see.' Her tired eyes filled with tears. 'You can't see the bars.'

Hellier crouched before her. 'We'll get you out somehow. You can't leave by the door?'

'Some unseen barrier prevents me.' Shiarn grabbed her shoulders. 'Has Jett got my necklace?'

Hellier creased her brow in thought. 'Jett has that thing now, after Seth was attacked for it. You're that worried about it?'

'As long as he has it and not Morgal.' Shiarn clenched her fist. 'Tell him to keep it safe and don't let anyone take it. It's wanted by a mage in the palace and he'll do anything to get it, even...' she took a short breath. *Rape.*

Grief billowed over Hellier's thoughts from Shiarn, at the centre was the man she encountered earlier, and worse than she thought at the time. She took Shiarn in her arms and fired out with rage, 'He did that for the jewellery?'

Shiarn drew away and wiped her tears. 'It's important for some reason, although I'm not sure why. He called it the Essenya.'

'Jett's not going to like this.' Hellier gripped her hands. 'And neither do I!'

'Whatever he thinks, he must be made aware people are looking for it.'

Hellier stood, ready to go. 'You must escape.'

'Yes.' Shiarn got down on her knees and searched under the bed. 'When you go back, take this with you.' She pushed a coloured bottle into Hellier's hands. 'I'm not sure what it's for, but Morgal wants it. Guard it with your life.'

Hellier screwed her face up in bewilderment at the glass, layered in three different colours. 'When I go back? Without you?'

'I can't leave yet,' Shiarn said, 'There is someone here I trust will help me find Ethan and Earona. I will send you word.'

Hellier chewed her lip in contemplation. 'Jett will be mad…'

'I can't leave anyway and that's the truth.'

'It will have to be.' She sighed with resignation. 'We are at the White Horse.' *But, what are they going to think about… what happened to you?*

'Don't tell them. Just tell Jett about the necklace. It's not a normal piece of jewellery, if he doesn't suspect that anyway.'

'I'll go before I'm seen.' Hellier started for the window, tying the bottle around her belt. 'I hate to leave you here.'

'I will manage.' Shiarn's smile was small, but genuine.

They shared a last hug. 'It's good to see you and now I'm going.'

'I know.' She pushed her towards the ledge and shut the window behind her.

Hellier climbed up into the night. In the west a faint glimmer of the rising sun appeared. She hung tight to the rope and pulled herself up. Once on the sill, she stepped into the dark room and dragged the rope through the window and wound it up. She took her wet clothes off and hung them on the chair to dry and crawled into bed to rest.

~ * ~

Sharp pounding vibrated the trapdoor, and a loud voice spoke. 'Are you alive?' Murky light hit Ethan's face through the barred window. Peering up like a captured animal, he pushed his fingers through the grate, unable to speak. The hatch was opened by Saybar, the old man from the cavern of waves. Behind him, two guards waited for Ethan to exit. Saybar said, 'Time to go.'

Ethan's blood had slowed in his limbs, and with his legs prickling with fire, he lifted himself out with his hands. A guard pointed a crossbow at him. They had nothing to fear, he could barely walk.

He got to his feet and they started off down the passage. His legs tingled to numbness and he fell to his knees. The guards dragged him the rest of the way back to the large cell. They threw him in and locked the door with a resounding slam.

Loc and Maddog grabbed an arm each and supported him to the adjoining chamber. Maddog's booming voice rang in his ears. 'You look pisspoor, boy.'

Old blood streaked Ethan's forehead, and he stared ahead without seeing.

Maddog lowered him down and Loc pushed a bowl of water to his lips. 'Here.'

Making his dry, cracked lips wet, his voice rasped. ''ave I been gone long?'

Gart came alongside and rubbed his legs. 'Long enough.'

'You been gone days and days.' Loc gave him a teasing smirk.

Maddog exclaimed, 'How the hell do we know?'

'Maddog told us where you might be,' said Loc, 'hell in a hole.'

Ethan stared up at the big man with profound understanding, and croaked, 'I know... now... I know.'

Anger flashed across Maddog's face, masking the sudden display of normalness. 'You think? I doubt it.' He abruptly hit Ethan's shoulder and lowered his voice. 'Wondered if you'd make it.'

'I was dying and didn't care.'

Maddog gave a sympathetic nod.

Gart interjected, 'We're all dying here.'

Ethan gave a strained moan and stretched back against the rock wall, his legs burning back to life. He looked around at the same ragged despairing faces. 'What happened to the girl?'

Maddog growled, 'Curse the bloody girl!'

'They dragged her off a while ago,' said Loc, 'she might have been dead, but you don't really want to know, do you?'

Ethan shrugged indifferently.

Loc pointed into his chest. 'You got to listen to me, lad, or you gonna get into bad trouble. You and Branan are the same, too strong-willed.'

Ethan ducked his head in defeat.

'Garutz is well and truly pissed.' Maddog laughed. 'He's cursing black and blue, he's got it in for you.'

Ethan gave a weak sigh.

'You better keep away from him,' ordered Loc.

'What?' Ethan replied, 'In here?'

'We'll see what we can do,' Loc said, 'we'll stick together.'

Garutz' wrath would eventually erupt, but the problem was, Ethan no longer cared.

40 - Cornered

The better the gambler, the worst the enemy
The higher the stakes, the deeper the fear

Olvarus Claw'Blade, Reader's Wisdom

After Hellier left, Shiarn paced her room, anticipating Morgal's arrival. Some time passed and still nothing. Dawn light filtered into her room and she turned to find Jonas appear in the doorway of her bedroom. Clutching her chest, she gasped with anxious fright. 'Do you have to? I'm already on edge.'

'My apologizes.' He held her arm, steadying her. 'I was in a rush.' Coatless and with his shirt half hanging from his trousers, he looked unusually flustered, and minus any wig, his brown hair was loosely tied at his neck.

Her shock was replaced with overt relief, 'No, I'm glad it's you.'

'I know what you mean.' He raised a brow, his eyes taking in her crumpled and loose-fitting dress of the night before. 'Your room was vacant earlier. I have been worried. You might explain why you are still dressed?'

'I could also say you have not visited your room.' Her eyes perused his crinkled attire from the ball. 'Perhaps you slept in a bed not your own.'

'On the contrary, I feel I haven't slept at all.' He continued the jest with a warm smile. 'Regardless, it will not do remaining in last night's gown, you must change. It is possible they might be here soon.'

'God above, who?'

He hurried her into the bedroom. 'I shall explain.'

She disappeared behind the screen to change.

'Can you manage?'

'Quite well.' Grimacing, she wriggled out of her loose gown, having been in it several hours. 'I hardly imagined you were Fáerinn, why didn't you tell me sooner?'

'I wasn't sure I would. In the end it was simply conceit. I wanted you to know.'

She hung her dress over the partition. 'How did you know I was?'

'A presumptuous guess, however, for one who is Fáerinn it is not too arduous to discern.' He paused reflectively. 'Your voice, your self-confidence, a peace in your eyes... although that was fleeting. But there is more pressing news,' he went on, 'I shall tell you outright, although it limits the surprise factor.' He paused, 'The king is dead.'

She stuck her head out to stare with shock. 'I can't believe it!'

'Adding to the dilemma, he was murdered. All is not well!'

'How do you... know?'

'That is not important.' His tone was grave, 'For you to be dressed in your evening wear would not bode well. You are watched and not by your usual keepers.'

Vulnerability swept over her once more. 'I hope you don't think I did any—'

'I do not. There might be others who will,' he replied, 'Presently, it is irrelevant who did it and there is no time to discuss supposed suspects.'

She came out in a gently-hued lime dress. 'You think they will suspect me?'

His self-assured posture vanished and he slumped, appearing tired. 'It is true, they might. I came to your room last night, tell me what has transpired.'

'Morgal.' Her voice lowered and her hands rubbed her cold arms, 'And it's quite a story. If not for a particular spirit in the tower I would not be here talking to you,' she finished breathlessly.

Jonas' eyes flicked open with immediate amazement. 'Who would have thought she was actually speaking the truth?'

She narrowed her eyes with suspicion. 'Yes, who would have thought it?'

His expression turned grim. 'I knew Morgal must have had you holed up somewhere. He must have secrets in that tower I know nothing about.' His mood became wrathful as he said, 'His ability to avoid death is intriguing me and I'm at a loss as to how to get him out of the palace. What has that man done now?'

'I'm unsure what he was trying to achieve but, he spoke with a sinister apparition who was becoming... real.'

'That's alarming.' His face paled. 'And nothing else?'

'He used Sasheya in this ritual and transformed her into smoke and put her in a bottle along with another poor soul. And I would have joined her.'

He creased his brow in brooding contemplation. 'Poor child. It has become quite dire and you could be in great peril.'

'Whatever he did wasn't entirely successful, I am still here.' Her face lifted with some cheer, 'And I stole the bottle. He will want it back. I would have given it to you, but one of my Kin, Hellier, came to me and I gave it to her. She said they are staying at the White Horse, wherever that is...'

'Good to hear.' He placed his hands on her shoulders and looked into her face. 'I haven't time to enquire how she accomplished such a feat. Some officials may arrive at any moment and you must be prepared. But first, can you tell them the prince was here during the night and left at dawn.'

She grumbled, 'He wasn't.'

'It doesn't matter; he was with someone else.'

'He needs an alibi,' she said, 'did he...?'

'He needs to not tell anyone where he really was. This is not the time for people to speculate, when the kingdom will be in disorder.'

She wrinkled her brow over the deceptive information.

'They will question you. It's to your advantage to say as little as possible. Steer clear of mentioning Morgal, despite wanting to blame him. I'm not sure what lies he will expound.'

'I gave up on any justice being done long before this.' Her eyes softened with affection. 'But you...'

He sighed wearily, as if he was the one burdened. Drawing a stray strand from her eyes, he said, 'From the start, you were thrown into deep water. Makes for gruelling swimming.'

'Makes for drowning.'

'I have much to repent of. Will you forgive me?' Smiling, he drew the back of his fingers down her cheek.

'This is not like you.' Shiarn blushed with a coy smile. 'Unless it is a new charm I'm yet to discover...'

'Remember what you said, you would like to know me better?'

She touched his hand and her eyes flitted up to meet his. 'I do.'

'I wish the same.' He lowered his face and kissed her.

She responded with more passion than she expected, and drawing away with her eyes down, she said, 'There won't be much chance of that now.'

'We cannot decide such things.' He smoothed his thumb across her cheek and said with a half-hearted smile, 'However, you do need to be careful what you say. There are some capable men here and if you find that hard to believe, watch out for Rachulles. He really has a problem with you.'

'Do I really need to know that? And you?'

'It's time to do something serious about getting Morgal out of here.' Concern hardened his face and his fingers caressed her hand.

'I just hope you can.'

He smiled with firm reassurance. 'I shall get word to your friends *and* watch out for you. Because I have not served you as well as I should have.' An abrupt knock caused them to look towards the main door. He whispered, 'They are here. I must say farewell before I would have liked.'

Shiarn was left on her own to face whoever was coming into her room.

~ * ~

Hellier was eager to leave and return to the Kin. Dario slept on, snoring away while she put on her servant's blouse, and skirt over her trousers. She packed the rope and damp shirt, along with the bottle, into her bag and was ready to go.

A sharp knock at the door startled Dario from sleep, and he hissed under his breath, 'Hide!' He yanked his trousers on while rushing to the door.

She kicked her things under the bed and crawled after them.

A woman uttered a soft greeting.

Dario responded, 'Vivella, why so early?'

'Something dreadful has occurred.'

Hellier assumed Dario might be holding her in a comforting embrace.

He replied, '...what is it?'

'Uncle Bas is dead.' Vivella sobbed. 'They found him early this morning.'

Who was this uncle she spoke of, Hellier's mind raced.

'That's frightful. How did it happen?'

She continued through her cries, 'He was killed, oh, Dario, I need you.'

An awkward silence spanned breathless moments. Eventually, Dario said, 'Go back to your rooms, I'll get dressed and meet you there.'

'Don't be long.'

Dario shut the door. 'You must leave immediately, a terrible thing has happened.'

She came up from the bed too disgruntled to care at that moment. 'Who is her uncle anyway?'

He stared with an odd look. 'You don't know?'

'No.' She pulled the wig back on her head.

'The king.'

Her mouth fell in shock.

Glancing at her with sudden apprehension, he said, 'You don't know about this?'

Heat rushed to her face and her fists clenched. 'You're not saying I—?' She had to admit her presence in the palace did look incriminating, swinging from a room at night, meeting a friend on the inside.

'I humbly apologize, of course, you didn't know. But regardless, we must get you out.'

No longer able to control her hurt, Hellier lashed out. 'And what about you and her?'

Dario looked away from her burning glare. 'I'm...'

She growled, 'You were kissing?'

He nodded with shame. 'There's no time to talk of it now, we must leave.'

People rushed through the hallways, but as they neared the servant's quarters it slowed and resembled normal routine again. They reached the laundry without conversation. Few workers were present, and they rushed to the drying room which had none. Fighting her angry tears, Hellier became more wretched as they went.

He took a basket and put her bag and damp cloak inside. He grabbed clothes pegged on the line and placed them in the basket, concealing Hellier's bag. 'When you go through the gate tell the guard you have garments for the tailor to mend, on Harlen Street, in Balydill. The servants and outside guards won't know what has happened yet, so you need to be quick.'

'You're staying?'

'I must for a while yet.' He kissed her cheek. 'Now, go out that door, put your best voice on and good luck.' He whispered, 'We can talk later.'

Ready to rage, her face was bright with passion, and she restrained herself from lashing out. 'Yes, we will.'

'I am sorry.' His face red, he kissed her and pushed her to the door.

She grumbled as she stepped outside, but changed her demeanour on sight of other servants. No time to express her hurt, and it was probably best she didn't right then.

Whistling a tune to relieve her nerves, she strolled to the gate, looming ahead.

A guard looked her over, more interested in her than her business. 'Where you off too, missy?'

She said, in her best Crissy imitation, 'I'm taking this mending.'

'Are you now?' He stepped closer and brushed his hand over her arm. 'What's your name?'

Another guard dashed to the one speaking and waited for his attention.

'Rosy.'

He smiled in a charming manner. 'I'll see you on your way back.'

She smiled sweetly. 'I'll say you will.' She waved and he turned to the agitated guard. Hellier walked down the street, listening to the servant's gate clang shut and she darted into the first lane she came to. She dashed to another and kept running, clamping a firm hand on her sliding wig while the other clutched the basket. Before approaching the alley at the back of the White Horse, she slowed to catch her breath.

Jett lead Thunder around the walk-about of the stables; obviously waiting for her. Yanking off her wig, she pushed past him and stalked inside to the stall at the back. Stick of the uncomfortable clothing, she dug in the basket for her own shirt. Too crinkled and damp to wear, she tossed it aside.

He followed her. 'Where... is she? And Dario?'

'She couldn't get out,' she snapped as she stripped the servant's blouse off and threw it away. 'Dario is staying... longer.' Her knees were pulled up to her chest and she scowled at the floor.

Jett's voice softened. 'I can bring you down a dry shirt?'

'Can you.'

He left the stables. Hellier ditched the grey skirt across the stall in irritation, and knees hard against her, she sat, half naked in the hay. Tired and sad, especially over Dario's betrayal, she let out a mournful sigh. Preparing to mask her feelings, she stared in a thoughtless trance while Lightning nudged her hair.

A clean shirt hit her face, jolting her from her daydream. She pulled it over her head.

Jett sat beside her. 'Well?'

'I've spoken to her.' Unsure where to start or what to omit, she said, 'She is a prisoner. Some type of magikal barrier was on the door. Earona and Ethans' fate were used as threats against her. And, there's a Mage, he wanted Shiarn's necklace.'

'So that's it.' His voice dropped. 'A plan was behind it all.'

'He's searching for it and will do anything to get it.' Despite Shiarn not wanting Jett to know about the attack, she continued, 'he hurt her, bad, because she didn't have it.' She became disheartened, recalling Shiarn's trauma. 'Must be a real powerful object.'

He studied her profile with a shocked gaze. 'You mean...' *he raped her?*

She nodded. 'It's not just jewellery. It's called the Essenya,' she kept her eyes on the ground and avoided his gaze, 'She told me to tell you, don't let anyone get it.'

After some moments of mournful silence, he said, 'How is she?'

Hellier hugged her knees in solace. 'Said not to worry.'

Staring in a fixed haze of rage, Jett said, 'I'll kill him!'

'You'll have to get in line.' *I met him in the hall.*

His face reddened with anger. 'He touched you too?'

'He didn't get that far.' She gave a brief chuckle at the memory. 'I hit him, deserved more than that though.'

His face remained set with fury, 'There's more?'

'Yes.' She reached into the basket for the coloured bottle. 'She gave me this to keep safe. Apparently the Mage, I think his name is Morgal wants it. I have no idea what it is for…'

Jett studied what appeared to be a regular glass bottle, but with the layers of colours. Red on the bottom, blue in the middle and the top was a muddy green. He pulled off the cork, but there was no change. 'Look's ordinary to me. You keep it for now.'

Hellier took it back with a maudlin sigh.

'There's more isn't there?' Jett asked.

'Yep. The king is dead, probably murdered.'

He cried with astonishment, 'Arse of the devil!'

'Dario thought I had something to do with—' She regretted her words and frowned with sullen regret.

'That's why he's not here?'

She kept the heartache from her voice. 'His friend Vivella needed his company. The king was a relative of hers.'

'I hope he doesn't think you had something to do with it.'

She nodded her agreement. *I know.* 'But Shiarn said she's made a friend in the palace, and she will send word.'

'Shiarn's resilient…' *But I can't come near to understanding what she's going through…* he looked up to the ceiling and expelled a long tired breath. 'All because of that cursed amulet.'

Hellier rested her cheek on her knees. 'Yes… '

'Now we wait for some word from her.'

~ * ~

Due to Mara's absence, Mother ordered Earona to take over her duties in the orphanage. She worked in the kitchen while the children played in the grounds outside. Their gaiety gave her some respite from her sullen mood, but she couldn't quite shake her hopeless situation. Her captivity was easier when it was two of them, but now… she really was on her own.

Counsellor Adarna informed her and the other girls it was time for a rest. Earona would have joined them outside except she spied a particular boy remain indoors. Mara spoke about him, and Earona made her own enquiries about Alfonso, blind since birth.

Most likely because of her dismal disposition, Earona went in search of him. He sat in the classroom with a fiddle under his chin, making a horrendous squeaking sound as he played it.

She sat beside him. 'Can I help you with that?'

The boy shook his brown curls, his non-seeing eyes looked straight ahead. 'Who are you? I don't know your voice.'

'I'm…' she said, 'visiting.'

'Why?'

Earona replied with hesitancy, 'I wanted to meet you.'

Alfonso barked, 'You wanted to have a gawk?'

'No. I... thought I could help you.' She got the sinking sense it was one of those times she should keep quiet.

'Help me with what? Find my mother? Give me a family? Get off your high horse, lady.'

Earona sighed with remorse. 'You're right, I can't give you the things you really want.'

He continued playing. The scratching on the strings was a toilsome sound.

She finally said, 'Can you play it?'

He snapped, 'I'm learning.' Several minutes later, he laid it down. 'You still here?'

'Do you get angry because you cannot see?'

The boy pressed his lips together. 'Every day.'

Earona wanted to give him his sight; the trouble was, what would people think of it? 'And if you had your sight would life be different?'

''course it would.' He creased his brow in thought, his glazed eyes darting around their sockets. 'I could learn this faster.'

'Why the fiddle?'

'It was my father's.' His tone softened at the mention of the parent.

A sob caught in her throat. 'Where is he?'

He shrugged.

His eyes were present, making the mending of the vision not a hard feat. If he needed new eyes, it was a different type of healing and one she never experienced before. 'If someone could restore your vision would you like that?'

Alfonso's hands suddenly clutched his fiddle in rigid expectation. 'You mean the Goddess?'

'Yes, that's right.' Giving credit to a deity they already believed in would work, although she wondered at the wisdom of giving praise to the Valáverïn. 'Now, close your eyes.'

He did as she asked and she stood behind him, covering his eyes with her hands. He relaxed under her touch and she felt his eye sockets. Her Ethos mended nerves and blood byways and the finer details around his eyes. Once it was done, she continued holding her hands over his eyes. 'This is important, keep them shut until I say open.' She removed her hands, hoping he would listen to her, and she dashed from the room. Outside the door, she sang, 'Open.'

Opening his eyes, he jumped up, crying with joy, and looking around the room at everything, 'I can see! I can see! Thank you, Niesta!'

Earona breathed a contented sigh and hurried down the corridor to the kitchen. Watching from the window, she saw him run outside, crying and yelling he could see. The delight on his face was a wonderful reward in itself. Children and counsellors gathered round him and he was tongue-tied trying to explain. Limping to the group, a boy came to stand outside the circle until a counsellor drew him in. His face screwed up with sadness and tears fell down his cheeks.

The other indentured girl came in beaming, and Earona asked, 'Why does that boy cry?'

The girl watched through the window. 'Oh, probably because he's lame. Still.'

Guilt wrenched her heart for the one who missed out. How could she stop at one? But even one was too many according to Fáerinn law. She always accepted this without question, believing it to be a noble rule to guard against Nayinn discovering their identity. Now she saw the reason for it, but for the first time she wondered if it was right.

The ringing of the orphanage bell broke her gloomy reflection. Counsellors and children came inside in a frantic rush, and Earona, out of curiosity, joined them in the main hall.

Breathless and flushed, Counsellor Adarna tried to hush everyone, and without the noise ceasing, she yelled, 'Everyone be still, I've very bad news. The king is dead!' Silence came and she took a breath. 'Mother heard it from the captain. As yet we do not know specifics, but he died during the night.' She put her hand on Alfonso's head and smiled into his new seeing eyes, with tears rolling from her own.

Earona had no sympathy for the man she never met. However, the women and children voiced great sadness and sobbed for their lost king.

~ * ~

Arms folded, Shiarn stared with cold disdain at the three men, walking into her room. She recognized them. Governor of Floris, Aristos Barygalone, introduced them; the king's brother, Provincial General Maustaton, was lean with neat grey hair, and the General of Floris, Domingo Rachulles was younger and dressed in a navy suit, his hair was dark and tied back. Aristos was elderly and with a slight stoop, and appeared to need a chair.

A serving girl came in past two armed guards waiting outside. With shaking hands, she placed the tray on the table and rushed to close the door on her exit.

Overwhelmed by the intimidating men, Shiarn remained in a rigid pose, but gained some comfort, knowing Jonas might still be in the room.

The Governor indicated for her to sit and she slowly complied. He started, 'I have not previously taken the time to find out who you are.' His deep voice was sharp with authority. 'And now it is time to ask those questions.'

She nodded and braced for his interrogation.

'We know your name, but tell me where you are from?'

'From Dunbloon, past the Allervium Mountains.'

His expression remained blank. 'And what is your business here?'

'I was travelling through on my way to Hakan-Kara and I was arrested.' Her irritation simmered at the stupid pervasive question. 'I didn't have any business here at all.'

The governor nodded. 'As you say.'

General Rachulles leaned forward on his chair and was not as polite. 'You arrive with nothing on you, certainly nothing for a journey. For some reason the prince advocates in your favour. Why is that?'

'Because I have done nothing wrong.' She raised her voice, matching him with equal discourtesy. 'Why are you questioning me now?'

Aristos put his hand up to Rachulles while the other general remained standing, listening to the conversation. Aristos said, 'Due to present circumstances we have only been able to investigate you more than we were first able to.'

She assumed the prince and probably Morgal did not want anyone to go near her.

Rachulles shot out. 'You should be in jail like those others.'

Trying not to retaliate over the injustice, her body was like stone.

'You can see the trouble you pose us.' Aristos reclined, but kept his studious eyes on her. 'It may seem impertinent, but have you and the prince had sexual relations?'

Her eyes shot wide with astonishment. 'That is personal.' She watched their unyielding expressions, expecting an answer. 'If you must know—' she blushed.

He smiled, but lacked any sort of mirth. 'I see, that explains much.'

Rachulles face tightened with annoyance. 'And this was in exchange for your freedom?'

She remained as stiff as a board, trying hard to say as little as she could. 'No, it wasn't like that.'

Rachulles retorted, 'It mustn't have been too hard for you.'

Maustaton, who so far remained silent, glared at Rachulles.

Rachulles continued, 'In other words, why have you been courted in such a manner?'

Aristos gave him a formidable look, and turned to Shiarn. 'Did the prince offer you freedom in place of,' he shrugged, 'companionship?'

It baffled Shiarn since arriving at the palace. Not until last night did she understand her relationship with Bastion, but she could disclose nothing of it. But, it wasn't only Bastion who wanted her. If Morgal's evil ritual was successful she would not be present. A perfect scapegoat for the king's murder. As it was, she might possibly land in worse trouble. 'He was displaying mercy towards me.'

'And he did that I presume,' Aristos said.

General Rachulles grunted his disdain and Shiarn scowled at his rudeness.

Aristos finally asked, 'What were you doing last night?'

'After the ball I was here and the prince came after that.'

'Did he stay the night?'

'Yes. He left early in the morning.' She exhaled deeply; relieved she irrevocably said her piece.

General Rachulles spoke with contempt. 'You served him adequately?'

She stared back, her eyes, slits of ice.

'I think we have acquired enough information for now,' Aristos said, 'you will remain sequestered in your suite. Guards are posted outside.'

As if it would be any different from normal, they had no idea how she was living.

He fixed his eyes on her with a commanding stare. 'You have not heard the news, the king has been murdered.'

She sucked in her breath.

'We do not know who did it, nonetheless, we will find out.' He continued, 'Under present circumstances the prince will not be able to visit. I hope you will bear it.' He chuckled at his own dull wit and stood to leave. The other two headed to the door.

'What is to happen to me?' She called to their retreating backs.

The two generals kept walking while the governor stopped. 'The death of a beloved king is a great blow, and murder no less.' He paused, 'My hope is justice is done, and politics will not stand in the way of that.' He left the room, shutting the door after him.

After they left, Shiarn collapsed on her bed, shaking and afraid. They actually thought she was the one who killed their king.

41 - News from a Stranger

Foreknowledge in the right hands, makes one appear wise
In the wrong, one is simply a cheater

The Latent Path

Later that morning, Jett left the inn to visit Pioter. His hand in his pocket, he fingered the smooth gold, circling the oval gem, and went over the conversation he had with Keanan. Now that he knew the potential damage the amulet could cause, he thought he better find out more about it. Keanan had leafed through the journal. 'There's not much on the actual medallion, except it is somehow linked to this object,' he pointed to a sketch of a globe above an altar, 'the Eye of Heaven, or the Chanin-Quyllar. Considering the jewel is called the Eye-key, or the Essenya, it probably fits into it somehow. Considering they are rooted in Fáerinn language, I can't recall anything on this Eye of Heaven, but if it was created during the First Age the records could be lost.'

'A key…' Jett glanced at the picture, 'that someone wants…and it's a Fáerinn name.'

'So it would seem.'

'What does it open? And where is this Eye of Heaven?'

Keanan read over the script for some moments. 'The location of the orb is unknown by the author. I haven't yet discovered what it might unlock. But I assume whatever it is would be in the land of Amin-Sayeda.'

Jett sighed with the lack of knowledge over something that was a danger to them all, and ran his hand through his hair. 'No good thing I expect. That's all we need, and it's wanted by someone who obviously knows more about it than we do.' Once more, his mind wandered to the gleaming sphere in his vision and he had to assume the girl was connected to it somehow.

'Well, at least we have it, and not them.' Keanan lifted his chin with conceit.

Jett gave a snort. 'Exactly.'

Keanan went on, 'It seems the Eye of Heaven protected Amin-Sayeda during the Age of Anarchy, creating a bastion of light and peace.' He nodded with satisfaction.

'Doesn't sound too bad… but in the end—' nothing in the vision portrayed any comfort, only an atmosphere of dread.

'Something catastrophic occurred.' Keanan speculated, 'Maybe it was stolen?'

'Whoever wants it tried to kill Seth, and Shiarn—' Jett stopped and studied the jewel, not ready to share Shiarn's violation with anyone. 'It's why Shiarn was taken to the palace in the first place. I'll keep it for now and hidden until we can figure out what to do with it.'

Jett contemplated reasons for the end of Amin-Sayeda, possibly if this Eye of Heaven was destroyed, the land would be overrun by disease or the anarchistic hordes that roamed the earth at that time. The mysterious object seemed to be one more problem added to all their other burdens.

Finally he arrived at the alley behind the tailors, and he entered by the back door. Pioter was surprised at his sudden appearance but glad to receive the rest of his payment and even more at the purchase Jett made. This time he carefully folded and looped the vivid aqua shirt over his belt and pushed it around to his back. 'Is this Meet still on?'

'Yes, chamber two. Must be a big turn out.'

'Chamber two, where?'

'The sewers.' He noticed Jett's grimace. 'Not pleasant, eh? You enter by three ways. Behind Yeo's Shoes in Racen Square, hidden round the back, or the docks by Massy's Fishing on the side or,' he creased his brow in thought, 'near here, The Blue Bird, out the back. They'll have people expecting you and they'll tell you where to go.'

'Everyone uses this method?'

'Most of them. Unless you bring them straight from the Rocks.'

'I see,' Jett said, 'How well do you know the Captain?'

Pioter gave him a suspicious glare and answered with resentment, 'bought me a long time ago. I'm supposed to be free now, but you never really are. You trying to figure out my loyalties?'

'I won't waste time with niceties.'

'I haven't a huge love for the man, so I'll give you a rundown of the place. All the unfortunates get jammed together in two or three cells. Either male or female. Some special wares sit with their traders. It's in an underground chamber, one of the pirates' store houses. Everyone brings their own guards. The Captain has the most,' Pioter said, 'and the doors are always locked.' He lowered his brow in warning. 'You can't just walk out. Go prepared is my best advice.'

'You've been a great help.' Jett gave him a wide grin. 'Can I ask a couple of favours?' Before stepping out the back door, Jett peered down the alley. Seeing no one, he left with an alert eye on the street. Travelling around Floris was making him more paranoid by the day. He walked the sloping alleys and heard the mournful ring of bells. He supposed they were finally announcing the king's death. He headed back to the inn with the thought they were in for an interesting day.

~ * ~

Jett sat at the bar of the White Horse while the rain fell in sheets outside.

Burgman leaned into him and said under his breath, 'Someone came looking for your girl.'

'What did you say?' Jett gave a brief glance at the tavern filling with people, realizing he shouldn't be sitting out in the open.

'Said she was here couple of nights ago, but haven't seen her since.' Burgman poured him a draught, 'you better lay low, I don't know what people they been asking around here.'

Jett winced at the news and took a swig from his tankard. For all he knew, the Captain might already know where she was, and him. 'Thanks.'

'You heard those bells?'

Jett nodded with a vague stare.

'Bad news — the king is dead.' He looked pale and distraught. 'It's not calm on the waterfront, that's for certain.'

Jett took another drink. 'Totally agree.'

'I don't know what's going to become of this kingdom,' he grumbled, 'what with threats of wars and the like.'

A man of medium height with a beard and pleasant smile approached the bar. Water dripped off his coat and he flicked back his hood revealing sandy brown hair.

Burgman spoke in his usual helpful tone. 'What can I do for you, sir?'

'Good day.' The man stood by the counter. 'Pity about the weather.'

'That's the sorrowful spirit of Floris,' Burgman replied. 'Would you like a drink?'

The man shook his head and discretely leaned across the counter, gaining Burgman's fixed attention. 'I'm looking for someone, a woman by the name of Hellier.'

Jett spluttered on his drink and covered his cough.

The newcomer, his brow furrowing with intrigue, observed Jett.

'Don't mind him.' Burgman brushed Jett's reaction away with a swoop of his arm. He leaned across the bar blocking Jett's view, and inches from the man's face, he remarked with convincing skill, 'The thing is, she was staying here, but now, I haven't see her in a while.'

The man, turning his attention back to Burgman, said with genuine concern, 'She's not here. Are you sure?'

'I'm sure. Haven't seen her in a few nights.' Burgman drew back slightly.

Jett gave the man a sideways glance. He appeared too polite to be associated with the Captain, and he lacked the thuggish mannerism befitting his henchmen.

'Perhaps she is here now. I have an important message for her.' His eyes caught Jett's interested look and he received his direct gaze. After several moments of concentrated staring at each other, the man gave him a relaxed smile.

Jett cut in with a blunt question, 'Who are you?'

'I might be asking you the same thing.' His light grey eyes never left Jett's dark ones. 'Because I'm sure I know you.' The man did a little bow and announced, 'I'm Kael and I come on behalf of a friend of Hellier. Perhaps your friend as well.' There was a devilish look in his eyes and in a teasing way, he continued, 'I shall continue seeking Hellier elsewhere.' He turned to leave.

'No,' Jett said. 'Come upstairs.'

Burgman shook his head and rolled his eyes, and muttered under his breath, 'Blimmin' tried…'

They climbed the stairs and Jett introduced himself, 'I'm Jett, by the way.'

'Ah, of course. It's not you I know, but your father, Aillas Storm'Hunter, and you must be Storm...' he frowned in thought.

'Heart,' Jett replied.

'That's right. Your mother was a Heart.'

Before opening the door, Jett responded with glad surprise, 'You are Gifted?'

Kael put his hand on Jett's shoulder and smiled with assurance. 'I am and I have come from the palace.'

A rush of emotions ignited Jett's adolescent fears; loss of control, the judgments, would he be striving to confirm his worth all over again? Or worse, would he be ordered back home?

Hellier was still asleep in her room, but Keanan and Marcus sat at the table, and Seth on the nearest bed. Jett did the introductions; informing them Kael was from Tellávare set them at ease.

After greeting them, Kael said, 'You have a large Kin.'

'We do.' Jett had no desire to waste time on chitchat. 'So what news on Shiarn?'

'You have heard about the king?'

'He was murdered.'

'Yes, a horrible thing. Everyone at the palace is pointing their fingers at the person they like the least. There are many suspects including the prince.'

Seth piped up. 'What does all this have to do with Shiarn?'

Keanan replied to Seth, 'I might assume Shiarn is under suspicion.'

Kael said, 'That's right, even though she hasn't been able to leave her rooms due to one man with a lot of power and influence, Morgal.'

'Hellier met him briefly,' Jett said.

'Has she? Well done on getting into the palace, I might add.'

'We had an acquaintance,' Jett informed him.

Marcus added, 'Turned out Dario was good for something.'

'Dario... I know of him. I always thought he was a dill.' Kael shrugged. 'Shiarn is currently under house-arrest.'

Jett said, 'She's been set up?'

'Possibly she has been used to take the blame. There are some who wish the prince harm and this won't help. A stranger in the palace offers a good cover. Certainly Morgal had plans for Shiarn which have not come to fruition, thank the Creator for that. Morgal was the one who predicted Shiarn would come to the palace.'

Keanan asked, 'How do you know this?'

'I have Kin in the palace who has spoken to her,' he declared. 'He's watching her too.'

'That does ease my heart,' Jett said, 'but now what? Surely she must escape.'

'We are waiting for something to happen.'

Jett's eyes smouldered under furrowed brows; they were forever waiting for something. 'What do you need from us?'

'There is nothing you can do, but wait.'

Jett asked with methodical precision, 'Another thing, do you know the whereabouts of Earona and Ethan?'

'Jonas, my man at the palace found out,' Kael said, 'the girls are indentured at the women's refuge at the Temple of Niesta and Ethan was sent to the Rocks.'

Keanan said, 'Is this temple in the city?'

'It's in this district.'

Marcus asked, 'Indentured? What's that?'

'A type of slavery, though it's easier. It's a contract that must be fulfilled.'

'Earona sold into a workhouse,' Marcus replied with relief, 'I could think of worse things.'

'It's better than the Rocks,' Kael informed him keenly.

'We will see what we can do about them.' Jett sighed heavily. At least the girl was with someone, although he could guess what Earona was saying and doing in front of her. 'It's Ethan I'm worried about.'

'The Rocks is a cruel place.' Kael cast a sharp eye around the room. 'Is your man stout of heart?'

Marcus chuckled. 'He's stout of body.'

'As tall as Keanan with a body like Marcus.' Jett smiled, reflecting on his lost brother.

Kael nodded. 'The strong get by.'

Jett queried, 'Is it possible he's been sold as a slave?'

'A man like that could bring a good price.' Kael scratched at his beard.

Jett asked, 'Have you heard of Tonius Shark?'

'He's a high ranking criminal of a sort?'

'So I am led to believe. He is my contact for the slave trade and we have a meet on tonight through the sewers.'

Seth and Marcus groaned. Marcus reproached with irritation, 'You didn't say anything about sewers.' Their complaints went unheeded by Jett.

Kael gazed at him with admiration. 'You have met with Shark?'

'I've met him...' Jett replied. Kael's surprise caused him to speculate whether he was walking into a trap and leading everyone with him.

'He must have taken a shine to you,' Kael said.

Jett grimaced. 'That won't last. We are gathering a reputation around the city so some of us will need disguises. If they see Hellier they will go berserk.'

Seth retorted, 'And I don't fancy being stuck underground when that happens.'

Neither did Jett like the thought of trudging through the sewers or being trapped underground. 'And I don't want every thug and lowlife coming after us and driving us out of the city which would probably happen.'

Kael said, 'Do you need my help?'

'No,' Jett replied with polite derision, 'I wouldn't want to endanger your life as well.'

'I'm sure you will figure it out once you get there,' Kael said confidently. 'Oh, by the way, only women are allowed in the Temple.'

Jett replied without batting an eye to his statement. 'Hellier will be going.'

'Hellier needs a woman's refuge.' Marcus cackled at his own humour.

Hellier interrupted by emerging from her room, yawning. 'What's all the noise for?' On glimpsing the stranger sitting in their room she blinked with surprise.

'You must be, Hellier.' Kael smiled. 'I'm Kael.'

Hellier raised her hand in greeting. 'Hello, Kael.'

Kael informed them, 'I'll be heading off now.'

'If we need to speak to you, is there some way of sending a message?' Keanan enquired.

'Send it to Lord Belleguarde at the palace, but it would need to be an emergency. I'll be seeing you soon, I'm sure.'

Seth exclaimed with awe, 'A lord, hey?'

'Oh, yes, he acts it too.' Kael chuckled. 'Perhaps I'll tell you about it one day or better still, he can.' He moved to the door. 'Take care this evening and good luck.'

Jett shut the door after him and with a purpose filled look in his eyes, said with devilish excitement, 'Now I'm in the mood for tonight.'

~ * ~

The underground chamber filled with guards. The prisoners were accustomed to their timeless dark world being intruded by the keepers, until the rarely seen officer, Talskin marched between his men. He shouted over the top of the prisoners' voices, 'Listen up you lecherous scum. You may or may not be pleased to know, we are clearing out the cells. Most of you will be leaving today.' He sneered at the men as he passed by the bars. 'No one out there cares about you troublemakers. In fact they despise you. We do them a favour by having you all taken off the streets so they can live in safety,' he declared, 'then we move you to a place that will make better use of you.' He turned back to the waiting guards. 'They can go now.'

The guards began taking out the prisoners in groups. They locked iron cuffs on their wrists and ankles and led them from the main cavern. Eventually Ethan, Loc, and Branan, and all of the Harn, except Gart, were chosen. Gart's separation from the Harn affected them, especially Branan.

The Harn said a hurried farewell to each other as they were shuffled out. Ethan said his own goodbye to Maddog, who was staying. Maddog said, 'If I ever get a chance, boy, I'll find you.'

'I don't know what to say—'

'Stick with them lot as long as you.'

Once outside the cell the prisoners were chained to each other.

Maddog hung his face out through the bars, his voice roaring across the chamber. 'Look after the boy.'

Ethan shook his head at him with fondness. 'You're a fine one to be asking, you know how tough I can be.'

'We'll look after him,' Loc shouted back, 'you look after Gart.'

'A deal,' yelled Maddog.

Ethan and the Harn were led through tunnels he had never seen, but eventually the rock passage opened up to smooth walls with better lighting.

42 - The Meet

When the storm of adversity passes over, the resolute are left standing,
And the wicked are washed away.

The Sleeping Sword

Dusk came and the Kin ate in their room while Jett discussed the plans for the evening. Considering he had no knowledge of the layout, but with a vague estimate of people attending, his decisions were limited. Essentially they prepared for every contingency with the focal point of their mission, rescue Ethan at any cost.

Seth put on the shirt Jett purchased for him. The vibrant colour was all the more remarkable because Jett chose it. Extravagant red embroidery was over the floppy collar, and the numerous pleats at the cuffs were matching crimson, even the lacing contrasted with the needlework. Pleased with his gift, Seth was still compelled to rummage through the basket Hellier stole from the palace. He put on the velvet jacket and matching emerald waistcoat. 'This will go splendidly.'

Marcus laughed. 'In a show for eccentric misfits.'

Seth, his long hair combed down for the occasion, paraded the room. 'You lack good taste, or any taste at all. I befit the appearance of a debonair lord.'

Marcus retorted, 'You will go for a good price, pity about the clothes.'

Pushing his chin out, Seth swaggered like an authentic snob. 'Indeed, I do believe I will receive the highest of bids, with or without clothes.'

Marcus snorted. 'Preferably with clothes.'

'Let's hope we don't have to find out,' Jett replied from across the room, as he strapped himself with two malreus blades.

Keanan carried the other valuable swords, and coiled rope was strung over his back. He rapped on Hellier's door.

Hellier took her time dressing in the plain wool dress that irritated her scarred back. She was not in a good temper to wear such divergent clothes, especially the wig. In a maudlin state, she replayed her night of passion with Dario, and how she desired to be with him again. But now she would have to crush that longing come what may. She exited her room with a grim frown.

Marcus grinned at her. 'Why so gloomy?'

'Dressed like this? You have to ask.' She glowered under her brunette curls.

Marcus shot back, 'Save it for tonight!'

'Let's just get this over with,' she huffed.

'All ready, let's go.' Jett headed to the door.

~ * ~

Through the dim streets they arrived at an alley behind "The Blue Bird". They stopped to tie Hellier, Marcus, and Seths' wrists behind them, and cloth was put over their mouths.

Jett lifted the sewer grate and laid it aside. An overpowering stink assaulted his senses. One lit torch glowed below showing an outline of a figure. With his keen vision, he viewed three armed men watch him jump down.

The tunnel was six feet and the same across. Worn stones spaced along the side suggested steps might have once run along the edge. High up the damp walls, jagged rocks protruded out, like a type of funnel, pouring out dirty water. Towards the end, rodents scrambled in the water, unaffected by the presence of humans.

One of the men approached Jett and glanced up the opening. 'What's the password?'

'Wasting away.' Jett repeated what Pioter told him.

'Straight down that way.' He pointed down the tunnel which Jett already surmised would lead in the direction of the Rocks. 'Three knocks and you're in.'

It was impossible for Hellier to jump down alone and not due to her prowess, but her skirt flying up. Jett hastily placed her on the edge of the sewer water. Taunted by the guards, rude remarks abounded regarding her anatomy. Forced to ignore their jeers due to her gag, she had to appear dazed and frightened. Marcus followed her, but he jumped down with constricted wrists. Seth however, needed Jett's aid and would have injured himself if left to his own skills. Keanan came up the rear, holding an unlit torch which he passed to a guard to light.

Due to their bound wrists, the pretend slaves took it slow on the wet stone. Marcus lost his footing in the sludgy water and grumbled through his gag. *You should have gagged my nose as well.*

The foul stink increased in potency as they walked the tunnel. Jett replied, 'Can't argue with that.' After passing tunnel openings on both sides, he halted at the end. He placed his hand on the blank wall and examined the variance on the joining stones. 'Hope you are ready for this.'

Keanan ungagged the slaves, but their ropes remained about their wrists. Their eyes shimmered in the torchlight with eagerness, if not some trepidation.

Marcus stated with exasperation, 'Knock on the door, will you.'

Jett punched the rock with the flat of his fist three times. They waited in silence unable to hear anything inside. Finally a clicking echoed from within the wall, then another. The heavy stone opened outward slowly, allowing Jett time to step from its path. Light from inside streamed through, hitting their eyes and lighting up their curious faces. Shadows from two men fell over them. Jett walked through into the underground cave structure. On first glance it appeared to be an old temple with remnants of colonnades and random broken steps.

'Stop there,' one guard ordered.

Jett recognized him as Mac, Tonius' worker.

A frown crossed Mac's dull eyes and he screwed his face up at Jett. 'You watch yerself in here!'

Jett pursed his lips together, holding onto a caustic reply, and watched the second pirate guard carry out a cursory scan of the male prisoners. Hellier received a languid pat to her inner thighs. His hands lingered up her skirt, and he gave a laconic chuckle to Jett and Keanan. Jett's chest tightened and he sought control of his temper.

Hellier squirmed. *I'm going to knee him in the balls.*

No longer able to restrain his displeasure, Jett said with cold wrath, 'Stop manhandling my property.'

Hellier's face screwed up in response.

The guard stared at him darkly, anticipating a confrontation.

'Hey!' Mac pointed at Marcus. 'I know you from some place.'

Out of the three slaves, Marcus had the audacity to glare. He shrugged, ducking his head from Mac, and Jett, whose annoyed stare was directed at him. *You better hope he doesn't remember you.*

Marcus remained stony faced.

Mac meanwhile stared at Marcus and creased his forehead in puzzlement.

The other guard ordered, 'Put 'em in the pen.' A collection of cells were to the right set back past the giant colonnades in the enormous cavern. Men and women prisoners were visible through the iron bars. Keanan lead them past storage racks to the holding area. An overseer pushed Marcus and Seth into a cell and they hedged their way through scores of scruffy looking men.

Hellier was taken to the next cell, and she walked in amongst women and girls, some only children.

~ * ~

Jett walked further into the cavern to view what he could of the chamber. Shaped stone formed the walls, and the roof was jagged rocks, some of which hung low. The roof slanted downward with the lowest point at the opposite side to the activity. Eight great pillars, wide enough for two men to embrace, reached high to the rock ceiling yet not entirely touching it. The cavern's length could not be determined due to the copious amounts of storage racks and crates.

A mixture of liqueur and whale oil combined with the earthy smell of the packed dirt floor and old rugs underfoot created an indiscernible stink in the stifling atmosphere. Innumerable crates, rugs and boxes of all sizes were everywhere, appearing to be dumped without any organization. The chaos could prove to be a hazardous drawback, Jett thought with frustration.

To the left of the cells and towards the other side was a platform. With fire poles pushed into the hard dirt, it was the most well-lit space of the cavern, and with good reason. Numerous spectators of varying descriptions sat in rows on a raised and carpeted area, observing the proceedings on the short stage. They appeared to be the interested buyers. Seated in the front row, an extravagantly dressed man in a yellow wig was deep in conversation with the Captain.

Jett watched, without any surprise, the man he roughed up, the 'Collector'. He should have known. The 'Collector' glanced at him and quickly turned his head from Jett's brooding look. After viewing him and the Captain speak, it gave Jett no encouragement regarding his plans.

Keanan, having placed his torch in a bracket on the wall, stood next to Jett. *I'm sure that does not bode well for us.*

Jett was not in a good temper to reply, but continued assessing the chamber.

'I couldn't see him.' Keanan kept his gaze steady despite the melancholy in his voice.

Jett nodded. It was disappointing, all of this trouble and Ethan was not here. But now they had to focus on the three in the cells.

How many are there?

Two guards were at the door behind them and another handful at the right of the chamber, but he could see no other obvious exits except gaps that appeared to lead to more caverns. He could assume there were ways beyond the layers of goods. A great amount of the armed men in the room were positioned about the seats and the platform. Scattered about the chairs were two score of men, half of them, Jett could safely assume were not armed or if they were would not have the skill to use a weapon to save their life. Overseers watched the cells. Two cells appeared to be overfull with prisoners, although one had only women and girls that he could see. *Nearly sixty.*

Keanan gave a disheartened sigh in response, but Jett choose to ignore it. There was no looking back and if they couldn't get Ethan they still had to get the three out of the holding cell. He noticed the back of the woman from the Captain's office. Her sabre drawn, she rested the tip on her boot, and with a flippant turn of her head, glanced at Sim slouching by a pillar at the back of the seating area.

Jett moved nearer and Keanan followed.

The Captain noticed Jett's presence, and he nodded his way. Jett's eyes moved from Tonius to the platform and a well-rounded man with a thick moustache, wearing a black cap and long coat. A sale was completed and guards, followed by a well-dressed man, took two girls from the stage and disappeared through an opening between the shelving.

Jett eventually responded to Keanan's growing nervousness. *There are more guards than I thought, but the prisoners are more than I hoped. Except...*

There are children and numerous women. Keanan's thoughts were vexed by the unexpected dilemma.

They'll have to keep back. It annoyed Jett too, but he had to leave that in Hellier's hands.

From the opening beyond the stage, a man in a dark cloak walked into the light. With his sharp vision, Jett watched him approach the seats. It wasn't the man that interested him as much as his companion. Jett suddenly paid more attention to the short, cloaked figure alongside him. A cloth hood concealed the person's face, but it was clear she was female. The man pulled on her bound wrists and she stepped forward, causing her stomach to be visible if only for a moment.

Jett swore under his breath. Could it really be her? It was only that day Kael told him she was in the temple. He scanned the growing crowd for any sign of Earona. She did not appear present among the random prisoners not in the cells and no other people had their faces covered. He assumed the man did not wish her identity to be known which was suspicious enough. Whoever she was, it would be a frightening and humiliating experience. He sighed at the depravity of it.

His fears compounded when the Captain greeted the newcomer and his eager gaze travelled up the girl's body. Their conversation seemed congenial until Tonius reddened and gestured with passion at the girl's stomach.

Keanan said, softly, 'No extra's in this business?'

'Even an unborn child must come with a price,' Jett said with contempt. 'Devil's arse!'

We're going to get her?

'Do you have to ask?' Jett burst out, unable to control his indignation at the amount of captured people. *Anyway, not we, I will go. You make sure Hellier and Seth get out.*

Captain Shark and the cloaked man turned their gaze on Jett and Keanan.

Jett returned a blank stare. Heat rushed to his limbs in wary preparation of Tonius walking towards him.

A ruckus was occurring in the slaves' pen. Prisoners yelled obscenities at the guards. Their rowdiness escalated and the overseer swung his whip through the bars. It only incited their fury. The slaves' tension was tangible yet the traders seemed to disregard the danger.

The prisoner's antics did nothing to halt the Captain's pretentious swagger. 'Good to see you made it.' His brow creased on closer inspection of Jett. 'We really must have similar tastes.'

Jett stared into his arrogant eyes. 'I might agree with you.'

His mood turned frosty. 'See anyone you know?'

'I—' Jett saw the subtle head nod the Captain gave the muscular short-haired woman. She lifted her sword and directed it at Keanan's throat. A man by the Captain carried out a similar motion on Jett. Jett cursed himself for not trusting his instincts when he observed the woman swinging an unsheathed sword. 'You can't be serious,' he stated in an irritated reprimand, more at himself than the Captain.

'This way you can get a better look inside the cell.'

A string of profanities was screamed by a prisoner. Other angry voices joined him, all vying to be heard by some scoundrel they despised on the outside.

Hopefully all that will break loose. Jett assured Keanan. *Soon.*

Indeed. Keanan looked down the length of the curved sword. *If we don't get run through first.*

Tonius spared the slaves a glance and frowned at the overseers. Meanwhile, Sim removed Jett and Keanans' weapons from behind and threw them near a pillar, and he tied Keanan's wrists behind his back.

'Shark, you're a flamin' cockpuller,' Jett leered, 'and that's not even close to how stupid you are.'

Tonius gave him a belittling smirk and opened his mouth to respond.

'You think you're the only one who can pull a swifty.' Jett's mouth curved into a wicked grin. 'And, I *have* seen something I know...'

A look of revelation crossed the Captain's face.

With half an eye on the cell, Jett watched the door near the platform open and the prisoners fall over each other to get out, with Marcus heading the pack.

Tonius turned to watch the fiasco. Hardened men, kept underground too long and suddenly let loose were clamouring for freedom. 'You bastard. Fern will hear about this!'

'Tell him what you like.' Jett gave him an ominous glare. 'You made the first move.'

Tonius gave a furious growl and leaving Jett, he drew his sword in defence of the rushing mob. The woman's sword stayed fixed on Keanan and she cast intermittent glances at the bedlam unfolding around her.

Jett connected with his Ethos and his eyes transformed to a fiery red. He dropped the man on him, sending him grovelling to the ground. Elbowing Sim behind him, he slammed his fist into the side of his head. His eyes still aglow, he crossed Sim's body with his vision. Sim cried out and scampered from his reach and Jett's line of sight. He stayed there and Jett retrieved his blades.

The woman on Keanan stared with wide-eyed astonishment at the scuffle. Jett closed in and she backed away from Keanan. Tonius shouted for her and she dashed away to aid him.

With his eyes fixed on the cloaked man, Jett started across the chamber to confront him.

~ * ~

Marcus and Seth were pushed into the cramped cell of male prisoners. Marcus did a speedy assessment of the occupants. Ethan was not among them. It was a bitter disappointment. Despite this major set-back, many able-bodied men were present. But, as it was, they were linked together in groups. A large cluster of thin looking men stood by the bars, sending hateful stares to those outside. Other crowds were of dark skinned men, and their faces reflected the same angry desperation. The overseer, his back to the prisoners, watched the platform.

Marcus made a way between the men with Seth following behind. *This will have to do. More loud angry men.* Seth thought. *How do I end up in these places?*

Chuckling, Marcus gave him a humorous look. He had no idea, but he would have preferred Seth be somewhere safer. That couldn't be helped. Marcus sidled up to the larger group of rough looking men. 'Any of you know Ethan?'

'Maybe.' A stocky, bearded man scowled.

A giant of a man hollered, 'I know him.' Straggly black-auburn hair went down to his waist and he spoke loud through a matted beard. 'Him and me are tight. We go way back.'

'Shut up, Maddog,' the other man ordered, 'you talk too much.' His plaited red hair, and beard were wiry, and bizarre tattoos patterned his face. 'Sure, we've heard of him, we've even met him.'

Marcus raised his voice in excitement. 'Where is he?' His Ethos started pulsing through his hands in preparation.

'Sailing,' Maddog sang, 'Sailing 'cross the mighty blue.'

'Maddog,' said the other man, 'I'm gonna shove my fist down your throat.'

'What's your name?' Marcus directed to the shorter man.

Another man, his dirty limp hair fell down his back, hissed, 'If we tell you, you gonna free us?' Anticipation flashed in his eyes.

'Name's Gart, that's Maddog and he's Fish,' Gart nodded at the one breathing down Marcus' neck. 'What's your plan?' Other men, overhearing their conversation, turned their way, their faces brightening with expectation.

'Tell me where he is?' Marcus spied their iron cuffs. That was the easy part. Avoiding the eyes of the overseer was more problematic.

'When we're free.' Maddog towered over Marcus.

Marcus stepped out of his radius. 'We're going to break out of here. Just don't get killed beforehand.'

Gart pushed Maddog out the way. 'If I'm out of here I won't be dying.'

Another man said, 'But how you going to do it?' And more of them joined the conversation.

'I'm going to open the door after I crack these off.' Marcus could set them free, but he would have to rely on someone untying him and Seth.

Gart whispered, 'You're his friends?'

'Yes.' Marcus kept his voice low. 'If you want freedom, we need your help to get us out of here.'

Maddog yelled at the overseer when he walked past, 'Spawn of a razorback devil!'

The overseer swung his whip, hitting the nearest man and not coming close to touching Maddog. The man who caught the whip with his bare skin shouted curses at the guard.

'Aye, I want freedom and I want to kill some bastards.'

Marcus had already taken hold of Gart's band and shattered the lock, but it was still too risky to move about freely. 'We need a distraction.'

Fish said with pride, 'We Rocks' boys are good at that.'

Across the way, an overseer opened the women's cell door and dragged out a southern-seas woman by her bonds. Screaming, she fought like a wild cat.

A robed prisoner held the bars and shouted in his own tongue. Then, he cried, 'You are the bastard son of a devil monster. You will perish in the fires of your sins, you obese fiend.' His profanities fired up Maddog, and he joined the foreigner in abusing the guards.

Gart finished untying Marcus and said, 'Distraction enough.'

After ordering Seth to wait at the back of the cell, Marcus moved amongst the men. His shattering ability coursing through his hands, he touched the cuffs one at a time. They cracked and fell away.

Seth ended up in the midst of the swaying angry men all cursing and calling for blood. *Holy Kahm, these an awful odour making me ill. Please hurry up.*

Toughen up, Sprout. Marcus smiled to himself as he discovered the men from the Rocks were the only prisoners cuffed. This fortune made the whole venture easier than he thought. After the iron rings had fallen to the floor they were free. He moved to the door nearer the women's cell.

'Oi,' Mac yelled at the sight of him. 'I remember you! Son of a whore!' His shouts added to the roar of the prisoners.

Marcus backed from the gate and disappeared into the crowd, making a beeline for the second door nearer the platform. A riskier route, and further from Hellier, but his only option. He stopped at the foreigner, shouting at the guard who took his woman, and said, 'Was that your lover?'

His cocoa-coloured eyes cringed with offense. 'She is still my lover.'

'Right.' Marcus covered the lock with his hand, destroying the metal within. 'Now you'll have a chance to get that bastard.'

'I will send him to hell.' His strong accent was difficult to understand, but his passion was clear.

Near the seats, Marcus spotted Jett and Keanan with swords at their throats. Crossbows were pulled out in response to the escalating noise, but it did nothing to deter the prisoners. The overseer lashed his whip and shouted to his off-sider. With a look of fury, he stepped up to the door. It flew wide and Marcus' fist met with his face. He fell straight back and lay motionless.

The men swarmed out, nearly bowling Marcus over. Those with crossbows fired a few, actually hitting an unfortunate target. They were not given another chance at firing. Howling like madmen, the freed prisoners went after the guards, and attacked indiscriminately, and using anything they could get their hands on. Some of the first to die by their hands, the fleeing crossbowmen.

Maddog, a giant seven foot man, announced his presence by lifting his arms and bellowing across the chamber. From the dirt floor, he pulled out a pole, fire included, and used it as a spear. A guard came at Marcus, and Maddog looped the pole around the man's neck from behind. Marcus punched his stomach and pilfered his weapon. Maddog wrenched the pole in, crushing the man's wind-pipe. He dropped, and Maddog swung out at the next victim.

Caught up in the fight, Marcus almost forgot Seth waiting by the gate. He called to him to follow and they ran to the second cell.

~ * ~

Hellier was nudged into the cell by the guard's hand fondling her backside. She gritted her teeth and recited Jett's earlier instructions over again, *don't do anything to single yourself out*. Punching the man in the face would certainly bring attention from too many eyes. She cursed him under her breath.

She groaned at the sight of the women and girls sitting on the ground, looking tired and afraid. A few lifted their heads, and their eyes reflected a bleak sadness. Girls as young as ten huddled together and more than half, dark skinned. At least most of them were unbound.

Hellier stood by the bars, staring with envy at the rowdy men in the opposite cell and wishing she could rip off the hideous wig.

A woman with rich caramel skin stood next to her and fired out, 'The pigs have taken my sisters.'

'Maybe we can get them back.' Hellier looked down at the woman's russet dress and coloured sash, and the rope binding her wrists.

She said in her strong southern accent. 'You have a plan?'

'A plan's in the works, but...' Hellier observed the weary looking women. 'These girls won't be much help.'

'I can fight.'

'Good.' Hellier turned her back to the bars and the overseer's gaze. 'But I don't want you to get killed or anyone here.'

'I will do what I can. My name is Jazmina.'

'I'm Hellier.' Hellier's skin ignited around her wrists, burning the rope to ash.

Jazmina watched, her tan eyes forming saucers. 'You are—' The gate opened and the guard grabbed Jazmina and dragged her from the cell, shouting and kicking.

Fists clenched ready to strike, Hellier could do nothing but watch her be yanked to the stage beyond the barrels and stands of rugs.

Women had noticed Hellier's rope disintegrating and they started gathering around her. She stepped among them attempting to remain concealed as she burned their ropes. They pleaded their desire for escape with restrained voices, and every question built with excitement.

Hellier gave instructions and pointed through the bars. 'When the cell is open go towards the door on this side towards the top. Don't stop. Run for it.'

The woman's voice was a trembling whisper, 'But the doors are locked.'

'They won't be.' Hellier stood by the gate once more with the women pushing in against her, even the children watched the guards with anticipation. Hellier's gaze was on the men in the other cell, getting more ferocious and noisy. Marcus moved amongst the male prisoners, coming closer to her side. A pirate shouted at him and he shifted away. She couldn't see Jett or Keanan, and she was useless until someone freed her. 'Flamin' arse, hurry up!'

Not long after, the male prisoners burst out of the cell with bellows and shouts and alot of confusion. At least the women paid attention to the ruckus, even the overseer ran off.

'But... how are we to get out?' A teenage girl asked.

'Through the far door—'

'But, we're still in this cell—'

It bothered Hellier as well. 'He'll open it.' Where the hell was Marcus? 'Soon.' Hands gripping the bars, she glared at the pirate approaching, a devious grin on his bearded face.

Keys jangling, he pushed one in the lock. His face was rammed into the bars from behind with a shaking clang. Blood trickled down his forehead and he crumpled to the floor.

Marcus stepped over him and turned the key in the lock, opening the cell.

'He almost did your job.' Hellier opened the door into the prone man.

'If I had known, I wouldn't have rushed over.' He grinned at the women, most of them under twenty, and waved them past. 'Ladies, please make your way to the exit.'

Seth shook his head with an amused smirk.

Hellier gave Marcus a condescending look, and ordered the girls, 'Go straight there.' The last to depart, a woman clutching the hands of two children. Hellier stooped over the pirate and took his sword. He groaned in defiance. She looked up at Marcus, 'You didn't kill him?'

'Didn't need to.' Marcus gave her a vexed look under his furrowed brows.

'Mmm?' She rolled her lips and clenched the blade she had taken.

'You don't need to kill everyone.'

'Maybe.' She eyed him with scepticism.

Seth crossed his arms looking them both over with exasperation. 'I don't know how either of you manage to kill anyone.'

'This isn't the time for lectures,' Hellier replied, 'I've got to find someone.'

'Who?!' Marcus cried.

'I'm getting them all out,' she stated.

Marcus sighed. 'Suit yourself. I'm going to open the door. Seth?'

Seth shrugged.

'He can come with me, he might be useful.' Hellier bounced the sword in her hand, ready to take off.

'You better take care of him.' Marcus huffed. *Or you're the one in trouble.*

'Hey! I'm standing right here.' Seth flung his arms wide and his eyes crimped with annoyance.

Marcus laughed and hit him on the back. 'Meet you at the door.'

Seth rubbed his shoulder and grumbled, 'Honestly, you're both as bad as each other.'

Hellier grabbed his hand, and pulled him along. 'Don't worry, nothing will happen to you.'

'It's not me I'm worried about.' Seth moaned.

~ * ~

The man cloaked in black, headed towards the far opening with his captive stumbling behind him. On reaching him, Jett pointed his malreus blade neck-high at the man's retreating back. 'Hand the girl over.'

Swivelling to meet Jett, the smuggler's sword was already raised. 'I believe trade has finished for the evening.' His hood fell back, revealing a bearded face and a malicious glint in his eyes.

'I didn't come here to spend coin.' Jett stepped closer, levelling his blade at the man's chest.

'It would seem.' With his own sword, he nudged Jett's weapon away. 'But I don't give away free goods.'

Jett lifted his second blade in defence and advanced. Still holding the rope, the man guarded against Jett's blows. Jett swept his strikes into him with relentless fury. Kept in a parrying stance, the man was forced to discard the rope and his hold of the prisoner. His long hair fell over his shoulder and his eyes danced over Jett, studying his movements. 'A sword fighter, I see.'

Jett had no desire to converse with the man he was trying to pummel, all the while thinking of his Kin waiting for him so they could leave. Smoke started filling the air. Towards the opposite side of the chamber, flames had taken hold of the storage crates. 'Blood 'n shite,' he growled to himself at the unexpected predicament. His opponent was exceptional with the one long blade, and with ash in the atmosphere, his vision was becoming impaired. Jett didn't have time to waste.

Tonius approached with his blade out and he pulled on the girl's arm, dragging her away.

'No, you don't.' The cloaked man withdrew from Jett and barred the opening through the rows of shelves.

'I seem to recall, Lucien,' Tonius smirked, 'finders keepers, isn't it?'

'This is clearly theft.' He grilled him with a fervent glare.

Shark stopped and yanked the girl to his body. 'Of which you know a great deal.'

'If anyone has a claim,' Jett said, 'it's me.'

'Ah, now you say. But it's too late for that.' Tonius glared from under his green hat. 'Let's be honest. It's nothing to do with ownership or money, it has to do with who has the girl.' He gripped her arm tighter.

The three men eyed each other, none of them wishing to back down, even as fire raged not more than twenty feet away. Heat warmed Jett's skin and the air was stifling yet he was too stubborn to leave without the girl, despite the standoff. The girl collapsed against Tonius, and her covered head lolled to the side.

Jett frowned at the Captain's unsympathetic demeanour. 'She can't breathe.' He contemplated grabbing her and making a run for it, but he would probably receive a sword in the back if not two.

Tonius pulled the cloth off her head, revealing her closed eyes and pale skin. Her red-gold hair, damp along her forehead, spilled over her shoulders, and cloth was across her mouth.

'If we don't end this, there shall be nothing to fight over.' Lucien's light eyes observed the girl with some concern.

A voice boomed through the smoke. 'Bunch of cockhead perverts!' The speaker burst into their tense circle. 'No more girls, you devil bastards.' The giant man picked Mara up and held her waif-like form under his arm. With his free hand, he waved a great axe at them and if they hadn't stepped back, he would have taken their heads' off. 'For Ethan!' He hollered and ran back into the smoke from where he came.

'You raving idiot!' The Captain shouted and swung his blade in vain.

'The ugly ones always end up with the girl. Well, that's that. It's been interesting.' Lucien sheathed his sword. 'But it's time to save my own skin.' He disappeared through the opening.

His hand over his mouth, Jett chased after the bushy-bearded man, gaining encouragement at the mention of Ethan. He left Tonius yelling and fuming behind him.

~ * ~

Once his keeper was gone, Keanan crouched to the floor, hoping to avoid the incoming men, pirate and prisoner alike. Jett was more abrasive than usual, and Keanan surmised he was upset about Ethan's absence. He was also annoyed Jett expected him to look out for Hellier and Seth, yet left him tied up. Thankfully, he dumped the other malreus blades in front of him before dashing away.

Keanan positioned a sword between his legs in a clumsy effort to cut his rope. While he attempted slashing the binds without injuring himself, he cast an eye over the fighting. The men's brutality sickened him. Working together like wolves, they used their hands if no weapon were available. The well-to-do customers ran madly from the escapees, towards the opposite side of the room. A gentleman in a cream suite was dead in his seat while another was slumped over his chair killed in mid-flight. Dead bodies congested the cramped walk areas around the chamber. A couple of prisoners had carelessly tossed aside the fire poles in favour of a sword. The fallen lights ignited the rugs, and it would not take long before everything caught on fire.

A shadow loomed over Keanan. The slight man, who took the swords, had a smug snarl on his lean face. 'Look's as if I'll be taking these off your hands.' He bent down and snatched the weapons.

Keanan struggled to keep his hands on one of the hilts. 'Get your hands off them, you villain.'

Sim chuckled under his breath.

From behind Sim, a voice chided, 'Pitiful, Kean. You'll never do it like that.'

Keanan resentfully lifted up his tied wrists to show Marcus he was immobile.

Sim backed away with one of Marcus' black blades in hand, while lowering the others to the ground.

Marcus pointed his stolen weapon at Sim's hand. 'Bets on you don't know how to use that blade.' He pressed the tip of his sword into Sim's skin, drawing a spot of blood. '…so, you better drop it before you find out.'

Sim hedged away and Marcus kept his reach on him.

'Marcus, you have to get the doors open,' Keanan stated, 'the fire — it will kill us.'

Storage crates at the right side of the chamber were ablaze and the seating area was next. All the black market wares were feeding the flames. Even Sim glanced at it with fear. The smoke was dense by the ceiling, and the lack of air and burning fuel was beginning to clog the air.

I know, but I'm not going anywhere without my blades. Marcus stepped closer, not taking his eyes off the small man before him.

Giving fervid glances towards the other side of the chamber, Sim dropped the sword and sprinted into the dark smoke. From the same direction, Maddog ran past them and headed towards the door. Under his arm was a girl hanging limply.

Marcus eyed him running past.

Jett ran up to them with his hand over his mouth and said to Marcus, 'Why are you still here?'

'I'm going,' Marcus replied with irritation. He threw down the plain sword and picked up his own, plus his second, and went towards the exit from where they had come.

Keanan said, 'I can't see Hellier or Seth at all.'

'I'll find them.' Jett cut him free from his rope. 'Make sure that man doesn't take off with the girl.' He ran across the room, dodging the flames, thugs, and prisoners.

~ * ~

The freed slaves gathered around the doorway, trying to escape the smoke. They bemoaned their impending doom with scared voices, and a small number of girls, huddling together, cried softly.

Marcus pushed a path through their cowering bodies. 'No need to worry, I have the key.' He laid his hands on the door and the people pressed against him in fearful anticipation. 'Girls, you're going to have to step back.'

'Move it,' Maddog bellowed, 'let the little man work.' They made space for Maddog, an axe in one arm, and a girl hanging under his other.

Marcus glowered at him, wishing he had time to pound his fist into his stomach. Instead, he focused on his job and sent his Ethos through the dense iron. After hearing the faint crack of metal, he shoved the door. No movement. With a dismal groan, he punched the iron, and shook his hand from the pain of it. Again, he touched the solid metal.

Maddog spat out, 'You gonna do something?'

Smoke clogged the air along with the smell of burning oil. Marcus didn't need the obnoxious giant adding to his aggravation. Ignoring him, he reached higher and discovered a second lock. After a few moments it cracked under his Shattering Gift, and he shouldered it open.

Cool foul air rushed in, and despite the overpowering stench of excrement it was a mild reprieve. The people scrambled out with shouts of joy. Marcus was glad to see the men were armed, he forgot to mention the guards they might meet further on. Most of the prisoners waited at the entrance including Gart, Fish, and Maddog. Maddog pushed his weapon into Gart and hefted the girl into a more comfortable position in his arms.

Marcus noticed her distinctive hair and fine features. 'Hey, I know her.'

'What's her name?' Maddog growled with suspicion.

'Ah...' Marcus wracked his brain for some recollection. 'Can't remember.'

'Bulldung!'

Concern masking his annoyance, Marcus stepped closer to view her still chest. 'You might want to take that gag off.'

Fish cut the rag with a knife and the girl gasped and moaned.

Keanan arrived at the doorway, coughing. Clearing his throat, he addressed Maddog in a polite tone. 'If you don't mind I will take her.'

Marcus rolled his eyes.

Maddog raised his bushy brows. 'Why?'

'I know who she is and it's in her best interests if we look after her,' Keanan said. 'Her name is Mara.'

'Maddog,' Gart growled, 'we can't be taking a girl. A pregnant one at that.'

Maddog gazed down at her and she struggled to wake. 'You'll not touch her!'

Let Jett deal with him. Marcus shrugged at Keanan.

Keanan coughed. 'Fine...'

~ * ~

Through the fighting men, Hellier spotted Jazmina on the further side. Lifting her annoying skirt with one hand, Hellier ran, with her sword in the other and her wig sliding off her head. Seth kept up behind her.

Prisoners fought pirate-guards amongst the seating area and around the platform. Barrels exploded near them, igniting rolls of fabric by the chairs. Countless crates and shelves of bottles were all potential fuel.

Seth watched the fire grow. 'That can't be good.'

'We'll have to be quick,' Hellier eyed the spread of the fire with concern, 'but first...' she squinted across to the opposite side. The man holding the woman's bound wrists was in combat with a dark skinned prisoner, dressed similarly to Jazmina. 'I have to help.'

Seth moaned. *I should have gone with Marcus.*

With a devious grin, she squeezed his hand and pulled him towards the combat near the wall and racks of canisters. Within reach of the pirate and his curved sword, Hellier recognized his bandana wrapped head, and motley beard.

In an attempt to stop her captor, Jazmina pushed him. Waylan Corps shoved Jazmina back, crashing her into the crates and sending bottles toppling down from the shelves.

Free to attack his opponent, Waylan swung into the dark skinned man, cutting his shoulder with a flick of his wrist. Grimacing, the man stumbled at the pain. Her wig gone, Hellier arrived in time to deflect Waylan's blade from piercing him through.

'You bitch!' Waylan shrieked, recognition giving his words angry passion. He thrust into her with unwieldy blows. She hit back with an intense need to strike him.

The smoke became thick, making the air near unbreathable. Flames were devouring the barrels to their left. With unflinching calm, Hellier continued her attack.

Suddenly, Waylan started for Jazmina, half slumped on the floor.

'Don't you dare!' Hellier warned with fire in her eyes.

He touched the rope, but gave Hellier a wary glance. He sprinted away and was gone.

Seth unravelled the man's sash and wrapped it about his wounded shoulder. Despite his dark skin, the man was pale, and rasping in the smoke. Coughing, Seth finished tying the material.

Hellier pulled the woman up, but she was dazed and unsteady. Flames lurched high, reaching the roof of the chamber and spreading at an alarming rate. Thunderous explosions were close and the air was becoming unbreathable. Hellier gave Seth an anxious glance, now worried about bringing him into the dangerous situation. 'We have to get to the door or you won't be able to breathe.'

Nodding and covering his mouth, Seth helped the man to his feet. *I can hardly breathe now.*

Through the roar of the fire, Jett appeared beside them and scowled at Hellier. 'What are you doing?! We have to get out. *Now!*'

'I know!' Hellier glared in return. 'But, we have to take them.'

'I can—' Seth muttered through a gagging cough, '—carry the girl.'

'No, I will.' Jett's tone was harsh, but he only got to them through a narrow gap, and the fire was nowhere near abating.

Hellier supported the man. His thin frame made him a light weight and Jett followed behind with the girl's arm over his shoulder. They stooped as low as they were able. Avoiding the main hub of the fire, the burning heat still touched their skin. It seemed the fire separated the huge space, and where they stood was the wrong side. Stock and wares of the pirate's black market operation fed the fire to great effect. Near the centre of the chamber, where it was not so cluttered with combustible stock, was a passage not yet consumed by fire.

'We have to run for it,' Hellier yelled over the noise, 'We can do it.'

Jett shouted, 'We have to.'

The wounded man took his full weight on his own legs. 'I can.'

Hellier replied, 'I'll take you.'

'Go through, Seth,' Jett ordered.

Without hesitation Seth sprinted through.

With a sturdy grip on the unsteady man, Hellier placed him by her side, opposite the flames and they dashed past. She ran back with singed skirts and took the woman from Jett's arm.

'Don't take your time,' Jett grumbled, and he jumped through the space free of flames.

Scorching heat pulsed in her veins, seducing her to enter. She smiled. Fire, teasing her skin, was an immeasurable delight. It was rare to encounter such a wild fire. Adrenaline charged through her heightened flesh. The desire to join with the ferocious drive of flames surged to a near uncontrollable level. The raging energy was vigorous in its need to consume more fuel. If it weren't for the woman under her arm, and her waiting Kin, she would abandon herself to the heated pleasure. Keeping a tight lock on the girl despite her wishful thinking, she cradled her close and ran through to the other side. She was confronted with more smoke just as dense.

The girl in Hellier's arms groaned, 'My sisters…'

Hellier saw no other girls, and she could say nothing in comfort to her.

~ * ~

Marcus and Keanan waited by the open doorway. Marcus peered into the smoke, but could see nothing. 'Where are they?'

Outside in the tunnel, a crowd of former prisoners gathered and they waited as if needing instructions. For the most part they were a small band of emaciated men and women.

Seth stumbled to the exit and stopped in the tunnel, coughing and heaving for air.

Jett arrived with the wounded man, and stifling a cough, he went to Maddog and Mara. Observing her greyish pallor, he held her delicate wrist and sensed her faint pulse. Her eyes opened to slits, but she remained silent.

Maddog watched her with care. 'She's lost in the Bosky.'

Jett raised a brow in puzzlement.

Fish studied Mara's face. 'A drug traders use to keep 'em docile. Screws 'em up though.' He lifted her eye lid. 'She's had a good dose. Must have made trouble.'

Jett glared up at Maddog, nearly two heads taller. 'We're taking her once we're out.'

Maddog snarled with a darkening gleam in his eyes.

'Good.' Gart butted in. 'Now let's get out of here.'

Nodding at the stocky man, Jett said to Maddog, 'You know Ethan?'

'We met him,' Gart started. 'If we get out of here, I'll tell you where he might be.'

'I'll hold you to that.' Jett turned to the group. 'Is there a Vlaus here?'

'I am he.' Crouched by the door with the other overly thin people, a man raised a spindly arm.

Jett gave him a measly glance. 'Stay with us.'

Vlaus nodded without questions asked.

'That's it?' Marcus asked Jett.

Jett's breathing was hard. 'That's it.'

Marcus grinned and pushed on the door to close it. 'I think we've made a fine impression.'

'One Tonius won't forget in a hurry.' Jett grinned in return, recalling Tonius' fury. He had a thought he would be more enraged by the loss of Mara than his men and wares.

The sound of the heavy door shutting, echoed up the tunnels. They were swiftly sent into absolute darkness.

Gart cried in disbelief, 'Didn't anyone bring a torch?'

Groans, and people cursing each other, fell dull against the walls.

Jett's impatience cut through the dark. 'Keanan, take the wounded girl from Hellier.'

'Gladly,' Keanan replied with annoyance, *but, you've forgotten we can't see in the dark.*

Jett shifted the girl from Hellier and settled her into Keanan's expectant arms. In the strange silence people started to panic.

'Hey!' Fish shouted, 'Someone took me weapon!'

Jett lifted Hellier's wrist and thrust the acquired club into her hand. *Light this and hold it. It might have the appearance of a torch at least.* He walked ahead of her, and with the club ignited in her fiery hand, she followed him, with the line of freed men and women trailing behind. Jett felt some responsibility for any repercussions from their escape. Tonius wouldn't let them walk out so easily, and not with the valuable merchandise.

Those following queried the sight of the bizarre burning club amongst themselves, but no questions came the Kin's way. Eventually, they stopped and the line of weary men and women gathered around a dead man. In the semi-light he appeared to be asleep and no one could ascertain whether he was a guard or an ex-slave, he had neither shoes nor a cloak.

'There were three guards.' Jett studied the sloping tunnel. 'Let's move to the next opening.' He took the unlit torch from a bracket and passed it to Hellier to use for real. They passed underneath a street opening, revealing the cloudy night sky. Curious glances were given to the outside, but no one made a move to exit by that route. They followed compliantly the single burning light and the taciturn stranger who despite his aloofness led them with a commanding presence. Another halt was signalled and Hellier held her light high, shadowing a grated exit. Jett shoved on the iron grate, straining his muscles on the locked plate.

'We need to get out.' The wounded man swayed and slumped against the damp wall. 'My Jazy.' At the mention of her name, the girl opened her eyes, and having regained some strength, she hoped down from Keanan's arms to embrace the man.

Jett's reply was blunt, 'We're working on that.'

Let a real man open it. With a flick of his chin, Marcus bade Jett step aside, and with a swagger he reached up to the iron door.

Jett rolled his eyes, and tightened his lips. *Just open the flamin' thing.*

Marcus' hand ran along the thick metal. Shards of rusted iron crumbled down, falling into the trickle of water. His mystifying actions opened the floodgate of questions. Jett and Marcus ignored them. The grate cracked and broke. Marcus shoved his hand out into the street. Hefty pieces landed with a sharp clank, and a shard missed Jett's head by inches. The night sky shone into their dark oppressive world and the divine smell of impending rain was a rich perfume.

Gart thrust past the observers. 'I'll go first.'

'I'll go too.' Marcus gave Jett an excited grin.

Gart tossed Maddog's axe through and he hauled himself up the narrow opening. Hollering a contemptuous challenge, he disappeared above and Marcus was not long after. The two men created uproar with their catcalling and farcical profanities.

Jett pulled himself up to view them. 'What a show. Pity about the noise.'

From below, Hellier asked, 'Do they need help?'

Maddog replied, 'That bastard, Gart, he won't want anyone interfering.'

The two remaining guards wavered, keeping their distance from Marcus and the precise strikes of his weapon. At a safe distance from Marcus' sweeping swings, Gart attacked from the side. One of the pirates fell from a serious slash across his torso and the other ruffian started backing away.

Jett's voice rang out in the alleyway. 'Stop him!'

The man was thrown forward, landing hard on the wet stones with a knife embedded in the centre of his back. Gart walked to the prone man to check his handiwork and remove the weapon. Jett hoped the man was dead before he could be found otherwise.

'That's it,' Marcus chided, 'get 'em in the back while they run!'

The group climbed up and lifted those who couldn't out of the tunnel as fast as they could manage. Once all were on the surface, the dead men were dragged and dumped below, but not before their pockets were emptied and every bit of decent material on their bodies fleeced. A few of the men from the Rocks gave a hasty thanks and were off into the night. The group belonging to Vlaus and the women and children looked to their liberator for further directions.

Mara looked like a doll in Maddog's huge arms. At times she opened her eyes, and her mouth appeared to form words, but for the most part she could do nothing for herself.

Gart said to Jett, 'You want to know about your friend?'

'I do.'

'We heard they were sailing to a place called Signet Reach.' Gart's eyes dulled with the news. 'Along the coast by the Arranons. For slave labour.'

Jett's face fell with disappointment and the Kin's initial mood of cheer at the success of the night's escapade was deflated in a twinkling of an eye.

'I was not chosen to go.' Gart looked past Jett in a reflective recollection. 'Now, I understand why.'

Jett was already calculating strategies to rescue Ethan. 'How do we get there?'

'Unless you have your own ship you cannot,' Gart responded pessimistically, 'You must go through the mountains.'

'It's off the record, no ships sail there openly,' Maddog added, 'there ain't no way you can buy a ticket.'

'Flamin' arse-ring of the devil.'

Gart said, 'Fate will keep him or not.'

'Damn fate to hell,' Jett growled.

'Don't worry 'bout the boy,' Maddog interrupted, 'I've met him, he's strong. Anywho, he's with the Harn.'

'Harn?' Keanan said.

'I am Harn!' Gart's fist pounded his chest in pride. 'Maddog is right. He is with my brothers, and they like him which is lucky.'

Jett stared with wonder at the stunted man before them. His long reddish hair was plaited and hung over his chest, and his beard was a straggling mess. Intricate blue and black patterns lined his face, arms, and hands. His body was not only broad, but thick with hardened muscles, and his face was solid with distinct bone definition beneath the tattoos.

'My thanks for tonight,' Jett said despondently. 'Have you a place to go?'

'Fish knows a man we can see. Me, Maddog, and Fish are gonna get out.' Gart's expression became downcast and he turned to Maddog with a scathing glare. 'Without the girl. It's time, Maddog. These are Ethan's people.'

Maddog stared into her face and his eyes became a soft blue. 'You keep her out of trouble.' He pushed her towards Jett.

Jett lifted his hands in refusal and nodded to Keanan. 'We'll take care of her as much as we are able.'

'I'll take her.' Keanan took her from Maddog and cradled her in his arms with gentle ease.

Not normally inclined toward formalities, Jett stuck his hand out to Gart. 'Good speed and safety to you on your journey.'

Gart grasped his hand. 'As well to you.' In Harnan he started, '*May our meeting not be an end—*'

The foreign words stirred Jett's memory, and he responded in the same tongue, '*but a beginning—*' Amazed he recalled the old chant, he continued without faltering, '*—and may our last word—*'

'*—be a link to our first and may our parting—*'

'*—be as a dream—*' Jett's tone softened '*—and our arriving—*'

'*—like the morning,*' Gart replied.

'And our day together shine the light of eternal fellowship.'
Gart let his hand go and narrowed his eyes. 'How do you know my language?'

'I read it somewhere. I gathered it was old.'

'As old as Stonharn.' Gart stepped away with his curious eyes not leaving Jett's dark ones, and with that, Gart, Maddog and Fish disappeared into the shadows.

Jazmina stood with support from her lover. 'Thank you and farewell.'

The dark-skinned man bowed while holding his clothe wrapped wound, 'We shall depart to our people.' The two shuffled off into the darkness of the laneway.

Jett approached the miserable group of half-starved foreigners. 'Who is Vlaus?'

A tall, gangly man stepped from the small crowd. Despite appearing to be in his thirties, Vlaus had fine grey hair. Like the others with him, he wore minimal clothing, and shivering, his voice quavered. 'How do you know me?'

'I know Vanya,' Jett replied. 'I will take you to her. Are these people with you?'

Vlaus' eyes lit up. 'Yes, this is my wife and her brother—'

'No need for introductions.' Jett gestured for him to stop, not in the mood for chatter. 'Let's go.'

'And everyone else?' Keanan's eyes shifted to the girls and handful of children.

Jett rubbed his eyes from the residue of smoke, and partly due to a moment of exasperation. 'They come with us to Vanya's.'

They were a cheerless bunch of people, creeping past the dark, peaceful houses of Floris. Fortunately for the escapees, Vanya's home was not a long walk. The group crammed into the yard at the back of the house. Jett knocked sharply. Receiving no answer, he banged harder.

Vanya's face appeared with a wary frown through the crack of the door. 'You have come back.' Smiling warmly at Jett, she flung the door open. Her eyes darted over those crowding in around him. 'Oh, dearest Amplora! You brought *him* back.'

Vlaus stepped forward and gave her a hug and a teary greeting. He attempted introductions. 'This is my wife, Ginnia.'

'Come in. All of you.'

A man's baritone voice boomed from inside. 'Vanya, is it your friend?'

'That's my husband. Hektor.'

Jett withdrew back into the shadows. 'We can't stay.' He turned to his Kin waiting at the gate.

'But, how can I thank you?' Vanya called.

Too weary to respond, he continued to the lane along with his Kin and they walked the cold streets back to the inn.

43 - Safer Place?

'We all swear by a good fight, the more in it, the more bloodier, the tougher the challenge, the better the win, but, there's one fight we never get involved with, the one where a man is fighting for his honour. You step into that, you might as well outright kill the man.'

Life of a Champion, Zab Thunder'Fist

Early morning, while the Kin were still asleep, Hellier crept downstairs to see Dario. After he answered her knock, she entered and quietly shut the door.

He glanced up at her from where he sat on the bed. 'I'm glad you came.'

'I had to…' She spied his packed bag. 'You're leaving?'

'It's for the best.'

Her voice cracked with fervent emotion. 'I'm leaving too.'

'Oh…' He creased his brow, looking confused and embarrassed. 'I'm sorry you have to go. I wanted to tell you, I didn't mean to hurt you—'

'It's not that really.' She choked back an angry sob. 'But, everything between us was a lie?'

With a mournful gaze, he looked down at his closed hands. 'No, it's not true.'

'Do you love her?'

'I don't think so…' His voice stumbled. 'Well, I do in a way, but it's not the same…'

Transfixed by the floor, Hellier roughly wiped her damp eye. Furious, she was caught between throttling him and begging for his affection.

He opened his hands revealing a silver trinket. 'I also wanted to give you this.'

She screwed up her mouth in vexation. 'I can't take that.' White silver, the pendant was a filigree leaf with a crystal strung in its centre. 'Isn't it your mother's?'

'Yes, but I want you to have it.' Offering it to her, he made a weak smile. 'To remember me.'

She gritted her teeth and picked up the jewel.

He took her hand and pulled her down to sit beside him. His shining eyes remained on her face, pleading for a kind look from her. 'None of it was a lie. You are the most amazing experience in my life.' His lips caressed the back of her hand. 'Never did I dare hope such a wonderful person like you would enter my life and give me so much happiness.'

She rubbed the jewel in her hand and her heart twisted into a sorrowful knot. 'I don't understand…'

Tears softened his eyes. 'I have acted most cruelly.' He sighed sadly. 'And truly, it is most unlike me to behave in such a heartless manner. That's why I want you to have the treasure.'

The leaf pendent was more beautiful than anything she would wear. But still, did she care for him that much to take such a valuable item? 'This is… special.'

'As are you.' He smiled with his usual merriment surfacing. 'Besides it's far too pretty for me to wear. She never left it for me especially.' He gave a lopsided grin. 'But I loved it all the same.'

She turned the jewel in her hand, admiring the delicate metal work. 'It's just like you…'

Raising a puzzled brow, he said, 'To give you gifts?'

'No, I mean, the pendant is,' she paused, 'extravagant. It would certainly remind me of you.'

'Exactly. Because you will always have a special place in my heart.' He closed his hand over hers, securing it within.

She put her other hand over his and tried to smile. 'I don't know if I'll wear it, but I will look after it.'

'I know.'

His remorse revived her heart, and she tucked the pendant away in her pocket. 'I haven't anything to give you.' With a thoughtful frown she stood and twirled one of her braids in her hand. She spied one of his tailor tools lying with his things, and grabbing it, she cut away a plait behind her ear. 'You can have this to remember me.' She handed him the long golden braid.

'A splendid treasure!' His eyes lit up as he took the hair and trailed his fingers over the blonde shades.

Hellier blushed and fingered the stub of hair at the base of her scalp. 'I've had that a long time. It won't be that useful.'

'It's a perfect gift.' His mouth turned down with a tremor. 'I'm far too unworthy for such a personal treasure. I don't know how I will get on—'

'You will.' A leaden weight descended on Hellier's heart as she recalled their intimate time together. 'And I will remember you with fondness even though I wanted to kill you.'

He blinked with sudden fright.

'Not really.' She pushed on his shoulder and chuckled. 'I only wanted to punch you.' She pummelled her fist into her hand. 'Hard.'

Dario made a lame laugh.

'But I didn't.' She smiled and caressed his cheek. 'But, I will thank you for all your help, especially with Shiarn, and everything else.' She kissed his lips and whispered, 'I had the best time, until I found out.'

'I hope one day you can forget about my downfall and only recall my love for you.'

She had opened her heart to him, but he broke it, too easily. The grief was painfully raw, but apart from the betrayal, she still loved him and it was more than a physical bond.

'Maybe.' She would miss him, more than she wanted to admit. 'No matter what, if you are ever in trouble I will come, if I can of course.'

~ * ~

Mara remained in a drugged sleep. Even with noise and prodding, she would not wake up. It was some comfort she appeared to be breathing easy and at times moving in her sleep. The Kin could do nothing, but hope she would eventually come to. While Jett and Hellier went to the temple, Keanan, Marcus, and Seth stayed with her. Jett was adamant she never be left alone in the room.

Hellier and Jett hooded up and started out for the temple. She gave up trying to assure Jett she could walk there on her own, he was determined to be with her all the way.

The refuge was connected to the Temple of Niesta on the boundary of Sybil's Rise and Balydill District. According to Burgman, Niesta was nearly as popular as Nesvar, God of the sea. Women travelled from all over Floris and the provinces to have their wombs and unborn babies blessed. Men were not permitted into the temple, except for the adjoining courtyard, and over the years it became more than a place of worship, but a sanctuary.

Arriving at the busy square, Hellier admired the temple. High, with a domed roof, the building would be about forty feet in width, and leading up to the front terrace were stone steps that might fit ten people across. The granite was unlike the common buildings but similar to older structures about the city. Thick pillars supported the terrace, and double doors were set deep within the raised level. Behind the temple, was a vast three storey complex and to the left, another two storey building. Overall, the compound was massive and the high encircling walls passed several streets. At the feet of the stairs were two statues; a pregnant woman and a woman with a baby on her hip and two children clutching her legs.

Hellier nodded at them. 'Not an encouraging sight.'

'It's life.' Jett shook his head with amusement. *Maybe you one day.*

'Look's flamin' uncomfortable.' Diverting the subject before Dario could pop into her thoughts again, she said, 'You are going to wait here?'

'I won't be sitting out here like a rat on a white floor, but I'll watch you go in. I'll come to the courtyard tomorrow, same time.'

'Right.'

She approached the steps. A man by the statues yanked her hood down, exposing her blonde braids and another man grabbed her arm. Struggling to walk up the stair, she was hauled back and a hand smothered her shouts.

'It's her,' one of them yelled.

She bit his hand and screamed for help. The man behind seized her waist and tussled with her flailing arms. Her calls for help created a scene and people stared with ambiguity.

Don't you dare show yourself, she pleaded with Jett, concealed amidst the crowd. *It's too risky for you to get involved.*

If you can't get away, I'll have to.

'Guards!' Two white robed women rushed down the steps, pointing silver spears at the men. 'Guards!'

'It's no good, they took that other man to the post,' the other counsellor cried, and she commanded the men, 'Unhand her or we will poke you and we have every right to do so.'

Hellier was thrown down and she stumbled onto the stone step. The man's hard wrinkled face frowned at the counsellors, and he thrust his finger at them. 'We know where she is. We'll get her and all of you.' He spat. They sauntered off, giving a heated glare to the crowd watching their departure. The women helped Hellier up the steps and through the door.

~ * ~

Jett watched the men walk down the street that would take them to Racen Square. *What a surprise,* he thought cynically. From a safe distance he kept them in view, praying they not split apart. On one of the seedier streets of Racen Square, he made his move. 'You dim witted thugs looking for someone?'

They halted and turned to see Jett. On recognizing him, they smirked. 'It's one of them.'

The other man took a lazy step forward. 'We'll get a fine price for him.'

His friend yelled, 'Let's get him.'

Jett scampered into the closest ally. A couple of adolescent boys darted from his path. The overhang blocked the daylight. He pulled his hood down, and unsheathing his sword, held it at the ready under his cloak.

Racing round the bend, the first man, his sword up, pointed it at Jett. 'You're the vermin who messed things up.' They drew closer and took an offensive position side by side.

'Come and find out.' Jett stood alert in the tight space, watching their guarded progress towards him.

The Captain's henchmen impatiently raised his sword to strike. The other queried, 'Why his eyes look like that?'

Jett sidestepped to face the one who noticed his glowing eyes. He blocked the incoming sword and his eyes bored into the man's neck. The injured man crumpled to his knees, gagging and clutching his burnt flesh. The other man lost his footing and stumbled over his comrade's body. With a startled look at Jett, he scuttled backwards on his hands. The man behind grovelled, still holding his permanently damaged throat. So far Jett didn't need to worry about him, yet that could change at any moment. He took advantage of the reeling man, the tip of his malreus blade touching his shirt front.

Cowering in fear, the thug whimpered, 'You're not going to kill me, are ya?'

Jett hesitated. But, as he studied the miscreant from within the shadows of his hood, he realized the more dire charge was to let him free. A spark of hate flared within, and with a do or die thought for those he loved foremost in the world, he plunged the sword into the man's chest. He lay on his back with a look of shock followed by wrath, but soon, all life disappeared from his face.

The second man attempted to rise, and choking for air, he lifted his sword. As far as the burn wound he was alive, as far as Jett was concerned it was a different matter. He cut into his back, and wishing somehow it was not so easy, he smoothly pulled it out. He wiped his sword and pilfered what coin pouches they had, in hope it would look to most like a simple robbery.

Scanning the alley for witnesses, he saw none, although he was instinctively aware eyes watched him. There was naught he could do, only rely on his face being hidden. Moving quickly, he left Racen Square.

A couple of streets later, he pulled out the dead men's pouches. A few gold coins, numerous silver, and he examined a gold ring and words etched on the band. He put them all in his own pouch. Small wealth for pitiful men who were now deceased. Not a nice business, but a matter of course, and somehow, he had not been remorseful at the deed. But now, a peculiar sensation unsettled him. All actions must carry consequences. He had to hope the Eldery didn't find out. It would only add to his growing list of offences in Floris. But, at least Hellier would be safe at the temple.

~ * ~

Other than servants under orders not to speak to her, Shiarn had no contact with any one. Even Regina was absent. Not until the afternoon did she receive visitors. The governor entered followed by General Maustaton. To her relief the other general did not accompany them. She was not encouraged by their hard resolute expressions.

Aristos held a scroll and he stood facing her. 'Our investigation has progressed where we can exercise our judicial rights.' He unrolled the crisp parchment and announced in a ribald tone, 'Shiarn Rose, you are under arrest on the charge of regicide. Punishment is execution by the removal of the accused's head. Plea of mercy will not be entered due to the severity of the crime. Date of execution will be determined by the Court. Any signed confession may prolong the decision—'

'Hold on!' Shiarn shouted, 'What proof do you have?'

Aristos cleared his throat and continued, 'As it stands, I am under no obligation to reveal such things.'

'But no,' Shiarn cried with disbelief, her eyes darting between the two men, in an effort not to plead, 'It's not true!'

The General, his lined face like stone, spoke. 'The prince was asleep and cannot vouch for your presence here.'

'What are you... saying?' His statement stabbed at her heart, leaving her stupefied. Could it be Bastion? Would he really betray her? Was this the trap she dreaded? And how much did Jonas know? Her chest seized up with fear. 'This is not justice.'

'We believe you have been sent by our enemies for such a purpose as this.'

At a signal from Aristos, guards marched in. Escorted by them, she left the room, leaving behind the miserable memories it contained. Her limbs were numb, yet she made them move. The blank faced guards led her through the corridors in silence. Her only prayer, she was not marched straight to a guillotine. They walked through the palace, and people stared, making their opinion obvious by their hateful glares. Their callous

332

judgments pierced her exterior layer of indifference. She walked in a daze, sinking deeper into her thoughts, no longer hearing their merciless remarks.

They finally left the palace and entered the world outside. The air was brisk under a light sprinkling. Her green dress kept the chill from her skin, but she shivered and stared up into the wet wind. Her heart turned cold, frozen by the words of loathing and accusing faces.

They arrived at a large stone building of two levels. Down where it was dark and the air clammy, a guard pushed her into a sombre cell. A high window did nothing to stop the chill and she assumed a pallet of straw with a ragged blanket was her bed. They shut the door, the sound echoed against the stone bricks. Left in the depressing shadows, an awful odour assaulted her senses. She listened to the last of the guards tramp up the stairs at the end of the passage. A deathly silence reigned. Leaning her head in her hands, she let loose a flow of shocked tears.

44 - Disturbing News

Do not faint at bad news that comes through a friend
For they will have a part in sharing its burden

The Latent Path

Flute music melded with banging crates and jingling bells on the street below. Sitting on a chair he dragged out onto the balcony, Seth breathed into the new white-wood pipe. Jett sat alongside him, humming softly and gazing at the bulging expanse of covering clouds. Inside and despite the music, Mara slept on. As the day progressed, Jett became more anxious for her well-being, but there was nothing they could do to rouse her. Keanan and Marcus took the horses out and Seth suggested it would take his mind off things to play. It worked to some degree till he remembered there was a pregnant Nayinn adolescent passed out in their room.

A pause came in their song and a rap sounded at the door. Jett approached the door warily. 'Who is it?' On hearing Kael's voice, he was ushered in.

'I heard some fine music.' Kael pulled off his hood and pushed his cloak back. 'Could it be you, young fellows?'

On the first day Jett met him, a youthful shine was in his eyes, on this day he had a sombre look. 'Seth plays,' he said, not wishing their music to be the topic of conversation.

Kael nodded a greeting to Seth, sitting rigidly on the bed, and his eyes observed Mara. 'Is she ill?'

'We saved her from the traders.' Jett scratched his head and looked sheepish. 'Apparently she's under the effect of a smugglers drug.'

Kael stood over her. 'Ah, I see.' He put his hand on her neck and she slept on. 'Hopefully she will pull through.' Mara had gained some colour in her face. 'I admire your compassion. But should you not tell the Watch?'

'It's the girl, who was in the jail.' Jett's tight smile met Kael's expectant look.

Kael creased his face in shock. 'She's very lucky then.'

Jett nodded. Luckier than he realized.

'Did you find him?'

Glad Mara was not going to be discussed, Jett replied, 'He's been taken to a place called Signet Reach.'

Kael said with a cognitive frown. 'Along the coast?'

'So we heard and because we don't have a ship, we need to pass over the Arranons.'

'I see,' Kael said, 'I've brought you more news to be concerned about.'

Jett gave him a dark look. 'Go on.'

'Shiarn has been charged with the king's murder and has been imprisoned.'

Seth gave a sudden gasp.

Jett's heart sank, yet he was not shocked at the news. 'I had a feeling it would fall that way.'

Kael nodded his agreement.

'What now?'

'She must escape.' Kael smiled like an old rogue. 'But with help of course.'

Jett was more pragmatic. 'When and how? And do you need our help?'

'One flaw of this mad plan, we do not know the day it will take place.'

Jett said with exasperation, 'Makes for difficult planning.'

Kael said, 'We rely on a particular event occurring which will serve two purposes, but we don't need to get into specifics. Can you free your Kin in the temple?'

Jett was doubtful of any way Earona could get out safely. 'I might need to wait for Shiarn.'

'You must think this through carefully,' Kael informed him, 'You know you must leave the city as soon as Shiarn is free.'

'We're on borrowed time as it is.' Jett's voice was full of malice. 'I don't know how we are going to reach Hakan-Kara and meet with Avare Garvel on time.' He gave a tired sigh. 'If at all.'

'I don't envy your position, but your Kin is more important right now.' He looked thoughtful for a moment. 'Shiarn is to be executed in about six days' time.'

Seth cried, 'So soon!'

Kael turned to face him. 'You really should be grateful it's that and not today or tomorrow, this way we have time.' With an intense look, he said, 'Let me stress this, you must leave the city and she must not be seen in Floris ever again.'

'The people are angry, I've heard them talking.' Lynching would be likely, and wouldn't be just one of them.

Kael indicated to Mara, 'If she is left here, she will be found, and they will find out who Shiarn is and all of you.'

Jett was already aware of that on many different levels. As well as the underground of Floris chasing her, so would the Palace. 'She's coming with us. I'll make sure of that.'

'Has Shiarn been hurt?' asked Seth.

'She escaped routine torture due to a confession.'

Jett raised his brows. 'She signed a confession?'

'Not exactly.' A mischievous glint appeared in Kael's eyes. 'It was done on her behalf.'

Jett peered at Kael with distrust. 'Perhaps things are going on we know nothing about.'

'It might look peculiar from the outside, but what can I say—' He shrugged '—it's politics.'

Jett brooded over Kael's evasiveness and pursed his lips in deliberation.

'How did your meeting with the captain pan out?'

His query broke the tension and brought a grin to Jett's face. 'We freed his slaves, destroyed his stock and some henchmen, maybe even exposed his secret chamber to the authorities.'

Kael chuckled with showy loudness.

'*And* we have a 'fine' price on our heads,' Jett directed to Seth. 'But the best of all, I like to think, we damaged that man's reputation. Even so, I don't think it equals what he did to my sense of pride.'

Kael shared a smile with them. 'His reputation is quite expansive.'

'It's another reason why we must leave Floris. I'm afraid every thug and lowlife in this city will get wind of where we are, and we'll be easy targets.'

'I agree. I have been discussing your situation with Jonas and on light of one of your Kin being so far from here it seems an even better idea. We thought you might like to go to Sommerlea, our family estate.'

Jett inclined his head with interest.

'In the Eastern Province, outside Parkvale.'

Jett pressed his lips together in thought of what sounded like a well meant proposal. 'Maybe…'

'Considering your harrowing time here, it might be in your best interests to lay low and plan your next step.'

'Are the Arranons accessible from that part of Coltrene?' asked Jett.

'Yes. I'll ask around about Signet Reach too.' Kael contended with a difficult pocket and tossed a plump pouch onto the table. 'You will need a wagon.' He said with humour, 'I haven't even asked what happened to your own.'

'That's another long story and a bad one.' And not one Jett wanted to discuss, he imagined some villager leaping joyously at the splendid find.

'You will need one when it is time to leave.' Kael gave the pouch a good natured push towards him. 'Here.'

Jett resisted the urge to push it back. In his position he had to take into account the whole Kin. He lifted the weighty purse in his palm.

'It should be more than enough,' Kael winked with a carefree grin.

'We thank you for this,' Jett responded solemnly. 'One day I shall return it to you.'

'For some reason I believe you, anyway, haven't done much yet, got to get her out, but we're nearly half way there. Oh, and Jonas says, buy Shiarn shoes and a nice dress, maybe two.'

Jett tucked the pouch into his belt. 'It's like that is it.'

'Let's just say, she has made an impression on him. Perhaps Shiarn will elaborate, but still, she is in the jail and it's not a pleasant place to be.' Kael added, 'Who knows, it might be tonight you see her.'

'Another thing,' Jett said, 'The man I mentioned, Dario, he knows we have ties with Shiarn…' His words were left to settle in the silence.

'He's not the smartest person, but he does have privilege in the palace. I shall keep my eye on him in case he causes any mischief.'

'And something else…'

Kael raised a questioning brow.

Jett's gaze flicked over Seth and settled on Kael. 'You mentioned knowing my father…'

Kael relaxed into the chair, and smoothing his beard, he looked past Jett in contemplation. 'In Baion over three decades ago. Seeing you brought back some memories. He and his Kin were hiring themselves out as mercenaries at the time, and we were living in a village on the lands of the lord who employed them.' He paused. 'But that's not what you really wish to know?'

Jett's brow deepened.

'You never knew him?'

'I know little about his travels.'

Kael continued fingering his beard, but he considered Jett with an interested gaze. 'Your father became well-liked by Lord Balendin. Internal fighting was a problem in Baion at the time, and Balendin had the coin to take on more men. Aillas was a good leader and Balendin eventually made him captain of his guard.'

'What happened?'

'I don't know. We left. Balendin wanted us to become a part of his court,' Kael said, 'and there were other things. Our paths had to separate.'

'And my father?'

'Aillas was an influential man. I could see him becoming a powerful asset to that lord and kingdom.'

Jett sensed Kael's sudden agitation. He wanted to delve deeper into the man's memories, but he was uneasy at the other man's reservation. 'But that was not to be?'

'It was only when I came back to Tellávare I heard news of his death.'

'It is said he went west?'

'I heard.' Kael frowned, but said no more.

Jett sensed Kael knew more than he was saying. 'Perhaps if I was to find this lord I might learn more of his whereabouts.'

'Balendin was a warrior, and most likely dead now, or near to.' Kael's tone bristled with an undercurrent of annoyance. 'But truly, you have more important things to do than track down an old man in another kingdom.'

Jett knew well the old recrimination over querying his father's disappearance. He sensed the walls of indifference rising over his need to know.

'I appreciate you are looking for answers.' Kael's voice softened. 'But I can't help you on that side of the search. I did know your father, and his charisma was far reaching, even to the King of Baion himself. It was a sad loss for Tellávare when he disappeared.'

'It was.'

Kael stood, and smiled at the two of them. 'You'll hear from me soon, and after, we shall meet in the comfort of Sommerlea.'

As if to break the sullen air, Seth gave a wistful sigh. 'What a delightful name.'

Kael nodded with a smile. 'This time of year it's starting to lighten up as it moves out of winter into spring.'

'I have great affection for the winter months. The trees don't sleep as much as what people might assume.'

Kael gave Seth a worthy pat on the back. 'I don't have to ask what Gift you have. You will find much in common with Adis, also a Naturist.'

Jett opened the door for Kael, and he said to them, 'Best of luck to you all and take care.'

~ * ~

Late afternoon, Mara sat up in bed and looked around the golden-lit room. It took her some moments to notice her aching muscles, and at every movement her head pounded. She scanned the room with confusion. On seeing the three unfamiliar men sitting at the table, she had a burst of fear. Apart from a curious glance her way, the men went back to their talk.

A dark haired man sat on the opposite bed and her eyes settled on him with recognition. She took a quick breath as she recalled his name.

'You've been asleep along time,' Jett said, 'There's food if you're hungry.'

'...I...' her voice cracked and she coughed through a raw throat.

He handed her a cup of water. 'Apparently the drug knocks you out.'

In faded scenes she could remember the man who took her, but nothing with any detail. Closing her eyes, she drank. She didn't know if she wanted to sleep or eat, her body was leaden and empty. On top of her lethargy was an unreasonable anger churning in her stomach. 'Why am I... and why are you… what... happened?'

'You were taken by a trader and we found you.'

She stared through him, and attempted remembering her rescue. Her memories were fleeting like a vapourous dream, but she recalled Jett's presence in a dark smoky environment. At the time she wondered if it was another nightmare. But now, he was right there. Her heart quivered with fear. It wasn't that he might send her back to her mother, although that worried her, it was something more sinister. She wanted to run out the door and flee from him. 'I can't stay... I'm going...'

'Go?' Jett's mouth hung open in surprise. 'Where?'

Mara shook her head and avoided his intense dark eyes. With her mind still addled, coherent words were difficult. 'Away.'

'You can't.'

Mara threw the covers off. Still clothed in her temple robes, she pulled her heavy legs around. Strength imbued her limbs and she stood with determination. After a moment of steadying herself, she shuffled to the door.

Jett walked to the door and put his hand on the knob. 'I said no.'

The men at the table paused to watch her peculiar behaviour. The auburn haired man spoke, the same one who patronized her back in Lanvin. 'It's best you stay with us. You'll be safe.'

Once again, she was a captive. With her hands clenching her waist, she faced Jett, 'I'm tired of this. You can't keep me here.'

'I am and I will.' Jett folded his arms with equal defiance.

'I have rights!' Blood rushed to her head at the exertion of her voice. 'I'm not your prisoner!'

'You are for now.' His mouth made a grim line. 'Would you rather be my prisoner or a smuggler's?'

She stepped back from him in a huff, but did not lower her stance. Something inside her was driving her fury, and with some irrational dread, it was him she wanted to get away from. 'No-ones!'

'Half of Floris is out looking for you, the bad half. As soon as you walk out of here, they will find you.'

'That's not my fault.' She tried not to whine, but really, she just wanted to be free.

He stepped closer and his arms crossed against his chest. 'I don't care whose fault it is. You would risk our safety as well as your own.'

She glared up at his black eyes and stormy expression. 'Who do you people think you are?'

'I want to know why you are wanted by them.'

'Really? That's too bad—' she ended with a yowl as Jett grabbed her arm and jostled her into the adjoining room. He slammed the door behind him.

She brushed his hand away and rubbed her throbbing flesh. Her head was near exploding and her eyes lit with rage. 'That hurt! You can't do that—'

Looming over her, he was rigid with anger. 'Tell me why I keep having to save you?' His eyes were unyielding as he watched her.

Mara's rage did not abate, nor was she intimidated. But, she could tell he was fishing for something more, as if she were supposed to understand his request. For all she knew it could be any number of things. 'How should I know?!' She threw her hands in the air. 'You should be asking yourself that. I never asked for any favours!' She stared him in the eye, her face twisting between vexation and anger. 'Anyway, you can't threaten me,' her eyes turned to slits of amber fire and she pointed at his chest. 'I know about you. All of you,' she spat with abrupt vehemence. She never meant to divulge that knowledge so soon. But this man continued to provoke her in ways that aggravated her state of mind.

'What do you mean?' His face paled with open wrath.

Obviously she touched a raw nerve. 'All I am is some possession, like useless baggage.' Without meaning to, she raised her voice to an irrational pitch. 'Carted around by criminals and reprobates, and weird... people. Drugged. Tied up. Beaten. Never allowed to do what *I* want. And she'll always be there hounding me for her own evil plans as if I'm just a... a... thing to be used. And now you—'

'What do you know about us?' Jett lifted his brow expectantly.

Mara took a sharp irritated breath. 'Were you even listening?' She folded her arms, refusing to say anything more on it.

He took a long breath and shook his wavy shock of hair. 'She couldn't stop herself, could she? I shouldn't be surprised, you were stuck with her for more than a day. It doesn't help any.' His voice grated with annoyance. 'It's all the more reason to not let you go.'

She took an indignant gasp.

Jett stepped even closer, making sure she couldn't sidestep him or avoid his drilling stare. 'Who would pay a great deal of money for you?'

If she didn't tell him something, she would most likely be stuck in the standoff until she fainted from tiredness or hungry, or both. 'If anyone, it would be my mother.'

'How would she know you are here?' He scratched his chin in thought. 'That doesn't make sense.'

Yavinia would have any number of ways. Although with the charm it would be near impossible to find Mara. That was aside from the man who kidnapped her. He did not seem to be connected with the witches or her mother. 'She'd be looking.'

'We had only been here a couple of days…' He spoke under his breath. 'I gather it's your mother who wants you for her "evil plans"?'

Mara ducked her head, wishing she hadn't mentioned it at all. She held onto Wendessa's leather wristband, finding comfort in the script. 'That's why I ran away.'

Jett's brow knotted together as he considered her. 'Do those evil plans have anything to do with the vision?'

She raised her eyes feigning surprise and opened her mouth to dispute the experience.

'Don't deny it,' he snapped. 'I did see it, although I don't understand it.' He rubbed his forehead and let out an exasperated sigh. 'Wish the hell I did.'

Her eyes narrowed with suspicion. 'Are you sure you don't?'

'What's that supposed to mean?' he barked.

'You were in it too! And you didn't look too… virtuous.' She snapped. 'It makes me wonder, who are you really?'

His eyes drilled into her and his shoulders were rigid. 'I have no idea what it means.'

Mara grumbled with a sulky pout, 'And I would rather not know at all.' She could sense his eyes fixed on her, studying her every expression. 'If you have to know something, my mother… uses the elements… like a magik user, and she wanted me to go with that man for a ritual to summon something. Maybe the vision was about that.' She scrunched her lips up, as if to hold her words in. 'But, I've never seen those women before…'

'Why by the devil was I in it?'

She shrugged with genuine puzzlement.

'Flamin' curses!' His loud tone made her jump. 'If the bastards found you once, they could do it again. If I have to tie you to the bed I will.'

She wasn't going to tell him about the witch attack in the temple, or that her mother might still be able to trace her, or at one time she would have done anything her mother wanted. That was why it was better to leave and stay on the run. She glared. 'Gods, you're just the same.'

'I said "if" I have to. If you behave I won't beat you.' He smirked.

Unsure whether he was serious or not, Mara glowered with a need to rant. 'You can't treat me like this—'

'You're saying your mother is a mage? And she's looking for you to use in a ritual?' Jett studied her eyes and face with a chilling intensity. 'What a shite position we're in.'

His scrutiny of her unnerved her and she turned her face away and sat on the bed. 'That sums it up.' Even so she had come so close to carrying out this ritual. She cocked her head with conceit. 'So, you really want to look after a pregnant girl who has a mage for a mother?'

'I don't like it,' he growled, 'But, I have to for now. Till I can figure out what do to with you.' He spread his fingers through his hair. 'What in hell's name does she want to summon?'

Mara gave him a poignant stare. 'Probably something from another realm.'

'Devil's arse, unbelievable!' After a strained paused, Jett said, 'Does this have anything to do with something called the Eye of Heaven, or the Eye-key?'

Recognition crossed her face and she couldn't suppress her shock.

'You know about it, don't you?' Jett pressed his lips together. 'It is related.'

'I've heard of it.' The ancient amulet was in the prophecy, and that she would be drawn to it, but not in a good way. It had the power to open a Gate, she knew that much. She also knew, the One could control it.

Out of loss and from chaos
Will appear the One who possesses the Key to Heaven
The Eye opens and controls realms of Dominions
The Mastery will cause enemies to flee

Could he really be the One, the 'wolf' that Wendessa spoke of? 'Do you have it?'

Jett creased his eyes at her question. 'Why?'

She recalled her attraction to the necklace worn by the redhead. Could it be the same? 'I'm curious.'

'It's a powerful object not fit for anyone.' He exhaled a weary breath and muttered, 'Why do we have to be dragged into this?' Despite his complaint, he raised his hand. 'You're not going anywhere.'

Mara pursed her lips together in a resigned pout.

He looked away, his face a mask of contemplation. 'If they know you were with Earona, they may target her for information.'

Mara covered her sudden gasp. They were seen together and even masqueraded as sisters.

'And after tonight she'll know alot more.' Jett rubbed his temples.

'You're going to rescue her?' Mara said, wide-eyed with astonishment.

'Not yet,' Jett said, 'she'll have to wait.'

~ * ~

Earona waited in line for her evening meal. Women were giving her curious glances, some stared openly. Earlier in the day, a woman was attacked on the street outside and was carried in with terrible injuries while the guards took the offender away. The counsellor asked for Earona's assistance. Now the woman was well and sitting at the table. It wasn't Earona's fault — what was she expected to do? She couldn't leave her maimed for life, she had to heal her. But now, the women talked about Earona's favour with Niesta. Gossip about her 'power' was spreading at a ridiculous speed. If Jett knew about it, he would be livid.

She concentrated on ladling the stew into the bowl, hoping no one would ask her outright about the woman's healing. The same warm meal night after night created a safe comfort. If she did stay seven years, it wouldn't be that awful... except... she let out a heavy breath and shuffled from the bench. Despondent to conversation, she searched for an empty space. She moved to the table, clutching her bowl and limp bread, hoping her stew would not be worn by the front of her dress due to those more anxious to get a seat.

'Blue...'

Jumping with fright, she turned at the familiar voice. With a detached alertness, Hellier leaned against the wall. Earona halted mid-step and stared with mouth agape. 'It's really you?'

'Don't make a scene, I'm not meant to know anyone here.' Hellier's eyes danced over the room, never stopping on her.

'How did you get here?'

'Not important,' Hellier replied under her breath, 'We'll talk later.'

Earona continued staring in a daze. 'Come to my dorm after dark.'

Hellier stepped away and joined the line of women waiting for a meal.

Earona politely pushed into a space at the table and watched Hellier saunter across the room to sit with the other free women. Full of questions, she could not wait to speak with her.

The room settled into a tranquil state as the last of the women drifted to sleep. Earona fought it off.

Don't go to sleep. Hellier crawled into Mara's empty bed.

How is everyone?

Hellier's eyes were bright in the darkness and she whispered, 'There's so much to tell you.'

'How did you find me? And do you know anything about Shiarn and Ethan?'

They think she killed the king.

Earona gave a frightened gasp.

'It's a long tale,' Hellier said in hushed tones. *She will have to escape soon and so will you. I shall speak to Jett tomorrow and hear about any new development.*

Amid trepidation, Earona queried, 'And Ethan?'

'Is not in the city,' she murmured. *He's shipped up the coast as a slave.*

Tears shone in Earona's eyes, and she sniffed. 'And Mara's gone too.'

Hellier stifled a snort of laughter. 'We have her.'

'You... have... what?!' Earona stared like a witless fish and interrupted Hellier's silent giggling. 'You rescued her and left me behind!'

'Shss!' Hellier put her finger to her lips. 'You daft ninny.'

Earona gave her a peevish frown.

'We saved her from some pirates.' She continued chuckling.

'It really wouldn't surprise me if you...' Earona grumbled. *She's with you while I'm stuck here. How unfair.*

'Jett will have a good laugh.' Hellier grinned.

Earona squinted an eye at her in suspicion. 'Anyway, it's best she be with you. She was attacked. I thought it was a witch...' but now, she couldn't be certain and the further it got, the more vague the memory.

'Really? You think? What does she look like?'

Earona frowned at her mockery. 'An old woman.'

Hellier's mouth formed a thin line. 'What have you got against old ladies?'

'I'm sure it was something.' On hindsight, even Mara didn't think the woman was threatening.

'The way Jett was talking, Mara is being hunted by the traders. But having to look after her is not something he wants to do. He's not happy.'

Earona whispered, 'As long as he does.' *He can be such a prig.*

No doubt this is hard for him. Hellier smiled. *Everyone scattered around and he has to find you all.*

Earona reddened at the insight. She thought of Jett's demanding and protective ways with fondness, not that she would even admit she sometimes appreciated them. 'When you see him, tell him — thanks.'

~ * ~

The lonely quiet of night descended into Shiarn's already colourless cell. A watery broth was pushed through the flap at the foot of the door. She had no appetite for the choicest of meals let alone old soup.

A moist repulsive odour was in the air and no matter where she stood she smelt it. It appeared to come from the walls and she assumed the cell had never been cleaned. She noted her clothing still had a vestige of elegance. Her pale emerald skirts were soiled in places and the white underdress hung past the skirt's hem. Wiping tears from her face, she realized she was probably smearing grime over her cheeks. If only the others could see her now, what an appalling sight she would make.

She upturned her metal bucket and placed it below her raised window to peek outside. Fresh air was pleasant on her face and a small luxury in the dirty world she was mercilessly thrown to. She looked up at what she could view of the night sky beyond the awnings. The rain had stopped, but the eaves continued dripping. She spied no stars only the grey of approaching stormy weather. A firm breeze hit her skin. She took a deep breath and tasted its strange scent.

In front of her face was an organized scrabbling. 'Hello, my dear.' A tender touch on her cheek startled her.

She could see nothing but the shimmering black of the courtyard. 'Jonas, I'm wretched.'

An unseen hand smoothed away unshed tears. 'It is a sorry state of affairs that is true.'

She pressed his hand onto her cheek.

'You will need trust me no matter what.'

She whispered, 'What is going to happen?'

After a moment of silence, he said, 'If they have their way, you will be beheaded within the week.'

'I trusted Bas. He said he...' Unable to form the words regarding what she understood to be the prince's treachery, she shook her head with disbelief.

'Words are powerful. Sometimes they are used to our advantage in a way we cannot see presently. His position was incredibly tenuous.' His voice was soothing yet he spoke candidly. 'They were going to charge him with the murder as well as you, and hence that would have done you and I no good at all.'

Suddenly questioning how much she could trust Jonas, she voiced her grief. 'And I am the one charged!'

'Ah, but you, my darling, have the greater chance of escape.' Jonas took a breath and said, 'You won't like to hear this, but it's in your best interest to be aware of what you are up against.' Her pale face creased with worry and he continued, 'I have discovered Morgal holds the only key to your cell. That is why I am out here and not in there. No one is allowed to enter bar him alone. It seems he is suspicious you will somehow escape, or disappear and therefore create trouble.'

Her eyes drooped and her voice filled with wrath. 'He wants the bottle I stole from him.'

Jonas stroked her hand with affection. 'He will not lay a hand on you again.'

Not desiring her emotions to tumble out unintelligibly, she said nothing.

His tone became downhearted. 'There is much commotion in the servant's quarters over young Sasheya's disappearance. Morgal has caused much suffering for many people.' He began on a lighter note, 'I have a query you may be able to shed light on. Not unlike Sasheya, Regina has disappeared. No one has seen her and none of her belongings are missing.'

Shiarn creased her brow, searching her mind for the last time she saw the woman; the banquet. 'I wonder if she was the other figure in the room with the altars.' She dragged her mind over the dreadful experience. 'Could it be possible she was the red smoke?'

'Of course,' Jonas agreed, 'that may bring an explanation to her disappearance and provide a justification as to why Morgal was interested in her at all. He needed her and Sasheya, and you, for this bizarre ceremony he performed.' He paused in a reflective silence. 'I wonder what devilish deed he has cast on the world.'

'It wasn't entirely successful, or so I assume.' She shrugged indifferently. 'It's the least of my worries.'

'True, your current dilemma is quite enough for us. The plan for escaping is hinging on a two things. All you need to be aware of is my friend, Kael, will assist your escape from the palace grounds. After this he will take you to your friends.' He paused, and Shiarn could not even hear his breathing. 'I think it's best if you make your way to my estate, Sommerlea, where you can rest and recuperate for a time.'

'And you will be there?'

'I will be there...' Uncertainty was in his voice. 'When I can...'

'I suppose I would need to talk to my Kin about it.'

'They appeared amicable regarding the idea.' He squeezed her freezing hand. 'You only need be ready.'

She managed a croaky laugh. 'I'm as ready as I'll ever be.' She had left nothing in her room and everything she owned was upon her.

He laughed softly at her effort to evoke confidence. 'That's the spirit. Now be brave.'

She kissed his hand, but the longing for an amorous embrace overwhelmed her.

45 - Don't be Fooled

Build up your fortifications is to lend strength to your brother's Keep.

Empirical Warfare Command

Yeon's Corner was a district situated on a gentle slope in the north east of Floris. Rural plots and old homes were along the narrow streets, clogged with sluggish animals and diligent traders. Marcus and Seth rode on Rose and Sunny, while Keanan walked by the horses' heads as they dodged carriages, people, and the occasional animal excrement.

Eventually they stopped at a shabby building with a splintered door and a sign, "Arjah's Wheels." Attached to it was an enclosure with a few wagons lined up. Wheels and odd pieces of wood were strewn about the yard in no order.

'Looks like the place.' Marcus walked to the fence and let himself through the gate.

Keanan, with Seth following, pushed the door open with his knuckles, not daring to place his hand on the fragmented wood to receive splinters for his trouble. A full bellied, long bearded man with caramel skin, rumbled a greeting.

'Good day to you…' Keanan started, 'Arjah?'

Arjah, in an aqua robe belted with a yellow sash, and his head wrapped in off-white cloth, bowed, and gushed with his ringed hand sweeping wide, 'I am Arjah, your humble servant.'

Keanan nodded a polite greeting. 'We have come to view your wagons.'

Arjah stroked his beard in consideration. 'My wagons?'

'That is what you sell?' Keanan raised a sceptical brow.

'Where did you hear about my undistinguished business?'

Marcus, deciding to view the wares himself, knelt by the first and looked underneath. The undercarriage appeared sturdy and suitable for their needs. He stood and the second wagon caught his attention. Painted a sky blue with bright animals over the sides, it was similar to the one they saw travelling from Lanvin.

A movement of colour from behind stopped him. He stepped around the back and caught a slender arm. A dark skinned girl fought against him, but he yanked her close, causing her warm hair to cascade over his shoulder and chest. Despite the plainness of her dress, and anger flaring across her face, she was attractive.

Marcus asked gruffly, 'What are you doing, sneaking around?' Suddenly a sharp point pricked the side of his neck.

'Shouldn't we be asking this?' A man's voice stumbled over the common language. 'Let her go.'

Marcus loosed his fingers and she dashed from his reach. 'Can you move the knife from my throat?' The blade was pulled away, and he turned to view his assailant. 'I know you. You were one of the slaves.' He rubbed his neck, still feeling the press.

'Ah, yes. My name is Faraq.' In spite of the wound, the lean southerner received the night before, his knife disappeared without a trace, in a flurry of swift fingers.

'I'm Marcus,' he responded. 'You made it to your friends?'

'True, but we still must get Jazmina's sisters back.' Faraq nodded at the girl sitting on a barrel, listening.

'Do you know where they are?' asked Marcus.

'We have our ideas. What is the reason for your visit?'

Marcus patted the coloured wagon. 'We need one of these.'

Faraq smiled at the exotic animals. 'You like?'

Marcus frowned at the extravagant creation with ill-concealed disgust. 'This one looks like it would cost alot.'

'It is true.'

'I've seen one like it,' said Marcus.

Faraq's body stiffened and he raised his fist. 'Where did you see this wagon?'

'In Ryne, a place called Lanvin,' Marcus said, 'He was travelling towards the Allervium Mountains.'

Faraq exploded with wrath. 'What did this man look like?'

Marcus answered with care, sensing his anger, 'A dark southerner, dressed brightly with a lot of jewellery.'

The woman spoke to Faraq in their native tongue.

Faraq shot out, 'Who was with him?'

Marcus concentrated on the brief encounter, but he could hardly forget. 'A boy.'

A string of harsh words poured forth from a glowering Faraq. 'What this man say to you?'

'He was in a hurry, he didn't want to talk.' Their inflamed interest in the man roused his curiosity. 'Who is he?'

'He is a dastardly fiend, a swindler and a devil.' Jazmina hopped down from the barrel and her hands waved in the air. 'A fat swine born of a yellow-bellied woman, he no good waste of skin.'

Marcus took a step back from the fiery-eyed enraged girl. Surprised one of such a delicate appearance could be so full of venomous passion. 'He must have done you over.'

She spat out, 'He sold me and my sisters.'

Faraq spat, 'We curse him and his ancestors!'

'He stole that wagon and he carries an artefact from the Randulan Temp—'

Shaking her arm, Faraq fired out in Abulian.

Marcus said, 'An artefact?'

Faraq stated, 'Nothing to do with you.'

'It doesn't matter. He's long gone, over the mountains.'

'It is the luck of Erantè we should get this from you,' Faraq said, 'he will not get away with this.'

Keanan and Seth walked into the yard with Arjah talking exuberantly at them. Arjah showed a look of fear at Marcus speaking with Jazmina and Faraq.

Faraq and Jazmina nodded a curt greeting to Keanan and Seth.

Keanan said, 'Good to see you looking well.'

She took a commanding stance. 'We owe you much, but still there is more to do.'

Keanan gave her an offhand glance. 'I gather you mean more slaves to rescue?'

'My sisters.'

'I assume you all know each other.' Arjah's query went ignored.

Keanan said, 'Do you know where they are?'

'A duke, Brytwold, has them.'

Keanan enquired, 'How would you plan on robbing a duke of his slaves?'

Faraq responded abruptly, 'We have our ways.'

Marcus patted his back in a light-hearted manner, understanding when a man had no wish to divulge his secrets. 'In any case, good luck to you. Now, let's look at this wagon.'

Jazmina directed her plea to Keanan. 'I beg you, can't you help us?'

'Be quiet!' Faraq burst out.

She turned to Faraq and said, in their native tongue, *It will be impossible on our own, they can help us.'*

'We cannot risk them knowing about us,' replied Faraq.

Keanan replied, 'We have our own troubles. Perhaps you can try going to the Watch.'

Faraq shoved her shoulder and shouted in Abulian.

Keanan's face reddened over Faraq's tirade. Startling them out of their heated exchange, he addressed them in perfect Abulian. *'There's no need for language like that or any form of aggression.'* They remained silent and he continued his business with Arjah. 'This is the one.'

Arjah beamed with pride. 'Yes, good condition, newly made.'

The wagon was covered with a waxed canvas over a square frame with side racks, and numerous hooks lined the framework. Inside, more storage compartments were along the bottom sides, and underneath two spare wheels, neatly packed away. Keanan glanced at the wagon next to it. 'That brings back a memory from the not too distant past.'

Faraq said to Arjah, 'They seen Samlomna on the road north.'

'That swine, he robbed me.' Arjah reacted with rancour much like the other two. 'If I could get my hands on him I would be very joyful.'

'He is far away now,' Keanan said with regret, 'We didn't know.'

Marcus added, 'On hindsight he did look suspicious.'

'It is not your business,' said Arjah, 'you could not know.'

Seth fastened the horses to the wagon while Keanan and Arjah exchanged gold and they were ready to go. Keanan placed himself in the driver's seat and Seth sat next to him.

Jazmina looked up to him, 'If you change your mind, we will be here.'

'Be careful with whatever plans you make,' Keanan said.

'We have our ways. I can get about and not be noticed.' Faraq lifted his head with brazen conceit. 'I'm just another darky to them. They don't know me from another.'

Marcus grinned at him. 'That must be useful.'

'It serves its purpose.' Faraq frowned. 'Your friend could be in dangerous peril though.'

Keanan looked down at Faraq with mistrust. 'Which friend?'

'I heard them speak this day. They are after the "black-eyed devil."' Faraq smirked. 'The Captain hates him.'

'I've no doubt he does,' Keanan said. 'We will pass that onto him, my thanks.'

Arjah said, 'He is a very determined man.'

'Who?' asked Marcus, 'Jett or the Captain?'

'The Captain does not like losing, I don't know about your friend.'

Marcus replied, 'The same could be said about Jett.'

Keanan pointed the horses into the street and they rode out. Marcus jumped on the back and gave a cheery wave as they left.

~ * ~

Jett spent the morning with Mara. A long couple of hours stuck in the room with a girl who didn't want to talk to him in a civil manner. He didn't think anyone could complain as much as Earona, but now she had met her match in the petite teenager. But, he had to admit in her favour, not being allowed outside or down to the tavern would be hard going. He wouldn't be able to stand it. He wouldn't even let her stand on the balcony much to her annoyance. She was just suggesting it to irritate him, he told her, because she didn't really want to go out there. His antagonism made her grumpier.

Keanan, Marcus, and Seth arrived back and Jett gave them stern instructions on guarding Mara, while she sat glaring at him. Hopefully they could entertain her better than he. As long as they didn't listen to her demands and let her out, he would be satisfied.

He arrived at the temple and glanced around the square before approaching the iron-gate, leading into the courtyard of the temple. He checked over his shoulder one more time. Over the last few days, his paranoia had augmented to unhealthy levels. He pushed the heavy door, swinging it open with a creak.

A quaint courtyard of flat steps and lawn had a long raised pond through the centre, and wooden benches, shaded by trees, were around the walls. Two women in blue gowns gave him short curious glances. Hellier came to him from the far end. Grinning like an adolescent, she took his hand and latched onto his arm.

Jett said, under his breath, 'What's wrong with you?'

Casting a peek at the women, she whispered, 'We're supposed to be lovers.' She led him by the hand to a bench at the far side, free of any eavesdroppers.

He sat facing her with a serious expression. 'Is she here?'

'Yes.'

'Is she well?'

'Well enough. Says she's tired. Probably from all the work she's doing.' She chuckled. 'And she's having bad dreams.'

'She's not the only one.' Jett thought of his own peculiar dreams, chiefly involving a mysterious dark hooded figure he was endlessly fighting.

'Any news about Shiarn?'

'She has been arrested.' He paused, letting the implication of his remark sink in. 'We wait for her to escape and then we get Earona out.'

'We will be leaving the city?' Her eyes dropped to the flat stones at their feet.

'As soon as possible, so you need to be prepared. Have you seen any way she could escape?' he asked, 'Keys perhaps?'

'Keys to the gates are kept by the Mother. She opens the front temple doors in the morning and closes them at night. One of the counsellors has a set and they are for the supply gate. A very organised and strict place. Apparently the person who abducted Mara picked the lock and now there are extra patrols going past at night.'

Jett sighed and a care-worn strain settled on his face. 'We will need Shiarn.'

'Did you discover where those men came from?'

No need to worry about them anymore.

Hellier gave him a vexed shake of her head and rolled her eyes.

Keep an eye on Earona as much as you can. He became restless, noting one of the women staring at him. 'It's possible they might come after her.'

'Could be some strange types here.' Hellier chuckled. 'She actually thought we stole Mara and left her here.'

Jett shook his head with a growing smirk. 'Tell her I did a trade, but then again, I don't know who I prefer.'

'She is grateful though.'

He shook his head and smiled. 'Always a first time.' He turned to her with concern. 'Are they suspicious of you?'

'I don't think so. I made up a story, I was a slave and I escaped, and you're earning coin to get us out of here, and...' A sheepish look came over her. *I said I was pregnant. As my disguise.*

It was Jett's turn to look vexed. 'That would explain the blatant stares I'm receiving.' He stood and looked down into her eyes, brimming with confidence. 'Hopefully all will go well and I will see you tomorrow with Shiarn. If not then at least without her.'

She walked him to the gate and reaching for the top of his cloak, she pulled him near and kissed him on the lips. A look of astonishment was on his face which changed to satisfaction.

Her cheeks tinged pink, she thought *got to make them believe.*

With a lazy half grin he left her staring after him with a glum expression.

~ * ~

Hellier walked past the inquisitive stares towards the yard at the back of the house, all the while brooding over the kiss. He reacted in the same blasé way he always did. It opened painful emotions and an old infatuation from her youth she thought she dealt with, or so she supposed. She sighed at the deception she was under. All this time her desire was dormant waiting for her senses to be vulnerable again.

Dario released the flood gates of her intimate desires, and a fire of longing emerged in her belly. She couldn't say what shape it would take, but she knew it would need sating somehow, whether by physical relief or a twisted form of denial. Kissing Jett was a definite mistake.

Staying at the refuge house provided an abundance of spare time to ponder her romantic experience with Dario. Beyond her walls, she wished to meet someone who could take away the undisclosed heartache she lived with. She decided when she saw Jett again, kissing would be completely off limits.

~ * ~

Outside, in the orphanage's courtyard, Earona hung the washing. After some time, she noticed the other girls had gone inside and she was left pegging out heavy sheets alone. It seemed even the distant noise of playing children disappeared.

'Can anyone help me?' An elderly lady, her back nearly doubled over, pushed past the washing.

'Oh, heavens!' Earona jumped back. 'You startled me.'

The woman's eyes widened with concern and she leaned on her walking stick. 'Sorry, dear. But please, can you come? A girl is injured in the barn. She needs help.'

Earona's heart leaped with worry. 'Shouldn't you tell a counsellor?'

'I have. She said to see you.' The woman beckoned her. 'But you must hurry.'

With some agitation, Earona chewed on her lip. 'I...'

'It'll be alright.' The woman nodded with a kind glint in her eyes. 'I'll explain to them.'

'I guess it's fine. I'm not really leaving the compound.' She followed the woman out of the orphanage at a quick pace.

As they walked, the woman said, 'A pity about your sister.'

'Yes.' Earona nodded. 'It is.'

'It could happen to any of us.' She gave Earona a sharp glance. 'Do you know who took her?'

'I don't.' Earona smiled at her in comfort. 'But don't feel afraid. I believe she'll be safe.'

At the furthermost corner of the compound they arrived at the barn that was strangely quiet.

The woman continued chatting, 'You sound so confident.'

Earona played with a strand of hair and glanced at the animal stalls. 'I'm... where is...'

'Come a little further.' Her pale eyes glowed with eagerness.

Earona followed her into the shadows past the crates of barrels.

'She's in a safe place, your sister?' She turned with a swift step to face her and her eyes caught Earona's in a penetrating stare.

'She is.' A comforting fog entered Earona's mind and she couldn't drag her eyes from the woman's strong gaze.

'She was fortunate to be saved. But I do miss the poor lamb.'

Earona gave a pleased nod.

'She's with your friends...'

'She...' Earona's heart raced, '... is.'

Her eyes lit with fondness. 'That's good to hear. I do hope to see her again.'

'I'm sure you will someday.' But how or why, Earona couldn't speculate on.

'Perhaps you could tell me where she is and I could visit the dear babe and wish her well.'

Earona tapped her chin in thought. Hellier didn't mention where the Kin were staying. 'She's at an inn, but I'm not sure where.'

'Hey!' A counsellor shouted from the barn entrance. 'What are you doing in here?' Counsellor Fidelia was a pudgy woman with a fierce countenance and not liked by the indentured girls.

Her cruel tone hurt Earona's ears and she snapped her head around to see her standing in the light outside. Attempting to form an answer, Earona stammered witlessly, 'I... came... someone was injured...' but who that was, she didn't know.

'How ridiculous.' Fidelia peered at her. 'You're in trouble again for slacking off and hiding in here.'

The criticism of her work ethic woke her mind up. 'But, I wasn't.' She turned to the elderly lady, but found herself alone. Spinning in a frantic circle, she saw no-one, not even a wisp of a moving shadow. Had she been alone all this time? Her heart pounded and she gulped with sudden fear.

'Get back to work!' the counsellor said, 'I'll be reporting this to Mother.'

'Did you see...?' Earona finished, breathlessly. Did she even see the woman herself? Had she imagined it? She left the barn, clutching her arms and shaking, and wondering what happened and what exactly did she tell the mysterious old woman?

~ * ~

The day passed in a strange blur and Earona hardly knew what to think on. Her thoughts were a tangled mess despite the woman fading from her memory. All she could recall was they spoke of her sister, who was not even her sister anyway. The incident, imagined or not, caused her to doubt herself and not want to speak to anyone.

Later that evening she lay awake in the dark dorm not even close to sleeping, but still feeling exhausted.

I spoke to Jett.

Earona hadn't noticed Hellier climb into Mara's bed.

We need Shiarn to get you out.

Earona let out a tired breath. 'Thought so.'

I should go back, but...

Picking up on Hellier's sad disposition, she said, 'What's wrong?'

I wanted to tell you. It's Shiarn, she...

Earona's own problems forgotten, she read Hellier's reluctant message. 'Raped?!'

'In the palace.'

Earona's wet blue eyes looked at Hellier with dismal defeat. 'Dreadful.' She sensed another sorrow. 'Something else happened?'

Hellier's thoughts came with reservation. *I've finally been with a man…*

Who? Jett?

Tears welled in Hellier's eyes.

'Oh… I'm sorry,' she soothed with a rush, 'but, who?'

'A man I met.' Hellier crudely wiped her check clean on the pillow.

'A stranger?! What in heaven's name is going on?! I need to get back to the Kin quickly.' Earona was indignant at Hellier's dejection, whose disposition was normally bright and carefree, this was unacceptable. 'How could Jett let you go and join with someone you just met, and leave you to feel this way?!'

Hellier gave a low laugh. 'He doesn't know of course.'

'Codswallop!'

'You can't tell him,' she demanded in a hushed tone, 'Promise?'

'I don't know.'

'It's too hard,' Hellier whispered. *He wouldn't care really.*

'I don't believe that.' Earona agreed with irritation, *fine, tell him when you are ready.*

'You'll be alright?' Hellier whispered. *Don't know if I should go…*

Earona was drifting off to sleep as she spoke. 'I can't really explain, but, please don't tell me where the Kin are or Mara…'

46 - Too Close

Forsake discretion for the sake of survival
Death gives no thought to circumstance

The Sleeping Sword

The Kin's room was littered with utensils, blankets, and general articles of camping paraphernalia. Keanan and Seth took on the task of sorting it. Out of boredom, Mara helped them, but she had no inclination to be organised about it. Keanan sat back perusing the items. 'I think that's all of it.'

Seth said, 'We can start putting some of it in the wagon.'

'I can help.' Mara's face brightened at the suggestion.

'No.' Jett fired out. 'You won't.'

Mara's face reddened and she stood suddenly. 'I can wear a hood. You're too paranoid!'

Jett stood over her. 'It's too risky. Sulk as much as you want, I don't care.' His point made clear, he looked over the piles. 'Did you get a dress for Shiarn?'

Keanan eyed the baggage and blushed with embarrassment. 'We did not.'

'I need a dress too.' Mara threw herself on the bed and grumbled, '... and a bath.'

'We will get you one too,' Seth smiled in reassurance, and said to Jett, 'Do you want one of us to come with you?'

'No.' Jett evaded eye contact with the pair. 'It's best I go alone.'

Keanan fixed a shrewd gaze on him. 'It's not prudent for you to go alone. There are men searching for you too.'

'So it's fine for you!' Mara griped.

Jett gave her a brooding stare, but said to Keanan, 'I know where I'm going and I'll move quickly.' He wrapped his cloak around his neck, shutting off any further questioning. 'I'll be back soon.' He banged the door behind him, leaving them staring with vexed expressions.

Seth cast a questioning look to Keanan. 'Will he be safe?'

'He thinks he will be,' Keanan said. 'He's worried about us.'

Seth gave him a puzzled look.

'If something happens to him his concern would be whoever is with him would be in trouble, possibly hurt and injured, if not worse.' Keanan went back to the stacking of blankets and bedrolls.

'But couldn't that person help him?' Mara said, 'That's silly.'

Keanan chuckled. 'That's Jett.'

~ * ~

Out on the main street, Jett withdrew into the shadows of his cloak and skipped over a dip of water. The crowds pressed on him, and in his current reclusive state he was not in a virtuous temper. On hindsight, he should have taken the back alley.

The Florisian's usual affability towards foreigners had slackened since the death of their king. An understandable occurrence considering his reign ended prematurely due to murder. The people were grief-stricken and angry at those from other lands; he heard it in the obtrusive language and the sullen conversations. Soon all of Coltrene would be in a similar state of lamentation. He couldn't blame them. If it was Judge Haldus he would be indignant. More than that, he would be livid and demanding justice. The Judge irritated him at times, but he was still their designated ruler.

Visiting Hellier made Jett apprehensive. The kiss confounded his belief in his neutral feelings. It took all his poise to hold himself together and walk out the gate. An understated change was in her personality that set him on edge. Something was amiss; she was softer, or more likely the problem was his. He was ruled by his inflexible habits and inability to change, or his unwillingness to. But, it was too impractical to begin a love affair in the middle of turmoil.

He switched from Hellier to Keanan's information from the Abulians. The Captain's schemes made him uneasy. He was disturbed by the amount of influence the arrogant bastard had in the city. After seeing the Collector as one of his clientele, there was no guessing who he was connected with.

Jett glanced at a couple of untidy brutes, leaning against a tavern railing. They gave him rigid stares as he walked by. He left the busy street and darted down a laneway that would bring him out to the square. Chancing a look behind, he prepared to see one or both men lurking there. No one followed and he continued at a steady pace.

Abrupt movement startled him and he stumbled backward from a mighty whack to his forehead. Dazed, he shook his head and his hand touched the open bloody wound. One of the thugs twisted Jett's arms behind his back; locking him hard, while the other punched his stomach. Winded, Jett hunched over the man's fist.

One of the lugs barked, 'Where's the girl?'

Jett grunted, 'Go wank yourself!' He could hardly breathe, but he wanted to vocalize his defiance at least.

'We're gonna find her with or without you.' The other man kept a tight rein on Jett's arms as he thrashed to free himself. The man's liqueur stained breath wafted to Jett's senses, but he kept his face down, hiding his eyes, intensifying in heat.

Jett constricted his stomach muscles in preparation of the second hit. Instead of the thump of a solid fist a sharp pain violated his flesh. Never had he experienced anything so physically adverse. Lifting his head with rage, his crimson eyes pierced his assailant's. The man fell flat on his back, writhing and clutching his eyes, before lying motionless. A thin wrist blade smeared with Jett's blood clattered to the stones from the dead man's slackened fist.

Dumbfounded at the sight of his inert partner, the man holding Jett loosened his grip. Jett dropped to his knees and swivelling his heated gaze, his eyes burned into the bewildered man backing down the alley. Fear was the guard as long as Jett was alive. But how long that would be, he was not certain. He should be grateful. If they were smart they could have tailed him, but they didn't have a brain between them. But then again, you don't need a brain to kill a man.

A feverish sensation travelled from his gut. He clasped his wounded stomach as if that would stem the blood pouring out, even so it seeped through his fingers. The pain was agonizing, more than he thought he could bear. He managed to stand, realizing he had to move or he would die where he fell. He spat up blood, tasting faintly of metal and sweat. The sight of it flowing from his body and leaking down his leg was a sure sign his life was ebbing away. He had to move with his Ethos' final bout of strength.

Dragging himself along the alley's wall, he paid no mind to the smear of blood and staggered out into the street. Swaying across the square, he pressed onto the gash in his flesh. It only seemed to cause the blood to pour out with more force. He knocked a lady sideways, making her gasp and scamper from his path. His steps were laboured and his legs induced him to topple over and be still. People walked by, appearing not to be hindered by the imminent death of another human. His breathing was difficult to maintain. Not being alert to avoid traffic, he prayed he did not trip, because he would not be able to rise again.

Dizzy and stumbling, he eventually arrived at his destination. The unfamiliar sights on the square were turning, making the gate a dark blur. He collapsed, knocking the door inward and he lay on the ground, unmindful to anyone, except... from a distant place he heard Hellier yelling.

He slipped into darkness.

In the void a square of light opened, and he fell into real nothingness.

~ * ~

Sighing with weariness, Earona sat back on her knees and examined her work. Due to her disobedience of neglecting her duties in the orphanage, she was back in the garden, getting dirty and aching knees.

Hellier stopped nearby and stared down at Earona, and said, 'Can you help me? But you must hurry.' The terror and lose of colour in her face was alarming. She spun away towards the door leading to the forbidden courtyard.

Earona had never seen her so distressed. Dropping her trowel, she walked after her without a thought. 'Why?'

I think... Hellier's thoughts came as she ran. *...he's dying.*

Who?

Counsellor Fidelia took a step towards Earona, sensing she was going to dash away again. 'Where do you think you're going?'

Hellier's words stormed back. 'My boyfriend.'

Boyfriend? Earona ran after her with all the speed she could muster. 'I won't be long,' she cried with weak conviction over her shoulder to the counsellor.

'Come back here!' Fidelia shouted, 'This is another report to Mother.'

Hellier and Earona dashed through the corridor, bypassing other workers and out to the free women's garden. Between them, the women heaved Jett's limp body into the courtyard and shut the gate.

Earona gasped and knelt by him, appalled by his blood and injuries. No life appeared in his deathly pale face.

Hellier touched his neck, 'I can't feel anything,' her voice rasped with fear.

Already connected with her life giving Ethos, Earona touched his wound. It was small, yet the internal damage was potentially fatal. She laid her hand on his stomach and another on his forehead, over an unsightly gash. She closed her eyes and concentrated on the mending of his body before Counsellor Fidelia could catch her and drag her back. Organs re-joined and arteries sealed. She had no time to deal with the lost blood. Floating from life, he drifted towards death. *You better not die, or I won't be pleased, and I won't forgive you.*

Some moments passed before thoughts entered her mind.

You're such a nagger...

Earona opened her eyes and smiled at Hellier. 'He'll be fine—'

'He has a knife wound,' a woman exclaimed at Earona's words.

Earona's voice wavered, 'It was superficial.'

Jett opened his eyes with languid contentment, his voice faint. 'Blue...'

Earona shook her head in admonishment and her voice trembled. 'What would you people do without me?'

His dark eyes, devoid of his usual sternness were vulnerable as he watched her. *I really don't know.*

Fidelia entered the courtyard and demanded Earona follow her to Mother for chastisement.

'I'm coming.' *What on earth are you doing to get hurt like this? I can't believe you nearly got killed! Don't let this happen again.* Earona could do nothing more for him in front of the women, but let her anxious and angry thoughts speak for her.

It's almost nice to hear you complain. I might have missed it.

She frowned at his nonchalance and said to Hellier, 'Stay with him awhile, I'm not sure if he can leave by himself.' *Well, I haven't. I even considered staying here.* She shifted his wavy black hair from his head wound to assure herself it was healing and finished with a quick pat on his cheek. She stood and crossed over to the counsellor watching suspiciously

Jett's thoughts settled in her head. *Maybe I'll rethink rescuing you.*

No you won't. You have to stay alive so you can get me out of here. Earona received a hard look from Fidelia as she walked past her. Black marks would certainly be against her name now. This would have no impingement on her peace of mind; her only concern was Jett and whether it was safe for him to be walking the streets.

Hellier supported Jett onto a bench. She dished out water from the fountain for him to drink and wash the blood from his hands and face. After satisfying himself with the refreshment, his back fell against the wall and he let his body recuperate.

They sat in a subdued silence for several minutes. Finally Jett breathed normally again and his voice recovered. 'That goddamn hurt like a ride to hell.' Breathing deep and steady, he rested, and sent his hurried thoughts to Hellier. *Will she get into trouble?*

'Probably.' Hellier said, testily, 'More important, what happened to you?'

He sensed her anger bubbling under the surface, and it annoyed him. 'I had a run in with some men.' *Part of the Captain's ensemble.*

Hellier cried, 'You left a blood trail?'

He paused pensively, grasping the significance of her remark. 'If they are smart enough to see it…'

'How are you going to get back safely?'

'I'll walk down the middle of the bloody street.' Jett's temper became heated at her reproof, but it was more than that, she was correct and it irked him no end. His irritation diminished on looking into her fearful eyes clouded with woe. He repented of his foolhardiness. *I have put you and Earona at risk by coming here.*

She tenderly touched his arm, also contrite. *No, I'm sorry. You had to come here. Nothing else you could do.*

We have to get out of here. 'I feel them getting closer.' He lent his head back on the wall and watched the women take short peeks in his direction. With surprise, they stared at the one who should not be sitting in their courtyard, alive and talking.

The sooner the better.

They sat together for a time, while Jett regained his colour and his body recovered. In the end he grew nervous and fidgety, voicing his concern he could no longer sit still and wait, he also had fears the temple would be watched. A vague advantage to the attack, the man might possibly believe him to be dead and so he should be.

After some time he stood, and opening the gate, he peered out at the busy square. He scouted the area for ominous looking cronies.

'You know I'd go with you if you let me.'

'That'll make it worse. I'll be as obvious as I can.' *My concern is I shall be followed to the inn.*

'Please take care.'

'Always.' He moved steadily out onto the pavement.

~ * ~

Earona was summoned into the Mother's rooms.

'I am most unhappy with your behaviour. You continue to be disobedient.' The old matriarch's face was stormy and her voice cold. 'This is the second time you have run from your duties. This time you dared to leave the house.'

Earona remained silent. No point trying to argue, Mother was right, she had broken the rules.

'You're getting a black mark. Do you wish to dispute this in any way?'

She sat with stony indifference, but a fire flared up inside. 'Yes, I do. If I obeyed the counsellor's orders that man would be dead.'

A devious glint entered the Mother's eyes and a small smile broke free. 'You did heal him? The counsellor present swore it was a serious wound.'

Earona's face flushed with the truth of it; she stuck her foot right in it.

'Stop lying, Earona.' Mother's demeanour softened and Earona noticed the change. 'You have a gift and it has not gone unnoticed. You have been with us a short time and already you have done much for us. Healing seems to follow you. You have been favoured by Niesta.' She observed Earona's perplexed expression. 'But you must honour our rules.'

'I will try,' Earona said nervously, wondering what the women of the temple really thought about her Gift and how much trouble she would be in back home because of it.

'And another thing,' Mother asked casually, 'how did that tall blonde woman know to come to you?'

Despite her smooth tone, Earona caught the query in her eyes; the question was an important one. 'Maybe she heard talk about me.' She shrugged, thinking quickly. 'Like others have noticed...'

'She must be very grateful you saved her betrothed.'

Earona nearly snorted with mirth at the lie, as it was, she restrained her chuckle. 'I'm sure she is.'

'Do you know her?' Mother threw in offhandedly. 'Your accents seem similar and I wondered if you came from the same place.'

'No,' she replied indignantly, hoping it wasn't too snappy. 'I'm not sure where she is from, but I know her now.'

'It's best you don't associate with free women, you might feel grievous they come and go as they like.'

'I can see that.'

'You are free to go, but please listen to Counsellor Fidelia.'

Earona shuffled down the hall, reluctant to return to her mundane work. Standing in her way, a woman leaned against the wall, eyeing her passage. Her brunette hair cascaded over her shoulders and the sleeves of her civilian dress were rolled up past her elbows. Far from friendly, the woman lowered her forehead and gave Earona a haughty gaze. Her voice had a lazy tone. 'Heard about your sister. Heard she escaped.'

'She was abducted!' The insinuation set her blood rushing.

'It's convenient, you have to admit.' She pushed her face closer and hissed, 'She's not here. Lucky bitch.'

Earona attempted passing her, but the woman barred her way with a hand on the wall.

She continued, 'You going to be joining her?'

'I...' Earona stared with sudden trepidation wondering how much the woman actually knew. '...don't know what you are talking about.'

'She's supposed to be your sister? Bet you know what happened to her.' The woman stepped into Earona's space, her dull blue eyes combing over her face. 'Maybe you even know where she is.'

Earona stared dumbfounded at the woman's confident assumption. She had to know more than she was revealing. 'I don't.'

'I don't believe you.' Her voice turned menacing. 'I think you know exactly where she is. You're going to tell me where or I'll dobb you in.'

Earona, mouth gaping, sputtered with indignation. 'Are you threatening me?'

'Just tellin' how it is.' The woman squeezed Earona's chin in a deathlike grip. 'You think about telling me and you'll sleep easier at night.'

'You can't be serious.' Earona froze under the abrupt pain.

'You're only getting one warning.' She let her go and walked away.

Earona was left rubbing her chin and sensing her vulnerable position.

~ * ~

This time Jett was extra cautious walking up the street. Hard to believe he had so easily let his guard down. No one appeared to be following, but this time he would stay on the wider street, relatively safe among the people. However, this meant he could not see any trackers.

He wrapped himself with his cloak, making sure his face was hidden. Blood covered the front of his clothes, making it impossible to suppress the extent of his injuries to the Kin. He pushed his finger through the hole of his new shirt with displeasure. His fingers rested on the smooth skin of his stomach and he recalled the acute pain he lived through, now gone but for the memory. Not an experience he wanted to have soon or again for that matter.

He neared Four Square and slowed his pace. With no burning rush to get back to the inn to be shut in with Mara again while Keanan and Seth went to the market, he sat under the trees, across from the tavern. The walk from the temple made him realize his body was still weak. The healing had not been complete. Leaning against the trunk, he watched passing traffic. His mood was reflective, probably due to his near death experience. He marvelled at how close he came to it and how fast it could take you. The sensation of dying would remain with him for all time.

He could see no one spying on the inn yet he felt compelled to stare until he saw someone watching, as if he willed some offender to be present so he could be rid of them permanently. He wondered if his desire to find trouble would increase the chances of it manifesting. Perhaps he was overly vigilant, but he didn't want to wake in the night to a sword tip nor did he wish to not wake at all. The Captain came close to ending his life that morning and he would be most unhappy to discover Jett had escaped his henchman.

Jett made slow progress around the side to the stables. Putting off the inevitable, he spent time with his horse. Eventually he went upstairs, only because the others had things to do and he would have to watch Mara. He groaned at the thought.

On sight of his bloodstained clothes, the Kin were mortified. His sheepish explanation he was stabbed did nothing to assuage their worry.

Keanan bristled with anxiety. 'It's getting far too close to the bone.'

'More like exposing the bone,' Marcus snapped.

Jett replied with irritation, 'I'm fine now. It could have been worse—'

'Worse! But you were nearly killed!' Seth cried. *Any worse you'd be dead.*

Mara stood, arms folded, staring up at him, her pretty face lifted in conceit. 'And you try to lecture me!'

'I'm alive and here,' Jett growled at her pompous attitude. 'If it had been you, you would not be so fortunate.'

Her eyes danced over him with gloating mirth.

'I've decided.' Keanan stood and faced him square on. 'You are not going there on your own, or anywhere for that mat—'

'I can get around on my own.' Jett stared him in the face. 'I won't have a flamin' nursemaid.' *Besides, it's better only one of us gets beat up.*

So you admit it's possible. Keanan said, 'It's too risky.'

'Keanan's right,' Marcus added. 'I'm coming with you, no excuses.'

'And we'll stay with Mara.' Seth nodded at Keanan.

Jett sighed. 'Great, Keanan and Seth watch Mara.'

'And there'll be no one getting beat up,' Marcus grumbled.

'It's settled then.' Keanan smiled, smugly.

'Fine.' Jett stared at them all. *Although I'm not happy about it.*

~ * ~

Earona no longer felt safe meeting with Hellier. Her movements were watched, and not only by the counsellors.

Hellier shared her thoughts in passing while waiting in the line for dinner, *Jett left in one piece, thanks to you. I'm meeting him again tomorrow.*

Good. Earona took a worried breath and clutched her bowl tighter. *But I really don't know how I will get out of here.*

You'll have to leave that up to him.

After all the candles were put out in the women's dorm, Earona lay staring up at the underside of the bunk. She cringed over the encounter with the woman, who she discovered was Gwyn. If Gwyn had any inkling she knew Hellier, she would be in trouble and Hellier would be watched as well. Earona was startled by Hellier nudging her arm. *They are suspicious.*

'I know.'

No talking. Hellier eased to the floor and darted vigilant glances at the women with views of the bed. The woman nearest had her back turned, fortunately, and was sleeping with a snore.

Earona leaned over and watched Hellier with a creased brow. *What are you doing?*

Soon, I'll be dozing, Hellier replied.

Earona continued with her confusion, 'You're sleeping under my bed?' She darted a glimpse at the woman across from her, moving in her sleep.

It's low enough to conceal me and I won't be here all night. I'll sleep light.

Earona's small giggle was loud in the settled dorm.

Besides, Jett wants me to watch you.

Earona threw her head back down on the pillow with weary annoyance. *I don't know how long I can continue like this.*

I'm with you on that. Hellier disappeared under the bed.

Earona once again lay looking at the top bunk and attempted sleep.

47 - Finally

Her verdant taste haunts my hungry lips
She flows with unattainable affection
An elevated well of vulnerable love
Which my soul endlessly thirsts…

Song of Evelonne Bloodflower

Shiarn woke from a restless sleep to the drafty grey-lit cell. Rain trickled through her window, covering the ledge and creating icy air. Gloomy during the day, the cell was a frightening prison at night. On top of her troubles, she hadn't seen Jonas since the night she was imprisoned, two days ago. Remiss, she never confessed her emerging affections for him, and her heart sank with misgivings for his welfare.

Past the cell window, flickering light danced against the opposite wall. Guards were accustomed to walking the corridor, but this shadow had no footsteps or voice accompanying it. A torch was placed in the bracket outside the door and a man chanted a simple sentence, followed with a more complicated phrase.

The notion of being violated again paralyzed her with fright. She could do nothing against him, but express the grave hatred she endured for the man.

After a jangle in the key hole, he let himself in, leaving the door ajar by inches. Morgal's eyes travelled up her body with abject infatuation, his depraved desires obvious.

Ready to unloose her wrath, she scowled. 'I can't believe you would come here.'

'No escaping this time,' he chortled with mean delight, 'and no hope of hiding.'

She crossed her arms and glared. 'What are you hoping to get from me?' She avoided his shrewd eyes that had seen too much of her.

'I'm glad you mentioned it.' He stepped closer. 'I've traced the Essenya and now I shall take the bottle you stole from me.'

She gritted her teeth, wondering how true that was. 'Really?' She strained a scornful smile, her voice dry with sarcasm. 'You're not getting anything.'

With a spring in his step, he cornered her against the wall. 'The question is what must I do to make you tell me where you put it?'

She was pinned and his sour breath assaulted her senses. To dash past him would only assure his hand touch her. 'You have done all you can to me and now I'm facing death.' In the negligible space she kneed his groin, doubling him up.

He seized her wrists and twisted her around. She fought against the torment of Morgal pressed against her back, bringing to bear the demoralizing memories of the first time he attacked her. He pushed her into the wall and she stretched her face away from the freezing stone. Water trickled down from the window, soaking the front of her already soiled dress. His face touched hers. His ugly washed-out skin repulsed her and his cold mouth rested on her cheek. 'You are a sweet bane in my life,' he whispered, 'I had no idea you would push so hard and resist so boldly. I only ever wanted simple things, things a woman like you can give. I gave you the opportunity to exist in luxurious comfort.' He smiled and she felt his teeth drag on her skin. 'I gather from your fighting spirit you wish for more, and I shall give it to you. Now, tell me.'

She cringed at his words and turned her gaze to the wall. His face a permanent scar on her memory. A creaking sound from behind startled her.

Morgal turned his head with an agonized cry. His body tensed and his hands relaxed from her wrists. He whispered a question she did not care to answer and she was free from his grasp. He collapsed by her feet.

Jonas appeared with a long bloody knife, jutting out from the folds of his floor-length heavy cloak. He took her hand and she stepped over Morgal with a relieved breath. 'I applaud your timing.'

'Punctuality is not a strong trait of mine.' He smiled. 'But, I did need him to be thoroughly distracted so he would not sense my approach. I was uncertain what he would be capable of,' he said. 'Have you been hurt?'

She rubbed her wrists and shivered. 'Not in the physical sense.' She stared down at Morgal's dead face, frozen in shock. 'Is he truly dead?'

Jonas pressed his fingers on Morgal's neck. 'I believe he is, though I have been wrong before.' He searched his pockets, taking a handful of oddments, including the cell key.

She stared at him oddly, but was too shaken to ask what he meant.

A pouch was on Morgal's belt and Jonas also took a gold amulet from his neck. 'We haven't much time.' He stood and placed his hands on her shoulders and gazed into her tear stained, weary face. 'It is cold out tonight. Kael will give you a cloak. Guards will come by soon. This is the only opportunity we have.'

Due to Morgal's death the barrier was broken and they walked from the cell unseen. Jonas locked the door behind them, leaving Morgal's body inside. Holding her hand, he escorted her through the corridors and upstairs. They glided through the prison, sweeping past guards like a night-time breeze. At last, a wide door led out to open air; cold yet refreshing and Shiarn breathed deep. Although soon enough, the cold would numb her limbs.

He led her near an alcove along the wall, circling the back of the military keep, and drew her shuddering body into his arms and wrapped his cloak around her. She could see nothing, but felt his finger resting on her lips. His endearing whisper brought a pleasurable sensation, foretelling of future romantic interludes. For a fleeting moment the current situation was absent from her mind. Then she realized he was saying goodbye.

'Kael is nearby. He will take you, as I have said.' With a press on her invisible lips, he stopped her speaking. 'I cannot go with you; there is unfinished business here at the palace. Leave the city as soon as you can. Do not be seen, this is imperative, or all will be in vain.' He paused before continuing with a heavy melancholy tone, 'You can say farewell to the intrigue of this palace, it has done you nothing but injury.'

She clung to his body not pleased he should leave her so soon. 'I don't know if I can say goodbye to you.' Finding his cheek with her hand, she ran it down to his open mouth, and he kissed it. 'I want to see you again.'

His body stiffened in her embrace and he kissed her gently. 'I have nearly forgotten, take this.' He put a folded letter in her hand and she pushed it down the front of her dress. 'It is from the prince, read it, but do not keep it, it's for the best.' He cuddled her cold body to his. 'I want to see you safe. Now I must leave; the chain of events has started. Stand here, Kael is in the shadows waiting, he will move, go to him quickly and conceal him.'

Shiarn whispered, 'Take care.'

His concealed body moved apart from hers. 'And you also.'

Feeling cold at his departure, she stared into the looming shadows of the building's wall and spied a shift of darkness by the alcove. She approached the hooded man. 'Kael?'

He thrust a heavy cloak into her invisible body and a kind voice ordered, 'Wear this.'

She wrapped the warmth around her. Holding on to his hand, they both disappeared from the world.

Kael said, 'Guards.' Two guards walked side by side not far from them, and continued on without turning. Once they passed, he said, 'I'll lead.'

They hurried past buildings, and rows of barracks. Kael's path was not straight, but seemed to dodge men and objects. Numerous soldiers were in the enclosure and the two snuck under their noses without hesitating. All the while he said nothing as they dodged and weaved, moving like the breeze.

Finally an official gate was in sight with guards on duty. Their chatter extended into the courtyard and carried into the quiet night. A fire in an iron drum warmed idle soldiers. Rain drops frizzled as they reached the highest flame and the steam obscured the street beyond the open gate.

At the sight of it, Kael stepped up his pace and Shiarn had to do likewise. With a swift glance over his shoulder, he started sprinting with a shout, 'Run!'

Gripping his hand harder, she balanced his weight with her tired body and ran.

In the distance behind them a trumpet reverberated, and again. The unusual sound broke the tranquillity of the night. Despite her tiredness she kept pace with him.

A guard was almost upon them from behind as he rushed to the gate. 'Lock down!' he shouted, 'Lock down the gate!' Orders and excited calls rang back and forth between the parapet and the gate's post, and the heavy iron-gate started its gradual descent.

Kael slid under it, half dragging Shiarn behind him as she bent her back, hoping she wouldn't be sprawled out on the hard stones. The two continued running until he turned into the shadow of a concealed alley. The gate announced its function with a menacing clang, resonating down the street.

Shiarn breathed heavy, sending steam out from her hot chest. From the shadows, she peered at figures on the walls organizing themselves. The pair took a moment to catch their breath from a run her body was unaccustomed to practicing.

With a tight rein on her hand, he whispered, 'We made it. Was close though.'

'Will he be safe?'

'Jonas?' The man alongside her chuckled and squeezed her hand. 'He'll be fine. You have to worry about yourself now. Although I must say, he's been in the thick of it for the last couple of days.'

She replied, 'He has said nothing…'

'I shouldn't say, but he was on the short list of suspects.'

She gasped. 'Not him. I was concerned Morgal would harm him and all along he was in danger of being arrested.'

He said nothing more on it and she left it, having the impression there was more to it.

They walked through the streets of Floris with only a bare light at an occasional building. For Shiarn it was a demanding walk, sudden inclines and short dips, and random rain.

'You are probably weary, and you'll need to rest well,' Kael instructed, 'You will leave soon, and they may have need of your Gift.'

'I'll be ready.' She cleared her throat and spoke with unease towards the stranger. 'So I'm really going to see them?'

'Your Kin? Yes, that's where we are going. Although they don't know it yet.'

Unable to see his face beneath his hood, she wondered if he were smiling at her awkwardness.

'So you really care about Jonas?'

'I…' Surprised at how much she did, and how concerned she was for him, she mumbled, 'I'm worried about him.'

'He's smart and thinks on his feet, you will see him again.'

After clearing the air regarding Jonas, Kael seemed more at ease to chat. Shiarn discovered he was the Avare of their Kin and Sommerlea and his Kin brought him the greatest happiness. No servants currently lived at Sommerlea; thereby offering some safety. Morias and Clara, were a couple of his Kin, but Shiarn was too exhausted to pay attention.

He halted in an alley, and threw his hood back. He whispered, 'Here we are,' with a spark of merriment in his voice.

~ * ~

Late into the night, Mara was already in bed, and the Kin spoke quietly in the warm room. Faint tapping broke through their low-key chatter. Jett moved to the door and the others watched with optimism. No-one was visible outside and he grinned with relief. After a moment Kael and Shiarn appeared inside and Jett closed the door behind them.

Untidy and soiled, her wild locks roamed free and unbrushed over her back, and her dress was ripped and stained. Despite that Jett had never been happier to see her in his life.

'I'll be off,' Kael said. 'Make every effort to leave in the morning. Good luck and I hope you arrive safely at Sommerlea.'

'Thank you for your help, Kael.' Jett closed the door after him.

Keanan took Shiarn in a warm embrace and she rested her head on his chest. Seth also hugged her, and Marcus followed. Even Jett gave her an affectionate clinch. Mara woke and gazed at Shiarn with sleepy wonder.

Shiarn gave her a bare look without any surprise and dropped onto the nearest bed. Seth sat beside her and she laid her head on his shoulder. 'Where is Hellier?' Her voice was weary. 'And Ethan and Earona?'

'Hellier and Earona are together, we will see them tomorrow.' Jett's demeanour was uncharacteristically gentle. 'We need your help getting Earona out.'

She nodded with closed lids. 'And Ethan?'

'That's more complicated,' Jett said, 'Not to worry about that right now, you need to rest. We hope he is well and safe.'

Arms high in an unabashed yawn, she said, 'Tell me, what have you been doing?'

They responded with humorous groans and exasperated mumbles. Marcus laughed at the Kin. 'Question is, what haven't we been doing?'

After Shiarn fell asleep, Jett lay watching her, pondering what he could say in recompense for her suffering. He sensed her discomfit and he had no words for the terrible trauma inflicted on her. Earona's feminine wisdom was lacking in this situation, and reflecting on Earona and Shiarn he drifted in and out of sleep.

Sometime after the room was still, Shiarn cried out. She sat up and glanced around the room in a daze.

Jett swung his legs over his bed and faced her. 'You will be safe now. You know...' *I'm sorry.* He took her hands, and her sad eyes searched for something in his. 'If there is anything I can say to make it better or go away, I would.'

'I know you would, but it's no one else's burden to bear.' *It's mine alone.*

As much as what I hate to hear that, I understand what you're talking about. 'But we can help you carry it.'

Shiarn looked at him with gratitude. 'I guess, but...'

Gaining a hint from her thoughts, he concluded, 'The pain is yours, the memories, the dreams.'

She sighed. 'Yes.'

'Now we must get some rest, tomorrow we have to escape this godforsaken city.' Jett stretched his body back underneath the warmth of his blankets.

Shiarn also lay down. 'I'm... so glad to be back, but...'

'But... let's get some sleep tonight and talk about things in the light of day...' He fell back into an uneasy sleep.

~ * ~

Jett flicked his eyes open and swirled his hands through warm water of a deep bath. Through the clear water black stone was visible at the bottom. He reclined on the carved underwater seat and surveyed the room with wonder. Rich dark wood furnishings were about the massive space, and the whole room opened up to a spectacular view of the night sky over the ocean.

In front of his bath, no walls blocked the panorama view, yet behind and to either side were black marble walls and thin columns. A sharp breeze blew from across the sea and onto his moist skin, bringing a tangible sense of another place. He appeared to be in a type of stone pavilion on a high cliff top. He dozed in the tranquil water, his body fading back into relaxed sleep once more.

A door opened at the back of the room. Hearing soft footfalls behind him, he opened his eyes with a dozy curiosity. A spicy scent preceded a striking woman in a sheer white dress parted to her thighs. She paused and gazed down at him. Spellbound, he stared at her mesmerizing beauty. Decorated about the middle with a gem encrusted belt, the dress had strings of multi-coloured gemstones dangling to her ankles. Around her neck was a similar necklace the width of her hand. A net of petite diamonds was over her long midnight hair. With intense green eyes etched with black kohl, and painted lips, she needed nothing to add to her allure.

She smiled languidly down at Jett as if they had always known each other. 'My love, you have finally arrived.' Her sultry voice intensified his transfixed state. She clicked long tanned fingers and two boys came from the shadows, carrying a tray with gold goblets and a crimson robe. 'Come, join me.'

He rose from the decadent bath using the steps at the end. The white clad boy offered up the robe to cover his nakedness, and the boy disappeared into the shadows from where he came. The beautiful woman took both goblets and passed one to Jett. He took it and spoke, his voice rough, as if he had to force his words out. 'Who are you?'

She took a step closer and placed a warm hand on his arm. 'I am Nya-Yun-Sioux-Sen. You shall call me Nya, or any other name that may bring you delight.'

'What is this place?' A sudden desire to caress her caramel skin overcame him, and instead, he studied her beauty with awe. Everything about her seemed too perfect to be true.

'There will be time for that. First let us enjoy some repose.' She stroked his arm, and barefoot, she glided across the marble floor to lie sensually on a golden chaise. Even her ankles were adorned with dazzling gems on gold chains held over her toes.

Rapt in her seductive authority, he trailed after. Her curves were a perfect form of loveliness under the transparent material. He sat on a similar lounge and watched her sip from her goblet. As yet unwilling to drink, he pulled his vision from her and looked into his cup. The rose coloured liquid smelt sweet, and not unlike her.

Her laugh was deep, embodying a rich melody. 'It's not poison.' She rested the goblet by her lips. 'Do not be frightened, Jett, drink with me.'

'How do you know my name?'

She leaned a hand on the lounge, and unperturbed, her bosom weighed heavy through the gauze. 'I know many things about you, knowing your name is really the least of them.'

The comment did not set him at ease. He stared into her sea-coloured eyes that changed to a bright grey. In the instance, her face reflected a sterner demeanour, almost as if a sudden change came over her temperament. He tried in vain to focus on the fleeting trenchant look, but it faded too fast for him to discern its unspoken thoughts.

Once more mesmerized by her majestic beauty, he drank from the cup without question. Sweet and cool, he enjoyed another sip.

She smiled with satisfaction. 'See, that was not so hard and you are still here.'

He gave her a half smile lacking conviction. 'Where is here?'

Nya rose, and her skirt slid up her thigh as she settled by him on the lounge. No longer holding a goblet, she placed her hand under his robe, pushing it aside and off his shoulders. It fell to the floor and he stood naked before her. She ran her fingers over the tattoo markings on his side before caressing his cheek, tilting his face to meet hers. Her passionate eyes revealed her desire for him. 'Does it really matter where we are?' She eased her glossed lips onto his. Her kiss was sensitive and no less potent.

He fought the desire to respond. An eternity seemed to spin, while he was frozen, trying to grasp reason – his thoughts of cold withdrawal seemed absurd – why should he not partake? All restraint seemed nonsensical and fleeting. Like drinking from the cup, he yielded to her lips, and relaxed at the touch of her searching fingers running down his chest. She reached into his depths and brought out feelings he never thought he would experience. Lovemaking was never so fulfilling nor had he ever felt such a connection where he could see no defining end between himself and the woman. He fell into her exquisite body and didn't want it to ever end.

They lay together, their bodies aglow with expired lust. She smiled with sated passion while he looked at her with underlying confusion. She held his face with her delicate fingers. 'It is time for you to leave, but we will meet again.' She kissed him firmly on the lips.

Jett woke with a start.

It took him a moment to recall where he was and many more before his racing heart was calm. He closed his eyes and tried to replay the scene with the beautiful woman from his dream; then he attempted to sleep without her.

48 - Leaving

Be as shrewd as a serpent. Be as meek as its prey.

Prophetess Janna Meadow'Fox, 4th Seat Elder

Morning light streamed through the doors leading out to the balcony in the Kin's room. The sound of objects being shifted, and subdued chatter, pulled Shiarn from sleep. Opening her eyes, she stretched and smiled at her humble surroundings. The night was over and she looked forward to leaving the city. Seth, already dressed in a vivid blue shirt, sang a cheery good morning. Keanan did likewise and continued packing. Mara was across the room, her back to her as she stared out the balcony door.

Shiarn peered at Seth with sleepy eyes. 'Any chance of a bath?'

Seth grinned broadly and sprang up from the bed where he sat. 'I think I can arrange that.'

'Can I come?' Mara turned suddenly at the request.

Seth gave Keanan a questioning gaze and shrugged. 'She probably needs too.'

Keanan studied the young girl. 'Indeed. But I'm not sure Jett would agree.'

Mara made an ugly face. 'What's that supposed to mean?'

'Holy Kahm!' Shiarn cried. 'You men worry too much.'

The boys purchased Mara a navy blue frock and Shiarn a jade linen dress, which she was eager to change into and be done with her soiled clothes. Seth walked to the wash room and Shiarn tagged behind unseen holding Mara's hand. With the rest of the Kin completing the packing of the wagon and eating breakfast, she felt free to squander her time refreshing herself.

Water was hauled in from outside to boil early in the morning. Shiarn sunk into the hot water with a pleased sigh. With only one tub there was not enough time for them both to bathe. Mara was content with a basin of hot water and some lotion for her hair.

Seth turned his back to grant them privacy and he chatted about the Kin's adventures in Floris. Shiarn listened while lathering her body with the soapy suds, not ceasing until the filth had vanished, even her hair had to be rinsed.

'Sorry, you're missing this, Mara.' Shiarn crooned. 'But I've decided to be quite selfish.'

Mara dunked her hair into the water and said half upside-down. 'I'm just glad to get out for a while. I'm their prisoner don't you know.'

Shiarn snorted with laughter. 'I don't know what Jett's telling you, but I'm sure they're leading you on...'

Mara grumbled her annoyance.

'No, it's true,' Seth said, 'He has threatened to tie her up.'

'He must have his reasons.' Shiarn lay back in the tub regardless of the cooling temperature. 'Seth, pass me that letter I brought down.'

Shielding his eyes, he turned with the sealed letter that had no formal insignia.

She procrastinated its opening, afraid of what Bastion wished to tell her. After a moment of silent debating, her inquisitive mind got the better of her. The script was perfect and as far as she could determine it was Bastion's own handwriting.

My dearest friend,

You must know it is a privilege to have made your acquaintance, and your kindness toward me is deeply appreciated. The troubles you endured, I suffer as a personal injury to myself, and the full responsibility of which is placed in my own hands. I truly hope the violation does not rest on your heart forever.

Our time together was short, nonetheless, we developed a friendship, and if the attraction for other pursuits had not been my undoing there would, I have come to acknowledge, been romance between us. Irrelevant to my feelings, it is uncertain whether our paths shall cross again, which brings me great sadness. You will not find a better companion in our mutual friend, who has offered me the utmost in aid and advice.

All shall be well due to your sacrifice. We now only desire you arrive safely at your destination. I wish you the greatest of speed and luck.

Your loving friend, B.

She stared at his eccentric initial and reread the letter. In one instance she thought she knew his character then it would fall away in the next moment. Yet, with his odd riddles of intrigue she developed a fondness for him. His words of sacrifice unsettled her, but she had no desire to delve into their meaning. At the heart of it she knew what he meant.

Heeding Jonas' instruction, she asked Seth to place it in the glowing embers beneath the grill. It caught light and she watched it fade into ash. With that she finally felt her time at the palace had ended.

~ * ~

In a booth at the back of the tavern, Jett and Marcus discussed the plan for the day. Keanan arrived after taking an overly large bowl upstairs. Jett said, 'The whole plan is depending on the smallest details.'

Marcus said, with self-confidence, 'It shouldn't be that difficult.'

Jett frowned with the knowledge nothing they did was ever simple. *No, it shouldn't be.*

Burgman approached them with a long face and downcast eyes. He placed a gnarled hand on their table. 'You really off then?'

Jett smiled up at him good naturedly. 'We are.'

'I forgot to mention, with you leaving and all.' Burgman's face reddened. 'Dario came to see you.'

Jett tensed with the sudden realization of how much Dario knew about them. 'When? And what did he want?'

'Yesterday, but you were out. He wanted to see you.' Burgman fixed a questioning stare on Jett. 'It was odd to see him, all dressed up fancy, hardly recognised him.'

Keanan fixed a studious gaze on Jett. *That doesn't sound promising.*

'He came for me?' Jett's chest constricted and his voice was strained. 'Not Hellier?'

'He asked for you then Hellier.'

Thankfully Burgman didn't know Hellier's whereabouts, though he was smart enough to deduce where she might be. Jett asked, 'Is he coming back?'

'He didn't say exactly,' Burgman said. 'He said he hoped to see you soon.'

'Very mysterious,' said Keanan.

I don't like it at all. Jett had a tight smile.

Burgman returned a jovial grin, looking relieved. 'Well, you have a nice journey. Where you off to?' He stacked their empty bowls with the flex of a hand.

'Through the west province and up to Ryne.' Jett was unruffled with the lie.

'North, eh? Have a safe ride. It's certainly been a season of storms with you here.'

'I agree on the bad weather,' agreed Marcus.

Keanan added, 'A most memorable experience.'

'We appreciate all you have done and we shall recommend your establishment to any we meet,' said Jett.

'Anytime you're in Floris you stop off here. If you happen to be in Aquila, go visit Bates, at the Talisman. We go way back, he'll know me.'

'I'll keep that in mind.' Jett caught a glimpse of sadness in his aged eyes, but he turned on his heel to the bar. Jett observed the tavern and the regular patrons before stating, 'Time to go.'

The covered wagon trundled through Four Square with Keanan guiding the horses. Inside, Mara and Shiarn kept quiet and hidden. Despite the covering flap, Shiarn remained invisible; the risk of her being seen, even accidentally, was too great for her to appear. Keanan gave her a sip of quartza, which caused a drug-induced euphoria to course through her body that would provide the energy to cover herself and Mara for a longer period of time.

Eventually the wagon stopped. Outside, amid clangs and ringing metal, a voice blared over the noise of the street.

What is going on? Shiarn thought to Keanan.

Keanan poked his head through the curtain of the wagon. 'We are at the temple and a patrol of soldiers are outside.'

Under her breath, Shiarn said, 'Looking for me I expect.'

Mara shook her head. 'No, they might be looking for Earona.'

'We're taking too long then,' Shiarn huffed.

The flap at the back of the wagon was lowered, hitting the side with a creaky bang. From her position at the edge, she saw the troop standing to attention on a large plaza.

Jett stood at the open flap. 'You must hide Mara and take her inside.'

'That makes it more difficult.' Shiarn took her hand.

Mara gasped at the sudden sensation of nausea. 'You mean make me invisible again?'

'I don't like it, but it can't be helped.' Jett stepped aside to let them through. 'No arguing about this, Mara, there's too many soldiers.' He looked at the empty air. 'Do not let go of Shiarn or you'll regret it. In more ways than one.'

'I'm not stupid,' Mara snapped as she passed him.

Shiarn looked into Jett's worried face. 'She won't, but, Mara, no talking or any noise.' Grasping Mara's hand, Shiarn followed Jett to an iron door. He held it open while they walked into a courtyard. Hellier approached Jett with a coy smile and Shiarn wondered if she were witnessing a special moment between them.

Jett's features were taut and he stated, 'It's time to go.'

'Now?'

'Soon as you can.' *Shiarn and Mara are here,* his thoughts reached them both.

I'll take them. Hellier said, 'Wait outside.' Her long stride took her quickly to the corridor leading into the refuge's gardens. *Come.*

They walked the passage and Hellier opened a door to another narrow corridor. Eventually they came to an open hall and Shiarn glimpsed the yard outside. So far only a few women were in their path, but with the soldiers waiting in the square it might only be a matter of time before they came in.

Earona scraped at the dirt in the garden. Other girls worked not far off, but none of them were as slow as she. Sitting back on her heels, she flicked her messy plait over her shoulder and wiped the sweat from her brow. She took a moment to observe the dark clouds threatening rain.

Your nails are filthy.

'Eh?' Earona looked around for the familiar voice.

It's me, Shiarn.

'Miss me.' Mara's voice was right by Earona's ear.

Earona jumped with a start. 'Oh, you're...' *both here.*

Shiarn thought, *there's no need to talk.*

Earona dropped her spade and noticed Hellier waiting on the terrace.

Also watching, Counsellor Fidelia shouted, 'Earona, get back to work.'

'Just having a stretch.' Earona lifted her hands above her head.

The counsellor glared with suspicion.

We need to go somewhere concealed. Shiarn thought.

I'll go to the outhouse. Earona nodded over her shoulder. 'Counsellor, I'm in need of the backhouse.' She bent her middle and wiggled on the spot. 'I...'

Fidelia's look could have curdled milk. 'Make it quick, you don't want any more trouble.'

Earona thought it was impossible to get into any more trouble than what she was currently in. Certainly escape was the maximum form of transgression she could perform and that was precisely what she was preceding to do. She dashed to the backhouse, realizing she had left her bag near the baskets outside. Inside the shed, she waited for Shiarn.

'You trying to get out of work again?' Gwyn leaned on the doorframe, blocking the entrance. 'Or maybe you're waiting for your contact?'

Earona hedged away from her and the exit. 'Not at all.'

'I've got my eye on you.' She rushed her and caught hold of her throat. 'You won't be getting away.'

Earona gagged at the pressure and attempted pulling her hand off.

We haven't time for this. Shiarn thought. *And I can't do a thing.*

'It's not... my fault...' Earona groaned with pain.

'What the hell are you doing?' Hellier yanked the woman's shoulder, dragging her off Earona.

Gwyn stepped away, her chest heaving with volatile energy. 'I knew it!' She glared between Earona and Hellier with insight dawning on her pale, freckled face. 'You and her, you're in it together!'

'In what together?' Hellier folded her arms and leaned back.

Gwyn's shapely brows lowered with contempt. 'You know what I mean. You're planning on escaping.'

Hellier took a step. 'What do you care?' Standing nearly two-heads taller, and in pants and a man's shirt under a leather vest, she was an intimidating sight.

Gwyn stood her ground. 'Because your friends are the ones who took the girl.'

Enough of the chat. Shiarn yelled in Hellier and Earonas' minds. *They might come at any moment.*

'Took the girl, eh?' Hellier replied, 'You don't know what you're talking about.'

'I know and I'm going to find her.'

Hellier's fist came up and punched Gwyn in the face.

Gwyn twisted sideways, clutching her reddened cheek. 'You damn bitch!' She swung at Hellier and skimmed her chin. Hellier grabbed her arm and Gwyn landed a hit in her ribs. The scuffle continued with Hellier coping one on her lip and in turn giving Gwyn a black bruise on the side of her head.

'What is going on here?' Counsellor Fidelia appeared at the doorway and took hold of Gwyn's arm while pushing Hellier away. Another counsellor was with her and she watched the skirmish with delight.

Gwyn pointed at Hellier. 'They know each other.' She turned with surprise at the space where Earona was standing. 'Where did she go?'

Counsellor Fidelia scanned the shadows. 'Earona! Show yourself. Mother wants to see you. Now!' No answer came from behind the partition. She said to the other blue-robed woman, 'Go and get her, I'll have to deal with these two.'

With her eyes fixed on Gwyn, Hellier wiped her chin. 'She's lost her mind.'

Gwyn pierced her gaze, her eyes creasing with menacing wrath. 'You're a demon liar.' She struggled against the counsellor's hold, but was restrained with a vice grip.

Hellier kept control of her own raging emotions that wanted to pummel the woman, realizing the precarious situation she was suddenly in.

The younger counsellor came back and shook her head. 'She's not in here anywhere.'

'I saw her come in. I watched the opening.' Fidelia pressed her lips together. 'Stay here. I'm taking these girls to Mother.'

'But,' Hellier cried, 'She's the crazy one. I don't know what she's talking about.'

'You're a bloody foreign bitch.' Gwyn hissed as she was lead outside.

Fidelia shook her head at the two of them. 'I don't know either. But fighting must be reported and is a punishable act.'

Hellier groaned and followed the counsellor up to the house to see Mother.

~ * ~

Shiarn took Earona's hand while Hellier distracted Gwyn. Earona's head stopped spinning and she regained her balance. She pulled on Shiarn until she came to the baskets of rhubarb and her bag.

Not that bag again, Shiarn thought.

I can't bear leaving it. Earona looped it over her neck.

Shiarn led Earona and Mara towards the women's house. Inside, the hall abounded with white and blue-robed women, flitting around in confusion. Mother paced back and forth, like a malcontent queen calling out commands and citing directives. Earona observed her and other potential hazards. It gave the room an added danger, not only could they crash into furniture but women as well, which was worse.

Keep to the edge. Shiarn whispered the same in Mara's ear.

The sight of armed men amongst the women caused Earona to pull up with a startled breath. A man walking down the stairs halted their movement. Captain Morran presented such an unwanted sight Earona's mouth was agape in a similar fashion to the other women watching his descent.

Mother stopped her pacing and with obvious annoyance at his intrusion, snapped, 'She won't be up there. I've sent someone to fetch her.'

He stood over Mother's lithe form and growled, 'And the other one has escaped?'

Her voice was low and wrathful, 'Escaped or abducted we can't say for certain.'

The captain snorted. 'She escaped. Who would abduct her?' He stared at the women fussing in the hall as if he might spy the girls concealed behind them.

Counsellor Fidelia burst in, hauling Gwyn with her and Hellier stamped in behind with her head down. Fidelia said to Mother, 'I can't find her out there. Counsellor Orela is still looking.'

'She's gone?!' Mother's voice turned cold.

Captain Morran looked over the counsellors and gave Mother a scathing glance. 'It's no wonder. She's an assassin.'

Mother responded, sharply, 'I find that extremely hard to believe.'

'She's fooled you and everyone here. She better be found or it could be the end of this place.'

What is he talking about? Earona listened with puzzlement. *Surely it's not this Raven again.*

Mara stifled a giggle.

Don't tell me he thinks you're an assassin? Shiarn thought with humour. *What a laugh!*

I had nothing to do with that. Earona thought with annoyance.

Mother turned on the captain. 'Are you threatening me?'

'I came to re-arrest those women, and by holy Nesvar, suddenly they are missing.' The captain's astute eyes slanted at the Mother and his voice was contemptuous. 'Can we assume that's a coincidence?'

His heartless declaration caused Mother to respond with outraged passion. She ignored the gathering audience and shouted, 'What are you implying? That I have sequestered them away somewhere?!'

The counsellor shook Gwyn and pushed her forward. 'This girl said she saw her in the outhouse. She's saying something about the girl who went missing.'

Morran's angry glare was directed at Gwyn. 'Is that so?'

Gwyn pushed Fidelia away and stood tall to meet his stare. 'That's right.' She cocked her head towards Hellier. 'She knows her. She'll know where she's going.'

'Bulldung!' Hellier growled. 'She's a blabbering bitch.'

Mother gave a weary sigh and looked at Fidelia. 'What happened?'

'They were brawling. Apparently about the girl who escaped.'

'I'll question them,' the captain said. 'Meanwhile my men can make a thorough search of the compound.'

'In that case, my counsellors can assist them,' Mother replied. 'Take these girls to separate rooms. We'll get to the bottom of this.'

Hellier gasped with abrupt panic. 'No...'

Oh, God, Hellier. Earona was yanked forward while trying to see what was happening in the hall. *What are we to do?*

Nothing we can do right now. Shiarn lead them along the corridor towards the courtyard. *I've got to get you out.* She came to an abrupt stop and the girls bumped into each other. Soldiers congregated near the entry into the courtyard, making it too dangerous for them to pass. Shiarn hissed, 'Curse it!'

'We can go through the temple.' Earona swung back down the passage and headed towards the inner door.

Numerous worshippers made walking problematic. Even so it was safer than a group of idle soldiers. Impossible to avoid contact with them, as one woman, then another, jumped in shock.

A full throated cackling rose up from a corner of the temple, gripping the room with alarm. An old crone with dull yellow hair and worn wrinkled skin, slouched on a stone bench. Earona gasped with recognition.

'Is that...' mumbled Mara, 'that woman?'

'The same, I'm sure,' Earona replied.

'Who is she?' Shiarn asked.

The woman stood and her stoop was an unfamiliar sight. A walking stick supported her; its carving was an irregular pattern of twisted hard knobs. Her eyes flashed with wicked intent and she pointed a bony finger at the unseen ones.

She can see us. Shiarn thought.

The woman narrowed her eyes at Mara. 'I shall take you to your rightful destiny.' She began chanting in a drawn out tone, 'Nazal-getar-baksarwaz-yahhamut.'

A heavy suppression seemed to fall, muffling the speech of all the women. They became immobile, like statues of flesh.

She's a cursed witch. Shiarn thought to Earona, *That's all we need right now. But, I think she can only see Mara.*

Earona said, 'I can't move.'

'Neither can I.' Shiarn groaned.

'That's odd,' Mara said, 'I can.'

Shiarn took a sharp breath. 'That's not much help. You can't let go of my hand.'

'Maybe...' Mara replied, 'but...'

~ * ~

Hellier was left alone in a room adjoining the Mother's quarters. She surmised it might have been a place for the sick with two beds and shelves of jars and bottles. Not interested in sitting down, she paced the floor, her anxiety building at every moment of her captivity. She pulled on the door handle. Locked. 'Flamin' bastards!'

The window was ajar, but not large enough for her to fit. She was stuck while her Kin waited for her outside. 'Ridiculous.' She pounded her fist on the door out of frustration. 'Stay calm,' she muttered, 'think.' She had to come up with a good story because she could only guess what the other woman was saying.

After what seemed a great deal of time, the rigid faced uniformed man entered the room, followed by one of his men. Hellier stood to meet him. Instead of being calm like she planned, she was tense with rage.

'It seems the one I came for has gone. If you have something to do with that, you better tell me the truth now, or you will face imprisonment if I find out you know her. I would have preferred taking you back to the barracks for questioning, but as it is, the head counsellor won't allow it.' He studied her body and his eyes fixed on her face. 'Sit down.'

Hellier folded her arms and looked surly. Despite not wanting to, she did what he asked. 'That girl has nothing to do with me.'

'I've been given some details about you, and some interesting accusations have been made. I would like to get to the truth. Why are you in this house?'

'I...' she paused, 'needed protection.'

'From who?' He lifted his brows in curiosity.

'Ah...' she avoided his probing gaze. 'The traders. I escaped and came here.'

Devoid of any surprise, the man's clear eyes remained on her face. 'I see. And who is this boyfriend of yours?'

'He...' Blushing, she glanced away. 'Was going to come and take me away.' Suddenly she could no longer control her agitation. 'Look, I haven't done anything! Why am I here?'

He ignored her outburst and continued, 'Who were the people you escaped from?'

She creased her brow. 'He had a glass eye and was big across the shoulders. Crinkly red hair. I don't recall a name.' She wasn't sure it wise involving some miscreant pirate, but at least it gave credence to her story.

He nodded with a blank expression. 'Why are you in Floris?'

'We were passing through, that's all.' She sat on the edge of the chair, gripping the seat.

'That's all? Mmm. And you know the missing girl? Earona.'

'I...' she hesitated. 'I met her here.'

'How about the other girl?'

'The one who hit me?' Hellier queried. 'Only met her today.'

'Why did you fight with her?'

Hellier reddened with guilt over her daft actions. 'She punched me first.'

'I find that hard to believe. Besides, it's not what she says.' He leaned back folding his arms with a smug grin. 'Perhaps your mannerism befits your attire.'

'What is that supposed to mean?' She cried. 'Besides, I don't care what she says. It's all lies anyway.'

'If what she says is true it's cause for locking you up.' His expression became sombre.

Hellier's lip lifted in derision. 'What is she saying?! She's a half-cocked loon!'

Morran stepped closer and stared down at her. 'Apparently you have friends who assisted the young girl's escape and have sequestered her somewhere in the city, and you helped Earona escape. You know where they are.'

Hellier gasped with indignation and sudden fear at the truth of it. 'How the hell can that be possible?' She jumped up, knocking the chair back. 'She's a flamin' kookoo!' she pointed at his chest and cried, 'You should be asking why she even thinks all this. I've got some accusations of my own. She's the one who took that girl.'

He pointed to the chair and shouted, 'Sit down!'

The soldier standing near the door snickered.

She grumbled with rage and righted the chair and sat with a heavy thump. She sat stiff, brooding.

'I'll find out for myself. Give me your boyfriend's name and where he is staying.'

'He's staying...' she searched her memory for that inn he mentioned. 'A place called, the Sleepy Dog, or maybe that was Sleeping.' *Curses, Jett is going to kill me.* 'His name is Jett.'

'What does he look like?'

'Black hair, tallish,' she pouted and crossed her arms, 'dark eyes, wearing black.'

A smirk twitched on the captain's mouth. 'Of course. We'll check his room and find him. You can stay here until we confirm your story.' He turned to go.

She stood abruptly, her arms flung wide and she shouted, 'Stay?! Locked up like this?!'

'Until we find out the truth you won't be going anywhere.'

'Flamin' arse!' Hellier yelled. 'That woman is lying. She's the one behind it all and she's blaming me!'

Captain Morran opened the door and his soldier followed him out. Hellier fumed at the door and vented her rage by kicking it and giving a cantankerous bellow.

~ * ~

In the temple, the women, civilian and indentured, could do nothing to stop the old crone chanting. The witch directed her staff at what must have seemed empty air, but Mara knew it was aimed at her.

Amid a burst of anger, Mara yelled, 'Stop!'

'You don't have the power.' The witch's voice resounded with brazen self-assurance as she shuffled back.

'You don't know.' Unlike Earona and Shiarn, Mara could move, but she couldn't reach the witch without losing Shiarn's hand.

'Azrak-watelnak-sarwaz.' The witch's voiced droned and her free hand flew in a circular motion.

Mara let go of Shiarn's hand. Now visible, she came at the witch and grabbed hold of her wrist, holding her down. 'I won't let you, old hag.'

The witch chanted another string of foreign words.

'Hellborn bitch!' Mara wrenched the witch's arm, toppling her sideways, and glanced with awe at her wrist band; the source of the augmented strength.

The woman's voice changed from cackling smugness to one seeped in venom. 'I'm taking you now.'

The statement only gave her increased determination to get away. Wrathful, her eyes turned to molten fire, and snatching the staff, Mara tossed it across the temple. She twisted the witch's arm and flung her away. The witch slid along the ground, hitting her head on the edge of a pool.

'We can move. Come on.' Shiarn took hold of Mara's hand.

Invisible again, Mara clutched her stomach as the baby tossed within, making her want to throw up.

'That was risky,' Shiarn whispered with a sigh, 'but it worked.'

Her heart raced, realizing what she did. 'Someone had to do something.'

'Hurry,' Earona said, 'I think she's getting up.'

The old woman sat on the floor with blood on the back of her head.

Shiarn hurried them along to the door.

Earona flung it wide with a loud crack. 'Oh, dear.'

'Can you get any louder?' Shiarn fumed.

Near the bottom of the steps, lines of military men looked up at the open door with puzzled expressions. Shiarn yanked the girls down the stairs and towards the wagon.

~ * ~

At the back of the wagon, Jett waited with Keanan.

'We can't stay here.' Keanan gave the soldiers on the square a concerned glance.

More soldiers trooped into the temple courtyard, and Jett was certain prying eyes observed their travel through the streets. Doubtless, Tonius Shark knew he had connections with the temple and they were probably, at that moment, spying out his passage. He had no desire to be near any alleyways. 'If we move too far it will create too many obstacles.'

We are here. Earona stepped onto the crate, left on the ground near the wagon opening.

Keanan thought back to the girls. *Thought you would be in need of this.*

Only you would be this thoughtful, Keanan, Shiarn thought joyously.

Jett creased his brow and glanced up the temple steps. 'Where's Hellier?'

Earona said, 'She got into a fist-fight.'

'She's being held for questioning,' Shiarn whispered near him. 'About Mara, I think.'

Mara was last and said on her way, 'Someone's looking for me, and they think she knows where I am.'

And she does. Tensing with anxiety, Jett rubbed his temple and grumbled, 'Flamin' unbelievable.'

The sight of a pair of soldiers strolling towards him did nothing to rid him of his sour expression. He walked to meet the armed men with forced pleasantness.

'Good day, sir.' The soldier nodded and started with self-assured authority, 'Why are you loitering outside the temple?' Clad in a red tunic and jerkin with metal straps, he was not unlike the men in his patrol, except he wore a silver helm.

'I'm waiting for a friend,' replied Jett, bluntly.

The soldier and his comrade stole a sombre gaze at the temple and fixed an unnerving eye on Jett. 'Your friend is in there?'

'She is on her way out. What is all the commotion about?'

The soldier studied him and Keanan. 'A prisoner has escaped and we are searching the area.' Staring over Jett's shoulder, he pushed past him and walked up to the wagon.

Jett trailed after with ill-disguised aggravation.

The soldier yanked the flap wide and peered at the empty space.

Amid growing exasperation, Jett watched him go through the compartments nearest the door as if it was his personal property. 'I don't know what you think you'll find in there.'

After glancing around, the soldier turned to Jett. 'You'll have to move your wagon and wait somewhere else,' he ordered, 'there's too much congestion here.'

Jett's manner was charged with mock responsibility. 'Yes sir, consider it done.'

The man paused with a warning glare. Jett considered it in his best interest not to push him further. The captain and his soldier marched back to his men.

'We'll start off,' Keanan said, 'and hope Hellier catches up.'

Jett gave an annoyed sigh. 'Guess we have to.'

~ * ~

For some time, Hellier contemplated setting the house on fire and walking out. She could do it, it would be easy. But the guilt of killing so many people would be too much to stand. What was the better option, massacre on a grand scale or Jett's wrath? She pounded the locked door and let her head fall on the wood. She groaned with painful anguish at visions of the soldiers finding Jett and wanting to know about him and his business. Would he even give the same story as her? She let loose a dismal gust of air.

Tired of pacing, she flopped back onto the chair. With her legs splayed forward, she tossed her head back and stared at the ceiling with a dismal groan. She had never been the patient sort and this was pushing her to the limit. Every type of dreadful image assailed her, and everything seemed to end in flames.

After what seemed another hour to her, the pompous officer entered with his bored looking man in tow.

Hellier rolled her head to view him and thought she really should be acting more submissive. His condemning glare made her sit up straight. She couldn't contain her nervousness and leaned forward. 'Well?'

'There's been an interesting change of circumstances—' he started.

'Yes?' She thought her heart might stop at the suspense. 'Did you find him?'

'Apparently Gwyn is not who she claims to be. It seems she is also known as Rudy Viper.' He crossed his arms and gave a resigned sigh.

The soldier interrupted with a teasing grin. 'Also, Miss Scarlet.'

Morran gave him an annoyed glance. 'Whatever her aliases may be, it discredits her account. She's known at the Watch for her involvement with some criminals, one of which a wanted smuggler.'

'And?' Hellier leaned closer. 'She did it, didn't she? She took this girl you are after.'

'Possibly. It would be in her line of work.'

'You can add kidnapping to her list of crimes, as well as making my life hell.' She huffed. 'What about me?'

He nodded at her. 'You are free to go.'

'Really?' Hellier stood slowly with wariness.

'She will be dealt with as will you if you set one foot wrong.' He glared with commanding severity.

She shrunk back with some sense she should kept her mouth shut.

The captain and his officer left the room. She opened the door with a sense she had to leave before anyone noticed her. After all she hadn't faced Mother over her fight and she didn't want to be stopped by her now.

She passed a handful of white-robed women as she dashed to the courtyard. It was not surprising to see soldiers congregating there. She slowed to pass them and smiled at their probing eyes sizing her up.

'Where are you going?'

She stopped and stared the soldier in the eye. 'I've got work at the White Horse. The captain said I could go.'

'Right then.' He waved her past.

Throwing her cloak around her, she pulled the hood over her head and left. The square was busy, and a troop of soldiers were idle around the fountain. People walked past them with their heads down. Her Kin and the wagon were nowhere to be seen. She mumbled, 'Curses, they left without me.'

Recalling the gate Jett mentioned they would use, she headed to Yeon's Corner in the east of the city. Lonely and irritable, her mind fell back to her time with Dario. Walking along the unfamiliar streets, she missed his overexcited chatter and his stories about the Florisian people. He had a way of easing her mind and making her feel — wanted. The traffic was slow on this side of town due to domestic animals and market carts, and every third step she skipped over puddles, as well as halt for patrols.

'Need a ride?'

The shoulder of the black horse nudged her and she smiled up at Jett. 'Only if you're on the way out.' She sprung up behind him.

'We're leaving. Come hell or numbskull soldiers.' *I can't get out quick enough.* 'I don't know what happened, but don't you remember what I said about controlling yourself?'

Hellier blushed, grateful he couldn't see. She had completely forgotten that discussion. 'Well…' Thunder's steady pace relaxed her as he started up the road. 'I had to.'

He cocked his head to give her a humorous glance. 'I've heard that before.' His tone turned stern. 'You nearly jeopardized everything.'

'You don't know the half of it.' She sighed. 'They didn't find you, did they?'

'Who?' He shook his head and grumbled, 'I don't think I want to know.'

Soon, he was in sight of the Sanchella Gate and a line of vehicles waiting to exit. A patrol had set up a post by the gate and soldiers were checking over every wagon, horse, and man, including barrels and crates. The Kin's wagon was further along the que and nearer the gate. Amid wary alarm, he watched a couple of soldiers speak to Seth behind their wagon before they moved away.

Jett rode past the annoyed travellers and up to Seth. He dismounted, leaving Hellier to trot the horse forward. His manner was brisk. 'What did they want?'

Seth replied, 'Too apologize for the delay.'

Jett eyed him sceptically. 'Apologize? I doubt they would consider it.' He lowered the wagon door and said to Seth, 'Sit on the flap.'

Seth did as he was told and Jett stuck his head inside. He whispered, mostly for Mara's benefit, 'You'll have to walk out of the city.'

Shiarn thought, *Are you mad?*

Jett replied, *You have to. We'll meet you along the road.*

Just when I was getting comfortable too. Earona whispered, 'You're probably right.'

He stood by Seth, giving them space to move. *Earona, take the pouch from my hand.* He sensed them touching him as they hopped down, and the pouch was taken.

'Flamin' hell!' Shiarn cried, *I slipped, hurt my ankle. Jumping from a wagon without the use of my hands is a feat and a half.*

Can you walk? Jett could do nothing to aid her nor did he even know exactly where she was.

A man behind shouted at them to move on, and the more Jett ignored him, the more incensed he became.

I can hobble, Shiarn thought. *Let's get out of here.*

Keanan finally moved the wagon forward and Jett waited with frustration as a pair of soldiers opened up the door of their wagon. An officer, in a suit of mail, observed Jett and his weapon with a shrewd eye. 'Name, please?'

Jett's reply went unheard as a proud white horse made a great noise on the pavement behind the officer. Despite the fuss, the officer only bothered with a short glance. Narrowing his eyes, Jett peered at the rider. Obviously a gentleman of some status with his curly white wig and lace shirt under a velvet jacket. The only place Jett had seen such extravagance was, strangely enough, in the underground of the city. Instantly on edge, he had good reason to be wary, he recognised the man from the night in the sewers.

The elegantly attired lord pointed a bejewelled finger at Jett, and with a scheduled flip of his hair, stated with all the pomp he could produce. 'My good Captain Lathewell, these are the villains I spoke off. These horrendous miscreants are the ones who stole my family jewels. You will find them in a beautiful box with my family crest.'

Captain Lathewell gave the rider a disparaging stare. 'Duke Brytwold, we will search their belongings as we are doing to everyone. If you don't mind, we'd like to get on with it.'

Women shouting across the street interrupted their conversation. After a moment, a terrible screech disturbed the controlled peace.

'Corporal Artus, see what all that noise is about.'

At the captain's order a soldier dashed out in front of the wagon.

The duke stared with candid conceit at Jett, and his malevolent expression was like a slap in the face. Jett comprehended the potential danger they were facing. 'There must be a mistake, I have never met this man before.'

Captain Lathewell placed his hand on the wagon and glanced inside. 'Regardless, we will check through your belongings. As you have probably heard the king's murderer has escaped and we are doing enforced checks of all outgoing vehicles and vessels. We are going to turn this city upside down till we find the criminal and anyone associated with her.'

Yelling across the street did not cease. Positive he heard Hellier's voice, Jett turned to look past the horses' heads.

Captain Lathewell indicated to a couple of soldiers to enter the Kin's wagon, along with extra instructions to search the riders for the duke's jewels.

Amid growing uneasiness, Jett surveyed the small square before him. Spying the man he was searching for, Jett gave a brusque nod to a green dressed figure slouched against a red leafed tree. The man returned the gesture with a smirk of inflated merriment from under his wide brimmed hat. Jett was right to suspect Tonius was behind this new peril.

It would not take the soldiers long to check over their wagon, Keanan and Seth were meticulous in their packing. Yet due to the additional search, including a going over of their personal baggage, the soldiers were not quick. After some time and an increasing line of travellers growing impatient and angry, the soldiers returned, empty handed.

'Searched, captain. Found no one in there, and nothing on their bodies.'

'Fine.'

'Anything else?' Duke Brytwold stared down at the soldiers incredulously. 'What about my jewels?'

'No jewels, sir.' Ignoring the duke, the soldier spoke to the captain looking annoyed by the whole situation. 'We searched their baggage and went over their persons. They aren't carrying anything like that.'

'This can't be. Search again. I demand my jewels be returned!' The duke's face flushed a bright red. 'And if they do not have them the guards must be checked. I demand satisfaction!'

Captain Lathewell responded, curtly, 'Duke Brytwold, if they haven't got them someone else might have. We shall keep looking.'

'This is an outrage! They are in a small wooden box, a very expensive box...'

The soldier said, 'Sir, we didn't see any box like that, or any jewels.'

'Some soldier must have it, check them all. You must search again! *I* demand it.'

'I swear,' Jett stated, 'I have nothing to hide.' The soldier had already touched on his pockets, and he lifted his arms.

Captain Lathewell glanced down the line of traffic before studying Jett with new insight. 'Duke Brytwold, everything seems in order.' He looked at Jett with surprise and said, 'You are free to go.'

Duke Brytwold sputtered with livid indignation. 'Someone will pay for this injustice.'

Amid gallant delight at their near escape, Jett grinned and waved two fingers at Tonius who appeared enraged.

~ * ~

After the guards checked her over, Hellier led Thunder past the wagon with a confident swagger.

By the roadside an old hag shouted, 'You can't get away that easy!' She pointed a bony hand at empty air towards the exit. 'Devilish curse on you!'

Grimacing, Hellier wondered if she could see the girls. She handed the reins to Marcus. 'I'll take care of her.'

The witch scuttled off with her elaborate stick in hand, her attention on the gate. 'Come back here you demon,' she cried, 'You can't escape your destiny, Hell spawn.'

People began murmuring at the woman yelling at no one they could see.

Hellier stood in her path, hands on her hips. 'Hey!'

'Akalla-tezquana-zelqua-sarwaz.'

Cries arose from the watching crowd, 'She's a witch! A witch!'

The witch stretched her stick at Hellier.

Hellier shouted, 'Damn, you really are a witch!'

'I want that girl.'

Marcus jumped off his horse and placed a hand on the witch's shoulder. He cried out in shock and withdrew a raw, red palm.

Hellier responded in Fáer, *'You can't have her.'* She could speak no other tongue, no matter how she strained.

A startled look crossed the old woman's face. 'She's a devil.'

Hellier grabbed the woman's fist holding the staff and pushed it down. It burned her skin, but she was unaffected by it. *'You can really talk?'*

The witch hissed with malice.

'You have failed here,' said Hellier. *'Be gone and don't bother us again.'*

'Maybe,' the witch growled, 'But, I won't next time.' She moved to the side and melded with the shadows, vanishing from view.

Hellier glanced about as if waking from a dream. Marcus mounted and clutched his burnt hand, and from the wagon seat, Keanan eyed her with concern.

She took River's rein from Keanan and without a word, mounted.

With satisfaction, Jett hopped up on Thunder. 'Shall we go?'

'Gladly,' replied Hellier.

Keanan pulled the wagon away and they trotted through the gate.

Still flexing his fingers, Marcus commented to anyone listening. 'Who would have thought Floris would be so much fun?'

'So much fun…' Hellier replied, 'I've decided I never want to have fun again.'

'I doubt we would be allowed back here anyway,' Keanan stated.

They passed the village outside the city and Jett signalled a stop. He dismounted and walked to the wagon and lowered the back end, and reached in for the crate. A soft pressure against his clothing caused him to lean back on the wagon. After a few moments he stuck his head in and looked at them, rubbing and stretching their hands. He looked Earona over with a charming smile; she looked well, and considering everything, healthy. 'It's good to have you back. You have my pouch?'

Earona dug around in her bag. 'See how useful this bag is.' She gave Shiarn a smug smile and handed Jett the heavy jingling purse. 'Here is your treasure.'

'You don't know how true that is.' He went on with sudden cheer, 'You also have an elegant looking chest?'

Earona rummaged in her bag again and brought out a box the size of a hand. 'A military man stuck his head in and hid this under those blankets.' She handed him the chest without viewing it herself. 'Very odd. Shiarn told me to take it.'

Shiarn crawled to him to gain a better look. 'Who does it belong to?'

Gold inlaid was on the top of the well-made box, and along the edges, gold was imprinted in the intricate swirls. Inside, on black velvet, were three rings, two with gems, the other was a thick gold band with a symbol inscribed. He whistled at the find. 'Some duke called Brytwold.'

'I remember him,' Shiarn mused with a half-smile.

'We better get moving,' Seth shouted from behind, 'Someone's travelling on the road.'

'He's a pompous ass and we are extremely lucky.' He closed the lid. 'Stay in here. Keep this safe, and always be ready to disappear.' He handed Earona the chest and moved out of the wagon and it began its rhythmic pace once more.

'What was that all about?' Earona relaxed against the wagon's compartment and opened the box again.

Shiarn chuckled and took the chest from her. She handled each piece, studying them closely. Even Mara fondled the rings with fascination, picking up the one Jett admired. 'The family seal.'

'Oh, my,' Earona gasped with surprise. 'That man wished to smuggle it out?'

'No, they wanted to set us up.' Shiarn frowned and tossed the ring back. 'It's best not to think what might have happened if they found this.' She reached across Mara and gave Earona a tight hug. 'I'm glad you are well.'

'And I, you.' Earona embraced her warmly. 'I heard you had an awful time?' She held onto her nervously, unsure whether the conversation would be difficult for Shiarn.

I can't believe you already know that. Shiarn blushed and folded her arms.

Earona placed her hand on Shiarn's ankle to heal her. 'We can talk about it later if you like.'

'I don't really want to talk about it.' Shiarn packed the box back into Earona's bag.

'I can't even imagine what you are feeling, so I won't say anything too daft…'

'Don't try to be sweet now.' Shiarn shook her head with fondness. 'About that argument we had…'

'I was a heartless duffer.'

'I have come to believe, it all would have happened at some point regardless of our actions that day.'

Mara sat looking at them with interest. 'I wonder…'

Shiarn turned to Mara. 'What was that woman about? And why weren't you affected by her spell?'

Earona gave her an arrogant smirk. 'Yes, do tell.'

'It's… I really don't know.' Fondling her bracelet, Mara said with exasperation, 'I'm just grateful we could get away.'

'She could see you,' Shiarn stressed. 'Why?'

Mara only shrugged.

Earona added, 'She was the same one as before. She's cunning.'

'You should mention it to Jett. I'm sure he would be interested.' Shiarn lay down on the blankets.

Mara replied with some irritation, 'Do I have too?'

'I'm glad we are all here, except for Ethan of course.' Earona told Shiarn what had taken place since their separation. Comparing their experiences of their short stay in the cells, they mused together, how it was more than long enough. She described life in the temple as gruelling, and Shiarn described life in the palace, detailing the richness of the dresses and the extravagant people, and how she developed a taste for fine wines. She dug around in Earona's bag and brought out the coloured glass bottle, explaining what would have been her fate if she hadn't been saved. Shiarn stared into the blue mid-section of the glass. Now she could appreciate why Morgal had to be taken out before they escaped from the city. His involvement would have led them to being discovered without any doubt.

Earona took it and peered through the red. 'Your friend is in here?' She held the glass up to her eyes and looked at Shiarn through it. 'How peculiar.'

'Yes, very. She went up in a cloud of blue mist and went in there.'

'I wonder what it means,' Earona pondered aloud, 'Where is she really? Truly fascinating.'

'I suppose it is,' Shiarn said, dully, and she settled herself along the floor of the wagon. Closing her eyes, she placed her hands on her stomach.

Earona folded the bottle in the cloth and placed it back in her bag. 'And Ethan has been sold as a slave?' she questioned, though Hellier already mentioned it to her.

Sighing, Shiarn kept her eyes closed. *He's a long way from here.*

Earona decided to leave her alone and even Mara was dozing on the floor. Her days were full of activity and now she had nothing to do. She climbed over the girls and pulled the front curtain apart and peeked outside. 'It's good to see you, Keanan, are you well?'

On hearing her voice, he spun his head around in surprise. 'I'm much better now you and Shiarn are back.'

Earona took in the landscape. They were travelling east from the city and the majority of land on the left was green hills with the occasional flock of sheep. On the right was sparse rocky green, and beyond that a horizon of deep grey ocean. She gave a cheerful wave to Marcus and Seth, riding beside Rose and Sunny, and they returned her greeting with equal joy. She could not wipe the happiness from her face. 'Where are we going?'

'Firstly, a town called Aylesworth, where we shall stop for the night. If we were earlier we might have continued on. You must keep out of sight and Shiarn will keep hidden. Then, less than two days to Sommerlea.'

'Sommerlea?' queried Earona.

'An estate owned by a Kin we met here. Shiarn made a friend of Jonas in the palace.' Keanan lowered his voice and cast a glance over her shoulder, 'I think it became more than a friendship.'

She risked a peek at Shiarn who appeared sleeping. 'Oh… romance abounds.' *Even Hellier gets to meet a man, and get intimate…* it was too late to restrain her thoughts.

'Hellier?' He asked with discrete shock, 'you mean with Dario?'

Her cheeks were flushed. 'You're not meant to know that.' Full of apprehension, she glimpsed Seth and Marcus talking. 'You mustn't tell anyone.'

He replied with exasperation, 'I wouldn't dream of saying anything, you can trust me and so can Hellier.'

Earona relaxed somewhat. 'And don't think it either.'

'I won't. In any case, she's old enough to make her own—'

'Codswallop!' She grunted her disapproval. 'The whole thing is entirely wrong! But I won't get into that now. I'm so happy to be back with everyone, except for Ethan of course.'

'That's a dilemma,' he said, 'We will do all we can to get him back.'

Parting from Ethan was terrible, and his physical pain from the torture remains in my mind.

Keanan said, despondently, 'He's a tough boy.'

She sensed his sadness beyond his attempt to comfort her. They sat in silence, watching the scenery pass by.

PART III

Dusk

Home in the Forest

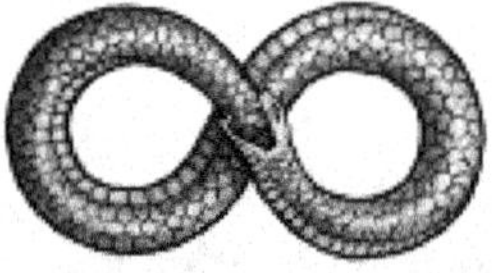

49- Signet Reach

Rollin' down Heaven Street
A Floris Watch I chanced to meet
Says he, "You're a Rocks rat by the mange of your hair"
"You're a Rocks rat by the stinkn' rags you wear"
Oh no, Watchman, that can't be me
I'm a deep water sailor from over the sea

Sailor Shanty

Ethan spent the voyage chained below deck, heaving up his empty insides and getting teased by the Harn. Their jibes over his less than sea-worthy legs was in good humour, but he failed to see anything funny in his situation. According to Loc it was a smooth journey. However for Ethan, sailing was turning out to be another torture. He hated every moment, and longed for their destination, wherever that was.

By the time the ship pulled into port, Ethan was feverish. He half-stumbled down the plank into a busy town. Ships were moored in an immense bay encircled by a range of mountainous cliffs. Stone buildings were at the feet of the rocks near the beach, and more cottages were on the outcrops. The place was teeming with people including chained prisoners unloading cargo and hauling goods.

The pirates separated the new prisoners into two crowds. As fate had it, Ethan was grouped with the Harn. Too ill to take note of his new surroundings, Ethan walked in a dizzy slant, with the Harn supporting him as best they could.

They arrived at a high barred gate and a rough looking man rattling a ring of keys. Eventually opening the door, he took them through into a giant cavern in the side of the mountain. They passed an empty cell and were herded into an adjoining one. More crossbows were aimed at the prisoners while they were unchained from each other, with their iron cuffs remaining fastened.

'You slaves will work the mines. Daegal will explain what you need to know.' The man with the keys told them. 'If you give us no trouble, we give you none. You all hear that.' After locking their cell, he and the others left through the main gateway, locking it behind them.

Rows of bunk beds with mattresses had the added luxury of blankets. Bowls and cups were under beds, and other items such as pouches and satchels hung from the bunks. The cell bars were embedded in and protruding from the rock walls, but they fell short of the high thirty foot ceiling. Despite being in another prison, the atmosphere of the empty cavern was peaceful. The men eventually lay on unclaimed mattresses to rest.

Ethan collapsed on the first bed, clutching his cramping stomach. Loc sat by him and laid a hand on his damp forehead.

Gailtram observed Ethan's ashen skin, shining with sweat. 'He looks deathly ill.'

'It's worst then I thought.'

Eventually the cavern grew dark with the new night, and the noise of chatter traveled into the chamber. The gate was opened and the other inmates filed in. Wary glances passed across their faces at the sight of the Harn.

An old pirate approached on the opposite side of the bars. A rimmed, black hat was over a white scarf, tied around his scalp. His shirt frills poked out from under a tight fitting jacket, and dangling at his sides, two curved swords. A grin appeared under his graying moustache and he paid close attention to the Harn. 'By Reddog's chest! You have arrived.' His voice was rough. 'My name is Daegal Segyorlefe. You begin your work tomorrow. If you please me, it will go well for you.' He stood with hands on his hips looking them over, but he stared long and hard at Ethan. 'That one, he does not look good. Will he live?'

Loc looked surprised by the man's genial manner. 'If he has water and food.'

Daegal creased his brow and shrugged. 'I cannot help slaves,' he paused, 'but maybe Kenric knows what to do with you.' He stepped away, and as if in after-thought, said, 'We are not like the Rocks here, but neither are we the Golden Crown.' He lifted his hat as he walked from the cells and sang a 'good night' and the keepers followed him out.

The inhabitants of the cell claimed their bed space, and it was clear, the old residents numbered less than the new arrivals. A thin man, nearing middle age with shoulder length brown hair and a neat beard of grey, stood above Loc and spoke in a crisp voice. 'I am Kenric.' He bent over Ethan and touched his neck.

'Name's Loc.' Loc looked up into Kenric's keen grey eyes. 'Think he's got waterdog fever.'

'Indeed.' Kenric studied Loc's tattooed face and with a keen glance at the other newcomers. 'You are all Harn.'

'We are.'

'However, he is not,' Kenric said. 'You are fond of him?'

'In a way,' Loc said, 'I made a promise to someone I want to keep.'

Kenric called to a small boy, not much older than ten years. 'Mouse, find some lemon and perhaps a cloth and anything else you deem helpful.'

'Will do Cap'tn.' The boy went quickly, making no sound as he scaled the wall and bars, and landed on the other side.

Kenric went to the adjoining cell and handed across a large jug. He asked a fellow prisoner to fill it. After a few moments it was passed back. Other men started passing bowls through the bars and receiving them back filled with water.

The Harn watched with greedy stares. It seemed an outreach of the cavern's rock in the joining cell had a flow of water. Soon the Harn stuck their bowls through, pleading for water.

Kenric crawled under a bunk and scrabbled underneath. He returned with a flask and brought it to Ethan's dry lips. Offering no word of explanation, he tilted Ethan's head, enabling him to sip it.

Loc asked, 'What is that?'

'It will help. If he does not recover they will take him out and hasten his death.' Kenric noted Loc's disapproving stare. 'Disease wipes out many slaves, so they like to eradicate it to prevent its spread, so to speak. In a roundabout pirate way it makes sense.'

'Where are you from?' Loc asked.

'I? Myself, and most of the men in this cell are Coltrenians.'

On top of the high rock crevice near the iron bars toward the rear of the cell, a shadow crept along. The boy stood on the top of the railing and with ease swung down to the floor.

'You have boys here.' Loc eyed three other young lads lying on the bunks.

Mouse pulled an orange from the pouch hanging across his chest. 'As you asked Cap'tn.'

'Yes, children… what a pity.' Kenric spared the lad a smile. 'They are useful underground, small hands, small bodies. At least it saves them from the brothels and other deeds just as indecent.' He looked through the pouch, and an older, white-haired man handed him a knife. 'Thanks, Bearn.' Kenric flicked the knife out, pointing it towards Loc. 'Word of warning.' He cut the fruit and placed it on Ethan's cracked lips, rubbing and wetting them thoroughly. 'We won't tolerate anyone doing them harm.'

Loc's brows deepened with indignation. 'You don't have to worry about that with us.'

'Good.' Kenric squeezed juice into the water and crunched up herbs he found in the bag.

'He should be right for morning, he's had the elixir,' Bearn stated, and moved away to lie on his bed.

Kenric noticed Loc staring with wonder at the items. 'A storage area is behind that.' He pointed to the rear of the cell. 'We make the most of it as discretely as possible. The flask is special and we save it for when we really need it.'

Loc said, 'Seems easy enough to steal things.'

'For some it is. Mouse and Berran are the only ones who can climb it.'

'You're at home here.'

'We have been here a long time.' Kenric placed the damp cloth on Ethan's forehead. 'Perhaps it's not a bad thing, having the appearance of being at home.'

'Did you hear that, Ruegar?' A redheaded boy called to another lad lounging on top of a bunk, his long legs hanging over the side. 'Looks' as if we're at home.'

A sandy haired, skinny boy yelled back, 'Whatever that looks like.' The boys hooted with laughter.

Loc ignored the children's banter. 'You haven't considered escape?'

Kenric busied himself with Ethan, helping him drink the medicinal water, and said with reservation, 'We have.' All eyes turned to Kenric, yet he said nothing further on it.

Loc and Gailtram tended Ethan as he faced a night of fitful sleep and raging fevers. By morning it had broken and he was able to acknowledge his surroundings and meet the other prisoners.

Kenric placed his hand on Ethan's neck. 'You are better.'

Ethan attempted standing, but his legs shook under him.

Kenric said, 'You will have to put on your best show of being well.'

'I can manage.' Ethan stretched his long legs out before him. 'Name's Ethan by the way.'

'Well, Ethan.' Kenric responded with a friendly smile. 'I am Kenric and I am pleased to have you in our living quarters.'

The Coltrenians were not overly friendly, but they were polite. They explained their work in the mines and general life at Signet Reach. Ethan had no desire to know how people lived at Signet Reach, he was eager to escape and as soon as he was better he would make this his mission.

So far Signet Reach had shown itself to be more civilized than the nightmare existence of the Rocks. The prisoners were led out of their cells and into the sunlight and herded into a hall where workers could eat their meals. The courteous atmosphere was unnerving. Ethan looked at his soiled skin and inhuman appearance and was appalled. But it was a welcomed change to eat at a table with a utensil. The porridge might have been tasteless, but it filled his stomach. Across the room he spied Garutz staring back at him with hatred. Ethan turned a blank face away from him.

After breakfast, the mining groups were led to their work areas. The Harn and the prisoners of the new cell were taken to another gateway in the side of the cliff. Six pirates were in charge of sixty men. Torches lit their way, and the guards, carrying at least two weapons each, if not more, led them down. Ethan was told there was a type of status among the pirates. Whoever had the most weapons was either more skilled at combat or simply wealthier. Either one brought praise.

Daegal, the chief pirate, sauntered in and looked the Harn over. 'My new men are an exceptional win.' His harsh accent rang about the chamber, 'And this big strong one is better, I am pleased.' He spared a passing glance at Ethan. 'We mine black-gold here and we are the best. Don't you let me down. I want to shove it up Masso's ass so far he'll fall on his knees.' He sniggered and wagged his finger at them. 'We mine the most black-gold and we stay on the top. Win for me, win for you. Kenric will show you the ropes.' He left without a backward glance.

Ethan wondered how so few men could mine such a great quantity, then he questioned if there had been more men before the Harn arrived. He overheard someone whisper, 'Masso's his main rival. Don't be fooled. Daegal can be a bugger when he's angry. If you waste his time it means he loses money. He hates losing money.'

'That's how it works around here,' Druce, a fit middle-aged man, said, 'if it can be bought, sold or stolen you're got a deal. Cursed Pirates!'

The pirate-guards took them deeper down one of the chambers. In a lot of places the tunnels were bolstered by old wooden arches wide enough they could walk two abreast. Ethan found it nerve wracking. He thought he could control the fear, yet as he went further in, it became more apparent the passageway, creaking with pressure, was unsettling him. With every step the narrow passages gradually descended. They arrived at another chamber. Tunnels branched off it and all of them seemed to slope down. Ethan became disheartened by the fact their descent continued without turning upward or leveling out.

After much walking he had to ask how far they were going. 'Fifty feet!' He repeated the answer in a shocked shout. But it had to be true, because they kept on walking down. He considered Jett and how much he would feel at home in a place like this, he might even enjoy it.

The elderly man, Bearn, said with cheer, 'This grand shaft reaches into the mountain.'

Something in his tone made Ethan think he liked being underground, and he wondered if he was sane. 'I know a man you would get along with.'

'He likes mining?'

Ethan nodded with inattention, realizing too late he was not in the mood to mention Jett.

They halted in a chamber with enough room for them to stand on one side. A table and chairs were present in the shadows, as well as cupboards and a beer barrel. Some of the guards leaned against the wall, looking as if they would rather be anywhere else then right there. Farther in, crates and boxes contained tools which the men collected before heading down the next passage.

'This is it,' Kenric addressed the Harn, 'We have a good tunnel farther down. The best stone is always in deep.'

The men went further into the chamber and through into a tunnel. Some started hammering at the rock walls and others chipped methodically at one piece of stone. Dull tones of men chattering and murmuring amidst the resonating sound of tools clanging on rocks filled the chamber. The keepers stayed for a while, and once they were satisfied rock was being heaved, they headed back to their area to chat and play cards.

Ethan observed the metal they were mining, surprised to discover it was malreus. 'They call this black-gold?'

Noticing his interest, Bearn said, 'It's fine, isn't it?'

'What do they do with it?' asked Ethan.

'Make jewels I suppose. Only the rich can afford this.'

Kenric stood at the center of the chamber and raised his voice with cheerful encouragement. 'Let's get a worthy quota today.'

Ethan watched Kenric tap a man, called Arth, on the shoulder. The two disappeared back down the passageway and into darkness. Not long after, Kenric reappeared alone.

As one of the biggest men present, it was allotted to Ethan to hack and pound at the stone to open up the chamber. Considering his body was on the mend, they allowed him to rest often and not cause himself anymore exertion, which he was grateful for. Near the middle of the cavern, water dribbled from the rock, enough for each man to fill the shared cup.

In the midst of the hard work, Ethan forgot he was under the mountain, but once they stopped for a break it was again prevalent in his mind. He noticed Arth had joined them again, luckily, as the keepers walked about, observing their work. The prisoners went back to hammering and fossicking into the rock, and the guards went back to occupying themselves with drink and gambling.

The men worked at a zealous pace, but Ethan once more noticed another man leave the main group and seemingly he disappeared. He wondered at it, but said nothing to anyone. The day came to a close when the guards came to collect them and order them up top. Apparently the day finished when the guards became hungry, which meant there was no true regularity to their shift. It was exhausting work although not unsatisfying as they looked over their load of black-gold.

The climb back up was laborious and more tedious than the downward journey. On their arrival at the main chamber, Daegal greeted them. He lifted a length of black rock, the size of a thick finger. 'Fine. Passable for today.'

To Ethan's amazement they were seated in the hall with a lukewarm bowl of fish broth and piece of bread. Apparently, the preferred meal at Signet Reach and the cheapest. Ethan was happy to down it all without any complaints.

50 - New Passage

You cannot long hide the diamond among the coal
You cannot long pretend a rock is a thing of beauty

Olvarus Claw'Blade, Reader's Wisdom

The Kin passed grassy hills on their way to Alyesworth. Grey clouds followed them and a vigorous wind from the coast. At the signpost they turned east, away from the road leading south to Belrorn. Aylesworth was a town of quaint dwellings lined up between the tree-spotted hills. Jett rode in front as they neared the edge of the town.

Flagrant cursing came from an approaching group of villagers.

With alarm, Jett pulled up alongside the road and the rest of the Kin halted. What appeared to be an incensed rabble came up the street towards them. Two men, broadswords at their hips, and wearing coats of mail underneath white tabards, looked to be outsiders amidst the villagers in their modest clothing.

Emblazoned on the soldier's shirts was a golden sun covered by a red ring with black script. The insignia of the Sentinels; holy knights sworn to eradicate evil from New Earth. Their interpretation of evil varied hugely from a Fáerinn's. Myth or not, Fáerinn rated high on their list of instigators of wickedness. Jett groaned at the sight of them.

Between the Sentinels was a scraggly haired woman in a plain brown frock. Gagged, and with both hands tired and looped onto an iron hook attached to a pole, she was pulled along, stumbling. Anger was in her eyes and not a hint of fear. A Sentinel followed them, holding a steel tipped staff, and chanting in a low voice.

'Good day.' Jett looked down from his horse with suspicion. 'What are you doing with that woman?'

'And a good day to you.' The man had sharp features and soft shoulder length hair. 'You do not need to concern yourself with this affair, however, on chance this scene will spark rumours, this woman is a servant of hell.'

'I see.' Jett displayed feigned surprise as did the Kin behind him, though theirs was less false and more genuine. 'It is good to know we can enter this town safely and not be assailed in any way.'

The Sentinel replied, 'True, this one will no longer trouble this world.' The woman pulled on the iron pole, trying to back up. He yanked on it, causing her to trip forward.

Jett asked, 'What will you do with her?'

'After the midnight ritual her spirit will be set free. It is the only way for her to be saved.'

Marcus thought to Jett, *should we tell them about the witch at the gate?*

Don't speak a word of it! Jett commanded.

The villagers lost interest in their conversation and started cursing and spitting at the woman. A mad look entered her eyes and she snarled at them through her gag.

They passed the Kin and the witch stopped. Swaying drunkenly, she stared at the canvas at the back of the wagon. She leered through her gag, her eyes narrowing as she turned to face her fate. The robed man kept his eyes fixed on her even as the head Sentinel pulled her to heel. The rowdy crowd followed the men escorting her out of their town.

The Kin drove their horses and wagon to an inn across the square. "The Green Hill" was attractive and near empty of patrons. The inn owner explained the townsfolk had been occupied with seeing off the witch and he had rooms to spare.

A fireplace and dark drapes made for added comfort in the room that only had beds for five. Once they were in they brought the invisible girls up. Jett and Keanan decided to visit the common room and talk with the locals to get any news of the road ahead. They ordered meals for themselves and those upstairs, including extra helpings.

Upstairs a fire warmed the air and the rest of the Kin talked about their adventures in Floris. Earona talked most of all. The Kin's chatter was disjointed with awkward pauses as if they forced themselves to speak. Earona wondered if they were really offering up what they wanted to discuss or perhaps they weren't willing to. It was not long before the evening came to a large uncomfortable silence and everyone wished only to sleep.

~ * ~

Long after the others fell asleep, Mara folded back the blanket and sat up. She had not slept at all, but laid in bed waiting. She glanced to Jett, he was in a dead sleep. For some reason, she thought he would wake, as if he would instinctively know she was up to something. She dressed, and wrapping her cloak around her shoulders, she left the room.

She left the inn by the backdoor and walked the street they came down during the day, taking the road out of town. Shivering in the chill air, she followed the pathway, winding through a spattering of trees and damp slopes. She rubbed her belly, trying to soothe the tossing infant. He did not want her to go. Neither did she want to, but a lead weight compelled her as if she were a fish caught on bait. She halted and vomited into the bushes. The desire to throw up only worsened as she moved closer. 'I'm just going to see, nothing more.'

A rhythmic chant came a short distance away and she stopped. In the light from long torches, the armed men stood around the woman fastened to the pole forced into the ground amidst a pile of brushwood. A knight prepared a flaming torch for the witch's funeral pyre. The woman smirked under her gag.

The voice, as clear as day, called for Mara's assistance. Mara knew what she was, and as much as it pained her, she was akin to her being. She only hoped the woman didn't know her or her mother in some way. She pulled the hood further over her face, and gripping the leather on her wrist, she walked through the shrubbery. Overcome with a burning need to speak and free the woman, she raised her hand and spoke. 'Alqua-elzat-varan-ezwa.'

The men spun with explosive wrath. A Sentinel came at her. Mara repeated the spell. It sealed the men's fate, crumpling them to the ground.

The witch drooped over her binds and remained still for some moments. She lifted her face and her eyes flashed with malice at the incapacitated Sentinels.

Mara scrambled to the nearest one, discovering he was unconscious and not dead as she first thought. For some reason it bothered her that she would care whether the man was dead or not. Finding a black knife on the pile of wood, she cut the bonds off the witch and pulled down her gag.

The woman breathed hard, and scratching her wrists, she hobbled over to a knight.

Staring at the lifeless man, Mara shuddered. 'I…' Why was she even there, helping this woman, except… she understood what she would be feeling.

'You only Slept them.' The witch gave her a pathetic stare. 'Should have killed them.'

'I can't.' Although there was a time she could easily have done it, now she didn't have the stomach for cold blooded murder.

The witch creased her brow. 'What did you say?' Her weak eyes considered her. 'Do I know you?'

'I saw your Element and I called you.' The witch searched the men's robes and pockets, taking what she thought useful. 'We do not have time to talk here. I'll kill them.' With a knife she found, she slit the throat of the unarmed priest.

Mara pointed the knife at her. 'No one else.'

The witch growled, 'These devils are our enemy.' At the sight of Mara's pregnant belly, she backed off. 'You!' Her face strained, she quickly turned to scan the tree line. 'What's a breeder doing out here?'

'What?' Mara cried, her face reddened with shock at the remark. 'Has my mother sent you?'

'Who are you?' The witch narrowed her eyes with suspicion as she stepped back.

'I'm…' Mara shook her head at nearly revealing her identity. 'No-one.'

'Liar!' Casting distrustful glances at the sleeping men, she said, 'You can't stay here. We'll talk on the way.'

For some moments Mara considered accompanying her. 'To where?'

'My Chapter.' The witch held out a bony hand, but her manner was far from inviting.

Mara stared at the offered hand, with a mix of longing and hatred. Suddenly overwhelmed with the desire to run away, and be done with Earona and with Jett. She stood rooted to the ground, clutching her stomach. The baby kicked with sickening force. She thought with rude selfishness he would only sabotage the flight by making her ill. 'I can't.' Besides, she was now enjoying her freedom and it would only be taken away from her once she made contact with another chapter, and eventually her mother would know. 'Go.' Mara turned from her with resignation. 'And don't harm these men.'

The witch vanished into the shadows. Mara waited some moments to be assured she had left before turning from the clearing. She wondered which Chapter the witch came from. At least Chapters were secretive and did not give information freely. Perhaps it would chance that her mother would not yet discover her location, and she would have more time to explore this new way of living.

Shivering with sudden fear, she held her stomach and questioned what she was really carrying inside. With a heavy heart, she dug out her charm, and gripping it tight, she took her time walking back to the inn.

~ * ~

Ethan's new surroundings were an improvement on the Rocks. He was reasonably fed, moderately warm, and hard worked, and he knew with some certainty what time it was. Despite this, he had no desire to live this way for any period of time. He had gotten the impression Kenric and the others had been doing just that and accepting it.

They were an odd bunch in the new cell. A handful were boys, the others were older men. The eldest being Bearn, with his head of white hair and a bony nose overlooking his bushy moustache. Kenric stood the tallest over them and they respected every word he uttered as if he was some king in exile. The Harn were unlike them in appearance, averaging a height of four and a half feet. In addition to their course thick hair and beards, they had stubby noses and solid limbs. The Harn looked up to Loc in the same fashion as Kenric's men did to him.

Ethan approached Kenric speaking to Bearn and Druce. He leaned on the bunk and stared down at their questioning faces. 'Kenric, I know you must be up to something and I want in.'

'Sit here, my lad.' Kenric tapped the bed next to him. 'You should not ask that before you know what you are asking for.'

Not being able to cram himself under the frame, Ethan tittered on the edge. 'I know you must be planning something.' He studied their guarded expressions.

'Maybe, maybe not.' Kenric turned a kind eye to Loc with his arm around Branan. 'Lost someone has he?'

'His mother's brother, at the Rocks.' Letting Gart go was a sad affair for the Harn and most of all for Branan.

Kenric replied, 'we all know how that feels.'

'Yes,' Ethan responded

'Can you guess how long I have survived this place?' Kenric asked with smugness.

'I don't know.'

Kenric remarked with pride, 'Nearly ten years.'

Ethan was dumbfounded. 'You sound happy…'

'Happy?' A twisted smile formed on Kenric's face. 'Do you know how many of my men have died in that time?'

Ethan shook his head with disinterest.

'All of them except Bearn, Druce, and Fariz.' The faces of the men he mentioned where a mix of arrogance and insanity.

Ethan was confused as to their true convictions. 'Quite a feat.'

'I don't plan on being here forever,' he said.

'How did they die?'

Kenric shrugged. 'Guards, accidents, disease, cave-ins, murder.'

From the bed above Ethan, Mouse's head hung down. 'Old age…'

'Suicide, you name it, someone's probably died from it.'

'It messes with your head,' Druce gave him a wild smile and tapped his head with a calloused finger, 'being locked up. Cursed too, this place.'

The men opened up and Ethan listened with amazement.

'They say this place used to be burial grounds of ancient mariners,' Bearn said, 'and them caverns back there was where they put their dead.'

Another man broke in, 'and their treasure.'

Druce went on, 'That's what they say and some of them pirates are searching for it.'

'But we ain't seen no bones,' said Mouse.

'Aye,' Druce added, 'nor treasure.'

'I know what I'd rather see,' Mouse replied.

Ethan butted into their chatter, 'You still haven't told me about your plan.'

The talk finished and they looked to Kenric holding a finger to his lips. He spoke to Ethan sternly. 'No one outside this cell knows anything.' By this time they were quiet enough to attract Loc over and a few other Harn. 'The question is,' Kenric asked Ethan, 'do you really want to know?'

Ethan shrugged. 'I will do anything to get out of here.'

'Anything?' Kenric questioned, 'Is that right?'

Loc ordered, 'Out with it, then we know what you're bloody talking about.'

'If I tell you, you cannot tell anyone else,' Kenric commanded.

Derryl, the redhead boy, piped up from some place on a top bunk. 'Or you end up like Bothman.'

Bearn ordered, 'That's enough, Der.'

Kenric chuckled. 'Under the rocks, like the others.'

Ethan stared at Kenric with astonishment, but had no desire to know any more details.

'Now, Daskar,' Kenric started, 'that old codge—'

'Aye,' a croaky old voice responded from a distant bunk.

'Is an old miner who's been digging black-gold all his life.'

Daskar retorted, 'Till the mongrels took it all and my mine and me for that matter.'

'And Daskar found this secret chamber in the tunnels.' Kenric leaned nearer to the men. 'And we've been digging in it for years now.'

'So you're digging a tunnel into the harbour,' asked Ethan.

Loc smiled with a sparkle in this eye. 'We could take a ship.'

'No, no.' Kenric shook his head with fierce denial. 'Always the ship. Many men have tried this.'

'I can sail a ship.' Loc glanced around at his men. 'We can all sail.'

Kenric straightened his back and declared, 'I can sail a ship and captain one quite well I like to still think, in fact, my very own ship the Golden Maid is still moored across the bay.'

Bearn cried, 'The bloody bastards.'

'Indeed. No, that way is guarded to the teeth. They are lenient here because they know in other ways they are unbeatable.'

'What then?' Loc asked.

'We go through the mountain,' Kenric exclaimed with passionate animation, 'To the other side.'

Ethan was lost for words.

Loc finally responded, 'I think, man, you have lost your mind.'

Kenric gushed, 'It's perfect. They would never suspect it.'

'"course they wouldn't expect it!' Ethan was shocked at the eager faces gazing at Kenric in admiration. 'It's daft. How would it even work?'

Grith said, 'You're all gibbering madmen.'

'I know it seems that way.' Kenric attempted to justify himself. 'Daskar is convinced there's a way. He worked under the mountains to the south and says they are full of caverns and tunnels and some of them are manmade.' '

Bearn added, 'And we've been storing supplies for a long time now.'

'Yes, tools and provisions.'

Fariz spoke up. 'We're convinced there's water through the mountain.'

Loc shook his head with dismay.

Ethan could not comprehend why anyone would willingly go underground. 'But that's not even through the mountain,' he said incredulously, 'that's flamin' under it.'

'Yes!' Kenric explained, 'But this tunnel is already heading up.'

Loc creased his brow. 'How do you keep direction?'

Kenric eyed Daskar with confidence. 'Daskar has a lodestone.'

'A damn risk,' Loc growled.

'Maybe it's a challenge,' Kenric replied in a more reasonable manner. 'You have not yet been here ten years.'

Loc sighed heavily. 'But is it the only way? What about over the mountain?'

'We thought of that. We have not had access to the higher levels, but we know from what we have heard there are no accessible passes there. If we come across any we will surely use them.' Kenric said to Ethan, 'We could really use a big man like you.'

Still stunned by the plan, Ethan said, 'I don't understand how you can do it. How do you all disappear without them knowing?'

'I've got an idea, but I'm not sure yet how to implement it affectively.' Kenric rolled his lips in thought. 'It's possible we can cause the tunnel to collapse to conceal our escape.'

Ethan frowned at him, amazed at how much thought he had put into the crazy scheme. 'You could kill yourself.'

'We're willing to go through with it,' Druce said.

'Talk to your men,' Kenric said to Loc, 'see if you can persuade them.'

Loc cried, 'Persuade them?'

'I know Harn stay together and if you are willing, they will follow,' Kenric said with wise cunning.

Tarcil, one of the Harn spoke. 'If the boy goes, I and my brother Dein will go.'

Ethan stared at him with puzzlement.

Grith added, 'Aye, if Ethan goes, I will.'

'Me?'

'They remember what you did for Branan,' Loc explained.

Branan came over to them and stood apart with his arms folded, listening.

'Are you skilled in some way, lad?' asked Kenric.

All eyes turned to Ethan with optimistic interest.

'In a way.' Ethan's reply was half-hearted, but he was more reluctant to commit himself to traveling under a mountain, which seemed ludicrous, than the revelation of his Gift. 'If you must know. I can move objects.' Number one rule broken; he would try his hardest to keep the rest intact. 'Without touching it.' Amidst their astonished stares and open mouths, he felt like a freak of nature. He wished he could go away somewhere, but he couldn't and that was the whole problem.

Kenric looked pensive, but not doubtful. 'I've heard some odd stories in my life, and believe it or not, this might not be the strangest tale.'

Mouse, his head still upside down from the bunk above, taunted him, 'Show us!'

Ethan was not in the mood to demonstrate, but he had to satisfy the eyes gazing at him expectantly. He connected with his Ethos and with an open palm he focused on a cup of water, lifting it a few inches off the ground.

The men gasped with elevated shock and astonishment, and they murmured amongst themselves at the sight of the supernatural.

'Can you do heavier things? Or higher?' Kenric said.

'I...' Ethan was reluctant to openly talk about his Gift. 'Maybe...'

Kenric scratched his cheek. 'But still, it could be useful.'

'I haven't said I was going underground.' He could sense the Harn staring at him and he realized they must all know what he did for Branan. 'I haven't decided anything.'

'You think about it,' Kenric continued with more confidence, 'Meanwhile, I'll think of a plan of how we can do it.'

~ * ~

Crisp lemon scent rose from the warm water washing over Jett's taut skin. His eyes crept open and he viewed his naked body yielded to the calm flow of the deep bath. The massive room had not changed from his previous visit, but this time the vision felt stronger or perhaps he was more aware.

A spicy scent preceded the beauty he ultimately desired to gaze upon. Her appearance had not altered although she now radiated potent arousing notions. She crouched with seductive precision and caressed his cheek. 'My love, you have come again.' She clicked her fingers and silent boy servants appeared.

Jett stepped from the bath. A boy helped him robe and after a short bow the child disappeared again. Another passed him a gold goblet and he too disappeared. Under her benevolent gaze, Jett relaxed. 'Nya.' He disregarded his semi-nakedness in front of the exotic creature and smiled at her as if he had to win her affections.

'You remember my name.' She smiled with leisurely coyness. 'That pleases me.'

He drank deep of the heady wine, his eyes never leaving her teasing mouth. In an attempt to gain enlightenment from the strange dream, he murmured, 'I can't imagine I come here simply for your pleasure. What do you want from me?'

'Not from you, it is *you* I desire.' Her moist lips made a seductive pout. 'Come, let us get more comfortable.' Taking his hand, she stroked it as she guided him towards the pavilion edge.

The scenery had transformed to a forest amid lush hills and in the far distance a great lake sparkled like a jewel in the grey night. On a low intricately carved bed, Nya lounged. White silk coverings contrasted with her tan voluptuous form; she bade Jett lay beside her.

He eased onto the luxuriant cushions and despite his actions, he said, 'I can't keep coming here.'

'There's no reason you cannot. It is natural that we should be together.' Her voice was sleek and a tender hand caressed his chest. She gazed down at him with open lust as her fingers moved up and down his lithe muscled torso. 'This is where you belong.'

He sensed the confused hesitancy in his thoughts and he strained to comprehend what was taking place. Entangled in the patterns of his spirit he knew the encounter was erroneous, but so far it was indiscernible as to why. He stared at her with bafflement. 'You speak in riddles. Tell me plainly what you want.'

She overlooked his perturbed state and concentrated her hand on his firm abdomen. 'You were born to rule and I am going to make it happen. I will serve you, every desire you want in every way.'

His fingers drew delicate circles over her shoulder and he whispered by her hair. 'Rule?' He gave a mocking chuckle. 'What shall I rule?'

'Nothing shall be held back from you,' she crooned, 'your throne shall be of the Midnight Order, but first…' her hand smoothed downwards. 'I must be called to the world of flesh where I can be closer to you.'

Jett's hand stopped on her warm skin and his throat tightened with apprehension. 'I'm not sure I know how.'

'Do not be concerned, you will know when the time comes.'

He continued frowning with a vague realization he needed to move and quickly before it was too late.

She kissed his chest, running her tongue over his skin. 'You are brooding on that girl. It is for your own benefit that I shall inform you - she has bypassed you and chosen another.' Her fingers walked down to his groin and moved with a discerning skill.

Jett paused on her odd words yet could do nothing to halt her seduction. Her persistent caresses and feathery kisses aroused him and excited equal passion from his body, but her reference to a girl was jarring. 'Hellier?'

'She has been with her lover. He has her heart, and she will use him for all she can get. As is the way with a woman like that.' Her tongue grew firm on his skin and arrived at her destination. 'Unlike her, I will never betray you.'

Her assertion brought a sad awareness of the reality of Hellier's relationship with Dario. Nya was right; Hellier was different and a distance was between them.

Disappointment pierced his heart like a knife. He was incapable of tossing away the grave sense of betrayal.

Nya whispered through languid kisses, 'But I am here, and together, loneliness will be far from us…'

Jett responded to her ardent searching mouth with new abandonment. A surge of turbulent passion burned its way from an angry place inside and he gave himself over to it.

'That's right, consume me,' Nya's sultry voice caressed his skin, 'You don't need them. Take me. I will be everything you need.' Her last words were swallowed up by the heat of his desire. Oblivious to any meaning that might be beyond her words, Jett obeyed her command.

51 - Dark Corner

Above all, guard your heart from deception
For it is the fount of your Ethos

Empyrean Ascension

The Kin woke to a frosty morning and much grumbling at the idea of getting up at such an early hour. They organised their belongings, and packed in a rushed breakfast of bread from the night before and cold mince cakes from the inn. Once outside, Jett saw the Sentinels coming up the street, but now only two. He busied himself with his horse's strapping, but gave them a curt nod. 'Good morning.'

The holy man looked at him with a stormy expression. 'I wish it were.'

Jett mounted. 'Did you have trouble with your business last night?'

'We lost one of our own.' The man's face reddened from long held anger. 'The hell spawn escaped us and she did not do it alone. Another of her kind was waiting and they murdered our holy priest.'

The other Sentinel walked to the back of the wagon. With a clean sweep of his arm, he yanked the canvas wide.

'What do you think you're doing?' Fury exploded on Jett's face and he turned Thunder around to confront him.

The empty wagon did not wipe away the Sentinel's look of suspicion. Ignoring Jett, he looked at the knight. 'Strange. She's not there.'

'Of course there's nobody there,' Jett growled.

The leader of the Sentinels scrutinized Jett. 'I see. Well, my regards to you.' The men marched away.

The wagon traveled awhile before the girls felt safe to reappear. 'Another witch to roam the earth.' Shiarn leaned back, releasing the girls' hands and the three appeared suddenly.

'Lucky you hid us in time.' After some moments of consideration, Earona said, 'But just think, he actually thought she was in here. Peculiar. She was going to certain death and she is freed, and they even manage to kill one of them.' She stopped talking, noting Mara was in one of her sullen moods and Shiarn was duplicating Mara's expression. It was going to be one of those days. Earona turned to Shiarn and placed herself across from her. 'Shiarn?'

Shiarn raised suspicious eyes at her.

'Have you noticed everyone's in a foul mood?'

Shiarn folded her arms. 'Jett certainly is or are you referring to someone else?'

Jett had bitten Shiarn's head off earlier when she disappeared to use the outhouse. It was unpleasant and Shiarn said as much to him, but he went on insensitively. 'You and Jett were extremely prickly this morning. I can't believe yesterday he was so cheery and now he's a monster.'

Shiarn's back stiffened against the compartment. 'I don't know what his excuse is, but...' *I've a lot on my mind.*

'Not only Jett. Marcus is not talking to me and Hellier's gone quiet as well.' She paused with a sudden frown. 'And what's on your mind?'

Shiarn grabbed Earona's hand and placed it on her belly. *Open yourself up.*

Mara watched the scene with a surprised gaze.

Earona felt the life force reposition itself and she whispered, 'From that man?'

'He was not a man,' Shiarn spat out. 'Most likely he has done it to scores of women.'

Earona's face paled with the appalling thought of how true that might be.

Shiarn breathed deeply. 'You have to help me.' *You have to take it out of me.*

'I...' The annihilation of life was the one thing Earona had sworn she would never do and for a Fáerinn woman to wish it was scandalous. 'I... have to think about it.'

Sudden tears dulled Shiarn's green eyes. 'Are you saying you would stand by and watch me birth his evil into the world?' She sobbed into her hands. 'I'd rather die.'

~ * ~

They passed slender trees and sloping hills as the morning waned and the sky cleared. Despite the warm day, Jett's cold disposition remained. He couldn't shake his bad mood, and it worsened as the day progressed. He couldn't determine where it came from, except everything bothered him; the Kin's chatter and the tedious journey. He rode on ahead, putting more distance between them. He reasoned to himself, he wanted space, but it was more than that. The revelation about Hellier and Dario grieved him, and created a festering wound he couldn't conceal. He retreated into his brooding thoughts and let his mind escape into his dreams, and the woman who now consumed him. If only he could forget Hellier's betrayal, and all of them, he would have peace.

But, they were there, following, and demanding his attention. They stared into his back with their inquisitive thoughts, but he shut them out. Their persistent murmuring increased his irritation. But, he wasn't going to disclose his private ruminations.

Engrossed in his dream-vision, he was startled by Hellier coming alongside him. He was avoiding them, but her most of all. Keeping his eyes ahead, he had no wish to speak with her.

She spoke with a nervous guilty titter. 'You really shouldn't be this unhappy.'

He snapped his head around and his dark gaze penetrated her light-hearted thoughts with a storm of chaotic emotions. 'And why shouldn't I be?'

She took an anxious breath. 'What does that mean?'

Despising her brazen interference, he cut her off with a warning. 'Nothing you need to be concerned about.'

She retorted, 'I'm asking because you're being a dick—'

'So you've come to insult me.' He pitched his voice with careless abandonment, 'Shall I respond in kind, you betrayed me - I know what you did with Dario. You're a liar. You used us and him, and where is he now?'

Hellier, her face reddening, gripped her horse's reins. 'What in hell's name—'

'No denying it.' Finished with the conversation, he growled, 'Opening your legs and letting him lay you for all your worth. As much a harlot as the other one.'

Hellier sucked in her breath and let her horse stop. 'You bastard. You can go to hell!'

'And you can leave me alone.' Jett's eyes crimped with satisfaction at her discomfit, but he could not smile. He stepped up Thunder's pace and moved further ahead, hoping to prevent any more unwanted conversation.

Hellier pulled right back, passing Marcus, and Keanan driving the wagon. Marcus, unable to catch her eyes, looked across to Keanan, with creased brow. 'What was that all about?'

Keanan watched Jett with distrust. 'I don't know, but I don't like it. Jett's had moods before, but that was beyond appalling.'

'How could he speak to Hel like that?'

'I will speak with him later,' said Keanan. 'Maybe he's truly upset about it.'

Marcus asked, 'Did she and Dario *really*?'

'Yes.' Keanan sighed. 'Now everyone knows.'

~ * ~

Jett's angry outburst wasn't a surprise to Mara. She sensed the difference in him since the morning. His eyes had darkened and a cruel expression had settled on his face. She had seen that type of face numerous times on those who worked for her mother. In the instance he looked at her, his eyes bored into her as if he knew what was in her soul, even more than she knew. A malicious presence was forming around him and she was glad she wasn't out there with him. With his look of wicked intent, it reminded her of the vision they shared. She was suddenly afraid that somehow that evil was now manifesting in him.

Even Earona and Shiarn stopped talking to listen.

'Son of a whore, how dare he?!' Shiarn growled.

Earona cried, 'I'm going to reprimand him myself.'

Shiarn snapped, 'Face him when he's like that?! No. You'd only make it worse.'

'Maybe, but...' Earona turned back to Shiarn and put her arm around her shoulders. This time Shiarn did not fight her off. 'Honestly, I know you don't want this inside you, I'm...'

Shiarn watched her with expectancy.

'It's… being able to heal is about life not death.' Earona's eyes softened. 'Tonight I'll talk to him.'

'I wouldn't if I were you.' Mara regretted her words as soon as she spoke them. But Earona always had that effect on her.

Earona stared wide-eyed. 'What makes you say that?'

'Just a guess.' Mara pressed her lips together. 'I'm not going anywhere near him.'

Shiarn eyed her with sobriety. 'That's quite foreboding. Do you know more about it than you are saying?'

The redhead was smarter than Earona, and Mara did not want to be on the end of her questioning. She evaded her scrutiny. 'Don't you think so too? … something is making him… angry. Like all of you are angry.'

Shiarn's frown deepened.

'There's no need for us to be that way.' Earona glanced between them and her eyes rested on Shiarn. 'How about we talk about something more pleasant? Tell me more about Jonas?' She made a cozy nest for herself amongst the bedrolls.

Distracted by her curiosity, Shiarn's cheek tinged with joy. 'Jealous, are we?'

Earona said, 'I admit.'

Her eyes darted from Mara to Earona, playfully. 'I'll tell you a little, but not everything.'

'As long as it's the good parts.'

~ * ~

Despite Ethan's misgivings about Kenric's plan, he woke contemplating the possibility of it working. There was no opportunity to speak with Kenric or Loc as they were herded into the dining hall. Not until they were back under the mountain, digging and hammering, did Ethan have a chance to speak his mind. While he swung at the solid rock with a heavy hammer, he said to Loc, 'What do you think?'

Loc pounded at the stone, breaking it apart with the blows. 'About the mad scheme?'

'Think it could be done?'

There was a long pause before Loc stopped to look at him. 'It's insane. It looks as if they'd be walking into their graves.' He continued pounding once more. 'But they'd follow you in.'

Ethan thought on the absurdity of the Harn wanting to follow him when he was scared out of his wits.

'And I will to…'

Loc's words startled him and he remained quiet.

As the day wore on, he observed the change in the Harn's attitude towards him. Quiet and reserved and less like the men he had met at the Rocks. The very short man, Morgan, stopped teasing him about his great size, and even Corma, who hated foreigners, eased his rough talk towards him. Even bad-tempered Branan spared him an uncharacteristic smile. Ethan did not like it and he was not comfortable with Loc, their leader, turning to him to provide guidance.

After hours of hard labour the men stopped for a water break. They sat in the dull light of the torches, talking softly in the muted silence. Ethan took the opportunity to walk down the passage within sight of the guards to study a wooden frame supporting the rock ceiling. The dark iron stone was not fragmented but in some parts was loose.

Kenric came up beside him. 'It could fall any day.'

'You sound hopeful?!' Ethan shook his head with shock. He turned to watch the guards at the table, or standing around, in ignorant bliss, presuming they were safe. In their sane reasonable world they were. How could they possibly consider men would attempt escape underground?

Kenric tossed his shoulders back and under his breath, said, 'We could always kill them.'

'No,' Ethan responded, 'there might be a way to bring it down.' But it still wouldn't guarantee the lives of the guards, but at least it wouldn't be murder.

'You thought about it.' Kenric nodded, giving Ethan a satisfied grin.

Ethan glared at him; he was right.

'You two get back to work,' Moss, the pirate guard, shouted and the two headed back into the tunnel.

Later that evening, Ethan sat with the Harn to discuss the escape proposition from Kenric. He had spent much of the day cogitating it, but he was reluctant to make a firm decision. The whole expedition seemed foolhardy at best and a death trap at worst. But he also came to realize if Kenric and his men were to escape they would all need to participate.

Loc's men discussed it amongst themselves; some fervently opposed while others were eager to take the chance and others had not yet been swayed either way. Ethan was unsure where he stood. He could not rationalize placing himself in such a risky predicament, and putting his trust in an old man he did not know was like asking for trouble. Kenric trusted Daskar, but Ethan did not know Kenric either, Loc he knew longer by a few days and Loc he trusted yet Loc was putting his trust in him. Everything was wrong and backward and he had no idea what was the wisest course of action. The Harn stopped talking and watched him.

Colour spread up Ethan's neck and into his face, and he stared at the rough faces of grown men, trapped. Looking over to Kenric's group, he lowered his voice, 'It sounds like the daftest thing I've ever heard.' The Harn nodded, appearing to agree on that notion, and he continued, 'I know you all want to get out of here, and I do too, but you have to make up your own mind. You can't be relying on me to make a decision for you.' He hoped for more response than the unyielding expressions he was currently receiving.

'I agree it is lunacy, but,' Loc paused, 'they believe in it.'

'What about you, Ethan?' The quiet redheaded, Conley, asked, 'What will you be doing?'

These Harn were sneaky, Ethan thought as he took a thoughtful breath. 'I don't want to be responsible for your lives.'

The men spoke to each other in their own tongue, Harnon. Ethan stared at them with frustration.

Loc said, 'They will go if you go because you can't go without them. If you stay, they will stay.'

'Loc,' Ethan whined, 'I want them to do what they want to do.'

'This is what they want.' Loc stared at him with puzzlement.

'Duan-Shai,' the old Harn, Arail, called out.

Ethan scowled and waited for an explanation

Loc flushed. 'An old name. One who has light, like a beacon.' More Harn repeated the name.

'Whatever it means,' Ethan had the impression there was more to it, 'you men could be walking to your deaths.'

A devious glint in his grey eyes, Stannar asked, 'You've decided?'

Ethan's chest slumped with a great sigh. He stared at their faces with the unique tattoos etched over their cheeks and foreheads. He didn't know all their names, but it seemed they all knew him. 'I want to get out of here.' He paused. 'But I'm not looking forward to going that way. I may have some skill at lifting objects, but I can't lift a bloody mountain.'

Loc chuckled. 'We're behind you '

After the Harn spoke together and men found their beds, Kenric and Ethan sat together. Kenric asked, 'What do you think?'

'How far in is the secret tunnel?'

'We broke through to a huge natural chamber. It's in about a hundred feet. We have seen tunnels there, but now it takes too long for us to work without our absence being noticed.' Kenric's eyes brightened with excitement. 'We have to leave soon.'

'Right.'

'Some of us have been cutting away over the tunnel arch. I think the best idea is burying the main chamber.'

'I agree.' Ethan dropped his voice. 'We cause it to collapse. Maybe I can help.'

'Brilliant,' Kenric interrupted, 'regardless if it kills the guards, they will assume we are dead.' He laughed loudly, waking nearby sleepers.

Kenric's preoccupation with the death of the guards gave Ethan some concern.

'Can you really do it?'

The rocks in the chamber would need some budging and shaking. 'I could shift them enough. I think.'

Overcome with enthusiasm, Kenric clenched Ethan's arm. 'I knew you'd be the answer.'

'Hold on.' Ethan bounced up, knocking his head on the top bunk. 'I'm not about to just do what you say, or lead this daft escape.'

'Indeed.' Kenric lifted his nose. 'We all work together, using our resources and we'll start tomorrow—'

Ethan raised his voice, 'Tomorrow?'

'Why not?'

'You need to assess the supplies, and I'll check the chamber again.'

'You may be right.' Kenric pressed his finger to his lips in contemplation.

They did not spend much more time talking before Ethan was trying to get to sleep. Again his dreams were dark holes between periods of waking minutes. At least in his dreams he got to wake up.

~ * ~

The rest of the journey Jett avoided conversation. If anyone approached him, his responses were abrasive and veiled warnings he wanted to be left alone. Hellier stayed away from him, and it suited him more than he thought possible. His bad temper continued gnawing at his sensibilities, till he had no control over the irrational rage.

A couple of hours before sundown, they reached Ginty's farmstead, where they hoped to spend the night. Jett's distemper had not diminished. It had blown up into an obvious ill-will towards his Kin. With no explanation, except his anger over Hellier, he was surly and unwilling to speak to anyone.

Keanan spoke to Ginty, a tall middle-aged man with a long beard, standing outside his house. Ginty pointed out his barn down the road in a shallow valley, and generously provided them with half a dozen eggs and some potatoes they could use. In exchange Keanan gave him some coin for his hospitality.

The end of the day had finally come and Jett was reluctant to spend the night with his Kin. It degenerated into sullen silences with little talking if any at all.

The only one to look him in the eye, Earona gave him a reprimanding frown. 'Jett, you can't go on like this and we can't take any more of your foul mood.'

Tired of his own antagonistic replies, Jett glared. He lacked any ability to put up with her probing. Ready to explode with irritation, and to prevent himself from reacting physically, he left the barn. Earona chased after him, calling his name. Fed up with her self-righteous arrogance, and their accusing stares, he walked out into the night.

Earona peered into the darkness. She could see the walled field, but no sign of Jett. He probably had no wish to be found.

Marcus came up behind her. 'He's not there?'

Startled by his sudden presence, she swiveled to face him. 'I want to talk to him.'

'He needs more than a talking to.'

She held her tongue, deciding there was already too much hostility between them all to begin something with Marcus. 'Someone has to.'

His usual merry brown eyes were anxious. 'I...' He stuttered, 'it's...'

A breeze blew her dark hair around her chin. She gave him a perplexed look and tilted her head in a questioning way. 'Yes?'

'It's a nice night out...'

She glanced up at twinkling stars peeking through grey clouds. 'Really? ...is something wrong?' Her forehead creased with worry. 'You're not acting like your normal self.'

'I aren't?'

She stared at him with humorous suspicion and stroked his cheek with her finger. 'You're taking an interest in the night sky. I wonder if falling ill in Floris affected you, perhaps it's given you a…' a sweet smile moved her lips '…softer edge.'

He frowned and colour spotted his cheeks. 'I didn't fall sick, I was poisoned, there's a difference.'

Her hand fell away, but she continued grinning at his awkwardness. 'I assume your body was strong enough to withstand such a thing.'

'I did.' The colour in his face did not abate. 'Thanks for caring.'

'I expect the whole thing was frightening.'

Marcus grumbled, 'It was.'

Earona lifted her hand, hiding a giggle. 'At least you admit it, but I meant for Jett and the others.'

'I'm sure *they* were worried about me.' Scowling, he turned away.

Catching onto his muscular upper arm, but not even close to circling it, she was surprised by the warmth of his skin. 'You know I do. Besides, I was worried about you the whole time.' She blushed. 'And everyone.' His glowing eyes pierced hers with a weighty seriousness and she felt compelled to add, 'You did fine without me.'

He faced her square on without responding.

She became nervous under his potent gaze. 'And maybe you are a little softer, what's the harm in that, at least you're not acting like an insane scoundrel trying to lose every friend he ever had.'

Marcus reached for her hand and held it. 'No, never.'

His touch was a shock that caused her skin to tingle to life. In the same moment, she spied Jett coming towards the barn and her hand fluttered from Marcus' hot grasp. 'Jett!' She waved.

Jett gave her a withering glimpse.

It would be harder talking to him than she thought. She gave a rushed smile to Marcus and sped to catch Jett up. 'Can we talk?'

'If you have to.' He walked away from her and back around the side of the barn.

Earona trailed after, trying to keep up. 'There's something wrong with you.' Through the shadows, she looked into his clouded eyes and shivers ran down her spine. It was not the Jett she knew.

'I'm exactly how I should be.'

Earona stared wide-eyed. Apparently he had no idea he was being mean, or was he intentionally speaking to everyone in a horrendous manner? After all they had been through it was hard to believe. 'It's Shiarn…' she went on half-heartedly, unsure if he should be privileged with the information, '…she has been Blessed.'

His eyes remained cold and distant. 'Nothing to do with me.'

'How can you say that?' Mortified by his heartlessness, she realized something truly was amiss within him.

'What do you want me to do?'

Why won't you talk to me? What's going on in your head? Receiving no response from his thoughts, she said in a huff, 'That's fine. I'll take care of it.'

'You do that.'

'Fine then.' She stormed off without a backward glance and Jett let her leave. She stamped into the barn, attempting to slam the large door behind her that came to a slow stop. Her rigid body shook with anger.

Keanan stood with authority and put his hands on his waist. 'I'll talk with him.'

She reached her hand up and placed it on his chest. 'I don't think it will do any good.' Recalling Mara's words from earlier in the day, she shook her head. 'Something is wrong… he had no thoughts and his eyes seemed...' she paused, 'darker.'

'He certainly has been saying terrible thoughtless remarks,' Keanan said, 'I wonder what we should do?'

Seth suggested. 'Don't speak to him at all. It only seems to incur his wrath no matter how trivial.'

'He can go drop dead for all I care,' Hellier plonked herself down beside Seth at the fire, her face still consumed with rage.

'I agree.' Mara sat by the fire nearly the whole evening and if not there, she stuck by Hellier or Keanan's side. 'And no one better make me be alone with him, because I refuse.'

Keanan said, 'Perhaps when we get to Sommerlea we can discover why he is in this state.'

'And we better do it fast. I don't think I can handle much more of this Jett,' said Earona. 'Kean, can I talk to you.' She led Keanan away amidst curious stares from the others. 'I wanted to talk with Jett, but that's impossible.'

Keanan sat on a square of hay. 'Something is troubling you?'

'Shiarn has been Blessed.' Her arms folded, she paced in front of him.

He gasped. 'What a time for it.'

'That's not all. She wants me to do away with it.'

His face reddened. 'I assume it's from her wicked ordeal.'

Sighing heavily, Earona dropped beside him.

'You're not happy with doing it?'

Earona growled a whisper, 'You're assuming I'm going to do it?'

Keanan did not hide his surprise. 'You mean you'd consider not doing it?'

Earona pondered his discernment in silence.

His tone changed to a kind-hearted understanding. 'View it in a different light. Shiarn is probably deeply distressed. See it as an act of healing not an act of destruction. Take away the ailment, the disease, and Shiarn's mind will be free of this pain.'

'It's none of those things, it's a life spirit. But…' Earona looked up into his caring eyes and for the first time began to think about doing Shiarn's will. 'She sees it as a great evil done to her. As much as I hate it, you could be right.'

'How could we expect her to carry around a reminder of what was done to her?'

'I've never killed before.'

'It depends on your perception.' Keanan gave her shoulders a warm hug. 'You only needed to talk with someone.'

Earona nodded and slouched with sudden weariness. 'What do you think is wrong with Jett?'

'I don't know, but I'm beginning to form my suspicions.'

'I want the old loveable Jett back, not this mean arrogant arse.'

'Loveable Jett, was there ever such a thing? However, you would have been surprised at how well he dealt with things in Floris, considering how short tempered he can be.' Keanan sighed. 'And now this. It's disappointing.'

Jett had not been seen by anyone, and he could not be found outside. After the Kin ate, they settled down in the hay to sleep without him. Earona's back was warmed by Mara, and Marcus lay across from her. She smiled at his shining eyes, and admired his suntanned face.

'Earona?'

Her eyes flicked open.

'Have you noticed it's getting difficult to read each others' thoughts?'

She had and she strained to hear Marcus' Ethos. 'I can't do it. I'm alone in my head.'

'A strange feeling,' he replied, quietly, 'Maybe it will pass by morning...'

~ * ~

With the Kin behind him and fading from his thoughts, Jett's night time escapades consumed his mind as if he had nothing else to live for. He needed release into that tranquil sanctuary and be drawn into Nya's embrace. Her face was ever before him, and everything and everyone was an ugly reflection compared to knowing her. A pit of self-gratification was swallowing him, and nothing could prevent the fall. His self-righteous attitude granted him the permission to indulge in the licentiousness and he was damning the consequences, and everything around him.

The natural spaces through the woodlands navigated his path. The air was chilly, but he heeded it not, and stepped recklessly, pushing past branches. Irrespective of his excellent vision, he stumbled and grabbed a branch to steady himself. Puffs of steam hastened from his tight chest, and his cold hands latched onto trees. He walked without direction, not seeing the moon or hearing the chatter of nocturnal beasts. His vision was claimed solely by a beauty the world could not produce. Absorbed by her erotic and pleasing touch, nothing else would satisfy. He would lie where he collapsed, and dream. Once more be overtaken by her affection.

He fell in a hidden patch on a gentle slope. A spreading tree sheltered his back, and stars peeked through the silvery slender leaves. He denied his wretched guilty thoughts drifting to the surface and cast himself into the familiar safety of his bitterness. This old emotion was encompassing and oppressively real. Oblivious to the woodlands' peace, he shut in his raging thoughts. Desiring to leave the despair of his earthly life, he would enter the divine tranquility Nya lavished on him.

An unfamiliar and discordant voice entered his mind. Its demands continued overriding any sense he might have made from the situation. Throughout the day the voice increased in volume and power, its message precise; its adamant wish, the breaking of the Kin and the elevation of Jett's own destiny. His trembling hands clutched at his throbbing chest and he moaned at the notion the Kin would end as if he had no part in their demise and they had already ceased to be. With unknown inner strength, he resisted the idea he would bring an end to them, but the turmoil gave rise to fear, fear of the persuasion of the voice. On top of that, and for some unexplainable reason, the young girl intrigued him, as if she held some secret knowledge of him and the dream. She kept away from him and out of his grasp, and now that he was away from her, he was oddly relieved. The idea of taking her with him, nearly pushed him over the edge.

As a last act of his conscious will he considered the Kin's welfare, and even the girl, and decided it best to leave and keep away from them in case the voice proved more powerful than his bond. He wrapped his cloak around him and nestled into the dewy floor, protected by a root infested overhang, to find comfort in Nya's embrace.

~ * ~

Nya became more radiant each time Jett set eyes on her, and once he did, he could not remove them easily. She lounged on luxurious crimson cushions on the floor, her dark bosom visible through the flexed cloth of her dress. With a coy smile, her lips hinted at sweetness to follow. 'My love, you spend too much time wandering the countryside. I missed you.'

Jett knelt beside her, yearning for her deepening fulfillment. She exposed her slender thigh and his hand glided up the silken skin of her leg. They kissed like ardent lovers parted for too long. He breathed against her lips, 'That time means nothing to me.'

Nya's smile lit her eyes with avid desire. 'Soon we shall be together forever.'

Her comment evoked a ripple of disquiet. It passed and he looked to the giant opening of the pavilion where a glorious night sky shone against the slanting green hills, similar to the previous night except a farmstead was below. In the distance, grey clouds cast a shadow on the horizon, heralding some approaching gloom, but of what he was unable to decipher. He stared blankly not possessing the words to express his thoughts.

Nya's delicate fingers brought his chin near. He lost himself in her rich sea green eyes. The colour changed to a lighter hue. She stroked his cheek. 'Those outsiders should have been your servants. Instead they despise you and will plot your downfall.'

Her statement made sense, but he had no words to explain why he should think this. 'Who is the girl?' The girl with the gold-fire hair, and amber eyes remained in his mind, even in the dream.

Nya's lip pressed together and she studied him. 'She… is a means to an end. To manifest the fulfillment of the dream.'

He creased his brow. 'You are the dream.'

'Oh, how much you delight me.' Her smile bedazzled him. 'However, it is unfortunate you did not bring her, in fact, I am disappointed.'

Her pout saddened him. 'I wondered at the notion.'

'Do not worry, you shall fetch her soon enough. In fact, she will come to you.'

'It would not be unpleasant to see her again.'

Her back stiffened. 'I see nothing special in her, except what she offers as her service.'

He gazed out at the sky in reflection of the young girl, her name was fading from his mind. 'What is her great skill?'

'Why, she is the Summoner of Souls, and you are the Master.' She gave him a peculiar look that he did not know the answer

The names unsettled him for some reason. 'Summoner of Souls…'

'My love, let's not talk on her anymore. She is not here, but I am.' She sweep her hand across his forehead clearing his hair from his eyes. 'We shall be finished with those others so you can be free. You know what needs to be done?'

'Find you?'

'Yes, and more. We must hope that it will not be too much longer.' Nya's lips brushed against his ear. 'Please take food.' She picked a glazed piece of fruit and popped it in his mouth. Overly sweet, the fruit dissolved on his tongue and he had another. Her hand moved across his chest and the other looped about his neck. 'They will have nothing to do with you now. The weaklings have no power to offer you. It will be a simple thing to eliminate them.'

Her statement hit a chord and he sighed, stiffening in her embrace. His thoughts on the matter dropped out of mind and he enjoyed the heightened sensation of her fingers on his body.

'You don't need them.' Her words came between the perfectly placed kisses on his chest. 'I will take care of your needs and when the Summoner manifests the Spell of Life, I will come.'

He frowned with apprehension. 'Will she do this?'

'The Summoner follows the Key which you already have.' She smiled up at him. 'Then you will have all you desire.' She devoted her attention to the task at hand and they spoke no more for some time.

52 - Lost Sight of the Road

Life is unpredictable and calamity gives no consideration to circumstance.

The Sleeping Sword

Throughout the morning, Ethan discovered that his Gift was not operating as normal. Amid grave anxiety, he would test it on something small, and without a doubt, it was getting weaker each time. Without the use of his power, he had to shift heavy stones with his bare strength. The fading of his Ethos disturbed him, and added to this new dilemma, Kenric desired to leave as soon as possible.

That evening he took Loc to the far side of the cell where the area was free of sleepers. 'You know when I helped Branan, my ability was a lot stronger…'

Worry shadowed Loc's face. 'I wondered about that.'

Ethan flexed his fingers and muttered, 'Something's not right.'

Loc creased his bushy brows in bewilderment. 'With you?'

Ethan shrugged. 'It's never happened before.'

'Are you ill?'

'I don't think it's that.'

Loc questioned, 'You think you'll get 'em back?'

'I don't know.' Ethan tried shifting a stone outside the cell. It rose a few inches, but no more. He considered it was linked to his Kin and he feared what might have happened to them.

'You think you can still bring down the tunnel?'

Ethan frowned at the sleeping men. 'I think it's possible, but…'

'Kenric is prepared to go with or without your power.' Loc squinted toward Kenric deep in sleep.

Ethan remained in quiet thought. He just didn't want to go into a dangerous place as a normal man.

'Maybe it will come back to you.'

'Did you look at their supplies?'

Loc's eyes sparkled in the darkness. 'Done. They need more, so we are going to strap some of that hard bread to our bodies tomorrow.'

Ethan nodded, so preoccupied was he with the loss of his Gift he failed to notice the Harn's absence during the day.

'They've found a big tunnel,' Loc said, 'and a large cavern beyond. It almost makes me think it's possible.'

Ethan landed a hand on his shoulder. 'At least you sound encouraging.'

~ * ~

Ethan woke sluggishly the next morning, and moved from his mattress with stiff limbs. The first thing he did was attempt moving something. His cup wavered off the ground by inches. A pitiful sight.

Supplies had been brought over in the night by the boys, and earlier, while the cavern was quiet, a few men concealed them under their clothes. Ethan marveled at how the pirates did not notice the missing stock.

Herded by the guards, the men headed towards the canteen. Lost in a cloud of exasperating problems, Ethan finished eating and pushed away from the table, oblivious to the man he collided with.

In return, Garutz shoved Ethan and sneered, 'Look at the dirty rat daring to touch me.'

Ethan snarled under his breath, 'Don't waste my time.'

'You think you can say that and walk away?'

'I'll say more than that.'

Garutz' fist met with Ethan's face. Ethan gave back the same. The nearest Harn caught hold of Ethan's arms. Pirates came and hauled Ethan and Garutz outside. They threw them to the ground amid jeering spectators exchanging bets.

Ethan got to his feet, suddenly losing the thrill for any fighting. Garutz came at him, having no such care he was on show. Ethan blocked his strike and leaped back with caution. Garutz rushed him again. Ethan remained calm, not wanting to throw himself into a blood match.

'You just a coward,' Garutz growled.

Ethan continued to dodge his advances. 'I'm no-one's pet.' Pirates started to lose patience and shouted obscenities.

'They'll whip you if you don't play.'

The statement made Ethan pause. Garutz threw a sharp punch to his stomach, doubling him over. Ethan attempted standing, but Garutz laid a kick to his side. For some reason, Ethan had lost his will to care.

'Enough!' A voice shouted through the crowd and Garutz was pushed away. With a cruel stare, Daegal raged, 'You bloody haulers! Purposely damaging my property!' He turned to his pirate comrades. 'Get out of here, you fiendish scavengers!'

A long haired pirate stepped up to Daegal, his yellow shirt bright against his billowing navy pants. 'You gone cold, Daegal. My man could pummel yours' to guts. The coin's there, any time you're ready.' The man walked away laughing, with Garutz following after.

Daegal spat on the ground and mumbled, 'Dirty mago, Masso.'

Ethan was led back to the chamber, now empty of prisoners. Daegal said through the bars, 'Those bilge bastards! I won't have my workers sabotaged like that. I'll have black marks and I will not forget it. If that happens again you will be out,' he pointed his finger at Ethan and flicked it at the main doorway. 'The only reason you are still here is they say you are a good worker. The only reason.'

'It's that bastard Garutz.'

'Everyone here is a bastard.' Daegal's expressive hands whirled in the air. 'I am a bastard, you are a bastard, aren't we all bastards, but I am the head bastard and I will make your life a worse hell than that bloody pot scum. We are the best and I'll not have you bring me down.'

'I hear you,' Ethan growled with more pain than anger.

'Respect, that's what I ask for,' Daegal huffed, 'and I will get it. Don't think you've gotten off either, I'll send a guard to fetch you.' He walked from the cavern and Ethan heard the front gate clang shut, leaving him in the silent cavern with his dismal thoughts.

~ * ~

Keanan woke to a drab grey dawn. A blur of mist shaded the farm fields, even the woodlands were devoid of colour. A short amount of time elapsed before the sad discovery was made. Jett was not outside nor was Thunder tethered with the other horses.

Breakfast was eaten in gloomy silence as Jett's departure took effect. Few words were spoken between the Kin and none of them seemed adequate to describe their heartache. Too add to their dilemma, they could no longer communicate through their thoughts. A distressing turn of events with no explanation in sight.

They packed up with haste with all their intent on making speed to Sommerlea, as if it could bring a solution or at the least some comfort. Riding past Ginty, Keanan thanked him for his accommodation and enquired if he saw Jett ride by. He had not, and once more they trotted back onto the dirt road.

Now in charge of the wagon, Seth arrayed a map across his lap while guiding the horses and called to Keanan riding alongside, 'Where do you think he is?' Seth gave the woods a grim study.

'At the moment we can assume he has for some reason lost… control.' Keanan scanned the conifers lining the road as if Jett might suddenly appear. 'I'm in charge for the time being, at least until he comes back to his senses.'

'Maybe there's nothing to be in charge of anyway.' A bite was in Hellier's words and she rode with drooping shoulders. 'Maybe we aren't even a Kin anymore.'

'We are still a Kin.' Keanan stared her down. 'It's not just about Mind-Speaking.'

Hellier glared at him. 'I don't like it, it feels…like a prison.'

Keanan gave a heavy sigh and suppressed his underlying anger. 'Let's just get to Sommerlea as quick as we can. Perhaps they will offer some insight to this problem.'

Inside the wagon the subject matter was no different. Jett's departure caused Mara an uneasy dread. On one hand she was relieved he was gone, because she didn't need to hear the mean remarks, or see him staring at her with his dark eyes of malice, but now she wondered where he was and what he was planning. The way he was acting was beyond what she had witnessed of his character. She found it frightening, even more so because Earona and her friends appeared oblivious to the repressive atmosphere. Something unpleasant was brewing around them. The continual bickering between the girls in the wagon was driving Mara mad.

Shiarn stretched her arms above her head, attempting to shift her body. 'I'm not enjoying this ride.'

Earona retorted, 'What is that supposed to mean?'

'You know what I mean.' She waved her hands in exasperation. 'Everything. Jett, you, this…' her hands glanced over her stomach.

Earona tilted her head back and snapped, 'It's not my fault.'

'Did I say it was?! Anyway, did you talk to Keanan?'

'He is in favour.' She paused. 'And I will… think more on it.'

A tense quiet followed and Mara decided to voice her own annoyance. 'Whatever is happening to Jett is affecting all of you in some mystical sense. I'm so fed up by it.'

Earona and Shiarn stared with surprise at her profound insight.

Mara went on, 'You two are testy and irritable. Always arguing, and those outside—'

'We have good reason.' Shiarn sat erect.

'But…' Earona frowned at her. 'How does that explain you?'

Mara had been on edge since the night at Alyesworth. Maybe Jett's descent into madness was affecting her as well? 'It's probably getting to me too. And I'm stuck here listening to it all.'

'And so am I.' Shiarn took an impatient breath.

Earona retorted, 'You're not the only one.'

'Have you decided?' Shiarn said.

Earona narrowed portentous eyes at her. 'I need to meditate and wait for some signs.'

Mara snorted with disdain. 'You never said that to me when I asked.'

'That was different.' Earona glared.

Shiarn stretched forward with outspoken interest. 'What signs?'

'That's personal, however I can say one has happened.' Earona crossed her legs and set a warning gaze on her.

A mischievous smile played on Shiarn's lips. 'What was that?'

Earona's left eye remained shut while the other stared at her. 'Jett.'

'That's not good.'

'I didn't say it had to be good.'

This time Shiarn remained silent.

~ * ~

The day would soon draw to a close with no sign of Jett. Keanan took the map from Seth and studied it. 'We have verged from the main road onto this old byway. It should lead to Parkvale although at some delay.'

Seth reddened at his mistake. 'What do you expect allowing me to direct you? I'm not the best map reader.'

No longer worrying about the map, Seth admired the airy woodland and shrubs of honey yellows along the narrow path. In places, the sun broke through the leafy trees casting bright lengths of magikal colour, otherwise the roadway would have been cold and sombre. The wagon crested a slope and they went down to a flat road that continued through the trees.

A lanky undernourished man walked out to the middle of their path. 'Halt!' His menacing voice boomed. Other men stepped out from hidden places amongst the trees.

Seth pulled up the wagon. Keanan and Marcus stopped alongside the horses.

The man continued in a lazy drawl, 'We've come to collect a chest you stole from a well-to-do duke and while we're at it, give us all your coins and the women in the carriage.'

Marcus dismounted and glanced at the man's leather armour and worn weapon. His lip turned up in disgust. 'You're flamin' crazy.'

An older man, stout of frame, remarked with gruff disdain to the initial speaker, 'You reckon these the ones that have it?'

The first man glowered at Marcus, but to the one on his left, he replied, 'He said they'd be coming this way. Yep, look at 'em, meets the description and there's supposed to be girls in there as well. We'll keep the women alive.' He raised his sword high and brought it down swiftly.

An arrow flew from the trees.

A shocked howl followed. Seth grasped at the arrow embedded in his upper arm. Grabbing Seth's shoulders, Shiarn dragged him down into the protection of the wagon.

Earona felt his wound. It was clean, but the arrow was set deep in his flesh. With nimble fingers, she tugged on it. Seth's anguished cries were too much for her to concentrate.

Shiarn crawled over Mara to the back of the wagon and stole a peek. 'More of them.' Without a backwards glance at the girls, she said, 'I'll go.'

Marcus had taken merited pleasure in killing the man in front, his only dissatisfaction was he did it far too easily. The second man was startled by Marcus' prowess and before he could escape he was thrust through. As Marcus fought, others jumped onto the roadway and into the fray. In between dodging the striking swords of a number of outraged men, Marcus was kept light on his feet by the flying arrows. There was not a thing he could do with the archer except retain dominance over his end of the fight. He had to assume Keanan would use his brains to give a fiery message to the man in the yonder tree.

Keanan fought with unconvincing skill against two poorly armored men. His flames came in unpredictable bursts. He stared down at his hand aghast, unable to comprehend why his Gift was no longer active. He lurched backwards from an arrow in his shoulder, and he growled like a wounded bear. With billowing adrenalin, he used his injured arm to fire up his opponent, shooting off a small flame.

The burley man's tattered clothes caught fire. He ran down the road in a blaze of howling agony.

Keanan swapped his sword to his opposite hand and fortunately, Marcus took charge of his other opponent, leaving him to focus his erratic power into the trees. He forced what little Ethos he had to create fire no bigger than a man's head, and sent it spinning into the tree. The flame lit up the branches. Leaves rustled amid a panicked cry followed by a thump. Keanan responded with a contemptuous yell, 'That will be your last arrow.'

At the back of the wagon, Hellier dismounted, keeping a steady gaze on the two men approaching her. With a grimace, she unhooked her wrist shield from Forest and with a pat sent her horse towards the wagon.

One of the men stepped in. An arrogant sneer appeared after a glance at her sword.

Hellier's sword lit up with flecks of fire. No time to be shocked over her fading power, she took advantage of the man's surprise and dodged his unfocused swiping. Her assailants wore smug grins, and one had the audacity to wink. They had nothing to show for such an attitude. Their sword skills lacked expertise. Although the two together kept her busy.

Blocking with her shield, she struck against the second opponent. Fire crawled up her arm from her partly blazing sword. The bulkier of the two spread his attention between her face and arm. Making the most of his inattention, she dragged her fiery blade along his side in a downward slash. Her opponent chanced a swing, cutting her upper thigh with a skin deep gash. She paced backward, repositioning her impetus, and driving the men to face her head on. The larger man came with a solid defense before gripping his open wound and doubling over in pain.

She disabled him more than she realized, and he was no longer a primary threat. She narrowed her eyes at the one striking hard with unwieldy blows. To her dismay more men were approaching from the forest. One, headed her way, and the other, towards the wagon. She could do nothing unless she wanted enemies at her back. Her leg shuddered with pain she obstinately ignored, and she swiveled to meet them head on. Aiming at the newcomer, her sword flashed and flicked from his block. She stepped in, targeting his chest. Small flames seared his skin, and the sword carved into his flesh. The other man contorted with pain and collapsed onto his knees.

The one still left, persisted with heavy handed blows, appearing to think sword fighting required brute strength and nothing more. She continued springing swiftly on her feet, evading his strikes and stopping his hits with her shield. Fighting the one was a joy after facing the two.

A stabbing pain hit her side, and she gasped with shock. The man gave her no break and she continued dodging step by step, regardless of the agony of her wound.

'Curses! I can't seem to heal him.' Earona laid Seth, now feverish, onto the blankets. With what Ethos she could stir up, she diverted the damage from the injury. No matter what she did, it availed nothing if the arrow was not removed. 'Stay still, I need to pull it out.' Her delicate fingers circled the shaft in preparation.

Seth nodded with a horrified look.

Mara's voice trembled. 'Can I help?'

'Watch the opening.' Earona tugged on the arrow and Seth squealed.

A man's bearded face appeared at the wagon door. Chuckling, he proceeded to climb in with sword in hand.

Mara pushed her palm towards him. 'Alqua-elzat-varan-ezwa.'

Disappearing from view, he landed with a heavy thud.

'Mara!' Earona yelled in shock. 'What did you do? And what did you do to Seth?' Life was drawn from him, enough to make him lose consciousness.

'I…' Mara stared incredulously at Seth's limp body lying across Earona's lap. In the sudden tense moment she forgot how much she relied on life to perform magik. 'Did I do that?'

'We'll talk later.' Earona edged the arrow out of Seth's arm, giving a wry smile. 'It's probably for the best you can't feel this.' She twisted and wiggled it until it was free. Seth moaned and began to stir. Earona said, 'Mara, what's happening out there?'

'Hellier is fighting two men…' Mara looked through the opening. 'I think Shiarn has caught a man.'

Shiarn clutched her jewel dagger in a forthright grip and slipped from the wagon shimmering in and out of visibility. She left Hellier to tackle the three rough looking bandits while she went to the newcomers advancing on the wagon. She had no idea if she had the stomach for killing, but she didn't want to see those in the wagon hurt.

After a brisk glance, she chose the one with a fierce look in his eyes. She locked an arm around his neck and brought him backward to her level. His sword clattered to the ground and he wrestled her arm clamping his airway. The presence of another man behind them startled her. No doubt he could see her outline. With peculiar resolve, she plunged her dagger into the captured man's back, holding it firm in assurance it had reached its mark.

The man behind drew back, his face a twisted mask of horror. The need to vent her rage had passed and she responded with rational thought. Withdrawing her knife, she pressed it into the stubbly skin of his neck. 'Run now and you live.' She steeled herself to dodge if he took a wild swing.

His eyes widened in terror and he took off into the forest.

No more men came through the woods, but the road was scattered with bodies. Hellier dropped to her knees and Marcus took charge of the last of the bandits.

Shiarn walked to the wagon, bypassing the body inert below the end of it. 'Earona, Hellier's wounded. Can you do anything?'

Earona's reply was faint. 'I'll try…'

Shiarn watched Marcus force his sword into his opponent's chest with a ferocity that unnerved her. Following a startling reflection, she realized she carried out a similar act moments ago. The man she killed was crumpled in the roadway. She had no business judging Marcus. Noticing something amiss with the man at her feet, she bent and touched his neck. 'This one's passed out.'

'I'll take care of him.' Marcus' voice was thick and his body tight under his shirt. He had the appearance he would have fought on unceasingly.

Shiarn turned her back on Marcus dragging the man to the edge of the road. A surreal calm encased the road. The violent windstorm had swept through and they rested in the aftermath, exhausted and shaken, but alive, luckily. Sounds of the forest tweaked with mellow ease, and a soft breeze flicked the leaves while birds jumped from branches. The tranquility was tangible.

Shiarn laid Hellier on her side and rested her head on her lap. The knife stuck out between her ribs and she touched it.

Hellier's cry escaped, 'Get it out...' her breath came in short puffs.

A prone man not more than ten feet away attempted to rise and throw his knife.

Shiarn shouted, 'Marcus.'

The man's dagger fell short as a weighty boot came down on his back forcing his face into the hard-packed earth. Marcus kept his foot there until the last of the man's breath passed away.

Bellowing came from the front of the wagon.

Mara wriggled off the dropped flap, supporting a large water flask. 'Earona is trying to heal Keanan,' she said in explanation of the sound and she handed Marcus the water which he took gratefully.

Seth sat on the wagon's edge, holding his bloody shoulder and surveying them. Without a word he meandered into the forest near the front of the wagon.

Earona came around from the other side, her hands smeared with blood. Keanan walked at a slower pace, pulling a piece of dressing around his shoulder, using his teeth and his free hand. Kneeling by Hellier, Earona yanked the knife out and flung it recklessly behind her. She placed her already red hands over more bloodied wounds and attempted with what she had to mend the torn flesh.

Meanwhile Marcus lugged each of the bodies to the roadside. Keanan could give meagre assistance, but he deemed it their responsibility to remove the corpses from the road. After the bodies were strewn with relative neatness, Marcus stopped to quiz Keanan with a look of concealed worry. 'How is your shoulder?'

'I have limited mobility.' Keanan's gloomy expression said it all. 'But it is better than what it was. I'm more concerned about our Gifts diminishing.'

Marcus frowned at his hands clamped into fists.

'This is more serious than I realized.' Keanan recalled the bandit's odd remarks and coupled with Jett's descent into madness, he continued with a disturbed look, 'If he's had anything to do with this.' He clenched his palm with a brooding rage. '...I'll kill him.'

'It could be someone from Floris.' Marcus laid his hand on his good shoulder. 'But if he is somehow involved, he doesn't know what he is doing.'

Keanan shook his head with controlled fury. 'This is more than we can handle.' With all he knew about Jett, it was inconceivable to think he would be coerced into abandoning them, but the truth was he had. Someone was controlling him, it was the only explanation.

Marcus chanced a glance at the others talking amongst themselves. 'It's possible that duke has men looking for us.'

Keanan shook his head, his face burning with fiery anger. 'It doesn't ring true. Why would he know about those in the wagon? And if we were followed, why wait so long?'

'We don't want them to think it might have been him,' Marcus replied under his breath.

Keanan's expression remained troubled. 'Maybe, but, he should have been here with us and he wasn't.' *That tells us more than we need to know.* He held his makeshift bloodstained dressing and viewed the quiet forest. 'And where is he?'

Marcus gave him a perturbed look. 'Wish I knew.'

Seth approached, a cluster of arrows under his good arm. 'They might be useful.'

'Good idea, Sprout.' Marcus gave him a cheery smile. 'You gave me a fright when you screamed like that.'

Seth nodded at them. 'Gave you a fright?' He attempted joviality, but a smile was absent. 'It hurt more coming out then going in, I can assure you.'

'The sun is going down and we need to camp somewhere,' Keanan said. 'Let's get as far from this as possible.' He forced a smile and said to Seth, 'Are you able to find us a place near water?'

'I will do what I can.' He dumped the arrows in a disorganized heap in the rack on the side of the wagon and walked a little way into the forest.

Keanan and Marcus turned back to the girls. With support, Hellier managed to get to her feet, and breathing heavily she held her bound ribs and examined her burnt sleeve.

Keanan frowned at her with apprehension. 'How was that?'

Hellier gave him a devilish smirk. 'The bastards weren't expecting me to actually fight back.'

Keanan gave her a tight lipped smile, it was obvious how close it had come; the fight would have ended with her on the ground.

'I often have that effect on men,' Hellier added, 'arrogant swine.'

'I hate seeing you with useless limbs.' Earona stood breathlessly. 'Maybe we should have given them a little coin...'

Marcus shook his head. 'I get the feeling they would have tried to do away with us regardless. They fought on until the end, even that one.'

Keanan added, 'He could have asked for mercy or at the least given himself up.'

Shiarn said, 'Simple, desperate, men.'

'We are dangerously weak,' Keanan said, 'My fire is nearly gone.' He stood alone in his thoughts detached from everyone.

Marcus broke the silence. 'Simple men who managed to take three of us out.' His unspoken inference sliced through their illusory triumph.

Hellier planted indignant hands on her hips. 'That might be so, but we did take...' she paused, staring over towards the bodies. 'However many there were... *all* of them.' She watched Marcus' reproachful stare and stated, 'Flamin' arse, you're right, we're useless.'

Seth approached from the roadside. 'I know where we can bed down for the night.'

They drove the wagon about a quarter of a mile down the road and stopped at another laneway more cramped than the previous one. 'It must be used to move livestock.' Seth justified to Keanan giving the road a dubious assessment. 'It leads to a creek.'

The prickly branches of the dense pines hung over the road leaving a minimum of space for the wagon to pass and in addition to the confinement it was bumpy for those inside. Eventually they emerged into a quaint clearing overlooking a flowing shallow brook. The water, spilling down from the Gravett Ranges, gurgled continuously. Across the water, green fields looked lush in the dying light.

'This is lovely, Seth.' Earona climbed from the wagon and breathed deep of the moist air. 'Worth that horrid ride.'

'The tranquility will be a comfort,' said Seth.

The last of the sun's rays gave enough light to wash by the water's edge and settle the horses with fresh meadow grass. They decided against lighting a fire, their position would be exposed for miles across the open fields.

It was a dreary evening and they ate out of necessity and from what little provisions they had remaining. The injured ones were in pain. Saved from serious damage, they still needed substantial healing to prevent their muscles becoming permanently impaired.

They huddled together on the ground in a protective circle, rugged up in cloaks and blankets.

'Whatever is happening with Jett is affecting all of us,' Earona said, 'We've been angry with each other...'

Seth contributed, 'Bad tempered...'

'Grumpy...'

A bleak sadness prevailed over Hellier's face. 'Like Jett.'

'Tomorrow we must get to Sommerlea,' Keanan spoke up. 'Hopefully all is well there and we can recuperate and figure out what is happening to us.'

'If our Avare has lost his mind and gone... crazy...' Seth stopped.

Marcus asked, 'What does that mean for us?'

Shiarn speculated, 'If our head no longer functions properly, we won't be far behind.'

'That does not leave me with a good feeling,' Keanan mumbled.

'We shall see what tomorrow brings,' said Seth.

'I'll be thankful if we can spend this night in relative peace,' Earona said.

~ * ~

Jett woke screaming in a cold sweat. Panting, he sat up, clutching his bare chest and heaving hard to catch his breath. He groaned at the unceasing and debilitating pain surging through his gut and over his body. A vague vision of fighting some wicked entity from the pits of darkness taunted him. The only evidence was the agony and his exhaustion. Something had been ripped out of his body, leaving him empty and with a foreboding sense he had lost some part of himself. He fisted the crimson sheet and his hand rubbed his aching heart. An intricate pattern of symbols was on his chest, and the interconnecting lines flashed like fire before fading away, and for a moment he thought he knew what they meant — but its meaning became illusive, like a dream he couldn't retain. As much as he tried, he couldn't capture the significance of the tattoo. Why would he have such markings on his body, it must be important…

'Jett.' Nya spoke, but not in her usual seductive tone. 'You are ali—'

'Where—' Pain contorted his face, and he glanced up with confusion. 'Where are my—' the word slipped from his tongue and escaped him. He searched his mind for some recollection, but it was absent along with other words and names. Throwing back the sheet, he sat naked on the edge of the bed in the sanctuary.

'My love, you're awake.' Nya's voice changed to a more melodious tone.

'Where…' Trembling, he held his head in his hands. Something wasn't right. Whatever dream he had woken from, left him depleted and without memories.

She sat beside him and drew circles over his back. 'You are here now and that is all that is important. You must forget them, they are not good for you.'

He pushed on his temples and tensed against her ministering touch. Her remark caused him some fear, but he couldn't figure out why. 'Not good… who?'

'The ones in the nightmare.' She kissed his shoulder and up to his neck. 'I'll take away the pain.'

The pain was easing, but he was unusually weak. He let her caress him as he attempted questions to his missing memories. But even contemplation was a chore. The black marble pavilion had a grey tint. He frowned as if seeing it for the first time. Above, the starlight had vanished. Dark clouds converged and cast a dreary glint on the walls.

'Now you are here, we will never be disturbed again.' Her moist lips trailed the skin under his ear.

Forcing out the words, he mumbled, 'But… who are "they"?'

'They are no-one.' She dragged her teeth down his neck with teasing reprimand. 'Don't think any more on it. It is not necessary to be troubled over anything now. I'll look after all your needs. You will never be alone.'

Her serene disposition settled him. Lacking any strength to capture his thoughts, the topic disappeared from his mind and he fell into her embrace with a needy abandonment.

53 - Sommerlea

*A joyous stream flows from a peaceful Heart
Many seek out its tranquil waters.*

Valfaèr, Elements of Arcane Power

Gentle bubbling from the stream roused the Kin to wakefulness. Mist covered the fields, although the bright sky signified a clear day to come. After refilling water flasks and consuming their remaining provisions, they readied the horses in silence.

Seth guided the wagon back onto the road and Keanan rode ahead leaving Hellier and Marcus lagging behind. Little discussion passed between them as they made their way to the next village and onto Sommerlea.

Halfway through the journey, Marcus rode up to Keanan. 'How far is it?'

Despite his glum disposition, Keanan tried to be civil, 'Not far, at least by afternoon and before that we shall travel through Parkvale, however we will not stop there.'

They entered the sprawling town of Parkvale around noon. Bigger than Aylesworth, it appeared better settled with cottages of stone. Incurious people bustled along the main street with carts and animals.

Further down the roadside, Jett was spied standing with a stormy expression. The reins of his horse were loose in his hand, and he glanced over the Kin, but didn't bother to acknowledge them. His face, an unusual pallor transformed to anger.

Keanan had spent the morning brooding over their misfortunes, in particular the conflict that left them wounded, and he was ready for a confrontation. He put his hand up to Seth. The wagon stopped, and he ordered Marcus, 'Don't say a word!' He dismounted Forest and approached Jett.

Scowling at Keanan, Jett turned to leave with his horse, who neighed at the approach of his herd.

With his working arm, Keanan punched Jett in the face, sending him wheeling back. Still boiling with rage, he came at him again, not knowing if he was going to hit or restrain him.

Jett jumped on his horse and turned away.

Waving his fist, Keanan gave a wrath-filled yell, 'You evil bastard!'

Jett rode away through the crowd, disappearing down another road.

Keanan's seething fury did not ease even with the well-placed strike. He mounted Forest and stared at Jett's departure with disapproval, contemplating whether he should pursue him. All his rational plans of speaking to Jett flew by the wayside at the sight of him.

'Are we going after him?' Wide-eyed with disbelief, Seth flicked Sunny and Rose to follow and they started moving again.

'Not at this time. He doesn't want to be found, I'm assuming. We are injured as well.' Marcus stared at him in unabashed astonishment.

'I'm sure I'll probably regret that later,' Keanan rubbed his knuckles, 'but it had to be done.' *If Jett is being controlled*—he sighed. 'If he's being controlled by an evil entity it's best they know we are aware of it. We will not tolerate being attacked. I want him to know.'

~ * ~

Inside the wagon, Shiarn peeked out in hope of seeing Jett in the crowd. She fell back from the edge. 'They've both gone mad!'

Earona scowled at the front of the wagon and Keanan beyond. 'That wasn't the wisest thing to do.'

'To be fair, he did have it coming,' replied Shiarn. 'And if it wasn't Keanan it would have been Hellier.'

'He needs our help,' Earona wailed, 'not fist-fights. He should have been captured.'

Mara squealed, 'You're joking, right?'

'Have him in back with us?!' Shiarn shook her head with fright. 'That would really piss him off.'

'But…' Earona's extreme sadness touched the two girls, 'did you see his face?'

Shiarn's brusqueness changed to a softer quiet. 'Yes.'

'Maybe he needs healing,' Earona said reproachfully, 'He left without a word.'

~ * ~

Not until Parkvale was behind them did Keanan's ill-temper diminish and he smiled sheepishly.

Across from him, Marcus smiled with brazen humor. 'I'd hate to cross you, Kean.'

'He's lucky he couldn't read my thoughts.' His self-righteous attitude dissipated and Jett's abnormal behavior caused more guilt than wrath. 'I don't often get that upset.'

'Fortunately for us.' Marcus looked ahead with a deadpan expression.

Soon the gentle hills tapered and the road became level. After some time a signpost appeared, indicating "Sommerlea" and "Haulton Estate". They trotted on towards the northeast, the direction of Sommerlea. Low-lying woodland fell away and the land opened up revealing flat yellow-green grass and dirty sheep.

They arrived at a wide open gate. Cast-iron letters over the gate signified they were in the right place. Rust confirmed it had not been swung in many years. A high stone wall disappeared into the trees on each side. On the gate pillars were statues of stags.

The roadway led past natural woodland with hints of cultivation. Lindens ruled each side and beyond, and between them, slender Rowans had clusters of flower-fruit beginning to show. Through the trees and bushy pines, rose the grey walls of the castle. The road broke through into a courtyard of flattened earth. Two towers fortified either side of the castle and would grant views of the countryside. Another wing was on the left at an angle to the main structure, and a third smaller tower was attached to that section. To the right, a newer, timber building stood apart.

Their wagon trundled in and the Kin responded with silent awe to the heartening character of the estate. Along the length of the front, a tiled terrace was supported by pillars, and short steps lead up to mahogany doors. With some trepidation at the high-brow dignity of the castle, Keanan dismounted.

A middle-aged rotund woman shuffled from around one of the adjoining towers. Carrying a basket of red apples and lemons, she stepped up onto the terrace and stopped in her tracks. Her eyes skimmed over Keanan and took in the rest of the party. She stared at their ripped shirts bearing remnants of blood, with suspicion. 'Good day.'

Keanan tried to ignore his appalling appearance, and smiled. 'Good day to you.'

Her puzzled eyes darted from each of them and her hand tried to keep in her escaping black-grey hair. 'Are you in the right place?'

'If we are in Sommerlea, then yes.' Keanan bowed. 'My name is Keanan, this is Marcus, Seth, and that's Hellier. I apologize for the inconvenience, but we have come from Floris where Kael kindly offered to aid us by permitting us respite at this residence.'

The woman's portly face coloured. 'Oh, Kael, well then, my name's Lelana. It's probably best you talk to Mory, he's round the back. Wait here.' She stepped away, then swiveled back, nearly falling off her feet. 'On second thought, come with me.' She walked around the right of the building towards the back of the barn.

On rounding the castle, the landscape transformed to an open lake valley. Sunlight sparkled on the water, and supple waves of deep blue fell onto the lake's reed laden edge. The house was set about a hundred feet from the water. Between the castle and lake, tiny yellow flowers were sprinkled across the grass. Amidst the overhang of willow branches was a contorted pagoda tree. Off to the right by the water's edge a dirt track peeked out from under leaning trees, by this was a jetty. Beyond the lake, woodland was at the feet of rock hills, the south end of the Gravett Ranges, which loomed as a distant grey and indigo spectacle.

Suddenly the sound of chopping echoed over the river. Lelana shouted at someone behind the barn. In front of Lelana and walking unhurriedly was a bulky chested, thick punched man. A mass of dark red hair hung by his neck and he had a beard to match; he smiled at them with friendly eyes. In his hand was an axe, and he extended his free one to Keanan. 'Name's Morias.'

Keanan carried out introductions again. After the four greeted him, Earona and Mara followed Shiarn out.

'Ah, so that's all of you.' Morias' voice was deep and slow and he paused to rest his axe against the wood. 'Explains the letters we received from Kael. Let's go in for a chat and maybe a bite to eat. Lel, get rooms ready, we'll have guests tonight.' Along with a hearty smile, Morias led them up a slight incline to a pergola. Every length of timber flowed with a weighty grapevine, tempting thoughts of lazy days spent under its alluring shade. A long solid table was the centerpiece and had probably hosted many an outdoor banquet over the years.

Hellier and Marcus offered to unsaddle and settle the horses. The rest of the Kin followed Morias into the house. The back door opened into an entry of dusty furnishings. Faded tapestries were on the walls, and two narrow staircases were in the middle of the room. The floors above were visible and everything was lit from coloured panes by the landing on the first floor. Morias walked down a hall, and near the end, he opened a door and they all entered.

At the far end was a desk, cluttered with parchments, scrolls, and an assortment of quills in pots. The opposite side had a carved mantle of similar wood. Comfy chairs and lounges were between short tables covered with books, and a vase of wilted flowers. Walls covered with book shelves bestowed a muted atmosphere that was stifling.

Morias' pulled the cumbersome drapes aside. Sunlight from the floor length windows cut through the murky shadows, revealing the lake and mountain vista beyond. Amid disorganized adeptness, Morias cleared scrolls off the lounges and allocated a pile of books to the floor. He attempted prying a bulbous, orange cat from the outsized cushioned chair. The animal dug its claws in, having no intention of budging from the comfiest location in the room. 'Old Toffee,' he blustered with embarrassment, 'he's a stubborn creature, he is.'

Shiarn placed herself on the edge of the chair and patted the annoyed cat. 'Don't mind him.'

'Make yourselves at home.' Morias darted apologetic eyes about the room. 'Sorry 'bout the mess. This place is too big, too many rooms for all of us.' He jiggled nervously and took a seat.

Keanan eyed the collection of precarious heaps of books with varying degrees of dust layers. 'I almost feel at home.' He sat at the end of the lounge and leaned back, stiffly.

Earona stared with a blank expression out the window. 'It's lovely.'

Morias nodded with a genuine smile. His attention turned to Mara, and he sprang up. 'Now, missy, sit here and put your feet up. You've been on the road many days.' He bade Mara sit in a chair, but not before fluffing a pillow to place behind her back.

Mara rewarded him with a brilliant smile.

Seth seated himself on the lounge. 'I'm completely at ease... except...' His face fell, revealing his misery, 'I'm not really.'

The door opened and an attractive woman with friendly eyes stuck her head in. Seeing them all, she entered. Her blonde hair had been hurriedly tied up and she wore a faded blue dress. 'Hello all. Really, Morias, you could have chosen a better room...'

'Everyone, this is Clara.' A hint of desperation was in his voice and he waved her in. 'Come in.'

'This explains the perplexing message we received.' Clara pulled up a chair and studied their disheveled appearance with a caring smile. 'You look as if you have had a troublesome journey.' Without waiting for a reply, she continued, 'You can have a wash shortly, but more important, some mending is in order.' Their unhealed wounds were noticeable as much as their damaged clothing. 'Can't wait to hear what happened to you,' she carried on, 'it's quite dull here with pressing, baking and the like... now, what was I saying... that's right, Kael sent two letters. One said we were to expect friends to arrive, and that he would come at a later date. The other was the formal letter sent to everyone about the king.' She mimicked with whimsical pomp, '"And the charged will be executed forthwith."' She glanced at each of them, and the Kin remained in silent reflection. Her curious blue eyes rested on Shiarn.

Shiarn eased the now purring cat onto her lap. 'There was a description of that person?'

'Indeed.' Clara stared at her intently. 'Oh, my, it's you?'

Shiarn grimaced. 'I'm a fugitive.'

Clara studied her thoughtfully.

'Kael and Jonas have been busy,' Morias directed to Clara. 'They are like us—'

'It would seem.' Clara gave him a warm smile and to Shiarn she asked, 'It's all very exciting, maybe you can tell us the tale?'

Her mouth tightly closed, Shiarn looked away and focused on the cat.

Keanan interrupted, 'We have more pressing things we need to discuss with you.'

The door opened again. Hellier and Marcus entered with Lelana carrying a sturdy tray with a teapot and cups. Morias hastily moved to take the tray and place it on the table. Lelana said, 'It's a regular party in here.'

'Yes, isn't it?' Clara said, 'How nice to have guests.'

Lelana headed for the door. 'I'd better start our dinner.'

'I'll be with you shortly, Lel.' Clara gave a welcoming smile to the newcomers. 'What a lovely looking bunch you are. You will have to tell me later if you have news from home.' She started pouring them a hot drink.

'Clara,' Morias called her to attention, 'Keanan was about to say something.'

Keanan said, 'it's about our Avare, Jett.'

Morias frowned and looked at each one. 'I thought there should be another one. Kael mentioned him in the letter. But he's not with you?'

Keanan gave a blank stare. 'He's not. Something is happening to his … mind.'

Clara and Morias looked at him expectantly.

'He's gone — mad.'

Earona gave Keanan an abrupt sideways glance. 'I'm not sure that's really it.' She took the hot tea and her voice grew steady. 'Something is making him nasty, and in some way it's affecting us.'

Keanan added, 'We can no longer Mind-speak.'

'And our Gifts have gone,' Seth joined in.

Clara was wide-eyed at the notion. 'Oh, my Heavens!'

Morias asked urgently, 'Where is he?'

Keanan blushed and avoided looking into the man's eager eyes.

Marcus replied, 'His horse came in as we were putting the others in your stables. I gather he must be around somewhere. We saw him in Parkvale.'

'We will have to find him. We can't let him fall into someone else's hands.' Morias said, 'I'll get Adis to scout for him.'

'Now I understand why you look so glum,' Clara said, 'I will look over your bodies and show you where you will be sleeping. We will help you with Jett. Avares are strong-minded people with many remarkable gifts at their disposal. I'm sure he will be fine.'

Her words were salted with optimism, but the Kin's despair was difficult to shake.

~ * ~

That evening they met Adis, the fifth member of Kael's Kin. A tall agile man with black hair braided down his back, and skin that had seen countless days in the sun. Imprinted on the knees of his buckskin pants were grass stains, and a twig hung off his jacket. Clara and Lelana teased him about his need to clean up prior to dinner. He replied with a wry smile, but said nothing.

They dined together at a table that would accommodate double their number. A small feast, prepared by Clara and Lelana, awaited their arrival. Two roasted fouls were among a salver of left-over meat, and two tarts, and an assortment of buttery vegetables. A carafe of white wine provided the refreshment. Silence reigned for a time while they ate.

Morias looked to Mara with a kind smile. 'Missy, I'm assuming you aren't with this group.'

Mara shifted in her chair with unease. 'I'm not supp—'

Earona added, 'She is for now.'

'How did that come about?' Morias charged on.

'It's complicated.'

Morias listened with a fond smile.

'You remind Morias of our children,' Lelana explained.

Mara asked with disbelief, 'You have children?'

Lelana said, 'They're all grown up now.'

'They went back home with Zander and Joel.' Morias paused and sadness came over his eyes. 'Kael took them awhile back now.'

Lelana added, 'Zander is Jonas' son and Joel is Clara and Kael's along with Kaela their daughter. They are full blood unlike our children. Without them they wouldn't be able to enter the lands there.'

At the mention of Jonas' son, Shiarn nearly choked on her food. After clearing her throat, she said, 'I had no idea Jonas had a son.'

'Zander is a dear young man and greatly missed here, as is all the children,' Clara replied, 'but we will see them again. Someone has to take on the property so we can disappear for a time and return to reinvent ourselves. Not many at the palace know of Zander,' she directed at Shiarn in explanation. 'Not that Jonas is ashamed, on the contrary, but it is less complicated in the long term. Our age is the hardest secret to conceal in the end.'

Morias went on to explain the predicament of Jett for Adis' sake.

Adis responded, 'We will search for him after dinner and bring him back.'

'Be careful,' Earona said, 'He might not be agreeable.'

Marcus added, 'I doubt he will be willing to come with you.'

'We're not going to ask him.' Adis gave him a wink. 'We're going to catch him.'

~ * ~

Later that evening, while Mara prepared for bed, Earona entered the room they shared. It was more Earona's idea than hers, and Mara didn't have the heart to argue with her. In a clean nightdress, Mara slipped under the warm covers. After making herself comfortable, she said, 'Do you think they'll find him?'

Earona sat on her bed, staring at the embers in the fireplace. 'I hope so.'

'And when they do, what then?'

'You're very inquisitive. Are you worried?' Earona yawned. 'That's a change.'

Mara shrugged, attempting indifference. 'It's just so unbelievable, I guess.'

'Yes...' The single word came out in a slow breath. After a drawn out pause, Earona said, 'That reminds me. What did you do back on the road in the wagon?'

'I don't know...' She had no plans to expose herself in that way, but the dire situation called for her to act. How could she even begin to tell them who she was, she herself didn't even know what she was now.

'I don't believe that!' Earona cried.

'My mother taught me.' If she didn't give her some information, Earona would hound her relentlessly.

'But, it was an incantation.' Earona scrutinized her with abrupt fear. 'Your mother's a witch?'

'In a way...'

'You can't mean...' Earona blinked with an expression Mara began to expect and detest, horrified shock. 'Wait! Did you have something to do with that woman?' She cried, 'Those men were looking for you in the wagon, weren't they?'

'I can't believe how you assume so much awful stuff!' Mara grumbled. 'Haven't you got more important things to whine about?!'

'Don't change the subject!' Earona said, 'Magik is not a casual thing, nor is it right. A cost is involved. Usually life is required in return for altering the elements.'

Mara knew all too well. 'I gathered that...'

'That's right.' She frowned with mistrust. 'It's best you don't do any more incantations.'

'But...' Mara lay on her back, looking at the darkened ceiling and sensing the chaotic storm within her soul, 'what if I can't stop it?'

Earona chewed her bottom lip. 'You must. Otherwise...'

'... otherwise, I really am a witch...?' her words were faint and directed at her own thoughts.

Earona turned on her side under the blanket. 'But you're right. I've got more important things to worry about.' She gave an extended sigh. 'But, it is serious and dangerous. To you and us.'

Mara creased her brow in genuine concern. She knew that better than anyone. 'Promise you won't tell anyone?'

'I'm not sure.'

Mara's eyes misted with remorse over the whole conversation. 'Please. I won't do anything like that again.'

'I guess there's no point now anyway.' Earona snapped, 'Just, I want your word on it.'

She had no desire to argue about it, and she shrugged. 'I promise.'

~ * ~

Ethan faced another day mining in the mountain. The loss of his power made him more hopeless, not that there weren't enough reasons to be miserable without the drying up of his Gift. He exhausted himself with his sullen pounding, and could not be dragged into any conversation. Anything he did say he growled in a terrible temper. By the end of the day the Harn had steered a circle of silence around him. Ashamed of his uncontrollable irritability, Ethan just wanted to be left alone. With all that was going on inside him he was becoming like one of them, hammering and chipping at the deep stone like any man. As much as he had a new appreciation for the average man he truly didn't like it. Loc was the only one to penetrate his obtrusive attitude. Ethan could give no explanation for his obnoxious behaviour except he was depressed about the loss of his Gift.

Ethan stopped hammering, and smoldered with irrational anger at Kenric approaching him and Loc.

Kenric said, 'Our plans are moving on.'

Ethan grunted, 'I'm not ready yet.'

'How long till you are?' Kenric gave him a calculating stare.

'I'll tell you when I am.' Ethan turned back to his work.

Loc put his hand up to pacify Kenric. 'We said we're in, but you have to back off. Besides, we need to carry down extra provisions.'

Kenric took a heavy breath. 'We will wait till then.' He walked away.

Loc responded under his breath, 'Pushy bastard.'

Ethan gave a tight lipped grimace.

Later on, Ethan went to sleep with an empty heart. Although the cell was full of slumbering, snoring men, he had an acute sense of loneliness. The more he lived this slave existence, the more certain he became, he would not see his Kin again. He found himself saying goodbye to them every day.

54 - Loss

Due to its practice of shifting between worlds, above the earth and below it, and of shedding its corruptive skin and taking on new forms, and its dominion over the misguided, it is considered the primordial deceiver. Balaam, overseer of the planes of hell.

Ei'myn Yamshõan-Shem script, Age of Night

Earona dragged herself from bed after enduring fitful dreams and broken sleep. The sight of the peaks of the Gravett Ranges across the lake revived her some, and she headed downstairs.

Everyone was already eating breakfast, and Morias and Adis joined them. Morias nodded towards Earona. 'We caught him.'

She stared in disbelief.

'He's down in the cellar, disarmed and secure.' Morias leaned forward on his elbows, his voice dropping. 'It sounds extreme.'

Keanan said, 'Did he give you much trouble?'

'He tried to kill us.' Adis' serious expression transformed to a wicked smirk. 'Fortunately, his Gift is also waning, although you might have mentioned he was a Charer.'

Keanan's face reddened.

'He could see us a mile off.' Morias waved his hand in the direction of the nearby forest. 'We found him skulking round out there.'

'There's a darkness about him,' Adis said, 'We put him in special chains that will work better than normal steel. But remain on guard.'

Earona stood, her hands clenching her hips. 'We have to do something.'

'Soon as we finish here I will take Clara to him first,' Morias said, 'She will know if he can be healed and give you the news.'

Earona had to be satisfied with that.

After breakfast, Earona joined the Kin outside under the terrace while Mara chased after Morias to help with errands about the house. Avoiding the anxious looks of the others, Earona sat in a gloomy silence.

Clara approached from inside with a dejected expression. 'I've seen him and tried to speak with him.' She pulled out a chair and sat. 'I don't know your Avare, but he doesn't seem… right.' She paused, 'His intentions are malicious and deadly, and he repels my touch. He's talking about a ritual and something about a Summoner.' Sadness dulled her face. 'Strangely, I don't sense he is possessed.'

A spontaneous sob escaped Earona. 'How awful!'

'What can we do?' Marcus said.

Clara stared down at the table. 'If only Spirit healing was available to us, it might have helped.'

'It's true.' Keanan scratched his bearded chin. 'Jett may be the only one who can know what's happening inside himself.'

'You can do nothing?' Hellier's eyes formed saucers as she looked between Keanan and Clara.

Clara gave her a grim frown.

'But we must consider how and why this has happened?' Shiarn probed them with a thoughtful gaze.

Keanan said, 'There must be a reason?'

Seth asked, 'Can we talk with him?'

'Oh, yes, but I doubt he is the man you knew,' Clara said.

Hellier looked at them with a determined expression. 'I have no desire to see him like this.'

'That's not right,' Earona snapped, 'You might be able to help him in some way.'

Shiarn stared morosely at the table. 'You might need to say goodbye.'

'Bulldung!' Earona cried.

Hellier's brow deepened, but no tears fell. 'If it's that bad, I would prefer to remember him the way he was.'

Marcus lifted his head and glanced at their depressed demeanors. 'We can't give up on him. He must know what's going on, after all this is Jett.'

The notion that it was, indeed, Jett, plunged Earona into a stale reflective silence. Afterward, no words could fill the empty space, and the Kin drifted apart and away from the table.

In a fog of considerations over facing Jett, Earona trudged up the staircase. Warm red light from the glass panes softened the landing. She stepped through a deep green and a translucent yellow, staring at each in a trance.

Shiarn waited like a breathing statue. 'Earona…'

Awoken from her sad reverie, Earona lifted her head. In a selfish veiled manner she was avoiding her. 'Yes?'

'Can we talk in my room?'

Earona puckered her lips and frowned. 'If we must.' She took her time following, knowing what Shiarn wanted to discuss.

Shiarn sat on the bed staring out at the lake, her voice strained with latent tears. 'Don't be angry I want this.'

Earona challenged her own emotions. 'I am angry you put me in this situation.' Every part of her was annoyed she would do the very thing she swore never to undertake.

'Why are you so selfish?!' Shiarn's eyes blazed. 'Think about the things I've done for you.'

She grimaced at her open hurt. 'It's not so simple… it's a life I'm about to destroy.'

Shiarn's face lightened. 'You're going to do it?'

Earona rubbed her temples with a shaking hand. 'I'm not happy, just so you know.'

'And I'm sure you will tell me about it for the rest of my days,' Shiarn grumbled.

'No,' Earona pursed her lips together, 'I don't want to even think about it.' Even though the deed would haunt her forever.

'You really can be infuriating.' Shiarn creased her brow.

Earona frowned with dark derision. 'I'm the one doing this remember. Anyway who knows if I can with my fading Gift.' She mumbled, 'It might be the last thing I do.'

Shiarn caught hold of Earona's fussing hand in a steadying clinch. 'Just try.'

'Fine. Lay back then.' Although not truly convinced it was the right thing to do, she did it for Shiarn. She suspected there wouldn't be peace between them if she didn't.

Shiarn leaned back on the pillow. Earona touched her stomach and finally discovered the miniature life. She lacked the power to analyze it, which was probably for the best. Instead, she cut the cord providing the embryo with Shiarn's essence. 'It's done. You should see about having a bath.'

'I will. Now I feel able to face Jonas.'

Earona studied her closely. 'Does he know of this?'

'No, and I would prefer to keep it that way. It's Jett we have to be concerned about.'

Earona became downcast at the mention of him. 'Yes, and I must go and see him.'

~ * ~

Marcus occupied a circle of space on the lawn, performing his customary fighting maneuvers. Earona stood under the terrace, observing his exposed torso and bronzed skin, and well-proportioned arms flexing swiftly. His balance was exceptional. Surprised at her flushed face, she shook off the attraction. After all, it was only Marcus.

He turned his head without his poise shifting. On seeing her under the vines he gave a dazzling smile.

Before she could blush any further she rushed over. 'At least you don't need your Gift for combat.'

His hands went to his hips and with years of familiarity he confronted her with a deadpan expression. 'Hey, you have all those herbs and potions, aren't they good for something?'

'That is different.' She changed the subject before he could twist her remark back on her. 'I want to see Jett.'

Marcus frowned at the house as if a dark menace lurked inside. 'And you want me to come with you?'

'Well, yes, unless you rather not.'

'I'll come.'

She spun away and he trailed after, pulling his shirt over his head.

Marcus held the lamp and walked ahead of Earona down the narrow spiral staircase. He said over his shoulder, 'Did you talk to Keanan about his visit?'

'Jett was saying some horrendous things, and Keanan didn't understand half of it.' Her voice softened, 'Poor us.'

Marcus shook his head. 'It's Jett we need to feel sorry for.'

Earona followed him into the cloying darkness of the basement. The lamp shed enough light to see, but the shadows over the barrels and crates cast eerie patterns. They followed the directions Clara had given and walked straight into the first room. Arched pillars sectioned off the rooms which were neat, unlike Clara's embarrassed depiction. The cellar was used often and appeared in good condition.

In silence they turned to the left and through into an adjoining chamber where a single lantern hung from a pillar. As she entered the storage area, Earona sensed the temperature soar in heat and an oppressive weight descended on her shoulders. Even with the presence of the two lights, the darkness was still dominant.

Earona gasped at the sight of Jett sitting in the shadows, chained to the wall, his head lowered. He lifted a deathly white face and stared through her and Marcus with his black eyes. The stubble on his face was a rare sight, and his clothes were soiled with broken mud from his travail through the woods. Sadness in her voice was hard to restrain. 'Jett…' She wanted to take him in her arms and hug him back to the man she knew.

Jett lifted his eyes and his voice boiled with contempt. 'Why do you useless pests keep coming down here as if you can change anything?'

'But, we want to try and make you normal again.' Everything about him was the same, his voice, his face, except his words were not Jett's. She had hoped he would look like an evil man, or at least have the voice of a demon. He was nothing like she expected. She rushed forward, wanting to hold him, but Marcus put his arm out stopping her.

'You foolish weaklings have no idea what's about to take place,' Jett's tone simmered with rage, 'and you will never know even as you die.'

Marcus said, 'What has happened to you?'

'I have become my true manifestation.' He raised his wrists and pulled on the chains of malreus. 'These won't stop my destiny.'

'What are you talking about?' Marcus' voice tightened with unease.

Jett hitched his knee up and put his arm across it. 'If you don't know, I won't be telling you.'

'Do witches have anything to do with this?' Earona said.

He replied, 'You underestimate their power and knowledge, as you have always done.'

She whispered, 'I wonder if you mean…' *the Fáerinn?* 'Jett, we want to help you.'

'You can keep out of my way.' Jett peered at her with a cruel smirk.

Earona pleaded with her hand outstretched. 'What is this Summoner you are waiting for?'

His voice lowered with disdain. 'You are too witless to know what walks among you.'

'I don't give a demon's arse about your plans, nor am I going to listen,' Marcus growled, 'I know you're not really Jett talking.'

Jett sprang up and came at Marcus, his fists clenched with rage. The chains clanked as he yanked on them, but Marcus was out of reach by inches. Jett breathed into his face and the two glared at each other. Jett said, 'If I weren't bound, you'd be dead.'

Marcus fumed, 'I'd kill you before you knew what happened, without a weapon.'

'You'd never touch me.' Jett's eyes became slits of pure wrath. 'And you sure as hell can't stop me.'

'Stop what?' Marcus said.

Jett finally said, 'Opening the Gate.'

Earona came between them and put her hand on Jett's chest. 'How are you doing that?'

'Don't touch me.'

Earona flew backwards from an unseen gust of power and landed on her backend with a shocked stare. Her heart pounding with fear.

Marcus turned to Earona, his face creasing with worry. 'Are you hurt?'

Earona shook her head. It wasn't her body that hurt.

Jett's gaze swept over them. 'It has begun. I will have dominion over you all.'

'Like hell!' Marcus barked with an anger Earona rarely heard from him.

Earona got off the stone and rubbed her back. She could do nothing significant to heal her muscles. She approached Jett warily this time and stood nearer to Marcus. 'Who are you really?'

He pierced her stare with a biting glare, and she shuddered with a chill foreboding. 'The Daemon Overlord who will own your souls.' He turned back to the wall and sat down, finished with the conversation.

'Overlord, my arse! I've heard enough.' Marcus spun to leave.

'Wait!' Earona said with tears choking her voice. 'How… Jett…'

He growled with contempt, 'You cannot stop it.' His eyes crimped with maliciousness.

Her lip quivered and she tried to control her emotions that wanted to vent on him. 'I don't care. I'm still going to try.' She turned from him, but swiveled back again. 'For Jett.'

Sneering, he shook his head.

She stormed out of the room with Marcus chasing after her. She couldn't stop the angry tears cascading down her cheeks as she ran up the steps. Once out of the stairwell, Marcus put down the lantern and grabbed her arms, halting her mad flight. 'Stop, Earona.'

Earona couldn't stop the tears flowing and she didn't want too. They had been controlled in Jett's presence, but now she let them free. In the narrow corridor, Marcus took her in his arms in a consoling embrace.

'I can't believe this,' she sniffled, 'He's lost… and everything… we are.'

Marcus continued stroking her dark wavy hair, trailing down her back, while his other hand held her firmly. 'And it's even worse. He's turned into some evil overlord who wants to open a Gate?'

'How did this happen?'

'I don't know…' Looking into her frantic blue eyes, he wiped her tears away with his thumb. He relaxed in her embrace and his lips pressed onto hers with tender desire. She responded and he delved deeper. Suddenly, he broke away. 'I'm sorry.'

Earona's eyes jolted open and she fixed them on him in incredulous shock.

'It's not the best time.' He flushed and backed away nervously. 'I didn't mean it.'

Her eyes flashed in protest and her hands went to her waist. 'What do you mean you didn't mean it?'

'I... I... no…that's not—' He blushed scarlet.

'Are you saying you didn't mean to kiss me?' She stared him straight in the eye and dug a steely finger into his chest. 'Next time you want to kiss me you make sure you really do mean it.' With her chin raised, she turned on her heel and stomped off.

He stood slack jawed, rubbing his bruised chest and trembling inside with astonishment.

~ * ~

Sommerlea would have been a peaceful haven for Mara if she hadn't been so disturbed by Jett's condition. As it was, she spent the day avoiding the house and people. Exploring the gardens, she attempted finding solace. It was only good for so long, until the anxiety became too great.

She supposed it wasn't the smartest idea to venture out on her own, but she didn't care and there was no one to stop her, not now Jett had turned. He was the only one who wanted her watched anyway. Even Earona didn't question where she went. She and her friends were too concerned about Jett, and she couldn't blame them.

Jett's fall was a grave blow to her too. They thought it must be possession of some sort, but Mara expected it was more serious than that. Now he was down in the basement she didn't want to go into the house, or anywhere near him. But deep down in her conscience she knew they were connected somehow – he was, no, he must be the One Wendessa spoke of. That was a near certainty. But she really didn't think it would be like this. She had to face the truth. If she stayed long enough, he would bring her down with him, back into the realm of hell, and even worse than she had ever experienced. She was only putting off the inevitable.

Already the pervasive dark was touching her mind. She lay on her bed, face down and still dressed, with her hood pulled over her head. In the darkened room she looked across to the half-eaten meal Clara left earlier. Mara had told her she was unwell and Clara fussed over her, touching her forehead and stomach. Partly true, the nausea was present, but the truth was, she had no wish to be downstairs with these strangers. Earona was the only one to pay her any attention while the others looked right through her, as if they didn't want to know her. On top of that, their gloomy disposition was depressing. Not that she cared what they thought of her, it only confirmed she was an outsider.

From listening to their conversation, Jett had transformed into an evil scoundrel and there was nothing they could do. It would only get worse; similar to the voice in her head getting louder. The indiscernible words began as a whisper, but since Jett was captured they took a more dominant place in her thoughts. Why they brought him into the house, she couldn't comprehend. It was lunacy as far as she could see. He was lost to the evil that was seeking her. She had thought he would be stronger to resist it, but she was foolishly mistaken. Now she had to get away from him before it was too late.

~ * ~

From the shadows of her dreams, voices pleaded for Mara to come, to follow. The wailing intensified and she clamped hard on her ears in vain. One voice echoed above the others, speaking right into her thoughts.

Come to me.

Arise to your destiny.

Release the souls from despair.

Unable to defend against the rush of malicious images forming in the shadows of her room, she screamed in silence and willed herself to wake.

Woken by a hand gripping her shoulder, Mara looked up at a figure concealed by shadows. Her voice trembled in rebuttal, 'No.'

'Another nightmare?' the figure replied, 'And you went to sleep in your clothes.'

It took moments for Mara to register the owner of the voice. Even longer for the haze to lift from her thoughts. 'Why is it so dark?' Her words came out like a rasping croak.

'Dark?' Earona glanced around the room. 'It's night.'

Mara pulled her cloak back around her. 'Not that.' The shadows seemed denser, and the candle was a tiny illumination in the gloom. Despite the heat in the air, she went to the fireplace and put wood on the dying embers.

Earona climbed into bed. 'Are you sleeping like that?'

She didn't want to sleep at all and had no intention of it. But she had fallen to it – like a spell. 'Is he… worse?' she asked with little hope in her voice.

'He's terrible… '

Mara kept her back to her and warmed her hands by the flame. Why should she be worried about someone she hardly knew, and shouldn't know? She should leave and never see him again, but what chance of that if he could haunt her dreams.

'Did you want to see him?'

'No!' Mara answered with more force than she wanted and she softened her tone. 'It's just… I'd rather not.' He scared her like nothing else, even more than her mother. He had become something not of this world.

'You sound afraid.'

Mara twisted around to see her. 'Aren't you?' She was amazed by their varying reactions, sorrow, confusion, anger, but none of them seemed frightened. Unlike her.

Earona turned on her back and stared into the dark. 'I guess I didn't want to be afraid of him. But after what he said today, I think—'

'What did he say?'

'He's says he's going to open a Gate.'

Mara caught her breath and tried to calm her racing heart. 'A Gate? What...?' Not that she needed to ask. *Curse it.* Had her mother the power to do such an abhorrent thing to him? It seemed a power that came straight from the underworld.

'It's not something you should know.' Earona sighed. 'But, it's a doorway between planes of existence. A forbidden pathway. Needless to say they should never be opened.'

'But how?' Mara squealed with fright, clutching her chest. She knew the answer. Didn't she know before she even met him? 'He's chained up, right?'

'Yes,' Earona said, 'but he seems to think he can do it.'

Mara spoke her thoughts aloud. 'He's got the power...'

'And we don't know how to stop it or him.'

There was a solution, but not one Earona would like; to kill him now, while they could. Mara muttered, 'You need to...'

'You can't think...' Earona's face paled and a tremor was in her voice. 'He called himself a Daemon Lord.'

'Oh my Gods!' Mara groaned. So that's who he really is. And what did it make her? She shivered.

'I know it's truly frightful,' Earona mumbled. 'He also said something about waiting for the Summoner.'

Mara felt the breath leave her chest in abrupt fear.

'Heaven only knows what that is. He wouldn't tell me.' Earona groaned, 'It's so... he's so... evil. Like his personality is completely changed.'

Mara sat on her bed and faced her, and mumbled, 'He's a devil...'

'It's heart-wrenching.' Earona's despair weighed her words. 'But is it reversible?' she queried to herself, 'Is he truly lost?'

'I... he should be killed...' Mara watched the fire, her emotions draining from her body.

'Oh my God! To even think such a thing —I can't...'

In the distance a door slammed, causing her and Earona to jump. A hot draft followed, blowing at their hair. The flames in the fireplace receded back to embers and the candle-light died. The room was enveloped in deepening shadows.

Earona cried, 'What's going on?'

'It's darker...' Mara, fully clothed, pulled up the blanket to cover her head. She watched the shadows shift and heard the sound of objects moving with a clatter. 'Something's here.'

'Holy Heaven!' Earona's voice shook.

The wind, carrying a foul odour, swirled around Mara and touched the covers with a tangible trail. She heard discordant voices similar to her dream. She hugged herself and withdrew into a tight ball. 'It's started...'

'What?'

'Whatever he wants to do!' Mara remarked with irritation. 'We probably won't get much sleep.'

55 - Confusion

All I hear is crying
From beneath this hardening skin
While my tired heart is petrifying
the rancid fever seeps in
to choke me within its grasp

Lament of Broken Stars

The next day, Mara dawdled across the lawn in a fatigued haze. She spent a harrowing night gripped by fear, watching figures separate from the shadows and listening to distant wails. No matter how bad it was, her dreams were worse.

'Mara!' Earona waved from the back terrace.

Too late, Mara was spotted before she could get to the gardens. Scowling, she trudged up the steps to meet her.

'Where are you going?' Earona looked grim.

She hadn't decided, as long as it was quiet and clean of foul air and gave her some momentary peace. 'Anywhere.'

'I didn't see you this morning. Did you get any sleep?'

What a stupid question. Mara had risen long before Earona, not that Mara woke up, more like got off her bed. 'Did you?'

'Not really.' Earona gave her a gaping yawn in response. 'It was frightening. I swear things were moving around the room.'

Mara grumbled, 'They were.' Small objects; picture frames, clothing, the porcelain.

Clara came through the doors in a rush carrying a bowl of apples, and with one of her dogs following.

'Clara,' Earona called with urgency.

Despite the concern in Clara's eyes, she smiled. 'It's nice to be outside in the fresh air and sunlight.'

Mara could guess where she must have been.

'How is he?' Earona reached down to stroke the animal's brown fur.

Placing the fruit on the table, Clara took a seat and a resigned breath. 'No change, except… he's becoming unbearable.'

Earona sat beside her and kept her eyes on the dog. 'I'm sorry…'

'It's hardly your fault,' Clara reprimanded a little too severely. 'But, I do fear he's getting more… evil.'

'You don't see him alone?' Mara continued standing despite the women making themselves comfortable.

Fear flicked in Clara's eyes. 'I wouldn't dare. I go with Morias or Adis. I have met mean people before, but he's inherently evil. His threats are atrocious enough, but when he speaks I have a foreboding sense…' she shivered and reached for an apple, 'they aren't threats, but he is speaking what will be.'

Mara trembled, knowing exactly what she meant. 'He's like something out of this world…'

'He's causing this eerie activity?' Earona said.

Clara looked at them with a worried frown and finished her mouthful. 'It's him. I can't even touch him now, and he doesn't appear to need food. The only reason we go down there is to check he's still there. I'm thankful he can't break the chains, although I wonder how long they will hold him.' She stopped suddenly and cast a look at her pet sitting by her chair, 'Actually, it's alarming he does not care to be released, or try to free himself, or make any demands at all. He seems unaffected by being our prisoner.'

Mara mumbled, 'Because he wants to be here…'

Clara nodded. 'I can only assume he's fulfilling his purpose of what seems to be opening a Gate.'

Earona sat hunched. 'It's terrifying, and we're just sitting here.'

'Indeed,' Clara said. 'The fear in the house is increasing too, as well as a tangible darkness.'

Mara had already noticed the deepening shadows. So he really was amassing power while they did nothing about it. She had to leave before it was too late. 'What's going to happen?'

'I can't even guess,' Earona whispered, 'Or maybe I don't want to.'

Clara nodded. 'Currently none of the options we have, have a pleasant outcome. I expect it is something you will need to discuss.'

Earona's eyes misted and she stared down at her feet. After a moment she lifted her head. 'Do you think witches could have cursed him?'

Clara looked across the water in contemplation. 'It's possible, I guess. Has he encountered any?'

'He hasn't,' Earona cast a gaze at Mara. 'But we have.'

Mara stared daggers at her, but remained silent, willing Earona not to say a thing about her.

'There was a witch in Parkvale a few years ago,' Clara replied, 'she was finally dug out. They can live under your nose for years without being detected. But the longer they are a witch the more evil and degenerate they become. Old Molly was in the village for years, yet in the end she was exposed. It was awful the day they burned her.'

Mara squeaked, 'Burn — alive?'

Clara nodded. 'Yes, child, it's not the nicest sight.'

'They can't be healed?' asked Earona.

'Not with our Gifts. Becoming a witch is more than an illness; you actually give yourself over to do work for darkness. I don't think you can change your mind afterwards. Once a witch always a witch.'

'Have people been burnt by mistake?' Earona asked.

'Undoubtedly!' cried Clara. 'I've still got some of Molly's things and odd bits of writings. What I could sneak out from under the villagers' noses. Wouldn't want them to think I cared too much. I'll show them to you if you like.'

'Anything is worth a try.' Earona gave Mara a stern glance. 'Mara will come too.'

'What?!' Mara had no desire to go into the house or look through a dead witch's junk. Probably stuff she had seen countless times before.

Clara smiled at her fussing. 'And after, you can help in the kitchen.'

'Fine,' Mara replied, 'But I don't know about the kitchen…'

~ * ~

Inside the house, Mara felt his presence surrounding her, and a voice echoing in her head. Her anxiety escalated and she wanted to scream at it to shut-up. She lagged behind Earona and Clara as they went up to the attic. Earona had pestered her enough she was obliged to accompany her. After all, Earona reasoned, didn't she want to help Jett if she could? But how could a witch's belongings help, she didn't know. The more she thought on it, the more it seemed a bad idea.

They followed Clara upstairs, eventually coming to a door that opened onto a flight of steps that brought them into the attic. Floor length windows lined one side of the room. Shelving and stacks of chests, and odd furniture, blocked sight of the room's end.

'It's a shambles.' Clara looked over the dust-coated room in the weak light. 'But I know where things are.' She stopped to examine a mustard coloured chest. Strewn on top, musky drapes and a worn feather cap. Picking up the cap, she studied the scarlet material beneath it. 'I could make a dress from this.' She hauled the chest across the erstwhile grime and with slight pushing from the girls, moved it near a window. 'This is it.' She lifted the lid. A stale odour with a rotten tinge hit Mara's nostrils. 'I'll leave you girls for a while.' She looped the scarlet drapes over her arm. 'Pack it away when you have finished.' She left the room with an armful of rediscovered odds and ends.

Mara cleared a place on the floor to sit.

On a closer inspection of the dusty planks, Earona reached for a cushion to sit on.

Sighing with resignation, Mara reached to the bottom and rummaged around. She picked up a handful of papers and flicked through them. Some of the language she had seen before, and she assumed it was a witch's chapter spells. She tossed them into Earona's lap. Next, she collected a fist full of sticks and studied the fine markings. Nothing new. This style of magik device was used by Wendessa.

'I don't understand much of this,' Earona exclaimed with frustration. 'It's a mixture of common and what I assume is this witch language.'

Suddenly curious by an object similar to what was used in rituals, Mara pulled out a curved black blade. She turned the bone handle over in her hands and clutched her moving stomach; she laid the knife beside the sticks.

Earona kept reading, 'Witches have groups called Chapters. This is about a particular one, Chapter of Torment.'

'You wanted to look through this.'

'It's dreadful.' Colour drained from Earona's face. 'Their task was to steal blood from the new life for the ritual of suffering.' Her mouth contorted with terror. 'It seems they were taking babies and killing them.'

'Horrible bitches!' Mara was shocked at the thought.

Earona glanced at Mara's neat display. 'That blade looks to be malreus.'

'What is that exactly?' She had seen similar weapons on Earona's friends.

Earona distracted herself with the papers. 'A type of metal.'

Amid building intrigue, Mara continued fiddling with objects in the chest and brought out a small satchel. She opened it and gagged from the putrid smell.

Earona stuck her nose in the proffered bag. 'Disgusting.'

Mara found another that appeared to hold dainty bones.

Earona peered into it. 'Most likely they were used for readings.'

Mara enquired with subdued fascination, 'These must be...'

'Probably. I should be telling Clara about that one.'

Mara put the bag of tiny bones on the floor with the other peculiar bits and pieces. She lifted an iron ring holding an assorted bunch of insignificant objects. Touching a finger bone and dried frog, she was reminded of Wendessa's odd little knick-knacks, and she smiled.

Earona shifted the pieces of paper. 'Oh, holy heavens! Look!' She held up an old parchment with a sketch of a snake biting its own tail forming a figure eight.

Mara bit her lip and her hands shook with astonishment as she tried to reach for the paper.

'It may be a sort of seal.' Earona ran her finger along the text and her voice trilled with excitement. 'Here, it says - the Curse-Mark of the Infernal is impossible to penetrate. Only one of the Order's Elite has the power to decipher and break the bane.'

A Bane, so that's what Wendessa and her friends did to her. 'But...what is... an Infernal?' Mara snatched the page from her and scanned the scrawled words, the blood draining from her face. '...and who is the Order's Elite....' She drew in a sharp breath.

Earona flipped over another page. 'I can't understand the language. I don't want you to be alarmed.'

'I'm....' Was she worried? Couldn't Earona get it? In the eyes of witches it was an affliction, but for Mara, it had so far changed her life, and even her view of the world. She grumbled, 'Bloody arse...' Now she had to worry about it being taken away, and she didn't have to wonder who was capable of that.

'I know it's not the best time to find out these things.' Earona sighed and rubbed her chin. 'What's that you have?'

Mara unknotted the cord of a small pouch and stuck a finger in. 'Ash?' Compact soot covered her finger.

'I'm beginning to regret looking at these things,' Earona whispered, gripping her stomach.

Mara nodded her agreement. 'Rayne is rolling and twisting. I think he hates it.'

Earona gave her a warm smile. 'You named him. That's lovely.'

'It seemed right to do so, and I…' she shrugged, feeling defensive, but not knowing why. 'I can if I want to.'

'Well, you have to. Someone has to…' Earona said. 'Anyway, don't blame him. Babies bones, talk of murdered infants. Of course he will be upset.'

Mara picked up the parchment Earona had discarded and attempted speaking the words.

'Don't, Mara.'

Mara stopped, but continued reading the script.

Earona enquired hopefully, 'Do you understand any of it?'

Parts of the language were familiar due to her lessons from Wendessa, but she had a sense these words were crafted for this particular Chapter. 'No.'

Earona went to the window and opened the glass panel, letting in the fresh air. 'I've had enough of dark arts. I need some daylight.'

Mara dumped everything back in the chest, but she lingered over the bone-handled blade. She placed it back in and the nausea left her. 'Fine with me.' She used the closed lid to rise to her feet. 'I don't want to find out anything more.'

Earona shut the window and followed her. 'A shame there wasn't more on that tattoo.'

'But – I'm cursed! Isn't that enough?'

'You seem quite normal most of the time.'

Mara giggled mawkishly. 'You mean sometimes I'm not.'

'No offence, but sometimes you get quite maudlin.'

'You have your moments too,' Mara retorted. 'I don't think you rate high on the side of normal.'

'Mara!' cried Earona, but she smiled.

'I think I fit in with the people around here.'

Earona turned and pointed at her. 'You really have no idea.'

After dinner, Earona helped Lelana and Clara clean up in the kitchen. Keanan was the only one to offer to help, but once everything was done and it was time for bed she was grateful for his presence. She was not looking forward to another night of frightening sounds and shadows.

Clara and Lelana said goodnight, and left Earona and Keanan in the hall.

Earona gave a gaping yawn. '…didn't realize how tired I was.'

'Before I take you to your room,' his voice was soft, 'I wanted to show you something.'

His gentle gaze suddenly alarmed her, and she almost squealed, 'Show me?'

He took her hand and stroked it. 'It may take away the tension, if only for a brief while.'

She looked at him with wide-eyed nervousness, doubting that was possible with all that was happening. Shrugging away her reluctance, she replied, 'It's not as if I can sleep anyway.'

'I promise you will like it.'

She smiled in return. Keanan was the love of Earona's youth. He was only ever kind-hearted with his rebuttals, but it left a recurring sting, made worse when another girl captured his heart. In the end she came to terms with his rejection. Now she had an awful suspicion a change had come over him.

He led her through the kitchen and into a semi-hidden door. He warmed her cold hand and they climbed one of the tower's winding steps. He shoved a door open in the floor and pulled himself out onto a platform. Extending his hand, he supported her up.

The moon shone between the luminous clouds and winking stars. Beneath them the lake glimmered and shadows of the highlands sprawled across the valley and dark forest carpet. Chilly air hit her skin and she shivered. Earona leaned against the tower ledge wishing she had her cloak so she could enjoy the vista in comfort. 'It's breathtaking.'

'But not as beautiful as you.' He moved to embrace her shivering body.

His tender manner made her stiffen in his arms with wary anticipation. She stared up into his sensitive eyes; watching her with familiar astuteness. '…this is a surprise… I…' Icy air blew across her face, making her shudder.

He ducked his head down and kissed her. The intimate touch stirred up all the old longings. She fixed her attention on him and pushed another more recent kiss from her mind. '…I—' She broke away and a sad pleading pervaded her words. 'Why now?'

'I realize it is not the most ideal time, and our future is uncertain, but… in the past I was immature, and foolish in not returning your affections.' He creased his brow at her surprise. 'Considering what is occurring to Jett and the Kin, I needed to make known my feelings.' Stroking her chin, he continued, 'Perhaps it is too sudden, but I wish you to know I would like us to take our relationship further.'

His words and caring caress conjured up many a wishful fantasy, but… as she tussled with the idea Keanan desired her, a stinging realization flung into her mind; how she wished it was Marcus to confess to her. Not for the first time was she grateful they couldn't Mind-speak. 'I… there is so much going on with Jett, with the Kin, I just don't… I'm… not ready…'

He moved his fingers across her cheek. His eyes clouded over at the mention of her pain. 'Does your reticence have something to do with him?'

Earona's head jolted upright with alarm. 'Who?'

'Marcus,' he stated.

How did he even know about that? Blushing, she said with surprise, 'I'm not sure what you are saying.'

Keanan creased his brow and brushed a strand from her forehead. 'My apologizes. I assumed you knew?'

Her cheeks flushed and she wiggled from his embrace. 'I don't.' But now she did and her thoughts froze at the revelation, yet her heart pounded with childish fear.

'Perhaps my discernment is wrong, and it's one of his moods.' Keanan's smile seemed forced.

Earona had a tinge of exasperation. 'Yes, probably, because I don't know what he's thinking.'

'He has said nothing, and that maybe an indication it's a passing thing.'

She could no longer contain her annoyance, over Keanan, and Marcus. 'Keep in mind, our Avare has turned evil, and we may be...' *Finished.* She paused, realizing she didn't want to ruin the moment in such a disheartening way. 'It's just... it's probably not the best time for this...'

'True.' A genuine contriteness came over him. 'But remember, I'll always be here for you.'

His kind words plunged her into more uncertainty over her feelings. Keanan was admitting his affections, while Marcus remained silent about his, if he had any at all. Trouble would arise from this shaky predicament and she had no wish to think about any of it. 'I know.'

He smiled, taking her into his arms once more.

~ * ~

Hiding from the darkness, Mara covered herself with the blanket. She tried fighting off sleep, but soon succumbed to a paralyzing slumber. Unable to move, she peered at the room shrouded in shadows. The dark seemed to have a life of its own as it shifted and formed the shape of unnatural entities. A presence entered the room, and a hot draft blew the curtains and rattled the panes. Voices assaulted her senses; calling and pleading for her attention. She wanted to scream but couldn't make a sound.

Floating out from her body, she rose through the covers. She struggled to wake, as she hovered above the bed. The shadows consumed her and carried her through the door. Amid terror she had somehow died, she was sped along by the hellish apparitions, past doors, and down stairs. Finally guessing their destination, she fought and kicked against hard appendages within the haze of darkness. 'No! I won't! I don't want to see—' the evil beings forced themselves into her mouth and held her tongue.

They rushed down a narrow spiral stair and into a boundless hot darkness. A glow emanated from her, enough to see him. He stood before a black square-cut throne, and his crimson aura, tainted with lines of black, was stark in the surrounding emptiness.

Slender bony hands pulled her limbs and dumped her at his feet. She crumpled to the floor, rasping with a swollen tongue. '...no... I won't...'

'I have been calling you, and it has taken too long. It was my wish that you come on your own accord, but you have been far too headstrong. However, that will soon change. If I have to break you I will, although I would prefer complete and willing obedience. Stand.'

Trembling in his ominous presence, and against her will, she stood, head lowered, and holding her shaking arms. She had never felt such dread in her life, not even her mother could produce such fear.

'You make it more difficult for yourself. For you need not be afraid. Look at me.'

His commanding voice pierced her soul, and any stubborn intentions she had to never see him. She lifted her face and stared with a hypnotic gaze. His eyes glowed with the same crimson fire, and with absolute authority over her. He cupped his hand around the back of her neck and with a steel grip drew her closer. 'It is time. I command you, come and stand before me.'

She fought to open her mouth in answer—

Mara nearly jumped off the bed at Earona's hand on her arm shaking her awake.

'You look sick.' Earona's voice was like thunder in the dark room.

Shivering from the dry sweat on her chest and back, Mara brushed away her damp fringe and tried to sit up. Her hand went to the back of her neck in fear.

Earona laid her hand on her forehead. 'And so hot.'

Mara tried edging away from Earona's hand, but her body was limp. She breathed, '...I'm... he was in my dream...'

'That's not a surprise, I've been having terrible nightmares too,' Earona prattled on, 'I could get Clara to look at you?'

Rubbing her neck, Mara shook her head. 'No.'

'I'm not convinced. Is your neck sore?' Earona got under her covers.

'I slept badly.' There was no use telling Earona, what could she even do about it? Mara pulled her hood over her head. She tried to ignore the pain around her neck and the sense he still had a hold of it.

'There's a lot of that going around.'

'I'll be glad if I never sleep again,' Mara muttered.

56 - Deception

A burden of sadness
Is carried in my heart,
It sets my tears on fire,
It burns my hope to a scarring ash

Lament of Broken Stars

Earona's nerves were on edge after the eerie night of unnatural wind and moving objects. She dozed in the predawn hours and on waking, remembered Keanan and his confession. She groaned at having to face him after they had kissed. She was already trying to avoid Marcus, and now she had to consider Keanan.

The Sommerlea residents and the Kin talked about more troublesome nights ahead. It had become serious with potentially lethal consequences, and they were forced to do something about the situation. Keanan had called a meeting with the Kin that morning and Earona had slept late.

In a sleepy daze, she opened the door to Keanan's room, knowing everyone would be waiting. She was not looking forward to the inevitable discussion, mainly because the Kin seemed to be so disagreeable with each other since Jett's demise. She sighed at the sight of them, watching her. 'Sorry.'

'Finally.' On the only chair, Shiarn sat with her feet tucked under her.

Earona scampered to the nearest bed and sat next to Seth. Marcus was on the second bed and Hellier paced between the two.

Keanan stood by the window, overseeing them all. '—now that everyone has seen him—'

Hellier shook her head with defiance. 'Uh-uh.'

'Except Hellier. We need to discuss what to do,' Keanan said, 'And considering last night and his intentions, it has become more perilous than the loss of our Avare.'

'His intentions?' Marcus said, 'More like threats. How can he do anything?'

'It does seem impossible, but he's so confident.' Earona shivered. 'And last night was frightful.'

'True.' Shiarn flicked back her fiery red curls. 'And he's acting like an arrogant sod.'

Earona folded her arms. 'More like a conniving demon.'

'There's more to opening a Gate than we know.' Seth blushed and added, 'So Keanan said.'

'Correct,' Keanan replied. 'Opening a way to another dimension is not a simple matter. It requires a process of rituals, or layers of locks to be opened, and an alignment of signs in the heavens and on earth.'

'Jett's change might be a part of this process?' Earona said, 'How many other things need to happen?'

Keanan gave her a perplexed grimace. 'No way for us to tell.'

Seth said, 'Jett said it's already begun.'

'Yes,' Shiarn answered with annoyance, 'and who knows when that was? I recall the mage at the palace conducted a ritual. I'm sure it was about a Gate.'

'And?' Earona eyed her eagerly.

'He summoned someone, or something, but—' Shiarn's eyes looked at a distant point. 'It didn't work the way he wished.'

Hellier said, 'You mean that bottle?'

Shiarn twirled a strand of hair in her fingers and gazed in thought. 'Maybe that's when it started?'

'There's been some strange things happening in the house, but,' Marcus spread his hands wide, his doubt obvious, 'can a Gate really open here?'

Keanan paced the floor and rubbed his temple. 'I wouldn't have thought so. It would need some type of dedicated structure.'

'Do we want to wait that long to find out?' Hellier huffed and came to a halt.

'I'm betting he's all talk.' Marcus leaned back with his arms crossed. 'And he can't do a thing till he gets this Summoner.'

'What the devil is that?' Hellier's fiery gaze danced over all of them.

'Who flamin' knows,' Marcus retorted, "Cos we don't.'

Shiarn's delicate brows creased with anxiety. 'Whatever it is, it's best he doesn't get it.'

Keanan ran his hand through his normally neat hair. 'And Jett is not forthcoming with any useful information. Curse him!'

'He's pretty much said we can't stop him,' Marcus stretched his feet out.

'Oh, right, and we should listen to him?!' Earona frowned.

Marcus shrugged. 'Hey, I don't like it either.'

'Sadly, he may be right. I've talked to Clara and Morias and they have never experienced anything like this and there is nothing in their library on it.' Keanan's mouth formed a hard line and he faced them. 'I've been thinking on this, and I believe the best option is taking him home.'

'What?!' Marcus jumped off the bed. 'You can't be serious?'

Keanan stepped closer and his voice was unyielding. 'I don't think we have much choice. We can't do anything to prevent the opening of a Gate and we don't have the ability to help Jett, and as it is our Gifts are gone.'

'You're probably right.' Shiarn tossed her head back and looked at the ceiling. 'As far as we know he may be lost forever.'

Earona stared down at the floor resigned to the topic although far from agreeing. 'But… we may never be able to leave home again if we return.'

'And we would be going back without Ethan…' Seth said.

'You really want to take him back?' Marcus shouted, 'In chains?! And without a full Kin? Blood 'n shite! As sure as I'm a Steel, they'll execute him, and if not that, they'll seal him away.'

A dreadful pause came over them at the harsh truth of Marcus' proclamation.

Hellier stepped up to him, her voice cold. 'Flamin' hell, we can't leave him here like this.'

'If we go back, we would most likely get a new Avare as well.' Shiarn tilted her head to view Keanan.

'True.' Keanan gripped his chin and his face reddened.

'I'll be damned,' Marcus snarled.

Keanan glared at him. 'I don't like it any more than you, but I see little choice in the matter.'

'We can't leave him here?' Seth looked up at Keanan, his eyes pleading.

'And what shall we do?' Keanan took an extended breath and regained his composure. 'We have impinged on the Sommerlea residents already, and now I fear, they and us will face further danger.'

Seth's head dropped at the truth of it.

'It's the flamin' curse.' Hellier's voice was a low menacing drawl. 'The curse of the Storm Clan.'

Earona gaped at the speaking of it aloud. A secret everyone knew, but no one dared talk about. 'Don't…'

Shiarn frowned at Hellier in warning.

'Whether it is or not, is irrelevant,' Keanan said, 'And doesn't help the situation—'

'They won't think like that back home.' Marcus directed his glare at Keanan.

'We should have seen this coming.' Hellier's voice remained wrathful. 'A long time ago.'

'But,' Seth paused, 'if he can't be saved, what happens to him?'

'In that case, he's better off dead,' Shiarn finished.

'Shut your flamin' mouth!' Marcus yelled.

Fist raised, Hellier fired back, 'Don't talk to her like that!'

Keanan lifted his palm to stop them. 'This is why we need higher counsel—'

Shiarn sprang off the chair to face Marcus and her arm swung wide. 'Do you want him to live like that, some pawn of the enemy? Would Jett want that? And if it's really still 'Jett' do we really need someone like that around, knowing all about us, leading us, or not?'

Marcus glowered at her and his voice teemed with anger. 'I don't want to be the one who decides his fate and ends it. Do you?'

'He's turned into an obnoxious evil fiend, who I currently can't stand,' Shiarn fumed, 'Saying things about me he had no right knowing. I wanted too…'

'Kill him?' Marcus taunted.

'I admit it,' Shiarn replied, 'it seemed he was provoking me.'

'He had that effect on me too,' Marcus relented, 'As if he wanted me to hit him.'

'Does he want us to hurt him?' Earona took a sharp gulp. Maybe Jett was trying to tell them something? Or was she just hoping that somewhere in there, Jett was still Jett. 'To kill him?'

Seth slouched beside her. 'It wouldn't be surprising.'

Keanan scratched his chin in thought. 'Would Jett actually be trying to get himself killed?'

'Damn him!' Shiarn's voice caught with a tinge of grief. 'That he would manipulate us and expect us to...'

'I know he'd prefer we did it than the Eldery.' Marcus gave an unexpected guttural chuckle. 'We'd be known as the mad Kin who killed their own Avare.'

'It's not funny!' Earona lashed out with her own hurt. 'Jett would never...'

Seth said, 'I can't imagine we would be able to deliver a killing blow.'

Hellier pointed at Marcus. 'He'd never let you.'

'I remember Jett saying once,' Seth said, 'he would face death to save the Kin...'

Earona put her arm around his shoulders to share his sorrow. 'Yes, he also said, if any of us died, he wouldn't want to live anymore.'

'Who knows, perhaps that is what he's trying to do,' Shiarn eyed Marcus, 'and maybe we should pay attention.'

'I don't think any of you understand the significance of what Jett is threatening,' Keanan cried. 'We need to put aside our own feelings and consider the broader dilemma.'

'If they can help him back home,' Seth implored, 'it's worth the risk of taking him back.'

'I don't give a demon's arse about a Gate, or what you do,' Hellier yelled, 'Take him back or kill him, I don't care. I'm out of here.' Her light and carefree disposition was gone, replaced by a callous expression.

Earona stared up at Hellier. 'What do you mean?'

'I'm never going back and I'll never be in another Kin.' Hellier stamped past her and left the room, slamming the door behind her.

'Hellier!' Keanan, his face lined with worry, called after her.

Earona clutched her stomach, suddenly sick inside. 'Why, when Jett needs us,' she wiped tears from her eyes, 'we can't be there for him?'

Shiarn shook her head with a grim stare. 'We don't know what he needs? Besides, the way it is, he doesn't want our help.'

'I'd rather free him and fight it out,' Marcus said, 'than see him go back home.'

Keanan threw his hands in the air. 'That's so typical. You'd prefer killing him than helping him.'

'No, if he has to die, I'd prefer fighting to the death.' Marcus eyeballed him in challenge.

'I think if Jett dies, I'd rather be dead.' Seth's tone turned melancholy.

Shiarn pointed at Marcus. 'Hellier's right. None of us, including you, would be able to kill him. He'd never let you. He probably wants to kill us.'

'All the better.' Marcus punched his hand.

'Holy Kahm, this is depressing…' Earona didn't think she could live without Jett as her Avare, and no one else could ever take his place in her heart.

'I can't disagree.' Shiarn threw herself back down on the chair.

'And we're not getting anywhere,' Keanan conceded.

Marcus turned to go. 'I've had enough of talking. If you take him back, you're on your own.'

'Damn it, Marcus!' Keanan yelled as Marcus walked out of the room, sending the door wide and banging on the wall.

Earona watched him stalk out with no desire to stop him. She had no idea that without Jett, the Kin would fall apart so quickly and with such terrible impact. It truly was the worst days of her life and all she wished to do was tell Jett about it.

Keanan looked at her with shrewd precision. 'Earona, what do you think?'

Her blue eyes, wet with tears, blinked at him. Every option was one of defeat and despair, with death the result, either theirs or Jett's. 'I…' her lip quivered and she burst out with a heart wrenching sob and ran from the room.

~ * ~

Later that day, Earona stared out at the lake and a lone figure sitting on the jetty. His blue shirt was bright against the dour grey water and he sat hunched over, with his ankles locked together. She contemplated whether to approach him. It would mean talking. Something she hadn't been good at lately. But sometimes other people's problems provided a needed escape.

She took a thoughtful breath and walked down to him. The boards creaked at each step she drew closer. As she neared, she noticed him staring at the water, but not seeing it. His white-sandy hair, normally tied up, was loose over his shoulders. The breeze swept it across his face in a way that must be annoying, yet he did nothing to move it.

'Oh…' his soft voice was not surprised by her presence.

'Hi.' She sat down beside him and shuffled closer. 'About this morning. It was…' she started – *an horrendous nightmare—* she stopped with a wistful sigh. 'I'm sorry about it…' she bowed her head. 'About everything…' *About him.*

'No. Don't.' Seth's tone bristled. 'I'm part of this Kin too.'

Earona suddenly doubted her motivations. It had never been like that before, but now everything she expected from the Kin had changed.

'Do you think we will get our Gifts back if we have a new Avare?' He looked down at his smooth hands fidgeting in his lap.

'I would assume so.' Earona glanced down at her own hands and rubbed them together. She missed her Ethos nearly as much as she missed Jett. She had read about Kins receiving new Avares after the death of their first, although a rare occurrence. She decided not to mention that detail. 'You miss it?'

He gave a slow nod. 'I'm cut off from everything. Kin and…' he reached his arm wide framing the woods to their right that bordered the lake. '…everyone. It's like I no longer have a purpose.'

'I know what you mean. I can't help anyone and I feel aches and pains.' Like she never had before. She assumed it was how everyone else must feel. 'So you think it's best to take Jett home?'

Seth shrugged. 'What else can we do? It must be better than the other option. He's completely changed and yet, he still seems to have Jett's memories and knowledge of us.'

'It's extremely disturbing.' That had saddened her more than she realized.

'His comments are spiteful in a personal way, and aimed to cause as much hurt as he can. It seems he really hates us.' He choked back a sob.

Earona wrapped her arm around his slender shoulders. 'It's not him.'

'I guess…'

A fire burned in her belly and her tone was fierce. 'He would never have hurt you or any of us. He was always worried about you. Someone had to be with you all the time…'

'I gathered that.' Seth gave a rueful smile.

Her hand tightened on his shoulder and her finger fiddled with the crimson embroidery on the sky-blue collar. It was a shirt that Jett had brought for him. The hole from the arrow was already mended. She was glad, as she imagined the shirt meant a lot to Seth. 'He cared about all of us, and he would hate this.'

'He'd be as mad as hell.' He snorted at his inappropriate humour.

'He would.' Earona's smile was sombre. 'But now…'

'He's gone.' His voice was stronger as if he had come to some resolution. 'Everything he was, was an illusion. That's what this evil Jett says. That other Jett was never the real one.'

Earona also arrived at this thought and she slumped with a disheartened sigh. 'But, no I can't believe it. We knew him, his good parts, and his bad. He was real. Maybe we were allowed to have him for a time, before…' Too many memories crowded in, causing her chest to tighten with sorrow. After all, they spent their childhood together, all growing up as a Kin. He visited her farm house countless times. Her family was large and her home chaotic, and he was comfortable there. Perhaps he could blend in. Jett was not an easy man to get on with, she knew that better than anyone, but he was welcomed. 'I wish I had been kinder.' He gave her his time and attention, even though she was at times a bit argumentative. 'But still… he's always been inclined to a bad temper.' She bit her lip, forcing her tears back. 'He wanted to protect us, always doing things on his own. He had good intentions…'

'Remember that time, me, you, and Ethan were lost in the forest while playing that daft game when we were camping.'

'You remember that? You would have been five?'

Seth nodded with a lopsided grin. 'We were lost for two days.'

Earona's mouth was agape. 'But that was terrible. Jett refused to get a Tracker.'

'True.' Seth smiled. 'He wanted to see if he could find us.'

'Oh, I remember, too well…' Earona grumbled. It was freezing and when Jett finally arrived, he found a makeshift cover of branches, made by Ethan with his hatchet. Seth was in a tree, and Earona had kept them warm and took the ache from their stomachs with her burgeoning Gift. But she still made her annoyance well felt. She almost laughed at the memory. 'He made me so cross sometimes.'

'Pushed to the brink of fear, I heard my first tree.' He sat straight and gave her a brief look of pride. 'And I was no longer afraid.'

'Yes…' Light entered her eyes at the memory of Seth discovering his Gift at such an early age. 'You think he knew what he was doing?' For the first time she considered it.

Seth lifted his head towards the mountains beyond the lake. 'I think everything he does has some purpose, even though we don't know what it is half the time.'

Earona followed his gaze, absorbing his wise remark. Jett never told them what he was thinking most of the time, and it frustrated her. 'Now he's not here to tell us what to do.'

'What is this curse?' His eyes glistened into grey as he faced her.

'My parents' Kin talked of it once when I was young around the time I found out Jett was my Avare. As far as I could work out, and it's mostly a rumour. One of Jett's ancestors did an awful thing, massacred some Kins, causing the perpetrator as well as his descendants to be cursed. Either before or after, I really don't know. Keanan probably knows more, but he will never tell you.' She shrugged with indifference. 'Whatever it was, something happened and it was a real event.'

Seth punched his thigh. 'But he shouldn't have to pay the price for someone else's crime.'

'True. And it doesn't look good that his father vanished mysteriously and his mother went mad.'

Seth watched the ripple of water for some moments. 'We should be grateful we knew Jett for a time.'

Earona rubbed his shoulder in comfort. 'And remember him like he was.'

'And mourn him…' Seth gave a heaving sob and hung his head.

~ * ~

Hellier battled her raging emotions all morning until she finally reached a decision and a semblance of calm. Although any peace she had was superficial and probably only enough to get her down there. Even as she descended the stair, she wasn't certain she was doing the right thing. It wasn't like her to back away from a challenge, she had to face him.

She walked into a deepening blackness with more trepidation. Forcing herself to remain steady, she went over what she would say and what she wouldn't. She wouldn't let her thoughts drift to their close friendship and shared memories, but she was well aware that could disappear at the sight of him. She had every intention of not seeing him, but now… she needed to see for herself, despite how it might tear her heart out completely.

Apparently a light was down there, saving her from needing a lamp. But on seeing the dark basement, she wondered if it was wise to come without one. If she had her Ethos, she wouldn't need to worry about such things.

Fear made her heart pound. The stagnant air was oppressive. An unwelcomed wind rushed through the rooms. But as far as she could determine there were no windows. She stepped quietly, guided by a distant glow of a lone lantern. She fought against the terror that caused her to feel like a child approaching a monster in its lair.

Once a good friend… but now – something else entirely.

She stopped in the shadows and watched him. He appeared asleep, sitting against the wall with his head lowered. She took a fast breath and absorbed his appearance, pretending it was Jett again. Why she thought he would look different was a vain hope. For tense moments she contemplated leaving, and keeping the vision of him as a memorial.

'Why are you spying on me?' His head remained down. 'You're too afraid to show yourself. That's surprising.'

At the sound of his voice the air in her lungs seemed to stop. Fighting back sudden tears, her trembling hand went to the sword at her back and she stepped into the dim glow. 'I'm not afraid. I was wondering if you were worth talking to.'

He looked up and pierced her resolve with his black-eyed gaze. 'None of the others were smart enough to arm themselves.'

'Maybe I understand the situation better.' The sword gave her confidence and she gripped it tighter.

He cocked his head and studied her. 'Why do you pests continue sneaking down here with no intention of fighting or killing me, and hoping I will do what you ask?'

She stepped closer to see him better. Stubble on his face made him appear rougher, and hateful animosity lined his face. 'Maybe we will kill you.'

He snorted and stood. The length of his chains was enough he could step towards her. 'You underestimate me.'

'They're making plans to take you back home.' Hellier resisted the urge to stand back from his familiar presence.

'And when their backs are turned you come and inform me?' He stared into her eyes without flinching. 'Makes me wonder about you. You hope to bait me in some way, or – you wish to join me. You will certainly be useful.'

'Or we will kill you here.'

'You're too weak and they're all cowards.'

Bursting with anger, she slapped his cheek.

He swept his hand out and grabbed her throat. His eyes glowed with an animalistic pleasure. 'Of all of you, you would have been the most suitable to my purposes.' His fingers pressed into the tender flesh under her chin.

'You're a bastard—' She grasped for air. '—always have been.'

'It seems I'm not the only one showing who they really are. But the truth is, you don't know anything about me.' His dark gaze fell to the leaf pendant around her neck. 'It's not like you to wear jewelry. Could it be a gift from your spineless cur?'

She rasped in defiance, 'Are you jealous,' she glared for impact, 'because I lay with him, and — I enjoyed it.' Maybe not the best time to provoke him, while he was choking her, but anything that would make him hurt would ease her torment. 'And I'd do it again and again—'

'Have your worm of a man.' He brought her close to his face and she twisted her face away. His voice hummed with wicked seduction. 'If that's how you play it - I'll take you with me.' His lips dragged across her cheek. 'I'll fill you up again and again.' Lust rippled through his voice and his lips curved with desire. 'When I'm sated I'll give you as a whore to the thousands.'

She wrestled to release his grip, but his arms were like iron. 'You evil bastard, I hate you!'

'You don't know what that means.' Holding her neck, he lifted her off the ground. 'But I'll show you. You will feel my wrath in a personal way.'

She had steeled herself for his hurtful words, but she was not prepared for his supernatural strength. 'You wish.' She choked inches from his face. So close she could see his lips twisting with malice and his iris' glowing crimson. Thankfully, they could not burn, because she thought she might be killed right there. 'You're…' she forced the words out. '…not Jett…'

'He is gone.' He threw her away from him.

She scampered up, rubbing and flexing her neck. His strength was incredible and he could have broken her bones if he had chosen to. 'Where is he?'

'Dead,' he snarled.

She frowned, masking her shock at his candid reference to Jett. 'You killed him?'

A wind started, centering on him and it increased in speed. Hellier wondered that his chains held, but perhaps that was a matter of time. Through the dark, she scanned what she could see of the room, and spied the short narrow stair leading to a hatch and outside.

'And I'll kill you all.'

The wind drove at her with palpable force and she pushed against it. She shouted, not able to restrain her anguish, 'You're nothing compared to him. He was a true leader.'

He directed his palm at her and the wind cut into her flesh like blades. 'You have not yet seen my power.' It blew her back with new momentum, swirling within it were wailing voices. The lone light flickered and died.

She lowered her head against the force and reached her arm forward to guard against the onslaught.

'He's never coming back.' Jett swiped his hand through the air and stopped abruptly.

Hellier staggered to the steps and up to the door. She found the latch and burst through. The wind swung the door with such force it slammed on the ground outside. She clamoured out from the evil pressure and bolted the door behind her. Heaving hard, she fell on her hands and knees. A smattering of tears was followed by an unrelenting flood of grief. With no chance of them being damned up, she let her tears flow onto the grass in shuddering sobs.

~ * ~

Mara walked between the trees on the overgrown lawn towards the entrance of Sommerlea. She had avoided the roadway, in case someone spied her. It would complicate things and she would have to talk to people. Not that she saw anyone herself. It seemed everyone was moping around, becoming more isolated from each other as the days passed. The presence of evil grew more oppressive, along with a blindness to its encroaching power. It was destroying all hope in the subtlest form. How she could sense

460

that, she couldn't say exactly, except she was given a margin of hope recently. But now… it was as gone as the man in the cellar. She recalled one of the paragraphs from the prophecy-

Out of darkness and from the abyss
Will the Summoner of Souls awaken the Demon Nation?
The Midnight Order subverts the Wolf and corrupts the Mouse
The One will rule them in the land of ruins

Could this now be coming to pass?

For some daft reason she thought he would be able to guide her, even protect her — now, it seemed a harsh joke.

She rubbed her neck and shuddered at the feel of his hand still on her, squeezing. His voice remained in her mind like an ache. His command must have done something in her spirit — because now she was battling an overwhelming desire to see him.

'Curse him! That he would end up like that,' she grumbled with irritation. The very thing she feared was unfolding around her. She would have to fight against the hell trying to claim her soul. If she could stop him, she would, but right now she had to focus on stopping herself. She patted the pouch of coins at her belt. She didn't take much, just enough. Under the cover of her cloak, a satchel held some food. She didn't care where she went, it didn't really matter, as long as she left the estate.

The tattoo on her chest throbbed and was nearly rubbed raw. Once again she scratched it. The urge to tear at her skin would not abate. Crying out, she stroked her throat again in recollection of his touch from the night before. She wondered if her body was going to fail her before she could even leave the property. Gasping with short moans, she stumbled forward in an attempt to reach the gate. She collapsed to her knees, clutching her neck and rasping for air.

Over ten feet away, the gate stood open. But now, she suspected, it was unreachable. Mara sobbed with unexpected anguish at her predicament. The sky darkened with an impending storm. Through her blurry vision, she saw dark shadows merging in the trees beyond the gate and walls. They melded into giant apparitions of creatures she could not discern. Even the statures became lifelike, with hideous faces and clawed limbs, ready to pounce on her if she stepped near them. Her way was barred. Had they always been there and she was only seeing them now?

She backed away, certain she could see their red eyes observing her movement. Leaving was not going to be easy, if she could even leave at all. He would see to it she never left. With shuddering pain and fear, she spun and ran back towards the house.

57 - Despair

Light attracts Life
Darkness does not abide any companions

Valfaèr, Elements of Arcane Power

Mara sat on her bed long after the house had gone to sleep. The embers gave off enough light to see Earona asleep in the opposite bed. It was not surprising Earona went to sleep so swiftly. Yet tossing and muttering in her sleep, she was far from restful. Mara stayed awake as long as possible, but an unnatural lethargy was dragging her body to sleep. The longer she fought it, the weaker she became and the more difficult to resist the voice. Encountering him the previous night, had left an impression on her and curbed her resolve. Most likely it was his plan, marking her in such a tangible sense; like a wicked desire she wanted to fulfill, but knew she would regret for an eternity.

If she slept, the hellish apparitions would come again. If she stayed awake, she would be fighting her inner convictions all night. Soon she would have no strength to resist either option.

Mara woke to a spindly arm hovering over her. She scrambled up the bed and away from the menacing sweep of its claws. Bulbous eyes gleamed in the dark and its blistering skin and deformed face was lit up from the grey moonlight. A blood-red tongue rolled out over pointed teeth. Too stunned to scream, she attempted moving from its reach.

Earona's scream filled the room.

The door swung open and Hellier ran in to meet the creature. Her sword swung at it and she shouted, 'Get your demon claws off her!'

The thing jumped off the bed and growled, exposing its sallow fangs. Its arm slashed at Hellier.

Mara snatched up her pillow and held it like shield. She peeked at Hellier fighting the monster, hoping she wasn't going to get cut by either of them. After a lot of growls and yelling, Hellier stabbed into the thing one last time. It dissipated into shadows from where it came. Mara sagged against the bed frame, but jumped at the sudden presence of Marcus at the door.

Marcus' worried gaze darted over them all, but stopped on Earona. 'Are you alright in here?'

'It's gone.' Hellier kept a tight grip on her sword. 'But who knows if there will be more.'

'There was one down the hall,' Marcus said.

Earona clutched her legs under the blanket and her voice warbled. 'What was it?'

'Seth's with Keanan?' Hellier ignored her and looked to Marcus.

'He is.'

Hellier started towards the door. 'I've got to check Shiarn. You stay here.'

'That's what I planned.' A hard gleam entered his eyes.

Hellier left the room and Marcus sauntered over to the chair.

Earona rolled her eyes at him making himself comfortable. 'What was that monster?'

Mara was vexed by his arrogance. Did he actually think he could stand against what was coming? She squinted at him and rolled her lips.

'A demon, probably,' Marcus replied, 'and his friends.' He leaned a sword against the chair, and rolled the hilt of the other, admiring the decoration.

Mara realized he was going to sit there, watching them, probably for the rest of the night.

Earona must have come to the same conclusion. 'Are you going to sleep there?'

'I won't be sleeping – you're sleeping.'

'Holy heavens!' Earona threw herself down on the pillows. 'I may never sleep again.'

A patronizing grin appeared on his face. 'Stop complaining and get some rest.'

Still dressed, Mara lay down under the covers. Eyes shut, she remained awake, listening to the slight movement of Marcus shifting in the chair. Her mind was a festering pool of endless recriminations and evil passion. Tense and churning with adrenaline, her body craved release. All she could feel was his presence enticing her, calling her to him. At each call, his tone became more demanding.

She groaned at his intimate hold over her senses. If she went to him, it would be her who instigated the death of these people. It would be her who made that decision, but could it even be considered a decision when he called her like this?

What if she just went to see him and nothing more? Her nail embedded into her tattoo and she wanted to gouge it out. She visualized his touch, and her flesh heated with need. A desire so strong her body trembled. It was beyond her understanding and more than she could control. Her breathing accelerated with a longing for some type of fulfillment, and she gasped.

Earona was asleep, but Marcus' bright eyes glanced about the room.

Mara sat up. With her head lowered, her red locks shielded her face.

'What's wrong?' His voice was flat in the silence.

'Alqua-elzat-varan-ezwa.'

Marcus fell back in the chair, asleep.

Clutching at her tattoo, Mara's breath came in rapid gasps and she ran from the room. Not needing a light, she dashed through the shadows. Strange noises of demonic creatures came down corridors as she headed downstairs. She sensed eyes watching her, but she sped by, hoping nothing would accost her.

Her hand stopped on the handle of the door to the cellar. Shaking, she pushed it open. Hot air hit her face, and she stepped with more deliberation down the stairs, guided by a dim light below. She hadn't been down to the cellar, but it didn't matter, she knew where he was.

A lone lantern cast a white circle of light and he stood on the outer in shadows. Anxiety had left her, and calm settled her mind, although her heart raced at his actual presence. His eyes were shut and he appeared asleep. Apart from his unkempt clothing and unshaved face, his presence took her breath away. She knew him and yet, he was a stranger. The mystery that linked them together seemed beyond the understanding of a human.

With his eyes still closed, he spoke. 'You have kept me waiting a long time. I have been patient, but I do wonder, why do you evade me?' To hear him speak in the uncharacteristic congenial fashion was jarring, and her heart jumped at the change of his disposition toward her. 'It's no matter. Finally, you have come to me.'

She paced on the edge of the light. 'Who—' she croaked and gulped. 'Am I really the Summoner? And who are you really?' She would maybe hear what he wanted, and leave. That's all, nothing more.

His dark eyes flashed open and he stared into her soul as if he had always known her. 'Why do you ask this? You know who I am, you have always known. I am your Lord, and you are my servant, the Summoner of Souls, who will fulfill my commands. Are you still being rebellious?' He stood and walked towards her.

Avoiding eye contact with him, she paced back and forth. 'But what do you want from me?' Her body fought against her better judgment and she stopped not more than three feet from him.

His eyes trailed her movement. 'You tire yourself with this needless questioning. You already have the answers within. You know who I am. I am the one who will set you free and protect you.'

She turned a horrified frown on him. 'But - I'm not going to do what you say.'

'That is because you have not yet been released.' He spread his chained wrist out inviting her to enter his space. 'Come to me. I will free you.'

Her body shook as the realization hit her. He would undo the ritual Wendessa performed on her. She would be doomed to that life of hell and destruction once more. Suddenly she knew what was at stake, her very soul. 'No, I don't want...' Her words faded away and she could speak no more.

He pulled the lacing of her dress front open, revealing the red interlocking snake. 'Look into my eyes.'

Her gaze travelled up from his chest to his face. She was trapped by his vision penetrating hers with an overwhelming sense he was going to consume her. His hand covered the seal on her chest and he spoke. 'Labarl-sharwin-margis. Ersha-ki-sudese.'

She gasped at the tearing pain. It seemed he ripped off her skin and was pouring hot oil on the wound burning her flesh. Instead of fire, she saw white light beaming out from her scar. Once the light had dissipated, she was drained and empty – there was nothing left inside that she could hold onto.

'Now you will see what you were birthed for. Verese-sheagierth-Aiya. Vassal of Wrath awake. Be weak no more. Submit to your true master.'

In her agonized state, his words echoed in her head. She had a vision of them standing on a pillar of rock surrounded by the abyss. No-where to run or hide. No-where left to go. This wasn't freedom. The wailing of thousands of souls, reached out from the pits below them, calling for revenge and the destruction of the realm of men.

He said, 'they await your awakening.'

Suddenly she recalled something very important to her, something that fascinated her. 'Have you the Key? I so want to see it.'

He held out the chain and pendant, its white gem seemed an unnatural light between them.

'You desire the treasure of the Eye of Heaven, it is a magnificent object to behold, but it is not the true power.' She attempted to hold it, but he withdrew it from her. 'It is not for you to possess.' He put it back in his pocket. 'First, I have a task for you.'

The surge of anger passed and she became subservient. 'What is your command?'

'It is time to summon her soul.'

An image of a beautiful woman in a white dress and jewels was before her, and Mara was overcome with adoration. 'She will join us. I'll make sure of it.'

~ * ~

In a cold sweat, Earona woke with a gasp and sat up, glancing around the dark room with some disorientation. Marcus was slumped in the chair asleep, and Mara – was gone. Earona tossed her blanket aside and rushed to Marcus. 'Marcus!' She shook his shoulder. 'Wake up.' Her hand cupped his face and she wobbled his chin. 'Where's Mara?' She lifted his eyelid, exposing his eye. 'That's strange…' she muttered, 'It's like he's unconscious. Oh, no.' Fearful of the encroaching shadows, she eyed the open door. 'I'll have to go myself.'

She padded down the hall in her nightdress and listened to the distant groans of a house under siege of hellish entities. Peering down corridors, she called Mara's name with a faint voice. It was Mara she wanted not the attention of some monster. She felt the shadows watching her passage and she quickened her pace down the stairs. Maybe Mara was in the kitchen? Possibly the den? Of all the places she could think of, she had an awful foreboding it would be the basement where she found her.

She neared the cellar door and hesitated, questioning her motives. Did she want to find Mara or see Jett again? She stepped through the shadows, realizing too late she had come without a light.

The air had an organic musky scent, and the heat increased as she entered the chamber where Jett was restrained. She pulled up short at the sight of Mara, and Jett with his hand on her shoulder.

'Stop!' Earona squealed with urgency.

Mara spun around with eyes like copper fire, glaring. She stormed towards Earona, and Earona stared dumbfounded at her scar-mark glimmering like fire. Mara shouldered her as she passed, 'out of my way,' and sprinted off into the darkness.

Earona's gaze made a slow curve to Jett standing outside the circle of light coming from the lamp that flickered with diminishing strength. Sweat dampened her chest and she swallowed hard, aware she was in the presence of someone from the demonic world.

He took a step forward. His body entered the light while his face remained shrouded in shadow as if it were a portentous sign. His eyes glistened and did not leave her face.

'What—' Earona's voice caught in her dry throat. '...did you do to her?'

'You came here alone. That's brave of you.' He brought his hands together and the chains clanked softly. Yet the sound was stark in the unnatural quiet. 'Although far from smart.'

The chains gave her some comfort, but his smirk made her question how presumptuous she had been in coming to see him. She clutched her arms despite the heat and teetered on her toes ready to run as if in the presence of a snake. 'It's... I like to see you, despite you being an evil creature.' There, she said it, bared her heart to the wicked devil. 'Because... I miss him...'

He sneered, revealing the white of his teeth. 'Your human emotions are disgusting.'

She gripped herself harder and felt the tears choking her throat. 'I don't care what you think.' The steel in her voice surprised her – but it was only to counter the tears about to drown her. 'Jett would never have done this to us. Why won't you remember?'

'I'll not entertain dead memories.'

With an abrupt sob, Earona's chest heaved and she stepped nearer to him, longing to see something familiar in his eyes. 'They're not dead to me. They are real and more powerful than you.'

He directed his palm at her and she dropped to her knees. She could do nothing to comfort her bones as a weight draped over her head and shoulders. She stared at her hands, flexing in her lap, hands that no longer healed, or even brought comfort it seemed. Tears came and shuddering gasps, and shame she would make herself so vulnerable before the instigator of her grief.

'Tears will not win him back.'

She sniffed loudly, but refused to wipe them away. 'Win him?' Her voice was a garbled mess. 'Then?' She gathered the courage to look up. It was Jett's body and his face, yet his eyes smoldered with a hate birthed outside her comprehension.

'You are the most annoying of all of them.' His hand gripped her head. 'I will erase those memories.'

She cried out from a stabbing pain entering her mind. It transformed to a biting chill numbing her flesh and making her nauseous. She opened her mouth to speak but was breathless. Air in her lungs was draining out and some dark substance was pouring into her mind, dulling her reasoning, making her forget...

A burst of fire propelled Jett's hand back. More flames lit up the room and sent him backwards. Ominous shadows manifested around him and repelled the fire.

Released from his hold, Earona slouched in a daze and was caught up in someone's arms. Her eyes opened enough to see Keanan, staring with a grim determination at Jett.

Keanan snatched Earona up while Jett was distracted by Morias' fire. As Keanan expected, the fire had little effect, but it was enough in this instance. He hedged backwards to join Morias.

Morias stood with axe and his hand at the ready. His deep voice hit the walls like a stone. 'We've come for Earona.'

Jett's mouth turned up in a spiteful sneer at Keanan and his eyes sparked with irritation at Morias. The shadows formed tendrils and swirled about him. His voice resonated in the confined space. 'What do you think you're going to do?'

'You shouldn't underestimate us.' Keanan remained calm despite his blood boiling with rage.

'That's right.' Fire spiked over Morias' palm. 'You don't know me or what we're capable of.'

Jett raised his open palms and the darkness took more solid shape. 'It doesn't matter what you can do, my power will have no rival in this world.'

Keanan's skin reddened with anger. 'We haven't been beaten yet, and you haven't won.'

The darkness whipped around and lashed towards them. 'You've all talk. That's all you've ever been.'

'You have no idea what we're planning,' Morias said.

Jett sneered. 'Come show me, because I am tired of waiting.' His voice grew in volume and appeared to correlate with the amassing shadows. 'And I am tired of these restraints.' He raised his hand and directed it at Keanan. Darkness formed sharp shards and shot towards him. Fire countered the attack, breaking up the black spears and sending them sideways.

Keanan breathed a relieved sigh and held Earona tighter as he backed away. Jett was becoming too deadly to confront without some defense. He left the cellar and the growing darkness. Morias followed him up the stair and he slammed the door behind him.

Keanan observed Earona's shallow breathing and closed eyes.

Morias gazed down at her. 'Take her upstairs. I'll get Clara.'

Keanan gave a short nod.

Morias put his hand on Keanan's back. 'He's getting dangerous. It's time to deal with him. Permanently.' His dark eyes drilled home his intention.

Keanan exhaled a long-held breath. 'I know. But can you do anything?'

'We might need to wait for Kael and Jonas.' He looked towards the door. 'But if we let him go like this, he's going to get stronger.'

'You are correct. It's him or us.'

'That's the best way to look at it.'

Earona remained motionless in Keanan's arms as he carried her upstairs.

On nearing her room, Marcus stumbled out, yawning. He became more alert on seeing Earona. 'What happened?'

'She was down in the cellar.' Keanan lashed out. 'You were supposed to be watching her.'

'Hold on, I was,' Marcus yelled. 'I… something strange happened…'

Earona opened her eyes and struggled to speak. 'Is Mara safe?' Her voice was a gravelly whisper.

'She's not in there,' Marcus said. 'I haven't seen her except for… she spoke to me and then… I can't remember.'

'We will look for her.' Keanan placed her under the covers.

Marcus stood over Earona, and his tone was wrathful. 'He did this?'

Keanan sat on the edge of the bed and caressed her dark fringe from over her face. 'We found her.' Devoid of colour, her skin was near transparent, and with her big shuttered eyes, she looked like a dead child against the white pillow. 'Hopefully in time.'

'The bastard!' Marcus growled. He placed his hand on her neck. 'She's cold… like stone.'

'She was near lifeless.' Keanan's face drooped with weariness.

With a half open eye, Earona looked at them and mumbled, '…Mara…'

Marcus replied, 'I'll go find her.'

58 - Prophecy?

Knowledge leads to understanding, and understanding begets wisdom
And wisdom is its own reward

Ei'myn Geí-Serenmãh

Earona stirred from a heavy sleep and discovered a weight lying across her chest. She opened her eyes to what she assumed was daylight in the dim gloom. A turbulent wind was hitting the window outside. Clara lay over her, trembling. Her braided golden hair hung over her outstretched hand. Was she crying? Earona attempted to reassure her, but found her limbs were lead. She tilted her head, but even that was a chore.

Clara eased up and wiped her damp cheeks. 'At last, you have woken up.'

'I…' Earona croaked from a parched mouth. '…what… is it?'

'Not a normal sickness.' Clara rubbed Earona's shoulder and sent a soothing warmth into her flesh. 'I've been restoring your life.'

Earona's mouth twitched with wonder. 'My life?'

'If Keanan and Morias had not found you in time, you would have become – an empty shell.'

Earona's gulp turned to a dry choke. Jett had intended to kill her.

'But still, you're weak.' She scrunched up her lip in contemplation. 'You may take time to recover.'

She was just thankful to be alive, although how long that was going to last she dreaded to think. Her eyes crossed to the other bed – empty and unslept in. 'Is Mara…'

Clara's sky-blue eyes glanced to the bed and back to Earona in sorrow. 'We can't find her. We looked all over the house and outside.'

Earona stared at the empty place.

'She may have run away. I hope she hasn't—' her forehead creased with sadness and she dabbed her eye. 'And the worst hasn't occurred.'

Earona blinked with disbelief, remembering the cruel look she received in the cellar. Mara had been different.

'Something will have to be done about him.' Clara's tone became gruff. 'Soon we won't be able to… he's getting stronger. We fear the malreus chains will no longer hold him.'

Goosebumps covered Earona's skin at the vision of Jett roaming free about the house. '…you mean?'

'I'm not sure it can be done without Kael and Jonas. Kael would never let me go near such a one who can drain a person's mind.' Clara gave her a careful glance. 'You don't need to worry about that. You need to heal from this.'

Earona stared back dumbfounded. What was the point of recovering if Jett was dead and the Kin fragmented? She closed her eyes and sunk deeper into the pillow.

~ * ~

Marcus pushed up the hatch to the open air. Hellier, her long plaits fluttering across her taupe shirt, stood with her back to him and leaning against the turret wall.

'Oh, it's you.' He hefted himself out onto the tower platform and shivered in the cold air.

She glanced over her shoulder and turned her face back into the driving wind. 'No-one else.'

He let the door fall shut and came to stand beside her. Stretching his arm on the stonework, he found it still damp from the stormy night. On a clear day he imagined the view was startling, but currently the lake reflected a grey haze from the rainy mist. 'Still looking for Mara…' It was only an excuse to come up here; he should have known Hellier would beat him to it.

'She's not here.'

Marcus shrugged and shook his wet sleeve with annoyance. 'I can see.'

'Can't blame her she's gone.' Hellier's voice resembled her weak pallor.

After several moments of silence and wind chilling his face, Marcus said, 'Reminds me of home,' he waved his arm through the air, 'cursed weather. Just like the plateau. But the view's not as impressive as the steeps.' Not until he started coming down to Melchior did he realize he took the plateau for granted. If Jett were with them, he'd probably be up there too.

'Home, eh…' Hellier breathed.

'Yeah, you remember… mountains, fog, snow, and the best fire-pit nights.'

'Home will never be the same.' Her tone was brisk, cutting off his reminiscing.

He took some time trying to figure out anything that might break her sullen mood. 'It will always have those people who care about you.' He thought on his own parents, elderly for Fáerinn, and his four siblings, all older than him.

'How can we ever go back?'

Marcus wasn't going to bite back, realizing she was only unfurling her grief.

After a tense moment, she continued, the distress building in her voice. 'He needs to be dealt with and we're doing nothing.' She spun on him, her jaw clenching and she threw her fist at her chest. 'I need to do something.'

He stepped back from her ire. 'We don't know how to stop him except kill him—'

'Exactly.' Her crisp blue eyes bored into his.

He narrowed his eyes, sensing his own irritation flaring up. 'You sound like you want him to die.'

She screwed up her face under his forthright scrutiny, and swiveled back to the lackluster view. 'I don't want him to live.'

He stared aghast. It wasn't that he didn't understand, it was that – Hellier was hurting more than he could see on the surface. Perhaps losing their Mind-speak had affected them more than they knew. 'I call your bluff.'

She faced him with her cheeks red and her hand raised. He wondered if she was going to punch him. She said, 'Do you really want someone like him, who knows all about us and Tellávare walking the earth? He knows too much – about… me.' Hot angry tears appeared and she kicked the wall with her boot. 'Isn't it like he's dead anyway?'

He had to admit she had a point and he replied in a sobering mumble, 'He's a foul-mouth demon that thinks too much of himself, I'll give him that.'

'If he's dead, I can mourn him properly and not like this. Seeing him, yet it's not him, but some…' she stifled a sob, 'mean-arsed devil.'

If Jett got to the stage where he was freely walking the earth, Marcus expected they wouldn't be around to witness it. 'When the time comes we will fight him and stand against what he's doing, whether we or he dies.'

She stared over the wall, but he suspected she wasn't interested in the scenery. 'That's fine for you and me, but Earona was nearly killed. And what if he kills Seth?'

Earona's near death had scared the life out of him, and made him aware how deadly Jett had become. 'Whatever we do can't involve them.'

Hellier snorted her admonishment. 'And they would agree with that?' She shook her head.

No, they wouldn't, and there would be more arguments all around, because they couldn't agree on anything. 'Curses,' he muttered, 'what a cock-up this journey has turned out to be.'

~ * ~

A continuous rattling from the wind outside caused Earona to open her eyes from a torpid sleep. Ashen grey tinted the room from the fading sun, and despite the storm, the air remained a sickly heat. Shiarn reclined atop Mara's bed, reading a book under the glow of the lamp.

Earona had been in bed for a whole day and night and she was only beginning to feel better. She dragged herself up onto the pillow. Her body was leaden and fatigued. At least her thoughts had cleared.

Too engrossed in her reading, Shiarn paid her no mind.

Earona observed the plain brown book and struggled to recall its title. 'Is that that journal?'

'Mm.'

'Any sign of Mara?' She asked everyone the same question.

Shiarn shook her head. 'She probably stole some coin and ran. Who would want to stay here, with all that's going on?'

Earona shook her head and it pounded from the movement. But Mara had been the one the witch wanted before all this and the one with the secrets. Maybe Shiarn was right. 'Is that interesting?' She pushed up the pillow and relaxed up against it.

Shiarn turned a page and took her time answering. 'Not sure yet.' Finally she looked over to her. 'God, you look awful.'

Earona combed her fingers through her hair, made lank by her cold fever. She looked at her bare arm. Her skin was dry and blotchy. 'Thanks,' she retorted, 'At least I'm alive.' She sighed. After all, he really had wanted her dead.

'At least you have some humour.'

'It's not humour—'

The door opened and Hellier walked in, shutting it quietly behind her. 'I'm here. What's with the secret meeting?'

'About time.' Shiarn waved her in.

Earona looked between them, sensing she was caught in some prearranged discussion.

Hellier stood between the bed and nodded at the journal. 'So that's it. That old stinking book.'

'We can't ignore the events in this journal having some significance.' She flashed the cover before their noses – *From Glory to Ruin, Amin-Sayeda*. 'I'm tired of us sitting on our arses and letting everything happen to us like we are a bunch of crying bubs.'

'Sounds like you're planning something?' Hellier's blue eyes brightened.

'Are you saying we should do away with him?' Earona said.

Hellier nodded at her. 'That's what Morias and Adis are planning.'

'I'm not surprised.' Shiarn shifted to sit on the bed. 'In theory it is the wisest action to take – but could it actually be done? I doubt it. It would take all of us and there would still be casualties, if not deaths. Thank Kahm, he doesn't have his Charer Gift. We would probably all be dead already.'

Earona fidgeted with her blanket and Hellier stared down at the floor.

'Morias' Kin is not made for combat.' Shiarn drove her point home. 'Imagine if Clara were killed? And Jonas and Kael came home to find their house destroyed and their Kin dead?' She shuddered.

Hellier's head shot up. 'That's likely no matter what anyone tries to do. That's why *we* should do it.'

'Kill him?' Earona gaped at her.

Hellier eyed them both with a malice Earona had never seen in her before.

'God, Hel,' Shiarn peered at her with surprise. 'You make it sound so easy. He's a flamin' demon lord!'

'Jett's not the only member of this Kin. We aren't brown-nose sheep, incapable of doing anything—'

'I agree.' Shiarn smiled. 'But it doesn't always have to be killing. So, I've been trying to unearth anything useful in this.'

Earona stared with wonder and Hellier squinted with skepticism.

Shiarn went on, 'I'm certain whatever Morgal was doing was connected with events in this book. He wanted the amulet I had—'

'That amulet?' Hellier tapped her finger on her lips. 'Seth had it and Jett ended up with it.'

'I know, I found out when I came back, but it slipped my mind.' Shiarn muttered, 'How convenient.'

Earona scratched her head. 'You think the amulet is making him like this? As if it's cursed somehow?'

Shiarn's lips pressed together. 'I know the pendant was important, but I can't say if that's affecting him directly. After all, I did possess it, as did Seth.' After a thoughtful pause, she said, 'Something Keanan said, got me thinking. We have been so focused on our feelings that our thoughts and reasoning is non-existent, or completely daft. We need to think.'

'Currently my mind is not able to think.' Earona's voice was a soft mumble.

Shiarn nodded at her. 'With all the big talk from this demon Jett, the truth is, he is currently bound and not wrecking chaos as he would like – something is wrong… '

Earona and Hellier stared in bewilderment. Earona said, 'Wrong…? I can't see anything wrong with that. Well, I mean the whole thing is "wrong"'

'Or, I should say, something isn't right.' Shiarn sighed. 'It would seem, from the perspective of an evil-being that the current situation is not in their best interest. This is all speculation, and more like a potential move from a game of King's Square. I believe something is occurring in Jett's mind making it harder for this demon creature to take over…' She let her words linger between them and went back to flipping through the pages.

'I see…' Earona said, 'But, we can't get into his mind? Can we?'

'No.' Hellier paced between them, staring at the floor. 'Maybe we can get this amulet off him.'

Earona watched her walking. 'It seems too simple. Would that really help?'

'It might piss him off.' Hellier gave a rueful grin; the first one Earona had seen in days. Perhaps Shiarn was really bringing hope to their situation.

'Here it is.' Shiarn flicked the book up in front of them, and her finger tapped on a drawing of the amulet in the middle of a circle. 'And here is a prophecy written in a temple in Amin-Sayeda apparently beneath the original of this sketch. The author of the journal, Zaki'is Fur'Mole, copied it down.' Her eyes blazed with pride as she read a few sentences aloud. The words, spoken in Fáer rolled off Shiarn's tongue like a song. She stopped. 'I'm too superstitious to read the whole thing here.'

'What the hell does it mean?' Hellier stopped short and crossed her arms.

Earona knew well that Hellier, like Jett, never appreciated the words of prophecy. But despite the ominous predilections, Earona's spirit lifted with hopeful anticipation and she sighed with melancholy. 'It's beautiful, but dark.'

'There is a distinction between good and evil,' Shiarn continued looking it over. 'And there are two interesting facts. It is written in Fáer by another race that by rights should not know our language, and also, the verses pertaining to darkness are in reverse slant.' She turned the book allowing them to view the script.

Earona studied it with confusion, and Hellier blurted, 'So?'

Shiarn cast them a condescending glance. 'Reverse script indicates the works of evil. But the forward slant is often viewed as the opposite, even in some cases, a counteraction.'

Earona caught her breath, recalling the writing from the witches' possessions also slanted backwards. 'Power in the words.' She sat straight, feeling revived.

Shiarn nodded with a sombre grimace. 'Yes, but for good or bad… I wonder.'

'And what do we do with it?' Hellier stopped pacing and gripped her sword hilt, preparing for immediate action.

'We should read it in front of him.' Shiarn stood from the bed. 'See what happens.'

'Now?' Hellier frowned at the two. 'With Earona?'

Having pushed the covers aside, Earona stood on unsteady feet. 'I'm coming.'

Shiarn considered her. 'It's your decision. But in honesty, what have we got to lose? We don't have an Avare, or our Mind-speak, and no Gifts.'

'The boys?' Hellier supported Earona's arm.

'No,' Shiarn snapped. 'It's more people to get in the way, and worry about. And I hate to say it, but if nothing happens, and we fail, it will leave them to… clean up.'

Earona gaped. 'That's frightful…'

Hellier shrugged. 'I'm not going quietly.'

'I really don't know if anything will change.' Shiarn held up the book. 'But I'm willing to try this.'

'At least it's something.' Hellier patted her shoulder.

With a tight smile, Earona said, 'You would be a good Avare, Shiarn.' She almost regretted it instantly.

Shiarn's eyes widened with comical surprise. 'That's the nicest thing you have ever said to me in my entire life.'

Earona scowled with sudden annoyance. 'That's not true!'

'If I was Avare…' Shiarn sang with a playful tune and hugged the journal to her chest. 'I would command that you all dress better and dance more. I would have one of you do my hair every day and a man for my pleasure.' She winked at them.

'You would hate it.' Hellier gave her a grim smile.

Shiarn gave a breathy sigh. 'I'm sure you are right. Looking after all of you would be exhausting.'

Earona snorted. 'Actually I don't think I—'

'Enough of this chatter.' Hellier started for the door. 'Let's go.'

59 - Find the Source

"The smallest spark is the brightest light in the darkest pit…"

Tiverbius Salt'Brew, Bard of Bards

He stood on the steps of the pavilion, looking out at the lake under the radiance of twilight. A sharp wind whipped at his black hair and he threw his head back to observe stars appearing. Fascinated by the spectacle, yet not having the sentiment to express his regard. The outside vista had not changed in some time. But even to that, he was not certain. The black-outs came with more frequency. He had no memory of falling or even going to sleep, but he woke on the bed, or the floor, and always with dark images in his mind and a debilitating pain that wracked his chest for some time after.

Nya approached from behind and ran her hand along his bare back and down to his pants. 'My love, you are out here again.'

She was the only warmth in this quiet world of cold marble and extravagant furnishings, and he was ever more dependent on her touch. She was the center of his world, inhabiting his thoughts and bringing solace in the lonely hours; his drink and food, and everything he needed to exist. Craving her embrace, he took her more often with a selfish wantonness. She was ever present – except for that one place where she was absent, his dreams. No, they were more like nightmares. 'I wonder what is out there?' his soft voice was carried away on the breeze.

'Nothing that would satisfy you.'

'They were in my dreams again.' He had woken on the floor moments ago, or perhaps hours. Time had no value and he had no way of measuring it.

Her hand tensed around his. 'You had a dream?'

'When I sleep.' He could recall no details or names, or anything except the feelings that remained. He mulled them over, imprinting them in his thoughts again, in case they disappeared like so many other notions he was sure he had. For the most part he kept them from her. It only seemed to darken her eyes with worry.

She looped her arms under his and held his waist. 'They are only dreams, nothing more.' And she kissed his shoulder.

He caressed her arms and considered her astute statement. But how could dreams leave him in agony, with a sense of loss. There were things he needed to know, and he struggled to form words for his queries. '…who are they?'

Her lips travelled up his neck to his ear. 'They can't be good, because they cause you such unrest. It displeases me.' She held his chin and turned his face to meet hers. 'What happened in this dream?'

He leaned into her body and brushed his fingers down the sheen of her cheek. 'I can't remember… except they spoke.'

'They were angry?' She pouted. 'At you?'

He searched his mind, recalling the semblance of heated emotion. 'Yes, and…' his brow furrowed and he concentrated till a glimmer of memory led him to feel… '…sadness.' Someone wept.

She ran her fingers through his hair. 'Dreams are only flippant emotions.'

But, why did they linger in him, affecting his reasoning and sinking his soul to despair? 'Why am I here?' His sudden question surprised him.

'It is your destiny.' She tangled her fingers in his and guided him back up the few steps. 'Your purpose is to take your place of honour.'

A chair carved from black rock had intricate embellishments of creatures and symbols he could not distinguish. He pondered if it had always been present, because he could not remember it as easily as the view. It loomed like a cold majestic object; its presence dominated the whole room. At every opportunity she enticed him to sit. Perhaps because she pushed so much, he was reluctant. He could think of no other reason why he would avoid it. He smiled at her warm eyes and shared his thoughts. 'We should leave this place.'

'Leave?!' Her eyes bolted open with surprise and she took a shallow breath. 'There is only death and pain outside. Besides, why would you wish to leave this sanctuary?'

He put mock sternness into his voice. 'The dream caused me to think I had some unfulfilled task.'

She lifted a brow in a comical fashion. 'I see. And what is this task?'

'I have to find…' he said with as much conviction as he could, 'someone.'

She caressed the carvings on the high back of the rock chair, and her mouth twitched into a beguiling smile. 'But you have found someone. It was I, you were searching for.'

He gave a short nod. 'Perhaps so. But, I want to understand—'

'You wish for understanding, sit at the center of all things.' The tone of her voice deepened. 'For me,' she whispered in a kiss on his other hand.

He laid his hand on the chair and the stone was oddly hot, as if a fire burned beneath it. If it could grant him answers, he would sit.

~ * ~

Shiarn followed Hellier down to the cellar with Earona tagging behind them. Groans and wails seem to come from the house itself, as if it were about to fall apart from the strain. But the girls arrived at their destination without any interference. Hellier had her hand on the cellar door knob.

'Wait.' Shiarn studied their determined faces huddling near hers. 'We have to be careful.'

'I know that.' Hellier glared with irritation.

'And I know you two. We are going to be in the enemy's territory,' Shiarn lowered her brow. 'Don't say anything that will provoke him.'

Earona huffed. 'What are we supposed to say?'

'Distract him enough so I can read this.' Shiarn held the journal out from her cloak. 'If it doesn't work, we need a chance of getting out.'

Hellier put her hand on her sword hilt. 'At least I've got this.'

'I said not to provoke him,' Shiarn hissed. 'Let's try to mislead him by acting meek.'

Hellier twisted her face in indignation. 'I don't know how.'

Earona made a fist. 'I'll try, but he can make me so upset.'

Shutting her eyes for a moment, Shiarn sighed with resignation. 'As long as I have time to read it. And remember, I'm not going to speak anything except this prophecy until I complete it.' She spread the book open at the saved page.

'Why?' Hellier said.

'I don't want any other words to interfere,' Shiarn said. 'It feels right that way.'

'We will do the talking for you.' Earona squeezed Shiarn's arm in reassurance.

Groaning, Shiarn hid the book away again. 'That's what's worrying me.'

Hellier opened the door and they proceeded down the narrow stairwell. Shiarn held the little lantern. The foul odour was stronger since the last time she was down, and it wouldn't surprise her if the darkness was more opaque. She started sweating as soon as she stepped into the cellar. The girls crept through the dark towards the faint glimmer of the other light.

Remaining out of the direct light, Jett watched them enter his chamber.

Judging the distance of his reach and making sure to stay out of it, Shiarn stopped. Earona, her skin still pasty, was already breathing hard from the walk down the stairs. She stepped to the left, while Hellier moved to the right, leaving Shiarn facing him.

Jett was cornered, not that he looked concerned. He smirked at the three and appeared amused. 'The traitor, the whore, and the whiner, come to taunt me with your insipid gibberish.'

'You should look at yourself.' Earona gave a grating cough. 'Who are you calling names? You're a despicable monster.'

'Your time is drawing to a close.' Hellier stood firm, her chest out, not intimidated in the least by his wicked demenour.

Shiarn rolled her eyes at them. Did they even hear what she had said? And she could say nothing to rebuke them – if only she could Mind-speak.

'And it has come now!' Earona cried before doubling over, leaning her hands on her knees to catch her breath. 'You're the one who should be afraid.'

Jett stepped closer and his black menacing gaze fell on her pitiful state. 'You look half-dead. I should finish the job.' Shadows formed from his palms and coalesced into sharp points. 'It is your time that has come.'

'Hurry and read it, Shiarn.' Hellier raised her sword at him.

Shiarn dropped the lamp upright and brought out the journal.

Jett's eyes raced to the book and his bearded face flared up with unexpected unease. 'What is that?'

'You're worried,' Hellier taunted, 'aren't you?'

All the time that the journal was in their possession, Jett had never read it. For once Shiarn was glad he was not an avid reader. She splayed one hand out to him and kept her voice devoid of her rising anxiety. Speaking in Fáer, she started,

'Heaven and Hell - collide.

Break the soul – divide—'

Red energy surged up from the floor and pulsed around Jett. With a fierce crack, the malreus cuffs fell apart and he was free. 'No you don't.'

Shiarn nearly faltered with panic, but was determined to finish come what may.

'Evil – Shadows the mind – no further.

Speak – Light of the Righteous - hear.'

Black-red power twisted around his arms and came at her from his outstretched hands. 'You whore-bitch.' The black shadows swirled around the room, creating a windy vortex.

His sudden loss of composure was a sign she was onto something, but his growth in power was incredible.

'Rule – Hatred spawned in one – cast down.

Arise – Conviction of Love – take place.

Abide – Iniquitous Wrath – no more.'

Thrown to the floor by an unseen pressure, Shiarn lay winded. The book tossed aside, and for some mystical reason, the page did not give way in the malevolent wind.

Jett's face stretched into a pale deathly mask, no longer resembling the Jett she knew. His hands groped to throttle her and he let out a vicious and unnatural growl from the pit of his belly.

'No!' Earona leapt in front of Shiarn and took the burst of power into her own chest.

Reaching for the book before the shadow could sweep it away, Shiarn snatched it close to her body. She stifled a curse and shouted into the air,

'Reside – Noble duty – reclaim.

'Reflect – Each own destined intention - decreed.

Light and Dark - Separate.'

Earona rose off the floor with the dense black circling her chest and crawling up her neck to enter her mouth. Choking for air, she could do nothing to stop its ascent.

'You've forgotten about me.' Hellier sliced through the solid mass of black connecting Earona to Jett.

Earona dropped to the floor encased in the black that was hardening to stone. She took long shuddering breaths.

Shiarn ignored Earona's wounded state and forged on, knowing she had to speak the last paragraph three times. The prophetic words gave her incentive. Her voice rose with supernatural authority as she shouted out the script.

Hellier stood between Jett and Earona, her sword ready to drag across his flesh.

'You can't stop me with that.' He stared her down with a malicious glare. The black tendrils rushed around the chamber, whipping at their clothing and hair and cutting into their skin.

'We're going to give it a good try.' Hellier stared back, her expression revealing nothing but a need to win.

Roaring with anger, he summoned more power. It poured out from his hands and swirled about them, slicing into their flesh like knives. Out of it, three pointed streams sped and weaved towards the girls.

Shiarn yelled out the last repeated paragraph,

'Call forth Soul's strongest desire.

Summon Mind's Heavenly path.

Herald Light's true birth.'

The last words of the prophecy echoed over the rush of his evil force, and everything in the room ceased its movement. Jett flew back and stopped abruptly a foot off the ground. His wrists went up to the side of his head as if he were pinned to an invisible wall, and his chin flopped onto his chest. The black-energy was frozen in mid-flight and a strange lull hit the chamber.

Shiarn rose to her feet awe-struck at the scene. The black tendrils hardened around Earona, but she had room to struggle up on hands and knees, and she spat bile onto the stones.

Hellier stepped up to view Jett suspended off the ground. 'Now what?'

Shiarn groaned and flipped through the pages in vain. 'What have I missed?'

'Are we meant to…?' Earona rasped 'kill him?! Now?!'

With her malreus sword glinting in the gloom, Hellier said, 'You have to admit, it's the perfect opportunity.'

'Holy Kahm… surely it isn't that?' Shiarn grasped at her stomach, ready to heave like Earona was already doing, but for different reasons.

Hellier directed her weapon at Jett's abdomen, making reading to thrust.

'I can't watch.' Shiarn turned her face away.

Earona, her arm held tight by the black stone, looked up, and gasped, 'Wait… there's something…'

A glimmer of white appeared from Jett's chest. Hellier jumped back and they watched spell-bound as it grew into a sphere that appeared to separate from Jett's body. It manifested into a human figure that lit up the chamber with its glowing core. Within moments, a beautiful woman in a sheer white dress, and rich dark hair, stood before them. Her form was translucent, but the multitudes of gems hanging from her sash was a dazzling light in the unnatural dark. Jewels also adorned her neck and her eyes held a mesmerizing sparkle – but it was the light emanating from within her that brightened the cellar, revealing every detail on the aged bricks and grime coated floor.

Her appearance was so unexpected, Shiarn blinked with profound amazement.

Hellier's sword was now pointed at the woman's chest. 'Friend or foe?'

The woman pushed past Hellier's weapon and touched the rock spears. Radiant light consumed them and they dissipated. She continued on and stopped at Earona. Reaching down to her, the top of the woman's hand glowed with a gem, shimmering like starlight. The stone binding fell away from Earona and disappeared. She placed her hand on Earona's shoulder and light spread over her body. 'I am not your foe.' Her voice was commanding yet it brought some comfort, despite her mysterious appearance.

Shiarn sputtered in surprised fascination. 'Who are you?'

Earona's face brightened with colour and she jumped to her feet, fully revived. 'Are you a spirit?'

The ethereal woman, appearing to glide across the floor, stood and looked at them with wise eyes. 'I am, but do not be afraid. You have finally read the ancient prophecy and have released me.' She bowed her head, and jewels glittered around her brow. 'I thank you.'

'Release you?!' Shiarn gasped. 'I don't know what you mean.' She flashed the journal at her. 'I wanted to help Jett.'

The woman nodded with recognition at the book. 'And you will. Once you sought for an answer it was revealed to you. The prophecy is foreordained for the release of Light, and also for halting darkness, and can only be read by one of your race.'

Shiarn said, 'That's good to know, I guess.'

'I want some answers.' Hellier pushed forward and eyed the woman. 'What have you got to do with Jett?'

The woman studied Hellier for several moments while Hellier became more restless. Finally she responded, 'If you want to know you will have your answer, however, I will not be the one who gives it to you.'

Hellier scowled at her.

'I don't understand—' Earona reached out for the woman's arm and her hand grazed the effervescent light. 'Are you here to help him?'

'That is the purpose of my release.' She stretched out her hand to Earona. 'You have many questions, and I do not have time to discuss them.' Her voice became more urgent. 'We must move fast. He is too weak to withstand her for long.' She glanced at Jett, his eyes were closed and his head still drooped down. Now that he was quiet, it seemed he was the Jett they knew once more.

'Her?' Shiarn said.

'She has manipulated his soul from the outset. Initially she used her seductive attributes to entice him, until the darkness could be birthed within—'

'Hold on.' Hellier butted in, 'Seductive attributes? Don't tell me he's been...' her face reddened, either from rage or embarrassment.

The woman gave Hellier her full attention. 'As you see me before you, she is the same image. A beautiful creation, offering everything a man could desire.' She laid a hand on Hellier's shoulder. 'Do not be anxious over this. I see an extraordinary destiny within you. I have a question for you, what is stronger, your hate or your love?' She paused, watching Hellier's puzzlement. 'Currently you do not have the answer. Do not be deceived, emotions are not light and dark.'

'That's fine and all,' Shiarn muttered, 'but who is "she" and what the hell are we supposed to be doing?'

The woman let her hand rest by her side, and her sigh was like a gentle breeze. '"She" is an entity of darkness, similar to what you have seen in him, although her powers are more subtle and they corrupt in a noxious way. She is hell in an exotic magnificent form.' A note of sadness entered her voice. 'Also, be sufficiently aware, "she" is a form of me.'

Shiarn stared with bewilderment, not knowing if she heard her clearly. 'She is you?'

'Oh, Spirit, I really don't understand and I do have questions,' Earona said, 'but will you save Jett?'

The spirit clasped her hands together and bowed her head in contemplation. 'Truly, now would be the moment to destroy the evil one.'

Earona gasped with fear. 'Is that the answer, to kill him...?'

'I knew it.' Shiarn grimaced.

'Possibly, it is the wisest course of action. Nevertheless, there is another path you can take that may one day prove the more difficult one. His inner battle is not yet won. Your presence here gives me hope. I will do what I can.' She turned to face Hellier and it seemed the question was for her alone. 'Do you wish to take the chance of having that Jett that you knew before, restored to you or shall you grasp this opportunity to end the evil? This way is sure and exact.'

Her face reddening, Hellier narrowed her eyes with suspicion, but remained quiet.

'Of course—' Earona cried.

Shiarn put her hand across Earona's mouth and looked at Hellier.

The spirit continued, 'There is always a risk that Jett may not return, and you shall miss this chance of destroying this demon.'

'Damn it!' Hellier's expression turned sombre, and after a breathless pause, she gave a sharp nod. 'Bring him back.'

Shiarn said, 'We will have to take the risk, and hope Jett knows what he is doing.'

'Will he be the same old Jett?' Earona asked.

'He will never be the same.' Her tone was heavy with sudden grief. 'However, if we are successful, he will not be in this evil form.'

'That's a relief...' Earona said, 'I think.'

'You said, "we",' Shiarn studied her. 'How?'

The spirit drew their attention with the brilliant gem on her hand flashing before them, and they gathered close. 'Listen to my instructions. You must retrieve a particular amulet and put it on his body. Ward of the Light Spirit will guard his mind—'

'Where is it?' Hellier demanded.

'The next chamber.' She stared past them through the arch and into the nearly lit room. 'On the first rack, third shelf, in a cane basket, I believe—'

'How do you know that?' Shiarn scrunched up her face in doubt.

'I foresaw it would arrive here.'

'All along.' Earona gazed with awe. 'Something that could have helped him was here?'

The woman's smile was kind. 'We are surrounded by answers, but oft times we do not know the right questions.' She nodded at Earona. 'You will know it when you see it.' She ordered her, 'Go now.'

Shiarn grumbled, 'Wish we had known about it sooner. Would have saved a lot of heartache.' The woman reminded her of the prophets back home, but she didn't appear to be Fáerinn. She pushed the lamp into Earona's hand. 'Take this.'

Wide-eyed, Earona scuttled off to the adjoining chamber.

'We do not have much time,' the woman said, 'And I must return to stop him making an eternal mistake, if he will accept my aid.'

'Aid him against yourself?' Shiarn scoffed.

'Yes, my evil form is intent on her own plans of opening the Chanin-Quyllar, except it will not be in its glorious form, but will be the mouth of hell, and Jett's life will crown the event.'

'What happens if we run out of time?' Hellier lifted her sword and rested it on her shoulder.

The woman observed him over her shoulder with a grim frown. 'He will awaken.'

Shiarn stared at Jett, remembering he was no longer bound, and probably more wrathful than ever. 'We better hurry.'

'I will trust you with the task.' Her light diminished as she shrunk to a glowing sphere the size of a fist. 'I will try to restore your master to you.' The light disappeared, leaving the girls in the oppressive darkness once more.

Shiarn snorted at the inference. 'Did she say master?'

'Does it seem darker?' Hellier glanced around the room.

60 - Search is On

Much can be protected when hope is the fortress

The Hidden Shield

He leaned his hand on the chair, his thoughts drifting in a strange haze of forgotten images. Frustrated, he strained to capture the memories, but they slipped past and left him empty. The chair would reveal all. Why did he linger - was he afraid to know?

'Jett, do not sit!'

Catching his breath, he halted. The speaking of the forgotten name caused his skin to prickle with alarm. Turning to face Nya, he queried, 'What did you say?'

Nya's lips drooped with shock, and annoyance was in her eyes. 'Say what?' She spread her delicate hands. 'You are mistaken.'

Hesitant, he stared at the empty room. 'Who was that?'

Her tan skin paled and an intense green entered her eyes. 'You were about to sit.'

Every muscle tensed with apprehension, he was suddenly unsure of everything. 'I…'

Taking a step nearer, she stood straight. 'It is the only way.'

He eyed her with confusion. As he watched, Nya appeared to separate into a perfect duplicate of herself. Nya's double stepped down from the dais.

Inhaling sharply, he gripped the arm of the chair and stared between the two women. 'Who are you?'

Nya held out her hand, beseeching his calm. 'I am your beloved.' She cast a steely glare over her shoulder at the second woman. 'And she is an imposter and our enemy. You mustn't listen to her. She must be banished.'

The second woman spoke with a voice like cold water. 'I bring warning, Jett. Do not sit on the throne.'

'No, don't listen,' Nya hissed and took hold of his hand, squeezing it tight. 'She doesn't understand.'

He looked between them in bewilderment. His love for Nya drove him to obey her – but the second woman was her mirror image. But something in her eyes was not visible in Nya, and she spoke a name he assumed must be his. 'Why should I not sit?'

Nya answered in a soulful plea, 'If you don't you won't have your answers and you will never be fulfilled.'

'Indeed,' the other woman replied, 'you will know everything and more than you would like.'

'Why should that concern me?' He frowned in curious contemplation.

'You will not be who you remember,' she said.

He gestured with frustration. 'I want to know who I am and the chair will provide me with those answers.'

'That's right,' Nya crooned, 'all the answers you need. We will find out together.'

He gazed into her eyes with adoration. He could follow her anywhere – to death and beyond – sitting in a chair would be a little thing.

'If you wish to know of your Kin, I can tell you of them.' The woman's voice was a painful ring in the marble room.

The word Kin startled him from his hypnotic reverie. He rolled it over in his mind and muttered, the odd, but suddenly familiar word, the word he had been searching for, '…kin…' It started a jumble of other words he could not distinguish.

'Don't listen to her, my beloved. It's only dreams. The chair will reveal all you need to know.' Nya finished with an angry snarl that surprised him, 'All she has is lies.'

He had never seen her features contort with such wrath.

'No,' the other Nya pointed at her, 'You are the one who has poisoned, with your devious devices.'

'If you sit, she will disappear.' Nya hung off his arm in placation. 'You will have your answers and we will be together forever.'

His dark eyes took in both women and he studied the chair.

Nya's turquoise eyes pleaded with him and she fell to her knees with a heart-wrenching sob. 'For me, you must…'

The other woman watched him with a stern demenour. A part of him wanted to believe her – the part evoked by his name and the comforting word, Kin. Yet he knew he must follow the desires of his love and assuage her sorrow. He felt compelled whatever the cost may be.

~ * ~

Earona dangled the light out from her face, but she didn't need it to see. With the radiant light from the ethereal woman, nearly every spot in the chamber was lit up. Shelves with wine bottles, and barrels took up the wall space. Within moments of appreciating the light, it vanished, leaving Earona in the near useless glow of the lamp.

Gulping, she stretched it out from her, hoping to find the right basket along the shelving. Amongst the earthen-ware bowls was a woven basket. She felt around inside. A mess of trinkets and odds and ends of items no longer needed. She pulled out a bronze buckle. 'Curses!' and threw it back down, and rummaged again for anything of significance. Her fingers skimmed over leather cords, feathered quills, more buckles, cutlery, darning implements, and a lot of wooden objects. 'This is ridiculous,' she whined, 'How am I expected to find this thing? Whatever it is.'

Shiarn shouted at her from the other room and a turbulent roar of some supernatural force followed.

'I'm trying.' Her reply was trill with her escalating anxiety. She upended the basket, sending the items to the stone with a tinkling crash. She cringed, hoping she hadn't sent the precious object rolling under the wooden rack.

On her knees she shifted through the things and tried to ignore the fierce activity in the adjoining chamber. Most of the horde was jewelry and a lot of it was ugly, in her opinion. 'What is this?' By the glow of the light, she examined silver glittering between braided cords. She brought it into the light, including the leather it was bound to. 'This is… Oh, holy Kahm!' The amulet, the size of her thumb was a detailed snake biting its own tail, forming a figure eight. 'The curse seal.' She gulped with nervous excitement. 'Could it be?'

Angry cries echoed in the room.

Earona quickly rose with the silver symbol in hand.

~ * ~

Marcus woke to his bed shaking. 'Flamin' hell.' He jumped up and grabbed his sword while grumbling to himself, 'Sleeping again.' With storm clouds outside, the room was in darkness, but the floor vibrated under his feet. The furniture bounced out of place and the window shook as if it would shatter.

High pitched screeching came from some place in the house. Not a human sound. He strapped on his double sheath harness and slid in his older malreus blade, and holding his newer blade, he headed to the door. 'What's going on?'

The hall was strangely dark. Within moments he knew why. Shadows lining the walls sprang to life with claw appendages and fangs. He cut into the apparitions. It didn't do much except turn them back into darkness. At least he was making a way through them, but the shadow creatures were relentless in fighting his passage.

He came to his destination. Earona's door was open and he burst in. 'Earona? Shiarn?' The room was empty. 'Devil's arse!' He ran out, not knowing where but with a horrible dread his search would end in the cellar.

The house creaked and the walls shook with such force paintings fell and furniture toppled over. He ran downstairs, fearing the house would collapse with them in it. On the ground floor, Seth met him through the dark. Marcus growled, 'What are you doing on your own?'

'You're on your own.' Seth pouted and folded his arms.

'I'm different,' Marcus retorted.

'Besides, I'm not.' He eyed Marcus' sword with apprehension. 'Keanan—'

Keanan ran into them. 'Something major is occurring.'

'I gathered,' Marcus said. 'Where are the girls? They are not in their room.'

Keanan frowned. 'Morias and Adis were upstairs restraining some hellish apparition, but the girls…' he looked towards the hall with the door leading down. 'Would they really go—?'

'Blood 'n shite!' Marcus dashed down the corridor with Keanan and Seth trailing after.

His mind was incessantly going over his conversation with Hellier. Would she really? He tried the knob. Locked. 'Damn it to hell!'

Seth crammed into the alcove next to him. 'You think they are… with him?'

Marcus shoved on the door, shouldering it with all his weight. It wouldn't budge.

'He's locked it somehow,' Keanan said.

Marcus kicked his rage into the wood, and growled his contempt. For the first time really missing his Gift. 'We have to get in. I think they are planning on killing him.' He punched his frustration on the door.

'They might get killed,' Seth cried.

'Might is an understatement,' Marcus snarled.

'And he has prevented us from getting in.' Keanan tried the handle himself. 'There is another entrance from the outside—'

'We'll get an axe if need be.' Marcus started off through the darkness.

~ * ~

Hot energy seeped out of Jett's body as he hung in a type of stasis environment. The shadows circled the room, as if they had a will of their own. More darkness flowed out of Jett at a faster rate. It careened through the air like a red-black wind.

'I don't like the look of this,' Hellier cried.

'Hurry up, Earona.' Shiarn was damp with perspiration and her skin heated up from the sultry atmosphere. She attempted staying clear of the hot blast that seemed to be consuming all the air. At least Hellier wouldn't need to worry about it, but Shiarn felt like she was melting. She collapsed on her knees under the weight. Pulling her hood over her curls, she glimpsed Jett lift his head and stare straight at her. His eyes were a threatening glare drilling into her soul.

Hellier shielded her face from the swirling black haze and started towards Shiarn.

Jett's top lip cocked in a wicked snarl.

Against her will, Shiarn trembled at his malicious attention. She clutched the book to her bosom as if that could offer protection against the enraged demon. She could only hope he was not able to move. She yelled for Earona again, the only one who could do anything to stop him.

Hope left her when he jumped down to his feet, and stepped towards her. He growled with volatile rage she had not seen in him previously. He was really pissed off this time. Kahm above, did they make the right decision?

'I won't let you.' Hellier's blade came down, headed for Jett's neck.

His hand shot out at her. Darkness billowed around his arm and created a wall between them, blocking her passage. His eyes flashed with hatred and he seemed incapable of speaking.

Shiarn stared at him, unable to draw her vision away or move from his path.

His hand caught hold of her neck and lifted her. It burned like fiery metal crushing her windpipe. Boxed in by darkness and his grip on her, Shiarn pushed on his hand. Compelled to stare into his face, she found it ironic her Avare would be the one to end her life.

'You thought you could do something.' His voice was like rocks and he ended with a spiteful growl, 'You were wrong.'

Unable to break away, Shiarn felt herself passing out in his stranglehold.

'We'll see about that.' Earona's cocky retort came from beside her. She placed the symbol on his wrist and wrapped the leather cord around until it was tight and tied.

Jett roared with a mix of rage and anguish. He fell, clutching at his wrist, and writhing on the floor in agony. After several moments his body went limp and he lay motionless. The hard dark tendrils attempted returning to his body, but bounced back as if repelled by his flesh. The darkness swooped around the room before disappearing into the shadows.

Earona laid her hand on Shiarn's back, and watched in fear-filled wonder. A smug smile welled up from relief.

Shiarn sputtered for air and grasped her throat. '...you...'

Earona patted her back. 'Can you breathe?'

'You...' Shiarn gagged. '...took your time.'

'God help me!' Earona was ready to slap her on the back. 'You don't know what rubbish I had to go through.'

Hellier crouched by Jett. 'What now?' She examined the loops of cord on his left wrist without touching him.

'I had to put it there. I wasn't able to stand to get near his neck.' Earona had to gather all her courage to walk through the curtain of darkness to find them. Then she was sent to her knees by Jett's presence.

'It's good enough.' Shiarn glanced around the room. 'All that hellish black is gone.'

'And it's not so hot. That's a good sign.' A broad grin spread on Earona's face. 'Do you think...?'

'He's not coming 'round.' Hellier's hand hovered inches from his face. Her hand shook and biting her lip, she withdrew her touch.

'Let him wake on his own.' Shiarn shuffled over and gazed down at him. His dark hair was a tangled mop and his beard needed a brush. Hanging out from his trousers, his shirt was a crumpled mess, and his palms were red and blistered. Pale and sickly, it seemed he could have been dead except for his deep breaths.

Earona crawled up beside her and whispered, 'Amazing that little thing stopped him.'

The silver amulet was half hidden under the black leather, and Shiarn answered, 'I assume it is no "little thing".'

'Whatever it is, it better be Jett waking up.' Hellier stood over them all.

~ * ~

Pure illuminous light exploded around Jett's body. In a blaze of uncontainable power it pulsed across the room before streaming into him. The walls fell away, and except for the black throne, all the furnishings disappeared. Light-headed, his mind emptied and he floated in a vacuous space. The only sound, the blood beating in his ears.

After moments of confusion, it seemed he fell into his body from a distant place. With every muscle aching from exhaustion, he sensed his mind stirring from a deep sleep.

Overwhelmed by a cascade of thoughts crowding into his head – each one important yet none of them staying in focus – he opened his eyes to the new pavilion. The comforting ambience was replaced by high pillars of black rock and twirling fire, and jagged fissures in the marble floor giving off a foul steam. The chair had nearly doubled in size and was formed from slabs of granite and black rock. Skulls and the figures of demons were in the stone, and it appeared bones were embedded in the base. Wrapped around the tall uneven backrest was a serpent, and flames danced over the top.

Wet with perspiration and shuddering, he collapsed on hands and knees, gasping for air as if he had been under water far too long.

The newcomer breathed a significant sigh. 'It is done.'

Nya, her face livid with wrath, turned on her. 'You meddling bitch, what have you done to him?'

The pain in his chest subsided, but his limbs remained leaden. He glanced at the women, identical, except for one piece of jewelry which he only now noticed. 'Who…' His throat was parched and he choked on his words.

Nya came to support him. 'I am your beloved and you are mine. The intruder has done this to you.'

It was true. His love for her remained, even in this new strange environment. But right then he had names rushing through his mind that he had forgotten. Looking past her, he swatted her hand away and stared at the other woman. Nya hissed her annoyance. He forced more control into his voice. 'Who are you?' It came out harder than he wanted, but she was the one to darken his sanctuary and cause images to bombard his mind. He wanted answers.

She bowed her head in greeting. 'I am High Priestess Nya of Amin-Sayeda.'

Nya cast her hands in the air and snarled, 'Look what she has done. My love, do not listen to anything she says. She has ruined everything—'

'Quiet!' His voice echoed against the stone and Nya pressed her lips shut in silent protest. For the first time, he noted her glaring with animosity. He looked back to the High Priestess. 'Is this true?'

'In a way. It is true I have ruined her plans. Your mind has been released and you are able to see with clarity.' She swept her hand across the transformed scenery. 'This is the truth.'

The walls had gone, leaving a clear view of a burnt red sky, swirling with clouds of vermillion fire. Giant snakes were wrapped around the stone pillars, and alternate columns were ablaze and whirring up to the sky. Around the dais, a massive serpent lay, curved around the base and steps. Whether it was asleep or simply stone, Jett could not distinguish. The scene was shocking and far from what it had been, but it was the visions in his mind of people he knew that evoked the most anguish. What he thought was the dream had become the reality. Life outside this cloying existence was distant, except he recalled each of them; their faces, their names. He sat back on his hunches and mumbled, 'My Kin?' The last he could remember, they were travelling out from Floris. 'Where are they?'

'They?' Nya rubbed his back, attempting to soothe his distress. 'They despise you and have become your dreaded enemy.'

Jett's eyes bored into hers with shock. 'You know who they are?'

Her voice, soft as silk, murmured, 'I wanted to protect you from them. They seek your downfall. Even now they plan to murder you.'

Her remark triggered a foreboding memory of terrible dreams of rage and sadness. 'Why would they…' he grabbed his head, attempting to unravel the memories. A vision of the girl weeping overcame him, and there were more.

'They have betrayed you.' Nya lifted her chin in arrogance.

'They have risked much to save you, even their own lives,' the High Priestess replied, 'You have not been killed because of their love for you.'

Nya blocked his vision of the other woman. 'My dearest, she is lying. They will continue to deceive you, because of their hatred for you. You can over power them and everyone, when you take your rightful place.' She knelt by him, and her hand, running down his face was refreshing in the hot air. 'I am the only one who has the love you need.'

Her words brought comfort, like a heady wine that brings strength to the heart. If his Kin had turned on him, what life would he have? Despair billowed up from his constricting chest and he wished to seek solace in her embrace.

'Right before me, you display your arrogant manipulations by continuing with your noxious lies.' The High Priestess' voice resonated with power. 'Jett, she has nothing but a false love for you. It is not you who she truly loves. You now have the freedom to decide what you will hear. Get up and see this domain.' She raised her arm, and a white gem on her hand radiated a peaceful ambience.

The speaking of his name caused his skin to tingle to life. It planted a longing in his heart for the truth. In the red-black tinted environment, his eyes were drawn to the brightness of the jewel on her hand. He noted this adornment was absent on his lover.

Nya weaved her fingers through his hair, and whispered in his ear, 'I am all you need, you will want for nothing, and no one will hurt you.'

The High Priestess' voice rose with authority. 'You have the strength to banish her and be free of her poisons. However, do you wish to be free?'

His mind shifted with unfamiliar scenes, and he struggled with the sudden bewildering emotions. All the while the white gem fascinated him. 'Why do you wear the jewel?'

'It is well that you are attracted to this. It is a power that cannot be possessed by darkness, infact evil despises it.' She glided her hand over the stone and gazed at it with adoration. 'The Peace-stone saved me. I was never intended to be her. The same way you don't have to be him.' Her eyes met his with profound insight.

Although he wasn't sure what she was talking about, he knew her statement was genuine. But, it left him with a sudden foreboding. 'Him…'

Witnessing the exchange, Nya latched onto his arm. 'This is what you're meant to be.' She flourished her hand across the dais. 'Not some dream—'

'But…' he shook his head, fighting against her intoxicating allure that brought out his lustful passions.

'If you have any feelings for your Kin, any love for them,' the High Priestess said, 'you must save them by banishing her.'

'No, don't!' Nya cried with anguish.

'They will all perish if you do not.' The High Priestess lifted her voice in warning.

His Kin…. They were a vague image, but the feelings they generated in his heart was overwhelming. Despite his love for Nya, he did not wish for these new affections for his Kin to vanish. Not again. With all the strength he had in his will, he finally said, 'Go.' His voice was a guttural order that he forced up from his gut. 'Nya. Leave.'

'No—' Sobbing, she fell on her knees. 'Please…'

Once the word was spoken, his tone grew bolder. 'Leave me. Now.'

She snatched up his hand and caressed it with her cheek. 'I won't—'

The High Priestess said, 'He has ordered it.'

Nya recoiled. 'My love…' Her tear-stained face was marred with anger. 'After all I've done for you. You'll regret this. I'll find you when I walk the Earth again. It was never you, he will always have my heart.' She jumped to her feet and pointed at her duplicate. 'I hate you,' she spat out, 'You will never have him. His soul is mine.' Her body transformed into a black outline and vanished in a wisp of foul smelling smoke.

At her disappearance, Jett sensed a burden lift and he stood. Although she had gone, her perfect likeness stood awaiting his attention. The same luxurious dark hair and voluptuous form beneath the white gown. Her familiar face brought him the resolve he needed. 'Who is she?'

'Lies and deception formed from the darkness in my soul. She is from me, but I am not her.' A light was in her eyes and her countenance was peaceful.

'Have I been dreaming?'

'It is more sinister than that. Come.' She turned from him and headed to the front of the pavilion.

He stepped down from the dais and over the serpent. With each moment apart from Nya, his head became clearer.

'Now she is gone, your mind will become yours again,' she said.

'Do you know what I am thinking?'

'Somewhat. I am, after all, in your Mind Palace.' She looked over her shoulder to see him dutifully following, and she smiled.

'My Mind Palace…' He frowned at the blistering red sky and fiery pillars. Skulls, snakes, and demon figures carved into the throne and columns, could only represent a vision of Hell. 'It wasn't like this before.'

'Previously, you were trapped in a lie.'

They arrived at the top of the step and Jett stopped beside her. Below them was a valley bordered by rugged rock cliffs that cast a gloom across the landscape. Creatures that appeared half man, half monster, stood on mountain tops, brandishing huge weapons. Waves of heat and a thunderous roaring erupted from below. It seemed the ground was moving. Flecks of pale grey and the glint of bronze was amid the shifting shadows. The valley was crawling with hordes of humanoid monsters, all pushing and heaving. Hands and weapons reached up, shouting as one horrid mass.

Jett swallowed hard at the fearful spectacle, and his voice was a bare utterance, 'What is it?'

'A glimpse of Hell.' Nya shivered and covered the Peace-stone with her hand.

'My mind's in Hell?' He cringed at the legion of armed demons.

'Now you see.' She spun from the view to face him

'The bed.' He squinted at her. 'The lounge… all a lie?'

'Initially those things were real, however; they were taken from you.' A sad note touched her voice.

His eye twitched as he controlled his rising nausea. 'But the chair?' Now that Nya had gone, his thoughts were taking a logical shape. 'Why did she want me to sit on it?' In hindsight, he realized she was constantly cajoling him to it and he was always evading her request. Perhaps he knew subconsciously the gravity of the decision.

'We have spent too long talking and you must return.'

'Tell me.'

She stepped closer and touched his forearm. 'There are more pressing needs, but perhaps it is beneficial.' She studied his unyielding expression. 'If you had taken your place on the daemon throne you would see and know everything, but affect none of it. For eternity.' She paused, letting the meaning of her words permeate his thoughts. 'You will understand the terror of this once you return.'

His furrowed brow deepened with shock at Nya's far-reaching scheming. 'Why did she—why didn't you warn me sooner?'

She stared with surprise. 'You were easily coerced by her enticements and eventually you were sent to death. However, with the Peace-stone I was able to save you from the void after you were defeated by your hatred and darkness. Your salvation was an unexpected and significant blow to her. You were never meant to return. He was the one who would sit on the throne and not you. Despite her cajolements, you were thankfully, reluctant.'

He sensed the truth of her statement, although nothing in his memory was left as evidence. 'Defeated by my hatred?' It evoked a chilling sensation in his heart.

She gave a crisp nod. 'The memory is buried in the place of death. She took over your Mind Palace. You have not been yourself. Nonetheless, I was able to restore what was left of your Spirit of Light. It is weak but it will grow again on your return.'

'I've been awake?' He rubbed the back of his neck. 'I remember vague dreams…'

'Once you awaken, your memories of the past week will be released to you.'

'I've been walking around for a week?! Flamin' arse of the devil!' He balled his fist into his palm. 'Why did she do this?'

'You have the power to command the Chanin-Quyllar, the Eye of Heaven, as is foretold.'

His eyes widened with surprise. It passed and he frowned with consternation. 'She wanted me to… hell on earth!' He took a short breath, recalling a conversation he had back in Floris. 'Mara…' her name shot into his thoughts with sudden clarity. He creased his brow in concern.

'She is in dire trouble.' Nya pursed her lips. 'You must stop her.'

Jett grimaced. 'Are they safe?'

'They are now,' she said. 'It was your female friends who released me and broke your chains.'

He glanced back at the lengths of chains around the room with new insight, and gave a wry grin. '… chains. I see…'

'Come. It is time.' She led him past the throne and a flaming pillar to the end of the pavilion and two doors. They stopped at the black door. Carved into it was the symbol of a snake biting its own tail in the shape of a figure eight. The door stood alone with nothing beside or behind it.

Jett had noticed a door previously, but he had not taken note of it. He drew his finger through the groove and his eyes widened with surprise. 'I've seen this symbol. On myself.'

'Ward of the Light Spirit. It is protection for your mind, therefore your soul.'

'It didn't work,' he muttered recalling the design on his own skin.

'It was an old Seal that would perhaps need renewal. It would seem it has been broken.' Nya paused. 'Or perhaps weakened over time. It is currently indiscernible to me.'

Jett clutched at his chest in speculation. 'Over time…? How could that be…?' The notion he had the mark for many years overwhelmed him with sudden rage. 'The bastards.'

'No, you must not think in that way,' she reprimanded. 'This Ward is unique in a way. Unlike others that keep unnatural elements out, it keeps Light in, containing it. It is a simplistic explanation for a Barrier that is quite complicated.'

'Containing it? And if it doesn't…?' Realization of what that meant set tremours through Jett, and all the degradation he had suffered in his life crashed into his mind. 'It really was me…' Finally he let loose a stagnant breath of dismay, 'God…'

She lifted his chin. 'It's true, but you can hold onto the light. You have been given the chance, and not just now.'

He searched her keen green eyes. 'I feel I don't know who I am…is this really me?'

'Maybe you don't know right now, but you will remember. They will help you.' She grasped his wrist and turned it over, revealing the same snake symbol glowing on his skin. 'I am unsure about the Ward on your chest, normally Seals can regenerate or even be renewed. If not, and this is removed, your mind will be vulnerable again.' She gave him a severe look. 'They have already found the halves of the Chanin-Quyllar.'

'Who are "they"?' his eyes creased with foreboding.

'They are your enemies, however,' her deep-sea eyes had a smug glint, 'they are not yet aware of this.'

'They'll know soon enough.'

She nodded. 'The ones grafted into Hell will not stop until the Gate is opened.'

He traced the silvery lines on his wrist with his finger. 'They won't be opening it.'

'They have ways of opening it without you. As long as they do not get the Essenya, they cannot reform the Eye of Heaven.'

Jett put his hand in his pocket. Empty.

'You possess it in the natural,' she reassured him.

He gave a frustrated sigh. 'They'll always be hunting it…'

'Your life is bound up in it for good or ill. As is the girl.' She ran her hand down his arm. 'But for now, you must leave here and awaken. You are the only one who can open the door.'

He stared at the door, devoid of any handle. 'Open it?'

'You shut it in the beginning to prevent your Kins' souls from being poisoned by her, in the same way you were poisoned. It also prevented the evil from using your power.'

He eyed the door, having no memory of that event.

'It was wise. They would have become your servants in wickedness. Nevertheless, there was a cost. They lost their Gifts, and their Mind-speak and all ways of communicating with each other.' Her voice softened with compassion. 'They lost you.'

'Curses!' He clenched his jaw and pressed his fingers into his temple, imagining his Kin without their Gifts. The agitation was rising with each new piece of knowledge. 'What's been going on out there?'

She lifted his chin and her eyes were gentle as she looked him over. 'It is best to think of him as the embodiment of your hate and rage controlled by Hell.'

He held her slight wrist, and grumbled, 'That's not encouraging.' When Jett was angry it was not good at the best of times, but controlled by Hell – his gut churned with apprehension. 'What have I done?'

'Only your return, and you, can reconcile it.'

He sighed and his gaze fell on her. 'I feel I've been with you all this time, and now, I don't really know who you are.'

'It is not me you have been with.' She smiled. 'But I have been with you.' Her hand on his cheek was a strong caress. 'It is ordained that I should aid you. In fact, I called this side of you into existence.'

His face crimped with bewilderment. It only gave him another reason to despise prophecy; powerful people playing with other people's lives. 'Damn—'

She put her finger on his lips to quiet him. 'Remember I know your thoughts here.' She smiled at his sour look. 'You are yet to know why I did.'

He held her hand and kissed her finger, and his eyes softened. 'As long as I see you again.'

Her eyes clouded with sudden sadness and she whispered, 'You must arise.' She added, 'Deeds of darkness will not withstand the offense of Light. Love unites – hate divides.'

He tightened his mouth in determination and pushed on the door. It opened and a warm yellow glow grew inside. Other doors within began to open and he walked through.

61 - Return

You cannot open the mind of another
Until you first open your own

Olvarus Claw'Blade, Reader's Wisdom

Groaning, Jett woke and curled inward clutching at his burning innards. Memories crashed into his mind's eye. With each scene he viewed, it revealed more of the missing pieces – all of them fitting together to form a horrendous image of malevolence towards the ones he cared about more than anything. How could it be? His words, his thoughts spoken with contemptuous cruelty had become an abhorrent reality. Recollections of violence bombarded his thinking. He had watched without any defense, as the fiend abused his memories and assaulted everything he held dear. Guilt tore at his conscience till he thought his heart would stop.

'At least he's not trying to kill us.' Earona's soft voice caused him to open his eyes to see the three watching him. The memory of what they did flooded in. Their bravery was astounding. He didn't know if he should be grateful or ashamed – but right then he felt grossly ill. It seemed a tight band was around his head and he cried out from his twisted insides.

Hellier lowered her sword and Shiarn shuffled closer. 'Maybe it worked…'

Jett rolled over and pushed himself up on one hand. Still groaning and his stomach on fire, he spat up black bile on the stone.

Earona crawled closer with her hands hovering over his shoulders.

'Be careful!' Hellier warned.

Turning his back on them, Jett rested his aching body, attempting to calm his stomach.

'No, he's in real agony.' After a moment, Earona placed her hand on him. 'Jett?' Her voice held a familiar gentleness.

'Don't…' His voice crackled from his parched throat. '…don't heal me.' He wanted to feel the pain, every throb and spasm.

'I don't know if I can,' Earona replied, 'I just want to know if it's you.' She squeezed his flesh that seemed more bone than muscle.

A heavy pounding came from the short flight of stairs within the half-hidden alcove. Marcus barged down the steps, black swords flashing, with Seth and Keanan rushing down behind him. He pulled up fast and stared at Jett, and Hellier's sword, with a mix of surprise and suspicion. He said to Hellier, 'You didn't?'

'Flamin' hell!' Hellier growled.

Seth peered over Marcus' shoulder. 'Is it… him?'

'Depends which him you mean.' Shiarn touched her red neck with her fingertips and gave a little cry.

'It's me.' He forced the words out, but could not follow it with any cheer. 'The real one…'

Keanan nudged past Seth and Marcus and exclaimed incredulously, 'But, how can this be?! Are you certain it is not a part of his deception?'

Jett heaved more of the foulness up from his stomach. 'I've got to get out of here.' A stagnant odour was clogging his senses. It was days since he breathed fresh air. Wiping his mouth, he struggled to stand, but his feet failed him.

'It's not a trick.' Earona supported his arm. 'It's really him. We did it.' She smiled, smugly, despite Jett nearly collapsing in her arms. 'She said we would.'

'She?' Marcus grabbed Jett's other arm and looped it around his shoulders. 'We got our powers back. I feared the worst…' he chuckled.

'It's really you?' Seth squeaked, his eyes wide with astonishment.

'I'm back.' Jett glanced at their fear-filled expressions. A fear he had put there. He didn't like speculating on the "worst" and realized it was best not to think on it.

'In that case,' Shiarn said, 'Earona, you could heal my neck. I hope the hell-awful thing isn't going to leave a scar.'

Earona gave her a quick gaze. 'It could always be a reminder…'

'You think I'm going to need one?!' Shiarn replied.

Jett let his head droop, not willing to watch Earona healing Shiarn's burned throat. He looked at his hand, also burned, and was appalled at how close he came to killing her.

They all trooped up the steps with Keanan trailing behind, still flustering with bewilderment. 'You haven't told me how you did this?'

Shiarn waved the book for him to see. 'I put some thought into it—'

'She read a prophecy from that journal.' Hellier grinned. 'And we – well, distracted him—'

'Thank Kahm it worked,' Shiarn said under her breath.

Keanan stared in astonishment as they came up from the cellar and out into the night.

'And a beautiful lady appeared to help us,' Earona added.

'Nya,' Jett grunted, 'She… saved me.' Her aid helped him more than he realized. He would be forever in her debt, and then he remembered he hadn't thanked her.

Earona nodded. 'And us too.'

'And the amulet helped.' Hellier inclined her head to the leather cord around his wrist.

Jett fingered the finely plaited leather. The wrapping, circling his wrist at least four times, was tied in haste. The silver symbol pressed into his skin but was still visible through the layers. This is what saved him from the throne; a place that would have damned him for eternity. The reason for Nya's deception and the symbol on his wrist triggered a memory. 'Where's Mara?'

'We don't know.' Earona's quiet voice caught in her throat. 'She's gone.'

'No,' Jett groaned. 'She's here.'

'We looked everywhere,' Marcus said. 'How do you know?'

'I know.' Jett sighed at the memory of the girl. She had courageously tried hard to resist him, but in the end, his power outweighed her immature strength. With remorse, he recalled the snake symbol she bore on her chest that was supposed to protect her, and keep the Light in, but he ripped it open. 'I... he told her to do something.' He refrained from the details; they didn't have to know she was trying to resurrect Nya's evil self. 'She's got to be found and stopped.' And who could tell what sort of horror Mara was dealing with in her own mind. A horror he had unleashed. 'Devil's arse...' in the state he was in, he could do nothing to help her.

'I'll go look for her.' Marcus helped Jett down onto the cool grass. 'Any ideas where?'

Frowning, Jett chewed his lip, attempting to sense her presence as he had done in his transformed state. 'She's hiding somewhere...'

Marcus shrugged. 'We'll start searching.'

Hellier, still gripping her sword, said, 'I'll go with you.'

Approaching from the shadows, a tall man with long dark hair, said to Marcus and Hellier, 'I will come. We may see Morias and Clara as we go.'

The three walked into the house and Jett cursed his frail body at not being able to help.

Shiarn nodded towards the amulet. 'You can't take it off.'

Jett turned his hands over and examined his stinging palms. The burning pain had become excruciating. 'I know.'

'But this,' Shiarn fell on her knees beside him and braced his shoulders with her arm, and with her other hand, she rubbed his furry cheek, 'needs to go.'

'What's wrong with beards?' Keanan massaged his own perfectly trimmed auburn show of hair, and gave her a sour look.

'On you it looks splendid,' she replied, 'On Jett – he looks like a seedy outlaw.'

Jett scratched at his face, and it darkened. 'I wonder if that suits me...'

'No, it doesn't!' Earona squealed with alarm.

'Here's the deal,' Shiarn started, 'I'll think about forgiving all the rotten things you said, if you take it off. Plus there'll be a payback one day, I'll just have to figure out what.'

Tears freely flowing down her cheeks, Earona grabbed both his hands. 'But me, I'm so grateful... I haven't any words...'

With growing remorse, Jett watched her lowered head and her hair falling about his hands, along with her tears. '... me too...'

Her Ethos poured over his burned hands with no chance of it being a slight healing.

Grateful I'm no longer a murderous demon... He lowered his face, sensing his own tears come to his eyes.

'Were you present?'

He pulled his hands away before she could heal anything else. 'In a way, although I didn't know it. But now, I remember. I wish I could say I don't.' He paused with a downcast expression. 'But the guilt is too great.'

'It wasn't you,' Earona muttered while wiping her red-rimmed eyes.

'I tried to kill you.'

Shiarn hugged his shoulders. 'She wasn't the only one, and you weren't the only one wanting to kill someone. We were given the chance of killing you—'

Earona frowned at her, 'But we decided to take the risk and hope you would return.' With a shaky smile, she wiped away more tears. 'And you did. Thank Kahm.'

Jett nodded his understanding. It was touch and go, and he was also thankful he had been able to make the decision himself. 'Thanks to Nya.'

Seth dropped on his knees beside him. 'You certainly have been horrendous lately, and creating a lot of murderous intentions among all of us.'

Jett made a short grunt of derision.

'Holy Kahm,' Keanan cried, 'You were downright evil. A demon lord spawned from the realm of Hell, in words and deed. I'll not coat it with sentiment. We nearly lost everything. In fact, we did lose our Gifts and Mind-speak. We were near defenseless and would have lost our lives in the end.'

Jett looked up at Keanan's abrasive tone. Everything he said was true, and there was more Keanan wanted to say, but he was restraining himself. He realized he would have to face him at a later time about those concerns. 'Somehow I did that. But I don't recall it.'

'You stopped our Gifts?' Seth said.

'I did. But not to make you powerless.' He paused. 'It was to stop the poison from flowing into you all.' He studied the four of them, his eyes glistening with sadness. 'You would have become my slaves, and just as wicked.'

Pensive quiet settled over them. Even Jett took some moments to comprehend the devastation their corruption would have brought. How he had the insight to understand the degree of evil invading his thoughts he didn't know, but he was grateful for the perception.

'How terrible,' Earona whispered.

'You messed up their plans,' Seth commented with a relieved smile.

Shiarn nodded with a broad smile. 'And it gave us a chance.'

'That's right, and if you hadn't...' Too awful to speak of... *It would be death and destruction.* Jett scratched the back of his neck and looked up at the top floor of the house. 'I think I know where she might be.' His muscles were reviving, but he was still weak. *I've got to try.*

Not finding Mara in the house anywhere, Marcus and Hellier followed Adis up to the attic. The house continued creaking and wailing, despite Jett being saved. Whatever Mara was up to, it was big. Previously, Marcus had already stuck his head in the attic looking for her, but at the time he didn't consider she wanted to remain hidden. The three entered, with Adis' holding the lamp.

They walked among rows of shelves and chests, and discarded bits of junk. Marcus whispered, 'You think she's—'

Adis put a finger to his lips. His eyes glinted with confidence and he beckoned them closer. He pointed towards the end of the attic.

Marcus and Hellier followed him past the lines of shelving. Soon Marcus heard the soft monotonous tones of a female voice. They neared ceiling high racks and a wooden screen, and beyond was the pale yellow of candlelight.

'A spell?' Hellier readied her weapon.

'Do not use that unless necessary.' Adis eyed her sword. 'I'll go first.'

They snuck into the lit cramped space. Mara was kneeling opposite, and between them were numerous circles of symbols. The blood-red markings took up nearly the whole floor and the candle was a small light in the oppressive dark that concealed everything except Mara and the markings. Eyes closed, Mara seemed oblivious to their presence and continued chanting indistinguishable words. A bowl with the remains of blood was by her side. Streamlets of dried blood were down her arms, and her palms, offered upward, were red. Her hair, damp from sweat, hung in the congealing blood. Her face had an empty deathly hue.

Shadows gathered over the symbols and they took shape, becoming a solid figure.

'Summoning something?' Hellier whispered.

'I'll restrain her?' Marcus cast a gaze at Adis.

With a sombre expression, Adis stepped forward. 'It might not be that easy.'

Hellier looked at Marcus and shrugged. 'Worth a try.'

Marcus smirked at her sheathed swords. 'I'll go.' He hedged around the blood, not wishing to touch the abhorrent emblems. The darkness around Mara intensified and spiked out at him.

Mara's eyes remained shut. She appeared to do nothing to evoke it. The shadows moved of their own will. The darkness restrained Marcus' wrists and shot out at Hellier.

The light disappeared, leaving Marcus in complete darkness. The shadows turned hard and propelled into his body, like a gushing wind. The roaring mini-whirlwind hurtled objects in the tight space. Cursing loudly, he attempted protecting his head and face as he inched closer to where he assumed Mara was. After some moments of pushing against the powerful force, a voice shouted above the chaos.

'Mara, stop this!'

Quiet followed and the wind dropped out.

Startled by Jett's voice, Marcus leaned on his knees catching his breath. Meanwhile the lamp was relit by Hellier, and Jett stood at the entry with Keanan holding him up.

Mara collapsed. Adis cradled her shoulders.

No movement came from her chest and Marcus wondered if she were dead. She had let enough blood for that to be possible.

Jett said, 'Is she...?'

Adis pressed his hand on her neck. 'Maybe...' He looked up at them. 'Clara's coming.'

Clara pushed past Jett and Keanan and rushed over. Taking Mara's wrist in her hand, she bowed her head in concentration. Some moments passed as they waited. Mara gave a shallow breath, although she remained unconscious.

'She's on the edge,' Clara said, 'I'll have to watch her.' She shared a fearful look with Adis. 'Take her downstairs.'

Clara, and Adis, carrying Mara, left the room with Hellier tagging behind them. Jett stayed behind with Keanan and Marcus. He stared down at the bloody circle and pot of dried blood with a look of grief.

'All that time, she's been up here.' Marcus nudged the bowl with his boot.

'It's fortunate we could stop her in time,' Keanan remarked, 'Not in the least to save her life, but also to stop whatever evil she was wishing to summon.'

'Right.' Marcus nodded. 'Glad we don't have to deal with more evil creatures.'

Jett gave a weary grumble. 'So am I.' He gave him an exhausted sigh.

62 - Burden Lifted?

Darkness will hold no fear
When what you see is peace

Valfaèr, Elements of Arcane Power

A change came over Ethan's body during the night. Upon waking, an inner surge of energy hit him and he leapt from bed. He opened up his Ethos, and caused a bunk, occupant included, to lift. His actions didn't go unnoticed and when Ethan joined the line exiting the cell, Kenric met him with a broad grin. 'You have your special gifting back, we can leave today.'

They all trooped out the main gate into the sunshine of early morning. Ethan stared up at the cerulean sky and fast slender clouds. The peace in his heart inspired him to rise above his crippling fears and seize the opportunity of escape, despite the risk. 'I'll have to discuss it with Loc,' he finally responded, 'is there enough supplies? And how long will they last?'

'We have been bringing down sailor rations. Enough for five days. We can always stretch that out.'

Either way, it didn't sound promising. Five days of provisions was not a lot and the idea of spending five days underground was not a thrilling prospect. Loc informed him the Harn were ready despite their verbal misgivings. Ethan knew he was the reluctant weak link.

An underlying tension was felt by all as they descended into the lower section of the mine. Despite the prisoners' nervousness, the guards treated them with the nonchalance, the same as any other day of boring routines.

Ethan eyed the chamber ceiling, gathering more confidence in the simplicity of the act. To pull the plan off and avoid injuries, all the men had to vacate the main chamber and access the hidden passageway at top speed.

After the pirate guards moved away and settled down to their games and drink, the prisoners dispersed. They went in small groups to the opening of the secret tunnel, leaving a few behind, pounding and smashing rocks. The chamber emptied of men and soon Ethan, Kenric, Loc and Gailtram were hammering at stone near the passageway.

Opening himself up to his Ethos, Ethan lifted the rock in the center of the chamber. The giant boulder floated down the tunnel, blocking the light from the torches at the guards' station. A faint shadow appeared on the ground.

Loc yelled, 'Guard coming!'

Ethan propelled the massive rock up to the dark ceiling.

Amid the cries of the pirates, the thunderous sound of falling rocks filled their hearing. The second rock fell from the ceiling, splitting on the first, and muffling the frantic shouts beyond. A tremendous cracking echoed in the confined space and the men scrambled into the cave opening in the stone. Dirt choked the air, and shards of stones flew at them. Rocks fell hard, scrapping their limbs, and leaving bloodied gashes.

Ethan was the last to force himself through the hole. On the other side Loc dragged his arms and Ethan scrabbled to get his legs clear. Shaking his dark brown hair, he loosened the dust, and the grit, from his beard. His face was a chalky grey. Loc, his eyes shining in the dusty gloom, mirrored his appearance. Flaunting a mad grin, Kenric crouched beside them, his eyes bright with excitement. 'Glory to Nesvar, we did it!'

'Aye,' Loc remarked, 'I wonder what we have done exactly.'

Ethan rolled his head back and released a deep sigh, realizing he held his breath during the escape. He said a silent farewell to his Kin and all he knew from Tellávare, feeling certain he had buried himself and everyone else alive.

Gailtram commented without emotion, 'We've buried ourselves, I'll wager.' He had not concealed that he was not keen on the idea.

With delighted abandonment, Kenric sang, 'Think what the minstrels will sing, what stories…'

With profound disbelief, Ethan stared at him. 'I don't give a king's arse what they say,' he snarled, 'I just want to get out of here alive.'

Kenric appeared to be deaf to his animosity and started up the tunnel. 'Come on then.'

With no way back, they had to continue or perish.

Ethan followed Kenric up the sloping tunnel. 'Let's get this over with.'

~ * ~

The rising sun cast a cold light over the lawn of Sommerlea. Jett sat on the dewy grass and shivered in the frosty breeze from the mountains. As much as he would have liked to, he resisted gazing at the lake sparkling in the new light. The water's edge seemed to come alive with the sun's rays, though it had been rippling through the night. In the distance a flock of water birds took flight; their gay squawking signaled the beginning of the valley's day.

Again he shunned the activity on the lake and concentrated on the task at hand which was almost complete. He spent the night in agonizing reflection, attempting to come to terms with the evil exposed in his own mind. No amount of heartfelt tears or sorrowful groaning could eradicate the guilt. The only placation he could scrounge up was the Kin had survived and he was restored to them. The evil Nya had not won in the end, but even so she had revealed a dark side of his soul. Fearing the rage lay dormant inside, he questioned whether he could contain it if it were ever unleashed again. The only assurance he had was the Ward on his wrist.

Soft footfalls were behind him. Tensing against the pain, he continued focusing on the sharp concentrated piercing into his skin and did not lift his eyes to view the approaching company.

A gentle voice queried, 'Jett?'

His task finished adequately, he dabbed his skin with the cloth and crooked his head to see the older woman, slender, and in a crumpled blue dress with her blonde plait half undone. He saw her briefly the night before, and he also recalled seeing her a number of times, nearly every day he was in the cellar. At the time, her kindness filled him with anger. 'It's Clara?'

'It is good to finally meet you officially, and in your right mind,' she said with cheer, 'And how remarkable! I'm so happy you're well. But have you been out here all night? Really, they should have shown you to a room.'

'I didn't feel like sleeping.'

She stepped closer to unashamedly gain a better view of him, and looked down at what he was scrutinizing with furrowed brow. The underside of his left wrist had a tattooed script, and she glanced at his open pouch of needles and case of ink pots. 'Ooh, that looks painful.'

'A good pain,' Jett explained in a relaxed manner. Tattooing was a soothing balm at times, numbing other pains that were far more destructive. He pushed up his sleeve to reveal more writing in a beautiful elongated script of Fáer.

She took his wrist and turned it, studying the markings. '"Hold True to Kin" Very interesting. I gather it is something only you will truly understand.'

'I don't know if it would have helped, but some part of me wishes I had some awareness.' And writing the words gave him some assurance, although he wished he could write on his skin everything about his experience. He already had markings on his side and back, but they were symbolic patterns and nothing in script. In his Mind Palace as Nya called it, he had wondered about the tattoos, but the evil Nya could never explain where they came from. Soon enough he forgot about them altogether.

She gazed up his arm and muttered, '"Your Kin will Guide Your Decisions. Fight for Them No Matter the Cost ~ Love unites, hate divides".' She gushed, 'It's quite profound, and absolutely true.'

He nodded, he imagined Judge Haldus' would be astounded that Jett would imprint his words on his flesh. 'A reminder.'

She stared at him, her eyes suddenly serious. '... incase he returns?'

If he were to lose his body and mind to hell again, Jett would leave his mark of resistance and defiance on his physical body. He turned his eyes away from her gaze. 'Among other things.'

'Like a stigma.'

'Yes...'

She gently turned his arm, examining the lettering. 'You are good at it.'

'Maybe.' Hammer had taught him the art, and he had practiced on himself, but most of his work he did on his Kin. 'But I'm not a master.'

'Not yet.' Not minding the damp grass, Clara sat beside him and bent closer. 'Oh!' She ran her fingers over the braids on his wrist and found the amulet. She gave a loud laugh. 'We picked that up when we travelled through the valley. Decades ago. Later on, one of the children wore it, till they tired of it and it was treated as junk. Lilliana braided the leather, that's why it's not even.' She chuckled at some memory. 'How wonderfully odd that it should become important and be so powerful. It must have had magic imbued in it somehow.' She placed a hand on his shoulder with a smile. 'I'm so relieved it helped and you were saved and our house wasn't destroyed by hellish fiends.'

He clasped his wrist over the leather. 'And you weren't all killed.'

'Yes, that too.' Clara looked out at the lake, but her merry expression had not left her.

'How is she?' He knew she must have stayed up with her all night, because, like him, it looked like she hadn't slept at all.

Clara looked away with concentrated thought. 'We really didn't think the baby would survive, but he's a tough little soul and has pulled through, although he needs to be watched. Earona is with her currently. She's not woken, but physically she is better. As for her mental well-being, I can only hope and pray she will be restored.'

Jett nodded with a grim expression.

'I'm glad she wasn't able to do whatever it was she was trying to do. She would have died if we hadn't found her.'

Jett screwed the lid back on the pot and avoided her gaze. He had the sense Mara would have returned but not in human form, as to what she would become, he didn't like to dwell on. 'Probably.'

'You…' She bit her lip. 'The evil one used her? Why?'

'It seems she has a special ability to summon dead souls.' He already knew she had some power about her, but he had no idea it involved raising an army from hell.

'She has that symbol on her body,' Clara looked down at his wrist. 'It's a Ward of some type? So she should be safe?'

'Mm.' Jett pressed his mouth in thought. Unlike the amulet, her symbol was a permanent scar on her skin, but he also had the same mark on his chest, although that seemed to have failed. Mara's was strong and impenetrable, and it would have protected her – except, he had broken it, speaking in Fáer. If he could affect the Ward, could others? 'It's to guard the mind – but, he opened it.' He bowed his head in shame.

'And you stopped her in time.' She squeezed his shoulder.

'Yes…' He owed his life to them, but he also knew they did it to protect themselves as well. 'It is my hope that the Ward can regenerate.' Or so Nya seemed to indicate.

'It's really quite fascinating,' Clara went on as if they were having a trivial conversation, 'All this happened within your mind, as if in a dream. With no one being the wiser it was going on.'

'A nightmare you mean.' Had Earona told her everything already? He shouldn't be surprised.

Clara made a fist and punched her palm, and said with much zeal, 'If only we could do Spirit Healing, I'm sure we could have helped you.'

Along with other useful Gifts, Spirit Healing was lost to the Fáerinn over two ages ago. Healers lived in hope it would return to them once more. 'I'm sure it would have.' The last thing he wanted to do was talk about it again, he spent time telling the Kin his experience last night, and it had exhausted him. Fatigued and hungry, he thought it best to divert her before she asked any more questions. 'How long have you been here at Sommerlea?'

Clara glanced at the house behind them, a grand sight across the green lawn. 'More than thirty years, with some travel here and there.'

'Before that you lived in Baion?' Although he mentioned it, he wasn't sure he wanted to bring up their past life. Kael had been reticent as it was.

'Yes.' Clara took a breath. 'Kael mentioned you. He said you resembled your father, and he was right.'

He nodded with surprise she would speak of his father so freely. It also proved Kael had already written of him to his Kin, or warned perhaps. On light of events perhaps that wasn't unfounded. 'Kael spoke to me briefly about him. He seemed reluctant...'

'He doesn't like talking about that time, and we really don't know much about your father's life in Baion. Baion became a place of grief for us.' She paused. 'But I know you must be searching in your heart. I will tell you what I can, but please don't speak of it openly.'

'I had the impression Kael didn't want to talk about it.' Jett stared at the ground with gnawing frustration.

'The truth is, it didn't have much to do with your father, and more to do with the lords fighting amongst themselves. In retaliation for previous attacks the lord opposing Balendin destroyed the village we were living at, Anstye. The villagers weren't even warriors. It was a massacre, innocent people and children were killed and everything burned. We lost our own child...' she finished in the barest whisper, 'We could do nothing, although we tried.'

He listened to her honest recount with remorse she felt compelled to share her sadness with him.

She continued, 'And Kael was angry.'

'At my father?'

'Not directly. Before the wars started, Kael wanted peace, but in the end it didn't matter. Lord Balendin was determined to advance his own plans and overcome his enemies. Aillas' was an honourable man committed to his lord.'

Jett nodded with some understanding.

'Balendin wanted us to come alongside him, but we decided to leave instead.' Clara's voice lowered. 'It's best Kael not know I told you this...'

Jett sighed with some regret. Clara was giving him selected details, enough he would not be justified in speaking of it again.

She gave him a small smile. 'And now it's quite ironic, Jonas has dealings with the King of Coltrene.' She paused, and looked across the water. 'He enjoys that type of subterfuge and the politics, but not as much as...' She hesitated, 'Suan.'

Jett looked on with puzzlement.

'She was our Kin, but she has passed. The pain still rises up, but time eventually causes the wound to heal, if you know what I mean.'

He didn't want to know what it felt like to lose one of his Kin, and he had come too close to that reality. The horror of it lurked under the surface of his thoughts, like a nightmare he could relive at any time. 'I think I know what you mean.' As it was, one of them was still out there, somewhere.

'Jonas can tell you more about palace life and all that, if you are interested.'

With a somber tone, Jett said, 'You miss Tellávare?'

'At times, but we have a life here now. This was the home of the children. Morias and Lelana have three. Lelana is Nayinn, but the children still manifested Gifts, and I have a daughter and son, and Jonas has a son. They travelled onto Tellávare.' Clara looked at the house and became light-hearted. 'I'm assuming you would like to eat and maybe wash.'

'I would appreciate it.'

Clara stared into his dark eyes and gave a mischievous smile. 'You are a lucky man those girls put their clever heads together and were able to help you. If not for them…' She finished with a shudder.

Jett remembered their courage in facing him, even Earona who had been spiritually wounded, stood against him. He was proud of their faith and determination, and he smiled. 'Those girls are fairly special.' Yet their risky endeavor nearly cost them their lives. 'But too head-strong.'

'Good on them they figured something out!' She stood and put her hand out for him to catch onto. 'Now you are better they might be more inclined to tell me about Tellávare.'

He gave her a half-hearted smile as she led him up to the house, still chatting away. He was not in the mood to relax, not yet anyway, there were too many things he had to get off his chest.

~ * ~

Near midday, Jett left his room. After cleaning himself up and putting on clean clothes, he felt somewhat better, but only in a physical sense. He only slept a couple of hours, and only because he couldn't completely relax. Memories of the last several days continued filtering into his thoughts. He dealt with one, then the next would assault his senses. There seemed to be no end or rest from the torrent of guilt. He suspected there never would be.

Down the hall, he stopped at the open door to Earona's room. Not feeling at liberty to enter, he leaned on the doorframe and crossed his arms, watching them. Earona sat by Mara's bed, holding her hand. Her eyes were closed and her head drooped, turning her hair into a dark wavy curtain around her face and over the girl's stomach. He wondered if she were also asleep like her charge.

She stirred at his presence and looked up. With a slow smile, she greeted him.

'You look tired.' He had to admit a lot of that was due to him.

'I could sleep for a week straight.' She beckoned him into the room. 'Now this house is no longer a demonic haven.'

He crimped his lips at her candid statement. They had a tumultuous friendship. It was not unusual for them to argue, or feel the brunt of each other's obstinate opinions. Perhaps it was because she spoke her mind he knew where he stood. He pulled up a chair to sit beside Mara's bed and across from Earona. Colour was in Mara's face and she was clean of blood, even her hair looked fresh. 'She looks better.'

'I know, thank Kahm.' Earona's concerned gaze switched to him. 'And you?'

He stiffened at her query, and his inner walls shot up. It was just... the memories were unrelenting. 'I'm adjusting.' He took a weighty breath. *The guilt is enormous, I can hardly dwell on it, or even start to explain.* 'I feel I've been running up a mountain again and again.'

Earona frowned with a piercing gaze. 'I don't mean your body.'

Jett kept his eyes on Mara, who appeared to be sleeping. 'I've never been so afraid of something – and it's something in me I have no control over.' *Dark and deadly, and powered by hate.* 'I escaped it by a devil's whisker.'

'I know.' She reached for his arm with a trembling grip. 'We all did.'

There wasn't much more he could add, he was still coming to terms with it. He expected they all were in their own way.

'I want to know, how did you – he — get that incredible power?' Her eyes creased with sincere curiosity. 'Is it, he, you?'

He still wasn't sure, but he could feel malevolent hatred underlining his initial decisions within the Mind Palace. It overtook him with an overpowering intensity. Eventually it killed him, and then something else outside his comprehension took control. It was as if, an entity had taken over his body, and mind, and his soul was left like a ghost. That was his rudimentary interpretation, for the truth was he didn't understand how it worked. What frightened him, who was the real Jett and who was the imposter ... He quickly wiped it from his thoughts. 'It was beyond a normal man. The wickedness had a will of its own.' Similar to his abhorrent actions and the words that came from his mouth.

'You certainly weren't a normal man.' Earona's tone became stoic. 'But why you?'

He ran his hand through his hair in puzzlement. The answer alluded him, although Nya had hinted at some reason. 'I don't know...'

Earona's gaze darted over him and her voice quivered. 'Do you think... the evil will come back?'

Her fear sent a shudder through his thoughts, and he growled his defiance, 'No. That Jett is not coming back.'

'But you don't know,' she said in an angry hush.

He scrunched up his lips at her pessimism. 'If it does, I won't be going so easily.' His voice simmered at her dubious stare. 'It won't be the same.' He gave a sigh and eased his rigid shoulders. 'I'd have more of a fighting chance.'

His contrite tone caused tears to well in Earona's blue-violet eyes. 'It was just so awful. We had no Gifts and everyone was arguing...' she sobbed. 'And you were turned into a vicious demon... and Hellier was going to walk out and never return, I think she wanted to kill you, and Marcus wanted to fight you to the death, his or yours, and...' she cried and rubbed her wet eyes. 'Keanan tried to organize us, but failed terribly... and Seth wanted to die, he was so morbid, crying all the time… and Shiarn was angry, and wouldn't talk to me…' she heaved a great sob.

'Stop!' Her flagrant expression of sorrow tore his heart with grief, and he grabbed her wrist, bringing it away from her face. 'It's over. I'm back now.'

Earona dried her eye with the back of her other hand and tried to smile. 'I know. A lot has happened to us. I wish we could go back to how we used to be.'

'I doubt that can be.'

Earona exhaled a long breath. 'I guess…'

Silence came between them, and finally, his heart pounding, Jett was compelled to ask, 'So Shiarn… how is she?'

'You..?' *You remember that?* She had a fresh stream of tears. 'She seems fine on the surface. I'm the one who suffers over the loss.'

'You didn't?' He gasped at the realization.

Her eyes narrowed, and her lips twitched with disbelief. 'Don't you dare – No!' She shook her head, refusing to acknowledge his surprise.

'She's no longer Blessed?' He blinked with blatant shock.

'Does that…' Her face paled. 'You would have advised… differently?'

Slow, he shook his head. So many layers of remorse and pain he had caused by his descent into evil. 'Maybe.' As Avare he had a higher counsel on it, but now he didn't want to speak on it at all. The deed was done. It only added to his guilt.

'I tried talking to you,' she snapped, her fist clenched the bed cover, 'You were an arrogant arse who didn't want to know!' She cast a concerned look at Mara, still asleep.

'I know,' he answered, gruffly, remembering the conversation with galling regret that he wanted nothing to do with the Kin. 'But, still, you surprise me, Blue.' He never would have expected she would do such a thing.

She put her hand up to his face to stop his admission. 'Don't.' Her anger did not diminish. 'I talked to Keanan. Do you think I should – No, don't tell me!' She shook her head at herself. 'It's too late.'

It's best that way. 'Who knows, it may have been the same outcome. Keanan is too pragmatic and Shiarn's very strong willed.' *You didn't stand a chance.*

Groaning, Earona flopped her head down on the bed, and muttered with scattered sobs, 'I can't believe… all that anguish… curses… no wonder I have this condemnation… I killed…'

'It's not your fault.' His hand hovered over her trembling head, remembering the last time he touched her there. He was intent on destroying her mind and everything she was trying to evoke in him. As if needing to break the memory, and right the wrong, he rested his hand on her hair, and let the soft strands caress his hand. 'Or anyone else's. I carry all the blame. I should have been there for you, for all of you. I should have been more…' What? He had no idea how his entrapment happened. How could he prevent it? Everything had been worked out in a complicated plan of deception. 'I'm sorry you are hurt and all of you. If I can make amends I will.'

Earona lifted her head enough to view his candid declaration. She mumbled, 'I know…'

Mara opened her eyes, and they widened at the sight of him.

Earona clutched her hand and sniffed. 'Don't worry. Jett has returned.' She smiled. 'It's over.'

Mara frowned at the both of them, her face awash with disbelief. 'Over?'

'It's finished,' Jett said.

Earona added, 'You will be safe now.'

Mara scrutinized Jett with a probing stare; her skepticism evident in her cutting tone. 'You really think I will be safe?'

'As safe as any of us.' He gave a non-committal sweeping gaze of her and Earona. From what he had seen of Mara's unique gifting, the truth was more frightening, she was far from safe.

63 - Weight of Guilt Remains

Rebuild the fortress with rubies and diamonds and every precious gem

The Hidden Shield

Halfway up the sloping tunnel the men loaded up with various supplies, of rope, torches, mining tools, and rations. Ethan might have been right in thinking Kenric was mad, but he couldn't say he was disorganized. While cuffs and shackles were broken off the men, and gear loaded onto backs, Ethan attempted to see their surroundings. Light from the oil lanterns stretched the men's shadows across the rock face. He had become accustomed to the still air of the underground caves, but here it was more stagnant.

A few words were shared amongst them about the collapse of the chamber. Sullen looks passed on their faces as the full extent of their situation came to light. Perhaps their fate was sealed as much as the tunnel and they were only walking dead men.

They left the chamber and came out into a larger cavern. Their lanterns shone on the high ceiling. Shadows extended over rocks and several levels of overhang. Chamber walls were a swirl of iron and russet, and the floor was black under a fine layer of dirt. On a slanting ledge above, Mouse waved his light. 'This leads up. It's a good size.'

Kenric led the group and Ethan came up the rear. The men climbed up the stone to the new passageway, making a slow, noisy trail. Mouse went ahead to check the tunnel for other openings. It was narrow, but high, and tight for the men with broad shoulders. The grey-iron stone was cold and oddly smooth. Overhead, was complete darkness, and Ethan could only imagine where the ceiling finished.

Two oil lanterns were in use, not including a couple of torch lights. With few torches to use, they had to be treated as priceless treasures. They walked along in silence with the occasional man muttering and mumbling to the one ahead. Ethan dreaded every moment, yet with gritted teeth he said nothing. The surface of the tunnel altered in places with large sharp stones preventing even passage. Gradually it rounded in a curved fashion and remained on a flat surface.

The boys' eagerness was needed motivation and so was their scouting information. The children walked ahead, calling back what form the passage took. Eventually informing them the tunnel branched into two, both appearing unhindered by rocks. A halt was announced and the men sat around the small cavern on outcroppings of ruddy stone or in the black dirt, waiting for Kenric and more importantly Daskar with the lodestone, to come forth and make a decision.

Cold shadows of the two tunnels loomed unpromisingly. Daskar looked down them one at a time and steadied the black cylindrical stone. It swung to the right and it was agreed that was the tunnel to take. Not that anyone had a better opinion.

Soon the new passage became a large chamber with wide rocks jutting upward to obstruct their path. The stale air grew to freezing temperatures. As Ethan exerted himself, his lungs became tight and breathing more difficult. He tried not to dwell on the amount of rock above them, but the oppressive air made it more prevalent.

Many hours of walking passed and most of it in a grim quiet. Idle chatter seemed out of place and Ethan had no heart for it. He noted they were steadily heading upward, but no one could say for certain how many miles they had already walked. Eventually they emerged into a monstrous cavern with a deep basin. All around were the usual sharp rocks pointing from the floor, but no obvious tunnels were apparent.

The men sat while Mouse and Berran went in search of a new direction. The two boys were agile enough to climb the rock ledges and search between the giant stones. After scrambling on a ledge made by thick boulders there was a sound of loose rocks falling and the two reappeared.

Berran waved to the men below and indicated a slab of grey-black rock set apart from the cavern's wall. 'We think there's a way through, beyond these stones.' His child voice hit the walls and went no further when he called.

Luz asked Daskar, 'What does the lodestone say?'

Daskar pointed to the space the boys suggested. 'That way be north.'

'If we have no choice, then we have to,' Ethan said, following the boys to view the passage with Kenric coming up behind them. The opening was the size of a crawl space.

'I'll go.' Mouse took the torch. With his petite size he was able to crawl through effortlessly. His light bounced in a shaky line through the tunnel. Finally his voice echoed back, 'It'll be cramped, but there's a small cave here. I'm looking it over.'

Ethan swept stones from the space, doubting whether he could safely enter through at all.

'There's another opening.' Mouse's muffled voice came back. 'It's small—' He made a startled cry.

Kenric shouted with concern, 'Mouse, what's that?'

A few fearful moments passed while the men waited. Mouse answered, 'The shadows were moving. Gave me a hell fright.'

Kenric said, 'We shall start coming through.'

Ethan shook his head at the size of the tunnel. 'I'll go last.'

It took some time for the men to crawl the distance. Their supplies were either dragged or shoved recklessly through. Ethan moved as many of the loose stones as he was able. Even so he dragged himself through on his stomach, hoping it wasn't going to cave in. His back scrapped on the ceiling, causing him pain. He eventually made it to the next chamber. A fine layer of dust covered a grey slate floor, and the walls were smooth.

Kenric said to Daskar, 'Looks manmade.'

'Too right.'

Mouse disappeared down the next tunnel. Once again they started into another crawl space longer than the previous one. Ethan waited for them to pass through. Again he shifted the stones to form an accommodating pathway for his size. The stones were looser and he could move the larger ones with ease. Before he knew it, he cleared a reasonable path and could wriggle through without touching the sides.

At the new chamber the men were unhappy to see no visible exits. Hefty pieces of rock stuck out from the wall at the opposite side. Ethan stared at it in dismay.

Kenric placed his hands on the chilled stone. 'Something has got to be here.'

Ethan came up to move the stone. Solid; he could only shift loose rocks about it.

Stannar pointed at symbols etched into the grey cobalt stone. 'Look at that.'

They peered at the markings, yet no one could read them.

Luz said, 'I suggest we start pounding at this.'

A cry came from the end of the chamber. One of Kenric's men, waiting in the darkness, rushed forward. 'Something's in the shadows.'

Mouse stated, 'I've seen it too.'

Those with torches directed them to the end of the chamber. Light cast long shadows against the walls. Nothing could be seen in the corners and no noticeable rocks stuck out for something to hide behind.

'We don't know what's living underground,' Bearn said, his voice trembling, 'Let's be cautious. Stay near the light.'

Meanwhile, Daskar put his ear to the stone and tapped a chisel. With a loud hush he silenced the men and tapped again. 'We hit here.'

They took it in turns to hammer and pound on the stone in between resting. Only a few could work at one time and it was thought best to conserve as much energy as possible.

The men huddled together or dozed on the slate stone floor, but it was still difficult to sleep with the constant noise. Air in the tense atmosphere was stifling, causing them to become short tempered. Daskar assured them it was empty beyond the layer of stone. They had no other option but to trust him.

After the men took numerous turns at cracking the slab, someone put a hand through into empty space. Ethan moved the larger loosened stones. Sure enough the beginning of a passage was revealed, although a tight one, but high enough to walk on two feet.

Mouse walked through first. The overhanging ceiling was five feet above his head. Waist high rocks, sitting on the earth as if a thousand years ago they landed from above, blocked the passage in some places. Mouse's light disappeared and reappeared as he clamoured over the boulders. After some time waiting, Mouse came back. 'The tunnel's blocked, but I think the rocks can be moved.'

'I'll come and see what I can do.' Ethan followed him back up the tunnel.

'We shall rest here,' Kenric said to the rest of them. 'No use going yet.'

Ethan looked with foreboding at the jagged rocks above, all the while relying on Mouse's light ahead to guide him. It looked as if it was a level pathway yet had collapsed due to the fallen stones. The passage narrowed, and he squeezed past stone outcroppings, and watched with envy as Mouse walked between.

At the end of the passage, a slight indentation was in the stone. Rubble and loose rocks needed to be shifted, but otherwise an opening was beyond. With the mining pick he brought along, he started hacking at the rocks. He kept at it until chunks of stone fell away. Once it was cleared, he breathed easier.

Mouse stuck his head and his torch through. 'Looks like the same tunnel but bigger.'

Ethan sat on the floor breathing heavily. 'I'll wait here, get the others.'

Mouse's eyes glistened with wonder. 'You don't have a light.'

Ethan stared up at the boy oddly, wondering how he knew of his phobia of the dark. 'Call them.'

Mouse shouted for the men to start down the passage. Standing again, Ethan pulled out the remaining stone with his Gift and let them drop from the hole. Eventually it was cleared and he and Mouse entered the next tunnel.

Ethan took the opportunity to eat what had been in his pack and drink a little. Not able to foresee what use his powers might have ahead, he took the time to doze. In his half asleep state, he sensed a scrabbling on the wall. Mouse approached with his torch, and whatever was there moved across the rock face.

'Something is there,' Ethan whispered.

Mouse held the light high, shining it on the rocks, revealing only bare wall.

Kenric entered the cavern. 'We should rest here.'

'Agreed,' said Ethan.

The great group crammed into the narrow chamber. They stretched out on the rocks and hard floor and breathed deep of the stale untouched air.

~ * ~

With the noon sun starting its descent, Shiarn sat under the shaded terrace after helping Lelana with chores around the house. Flute in hand, she watched Marcus and Keanan sparring with Hellier on the lawn with mock weapons. Clara came to the table carrying a tray with a pitcher and bowl of fruit. The day was turning out to be lovely, and now Jett was back to normal, she could appreciate the surroundings. Everything seemed right – except, they were far from their destination and they weren't a full Kin.

Clara pulled up a chair and looked at the fighters. 'Morias will be out soon, he would love this.'

Shiarn lowered the flute. 'He will fit right in.' A black cat rubbed against the table leg and leapt up beside her. She scratched under its chin and he pushed on her hand for more.

'That's Sanoe.' Clara ran her hand along the cat's back and relaxed into her chair. She cast her eyes onto the lawn where Hellier faced Marcus and Keanan with wooden swords brought up from the cellar. 'I must say, your Avare isn't so bad after all.' She gave Shiarn a cheeky wink. 'He seems quite charming.'

Shiarn laughed. 'You have seen him at his worst. Anything else would make him look holy.'

Clara's laugh was exuberant. 'I suppose I shouldn't joke. I guess I'm just so relieved.' She patted her chest and took a gasping breath. 'Overwhelmingly relieved.'

'Yes, the whole thing has been an extraordinary experience I never want to repeat.'

'You really are extremely intelligent to have figured it out and saved him and us.'

Shiarn cast her a surprised glance. 'It wasn't only me. I had the initial plan. But thank you for saying.' She occupied herself with the purring cat, and recalled the spirit woman's words about seeking an answer. Sure enough it was there all along. 'I only hope... if it happens again, we will know what to do.'

Clara nodded and did not seem surprised. 'At least you know it's possible for him to remain himself, somewhere.'

'True.' Shiarn paused. 'But I still never want to try to make decisions like that again.' She was still pained by her own personal trial and decision. Not for the first time she pondered what it would be like to have a new life inside her body. As the idea took shape, she threw it down in denial. Not now, and not with that man. She couldn't stand it, and she couldn't bear loving it.

'Thank Kahm, no one did anything drastic,' Clara said.

That wasn't entirely true. But the worse, Jett dying or them, could have happened, so easily. But she had a gnawing fear, they had come across an evil that could possibly terrorize them again one day. 'Yes...'

Down on the lawn, Marcus raised two swords and paced about Hellier equipped with a real shield and wooden sword. With Lightning strokes he worked her hard, provoking her to extend her reach. Morias marched through the back door. Disregarding the girls at the table, he headed straight to the combatants, carrying a staff. They heard his rumbling voice travel up to them. 'Would you like help, Hellier?'

Hellier, her gaze fixed on her two opponents, responded with a curt nod.

'Aha!' Clara cried.

Hellier started swinging at a furious pace, landing hits on Marcus. In return for her daring he allowed himself no slack in his own strikes, landing a heavy hit on her side. She came at him with more determination.

Clara chewed an apple while watching with animated amusement. 'I believe they will be calling for a Healer.' She ended with a quiet giggle.

'They'll take a few more before they confess that,' Shiarn bantered.

Marcus stopped and shared some words with Keanan, and they both came towards Hellier from different directions.

'They are very good.'

Shiarn gave them an obliging glance. 'They thrive on it.'

The back door swung open and Jett came out from the house. He walked past Clara and Shiarn with a leisurely nod. 'Good day, ladies.' He glanced at Shiarn while stroking his smooth hairless chin, and he passed on down to the grass.

'I said I'd think about it,' she called after him with a teasing grin.

'Oh, my.' With a broad smile, Clara stared at him as he approached the group. 'That's a nice change.'

Shiarn shook her head and couldn't wipe away her smile. 'Don't be fooled. He's on his best behavior.'

Clara stretched and stood up with reluctance. 'It's marvelous sitting here, but I should check on Mara and Earona and help prepare dinner, and other chores are waiting.' She sighed forlornly.

'And I shall help.'

'Wonderful.' Clara smiled down at those on the lawn. 'For tonight we have a new guest.'

~ * ~

Jett watched his Kin spar from the edge of the lawn. The light sky became heavy with dense cloud and the wind brought a chill from the mountains that prickled his skin. He would have liked to have joined them, but he felt drained and lacking energy. Nya said his spiritual power would eventually recover, and he would most likely need physical rest.

The fighters, finally exhausted, came to the table for water and a piece of fruit. Marcus and Hellier wandered inside in search of Earona for their newly acquired sores while Morias chatted to Jett and Keanan.

Still breathing heavy from the demanding sword play, Morias said, 'I haven't been worked like that for some time.'

Keanan swallowed a mouthful of apple and gave him a wry grin. 'We seem to get a lot of practice.'

'We have trained for years,' said Jett, 'Marcus is one of the best in Tellávare.'

Morias jested, 'And Hellier, I've never seen a woman fight like her.'

Both men laughed and Keanan said, 'It can be a disturbing sight.'

Morias added, 'Certainly there are female fighters, but she has great skills.'

'She's needed them,' Keanan replied without a thought.

Morias turned his warm gaze on the two, 'You boy's fish?'

'We can,' Jett answered reluctantly, fishing was not a sport he was fond of, 'but not well.'

'I've got my rods down in the boat.' Before Jett could decline, Morias walked them to the jetty and informed them the buckets were in the boat and a pot of bait. 'Everything you need is in there.'

Keanan and Jett hopped in while Morias pushed them out and Keanan paddled through the gentle waves. Jett watched incredulously as Morias picked up a third rod and walked down the side of the lake.

Keanan pulled the oars in. 'You get the impression he was trying to get rid of us?' He attached a moist bug onto his hock and threw out his line.

Jett did the same. 'I believe you are right.' The placid bopping of the boat settled him and he scouted out the distant ranges. The oncoming grey clouds shadowed their lavender and blue majesty and he looked on in appreciation of their presence. It brought to mind the view from his Mind Palace, and how he had taken it for granted, not even aware of its unique bird's eye position. 'It's an amazing sight.' The lap of the water against the boat infused the air with tranquility and the men sat in a reserved silence.

Not having the heart to reach into Keanan's mind for the topic bothering him, Jett broke through the growing strain with a despondent sigh. 'Just ask me won't you.'

Keanan turned and studied Jett's profile. 'Amongst other things, I want to know, when did it all begin?'

Jett risked a sideways glance at Keanan's flushed face before going back to his line. His tone was blunt and uncommitted. 'Really, is that what you want to know?'

Keanan fixed a pair of frosty eyes on him. 'You wanted to kill us back then, with those bandits?'

Jett lacked the compulsion to discuss it, he remembered it clearly enough. It was one of the shameful parts of the whole damnable experience, mainly because he could recall he had reasonable thought at the time. Keanan continued with his delving stare and Jett realized he was not going to let it go so easily. He owed him an explanation and much more besides. He replied with exasperation, 'Why do you want to know that?'

'I want to know why this happened to you,' Keanan sputtered with restrained anger, 'How were you corrupted?'

'How? Far too easily.' He stared back, his eyes ablaze with passion. 'Why? Somehow I had the power to bring up hell, and she wanted to use that. And if you want to know, that frightens the Ethos out of me!' His unconcealed shame forced Keanan to stare into the murky green of the water. Jett ignored the retraction of his stabbing glare and exclaimed, 'And I never want it to happen again.'

Keanan's annoyed gaze followed the moving fishing line.

It was a hard touch of reality, but it was best he find out from Keanan rather than the others. After a few awkward moments of silence, he said, 'The robbers were trouble?'

'We weren't aware our Gifts had faded, and we had no Mind-Speak ability.' Keanan's anger erupted within his sincerity. 'Seth was punctured by an arrow as was I. If it hadn't been for Shiarn, Hellier would not be with us today. As it was Hellier caught a flying dagger with her ribs while facing two other bandits.' His articulate voice ascended with pent up heat and he attempted a calmer pitch. 'Earona's fading Ethos was of adequate help. But even so that was nothing compared to what you would be capable of doing to us.'

The image of his Kin facing attacks in such a vulnerable position left Jett feeling ill, in fact he regretted asking about it. He recalled meeting the seedy character in the tavern and telling him about the travelers and the treasure belonging to a certain duke. Jett had wanted his Kin destroyed, but the girl they were to bring to him. He couldn't say why at the time. Not till later did he understand. Eventually it would be him who would break their lives and bring their souls into captivity. The memories were an abominable glimpse into the essence of a demonic character.

Keanan continued, 'And this was while we had a pregnant girl, and Earona trying to heal Seth, in the back. But that turned out to be nothing, because it was you who nearly killed Earona, and Shiarn, and eventually it would have been all of us.' Jumping up, and making the boat lurch, he revealed his rage. 'How, by sacred Kahm, did you come to have so much hatred for us?'

Jett tipped sideways from the sway. He stood to confront him, his own anger rising with irrational fervor at his honest outburst. A great reservoir of hate was inside him, and he couldn't deny it. Even Nya said his own hatred defeated him. 'There's hatred, but not for you or the others.'

'Bollocks!' Keanan shouted. 'How do we know it's not there festering in your heart—'

'What the hell is that supposed to mean?!' He was already deeply shaken by the revelation of the evil within him, but to have it presented to him in such blatant terms crushed his confidence. 'You think I'm going to change again? Just like that?'

'We, you, should have paid more heed to the prophecy.' Keanan threw his hand into the air, and the boat rocked under their feet. 'We should have foreseen something like this was going to occur.'

Jett's arms tensed with the need to lash out. 'You're worried about that cock-arse prophecy?! Did it mention this?' He stabbed his finger into the leather cords on his wrist, indicating the Ward. 'What do you think, I'd sit at home on my arse—'

'You don't understand.' Keanan drove his finger into Jett's chest. 'Where did the leverage come from? Where did this evil-you originate from? Did those contemptuous remarks and acts come from nothing?'

Beneath Keanan's anger, Jett sensed an undercurrent of hurt – but he was too incensed to speculate on the hateful words he had spoken while transformed. 'I don't know how that evil… character came into existence,' he shouted, and his voice carried across the water. 'But you should know it's not me.'

'But has it been there all along waiting to reveal itself?' *Have you always hated—* Keanan shook the condemning thoughts from his mind.

Jett fumed at how close his words came to his own fears. He reacted with the same defensive rage at his inference. 'It wasn't like that! I'm not like that.'

Keanan said, 'Trust has been compromised, and we are left to wonder…' His tone turned to steel. 'You would think you would be—'

'Wiser?' Jett narrowed his eyes. *If I hadn't been born so prematurely, you would be the elder, like you wish—*

You are the Avare and that's the way of it. Keanan eyed him down with a stern glare. 'Being wiser would help. No, I mean more open…'

Jett snorted with derision. *You're got no idea.*

Keanan stiffened with indignation. 'I was the one left to make the decisions—'

'Right,' Jett threw back at him, 'Your decision, take me back to Tellávare.'

'How did you know that?' Keanan eyed him with suspicion.

Jett scratched the back of his head, recalling his encounter with Hellier. Like everything else, it evoked terrible guilt. 'Someone must have mentioned it.'

'It was the best option at the time—'

'It would not have worked out like you think. It would have been the worst option,' Jett said, 'Aside from the fact, you might not have made it, I would have done a lot of damage there, and there would have been no guarantee you would become Avare. They could have been scattered over different Kin, and none of them would be allowed to leave again.' He muttered, 'I would have hopefully got what I deserve.'

'Nevertheless, it would have been the right thing to do.'

'Curse the "right" thing. It's you abiding by the book,' Jett cried, 'And being "righteous" before your superiors.'

'Damn you!' Keanan flashed his fist in Jett's face. 'You would have preferred getting killed and making us murderers, or more than likely, killing us outright, which was your plan. We either get the blame and the negative reputation for such a wicked deed, or be known as the Kin murdered by its Avare.'

Jett stepped back from Keanan's upraised hand, remembering when he had used it against him recently and that he was capable. 'I don't like it, but—'

'That's the selfish way out,' Keanan growled. 'You would let us wear that, and we might never have got our Gifts back. On top of that, no-one back home would believe it—'

'They'd believe it.'

They both stared each other in the eye.

Keanan finally relented with a gruff sigh and threw his hands in the air. 'You're right. Why should I defend them?' He carried on with sarcasm, 'It would be the most scandalous event in our age and hence never spoken of or written anywhere, for public view anyway. All explained and justified through the 'curse'.'

Jett's eyes turned dark, and fire burned in his mind, seeking an outlet. 'You're going to bring that up?' He wished he wasn't standing on a precarious surface, where he couldn't land a blow, but neither was he able to walk away. Curse that Morias for sending them out onto the water.

'You know what I mean.' Keanan cocked his head, knowing he had scored some win. 'Does this event disprove it? I think it goes a long way in explaining things.'

'Nothing I can do.' He gave him a threatening glare. 'Whether it's true or not.'

'That is reason enough to be concerned,' Keanan went on, 'Because it is probably what they are expecting. If they do find out about this back home, it could have serious repercussions for you.'

'I don't give a demon's arse about it and I'll deal with it when it happens, but—' he paused. 'Curse it, you are right.' He would have eventually killed them all without regard and gone on a death rampage. Everything Keanan said was right. If Nya's wish had come about, she would be walking the earth with him, and no one would be capable of stopping their plan to open the Gate. His sigh was a loud grumble of defeat. 'It's one of the reasons I wouldn't want to be taken back home.'

Keanan nodded, and seeming appeased by his humble response, he backed off. 'Despite everything I may say and think, you are still my Avare, therefore you have authority over me.'

'Hell, Keanan.' Jett combed his fingers through his hair and relaxed his stance. 'You don't have to be a pompous arse about it.'

Keanan grunted his disdain. 'It aggravates my peace of mind that we may be faced with this dangerous situation again. What would you advise we do if you become... that again?'

Losing his momentum for arguing, Jett sat, and the boat jolted under him. 'It's not something I can simply tell you. I hope you will all know what to do.' He picked up the line again. 'But, I want you to know, if you really had to kill me, I wouldn't feel a thing.' He gave him a grim smile.

With his eyes on Jett, Keanan sat beside him. 'You think that makes it easier?' He shook his rich auburn hair. 'What about how we feel?'

It would be easier for some than others. Jett looked away to the mountains once more and took a fresh breath. 'I would trust that you do whatever you can to protect the Kin, and especially home. That's the most important thing.' *Although they might disagree – stubborn bastards.*

Keanan let loose a dry chuckle. 'You know it wasn't so much the lethal attacks, but your malicious use of your intimate knowledge of us that has done the most damage to our bonds.'

Jett hung his head with remorse at the truth of it. 'I know…' It ached his heart when he went over some of the defamatory and outright cruel words he spoke. It took him years to earn their trust, and he had come near to destroying it utterly. 'It pains me…more than I can even express.'

'I have my own regrettable behaviour to deal with.'

Jett gave him an incredulous glance. 'That? You think that's bad?' He rubbed his chin in memory and chuckled. 'I can't believe *you* actually hit me.'

'Surprising indeed.' Keanan turned his fist before his face, studying it with a frown.

'You know I…' Jett fixed his gaze on the distant peaks and for the first time gained some perspective on how he was seduced. 'I was angry at the world. I believed in the surreal dream of pleasure and I retreated from the old familiar rage on the outside. I had no discernment the two were connected – they were in fact intricately linked. The one drove me to the other like a vicious circle of destruction, until it killed me.' His downfall had been swift and complete. *I was chasing the dream and running from the pain of the world.*

Keanan's voice turned contrite. 'I expected we might have given you a hard time over the years.'

'Maybe.' He chuckled. 'No, it's my own weakness.'

'And everyone has them.' Keanan watched him with a sparkle of wit in his eyes. 'But, I may have some malreus chains crafted.'

Anger pulsed through him at the thought of being restrained. He let it go along with the cool breeze hitting his face. 'They did their job.' He cast him a warning gaze. 'For a time.' *I wouldn't rely on them solely.*

Ignoring his remark, Keanan went on, 'I expect it will take time to heal this.'

Jett was conscious of his encouragement, but he could not be completely convinced. Moments passed in a contented silence as they watched the water for any sign of fish. Jett cleared his throat. 'So Hellier and Dario really were together…' His words tapered off and he looked across the lake with embarrassment.

'You made your thoughts known on that one,' he remarked with indignation, 'What was puzzling, how you even knew of it? She actually accused me of telling you.' He softened his tone. 'It is quite true, though I must add, what you said was all untrue.'

'The evil spirit baited me with the information…' Jett did not remove his gaze from the mountains and his voice was rough amid the holding back of the heartache over Hellier's own admission. *I've been arrogant.*

'That's the least of it. You were a demonic arse of a scoundrel!' Keanan indicated the script on Jett's wrist. 'Did you have to do that?'

With his finger, Jett traced the black lines on the underside of his wrist. 'A reminder of what is important… and I like to believe it's an imprint on my spirit. I'd do it all over my body if I could.' He pulled up his sleeve, revealing the whole quote.

'A worthy verse. Hopefully I won't need to remind you of it.'

Tired of talking about himself, Jett turned to the bow of the boat and the east, the direction of the ocean he could not see. 'I like this place, but I'll be glad to see Ethan again.'

'True, we need to rescue him. Then, onto Hakan-Kara.'

'You don't sound as thrilled as you once were.'

'Our momentum has been impeded,' Keanan justified, 'I'm sure when we do have Ethan we can get on track.'

Jett was less inclined about it during their time in Floris and after a taste of independence he found he liked it. Although he couldn't prevent the damaging exploits arising from the missing Kin, one still missing, or stop his descent into hell and becoming a daemon fiend. Sighing with exasperation, he had to admit there was probably a need to be under the covering of another Kin.

'First things first,' said Keanan. 'When the baby bird is pushed from its nest, does it not have wings? Does it know how to fly? It asks; what are these wings for? And all the while the answers are in its nature, to be what it is purposed to be. Instinctively it stretches wide its wings and clumsily takes flight and comprehends its nature.'

'I'm not sure what you are referring to…' Jett responded to Keanan with a fond half smile. '…my errant nature or that we fly ineptly.'

'My friend.' Keanan's expression changed from serious to having a merry gleam in his eye. 'I refer to all of us. You may be of the opinion you are the epitome of this odd flock, but you are gravely mistaken. We fly together or not at all and it does not matter how as long as we do.'

'Well said and to that I can readily agree.'

In the hour, out on the water, they had no success at catching fish and they paddled back to the jetty. Morias greeted them, and boasting his own catch, swung a line of fish before their noses. A delighted grin spread his red bearded face. 'These will cook a treat.' He stared at their empty bucket. 'You didn't do much fishing?'

'Ah, no,' Keanan replied.

Jett gave him a broad grin. 'You've caught enough for all of us.'

'Guess they weren't biting out on the lake today…'

64 - Danger Returns

The body's rest will not grant you peace
True peace comes from the wisdom of choice

Fellowship of Healers, Age of the First Born

After a night of restless sleep, Jett sat on his bed dangling the Eye-key on its fine cord before his eyes. The powerful item was a weight in his mind again. The white gem, the size of an eye, shimmered with various depths of silver. Framing it, in an almond shape, was pure, perfect gold. The craftsmanship was the best he had ever seen. He handled it with a timid touch. No visions appeared, but an anxious foreboding made his heart race. The thing was beautiful – but dangerous, and worse, cursed. He hated having it, but no one else could be trusted to safeguard it. He had the impression the amulet hated him in the same way, and would have preferred him in the demonic altered state.

Staring into the gem, noises pervaded his mind. Distant tumultuous voices and angry cries grew in volume. A voice, stronger than the rest, flew towards him. The incongruent dulcet tone was a presence in this thoughts. He frowned with perplexity. Was it his own voice – or…

His eyes flicked open to see light expand within the gem. Pain struck his eyes that glowed with his Ethos fire without him realizing. He flinched and rubbed his temple. He covered the Eye with his fingers and squeezed it with irritation. "They" would be after this jewel – and he was stuck with it. 'Bastard of a thing.' He shoved it back into his pocket, and tried not to think – that he possessed an object that would grant an unknown enemy the key to bringing hell on earth. Heaving a tired breath, he stood.

Jett entered the den with a need to put aside the recent conflict and his own descent, and concentrate on finding Ethan. The sooner they united, the better he would feel about dealing with the amulet.

Keanan and Morias were already present and looking over the maps. The ease of the two men conversing as if they were old friends, evoked a poignant memory of their encounter with Jett in the cellar. Jett had seen a different side to them. Strong men with the same Gifting, and ready to defend the weak against a heinous villain.

Shame caused Jett to recoil at Morias' hearty greeting. Jett responded with politeness, but his guilt remained in a shut-out recess of his mind. The Sommerlea residents were kinder than he realized, far too gentle to have encountered someone like him. Partaking of their hospitality, he felt responsible for causing them such a troublesome time.

Keanan sat at the desk with Morias looking over his shoulder. Spread out was a collection of old and new maps. Morias waved Jett to come near.

Jett stood at the front of the desk.

Morias drew a gnarled finger along the Arranons and stopped at a mark on the coast. 'It's not named, but I'm willing to wager, Signet Reach is around this cove.'

Keanan lifted a map from underneath. 'But this has the location marked further north.' He pointed to a third map alongside. 'And this, another location.'

Jett flicked between the two maps with a frustrated grumble. 'And you think it's there, Morias, even though it has no name?'

Morias took a few moments to reply. 'True, it doesn't. But this new map came from Jonas through the palace.' He looked puzzled. 'This map is older.' He pointed to the one with Signet Reach further north. 'The new map has been produced after this one.'

Jett pondered the odd occurrence. 'As if it doesn't exist anymore.'

'But, we know it does,' said Keanan. 'The man we met spoke of its existence with certainty.'

Jett sighed with weariness at the dead-end. 'Is there a way up to the mountains?'

'Some roads,' Morias said, 'and one main road through the valley.'

'What's all this?' Jett pointed to the land they would have to travel to reach the northern ranges of the Arranons.

'The valley pass that takes you to Baion,' Morias replied, 'Unofficially Coltrenians consider it theirs while the Baions' probably think it belongs to them.'

Jett's heart beat with sudden fear as he pulled a tattered parchment from beneath the pile and read the slender words. He muttered with gut-wrenching surprise, 'Valley of Amin-Sayeda.' They were sitting on its doorstep all this time. *I don't like the look of this.*

'Ah, so that's where it is,' Keanan exclaimed.

Morias answered, 'An old name that faded out of history when the inhabitants perished.' He contemplated the strip of land. 'We came across this map in Baion.'

Jett pointed to a cross in the valley.

Morias looked at it closer. 'Mm, maybe their city. It'll only be ruins now though.'

Further north was a tiny triangle not far from a main highway. Jett speculated to himself, 'I wonder…'

Keanan said, 'The maps in the journal were rough, but perhaps it is the pyramid from the sketches.'

Jett wasn't sure he wanted to know, and he didn't think it wise to go near it if the enemy, the High Priestess spoke of, had reformed the Eye of Heaven. But, if they were to find Ethan he might not have a choice.

Morias' deep voice cut through his contemplations. 'Now I think of it, it might be best you avoid that main road and make through the forest on the south side. It'll be a longer journey, but safer over all.'

'Probably for the best,' Jett muttered under his breath.

Morias straightened up. 'I heard you had an encounter with Skar and a Narahk. That's pretty unheard of these days.'

Jett's eyes skipped between the two and landed on Keanan with suspicion. He wasn't in the mood to bring that up, and now he realized Keanan and Morias had gotten friendly on many levels. 'It was a surprise to us too.'

'At the time it was.' Keanan leaned back and folded his arms. 'On light of recent problems, perhaps we could assume it was more personal.'

Morias looked to Jett. 'They were after you?'

Jett pursed his lips at Keanan. Recalling the Narahk's attack, Jett had the impression it knew what or who Jett was. If not for Marcus… 'No… it wanted to kill me.' Mara was the objective, and now he could understand why that might be. 'It came to take Mara.'

'Sounds as if the whole town would have ended up dead,' Morias said.

'True,' Keanan said, 'if it weren't for Earona.'

Yes, Mara would have ended up among the dead. 'So the Skar or Narahk couldn't have done that….' Jett stopped with a deepening frown.

'It would seem.' Keanan raised his palms. 'Someone else in the area had to be feeding that creature with dark magik.'

Jett grumbled to himself, 'It doesn't make sense…'

'Not much of this does,' Keanan replied in a huff, 'and currently it is irrelevant to what we want to achieve.'

'I don't know much about this sort of thing, but you did kill a mage's servant,' Morias said, 'if he wasn't aware of you before, chances are he will be now or at least of something or someone who did this to him.'

Jett was not surprised by the observation, it had been on his mind since it happened. Floris offered some sense of security, but now the open country posed a whole range of new threats, not least his own clash with the dark powers of hell.

Keanan's mouth turned down. 'That makes me feel so much better, Morias.'

Jett went to the window with a cocky grin at Keanan's words. *It's just our luck I guess.* His eyes wandered down past the lawn to the tranquil water of the lake.

Keanan retorted to Jett's back, 'I find nothing amusing about our situation.'

Jett sighed at Keanan's high-brow staidness. 'You're right, there's nothing funny about it,' he could see nothing but troubling repercussions, 'but there's not a lot we can do right now.' He continued admiring the gentle water. 'Kean, you need to get out of here and so do I. Let's get some fresh air.' He turned toward the two men staring at him in bewilderment.

~ * ~

Pipe music rose from the outdoor terrace and floated down the lawn in a wistful melody. Shiarn paused her play and nodded at Clara as she pulled out a chair beside her. Clara shaded her eyes and looked down to the lake. Down by the water, Jett, Keanan, and Marcus sat with legs dangling over the side of the jetty. The three stood and unbuttoned trousers and pulled off shirts. Unmindful of the women sheltering under the pergola, the men, amid jeering banter, jumped off the boards.

'Glory heavens!' gasped Clara, her blue eyes widening in surprise.

Keanan was down to shorts whereas Marcus and Jett had stripped completely. Shiarn cast the boys a disparaging glance, but it was too far to see anything that may embarrass them.

Clara stared with slight awe. 'What good looking boys!'

Shiarn gazed at her with humorous scorn. 'Wouldn't they love to hear that, but it would only go to their heads.'

'I wouldn't dream of saying anything.' Clara's cheeks brightened. 'Imagine!'

The boys leapt from the jetty several times before contenting themselves with swimming. Shiarn watched with envy, wishing she had thought of it before they took the initiative.

'They truly are unfussed by it,' Clara commented.

'When they are in a group they have no fear. Alone, that's a different matter.'

Clara smiled at the merry scene. 'I recall Kael, Adis and Morias being so uninhibited.' She watched them swim out into the lake. 'Jonas not so much.'

Shiarn attempted seeing Jonas naked and swimming and her cheeks flushed. 'He certainly doesn't seem the type.'

Clara cast an inquisitive eye on Shiarn. 'You became close to him at the palace?'

Shiarn gave a mournful sigh. 'If it weren't for him I don't think I would have survived it or Morgal.'

'Jonas has spoken of this man,' Clara said, 'he's far more evil than I realized.'

'It was he who wanted the amulet that Jett has.' Shiarn became hesitant at disclosing the information. 'He conducted an elaborate ritual that took the life of a friend. I'm sure it had something to do with the Gate Jett spoke of.'

'Perhaps he is involved in this?'

'He's dead now.' Shiarn's tone was curt, she wanted everything to do with him, dead, even memory – if that were possible. 'Nothing more he can do.'

Clara's eyes widened. 'Jonas did…'

Shiarn gave a decisive nod. 'He really had no choice.'

'He doesn't do things without good reason.' Clara reached for her hand and held it with wise counsel. 'He has valued his position in the palace for some time. We never really appreciated what he did there.' She sighed penitently. 'At times we had differences over this topic. I've since been humbled and I will never discredit Jonas' work again. In fact, I will lavish praise on him for his worthy behaviour next I see him.'

Shiarn listened with interest.

'Initially he was not committed to palace life in the least, unlike Suan, but when she died that changed. He threw himself into his life as a lord. I think he was attempting to assuage his guilt over her death, and eventually discover the culprit who murdered her.'

'I heard a rumour about his wife. When you mentioned his son I knew it must be true.' She recalled Jonas' self-assured manner, but now she questioned how much of what she knew of him was a mask. 'How sad.'

'Extremely. She was young, we all were, but thankfully, they were Blessed with Zander.'

'It must have been a terrible tragedy.' Shiarn gazed off towards the lake, wanting to know more, but unsure how far to push.

Clara studied Shiarn. 'She was poisoned at the palace. Jonas disliked the palace, and I wasn't there with her.' Her face darkened with the revealing of years of strain. 'How could he think it his fault, I'm the one who should have helped her.'

Shiarn exclaimed with surprise, 'But it's no one's fault, the murderer is to blame.'

'Oh, yes, some poor devil of a servant they beheaded.'

Shiarn's stomach churned at how close she came to sharing that fate. 'Justice done?'

'No, we don't believe he did it.' Clara shook her head. 'Suan was an attendant to the first queen and on that day she was also murdered.' She paused. 'Suan's death was trivialized besides that of the queen.'

'You think they never got the true murderer?' Shiarn fixed shocked eyes on her at the startling revelation.

'We had doubts. Jonas' suspicions were validated as he spent more time in the palace. The death of the next queen was said to be suicide, but…'

Bastian's mother. So it would seem Bastian had a right to be perplexed about the truth of the event. She leaned forward, hungry for information. 'Also murdered?'

'Jonas certainly came to believe that. He was on good terms with Lydia, in fact they spent much time together. Her death only added to his loss.' Clara distracted herself by watching the men. Their raucous behaviour made her smile. 'For me it is inconsequential. Suan is gone.'

'I'm sorry. Jonas never mentioned anything.'

'He wouldn't.'

'The more time I spend away from him and that opulent lifestyle, I realize how little I know him.' Shiarn pondered Jonas and the idle days with the occasional intense banquet or party. Like a heady dream difficult to recall. The nightmare however was toxic and never left her.

Clara enquired with a searching look, 'You are fond of him?'

She fiddled with the pipe in her lap and observed the boys splashing in the water. With reluctance, she voiced her feelings. 'I fell in love with him.'

Clara's smile disappeared. 'You seem unsure.'

'Such a short time and…'

'If Jonas revealed feelings for you, you can be assured he means it.' A soulful plea was in Clara's voice. 'I don't want to see him hurt again.'

Shiarn recalled his enigmatic manner, his inner strength, and clever wit. All these excellent traits could not be outdone by his debonair composure. Her affections for him remained despite her lack of knowledge of his background, and at the sight of him her desires would be flagrantly apparent. 'It's… I don't know where I'm going to end up.' Her sigh was full of weight; finally she gave voice to the bleak truth plaguing her.

A sparkle of admiration was in Clara's soft blue eyes. 'Jonas would be more understanding than you know. It's best if you enjoy your time together, because you never know what might befall.'

'Sounds ominous, but good advice.'

'Oh, dear.' Her palm slapped her forehead. 'I've just remembered. Kael and Jonas will probably be arriving soon, maybe even tomorrow.' Her face flushed pink. 'I sent them word about our situation here.'

Shiarn chewed her lip at the thought of them racing home to deal with Jett to find all was well. 'They will be needlessly worried.'

She stifled a chuckle. 'They will be, and they will arrive and we will be sitting at our leisure, enjoying the company. But it will be nice to have them home.' She gave a wistful sigh.

'Yes…' A grin spread on Shiarn's lips.

Earona approached the table with a delighted smile at the sight of them.

Before she could make herself comfortable, Shiarn said, 'I wouldn't come out here. Some bares are in the water.'

The boys climbed out of the water and lay on the jetty to dry.

Staring out at the lake, Earona went a lovely hue of pink. Her smile faded and her slight shoulders stiffened.

Clara commented, 'the "bares" have migrated to the jetty.'

'I hate when they do that.' Earona pursed her lips in irate indignation. 'Why here?! I certainly don't need that right now.' She turned on her heel and stormed back inside. They heard the bang of the door as she entered.

Shiarn explained with careful respect, 'Earona values her modesty. Maybe too highly.'

'Oh, bless her,' Clara replied. 'Anyway, I'm a great believer in things happening as they should. Just look at your Avare. What a marvelous turnaround.'

'That nearly killed me with stress alone.'

'It certainly wasn't good, but…' Clara smiled with motherly kindness.

'We did survive,' Shiarn cried with triumphant.

Clara nodded with rapt agreement. 'Thank Kahm he didn't kill any of us. But I have this frightening sense we managed to divert the most horrendous of events from occurring on New Earth, by the slightest of margins.'

~ * ~

After swimming and a midday meal, Jett strolled through the gardens bordering the front of the Sommerlea estate. He could discern the occasional flat stone marking the path in the long grass and flowering bushes, and through vines attempting to suffocate trees that grew untended. The wild state of the peaceful garden was a welcome change after the last few days in the underground airless chamber. Determined to ignore his condemning thoughts, at least for the afternoon, he listened to the birdcalls and whispering leaves, and breathed deep the scented air, and made his way to the pond Clara mentioned.

The path opened up beneath the trees into a hidden patch of green with a lily swathed pool. Reeds and fragrant flowers among the rocks brightened the water's edge. The water rippled from a fountain statue, and was alive with speckled light from the leaves above. Trees and coloured shrubbery encompassed the alcove, giving the impression he had entered a secret refuge.

Walking closer, to gain a clearer view, he stopped, sensing a presence behind him. He turned to see her, sitting on a bench of carved branches. Hunched over, her fiery-gold hair hung over her folded arms and down to her stomach. Her eyes were on him, under her dangling fringe, but in a distracted way – perhaps hoping not to be noticed.

He said, 'I didn't know you were up.' Although, she was the last person Jett wanted to see, she was probably the one he needed to talk to more than anyone else. 'Good to see you are better.'

'I wouldn't call it that.' Mara stared past him with a blank expression and gripped the edge of the wood, preparing to rise. 'I'll go.'

'No.' Jett put out his hand, but softened his tone, 'I wanted to talk to you.'

She eased back down, but her hands remained rigid on the chair. 'Why?'

Stepping closer, he creased his brow at her animosity. Despite him being himself again, she still didn't trust him. 'Don't you think I should?'

Her shoulders rose in a stiff shrug and her voice was sour. 'You're not going to apologize, are you?'

He cringed at her cynicism. 'It's been on my mind, and I am.'

Her amber eyes flicked to the pond and her face became a brooding mask.

'Do you remember?'

'No!' Her voice was a cutting rebuke.

He observed the strain across her face as she replayed some memory.

After a moment she responded to his intent stare, 'I'm good at forgetting.'

He gave a weary sigh, wishing he could say the same. 'Can I ask you - who gave you that tattoo?'

Her hand pressed on her chest and her gaze remained on the water. 'It was… Wendessa.' She took a breath and bit her lip. 'I didn't realize how important it was.'

Jett came closer with a scrutinizing eye. 'You know what it does?'

'I know now.' Her lips screwed up with scorn. 'It's a curse-seal of some type…'

His breath caught in his chest. It certainly was another way of looking at it, and the reference could explain a lot about his own life.

She continued, her voice a faint whisper, 'Guess it's true.'

He rubbed his chin in thought. It seemed she wasn't yet aware he also carried the mark, on his wrist and also on his chest, although he wasn't sure how effective that one was anymore. Yet, Nya's definition of the symbol was different and he wondered at the discrepancy in her remark. It might be viewed as a curse by those with evil intentions, but it also offered protection against those same types. A protection he broke through. 'It seems to keep the curse sealed…' his words tapered off as he realized the significance of the remark.

'Maybe, but, it all came out in the end.' Her voice was cold with spite.

Now her contempt was revealed. He was suddenly concerned that perhaps her Seal was not regenerating. It was best to step cautiously around her. 'Try not to make any decisions in the next few days as you recover, and if there is anything you need to discuss about what happened come and find me.'

She hung her head and was quiet.

He took a thoughtful breath. 'I will be honest, I don't understand the connection we have. But it's there, and it seems outside our control. You both repel me and attract me in the same instance. Even so, it doesn't help that you aren't telling me everything.'

She peeked up with a squinting gaze. 'Are you always going to be able to control me?'

He scratched his head in thought. 'It never occurred to me, but, I doubt it.'

'I won't do what you say anyway.' She clenched her fists on the bench.

Starting to warm to her antagonistic attitude, he smiled. 'Exactly.'

She screwed up her face. 'I nearly died.'

'I know.' Jett gave a deep breath. 'You told me your mother wanted to open a Gate and summon something. I assume she is a part of all this? Tell me more about her.'

'She's…' Mara looked away towards the fountain and its soothing flow. 'I think this is what she had planned for me. No, I'm certain.'

'And you were supposed to travel with that stranger at Lanvin. Yet somehow she knew or even instigated my compromise and eventual fall?' He finished with an angry tone as he realized the depth of the plan. 'She's a mage?' He folded his arms in thought, attempting to understand what he and his Kin would be confronted with.

'I don't care about her plans anymore.'

Her nonchalance surprised him, and he replied with abrupt anger, 'You should start.'

'What do you expect me to do?!' Mara's knuckles turned white, clenching the bench, and her eyes pierced his with glowing ire. 'You think I have anything to do with what she plans? As if I have a say? I wanted to get away from her, and find…' She jumped up and pointed at his face, and cried with brutal honesty, 'You should know about all this more than any one—' an angry sob escaped her, 'she could probably control me anyway like you did. You made me— evil– and now I…' she pressed her lips together.

With irrational annoyance he proceeded to grab her wrist. Inches from her, he stopped with a beat of fear at what he might see from the touch. 'You're wrong, I don't know. I feel like I can't swim and I'm drowning for lack of knowledge. Why should I know? It seems you know more about it than I. And you tell me nothing.' His tone weakened. 'But you are right on one thing, I know what I did to you, and what I am capable of doing, to you in particular.' He lowered his hand. 'It's because of that…' he put determined force into his words, 'it's best you and I keep away from each other from now on. You will stay here when we leave.' His voice was steady but his heart raced with anguish over the decision. Some part of him wanted to watch over her, as if it was a physical need to know what she was doing… but if they had to travel through Amin-Sayeda he didn't want to risk her getting involved in anything to do with the Eye-key. It was already bad enough he had to travel with it.

Mara stared at him aghast. 'You wanted to bring me along, remember?!'

'I had too then.'

Her face became an obstinate scowl. 'Anyway, I go where I like.' She planted her feet and her hands swung out wide. 'I won't be staying here, just because you say so.'

Jett crossed his arms and growled, 'You *will* be staying here. You can't wander off anywhere you like. You have people looking for you, especially your mother. On top of that, it's wise that we not be together.'

'You think that will stop anything?' She stared up at him, her eyes darkening with resolve. 'You're an arrogant arse who has no idea, and besides, you can't tell me what to do.' She spun on her heels and stormed across the lawn.

Cursing under his breath, he watched her break into a run through the trees. She was more upset than he thought she would be. She did need protecting, but he didn't think he could provide it for her. Trouble would surely come if he and the girl were near each other. He had to hope those at Sommerlea would keep her here and safe.

~ * ~

Hours could have passed or minutes for all Ethan knew, but soon they were ready to set off again. In muffled silence they walked in single file. The boys bounded ahead, and soon two returned to report the tunnel continued with the same confined overhang. After consulting with Daskar and his lodestone, he told them they were more or less moving in the right direction.

Ethan decided to walk with the boys. He was in need of their enthusiasm and thirst for adventure. For the boys, it was a venture into the unknown, but above all, it was better than a slave to the pirates. To Ethan, it was more like a grave.

Mouse's firelight paused up ahead and Ethan hurried towards it. After a bend in the passage, Mouse gave a startled cry and his light disappeared.

Ruegar and Branan fell to their stomachs after sliding on the loose shale. Ethan skidded up to them, almost sending the two over the edge. He watched Mouse's light fall into pitch darkness and vanish. Ethan called over his shoulder, 'You better halt.' Without the guiding light, the men behind Ethan stopped and waited in near darkness.

A faint yell came from below the ledge. Stumbling on the shifting stones, Ethan nearly toppled over the edge as he assumed Mouse had done.

Over a continuous roar in the distance, Branan shouted, 'I've got him.'

Ethan crawled his way across the sharp stones in search of the edge. A torch had been passed to the men at the front and the light revealed the immense cavern they had entered. The roof was in unfathomable darkness and the bottom lay unseen miles below.

'Hurry, he's slipping…' His arm wedged between the rocks, Branan held tight to Mouse's hand.

Prostrate on the loose stones, Ethan cried, 'Don't let go.' Leaning over the lip, he touched Mouse with his Gift and moved him above the ledge. Mouse floated to the opening they came from and reaching hard ground, he pressed against the wall.

Rushing and crashing sounds boomed off the uneven rocks of the chamber. The men could see no farther than fifteen feet in and beyond was a chasm of absolute blackness. Yet, a change in the atmosphere was palpable. Ethan breathed deep of the fresher air.

After a pause, Kenric commented, 'That's water.'

A narrow ledge by the wall of the chamber appeared safe to travel. Ethan said, 'It might go around.'

'I'll see if it does.' Derryl stood in front of Mouse, his fiery hair matted and nearly grey, and his hands rested on his hips. 'Give me a light.'

Ethan shook his head dubiously. 'I don't know…'

Derryl said, 'Move me across?'

The darkness was thick, but it was possible. Ethan said, 'You'll need a light.'

Once Derryl had light, Ethan stretched his hand out to the boy. He floated out from the edge. After a flurry of movements he relaxed and swung his legs and grinned. Eventually his tough little voice shouted, 'I see it.'

The old man, Bearn, called, 'What you see, boy?'

'Waterfall.' His light hovered against a spraying blanket of water. 'It's spitting on me.'

Bull's voice thundered across the cavern. 'What about a pathway?'

'The ledge goes around.'

'Can you see a way through?' shouted Kenric; his words reverberated around the cavern.

Derryl's voice came from over fifty feet into the giant cavity in the mountain. 'It might, can't say for sure.'

'I can't send him any farther.' Ethan concentrated on bringing him back.

Derryl came back with a look of exhilaration. 'Always wanted to fly.'

'So we take the ledge,' Comgel said.

'It's the only way,' said Derryl.

Their scant light did nothing to reveal the chamber's magnitude. Ethan was left to imagine the enormous size of it. The ledge curved around the edge of the chamber on a downward slope. The sound of water thundered in their ears as they persevered with the tedious walk that circled the chamber.

Another halt was called. Farther up, a hole in the rock was large enough for men to enter although it was lined with abrasive stone. Three feet off the ground, the opening seemed to be happenstance and lucky. The line of men filled the new chamber and on closer inspection it was larger than they first perceived.

Their lights flickered off the ceiling. Dense shadows stretched downward to meet an end wall. The cavern appeared to drop into more black dust and smoother stones. The atmosphere changed back to the dank moisture and stagnant air. Even in the dim light their tired and soiled faces were evident, and dull eyes showed more fear than their words would express. They sat under a ceiling of intricate stalagmites, and had no qualms about lying down in the fine black dust.

The men ate sparingly and made do with the little water they had left. Ethan wondered whether he should attempt gathering water from the falls outside. No one suggested it so he disregarded the idea and drifted off to sleep. He woke later to the subdued conversation of sombre men. For a time he thought he was back at the rocks until he viewed the low ceiling, but he turned over with a stiff groan at the men's discussion.

The Harn, Con, said to Brith, 'I've seen it again.'

'Aye,' replied Brith, 'I don't disbelieve you, but I can't see anything.'

Gailtram cut in, 'You talking about the shadow?'

'Aye,' Comgel joined in, 'looks as if it's moving.'

'I've seen it too.' Ethan sat up to join them. 'And more than one.'

'What is it?' Bull asked.

Ethan shrugged with uncertainty. 'I don't really want to know, as long as it doesn't come near us.'

'They're looking for it now,' said Rad.

Branan, Grith, and two of Kenric's men scoured along a side of the cavern with a torch aloft.

'It probably doesn't like the light,' Ethan commented.

'We need to light more,' Gailtram said.

Bearn approached at Gailtram's words. 'We go easy on the torches. We can travel closer together.'

Gailtram lowered his face. 'Doesn't comfort me, but if it's necessary.'

Ethan noted various openings in the chamber. He glanced around for Kenric and Daskar. Both appeared to be missing from the chamber. 'Which tunnel?'

'Not sure yet,' Bearn said, 'They're figuring it out now.'

Many of the men were restless and on edge. All were committed to the task whether they lived or died, they only wished to know what it was to be and the sooner they found out the better. The dust-covered men looked the same. The only defining factor between the Harn and Kenric's men were the difference in stature. Ethan was unable to tell one Harn from the next, but he was known by all. He searched for Loc amongst them. Having spotted him, he stood by his side.

Loc said, 'I've seen one of them creatures. Hold still for a time you can see it. It doesn't come into the light.'

Ethan affirmed, 'We stay in the light.'

'I've never seen anything like it,' Loc stated with wonder, 'Black and hard looking, almost like bone.'

Ethan replied, 'and I've never been underground like this before.'

An argument started on whether they should enter the nearest tunnel and evidently, based on appearances, the easiest to travel.

Kenric stood between them and shouted in a bright and orderly tone. 'That is the tunnel we seek.' He pointed up to a four foot black opening they could barely see, nestled above an outcrop of smooth stone.

Looks of dismay and blunt refusals passed over the men's weary faces. Again they stubbornly studied the tunnel before them which was man height with level footing. The higher level would require climbing and more back breaking crawling. Daskar was adamant, the higher tunnel was the way and he could not be swayed to any other opinion. Ethan could not comprehend why he was so certain about it. Daskar replied, it was his instincts from decades of underground mining.

Mouse had already clambered up to the opening. He called down, 'It's narrow for a short way, but a decent size. Even Ethan could fit.'

Finally they were convinced and only because they couldn't justify their own opinion on taking the easier tunnel, except to say it was easier.

Once more the arduous task of moving over rocks and through a small opening began, while lugging all the gear behind them. Soon, the constricted tunnel widened, and walking became less taxing. The stone of this new passage was an intense sienna colour that crumbled with firm pressure. After walking a distance, it once again reverted to a narrow fit. It became worse, and the men had to walk sideways with backs pressed against the fragmenting wall.

Ethan found it excruciating and wished to have this particular tunnel behind him. He shifted at a slow speed and only as fast as the man in front, that was sluggish at best. All the while he felt he was walking in a tomb.

Shouts travelled down the length of men as they communicated what was occurring ahead. They halted while stones were cleared away and a large rock was climbed over. The men up front were endeavoring to fit through a four foot high gap raised three feet off the ground. Curses abounded, and bellows from annoyed men added to the already explosive atmosphere. They shoved and dragged their bodies through the gap. All needed what help they could get from the men pulling on the other side.

Ethan bore the worst of it. The stone was stuck fast in the underground rock. He cursed his great size and not for the first time. He thought he would never be proud of his large build again. However his body did drop through after much heaving and pushing, as if the stone gave birth to a grown man. He paid the price of it with cuts and bruising. He collapsed on the dirt of the cavern and crawled out of the landing space. The chamber tapered down into a low cave with a ceiling only four feet high. He groaned with the ache left from the sharp stones and hoped somehow the new cave would rise as they moved deeper in.

Mouse walked to him without needing to stoop. 'Come see this.' He led Ethan a short way to a huge span of water with the ceiling only two feet above it. The colour of the water was indistinguishable and as still as a pane of glass.

'Is it drinkable?'

Kneeling by the edge, Mouse dipped his hand in and brought it to his mouth without fear. 'Tastes clear.'

In the dull light of the torch the water was dark, but it was fresh. The men slouched under the roof, drinking their fill and topping up their water-skins. Ethan rested while men continued emerging from the crawl space. Taking time to catch his breath, he wondered where Loc was.

A shrill scream rang out, sending fear into Ethan's heart and filling the chamber with dread. He sat upright, knocking his head on the low hanging stone. Another fervent cry, and shouting men burst out from the tunnel. Doubled over, Ethan rushed to the opening with the others. There would have been less than five men still waiting to come through, Loc being one of them.

Derryl scrambled back through the high opening, and Mouse, even smaller, followed after.

'Lads, don't be going through!' Druce yelled as he held Ruegar and Berran back.

Ethan stood helpless with the others. Two Harn pushed their way through the gap and fell onto the floor amidst anguished questions from those waiting. They puffed and gasped. 'It's them moving shadows.'

Ethan asked, 'Loc?'

'In there.'

'Devil's bollocks,' Ethan cursed.

Another Harn came through followed by another, but still no Loc or any sign of the boys. Ethan stuck his head in through the gap. Fine scrabbling was over the rocks. He shouted down the passage, 'What do you need?'

Loc answered, 'Fire!'

Mouse's scared voice cried, 'Too many.'

'I'm coming in,' Ethan called.

'No.' Loc swung the one torch overhead. 'We're coming to you.' The shadows stretched across the ceiling of the tunnel. It wasn't one or two, but numerous bony creatures scurried across the rock face.

Ethan stuck his arm through in mounting panic. 'I know what to do.'

'Aye, I figured.' Loc did not remove his eyes from the shadows as he swayed his light high. 'Derryl, climb out.'

Derryl scampered through.

Ethan opened himself up to his power and took the torch from Loc. He moved it out above Loc's head and with agile skill Mouse came through the gap. Once Mouse was clear, Ethan said, 'Come on, Loc.'

Loc clambered through the stone in a mad dash to escape the shadows. Ethan moved the torch towards the ceiling. Their huge eyes shone silver in the light and long needle teeth protruded from open mouths. Their skin appeared hard and they had pointed ears flopping down. They made no sound except for the scratching on the stone. Even though there was near a hundred, they moved as one mass.

Ethan took hold of the torch and spying a hefty rock on the ground of the tunnel, he moved it to block the hole. For several tense moments he watched the opening for any further movement.

Stannar cried anxiously, 'Where's Var?'

'He's gone.' Shaking his head at them, Loc sat on the ground breathing hard.

Confused stares and disbelieving gasps met his unexpected words. Loc finally stated, 'Those things are deadly.' A trembling terror was in his eyes. 'A horror from deep in the earth. They bit Var and weren't going to stop.'

Ethan gave him a grim frown. It was bad enough stuck underground, but now they had to contend with strange killing beasts.

'It's like...' Loc muttered, 'we've entered hell.'

Ethan said nothing; this had been his thought all along although he had not worded it in such a blatant way to anyone, but himself.

65 - Surprises

Who is really free?
Are we not all confined in our personal cells?
With the walls, of duty, physical limitation, fear, and doubt
And overhead, the weight of remorse, always opposing advancement

Olvarus Claw'Blade, Reader's Wisdom

Earona dragged herself downstairs to face the new day. The sun was up for some time, but after a deep sleep, she had lingered in her warm bed for too long. Since Jett's return, she started dreaming of the boy from Lanvin again and with increasing detail. Mal was the center of her sleep, like a solid figure always present against a coloured blurry background.

On top of her unease, Keanan was intent on snaring her attention to the extent Marcus avoided her as if Keanan had some unspoken rights to be solely with her. It ruffled her peace of mind. No wonder she lacked the desire to get up that morning. 'I wish everything would go back to what it was before,' she mumbled as she went downstairs.

She breathed a relieved sigh at the empty kitchen, having no patience to talk to anyone.

Hellier strolled in and gave Earona a pleased smile. 'There you are.'

Earona snapped, 'Yes.'

'Could you braid my hair?' Hellier looped a white-gold braid around her hand.

Her loose plaits, sweeping across her back, needed re-braiding and no one was more adept at it than Earona, or perhaps no one was as generous with their time. 'I'll do it outside.'

Hellier and Earona sat on the grass near the twisted pagoda overlooking the reeds of the lake. Clouds blocked the sun, making the air humid, and the murky water rushed to the shore in more frequent succession. Apart from the girls and the chatter of ducks it was quiet.

Earona yanked on Hellier's hair, straightening her head.

'Flamin' hell.' Hellier's face reddened with annoyance.

Perhaps she used too much force, but she was unraveling braids in place since Tellávare. 'Isn't it time you let your hair down?' *I ask this every time…*

Hellier stroked a fly-away strand with reverence. 'It's family tradition.'

'It's good to see you happier...' Earona said, 'and all of us.'

'You think I'm happy?' Hellier muttered.

Perplexed, Earona took the comb Hellier pinched from Shiarn and pulled it through her long nearly white hair till it was tamed and sitting in thick waves against her back. 'I don't understand you—'

'You don't have to.' Hellier ran her fingers through her wildly crimped hair. 'I just need time to think...' Abruptly she got to her feet and started off towards the water.

With annoyed astonishment, Earona watched Hellier plonk herself down at the end of the jetty.

Jett watched Hellier sit on the jetty as he came to sit beside Earona on the lawn. Not that Earona was the one he really wanted to talk to.

'Oh, it's you.' Earona let her breath out in a rush.

'You were expecting someone?' He gave her a swaggering grin, it changed when he felt her bad temper and he became less merry.

'No-one really...' *Someone else.*

He enquired shrewdly, 'Keanan?'

'What?' She gave him a stunned grimace.

His eyes drifted to the storm clouds illuminating the brilliant shades of lilac grey in the distance. 'I sense something going on.'

'It's complicated.' She sighed and pulled her knees up and held them tight. *He kissed me.*

'Keanan?' Jett's head jerked to witness her sudden timidity.

'Yes, and...' Earona stared at the grass, her face colouring. *Marcus did too.*

'That's a shock.' *I can see I've missed some things.*

'I reacted badly,' Earona mumbled, 'Now I don't know what to do.'

He chuckled at her stiff composure. 'Don't do or say anything. Make them squirm.'

She moaned, 'So easy for you.'

'You should wonder, why is Keanan now interested?'

'What does that mean?' Her face turned sour.

'You know.' When they were younger, Earona's sadness at Keanan's rejection wasn't a secret. The Kin stepped warily around the two, as no one wished to take sides. *His decision was determined by his arrogant disposition.*

Her shoulders flew back with indignation. 'People change.'

'I guess even he can change.' He gave an involuntarily chuckle at her presumption and contemplated Hellier looking into the water. 'But as you know, I'm not the best at giving advice on matters of the heart.'

Ignoring him, she said, 'Perhaps something will... happen.' *Maybe someone else will...*

Jett's manner was gruff. 'You either decide which one, or leave them both hanging, but don't get caught up worrying about them.'

An anguished groan came from her chest.

'I guess that's why Marcus seems to be avoiding you.' Now he better understood the awkwardness between them all.

She blushed at his statement. 'Oooh.' *Maybe you could tell—*

'I'm not going to say anything on your behalf.' He put his hands in the air. 'I'm not going to interfere again. Not after last time I got involved with you and Keanan.'

She let out an exhausted sigh. 'I suppose.'

He sensed the fatigue in her voice. 'Something else?'

'I'm tired lately. Seems to be getting worse.' She gave a gapping yawn. 'Perhaps it's lack of sleep over the last week.'

He creased his brow in cogitation. 'It's true. Sleep hasn't been easy.' Not being able to wipe the worry from his face, he sat, lost in a vision from his own sleep.

'I've been having the strangest dreams since Floris.'

He gave her an alarmed stare. 'Dreams can be deadly – so I've discovered.'

'Seems daft in the light of day,' she said, 'I've been dreaming of a boy I met in Lanvin, Mal.'

'I remember him.'

'He was the reason we went through that cursed hole. Well, I was the one who went through and that silly lot followed me.'

He gave her a sly half grin. 'I wondered what occurred and that clears that up.'

'He ran through and disappeared and I foolishly ran after him and so forth and then here we are.'

He gave her an amused look.

She continued with irritation, 'I had no idea it was there!'

'Anyway.'

'Mal was there when I came through and he disappeared back through the senyu.' *I inadvertently sent him to his death or at least into terrible peril.*

He sympathized with her gloomy thoughts. 'Those structures are a menace.'

She nodded her agreement.

'You've been dreaming of this boy?'

'Yes, and he's saying the oddest things.'

Although he tried to conceal it, urgency pervaded his questioning, 'And where is he in the dreams?'

'Some places I've never seen, sometimes in Tellávare.'

His tone became stern. 'What does he say to you?'

'I'm sure he's trying to tell me something.' She creased her brow in concentration. 'He said something about building something… Oh, that's right, his palace.'

Jett listened with alarm.

'I recall him speaking about a beautiful lady…' She caught her breath. *Could it be…?*

'What?'

'She scared him off.' A strained look was in her eyes. 'I wonder if it's the spirit from your dream?'

He was as concerned as she at the idea. 'A beautiful lady, there might be a link. This news is disturbing, Blue.'

'I tried to talk to him, but my mind is too foggy.'

'You have to be careful,' he warned. 'And don't trust anyone.'

'Do you know how hard it is to even know I'm dreaming?'

He stared down at the writing on his wrist with full comprehension. 'I know.' The world of dreams was complicated and fraught with danger, but his experience had been different, he encountered spirits. 'Tell me if you dream of him again. Possibly he is dead.'

'What an awful thought!' Using Jett's shoulder, she steadied herself as she rose from the lawn. She looked down at him with sadness. 'But I will tell you.' She looked toward the jetty.

He followed her gaze. *Do you think she's avoiding me?*

'Probably, but she has to come in eventually.' She started back up to the house.

Jett sat watching Hellier for some time and she was not budging. She hadn't spoken more than a few words to him since he returned, and she avoided being alone with him. He was driven mad by her evasion, because he knew it meant she really needed to talk to him. Finally he decided it would have to be him going down to meet her.

His gaze set on the lake, he walked the short pier towards her. She lifted her head as he sat beside her, but did not look up at him. He started, 'Hey…'

'Water looks good for swimming.' Her tone was dull, similar to her eyes that were usually bright.

He scanned the lake, reflecting back the graying sky. 'I suppose.' After a thoughtful pause, he realized there was no noble way to start. 'I've been worried about you.'

'I'm fine.' Her answer was a quick rebuff.

'Really?' He tried not to sound sarcastic, reminding himself he wasn't there to debate her feelings. 'How is your side?'

'You know about that?' She tilted her head and glanced at him with suspicion.

'I do.'

Her hand circled her ribs. 'Another scar.' She shrugged. 'Seem to be getting a few.'

His face darkened with anguish at her subtle inference. 'I know you don't want to hear this, but I'm sorry you had to face—'

'No, don't apologize.' She stared straight ahead and streams of golden hair blew across her face. 'It makes it seem like it was you. It wasn't you… it's best to think of it like that.' Her tone was more a question than a statement. 'Everything is good now.'

Her curt remark shut down any further talk on it – but he wasn't letting it go that easily. He studied her profile with vexation. She couldn't even look at him, and she was blocking any remorse he wanted to show. He snapped, 'No. It's not.' Now he was getting mad at her.

'No, I'll tell you if it is or not.' Anger erupted in her words, despite her calm composure.

'I said things to you…' His voice was raw and he tried to gain eye contact with her which was not forthcoming. '…and whether it was me or not, there were words that should never have been said…' His attitude on the road to Parkvale left him with more guilt than what would come after. Probably because he still had some sense remaining at that time, yet in spite of that, no concept of his changing nature.

And so did I. 'But you had an excuse.' Her voice was a breathless whisper.

It took him a moment to perceive her heartfelt remark. He gave way to a weary sigh. 'Your excuse was better than anyone's.' Her verbal attack left him with a depressing wound in his heart, he couldn't deny. But he knew she must carry a similar wound.

'I want to forget about it.' Her voice cracked in warning.

'Then why can't you?' Angry remorse filled his thoughts over her stone-wall indifference.

'You— you don't understand,' she spat out, but her tone became quiet, 'I don't want to talk about it.'

'Will you tell me if you do?'

She hesitated. 'If you needed to know.'

His dark penetrating gaze rested on her inscrutable stare and his tone remained irritated. 'That's a cryptic answer if ever I heard one.'

'You really should...' With an open burst of hurt she thought, *men haven't been the best company, and I can't...*

He was not prepared for the flash of heartache her words brought to his thoughts. Pain, he had a hand in creating, but it wasn't only from him. He stared at her face, suddenly her beauty appeared fragile and her customary cheery grin was no longer a firm fixture. Her distress put him in his place, giving him a new comprehension her anguish ran deep. But now he had the awareness more was troubling her, and he could do nothing to console her.

After some moments, she said, 'And that thing is going to keep you—safe?' she nodded at his wrist.

'So I've been told.'

'What if it's gone?' She went on in an incriminating tone, 'You haven't said what we should do if that happens - again?'

He retorted, 'You do whatever you need to do.'

'Curse it,' she snarled, 'That's so helpful.'

'I could have killed you—'

'But you didn't,' Hellier replied.

'No...' Because he – the demon had plans to use her once the transformation was complete.

'For what it's worth I'm glad you didn't.' She made a small smile.

He realized it was her way of bridging the gap. 'For what it's worth,' he returned the smile. 'I'm glad you didn't.'

'You're just lucky.' Hellier stood and looked down at him with a serious gaze. She wagged her finger at him. 'I never want to find out if I can do it or not.'

'Agreed.'

~ * ~

Late afternoon, Jett entered the house from the back. Laughter and chatter came from the main lounge room. Kael and Jonas had arrived, and with some trepidation, Jett steeled himself to meet them. Through the front doors a chest floated inches from the upturned hands of Kael. His merry eyes caught sight of Jett and he gave a jovial grin. 'Jett! Good to see you are… normal.'

'They told you?'

'Somewhat. The important part, you have been freed. That's a great weight off my shoulders.'

Jett tried to smile. 'And everyone else's'.' Now it all rested on him.

'You go in,' Kael said, 'I'll be there shortly.'

Clara and Shiarn sat on the lounge by the window. Opposite them, sat Morias and Keanan, and Marcus leaned on the edge of another chair. Standing in the center of the room and occupying the attention of all, was a tall good-looking man, in a frilled shirt and navy trousers. His hair was longer than his shoulders and held neatly at the back of his neck. This, Jett presumed, must be Jonas.

Jonas stepped towards him with an outstretched hand. 'Jett, we finally meet.' He took him in with a discerning gaze. 'Thank the heavens, you are well. You have survived a remarkable experience.'

'Jonas.' Jett grasped his hand. 'It's true, but I have recovered.'

'Fortunately for us and you.' Jonas motioned for him to sit in the chair near the door. 'You can take a seat if you prefer, however, I shall stand. I've been in the saddle too many days.'

Unable to be comfortable sitting, Jett leaned on the high backed armchair by the door.

'I have met Keanan and Marcus, but where are the others?' Jonas said.

Clara replied, 'The girls are coming.'

'And Adis is out with Seth,' added Morias.

Kael entered and clapped his hands together in a festive manner and enquired with infectious good cheer, 'It's splendid to be back and everything is fine. It makes me wonder if it was a ploy to get us home.'

'No, it was real enough.' Clare continued, 'Although… you are back and I'm glad.'

Lelana shuffled into the room, bearing a tray of refreshments. To the newcomers she showed merry affection. 'How was the palace since the king's passing?'

'Now *that* is a prelude to a lengthy conversation.' Jonas placed a steady gaze on his Kin and his words glided out with a dramatic flair. 'And there would be much to say on it, but I believe events here have been far more riveting than anything the palace could offer. News from the city would be rather humdrum, I'm afraid.'

'After everything, some trivial gossip would be a joy.' Clara finished with a tittering giggle.

Jonas' articulate speech contrasted with the laid-back mannerism of the other residents of Sommerlea. Jett had to admit there was a quality he envied in the man, natural charisma.

'I do have some gossip, although whether it is trivial is debatable.' Jonas' eyes swept over the room and rested on Jett. 'Aside from the near catastrophe here, a question has been on my mind. Despite probably knowing the answer, it was become insufferable to my inquisitiveness—'

Kael's comical moan interrupted him, 'Don't I know it. And I hope you can tell him what occurred.'

A devilish smile played across Jonas' handsome face as he eyed Jett. 'A certain duke, Brytwold has been excessively riled up by an incident at the Sanchella Gate.' He raised his brow at Jett's Kin. 'Describing some "conniving brigands" I quote, that stole and made off with a priceless heirloom.'

Jett responded pleasantly, recalling the arrogant man by the gates. 'You heard about that?'

'Indeed!' Jonas laughed.

'We have a small chest of his.'

Jonas chuckled slyly.

Shiarn continued, 'It was planted on us. Lucky we found it otherwise we would have still been stuck in Floris.'

'Or worse. The duke is a powerful man amongst the right people.' He set a warning gaze on Jett. 'He will certainly not forget you.'

'He won't be the only one. We are wanted by the underground society of Floris. Especially me. This duke is connected to the slave trade in the city, if you'd like to know.'

Jonas looked to Kael. 'Perhaps it is worth us inspecting their wares and becoming prospective clients?'

Jett eyed Jonas' flamboyant attire. 'It's a dangerous environment.'

Jonas jested with a blank expression. 'I imagine it is, if there are people like you involved.'

Marcus and Keanan laughed loudly. Jett was indignant before grinning at the recollection of the fiery night in the sewers.

Clara sat upright on the edge of the chair. 'It's good it all worked out and you are free.'

'We were extremely lucky,' Keanan said.

Hellier, Earona, and Mara walked into the room. Hellier smiled at Kael and Jonas, and took a seat.

Morias waved at Earona and Mara to come further in. 'Introductions are needed,' he started, 'That's Hellier and Earona and Mara. Kael and Jonas. These two girls were the ones staying at the Niesta Work-House—'

'Mara?!' Jonas interrupted with astonishment. He stepped across the room to meet the petite, golden-red haired adolescent, his eyes discretely drifting to her stomach. 'Could it be Princess Mara?!' With a worried brow, he searched her flickering eyes and flushed face.

'I can't believe you recognize me.' Mara had a disagreeable pout. 'I can't recall your name.'

'Jonas Belleguarde.' He bowed his head. 'I cannot forget a face, and not one as sweet as yours. Last summer I accompanied the Prince to the Alabaster Palace. However, to see you in my own home…' Confused by her presence, he took her hand and looked her over.

Mara's sigh was full of resignation. 'It must be… strange.' She cast a glance over to Jett and Earona.

Jett glared, his anger was building, like a fire laid with new wood.

Earona stared wide-eyed, her face paling.

'Mara's a princess?' Morias remarked, 'Well, I'll be the cat's fifth leg.'

Clara cried, 'What a wonderful surprise!'

'It's a surprise, but I can't see it being wonderful.' Jett's brooding expression was directed at Mara, but she kept her eyes away from him. To Earona he sent his heated thoughts, *I hope you didn't know of this.*

She told me nothing.

'What have you people been doing?' Jonas' cool composure faded and he lifted his hands in frustration. 'I don't think you understand the ramifications of who she is.'

'I know,' Kael replied dryly, 'Now.'

Jett seethed at the revelation. 'Mara said nothing.'

Keanan glanced at the others. 'We didn't know.'

'A lot of things make sense now,' Shiarn said, 'Why she was abducted for one.'

Mara's face heated and her hands made tight balls. 'I was under no obligation to tell anyone.' She made a sweeping gaze, but Jett knew the comment was directed at him. 'It makes no difference at all.'

Jonas tapped his chin with a perplexed expression. 'I have heard that your mother, Queen Yavinia and King Rikard, are searching for you. Your disappearance is not common knowledge, nor is it official. Currently you are the legitimate successor. As you may know there are two others who would have a claim. Needless to say, it is imperative you be found.'

As those in the room began to comprehend the impact of her identity they stared at her anew with shocked and stunned faces.

Jett drilled Mara with a piercing stare. 'You should have told me.'

Mara's tone was equally sharp. 'Would that have really helped?'

Jett's fury turned to frustration. No, but it would have given him a better perspective of why she was wanted in Floris. She certainly wasn't a homeless waif with unique powers – he should have expected as much.

Morias seated Mara on the lounge and Lelana poured a short drink for Jonas.

After taking a delicate sip, Jonas said, 'It is good to see you are still safe and well.' Not able to remove his eyes from her young face, he shook his head in wonder. 'All along under my nose at the palace prison and the temple. Not a skerrick of an idea ever alighted into my curious thoughts it was you. What a marvelous feat of subterfuge!'

'If you had seen the state we arrived in, it wouldn't surprise you at all,' Mara replied.

Jonas nodded. 'True. Your disguise was real enough. As well, your disappearance from Aquila was concealed from public knowledge.'

Morias said, 'I knew there was something special about her, she has a dignified air.'

'No one has ever said that before.' Mara smiled without cheer. 'Must be palace life…'

Kael interjected kindly, 'We believe your step-father has sent people to search for you.'

'They are, and here you are in our house, of all places.' Jonas studied her. 'But the question is, why are you here? Why do you not reveal yourself and go back to Ryne?'

Mara responded, revealing a daring air of arrogance, 'It's more problematic than that.'

Jonas appeared troubled and addressed her with kind regard. 'So I assume.'

Jett staunchly folded his arms. 'We discussed taking Mara home, but I had no idea it was the palace in Aquila.'

'Perhaps it might have worked at that time,' Jonas replied, 'However, now I fear it will not be that simple. The word is, they believe she has been kidnapped.'

A malicious glint fired up in Mara's eyes. 'That's not a surprise. But, she knows… that's not true.'

'I see. Well, it is the right political move on their part. The queen can then place blame on whoever will attempt to stand against them.' Jonas studied her. 'It seems the king is genuinely searching you out. It is interesting to note, there has been no hint whatsoever you are with child. Perhaps this adds the layer of intrigue we are missing.'

'King Rikard is searching without informing any of the nobility?' said Kael.

Jonas pondered, 'Correct, although if we have gained knowledge about this, then surely they have also.'

Jett considered his encounter with the man at the Meet who had kidnapped Mara. The criminals of Floris must know of Mara's lineage. Who were they working for, he wondered? 'There are some unscrupulous men looking for Mara, and it would seem they know who she is.'

Keanan gave him a thoughtful frown. 'I still don't understand how they would have knowledge she was even in the city at all.'

Kael said, 'Could it be Rikard was the one who would pay these men?'

'Possibly,' Jett recalled his meeting with Shark, and his mention of an important person seeking Mara. 'Although she was brought to the Meet as merchandise, to apparently be sold to Tonius Shark.' He could now see the reason for Mara's kidnapping was more diabolical – something that involved him and the Key. He assumed Mara's mother had more to do with it, but he was reluctant to speak on her in front of so many. His eyes scanned Mara, suddenly wary of any volatile reaction.

Mara's gaze scattered over all of them, but ended on him with a defiant glare and a sulky pout.

Jonas continued, 'It stands to reason, if the news is shrouded in darkness, those who dwell in such will be well-informed. I expect we would never know if it came down to it, but still, it would be scandalous for a king to pay for his relative.' He sighed as he considered her. 'As it is, Mara is here and safe, and we are in charge of her, which brings about a whole gamut of problems and repercussions. I will need to determine the best plan of action.'

After some moments, Morias broke the stern air with a kinder tone. 'Have you got a boy back home you're worried about?'

Mara smoothed her hand over her bulge. 'Not really.'

'Perhaps we shall leave that for a more private conversation,' Clara said to Morias, saving Mara from her obvious unease.

Adis and Seth came through the door. Adis gave Kael and Jonas an enthusiastic embrace each. Jonas gave Seth a genuine smile and said, 'More of you.'

Adis chatted with the newcomers about their journey and the day to day running of the winery.

'The day is getting on and I still have chores to do.' Kael spared Clara a glimpse at the word chores and gave a sheepish smile. 'We can discuss the last few days later.'

'That's right and I want you to move those boxes from the hall,' Clara instructed him. 'Earona and Mara will help me in the kitchen.'

Kael grinned happily. 'Ah, the lady of the house has spoken and I am put to work.'

'You be careful with her, Clara.' Jonas indicated to Mara as the girls left the room. 'We don't want anything untoward to occur while she is in our care.'

Clara smiled at Mara's back. 'Not to worry, we've gotten through the worst of it already.'

Jonas replied with a knowing nod, 'You need say no more.'

The party dispersed into their separate directions, either out into the front courtyard or the back of the house. Shiarn stood on the stairs and watched Jonas approach. She wore a reserved smile, but her eyes were aglow with happiness.

'That leaves you and I.' Jonas slipped his hand over hers and led her upstairs.

~ * ~

Shiarn stepped into an open suite of rooms overlooking the lake. Solid furnishings were covered with velvet cushions. A cyan rug with a tree in various shades of green was the focal point of the floor. At one end, a step led to a raised dais and a sumptuous four poster bed. Two great windows had cushioned seats with a view of the lake vista past the heavy drapes. Cut wood was at the ready and fresh white flowers would have been placed there by Clara earlier.

Jonas pulled the door closed and Shiarn turned to face him. He smiled down into her expectant green eyes. 'I am glad you arrived safely and you overcame your predicament.'

'And I too…'

He pressed his lips onto hers in hesitant expectancy. She did not resist and he continued with a controlled firmness. He broke off, yet his mouth lingered above hers and he ran a finger over the side of her face, feeling her velvet skin. 'Before I commandeer you for my own selfish passions we need to talk.'

An understated gravity was in his words that set her on edge.

'Come, sit.' He took her to the blue upholstered lounge where he sat.

She curled her legs up and sat facing him. 'It's bad news?'

'I wanted to tell you first.' He reached for her hand and delivered his words with poignant bluntness. 'Morgal is not dead.'

A shiver of foreboding caused her to grip his hand harder. 'But how?'

'I fear he has power we do not know or even comprehend,' Jonas murmured. 'After your escape, all went well. Morgal was found in the cell and orders were given previously it was not to be opened under any circumstances. That was instigated by Morgal before he came to you. So it did cause some trouble, because I had the key - which I eventually returned. Nevertheless, Bastion was notified Morgal was dead and not being convinced, he came to see for himself.' He chuckled at the recollection. 'Consequently, the prince charged Morgal posthumously with conspiracy to regicide and aiding an escapee.'

A spark of joy flashed across her face. 'Brilliant—'

'Indeed,' he agreed. 'But on hindsight it may have been more beneficial to not have done away with him and perhaps he would have stayed in that cell, and faced the block.'

Shiarn gave him a puzzled stare. 'You did kill him?'

'I'm certain of it. Even Captain Morran confirmed it. By morning Morgal had no official posting and his quarters were cleared out by Kael and myself.' He smiled tightly. 'We even have a portion of his work here with us.'

She was horrified at the thought.

'We took journals and parchments, very interesting documentation. He simply had nothing left that we know of.'

'And...'

'He was unwisely put into a box ready to be carted to the burying fields,' he declared vehemently. 'And like the sly demon he is, waited for an opportune time to escape.'

'But... I don't understand?' Fear continued to bubble, rising into unconcealed terror.

'Kael and I have gone over his paperwork and we believe he has a style of magik that allows him to store, what he refers to as his life essence.' He creased his brow at her sudden wide-eyed stare. 'It seems this grants him a type of resurrection ability.'

Sickness rose from her stomach, making it difficult to swallow. 'No...'

'I'm sorry.' He stroked his chin while considering her. 'I have an idea what it might be. His unspeakable actions towards you and other women have a more sinister explanation.' His tone softened and his face flushed, 'So I must ask, are you with child...'

'No...' With a fluttering hand she touched her abdomen with a mix of relief and fear. 'Not anymore.' She choked back the tears she had pushed aside.

He folded her in his arms and patted her floating curls, soothing the rush of emotions. 'It's a painful thing...'

'I had hoped it was for the best... but...' Her tears gushed out against her will. He held her without speaking a word and she said, 'I'm sorry — acting like this.' Swiping at her cheeks, she attempted a chuckle. 'It's not like me...'

'You can be whatever you need to be,' he kissed her forehead. 'I make no judgements over any decision you might have made.'

Heat spread up her neck at his touch, but also a pang of remorse she didn't wait a little longer. After a moment, dread caused her to freeze up. 'Could he know where this essence was?'

Concern clouded his eyes. 'That is my fear.'

'I can't believe that man still haunts me...' Her voice trembled, despite her brave front.

Jonas took a tendril of her fiery hair and twirled it around his finger. 'If he is nearby we shall find him. Adis will scout the area. We will do what we can.'

She sighed with resignation.

'Not too fear,' he said, 'After all, you have already defeated a terrible foe.'

She gave him a tight smile, but inside she flinched at the idea of Jett being a foe. 'You're right.'

'I have remembered something I was to give you.' Jonas went to the chests left near the door. 'It might bring you cheer.' He brought back a slender box and placed it in her hands. 'I wish I could say it is from me, but no, it is from the prince, well, the king.'

Opening it, she gasped with delight at the rich sparkling emeralds set in a beautiful silver chain, plus the matching earrings. 'From Bas,' she uttered, 'Why?'

'He is an expert in generosity.' With a warm gleam in his eyes he watched her touch the necklace. His tone became sombre, 'You did much to aid him and he considers himself forever in your debt.'

'I enjoyed his company despite his diffident manner.' She smiled at the gems, but even so, she was not convinced Bastion did not know what would eventually transpire. 'I guess I will never see him again to ask about his involvement.' Despite what she pretended to see, his actions still betrayed her.

'The chances of seeing him are more than slim or even entering Floris.'

'I wonder if he will ever marry,' she speculated.

'Now that he is king he can do whatever he pleases.' He laughed. 'To a certain degree.'

'That is wonderful, I think.' The necklace forgotten, she turned a questioning gaze on him. 'Did you find out who murdered the king?'

'No.' He creased his brow while his eyes lingered over the jewels. 'So far it remains a mystery.'

She noted his evasive manner, knowing he was too smart for that to be. 'Mm, well, that's a surprise...'

'I am certain it will be unearthed, at some point.' Jonas rose from the lounge. 'I must also mention he sent a few gowns.' He chuckled in response to her shocked expression. 'They are in a chest downstairs.' He explained, 'He had no need for them and you would never use them in the palace.'

She held firmly to his outstretched hand and stood. 'Bastion has been benevolent towards me, perhaps he wishes to make amends for his actions.'

'Perhaps. But, Shiarn...' A slight colouring was in his cheeks, and his rueful tone was unfamiliar, 'You have done more for him than you can imagine. As far as I am concerned you deserve more.'

She looked directly into his eyes that suddenly appeared vulnerable. 'And you?' Her voice was gentle, 'How did you fare at the palace?'

He pressed his lips tightly, but did not avoid her probing stare. His solemn gaze spoke more to her than any answer. 'You have also helped me greatly.' He took her hand and held it warmly. 'The storm has passed and we are both here.'

Shiarn wanted so much more. 'That's very cryp—'

'Shs.' He touched his finger to her lips and he lingered there. 'I've an idea that might lighten your mood. Why don't we take ourselves to the upstairs terrace with a bottle of fine wine and have a game of king's square?'

'What a marvelous way to spend the rest of the day.' She grinned at him, her charm brimming over. Forgetting about Morgal, she added with flippant ease, 'And you can tell me about your son.'

'Ah, yes.' His good humoured grin did not waver. 'I knew it would not take long for the women of this house to barrage you with my secrets. We shall most definitely speak of him and also of your recent heroic deeds, of which I am quite eager to learn more.'

66 - Touching Hope

"…Swaggering, he's a strutter true, thinks he's sir wonder'full
Skull it fast, can't be surpassed
Four rounds down and prancing

Have another, have a third, he'll be foreva' slurred
Roll it back, can see no lack
Five rounds down and preening…"

Ten Rounds of a Drunken Mirth

By evening a thunderstorm was rumbling across the Gravett Ranges. Lightning flashed above Sommerlea and rain fell in heavy bursts. However, within the manor house, a fire warmed the residents in the sitting room where they had gathered after dinner. The chatter had grown into a harmonious hum of conviviality.

Jett was uneasy in the merry atmosphere, and despite his Kin attempting to draw him in, he couldn't relax enough for trivial conversation. The presence of Kael and Jonas unnerved him, most likely because they said nothing about his transformed state, or even questioned him. He had the impression they were circling the issue and at some time they would make known their opinions. After all, Jett was now talking and dining with the ones he planned to kill only days ago. It left a bad taste in his mouth. He assumed it did the same for them.

He watched his Kin, observing the slight changes in their interactions with each other. Earona blushed and fidgeted at Keanan's over-attentiveness while avoiding Marcus' uncomfortable glances darting her way. Shiarn, dressed in a fine green gown, and holding her fourth cup of wine, was absorbed with Jonas. Seth, clothed in his bright blue shirt from Floris, and his cheeks glowing, was beaming. He seemed the only one genuinely happy. But it might have more to do with spending time exploring the woodlands with the older Naturist. Then there was Hellier… standing between the couches, her long unbraided locks, pure white-gold, hung by her slender waist. Her hide pants were a snug fit, but with enough room to move. He sighed at her reticence towards him, and wished he had the liberty to run his hand down her hair, and relax in her presence.

Mara sat, much like him, quiet and apart from the chitchat. She also watched everyone, but avoided his gaze. With her chin jutting up, she made sure he knew she had no desire to talk to him.

Jett wondered if he would ever feel at peace again. His hand reached for the leather cord at his wrist, but stopped from grasping it. He didn't want to bring attention to it here, and he certainly didn't want to announce how reliant he was on the silver token.

Jonas rose from his seat and holding his goblet aloft, he cleared his throat.

Jett tensed with apprehension.

An unhurried hush settled over them and Jonas said, 'If I might have your ears for a moment I should like to speak.' After a poised pause, he said, 'As the certified master of this estate,' his shrewd eyes went to Clara, 'it is my privilege to propose a toast and acknowledge the true worth of this evening with a handful of dignified remarks. I also believe I speak on behalf of all Sommerlea residents.' He exhaled gracefully and glanced at the humorous expressions. His composure became less formal yet his self-assurance did not falter. 'First, however, I admonish you all to display your uttermost in outstanding behavior for tonight we dine with royalty.' He gave Mara a brief bow and charming smile.

Her gaping mouth turned into an embarrassed grin.

He continued, 'I trust you are all now enjoying your respite at Sommerlea and if you are not, then, I'll have to say there are worse things.' He chuckled dryly. 'It is quite stupendous having you with us and not least is it extraordinary, nevertheless, I shall not keep on.' He tilted his goblet with an elegant twist of the wrist. 'Let us lift our cups in honour and celebration of new and old friends, and ongoing peace and fellowship.'

Everyone agreed and a brief silence followed as cups were lifted.

'I shall not drone on,' Jonas relaxed his stance as if he might keep talking into the night, 'As you know I am relentless in my pursuit of fine aristocratic idioms. Although I deem myself to be tolerably self-effacing there remains a desire to cultivate the characteristics customarily befitting those of noble birth—'

'You've just had too much good wine.' Morias roared with deep belly laughter.

'Don't get me started on that, dear fellow.'

Morias waved him to sit down.

Clara gave him a beaming smile and laughed. 'Jonas, you do go on.'

Jonas took his seat and smiled at his own buffoonery.

With eyes suddenly cast on him in expectation, Jett stood with reluctance. But with a wit driven smile, he held his goblet before him. 'I must apologize, I lack the stately speech that comes with such a grandiose position.' He gave Jonas a jocular grin. 'But, I hope I am humble enough to offer you what I can, a sincere thank you, for your kindness and patience in accommodating us, and your hospitality for even one such as I.'

In satire, Jonas responded with hurt features. 'I have encountered this style of brazen humour, I see it must run in your Kin.'

'I only take credit for subtle wit,' Shiarn piped up, and eyed Jett.

Jonas gave her a tight lipped grin. 'Such a bold declaration, truly, I'm not sure it suits one as modest as you—'

'A man should espouse honesty, however it is a woman's prerogative to be intrepid,' she said over the lip of her cup with a teasing smile.

'You admit you choose.' His eyes glinted with merriment. 'In that case, it is a man's liberty to be forthright—'

'It is a gentleman's duty to be chivalrous—'

Jett cleared his throat. 'Pardon me for interrupting your carefree banter, but knowing my Kin, who can provoke the leg off a mule,' he avoided looking at Earona, easily included in his statement, and watched Shiarn raise her brow at him. He went on with a conceited grin, 'If I don't speak now I might be waiting all night.' His words were met with genuine laughter, including Shiarn and Jonas. 'All the same, and apart from any boasting,' he eyed Shiarn, in hope she would keep silent, 'We are more than privileged to have met you, and I would like to drink to our new ties. May they endure whatever may come.'

Once again the speech was heartily agreed upon. Clara, sitting on the arm of Kael's chair, clapped her hands and said above the growing noise, 'Now everyone is in a better frame of mind, you can play some music.'

Seth passed around their instruments gathered together by the chair. Shiarn took the pipe, and Marcus the double drums. Keanan strummed one of the lutes while Seth took the other. Earona, sitting beside Keanan, rested her harp on her lap, and Hellier prepared her violin. Eventually lively tunes swept through the living area.

After playing for some time, Mara excused herself to go to bed, and Shiarn handed the pipe to Seth. With cheeks radiant, she suggested an amusing song. "Maiden's Wishful Thinking."

Jett smiled at her near drunkenness, and admired how attractive she was in the emerald dress that illuminated her red curls.

The tune was fast and Clara and Kael stood to dance between the couches. Shiarn sang another, with a rudeness that induced red cheeks and chuckling. Shiarn suddenly turned to Jett, her hand outstretched, 'Let's sing.'

Jett waved her hand away. 'Not tonight.'

Shiarn pouted and flicked her hair from her eyes. 'I'll have to do it without you.'

Jonas responded with a surprised look at Jett, 'You won't sing?'

Seth piped up, 'It's a shame. He's very good.'

Jett frowned at Seth, realizing the youngster probably had one too many wines. 'Anyone can sing.'

'Not like you,' Earona said with a teasing grin.

Shiarn latched onto his arm and attempted hauling him to his feet. 'Come on…'

Far from wanting to sing, he dug his feet in. 'No.' He noticed their disappointment and added, 'I'm not up to singing such… joyful tunes. I may sound too melancholy. Another night I will.'

Shiarn stepped back with her hands on her hips. 'Fine. Sulk away.'

Kael laughed at her, and asked Jett, 'So, the reluctant singer?'

Jett replied, 'Shiarn had always been singing, and Earona started learning music when we were children. It was her opinion we all must learn an instrument.'

Earona screwed up her face, 'Jett played the lute, but he didn't like it as much as singing. We were surprised at how talented he was.'

Jett shrugged. He enjoyed it too, most of the time. Although he had to be in the mood.

Marcus smoothed his hand over the drum. 'Earona made us all troop over to the Music Sanctum for lessons. Me, Hellier and Jett came down from the plateau.'

'That's right,' Earona added, 'And Ethan, Seth and myself came up from the valley. Keanan and Shiarn were already in the city, so travelling to the Sage for regular practice wasn't so difficult for them.'

Kael creased his brow in contemplation of the name. 'The Sage…Oh, yes, I've been there.'

'One of our childhood playgrounds,' Marcus said with a playful glint in his eyes, 'A tavern.'

Keanan added, 'The only place that allowed us to play what we liked, no matter how bad we were sometimes.'

Shiarn sat on the arm of the lounge by Jonas. 'And sometimes they were awful.' She chuckled, 'The Sage is my parent's tavern.'

'A publican's daughter.' Jonas smiled sweetly at her. 'Now, that explains a great deal.'

'It may at that. I've debated, crossed words, cajoled, and comforted, every type of scholar, jokester, drunk, and leech I've ever come across there!' She lifted her head and grimaced.

Jett smirked. 'I'm sure it's been a trial, with a stream of admirers at your door.'

She eyed him coyly. 'And of course, I'm well acquainted with the sweet talkers, but the worst, those bloody miners.' She pulled a face at him.

Jett chuckled. 'Can't be beat for slanguage—'

'Can't be understood,' Shiarn blurted with a laugh.

'If Shiarn has met her match, I shall be suitably impressed,' Jonas added.

Shiarn shook her head with a conceited expression. 'I admit nothing.'

Keanan said, 'She can't be matched for singing.'

'True, I have been singing since I could talk.'

Marcus barged in, 'And that's how long the Sage has been putting up with us.'

'You maybe.' She retorted with whimsical conceitedness, 'But I am renowned for my magnificent singing voice.'

'It's good to see you do not hide your talents,' Jonas remarked with a smile, 'or your distinction.'

Jett leaned over and contrived a whisper, 'She enjoys this too much to ever be demure, and she cannot be anywhere but the center.'

'A trait I understand completely.' Jonas' sparkling eyes were fixed on Shiarn.

From across the room, Adis opened sleepy eyes and commented, 'It doesn't make sense to me that Concealers always seem to want to be noticed.'

Laughter and agreement met his wry remark. Once the noise died down Keanan said to Shiarn, 'How about, Love Yields. The harp is perfect for it.'

Earona's cheeks brightened at the compliment.

Shiarn nodded, and her cheeks also tinged. But Jett suspected it was due to her high spirits, and not unease over the love song.

The Kin paused to let the delicate sound of the harp rise above the other tunes, filling the air with the romantic melody and Shiarn singing in Fáer.

'Bright as the warmest sun
Shine ov' leaf and flower true
Reign in heart and song.
My love's fairest voice ensues.
Remove not your bright tune
And shed light on my bleak fields
Come unto me
As I wait and love yields.

'Heat my silent inner part
The lengthy rays of affection.
And I, a flower, loving heart
Seek your song above all perfection.
Wither me not my ardent one
And shed your light on desolate fields
Come unto me
As I wait and love yields.

'Beneath my winter skin
Desire in me to make
Our burning hearts akin.
Need for love do not forsake
All promises I shall fulfill.
If shed light would ravish my fields,
Till you come unto me
I wait and love will yield.'

An enchanting love song and not hard to miss the exchange between her and Jonas.

Earona, her face red, cast anxious glances around the room, and she introduced another tune.

Jett was thankful the evening did not continue long after and the party soon disbanded. He was one of the first to head upstairs to bed.

~ * ~

Mara had changed into her nightdress and lay under the covers, staring at the ceiling. The last two nights she had finally been able to sleep, but she still couldn't take part in the frivolous merriment. They carried on as if the horror of the last week hadn't happened. For her, the turmoil continued, and he, who had been the embodiment of evil, was in their midst. Unlike her, they seemed oblivious to what may be lurking under the surface.

Over dinner they made a great fuss of her. But she suspected, they only wanted information about Ryne. She gave them nothing that would satisfy, and only leave them more intrigued. As a princess she had some prerogative she liked to think. Her detachment over the whole horrid affair with Jett became more apparent. Fortunately, Jett was the only one who knew how intentional her part in the ritual was. A sour look was on his face throughout the evening. He was probably furious she didn't tell him the truth. It only increased her resentment, no matter how irrational it seemed.

She shivered in her warm bed, recalling his eyes, like pools of darkness, turned towards her. Her skin had flamed to life and she revisited standing in his presence again. They had shared a peculiar intimacy she didn't understand. His touch haunted her. She pressed on her tattoo, replaying the sense of release from his hand. It no longer ached, nor could she feel its mark. She recalled his words from earlier that day, about how they repel each other but also attract. It seemed odd at the time, but now she could see and feel it herself.

She again wondered what would have happened if she had been successful at resurrecting that woman? Where would Mara have stood in the powerful threesome? Would she have even been alive, because she was near death at that time? How she knew the incantation, she didn't want to speculate on. Rayne had been strangely quiet throughout, but she now knew he was slowly dying within her, and was nearly dead when they found her. The one thing able to stop her was Jett's command. Not until she woke later did she remember it was his voice that shook her out of the nightmare.

She heard Earona talking to a man outside the door. Eventually Earona entered, and threw herself across the bed and moaned into the covers.

At times Earona's complaints offered a distraction, but mostly, Mara enjoyed teasing the up-tight girl. 'Were you kissing?'

Earona lifted her red face. 'No!'

'Then you should tell him you're not interested.'

'How do you know I'm not,' Earona huffed.

'You would have been kissing.' Mara had observed Keanan's face light-up when Earona spoke to him. Surely it was obvious to everyone else, especially Earona.

'It's hardly been the time or place for such things.' Earona sat up and rested her face in her hands.

Mara shrugged. 'Is there ever?' She stared down at the bump under the blankets, recalling those few nights of what normal people call love-making.

'Anyway, I might be interested. I need to take it slow and not do anything I might regret.'

'Like this you mean?' Mara pointed at her stomach.

Earona narrowed her eyes. 'Not exactly. Anyway, how about your recently revealed identity? Why would it have been so hard to tell me that?'

'Not this again.' She had no patience to listen to Earona gripe on about it for the umpteenth time. 'It wasn't important.' It was irritating enough her secret was revealed, and now to everyone.

'It is.' Earona folded her arms. 'We could have been in serious trouble for having you.'

'I would have figured something out.'

Earona threw her hands in the air. 'So many lies—'

'It's nothing to do with you,' Mara spat out with sudden vehemence. 'I don't have to tell you a damn thing.'

'I disagree. It means your mother is the queen,' she lowered her voice, '…who will be looking for you, with soldiers, and… witches?'

'Just because she's a queen doesn't mean she's not a bitch.'

'Oh, my heavens!' Earona cried in a sudden panic, 'You were up there,' she waved up at the ceiling, 'chanting a deadly spell, bleeding all over the place, and almost dying, and it probably would have destroyed us.' She gasped, 'And you're a princess of Ryne and you're pregnant!'

'I had no control over that.' Mara's voice was a cold rebuke. 'Any of it.'

She continued her lecture, 'And I'm the one who knew about your wicked mother and that you could do spells.'

'A spell,' Mara corrected.

Earona stood, gripping her waist, and said with fiery passion, 'That you cast on Marcus? After you said you wouldn't.'

'That—' Mara studied her, wondering how much of the truth she knew, if any. 'I was in some sort of trance from hell cast on me by your *friend*. Besides, he got better, right?' It was near enough right and the best explanation aside from the truth - she wanted to do the bidding of a demon.

Earona gave a frustrated wail and sat on the bed. 'That's not the point. And I know Jett - he made you do it. But…' Her voice became strained, 'I fear your knowledge of magik puts you in danger, because you can be used by demonic beings. Also your mother has connections with witches and will be determined to get you back.'

'Puts you or me in danger?' She retorted.

'All of us.' Earona let out a short breath. 'Oh, my goodness! Does Jett know any of this?' She let out a pained moan. 'I'm in such trouble.'

'I'm not talking to him about this,' Mara growled. She had no desire to share anything more with him, and on light of his decision to leave her at Sommerlea it seemed pointless.

Earona frowned with annoyance. 'It might have more to do with him than you think.'

'He's not that innocent.' Mara pouted in protest. 'Anyway, I had nothing to do with that.'

Earona extinguished the candle light. With her back to Mara, she wiggled out of her dress. 'It's just…' her tone became a soft whisper Mara could barely hear, 'I think he should know…'

'Gods, don't talk about me to him,' Mara cried, 'No-one has a right to know.'

Earona pulled back the covers and climbed into bed. 'Jett has some right to know,' she grumbled, actually he had every right to know, 'And this whole journey is turning into a disaster…'

'But that thing with the demon is over now.' She sat up and glared through the dark. 'I don't want everyone coming at me with their self-righteous opinions, or deciding where I should go.'

Earona lay on the pillow, and her eyes were glistening lights staring across at her. 'But, I don't know if I can stand it.'

'I don't want him knowing…about the witch stuff,' Mara moaned. She fell back down and turned her back to Earona.

~ * ~

Added to the sombre mood of the men, was an urgency to keep moving no matter how tired they were. The loss of Var was a serious blow, creating an extra grievous burden for the men to carry. Even those who voiced objections to the directions went along without complaint, as if committing themselves to a last resting place.

The plan of escape had transformed into an indomitable need to stay alive. The only strategy with any hope of results seemed to be keeping near the lights and staying together. If it weren't for the boy's eagerness, the men might have decided to sit in a chamber and come to a slow painful end. Even Kenric, who showed so much enthusiasm, was less driven by his cheery nature. Even so, he never lost his single-minded determination they would continue till they could go no farther.

The low roofed chamber they entered had various openings, none of which looked appealing. Daskar studied the tunnels with his torch swooping along the rock face. Eventually choosing one that appeared the same as the others. Again Ethan wondered why Daskar thought that particular tunnel would be more advantageous than the others, but he had no energy to question him.

It was a crawl space, forcing them to move on all fours. Ethan found it hard to breathe in the stifling air as he labored through the tight enclosure. Half the men were through when a halt was called by Daskar up front, causing them all to sit in the cramped place.

Ethan sat in the dirt, his back hunched against the wall, and head slumped forward. Muffled shouts went up and down the darkened line. Apparently a small cavern was ahead and Daskar was searching for a way through. In the dark, Ethan voiced dismal yet honest fears to Loc beside him. 'You think we'll get out of here?'

'It'll be nothing short of miraculous.'

'Wish I could feel the breeze again…'

'Aye, sea breeze and the sun…' Loc's voice tapered off.

'Did you know Var well?'

'Well enough.'

Ethan heard the sadness in his voice and needed no light to see it.

'If I live I will say goodbye to his spirit, if I do not I shall greet him.'

Ethan nodded in heartfelt agreement.

A sharp cry and yelling from ahead spread alarm through the waiting men. Unable to do anything, Ethan waited until word came. He decided, next time he would go at the front of the line.

'There's another tunnel.' Someone passed the word along. 'Bearn's fallen through.'

Faint chuckling from one of the boys was an alien sound. Obviously, Bearn was not injured – or so Ethan hoped. At a slow pace, the men moved on hands and knees, pushing their packs in front of them.

Ethan neared the chamber. The tunnel extended through the chamber. The only opening was a slight hole made larger by Bearn falling through. Loose stones still trickled down to dull light below. Stannar and Bull held a rope that dangled down.

Gripping the rope, Ethan hoped the strong Harn, Bull, could support him. He lowered himself amongst flaking shards and dust through the opening at the top of a wall of what seemed to be a corridor. He jumped down and moved to the light and the men seated on the floor.

Daskar touched a flat square stone embedded in the floor. 'Someone laid this.' Many more like it, were in a uniform pattern down a square corridor as far as the light let them see.

'That's a good thing?' asked Gailtram.

Daskar responded, 'Mean's we might be getting near the outside.'

Ethan glanced down the passage in genuine surprise. 'Who would live here?'

Daskar shrugged. 'Whoever, they don't live here now.'

Ethan replied, 'I don't blame them.'

Rowdy noises came from the tunnel above as the last few men came through. An exuberant shout came from the chamber above. Bull slid through followed by Luz, a hardy man with an obnoxious personality, and he clutched something small and black in his hand. 'I've got one,' he bellowed as he fell through the gap with numerous rocks following.

'Is it dead?'

'Aye, dead as dead can be.' Luz threw it to the floor. The size of a cat, its limbs were long and spindly with needle sharp claws. Kenric prodded its smooth mat-black flesh with a chisel.

Bull said, 'One down for us.'

'Doesn't look too threatening,' said Kenric.

'Not one on its own,' replied Loc, indignant, 'but many of them working together… is lethal.'

Ethan said, 'We need to be cautious.'

After a short discussion about the direction the lodestone indicated, they started down the new tunnel. Large arches of carved stone were at intervals along the corridor. Despite the piles of rubble, they could walk two men abreast. The ceiling was at least two feet higher than Ethan, which meant walking was a new pleasure.

Leading the group, the boys halted to observe a man-high heap of loose stones. Mouse stood on the limestone debris, peering over the top. 'Another tunnel.'

Branan looked through the hole alongside him. 'Like the others. Dark.'

The men stopped for a rest and a few poked their heads over the stones to see for themselves. Daskar and Kenric finally pushed through the gathering, and Daskar ignored the slight opening. 'We keep moving forward.'

Stannar examined the rocks. 'Don't you wonder about these heaps of stones?'

'It's unstable.' Daskar shrugged. 'We have to move quick.'

Dismayed looks passed between the men and they quickened their pace. At the front, the boys stopped at the choice of openings and waited for instructions. Daskar came and decided on a direction. The tunnel facade was unchanging except for the differing piles of stones. In some places, holes were in the ceiling and at one point, half the passage was collapsed. But at least they were walking upright on level ground.

So far there was no sight of the shadow creatures although those at the back swore there was scratching on the ceiling. The men continued to be cautious, but Ethan's steps lifted and he became determined to persevere without grumbling.

With what seemed to be numerous turns and the clearing of large stones and loose rubble, the men assumed they had walked for hours. Once again, the boys, excited by the change in the environment, travelled farther ahead despite being instructed to stay close. Led by Mouse, they chuckled and chatted to themselves. Breaking through the solemn talk of the men was an odd rumbling from above. Stones started to fall into the tunnel. Frenzied shouts became a mess of confusion.

'Boys!' A low muffled bellow came from Grith.

Ethan pulled Mouse towards him with his Gift, and he caught Derryl and Berran as he flew backwards to safety. Rocks tumbled down in front of the boys at Ethan's feet. The men behind him crouched in anticipation of the stones settling. Ethan stared at the high mass of rocks with growing panic.

Berran's soft voice quivered, 'Ruegar…'

Kenric rushed ahead and slipped with a shout, 'Not Rue.'

'Ruegar!' Bearn yelled at the stone.

A faint cry came from beyond the barrier of rocks.

'Start digging.' Mouse pulled stones away, causing more to topple down.

'Wait,' Druce cried. 'We need to be careful.'

Berran cried, 'He's got no light.'

Ethan started to shift the rocks from the top. A few fell while others remained in place. 'I'll do it.'

A few of the Harn spoke to Ruegar to keep his spirits up and Ethan focused on clearing the rocks. The caved-in area was thick, but he eventually made a space. With the light shining behind him, he saw Ruegar's outline covered in dust and looking like a ghost in the firelight. Ethan moved a space for him to climb through.

Daskar stuck his head over. 'This is the path. Might as well keep clearing.'

'But this way might be unstable.'

Daskar's old eyes responded with a hard stare. 'Don't worry 'bout that. It's *all* unstable.'

It was a statement Ethan took no delight in hearing.

With only cuts and bruises, Ruegar climbed over the rocks and back into the safety of the group. The men cleared the rocks together with as much care as time would allow. But, the setback caused a gnawing concern over the wasted time as the oil and torches burnt away. They were not as worried about the dwindling food as their light diminishing; a constant anxiety on their minds.

Finally a pathway was created and they started down the straight passage once again. This time the boys walked with caution amongst the men.

67 - From the Dead

Do not miss the opportunity you are given of defeating your foe

Empirical Warfare Command

Unable to get back to sleep, Earona lay awake for some time. Her heart raced with building anxiety. As if Jett had turned again and was back in the cellar, and she was stuck in that despairing state of mind. She attempted soothing her body with her Ethos, but that didn't last. The trouble was, her problem wasn't physical.

One of her woes, her apparent relationship with Keanan. She wasn't certain what she wanted, but she wanted to decide on her own. She couldn't determine if Marcus was hurt or embarrassed. Either way, she felt guilty over her deception. But her disastrous love-life couldn't compare with the remorse of destroying an innocent life. The guilt of killing the embryo seemed to grow in potency each time she dwelt on it. And now, adding to her troubles, she was concerned over Mara, even more so after discovering that people in Ryne and her evil mother were searching for her.

All these dilemmas were present previously, but none of them had come close to her heartache over losing Jett, and the Kin fragmenting. Now he was restored, everything else was flooding in. No sooner did she wrestle one thought, the next broke her nerves till her head was a thumping mess. She gave an involuntary groan and sat, clutching her chest, fearing her heart would stop.

Pretending to sleep was no longer doable. Relief had to be reached or she would go mad. It was now or never. Watching Mara sleeping, Earona sat on the side of the bed, and listened to the stormy rain and rattling window. Then, she left the room.

~ * ~

Wind swept past the windows, knocking erratically on the glass panes. Shiarn lay under the blankets listening to the whistles of the storm. She surmised an annoying flapping sound was coming from a distant loose shutter. She cast an affectionate look at Jonas asleep beside her and smiled with delight. Until last night she was uncertain whether it was her own feelings, but there was no denying it, he felt the same way.

A breeze seeped into the room. She eased herself from under his arm to investigate where the draft was and remedy it. Her gauzy nightdress did nothing to ward off the chill, but she would not be long from the bed's warmth.

A shift in the shadows startled her. He moved with wily speed, grabbing her around the mouth and chest. She knew who it was without seeing his face. Her whole body was alerted to his vile presence. Straining against his clutches, she had no doubt she would rather die than have him touch her again. He restrained her against himself and breathed on her cheek, 'Make this easy on yourself.'

Shiarn's eyes reflected a hate filled terror.

In a depraved tone, far from his usual silver-tongued speech, Morgal said, 'I've got something for you.' He clamped harder on her mouth and chanted under his breath.

Jonas tossed on the bed and discovering she was not there, he woke. Shiarn kicked out behind her in an effort to distract Morgal or at the least warn Jonas.

Morgal arched back, but was unaffected by her striving and continued casting.

Jonas rose and charged at him. He attempted invisibility, but the ghostly outline of his figure revealed his position. Cackling brashly, Morgal shoved Shiarn aside. She floated a foot off the floor in a type of invisible sphere. Unable to move or be heard, she trembled with fear as she watched Jonas and Morgal confront each other.

'She will be my captive, but for you I have a gift I spent time making.' Morgal raised his hand to Jonas.

'You can't escape here!' Jonas' voice was enflamed with wrath.

Morgal gave a malicious laugh. 'This is for your interference at the palace.' From his palm a rounded flare of a luminous olive substance spurted forth. Its shimmering surface lit up the room as it spun towards Jonas' chest. The force of the unnatural object threw him backwards and it disappeared into his body. He crumpled and lay motionless on the floor.

Pounding on the barrier, Shiarn's heart plunged at the sight of Jonas' inactive body. Her scream went unheard within the seal. Morgal turned his conniving laughter on her. 'I was surprised to find him at the core of this, but once I found you it made sense,' he ranted. 'Now we shall be leaving!'

To her horror he was planning on taking her away. He began his chanting once more, putting their departure into effect, and she could do nothing.

~ * ~

A noise in his room pulled Jett from sleep. He opened an eye to see a figure in white feeling her way, half blind, to his bed. 'Earona?'

'Are you awake?' Her remark was loud and flippant.

'No,' he grumbled his protest into the pillow. Lying on his stomach, eyes closed, he felt her sit by his head.

'But, you are.' On the cold drafty night she came without cloak or shoes, but thought it fine to tuck her legs under his covers, nudging him aside to make herself comfortable.

God, do you have to?! He tugged on the blanket, claiming his share, and he shifted his waist away from her shivering limbs. 'Mind where you stick your freezing feet.'

She made a fuss rubbing her toes together. 'But it's cold.'

You have a bed, don't you? 'What's wrong?' he muttered, closing his eyes again. 'Bad dream? You don't need to tell me in the dead of night.'

'No.' She looked across to the slight parting of the curtains and the clouded night sky beyond. 'I couldn't sleep…'

He pulled the blanket to cover his shoulder. *Not my problem…*

She grasped her hands and took a prolonged breath.

Sensing her turmoil over Shiarn, he queried, 'It's still troubling you?'

'It is and will forever I expect.' Her voice was strained. *I'm the one who killed… I didn't even have the power to identify its gender.*

'It's not for you to carry.' *I must bear it…*

After several moments she faced him, her eyes damp with sadness. 'I did it, no one else.' *And you tell me it wasn't right.*

'I regret saying anything.' He sighed with remorse and his eyes clouded over as he remembered. 'I should have been the one talking to Shiarn, not you, or Keanan. Yet, after saying that, she won't talk to me about it.'

Earona flushed. 'She's not the only one not talking.'

He gave a muffled grunt. *It's done, and I don't want to go over it.* Perceiving her train of thought switch to a more trivial topic, he thought, *you're the one who needs to say something… stop avoiding him.* He closed his eyes, and tried falling back into sleep.

'Me?! But—' she squeaked, 'I'm the one being avoided.'

Jett covered his ears with his pillow and groaned into it.

'Fine. I admit I have been avoiding certain people, but some people *have* been avoiding me.'

'I'm fast getting tired of it,' he muttered, 'Marcus in one ear and Keanan in the other and you pestering me in the night.' *Why the hell am I in the middle of this?*

Her voice elevated in alarm. 'Marcus talked to you about it?'

He flung the blanket off her and him, exposing the tattooed markings on his side, and he pointed at the door. 'That's it, out.' The Eye-key hung from his neck and swayed over his bare chest as he propped himself up on his elbow. 'Sort it out, on your own time.'

'You're wearing that?' Earona, her eyes like saucers, stared at the amulet.

He clutched the pendant, hiding it in his clenched fist. 'When I sleep.' He spoke before she could drill him for more information. 'Are you finished?'

'No…' she bowed her head and looked down at her hands. *There's something I wanted…*

He gave an irritated sigh, realizing sleep was getting further from happening. 'What is it?'

'It's Mara.' Earona clutched her arms and shivered. 'She's… well, I think… but I'm not sure…'

'Spit it out.'

'She cast a spell.' She took a gulping breath.

'When?'

'On the road to Parkvale,' she whispered with a tremor.

It shouldn't be a surprise, it was just another thing Mara hadn't told him, but he brooded over the revelation. Frowning with annoyance, he said, 'From what I've learned of her, it is not unexpected.'

Her back stiffened and she took a stilted breath. 'And…I'm fairly sure she set that witch free.'

That was not expected. 'Why?' He grumbled to himself, as if he should have an answer. But there was more that was unsettling her. 'There's more isn't there?'

Earona bowed her head and mumbled, 'In a way, but that could be because you had control over her…'

'Tell me and I'll decide,' he answered gruffly.

'She cast a spell on Marcus.'

Jett snapped, 'Blood 'n shite! I won't tolerate magik being cast on us.'

'Can't you see?' Earona cried in a fervent whisper, 'You used her – well, not you – but, he did, and they, Hell, must have known she had special powers and all along she is… like them. Like you were.'

His menacing glare turned away. She was right, he must have known, but didn't want to see. It did explain her deceptive nature, and antagonism towards him, and everyone else.

Earona continued, 'But—'

'She's a flamin' witch,' Jett fumed, 'with everything that's gone wrong that's all we need. Some things make sense now. I should have seen this.'

She laid her hand on his arm. 'Her mother is not normal, and also a witch attacked her in the temple.'

'Why didn't you tell me this?!' Jett's tone became irate.

Earona matched him with her own annoyance. 'How could I?! You were a monster.'

'Flamin' hell, maybe you could have tried after.' His voice turned grim, 'It could be worse than you think, her mother is a mage, or possibly she is a witch - and now I find out Mara's the same. All this makes me wonder, what is her true game with us?'

Earona gasped at his candid remark. 'No, you don't think…. But she's not been hostile to us.'

'You have no idea what's going on in her head,' he growled. 'I certainly don't.'

Earona stared away and her expression became anxious. 'She's the Summoner, isn't she?'

Jett considered whether to reply, but after a moment he shot out, 'Yes.'

She gasped with shock. 'Oh, no!'

'That's right.' He sensed the anxiety building once more. 'And that's why it's best she stay here.'

Earona turned to face him with surprise. 'She can't. She's…'

His shoulders tensed, preparing for the debate. 'According to you, she's probably a witch, and now, we know she is a princess wanted by Ryne, plus a bunch of merciless cock-suckers, and she's pregnant. Aside from all that, she is the Summoner that demonic power was waiting for.'

Her face drooped with disappointment. 'It truly is a terrible burden she must be carrying. No wonder she wants to get away… but,' She grabbed his arm in supplication. 'I really think she would be safer with us.'

'With us or with you?'

'You're worried about it?' She stabbed her finger at his chest. *That you might hurt her.*

'Devil's arse!' he yelled, 'I've got good reason to think that.'

'It shouldn't be just about you.' She narrowed her eyes with recrimination.

'It is unreasonable to think she should come with us. They will take care of her here.' He attempted bringing sense to the issue spiraling out of his control. As usual her questions drove him mad, even more so because she was arguing with him in the dead of night. 'If she is a witch, it's even worse.' His voice seethed with building anger. 'Imagine how much she knows.'

'That's more reason she shouldn't stay here,' Earona cried, 'She will only run away, or—'

'She's a bloody princess. And you can add liar to her list of crimes.'

Earona made a face. 'You saved her before.'

'I have no regrets about that—' His face lined with pain, he clenched his chest, suddenly throbbing.

'What is it?'

'My heart's going to explode.' He jumped from the bed, dressed only in his under-shorts, and rushed to the door. '…it's Shiarn!'

'She's in Jonas' room in the adjoining wing.' While she spoke, he dashed into the corridor and she jumped off the bed and followed after.

~ * ~

Jett dashed into what he supposed was Jonas' suite with initial uncertainty. It was quiet but with his night vision the scene became clear. Shiarn appeared to be yelling from a position a couple of feet off the floor, making gestures towards Jonas lying motionless.

Morgal watched Jett enter. Despite the grime smearing his twisted face, rage was plainly evident. No pause in his chanting, the acerbic tones of the unknown language increased in vehemence.

Jett halted the mantra by burning a significant hole in the mage's forehead. The mage dropped like a dead weight, leaving a wisp of smoke snaking upwards. It was a decent size burn and one Jett had brooded over since learning of Shiarn's assault in the palace; actualizing his fantasy brought him a great deal of gratification. Rubbing his temples, he cringed and bowed his head. He ached from the sudden intensity such heat could induce.

Earona rushed in and witnessed Shiarn collapse to the floor unconscious. She glimpsed Jonas' inert body. 'We need Clara!'

'Where?' He ran to the door.

'Two doors down.' She let loose her Ethos and attended Shiarn. Startled at the mage sitting upright, she gasped, but was not quick enough to evade him. He wrapped his hands around her neck in a deathlike grip. *Jett?!* Clutching onto the mage's hand, she could not budge him with her strength, and her Healing Gift had no effect on his flesh.

Help! Choking for air, she screamed in her mind. *Can you hear me? Help!* Lights flashed in her eyes, and sensing herself passing out, she wondered how long it would take to suffocate.

Racing into the room, Jett landed on his knees, bowling the mage on to his back. The mage did not release her, but yanked her down with him. Jett drilled his knee into the underside of Morgal's elbow, loosening the hold on her throat. Wrenching the mage's other vice-like grip from her neck, he snarled, 'You cock-arse demon! I will kill you!' He latched onto the mage's throat and crushed the air out of him.

Nauseous and light-headed, Earona fell from his grip. Rasping, she held her neck, and soothed it with her Ethos, until feeling returned.

Finally Morgal lay still and Jett relaxed his hold. Looking to Earona, he took a breath and touched her neck, examining the red bruising. His voice was shaky. 'Can you breathe?'

She gave a short nod. *It's healing.*

Jett raised his brows with apprehension. *I did hear you. Like a pain in my head.*

Earona breathed deep with relief.

Jett reached for the coloured bottle that rolled out from Morgal's robe and turned it over in his hand.

It's Shiarn's. He must have tried to steal it.

Jett gave her a puzzled frown and set the bottle upright.

Clara and Kael rushed into the room. Kael moved Jonas' body to the bed while Clara touched his chest. She said, 'His breathing is weak. Earona, I need your help.'

Still caressing her throat, Earona went to the bed.

Jett lifted Shiarn's body, laying her beside Jonas while Earona rested her trembling hands on his motionless body. The taint within him was like nothing she had ever felt before. A fetid substance was destroying his organs at a rapid rate. 'What is it?'

Clara's face was a deathly white. 'Poison.'

'But it's growing.' Earona stroked his foot.

'I need to transfer it into something.' Clara's hands wavered over Jonas' head.

'Use Morgal, he appears to have some life.' Kael called to Jett who was dragging Morgal out of the room, 'Bring him back in.'

'You heal Jonas,' Clara said to Earona, 'I'll focus on redirecting the poison.'

Jett hauled him back from the hall and dropped him by the bedside.

A green tinge came over Jonas' skin and his breathing slowed. Earona and Clara knelt on the floor, one holding his foot, the other his head. Earona healed Jonas and watched with amazement as Clara drew out the poison, and with her hand on Morgal sent it into him. Soon it had disappeared from Jonas, and Clara, her face red with exertion, panted from the task. Morgal's skin turned a pale green and he passed out.

'If this doesn't kill him I don't know what will.' Jett walked around to the other side of the bed to check Shiarn who looked asleep.

Clara pointed at the door and puffed. 'Take him out.'

Morgal's body lifted and lay straight as if carried on an invisible bed. Kael directed him out of the room. Jett followed Kael, and Morgal's body, hovering a few feet off the floor, to the entrance of the house and outside. The mage's arms hung like weights, almost touching the ground, and he appeared dead. But, Jett had been mistaken earlier, and he kept his eyes on the mage's face.

They walked across the green in the silvery light of pre-dawn to the line of trees. Jett shivered in the morning chill. Still wearing his under-shorts, he realized he was not dressed to be outside, or to be facing a cornered mage for that matter.

Kael said, 'We'll take him into the woods.'

Jett wondered exactly what he had planned. Simply killing him wasn't enough. 'You got something in mind?'

Kael looked over his shoulder and his eyes scanned the grounds. 'Maybe.' He muttered, 'If he gets down here in time.'

A few steps under the overhang of branches Morgal's eyes sprang open. His body, still a repulsive pallor, moved. He fell to his feet and pulled away from Kael's Gift.

Jett's eyes shone red and he made ready to pounce on him.

Kael lifted his palm in authority. 'You have nothing left, Morgal.'

Morgal's hair covered the side of his face in a black sheet, and his eyes had a weak gleam. 'Don't assume so much.' He spoke in a grating cough.

Jett stepped closer, his eyes burning into the mage's neck. This time he seemed unaffected.

'It won't work again.' Morgal switched his hate-filled glare to Jett, and his eyes lingered on his chest. 'Now I see. You're the one.' A chilling grin of victory changed his demenour.

Jett glared with fury at the man who was alive and daring to speak to him.

The mage's voice grew in strength. 'She's your friend...' he laughed, 'maybe more...'

Furious, Jett swung at his face with a straight punch. Morgal dropped to the ground and lay twisted in a ball. Inches from kicking the mage's stomach, Jett was stopped by Kael's hand on his shoulder. Kael said, 'It won't do any good.'

Morgal's eyes stared ahead and his body seemed empty of breath. Suddenly a voice came through the open yet motionless mouth. 'This is not the end of it.'

After a tense moment, Kael crouched by the body. 'He looks dead.'

'I've thought that before.' Jett's fist remained clenched. 'Curse him!' The body's features no longer resembled the mage he had strangled upstairs. It seemed another man was laying before them.

Kael said, 'It might be the poison...'

Morias rushed up to them and stared down at the body. 'He's dead then?'

A putrid smell came from the body. Its muscles rotted before their eyes as if it had been dead longer than a few minutes.

Kael pointed at the body and said to Morias, 'He's dead. Whether it's Morgal or not is another matter.'

Jett shook his head. 'It's magik somehow.' He whirled around, looking into the shadows of the trees, with a sense the mage wasn't dead at all, wherever he was. And now he knew, Jett possessed the Eye-key. 'Arse of the devil!'

68 - No Answers

Luck is but a word to explain the mystery of fate

Journal of a Roving Savant, Zaki'is Fur'Mole

Dull morning light from the den's window was enough to view the maps spread across the bulky desk. Kael sat, shuffling through them and Jett looked over his shoulder at a new map brought back from the palace. Jett said, 'This is better detailed.'

'It's from the royal cartographer.'

'But,' Jett scanned it. 'There's no Signet Reach on this at all.'

Kael said, 'It would seem it does not exist.'

Placing a heavy hand on the desk, Jett said, 'In effect you have found out nothing?' All his plans were centered on the location of Signet Reach. Once again he was going around in circles.

'Many years ago, before the treaty of the empire, a type of settlement was created to make warships.'

'Warships?' Jett frowned with surprise, having some knowledge of the war between the two largest kingdoms in New Empire, 'Against Ryne?'

'There's a rumour Signet Reach is linked to it.'

'Hope this new king has the sense to look into it.'

Kael nodded. 'He will have a few nobles to get through. Let's just say, he must charm his way into their confidence before he can gather that type of information.'

Jett responded with an exasperated look. 'I gather that's difficult?'

'The biggest threat is his sister. She has followers in her province, but as yet no one has been defiant.' Kael rubbed his bearded chin in thought. 'She voiced an opinion that was not to the old kings liking.'

Compelled by his curious nature, Jett said, 'What was that?'

'Her contacts in Ryne wished to form an alliance against King Rikard. Basylus didn't agree, but he changed his mind in the end.'

'Someone was influencing him?' Jett questioned.

'Maybe.' Kael paused. 'Morgal may have had something to do with it. Perhaps once we analyze his work we may find out.' He brushed the air with his hand, waving the conversation aside. 'Anyway, it's complicated and involves internal politicking which you might find wearisome. I do after many weeks of it. And you need to begin the search for your Kin.'

Jett returned to the map and spoke amid lost confidence. 'Any suggestions?'

Kael took a long breath. 'Looking at these other maps, the northernmost point of the Arranons seems the best route.'

Jett measured the range of mountains lining the coast on the southeast; a fair distance. 'Any way through these mountains?'

The door opened and Adis walked in followed by Seth.

'About time.' Kael waved them over.

Adis approached the desk with a nod in greeting, and his long black braid hung over his shoulder as he studied the position Kael pointed to. Seth hung his head over the desk, also viewing the stretch of land.

Kael asked, 'Any pathways through here?'

'Not really.' Adis' finger followed an invisible line. 'The Arranons are rugged here.' He pointed at the middle of the ranges. 'Here is the temple of the Righteous. I don't know if they have a pass. My guess is you'll never know as membership is very exclusive.' He dragged his finger up the northern section of the Arranons. 'Passable here where the mountains ease.'

Kael said, 'Three days journey to the top of the ranges in the high north?'

'More all up, that's doing it rough and only to the mountains. No villages along here.' Adis indicated the length of land with no title.

'Amin-Sayeda.' Jett's voice ran with graceful ease over the familiar word.

Adis gave him a peculiar stare. 'It's disused and overgrown now.'

Seth pointed at crosses marked on the map. 'What are these?'

'Probably old temples,' Adis replied, 'These adjoining lands are the beginning of Baion and the first town is Gearoidin Gate.' The map was blank after the marking of the town. 'This road is a by-route between the kingdoms and is good to travel,' he informed them. 'The people that lived there liked making roads and there are many in the valley.'

Kael carried on, 'This is the road Duke Haulton is watching.'

'He must have scouts out there,' Jett speculated.

'I hope so,' Kael responded. 'He's practically the front line of this province.'

Jett considered him with a new perspective of Sommerlea's position. 'As are you.'

Kael exhaled with a note of annoyance. 'And us.'

Jett studied the map again not wishing to scrutinize a problem that was most likely an unpleasant topic.

'We'll have to prepare supplies,' said Seth. 'Will we take everyone?'

Ignoring Seth's question, Jett said to Kael, 'How far into Baion are Ryne?'

'Ryne attacked their Royal city, Everingham in the north, and their royalty has been displaced.' Kael reclined back in his chair. 'That information came through to the old king via an informant over a fortnight ago.'

'I knew that.' Jett went on, 'A woman in Floris told me Everingham had been taken. She was very concerned.'

Seth added, 'A woman of many talents. I wonder how Annabella knew.'

'Yes, I wonder.' Jett creased his brow, puzzling over the woman's knowledge.

'Who is this?' Kael looked at them expectantly.

'A herbwoman…' Seth explained, 'with a shop near the docks. She saved Marcus from dying…' He chatted about their experience with the insightful old woman.

Jett drifted to the window. Marcus and Hellier were on the lawn, fighting each other again. She moved around him with a larger shield than she was accustomed to while he used the two wooden swords. Their fast pace and smooth strokes became a dance that seemed to last for minutes without either of them landing any hits.

'Jett?' Seth brought him back to the present conversation. 'What do you think?'

Jett turned to him with a grim expression. 'I don't like it, travelling all that way to perhaps meet oncoming troops and arrive at the top end of the mountains to pass it and discover Signet Reach is still inaccessible. But – it seems the only option.' He followed it with a half-hearted smile. 'And I'll take everyone.' He had no intention of leaving anyone after spending weeks to get them back together.

Kael nodded his understanding.

Jett went to the lounge and stretched his legs. Watching Hellier aggravated an old topic, and he directed a questioning gaze at Kael. 'I must ask if you had any problems with Dario.'

Kael gave a hearty chuckle. 'We didn't know what to expect, so we watched him on the day and following. He spoke to no one about Shiarn or anyone of you, except he did mention Hellier. But even that was minor, and in the end he seemed trustworthy enough.' He continued after a pause, 'We were ready to deal with him at the slightest inclination he would talk.'

It still didn't change Jett's sentiment towards him. He was glad to see the back of him.

Seth shook his head with embarrassment. 'It seemed quite loyal in my eyes, especially in regards Hellier. They got on brilliantly together, even to the point of becoming—' his eyes flicked wide and his cheeks brightened '…good friends.'

'Hellier made such an impact on him, he actually told Vivella he made a special friend for life,' replied Kael.

A fire burned in Jett's belly at the vision of Hellier and Dario in an intimate embrace, even in love. He never trusted Dario nor did he even like him. Now, even despite Dario keeping their secret, he wanted to kill him. He remained silent not wishing his jealous views to be examined here.

'Well, he did fall in—' Seth closed his mouth at Jett's dark stare.

Jett's invidious thoughts stabbed Seth's mind like a barbed knife. *I don't want to hear a thing about him.*

Adis said, 'I guess you will need supplies and provisions.'

Jett shifted his brooding eyes from Seth. 'We will.'

'Seeing as you are just going to chat,' Adis said to Kael, 'I'm going to arrange provisions for your journey. Seth will help me with what you need.' The two left the room.

The door shut and Jett was left in a vacuous silence, where the need to speak was suffocating. He said in a casual sweep, 'So, they told you what happened?'

Kael sat straighter in his chair and leaned forward. 'Yes. Lucky for all of us, you were saved. It seemed to have happened suddenly, almost from out of nowhere. Do you know what caused the… possession?'

Jett detected the doubt in Kael's tone. But he couldn't blame him. Jett had escaped, they all had, by the finest of chances. 'The evil spirit had a way into my mind and was poisoning me.' To the degree his mind died. If it wasn't for the prophecy from the journal, he would have remained so.

'Can this evil spirit return?' Kael questioned.

'It's not going to return.' Jett delivered a penetrating gaze.

Kael's eye twitched, but an enigmatic smile appeared. 'That's good. And I'm relieved Mara is still here with us. Even more so, considering who she is. If she had died, I dread the consequences.'

'The consequences would have been deadly.' Jett's voice dropped. Kael would have been coming home to a house on fire, at the very least.

'Very fortunate, indeed.' Kael scrutinized him. 'For both of you.'

'For all of us.' Jett frowned at his nonchalance over a situation that could have seen the death of them all.

'True indeed. Although, I was coming home to stop you.' A cold glint entered Kael's eyes and his voice became threatening.

'I'm not sure it would have been so easy.' Jett recalled the violence used against his own Kin. He could have killed them without effort, yet he toyed with them, contemplating how best to use them.

Kael broke through his mournful recollections. 'I would have done it,' he said with frightening conviction.

Jett's brows arched in surprise at his confidence.

'There are more ways than one to kill a demon.' His smile gave Jett a cold shiver. 'No need to go into details, but I will do whatever it takes to protect my Kin and home.'

Jett gave him a submissive nod. 'I understand. I would do the same.' *And more.* He returned a melancholy smile, remembering the abhorrent plans, and words he spoke in his transformed state. Kael's actions would be more than justifiable, they would be noble. 'I'm glad.'

'Good.' Kael's smile became warmer and he bounced forward in the chair. 'Clara mentioned you spoke of a Summoner, I assume that was Mara?'

'It was.' He hated dredging the information up from his tainted memories.

Kael nodded as if already aware of the fact. 'It's probably best if you and her are apart.'

It irked him the older Fáerinn would make decisions on his behalf. He never liked being told what to do, even if it was sound advice. 'I know, but—' he lowered his brow and caught Kael's eye. 'There are people looking for her.'

'She is wanted by Ryne.' Despite that, Kael didn't appear worried.

'Worse than that.'

'It's true, I don't particularly like the idea, and it's my hope she won't stay here overly long.' Kael sighed. 'When Jonas decides to join us we can discuss that.'

Jett stretched back on the lounge. 'I'm hoping we can find Ethan and come back through without any trouble.'

Kael creased his brow with concern. 'There's no preparing for what you will meet at Signet Reach.'

Jett gave a grumbling sigh. 'That will be an entirely new dilemma.'

The door opened and Jonas sauntered in. He eased himself onto the lounge opposite Jett, completely unruffled by the earlier attack and his near death.

Kael said with cheer, 'You're in good condition despite everything.'

Jonas reached his arm along the back of the tawny gold chaise. 'I'm quite well, thank you for asking.'

'Well for now,' Kael said, 'For all we know, he might be still alive.'

Jonas cleared his throat, and his bright gaze took in both men. 'Quite possibly. He is not a foe who can be killed like a normal man. However, on this occasion he has not won, and I hope he is significantly impaired.' He looked across to Jett. 'Many thanks for your aid. Without your intervention I fear the worst may have occurred.'

'No need for that, Shiarn is my Kin. Anyway, you have done much for us.' Jett acknowledged his appreciation with a friendly smile, hoping he didn't have to recount all the evil deeds he had undertaken in the last week. 'It's the least I can do.'

Kael remarked, 'It is a wonder you were there in time—'

Jett interrupted, 'Luck I'd say.'

'I'm not a big believer in luck,' said Jonas.

'And in regard to wonders,' Kael spoke over the top of them, 'Mara.'

Jonas eased forward. 'Princess Mara has put us in a difficult position.'

'She should be sequestered, and word sent back to Ryne she has been recovered,' Kael replied with a dry note, 'and escorted back to their palace.'

'Exactly.' Jonas ran his finger along his chin.

Knowing how she would react to that, Jett spoke in her defence. 'She wouldn't be going willingly.'

'When one becomes a member of the royal court,' a smile played on Jonas mouth, 'there is little choice in what one wants to do. But—' he gave a melancholy sigh. 'I know, and I agree. She has voiced her opinion on this, and muttered something about her "wicked" mother wanting her baby.'

That information was news to Jett. As usual Mara was not being honest, or not honest with him. 'Why?'

Jonas shrugged. 'It is feasible to assume the queen wants to cover it up. Yet, even so, Mara will not inform us who the father is, not even to Clara.'

'Clara said the father is not a boy but a man,' Kael said, 'Apparently she was in love with him.'

'Bollocks!' Jonas postulated with indignation, 'She's only a child. She would hardly know the meaning of the word.'

Jett frowned with annoyance. He found it hard to believe Mara would be manipulated in such a way. With her rebellious opinion, he would wager she had more of a part in it than they realized. 'The child would be the heir?'

'Possibly, depending on its parentage perhaps,' Jonas said, 'although it could be disputed. Currently, Rikard and Yavinia have no children together, and Mara his is step-daughter. However, he has made Mara his ordained successor.'

Jett rubbed his neck in contemplation. 'And Mara's child would do well enough as an heir, and even more so if it's a male?'

'Indeed,' Jonas said, 'Even better if the queen could claim it was hers. Count Duruick, Rikard's cousin, has sons who would contend for the throne, if they aren't already. I sense we are caught in a complex family drama on a royal scale.' He ended with a poignant sigh.

Kael chuckled. 'Will you tell Bastion?'

'I am undecided. Although I dislike keeping the secret,' Jonas replied, 'Who knows what he would do with the information, he can be annoyingly unpredictable.'

'Whatever we decide, we can be clear on one thing.' Kael's gaze swept over the two men. 'She must not travel with Jett and Kin into the valley.'

'I agree.' Jonas' expression was firm. 'She must remain here and not travel the countryside. However, it is a shame, as it would offer a solution of a sort, but not a wise course of action for everyone involved. Besides the consequences of being discovered with her, would make it a dangerous venture. There is also the potential she may be used—'

'We've been over this.' Jett's tone was more curt than he liked, and given he was in agreement, it still irked him.

Jonas gave them both a warning gaze. 'She must stay here, out of sight, and safe. While here, I am hoping she will open up to Clara and Lelana, and tell them more details. We might be able to find people in Ryne who could support her. Although… we could inadvertently be starting something we may come to regret.'

Kael thumped his fist into his palm. 'Why would she conceal his identity from us?'

Jonas' eyes rolled to the ceiling in thought. 'She's protecting someone important.'

'Not just a scandalous officer or lustful servant?' Kael raised his eyes.

Jonas gave Jett a curious glance. 'You found her in a small village on the edge of Ryne? Was she planning on meeting anyone there?'

He had no idea. The only one who came for her was the Narahk. Suddenly he was reluctant to speak of how willing Mara had been to go to the evil entity. 'She ran away from her mother and was staying with her grandmother as far as I know.'

Jonas squinted at him with doubt. 'And that's where you were attacked?'

'We were.'

'And did they want the girl?'

'We believe so.' Uncomfortable under the scrutiny, Jett moved restlessly.

After a tense moment, Jonas took his eyes off Jett and exhaled a weary sigh. 'On learning of her actions here, and your own, it becomes more perplexing.'

'That's why she's going to stay here,' Jett lowered his voice with impatience.

Kael gave his response a hearty grin. 'That's settled then.'

'You are leaving soon?' Jonas gave Jett a rigid smile.

'Perhaps a couple of days.' Jett returned a tight smile of his own. The sooner he left the house and Mara, the sooner he could put those memories behind him.

A look of happiness alighted Jonas' face. 'Time enough to enjoy your company. The better prepared you are the better off you will be.' He turned pensive. 'We wish to see you all again.'

'Yes, safe and sane.' Kael ended with a hearty laugh. 'And we'd like to meet your lost Kin too.'

Jett smiled at his brazen humour, knowing it would be far different if the reverse were to happen.

69 - Trouble Afar

There is a force outside a man's understanding that compels him to life a significant life

Tome of the First Born

Along the slope down to Lake Lowanna, the late sun touched the leafy trees and wreaths of vines, covered in a petite white flower. Fresh pine and faint birdcalls were in the cool wind. An incessant grunting and rustling from a bush broke the pleasant lull of the woodland. Through the covering of low branches, an arrow stuck out targeting the black boar.

A high pitched bird cry came down the hill's decline. Ignoring the screech, Seth turned back to the loitering pig.

Adis, a few paces behind, gazed upwards. 'Must have some prey.'

An unexpected roar startled them. Seth's arrow flew amiss and the pig took flight through the bushes. A second roar was amplified by the mountains behind them.

'I know that voice.' Adis stepped under the overhang of branches. 'Come.'

Seth dashed after him with a wondrous look on his face. 'We're going after a lion?' Over the last few days, Adis taught him much in regard to his Gift, but this would be burgeoning on one of the strangest lessons so far.

Adis stepped over layers of spindle, without a sound, while equipping his long bow and nocking an arrow. He pulled up in the semi-protection of squat bushes, and looked out at the source of the snarling.

With a faint rustle and broken twigs, Seth raced up behind him and stopped still. On the hard earth road at the bottom of the short incline was a fallen horse. Upon the beast's rump a mature mountain lion rested its extended claws. Sharp teeth tore the horse's flesh while a bird landed on the dead animal's head. The golden-brown lion gave the bird a guttural growl, but otherwise was not bothered. His heavy claws pushed the horse to the side revealing movement.

'Holy Creator!' Adis crouched, peering at the horse. 'A man is under it.'

Seth stepped closer, risking being seen by the lion, yet the beast seemed oblivious to any movement from the forest. 'Alive?'

'I don't know what old ginger is doing out here but it's time he went home.'

Seth stared at the older man in fearful awe.

Adis stood with his bow cocked at the ready. 'Come behind me and get the man out from the horse.' He moved at a steady pace down onto the road, his arrow never leaving sight of the cat. His tone was deep and soothing. 'I don't want to shoot you, Ginger.' He neared the horse's neck and the bird flew to a nearby branch while Seth made a cautious path towards the man.

Crooking its massive head, the lion let out an intimidating roar.

'You can have the horse,' Adis continued in the same calming tone, 'I just want the man.' He rested his boot on the saddle and confronted the great cat head-on, without his arrow leaving his target.

The man's leg was pinned under his steed. His eyes opened and he mumbled something indiscernible.

Seth decided to ignore the fierce lion and his own trembling heart. If he paid attention to either he would achieve nothing. He crawled to the man and held his arms tight.

'It's a deal,' Adis said, 'You don't move and I won't shoot you.'

Seth yanked him from the horse, and pulled with all his strength. The man cried out in pain. A powerful claw swiped at Seth. He hauled him free at top speed and fell backwards in a heap with the shuddering man on top of him. His hands shaking, Seth dragged him into the partial covering of the trees.

'You enjoy your meal.' Adis backed away, his line of sight never leaving the animal.

Its luminous eyes glared at them and not until Adis disappeared into the woods did it begin to redden its mouth on the horse.

Seth went from dragging the man to supporting his torso into better covering under the trees. He persevered with his weight, but his height made awkward handling. The man groaned and stretched towards his leg where a bone pushed out from his skin.

Their horses were down the hill, near the beginning of the slopes. Seth puffed hard, supporting the wounded man's tall body. 'We will get you help, hold on.' The wounded man seemed to be a soldier, dressed in a red shirt under a sleeveless tunic, half red, half yellow, with an emblem of a lion in the center. All of it soiled with blood from an untended gash on his shoulder.

The sun was setting and the shadows of the forest expanded around them. Adis came through the woods on Forest and leading Lightning. He dismounted. 'Get in the saddle, I'll pass him to you.'

Seth mounted and Adis hefted the injured man up before him. He slumped against Seth's chest, his blood dampening his shirt. In the moment, Seth was thankful he was not wearing his best clothing.

Adis leapt into Forest's saddle. 'We must be quick, think you can manage?'

'Yes.' Seth rode out to the road and they galloped down the hill. The road opened up and they raced towards Sommerlea with the expansive estate of Haulton on their left. The fortress was well placed amongst the rocky hills, and they rode hard across the bridge taking them through the vineyards of Sommerlea.

The man fell in and out of consciousness. Seth eased his riding when his groans became pitiful. Seth's concerns were centered on him staying sturdy in the saddle as the man swayed in the mad dash to the house. The horses were still cantering at a fast pace when they hit the pathway by the river. Adis pushed Forest into a fast gallop to the lawn, and he jumped from his horse with all speed, calling for Clara.

She came out the side door with a questioning look while Seth rode up with the injured man. 'Bring him in,' she ordered.

Sweat poured from the man's face and his agonized moans were louder when lifted down. Adis cradled him in his arms and Clara followed him inside, and said, 'Take him upstairs, everyone is gathering for dinner.' The three went up and Clara led them to a spare room. 'Seth, go and fetch Kael.' She sat on the bed beside the injured man and Seth dashed away.

'He's not one of Haulton's men,' Adis said. 'We found him on the road. His leg's broken and he's got a wound on his shoulder, maybe an arrow.'

Clara pushed up his pant leg and touched the bone extending through the skin. She laid her hand on his flesh near the wound.

His fitful cries lessened and his words became coherent. 'Prince Aric… needs aid,' he breathed out heavily. 'I have to get to the king.'

Digging into his flesh and through congealed blood, Clara wiggled what was left of the arrow from his shoulder blade, giving him whispered apologizes in reply to his moans. He laid his head back on the pillow and closed his eyes.

Meanwhile Kael entered with Seth in tow and he took the seat and pulled it close to the bed.

The man was young, but this had been concealed by a scraggly beard and a weather-beaten face. His lips were cracked and dry and his eyes were dark circles.

Clara spoke softly. 'He is fatigued, parched and starving. Things needing natural remedies.'

Adis informed Kael, 'He's speaking of the king.'

Kael looked to Adis. 'You found him on the road?'

'Yes, under his horse.' Adis did not elaborate further.

Clara turned to Kael. 'Who is Prince Aric?'

The man's eyes shot open. 'Prince Aric is in dire need.'

'This is serious indeed,' said Kael. 'Prince Aric is the son of King Garrick of Baion.'

'You are well now. I'll get you food and drink.' Clara looked down at the man with kind compassion and laid her hand over his cold one. 'What is your name?'

The young man's voice croaked. 'Hayden, but there's no time.'

'Hayden, I'll prepare something for you.' Clara cast a worried frown at the young man and the two men. 'I'll get Jonas.'

'Seth, we better see to the horses,' Adis said. 'We shall leave you to it, Kael.'

The two men left the room and Seth said with a breathless thrill, 'That was incredible. What an awesome lion.'

Adis nodded. 'He is—'

'You know him?'

'He lives up towards the north, in the mountains where he is master.'

Seth replied in wonder, 'You showed no fear.'

'You can't, he senses it. We have met before.' Adis was reflective. 'With old Ginger you have to negotiate.'

Seth's eyes widened attentively to his prudent wisdom.

'He must have followed the man as he rode,' Adis said. 'We need to go back and move the horse.'

'Go back?' Seth gaped at the man's audacity. 'I guess it's in the roadway.'

'Not only that. It's the saddle and bag. First we fix the horses and have a bite to eat ourselves.'

~ * ~

'Where am I?' His voice cracking unevenly, Hayden took short glances around the comfortable if not sparsely furnished room before setting his eyes on Kael.

'You have crossed into the westernmost boundary of Coltrene and are in Sommerlea,' he said cordially. 'And my name is Kael.'

'I'm in Coltrene.' Lying back on the bed, he appeared to relax somewhat. 'I made it.'

'You have come a long way?'

Hayden nodded, closing his eyes. 'I must get word to the king. I have ridden hard for a night and a day,' he took a deep breath. 'My horse was fast but it could not continue on.'

Kael listened with patient interest.

'The lion was following…' Hayden's voice was irregular. 'But the horse dropped before it pounced.'

'A lion?' Kael lifted an enquiring brow.

Hayden's voice was labored. 'The man was beyond brave.'

Kael nodded. 'Now, save your energy.'

Hayden closed his eyes and appeared to sleep.

Jonas entered the room and took a chair on the opposite side of the bed. Jett followed him in, intrigued by the new visitor, and concerned by the sight of Seth's shirt front stained with blood. He stood back, behind Kael.

'Hayden has ridden all the way from Baion.' Kael spoke to Jonas, keeping his voice low. 'He speaks of Prince Aric.'

Hayden's eyes flicked open and he sat up a little straighter at the sight of the new faces in the room.

'Hayden, this is Jonas and Jett,' said Kael.

Hayden nodded to each in turn and his words tumbled out with impatience. 'I cannot stay here, I must be off.'

Kael placated him with a raised hand. 'Slow down.'

Clara came in with a bowl of steaming broth. She nudged Kael out the way and placed it in Hayden's dry hands. 'You'll feel better after this.' She ran her hand over his clumped hair. 'You have come far and you will be rewarded with rest and food.'

Hayden took the bowl and drank it, his eyes revealing his heartfelt appreciation.

'And soon I shall bring you up something more hearty so don't worry about missing out.' She smiled as if a long lost brother had come to visit. She gave his hand an assuring squeeze and left the room.

'They have taken Everingham and are moving across our lands.' Hayden began, 'we retreated from Thornmere… our forces were separated.'

'You speak of "we",' Jonas asked, 'the prince?'

'I do. We had no warning. They came on Everingham and we believe King Garrick was killed.' His voice rumbled with unspent sorrow. 'The prince was at Eltringsom with his siblings. But we feared being held in a siege so decided to ride south. We spilt our forces and we rode to Mount Cirrus. The nearest town is Gearoidin where we hope General Clemeus still has troops.'

'Terrible news,' Kael said.

Leaning closer to the man, Jonas enquired, 'Where is the prince?'

'At Havenside at Mount Cirrus.' Hayden paused to observe any recognition from the men.

'An old mountain fortress,' Kael said.

'Old, but strong.' Hayden leaned back on the pillow.

'The prince is under siege?' Jonas questioned.

'As of when I left, maybe a thousand Rynian troops. We are only eight-score, but able-handed.' Hayden turned his gaze away.

Kael regarded him with admiration. 'How did you escape?'

'A cliff door in the rocks of the fortress. I climbed down the rocks at night and stole a horse from the soldiers.'

Jonas nodded his head, appraising his courageous venture.

'Are they aware you escaped?' asked Kael.

'I was shot.' Hayden felt his healed shoulder. 'But they didn't pursue me, perhaps thinking I was dead…'

Kael had disbelief on his face. 'You climbed the mountain at night?'

'I did.'

'A brave act,' Jonas remarked, 'If not a touch foolhardy.'

The man shrugged in a defeated manner. 'It was the only way to assure escape.'

Jett regarded the man with warm esteem. Anyone who could climb down a cliff at night, face possible capture and death, and race through the forest, had his respect. 'Are all your comrades as brave?'

Hayden stared into Jett's dark eyes as if gauging his intentions. 'Yes, and more so than I. I am here and they are not.' He studied him with a steely gaze and Jett did not remove his stare and Hayden continued, 'Men are capable of bold deeds when all they hold dear is threatened.'

Jett nodded his approval of his commendable avowal.

Jonas asked, 'And you seek aid from Coltrene?'

'If they have taken Havenside and manage to take Gearoidin, Coltrene will have a great force with supplies marching down your east road, faster than you realize.'

Kael and Jonas looked at each other with a silent exchange.

Jett finally enquired with curiosity, 'How long can the prince hold out?'

'If the Rynian's send more troops… not long.' Hayden's face lowered.

Jonas creased his brow in deliberation. 'The king would never get there in time.'

'Haulton?' Kael offered thoughtfully to Jonas.

'Perhaps.'

Hayden stared mournfully down at the bed. 'The prince is a brave young man but he is ready to face them.'

Jonas looked to Kael with grave concern. 'Prince Aric is only about fifteen years of age.' He turned back to Hayden. 'What of his siblings?'

'We are hoping they the princesses' are at Gearoidin and the youngest prince was thought to be at Everingham.' Hayden's eyes misted over and it was all he could do to prevent himself from crying.

Jonas speculated sadly, 'It seems Prince Aric is now king.'

'But of what?' replied Hayden.

Kael studied the young man. 'You are also quite young.'

Hayden replied with pride, 'I'm two years older than Aric and the youngest of the men present.'

'Well, Hayden, you have done well,' Kael consoled him.

'I mean you no offence, sir, but as yet I have done nothing.' Again his eyes were downcast. 'I have only informed you about the decimation of my homelands.'

'Do not despair,' Jonas comforted him. 'It was a wise decision nonetheless to send you to Coltrene and here you are and we are well informed.'

Hayden nodded, and suddenly appearing anxious, said, 'My letter. It's in the saddle bag.'

Jonas directed to Kael, 'Didn't Adis bring it?'

'Mm,' Kael answered tediously, 'I have a feeling he was busy.'

Hayden declared with dread, 'He could not!'

Kael turned his attention to Jonas and replied with mock affection, 'I think that old cat was there.'

'Ah, I see,' said Jonas. 'Well, I will need that letter.'

'I'll go,' said Jett.

'I and Adis will also go,' Kael said to Jett.

Hayden's eyes pleaded with them. 'Is there any chance the prince can be saved?'

'I cannot say.' Kael gave him a serious look. 'We can speak with Duke Haulton and discuss sending men out there.'

'How far is Havenside?' Jett enquired of Hayden, ignoring Kael's unexpected glance.

'Hard going under two days, but that will kill your horse. Maybe three days through the valley and to the end of the Grey Stone Peaks.' Hayden looked at Jett with hopeful eyes.

Kael answered, gruffly, 'There would not be much you could do against that many armed men.'

Jett creased his brow in consideration and stared into the boy's eyes, seeing an optimistic belief that somehow help would come.

'Any help would be appreciated. Our men are more than eager to fight and I know they will take this course, in the end.'

Kael stared at Jett judiciously. 'It would be fraught with difficulties.' His voice was stern. 'And you have more than your share of problems right now.'

Jett stood, arms crossed, observing Jonas' opposing expression. 'Of course.' This was the type of confrontation that always caused him trouble in Tellávare. He was not good at accepting orders from anyone, in fact it seemed to incur the opposite effect, but he was not about to argue it there and then. 'We already have a weighty task before us.' He put his hand on Kael's shoulder in reassurance, in doing so he sunk any hopes the young man might have had.

Kael said, 'Hayden, do not despair yet.'

Clara came in with a tray of food and a pile of folded clothes and Kael stood to leave. 'And we will bring your gear back and get word to Haulton and we can talk again later.' He sighed at Jonas. 'Looks like we shall be leaving sooner than we had planned.'

'We will be taking young Hayden with us,' Jonas said, 'but, first we shall pay a visit to Duke Haulton in the morning. Then onto Floris.'

Kael directed at Jett, 'You will be ready to leave tomorrow?'

Jett glanced with unflinching self-confidence at the two of them. The last couple of days had been well spent, but he was ready to begin the next journey. 'Yes. We will depart early and start into the valley and up towards the eastern mountains.'

PART IV

Darkness

A Land with no Master

70 - Departures

Deceit is an offspring of wickedness
But an honest heart begets righteousness
Wealth spawns greed
While hardship births benevolence

Ei'myn Geí-Serenmãh

Weary and hungry, Ethan and the men laboured on through the tunnels. They passed numerous openings, speculating where they might finish, and panicking on whether they were lost in the labyrinth of passages. Added to their complaints, men at the back sensed unnatural movement in the shadows. Unnerved by the scratching on the rock walls, they quickened their pace with no real sense as to where they were headed.

The last of the line passed. With Loc beside him holding the torch, Ethan observed the moving shadows on the ceiling. He prodded the rocks above with his Moving Gift. Looser than he realized, they tumbled down along the corridor. Amid the falling stone, sharp needle teeth bit into his arm. Loc attacked the creature with the torch, and Ethan flung it into the wall. It crumbled into a ball of flame. With a grateful nod to Loc, Ethan rubbed his punctured arm.

The other men raced back to them.

Stannar patted Ethan's back, sending the dust flying, and with sarcasm said, 'No one could have done it better.'

'I don't know how long that's going to keep them away.' Ethan turned from the blocked path to survey what he could of the passage.

Men were scattered along it. At the end, Kenric shouted, 'Come everyone. See what we have found!'

A large chamber, its smooth walls disappearing into the darkness above, and embedded in the walls were horizontal streams of gems. Gold, diamonds, rubies, and black gold. Other lines had greens, blues, and pink, all in layers up into pitch black. The men stood in awe of the jewels shimmering in the torch light.

Shunted out of his daze, Ethan left the room, clutching his throbbing arm and looking for a way out. No other exits were present. The realization hit him and he sat outside the doorway, head in his hands, and groaned. His wound was trifling compared to what he had done with the tunnel. Loc and Gailtram sat beside him in a wretched silence. The Harn also slumped to the floor while a few started digging at the rocks of the blocked passage. The rocks fell in a continuous shower for several minutes before the men started again.

Ethan contemplated helping the Harn clear the collapsed tunnel, but his limbs were a dead weight. After some time, he stood. The Harn looked at him with despair and he didn't bother trying to conceal his own sense of defeat.

The repetitive tapping continued in the gem encrusted chamber, but over the top, Branan yelled in Harnan. Loc and Gailtram rushed into the chamber, followed more slowly by Ethan.

Branan waved his fist at Daskar and cursed.

Ethan asked, 'What's he saying?'

'He's got a map.' Loc glared at Daskar with surprise. 'A map!'

Branan, his arms flailing, spoke to the Harn, in heated dialogue.

Ethan watched Daskar's eyes light up with fear at the sight of the Harn encircling him. A rolled up parchment was in his hand.

Daskar took an unsteady step backward. 'We were gonna tell you after.'

'*We?*' growled Stannar.

Daskar squirmed, but turned to stare at Kenric.

The men raged with deadly threats. Even Kenric's men gathered in astonishment at the shocking revelation.

Kenric was shoved forward. He lifted his palms, as if it would placate the enraged men. 'Everyone stay calm.' He spread his hands at the gems. 'I wanted to tell you after we found this.'

'You're a low-life scoundrel!' Luz shouted.

Bearn's crinkled face blazed red. 'How could you do this to us?'

Ethan snatched the map from Daskar and unrolled the scroll. Numerous thin and tiny lines crisscrossed the aged parchment. It was complicated but not unreadable.

Loc examined it over his arm. 'It appears to have a way out.'

'You've as good as killed us, Kenric,' Ethan cried with malevolent annoyance.

Kenric's eyes lit up with unusual ferocity, 'Not I,' and he pointed his chisel at Ethan's face. '*You* collapsed the tunnel. We could have cut some treasure and left.'

Overwhelmed with wrathful intentions, Ethan could not speak. He pushed the map into Loc's chest and stomped out into the darkness to prevent himself from killing Kenric with his bare hands.

Loc spoke in the chamber. 'If we were heading in the right direction it wouldn't have mattered…'

Ethan tuned out the argument and sat against the wall beside the stones barring their escape. More commotion came from inside, but he heard no clear words. In the semi darkness he started moving stones from the pile. The yelling continued, but through it all he heard someone approach.

Ruegar sat on the rubble. 'You going to clear this?'

The tunnel was blocked solid, all hope was a farce. 'I'm not sure it can be done.' He wondered if it was right to mislead him now. 'Where you from?'

'Sanyar, on the coast, west of Floris.'

Ethan nodded. 'You have family there?'

'Ma and my sisters…' Ruegar's small voice trailed off.

Ethan was unsure what to say to the boy who had obviously suffered much after living a short time.

Ruegar's voice was a bare whisper. 'You?'

Ethan had no desire to dwell on it and he continued shifting the stones, this time with more resolution. 'I've got family. Parents.'

'We shouldn't give up?' Ruegar looked to Ethan, searching for reassurance.

He attempted smiling at the child's dirty face that begged for hope and he began moving the stones. 'No.'

~ * ~

Jett, having already been downstairs to help equip the wagon for departure, stood in his room one last time, staring out at the sapphire lake and mountains beyond. The previous evening he helped remove the horse carcass and the pouch. Not much was in the bag except the sealed letter addressed to the King of Coltrene and a map of Baion. Jett had spent a short time examining the map. Not as long as he would have liked without raising unwanted interest on Kael's part. Jett was of the mind it would be ill preparation if he did not acquaint himself with the territory and potential hazards he was leading his Kin into. He got the impression Kael would not believe this reasoning if he were to mention it and he had no wish to cause him angst over it. Besides, Kael was correct.

He still had mixed feelings about the decision to leave Mara behind. Was he being selfish, as Earona put it, by leaving those at Sommerlea vulnerable to anyone wishing to abduct Mara? He reasoned, Kael wanted her to stay, so in the end his opinion would not have mattered, either way. As it went, his mood lightened by the decision, and he looked forward to not thinking over the Key or Mara. The most concerning issue was how safe she would be left at Sommerlea. He would have to trust them with her care, because there was nothing further he could do for her.

Jett buckled his double belt harness, swords already sheathed, around his waist and over his shoulder. He threw his cloak over the blade at his back and glanced at his black shirt, purchased in Floris, and noticed the mended tear. Most likely Clara. He couldn't imagine it was the girls of his Kin. With a last sweep of the view he left.

Downstairs in the entry hall, Kael and Jonas, also attired for departure, waited for him. Kael said, 'Good luck to you and may Kahm keep you and give you guidance and strength.'

Jett clasped his outstretched hand. 'And I pray you have all manner of luck with the duke.'

'Ah, the duke,' Jonas commented with a raised brow, 'What a dreary challenge first thing in the morning.' He also took Jett's hand in a firm clasp and his other covered them both. 'Now then, I presume I don't need to say this, but, you will take care?'

Jett reflected back an arrogant confidence. 'Always.'

Jonas narrowed astute eyes. 'You won't take any unnecessary risks?'

'No.' Jett's reply became jovial. 'Only necessary ones.' He relieved the tension by giving a low chuckle. 'I'll take care of them.'

Jonas responded in good humor, 'I know you will.'

Kael said, 'Come, they are waiting outside.'

The three walked out the front doors to a full courtyard of two wagons and numerous horses. The Kin had already said their goodbyes to the Sommerlea residents and were mounted on their steeds, with Keanan heading the wagon.

Jett walked by Seth seated on Forest and patted his horse, Thunder. The impressive black stallion pawed at the ground in anticipation of being on the road again. Instead of mounting, Jett took a moment to say his farewells to those under the terrace.

Clara's cheeks dampened with blatant tears. 'You all come back safely, as soon as you can.'

'That's right, we'll be waiting.' Morias put his arm around Lelana and squeezed her close. 'But not without your Kin.'

Jett smiled at them in reassurance. 'I'm sure we will find him.' He approached Hayden, leaning up against Kael's wagon, and put his hand out to him. Hayden gave him a firm clasp. Jett said, 'I hope you get aid from the duke.' He paused. 'I also hope your prince endures.'

'As do I.' Hayden searched Jett's eyes. 'He will hold on longer if he has hope, as I hold on.'

Jett studied his face that had aged beyond its proper time. 'All the same, I wish you the best.' He turned from him and saw Earona peering from the back of the wagon, and he called with haste, 'Where is Mara?' He had caught a glimpse of her much earlier, but she had dashed away before he could speak to her.

Earona frowned with irritation. 'I saw her earlier. She was in a foul mood and didn't wish to say farewell to anyone.'

He shook his head with annoyance. More likely, she was avoiding him. Just like that, he was leaving her behind, was her words to him. He wasn't certain whether it was right or not, but he felt it had to be done. He took Thunder's reins from Seth and stroked the black horse's neck before settling in the saddle.

'We shall see you on the road soon,' Kael called from the second wagon.

Jett gave him a nod and indicated for Keanan to ride out the gate.

Earona and Shiarn caught glimpses of the grape vines from their position in the back of the wagon, as they traveled towards the bridge. At a distance, Kael and Jonas came up behind, as they made their way to Duke Haulton's estate.

Shiarn tied the canvas to the side to get a clearer view. 'I hope they keep well.'

'*They* will be fine.' Earona contradicted her own fearful thoughts. 'It's us you should be worried about,' she finished with a sad sigh, 'and Mara.'

Shiarn fell back on a pile of camping utensils and cursed under her breath. 'The little she-devil didn't even say goodbye. After all we did for her.'

Earona pouted with disdain. 'That's in poor taste.'

'Ha!' Shiarn pulled herself up from her cramped position. 'I'll say the same to Jett if he gives me a hard time.'

'I guess Mara will be safer here…' Earona managed a small smile. Jett was probably right.

They reached the bridge and Shiarn leaned against the wagon door beside Earona. Jett stopped his horse, allowing Kael and Jonas to catch him up, and he rode alongside Jonas. The land to the girls' left opened up, revealing a stream running down from the rocky green slopes. The walled enclosure of Haulton's estate stood like a mighty fortress. Wide towers and parapets lined the walls, and within were numerous buildings.

Earona's attention was dragged from the castle to see Jonas blow a kiss in their direction. 'How romantic,' she gushed with delight.

Looking to Jonas, Shiarn lifted a newly acquired ring to her lips. Jonas and Kael, with Hayden accompanying them, turned into the roadway leading up to the gateway manned by Duke Haulton's patrol. 'I can think of a hundred more romantic gestures.' She sighed. 'Anyway, we said our real goodbyes privately.'

'At least you get to do that…' she said with a begrudging tone.

'You've had plenty of time to talk to Keanan.'

'I know.' She stopped her with a raised hand.

Shiarn stared with a puzzled frown for moments. It was followed by bubbling laughter. 'I don't know who to feel more sorry for.'

Earona blushed and her face puckered. 'If you haven't noticed, I have not asked you for any advice.'

'Fair enough.' Shiarn smiled. 'But I'll be waiting.' After some moments passed, Shiarn said, 'Thought I would tell you, I took some of the herbite from your bag.'

Earona turned her gaze from the passing greenery to heed her abrupt statement to eye her satchel. 'I'm surprised there was any left. That bag has been gone through countless times. You probably need fresher herbite than that.' Herbite was a bitter herb used in Tellávare as a method for preventing conception. Due to Fáerinn eggs being precious, women took every opportunity of securing them for the right time. She scrutinized Shiarn from under dark brows. *And if you happen to fall pregnant that's something I won't be able to help you with.*

Shiarn's face twisted with angry consternation. 'Is there really a need for that?'

'You—' Earona put a halt to her retort. 'I'm—sorry.' She laid her face into her hands.

'It's done.' Shiarn rested a hand on her shoulder. 'No point thinking about it. In fact, I wish you wouldn't.' *I don't want that man in my thoughts in any form.* 'Now that I know he's probably still alive. Curse him.'

Earona remained silent, knowing this to be true. But, she was at a loss as to how to counter her own remorse. 'So, tell me, are you in love?'

A grin emerged on Shiarn's face. 'Feels like it.'

'You're so lucky.' Earona sighed like a pining adolescent.

A gloomy change came over Shiarn's face. 'But now, I'm unhappy.'

Taking Shiarn's hand, Earona looked into her anxious eyes. 'I think I understand.'

'I'm not sure when I will see him again.' Shiarn gave a pensive stare. 'I had no idea how problematic it would be to find love outside the Kin.'

Earona squeezed her hand with affection. 'I'll be here if it gets too difficult.'

'God, you and I stuck in this wagon together again.' She groaned. 'What am I thinking?'

Contemplating the rising forest, Earona said, 'I wonder what is past those mountains.'

'"Through the tranquil valley, over rushing stream,' Shiarn sang,

'"See the awesome ranges loom, above a sea of trees,

Time has passed but they still reign supreme.

Time has come for us to pass,

Beyond the familiar to unearth a world that's vast."'

'I hope it's not too vast.' Earona slouched against the compartment at the thought of the long journey.

Watching Jett trot up to the wagon, Shiarn cupped her chin and leaned on the squat door. 'I don't care where we go, as long as we find Ethan. He's missing all this fun.' *Poor sop.*

'I agree.' Jett's voice brimmed with excitement. 'And now, next stop — somewhere in the valley.'

~ * ~

A few Harn, including Ethan, continued shifting the rocks from the collapsed tunnel with a frail hope it could be cleared. He listened to the details of Kenric's betrayal. Years ago, Daskar found the map and the lodestone on a skeleton in a cave hole. He and Kenric kept it secret even from the men in their own cell. Kenric's eagerness to move through the mountain and his overconfidence it could be achieved was better understood. Although nothing about his deception made sense. If only the two had been honest, they could have been nearer to freedom.

'He's gone mad with greed.' Bull hammered into a boulder in the middle of the pile. 'The Gold Curse.'

'Aye,' Morgan agreed.

Ethan said, 'I'm surprised he's still standing.'

Luz replied, 'Barton cuffed him a fine one.'

More Harn approached to help with the mass of rocks. After a time and in between the pounding of the stone, they heard hammering from the inner chamber. Ethan looked with shock at Con, who had just joined them. 'He's still at it?'

'He's not right in the head. Him, Daskar, Fariz, they think this can be moved.' Con nodded at the rubble.

Ethan shook his head with weary dismay. 'It's dense.'

Loc nodded in agreement. 'It would be a bloody miracle.'

Ethan looked down at Ruegar, listening to their dismal conversation, but directed his question to the men. 'How are Mouse and the other two taking it?'

Grith replied, 'Hard, as have all Kenric's men.'

Luz said, 'Let's see what can be done with this.'

The tunnel had been unstable at best and now with the hacking and hauling of the stones it doubled the danger of the roof caving in. Somehow Ethan managed to bring down giant pieces of mountain rock. It was a surprise they weren't buried alive, although the possibility of that still remained. It was more back-breaking labour and the men were aggravated and exhausted. They rotated the workload allowing rest time, but the mental anguish of being trapped alive was a drain. No one spoke of it, but every mind was occupied with it. In the hours they were smashing away, the men would have moved about seven feet into the rock. It was not a lot and time was running out.

71 - Valley Road

Climb the majestic summit, feel the windstorm blow
Strengthen body and soul, prepare men for war and woe
Touch the heart of the mountain, journey where no man goes
Time has come to herald the end of an era
And we have come to fulfill that reign

Crimson Sky

By noon the dirt road the Kin traveled, merged into a roadway of flat stones wide enough for two wagons to ride abreast. They rode between cedars and airless groves of redwoods and lofty pines.

Shiarn crawled out to the front of the wagon, leaving Earona dozing within, and sat with Keanan. The fresh air was a welcomed change and besides, she needed a break from Earona. Earona always managed to annoy her with her repetitive conversations. To add to their boredom, Jett said they weren't to play their instruments because he did not wish to attract any attention.

Keanan gave her an inviting smile. 'How is it back there?'

Shiarn chuckled. 'I'm out here, aren't I?' After noting his meditative disposition, she became immersed in the scenery. Marcus and Hellier rode ahead while Seth was nowhere to be seen and Jett was coming up behind. 'The forest is different here.' On her left the tops of mountains, towered over the valley.

'Wet and overgrown.'

She contemplated his blank expression. 'What do you think we shall find at Signet Reach?'

His neatly grown auburn beard suited his fair skin, and his wavy hair was getting longer by the day, however his drawn-out eyes did not suit him. 'Lowlife thugs, pirates, and slaves. Sounds perfect.'

'I guess we shall know more when we get there.'

'That's another matter,' he grumbled, 'I'm not certain how it can even be achieved, finding this place.'

Shiarn attempted to generate some cheer. 'We need to try to do something.'

Keanan slumped under the burden. 'It is true, but—' *we should have gone home for a Tracker as I had suggested.*

I couldn't imagine Jett going back or letting you. She was immediately struck by the awareness something else was troubling him besides the looming endeavor of finding Ethan. Questioning whether she should even enquire after his problem, she cleared her throat to speak.

He faced her with a suspicious stare. 'Yes?'

She hid her apprehension behind a warm smile. 'I was wondering how you are?'

Keanan's eyes went back to the road. 'Well enough.'

'I mean…' She flicked her head towards the wagon opening and glanced at Earona, dozing on a bedroll. *With her?*

He studied the reins, clenched in his white knuckles. 'I'm not exactly sure, but I know what I want—'

A frightened squeal from the wagon interrupted him.

Shiarn swiveled to see within the wagon. Stunned, she rolled her eyes and shook her head with disappointment. 'Why am I not surprised?'

From within, Earona snapped, 'I didn't plan this, Shiarn.' She cried, 'How did this happen?'

Mara heaved herself out of the long compartment, and pushing up pillows and pots, she gasped for breath. 'I had to.'

Earona caught her arm to support her out of the long compartment.

Keanan raised a curious brow at Shiarn. 'Did I just hear Mara?'

Shiarn grimaced at his unyielding glare. 'This journey just got a whole lot more risky.'

He twisted around to see the girls within the wagon. 'I suggest you tell Jett. Now, and not later.'

Breathless with shock, Earona cried, 'You shouldn't be here.'

Mara's ashen face glowed with perspiration and she exhaled loudly.

The wagon came to stop. Amid a great deal of apprehension and her heart beating erratically, Earona's hands shook as she lifted the back canvas, high enough Mara could be seen. She pointed at the girl and shrugged in bewilderment at Jett, riding some distance behind. He rode closer, a mix of emotions crossed his face; initial disbelief to an intimidating reproachful scowl. He arrived with a menacing frown.

Earona felt the heat of his rage, and she cried, 'I didn't know.'

Ignoring her, Jett's dark enigmatic eyes scrutinized Mara. Her face was a sickly colour and she gave him a tight lipped sulk. He glared with fiery umbrage. 'Why by all the hells are you here after I told you, you weren't to come?'

'I couldn't stay.' Her tone was icy and she gripped the lip of the door, stopping herself from swaying backwards.

'That's not my problem! You've deceived us and those at Sommerlea,' he barked, 'Do they even know where you are?'

Mara's eyes lit up in hostile rebuke. 'They will figure it out.'

'Bloody bollocks! It's reckless and selfish,' he raged, 'we're heading into Kahm knows what, any and every sort of danger. And a whole flamin' kingdom is looking for you. Devil's bloody arse, you had to end up with us!'

'I don't have to stay with you,' she bit back.

Earona looked between them with amazement that Mara had the nerve to stand up to him.

He stared Mara down with a wrathful expression. 'Kael and Jonas will be making plans in regards to you, assuming you are safe at Sommerlea. And you'll be missing, and they'll evoke suspicion, and maybe even put in danger. Who knows what the consequences might be for them. By all the hells! I'll be the one facing any reprimand if something happens to you. Damn it, why are you so pig-headed?!'

'It can't always be about everyone else.' Pouting, she folded her arms and remained stiff.

Earona turned an arrogant gaze on him and gave an agreeing nod.

'It can't always be about you.' He pulled Thunder back from his stamping, and growled, 'I'm in half a mind to ride back and deliver you to them.'

'I'll run.'

An irritated roar erupted from his chest. 'Don't push me! No. If you are here with us, then you are my responsibility and you will do what I say.' He glared, giving her no leeway to respond. His bad temper turned on Earona with a fierce look in his narrowed eyes. *You better not have had anything to do with this!*

I've nothing to do with it! His anger put her on the defensive, regardless of her non-involvement, but she held her tongue, knowing it would only provoke his rage. And this time he had a right to be mad.

Jett shouted, 'Head off, Keanan.' He waited behind, leaving some distance between them.

Earona let the flap fall, and burst out with stormy passion, 'Why are you here?'

Mara fell back on her bottom, her arms still rigid against her chest. 'He's such a swine.' Her eyes flashed with pain.

Earona sighed and rested against the wagon compartment. 'He can be, but… he is right.' She watched Mara's silent tears roll down her cheeks. 'He doesn't mean to be like that.' She attempted consolation, 'He makes me blubber sometimes too.'

'I couldn't be with them, but—' Mara wiped her tears away. 'I don't belong here either.'

Earona rubbed her shoulder. 'It's just difficult right now…'

'I shouldn't have come.' Mara edged away from her. 'I should have gone alone.'

'Gone where?'

Mara shrugged, and murmured, through her sniffles, 'I don't know… away.'

'When we get back we can work out where you will be better off and maybe they will work something out for you.'

She sniffed, 'Maybe…'

'He's certainly a rotten pig about it.' Earona gave Jett's uncaring attitude a reproachful scrutiny. Mara's pretty face was still pasty and within moments she became limp. 'You've been in there all this time?'

Mara whispered, 'I Slept my… mostly.'

Earona gave her a steady look. 'You could have suffocated.'

Irritation peeked in Mara's eyes. 'I don't care…' She lurched back in a mild faint.

~ * ~

After the appearance of Mara, Jett was thrown into a foul mood. The others had responded with astonishment, unsure how to interpret the intentions of the girl. She was becoming more of a mystery the more they discovered about her. For Jett, he knew more than enough.

Pillars by the roadside marked tracks leading into the forest. Inscriptions were in the stone, but Jett was unable to read them. A couple of hours before sundown, Seth came out through the trees with a pleasant grin and a wild pig, and news of a nearby clearing. He guided them to a path on the left, of broken-up paving and gnarled roots, until they arrived at what was left of an old village. Decrepit stone buildings were scattered amongst the trees. Seth pointed out a gap through the leaves, indicating a stream beyond.

Jett instructed them not to roam far and nowhere alone, 'Especially you, Seth,' he ordered with a pointed finger.

Too incensed over Mara, Jett kept away from her and Earona. He helped Marcus with the horses, under a layer of impenetrable silence. No matter how much Marcus tried, he couldn't coax him into conversation. He gave up, but didn't seem to mind the quiet. Jett preferred it that way.

Mara kept close to Earona which was a good thing, because Jett wasn't sure he could rein in his temper if he had to speak to her. Every time he considered her presence, it infuriated him. She brought to mind the evil plans during his transformed state, like a cavernous pull on his sanity. His anger threatened to erupt, revealing his lack of control. Right then, he needed to harness that rage. At least she was avoiding him. Perhaps she could sense his rage. Then again, it wouldn't be difficult. On top of his irritation, he now had to consider her safety as well as his Kin. He let loose a cutting curse, causing Sunny to shake his mane at him. Under his breath, he grumbled, '…a flamin' princess.'

~ * ~

After several hours trying to shift rocks, and not appearing to get any freer, Mouse, the smallest of the boys, ran through the darkness to the men and tugged on Ethan's arm, pulling him up. 'Hurry, I think we found something.'

With a groan of protest, Ethan was dragged along. He had no desire to look at the gems, or face Kenric. The other boys stood waiting at the far end of the chamber. Daskar and Kenric continued chipping away, along with a few of his men. Ethan walked past them, giving his attention to the boys, staring up at the blackness.

Mouse's eyes bulged with excitement. 'Something's up there!'

Ethan peered into the dark, seeing nothing. 'What?'

'We threw the torch up,' explained Derryl, 'Send me up.'

'No, send me,' Mouse whined, 'Der's been flying.'

Ethan's power connected with Mouse's body. They passed the boy a torch and he floated up. Legs swinging, he gave an exhilarated whoop. Nearly fifty feet up was a dark circular opening in the wall. Mouse gave a happy shout as he caught the edge of the hole and lifted himself through.

Bearn, who had been slouched near the entry, came over. He cried with an abundance of pride, 'Good on you, boys.'

Kenric spared them a glimpse and kept digging out the jewels from the wall.

Mouse's light moved and faded as he disappeared into the hole. Finally he reappeared, his grin large enough Ethan could see it from below. Mouse said, 'It's like another chamber. The same type corridors. It's like a special room.'

Ethan nodded, his hope rising. 'Ruegar, go tell the men, hurry.'

Ruegar sprinted off before Ethan finished.

Ethan considered the men pouring into the chamber and whether he could move them all up. On seeing the light above them and Mouse's face poking out from the rock, the men's eyes lit up.

Gailtram asked Ethan, 'What do we do?'

'I'll send you and Stannar up,' Ethan said. 'Take rope, I'm unsure if I have the energy to move everyone.'

Gailtram nodded. 'Move those who can't take the rope.'

'Agreed.'

Bearn and Druce approached Kenric. He stopped hammering to observe what they had found and he nodded. 'I knew there'd be a way.'

Bearn shook his white haired head and his voice rasped in anger. 'You're a bastard who only gave a damn about yourself. What about the boys, did you think of them?'

'This is for them and all of you,' Kenric droned, 'We won't have anything on the outside, nothing.'

Druce replied, as he walked away, 'I'd rather have nothing and be out there.'

Once the two were moved above, the rope fell down against the wall. Those who could climb did so, while Ethan took a rest and ate what was left of his food rations. The boys sat with him in hope they would be lifted up first, but he knew they were light enough to be lifted by the rope. Their enthusiasm caused him to remember his first ride through the air. For Fáerinn children it fast becomes an everyday experience, even so the initial thrill never leaves. Berran, his white blonde hair matted with cave dust, pushed in close. Ethan put his hand around his shoulders, and looked at each boys' grubby face. 'If I have enough energy I will fly you up.'

The four men, hammering at the walls, were unwilling to budge from their tedious work of extracting the gems. No amount of persuasion could induce Ethan and the others to wait for them. The compromise was a small share of the provisions and the rope left dangling. It more than suited the men. Once all were in the above chamber, Loc said, 'We don't have the map.'

'Not so.' Bearn pulled a raggedy piece of parchment from his shirt pocket. 'The craft of my youth never truly left.'

Druce patted him on the back. 'Bearn, you old dog.'

Bull asked with a gleam in his eye, 'He doesn't know?'

The old man laughed merrily. 'He don't know yet.'

'Well then, let's get going.'

The walls of the new room were a lighter stone and smooth from floor to its eight foot ceiling and paved with large flat stones. One out of the two passages was not blocked. Amid renewed optimism they started down the corridor. The group walked at a fast pace while Bearn consulted the map under the light held by Ethan.

~ * ~

The Kin gathered around the fire, their shadows loomed like giant specters against the ruins. After a day of riding it was a comfort to sit on the spongy ground-cover and be still. His back against a stone, Jett was lulled by the hypnotic play of flames, as the Kin conversed around him.

Keanan finished his recount of their exploration of the ruins, 'It might have been an important township in this ancient civilization.'

Marcus lounged on the grassy floor. 'Anything worth looking at?'

'Nothing that would interest you.' Shiarn chuckled.

Earona, wrapped in her blanket, looked at Jett across the fire. 'You know the name of this valley?'

Absorbed with the light, Jett was reluctant to speak. '…Amin-Sayeda.'

She puckered her lips with thoughtful interest. 'Who lived here?'

'The Sayen.' Keanan spoke with furrowed brow. 'As mentioned in the journal.'

Marcus looked to Jett. 'That man from Baion came up that road?'

'True,' Jett replied with preoccupation, 'from Mount Cirrus.'

'Which is?'

Jett waved behind him, in an easterly direction. 'End of those mountains.'

Seth said with gravity, 'Annabella was right, their lands are at war?'

Jett dulled his thoughts with the crackling flames, but the question brought the topic to his mind. 'It seems.' He avoided Seth's probing gaze. 'Ryne have overtaken their lands, and Baion's remaining monarch is held in a siege.' His expression turned sombre as he voiced aloud the situation. Until then he hadn't decided whether he would talk to them of it.

Earona asked with disquiet, 'What does it mean?'

Shiarn answered with impatience, 'No more Baion.'

'And, Ryne will be in a better position to invade Coltrene.' Keanan cast a blatant eye on Mara. 'If that is their plan.'

Jett nodded, letting them speak without the interruption of his own opinion.

Marcus shifted to a sitting position with unease. 'Blood 'n shite.'

'Sommerlea would be in their way,' Hellier said.

Keanan asked Jett, 'Is there no military left to defend their king?'

'There might be troops at the town, Gearoidin Gate, about half a day ride from Havenside, but they were unsure if they were also under siege.'

Keanan replied, 'You studied the map well.'

'What is to become of them?' Earona burst-out.

'Kael and Jonas were to notify the closest border lord, and possibly he will send a relieving troop.' His thoughts full of doubt, Jett continued, 'Or Coltrene will begin to make plans.'

The Kin spent dismal moments visualizing the outcome of an invading Rynian army marching through to Coltrene.

Seth interrupted their sinking thoughts, 'It seems hopeless.'

Earona wailed, 'Is there nothing that can be done?'

Keanan looked across to Earona's pleading eyes. 'I imagine many troops would be involved. It would take Coltrene days if not weeks to mobilize its forces.'

Jett sighed at the despondency going back and forth in the thoughts of the Kin. 'Coltrene might be moving an army to meet Ryne on its border.'

Marcus said, 'How did this happen without anyone knowing?'

Breaking the stilted silence, Mara's sullen voice came from the folds of her blanket. 'The queen is manipulating things behind the scenes.'

Jett lifted his eyes from the fire in suspicion. 'How much do you know of it?'

'I'm…I know the sort of person she is.' Mara kept her face fixed on the dancing flames. 'Before I left she had visits from mysterious strangers which included Blood Writ priests from the Marsoud temple. I overheard them speak about creatures, I think they were called the Zherans.'

Earona peered at her over her own blanket and cried, 'Why didn't you mention this before?'

Mara drilled her with a fervent stare. 'I only recalled it now, and really I don't know what they are.'

Jett narrowed his eyes with doubt. 'What did these "mysterious strangers" say of it?'

Mara snapped, 'I tried eavesdropping but didn't hear much.'

Keanan shook his head with shocked dismay. 'It seems the queen has access to those with knowledge of dark forces.'

'Creatures from the time of Wrath…' Jett muttered under his breath. Along with what he knew of Mara, it created a new dimension to what had befallen the lands of Baion.

Mara asked, 'What are they?'

Jett's piercing gaze made sure she understood. 'You don't need to know.'

Mara's brows darkened with annoyance.

'So…' Hellier piped up through the cold tension that followed, 'while all this is going on we are more or less headed into it?'

'In a way.' Dragging his eyes from Mara's pinched expression, Jett gave a weary sigh. 'We shall ride up this road until it meets the crossroads. We take the east road and make our way closer to the Arranons.' He glanced at their tired faces. 'Traveling through the forest should keep us away from any movement of the Rynians. It is late, we need to sleep. We put out the fire and keep a watch.'

Earona said, 'But what about the Baions?'

Jett stood. 'There's nothing we can do for them.'

Shiarn said, 'We have to find Ethan.'

'We must,' Jett added.

'Perhaps after…' Earona looked into his eyes for some glimmer of hope.

Jett reached down for her hand and pulled her up. 'When we find Ethan I think I'd be willing to do anything.' *But…*

'It may be too late for them,' she whispered.

'You can't help everyone you come across.' Jett's tone turned sour. His uncaring opinion was normal, but this time more troubling matters were on his mind.

~ * ~

Ethan and the Harn reached another chamber with random paving, but the same white walls. Two corridors led off it. Bearn scrutinized the map and the boys dashed past. Berran slid into a half concealed black hole. A weighty thud followed. Ethan and Luz leaned their heads into the hole.

'I'm fine,' Berran's small voice came from below, 'give me a light.'

Ethan passed him a torch, while stretching his arm in front of Mouse, preventing him from jumping after Berran.

They could hear scrabbling over rubble. The men looked at each other in puzzlement.

'It's amazing!' Berran finally yelled.

Ethan jumped down, deciding it best to view the area himself. He landed on what appeared to be a pile of broken slabs. On closer examination, it was a cracked sarcophagus. Standing amongst the debris, he observed the new surroundings. Decorated pillars were in the corners of a narrow chamber. Coloured inscriptions and pictures adorned the cream walls. A musky foul odour was unlike all the other caverns they had passed. He breathed shallow, not wanting to fully inhale the unclean air.

He circled the room, viewing the ancient murals on the walls. He could not discern the era of the writing nor could he understand the symbols. The images were lucid scenes of dark skinned people dressed in sheer gowns. Seemingly, they narrated symbolic episodes of the lives of the people who must have inhabited the underground tunnels. Rows of majestic black clad soldiers, all armed with axe and sword took up one wall. In between these warriors, a woman prevailed as a beautiful monarch clothed in red. On top of a pyramid, appeared a white ball. He stepped closer, and noticed a sort of ivory and gold sphere in its center. Peering closer still, he realized it was similar to the amulet Jett gave Shiarn. Ethan found the picture perplexing.

Berran shouted, 'You've got to see this.' His face flushed, he waved at Ethan to come through the door.

Ethan dragged himself away from the other scenes to follow the lad through a broken hole in the chamber. The door was framed by jagged rock and did not appear to be a doorway at all, but a hole blasted in the stone. It made him wonder what had occurred in the tomb. He glanced at the empty sarcophagus again with a stab of fear something or someone had destroyed it. As he continued studying the cracked slabs, his eye was drawn to a carving on the wall next to the remains of the door. He circled the figure eight with his finger in fascination, certain it was the same shape as the medallion taken from him. It looked to be a keyhole of some type. But a key to what, he could only speculate as the tomb was empty.

In wonder, he moved from the destroyed coffin and entered a chamber with an end he could not see and a ceiling that loomed into darkness. The impressive size of the chamber was not what held his attention, but the two lines on both sides of the massive stretch, of seven foot faceless statues. In the torch-light their black armour was like dense shadows. Each one possessed a half-moon axe, a bow, and an exotic curved sword, all made with malreus. Ethan exhaled sharply, awestruck by the realization the pictures within the tomb were these same warriors.

The peace of the room was disrupted by the Harn entering the chamber. Their expressions were similar to Ethan's. Unlike Ethan they noticed the waist high ceramic vases overflowing with gems. The boys wasted no time. Bypassing the jewels, they went after the weapons.

Ethan slid out an axe and examined its black gleaming surface of a superior malreus. He balanced it in his hand; a good weight. The men stuffed their pockets with jewels before they undressed the statues and pilfered their weapons.

Bearn walked to the end of the room. His light revealed an opening. 'Let's keep moving.' He poured over the map and said, 'I'll wager they made a mistake. This is the Chamber of Treasure.' He considered the men dressing themselves and cramming jewels into bags. They had for the most part dropped their picks and chisels and were equipped with swords and axes, and were putting on helms and armour. Lacking the strength to carry armour, the boys slung bows over their backs and the quivers dangled by their knees.

'Is it wise to be robbing what appears to be someone's tomb?' Bearn asked with satirical seriousness.

Con said, 'There's no one in the tomb.' In his hand was a long axe and over his armoured back a curved sword was attached.

Slung over his back, Grith wore a black shield with bright gold worked into its surface, and a sword was beneath it. He displayed his usual cynicism. 'Aye, that's a worry, ain't it?'

'That's why we should be taking what we can,' Dein, similarly attired to Con, said in earnest.

Bearn shook his head comically at the sight of them. Noticing Druce among them, carrying a sword and tying on a black vest, he remarked, 'You too? Truly, are we just like Kenric?'

'I'm not going to miss out.' Druce grinned devilishly. 'This stuff will be worth a fortune.'

'If everyone is ready we shall keep moving.' Bearn looked them over. 'We don't have much food.'

'More important,' said Loc, 'We don't have much light.'

'Right then.'

~ * ~

Stars sparkled between clumps of clouds, and the breezeless air was cool under the trees' night shade. Jett, his knees drawn up, leaned against a pine sheltering their camp, and nestled into the shadows with a view of the sleeping Kin. Earona, swathed in her blankets, rose from her sleeping place and tip-toed towards him.

Jett sighed with exasperation as she plonked herself near his feet. He remained under the shield of his hood, and his hushed tone was harsh. 'I don't want to hear it. You know why I don't want her here.'

She gave him an accusing glare, but did not respond.

'You seem to forget where we are going. It's hard enough you are coming. But she is being hunted by those slave traders,' his voice increased with wrath as he expressed his fears, 'and probably the ones who have Ethan. I'll be leading her right to them.'

She dropped her head and stared at her hands. 'I real—'

'This on top of her being wanted by the King of Ryne,' he grumbled on, 'What if we are caught with her?'

'She can speak in our defence.' Earona looked up with a scowl.

Jett grunted his irritation. 'I doubt it would be that easy. Someone will need to be blamed.' He continued, 'And worse than all of them, is the entity that sort her out in Lanvin.'

Earona gasped with her hand over her mouth. 'What was that?'

Jett gritted his teeth, realizing it hadn't been discussed.

'You aren't talking about those Baskharefs?' Her blue eyes widened in the moonlight. 'It's something worse?'

'Yes.'

'But, but…' she stammered, 'if she were left at Sommerlea…'

'Don't need to worry about that now.' His tone turned grim. 'Something else is bothering me, how much does she know about us?'

She stiffened. 'Probably more than she ought.'

Jett spoke with cold rage. 'She knows of Tellávare?'

'She knows we have Gifts, well, me and Shiarn at least,' she responded with a trembling voice. *Oh, probably Ethan too.*

His voice was severe under the shadows of his cloak. 'Considering what and who she is it's enough. Not only have our secrets been revealed, but to one such as her.'

Her cheeks red, Earona lowered her gaze.

'We have left a trail of ourselves across the land, starting from Lanvin, and who knows what people have seen in Floris.' He paused, 'Even my actions in the city may cause condemnation from home,' *but if they hear about my corruption in Sommerlea and a possible Gate opening, the consequences will be dire.* 'There's also your Gift glorified in the temple.'

'You know?'

'Shiarn mentioned something about it.'

She sighed, pursing her lips together. 'I really did forget about that…'

'The implications could be disastrous.' He looked away, not wanting to be too judgmental. His decisions would leave an obvious trace of the supernatural any Fáerinn could discern if they were looking. 'If the Eldery found out about my demonic descent and the manifestation of power, they have the right to call us back.' *I'm sure that potential trouble will raise its ugly head in time. Damn that cursed prophecy—*

'What prophecy?' she glared expectantly.

He grimaced. 'Tch.' He no longer had the paper it was written on, recalling how he lost it. It was one of the only things that didn't evoke shame. After some moments, he decided she had to be told, now. 'We were given it by the Seers. It wasn't encouraging…'

'Is it really…' She sucked in her breath and held it for some surprised moments, '…awful?'

'That's open to interpretation.' He added, 'If you must know, to some it is.'

Earona stared at him, her bright eyes bulging with apprehensive shock, and she squeaked, 'Why didn't you say something?'

'Because,' he sighed, 'of how you are reacting right now.' *You're scared out of your mind and you haven't even heard it.* 'I don't want you to be worried about it.'

'Worried?! Of course I'm worried!' she wailed. *And scared.* 'And angry! You were dishonest.'

'No, I just didn't tell you.'

She tilted her head back and took a calming intake of air. 'Fine then. Well, tell me what it is.'

He lowered his brows at her in consternation.

'On second thought, don't.' Gripping his arm, she added, 'I don't want to know, do I?'

'Probably not. The Circle didn't want us to leave because of it—'

With her hand over her mouth, she gasped. 'It is bad!'

'And with the near destruction of the Kin and now travelling in the opposite direction of where we are supposed to go, and into a potential war, is not going to help, and having the runaway with us could worsen the whole situation.' He contemplated Mara once more, as he had been throughout the afternoon. 'And why is she here with us? I don't like it. She would have been safer at Sommerlea.' He lowered his voice. 'I'm not even free to speak about anything in front of her.' After a broody pause, and before Earona could respond, he went on, 'She knows too much.' *Too much about me.* She knew far more about his demonic transformation than she was saying. 'Flamin' arse, she shouldn't even know about dark magik, or Zherans. But she does.'

In a weak whisper, she said, 'Has she anything to do with the prophecy?'

'Who knows? I really don't care. I'm more interested in her motivation,' he eyed the camp, spying the girl asleep. *The prophecy will be, come what may, but this, I should be able to control.*

She looked him over with shock, her blue eyes glowing like pools. 'But why shouldn't we trust her?'

'Because of what she can do.'

Earona frowned pensively over his words, *could you be right? No, she can't be dangerous…*

He observed her silence and shook his head knowingly.

She whispered, 'She doesn't have evil intentions.'

You don't know half of what she is capable of. 'You suspected something back in Lanvin.' His scowl remained fixed on her turned away face. 'You knew about that scar-mark?'

She frowned with vexation. 'I had no idea it was significant in anyway,' *besides, I really didn't have much of a chance to tell you.* 'But, the spirit called it a ward. Doesn't that mean it will help her?'

Despite that, he had been able to overpower it. 'Provided it has regenerated.' He contemplated how dangerous she could be if she were controlled again – with the ability to summon the dead. But could she do it without him?

'I was thinking…' Earona started with a sharp whisper, 'Why don't you put that symbol on your skin too?'

As usual her questioning drove him mad, even more so because in this instance he couldn't speak of it so freely. 'I—' He seriously considered telling her the truth, that he already wore the mark on his skin, but that would mean letting centuries of secrets loose. 'Tried.' He threw his hand down on his knee in frustration.

'But…' Earona blinked in disbelief. 'It would be easy for you?'

The question was feasible, he had been tattooing for years, even creating his own style of design. But this was more than a simple pattern. 'It needs to be made by someone with authority. I assume a ritual would be involved.'

She nodded her acceptance, her eyes forming starry saucers. 'I wonder who did Mara's?'

'Her grandmother.' He added, 'I assume the woman at the place she was staying at.'

Crawling closer to see Jett's staunch face, she whispered, 'I'm sure Mara would help, if she could.'

He sighed at her eagerness. 'That's not important. I'm concerned her motivations are not genuine. If she deceives us the consequences could be deadly, and for those at home too.'

'She has not shown any maliciousness towards us.'

Jett's voice was gruff. 'There'd only be one time.'

Her hand went to her hip in protest. 'Well, it's fine for you.'

He glowered at her low remark. 'Unlike me, there's something in her past that we don't know about. As you say, the ability to cast spells.'

'It's true I guess, but… she's still so young.' She said in a fervent whisper, 'Try to be civil. She thinks you hate her.'

'She's in good company then.' He noted her disdain. 'But I have said she is my responsibility and I will be watching her, and I don't give a devil's arse if she's royalty or not, if she makes me think she has some ulterior motive I'll take drastic action.'

Frightened by his menacing words, she fell back. 'Heaven's peace, she's only a child!'

'Doesn't make me any more trusting.'

'Please don't make me think something awful is happening to you again.'

He snorted with derision. 'Are you going to say that every time I say something you disagree with? God, I hope not.' *Alright, I will try to be more pleasant. To her.*

She smiled smugly, and abruptly wrapped him in a blanket covered embrace, and said with whimsy, 'I guess it's people like me that make up for people like you.'

People like me? Unmoving beneath the curtain of wool, he muttered, 'If it weren't for you I doubt we would even be here hundreds of miles from our destination.'

'Meany,' she snapped and drew back. *And Ethan wouldn't be where he is…*

'I heard he had a rough time in the dungeon?'

'I found it horrendous.'

Her guilt left a ripple of pain in his thoughts. 'Who is to say what might have been or not. This is where we are now. We will get him back one way or another.' He ordered, 'Now, go to sleep and don't think I've forgotten what we spoke about.'

'Of course not. Night.'

'Night to you too.'

With a slight smile of affection, Jett watched her huddle off, still enfolded in her blanket.

Earona fell upon her cushion beside Mara. The movement of Marcus' head startled her, and he whispered, 'Was he giving you a hard time?'

She could barely see his expression, but felt he was asking in good humour. 'Nothing out of the usual.'

He nodded as if he needed confirmation.

After they said goodnight to each other, Earona had a broad grin on her face. She had shared a brief conversation with Marcus albeit a few words, but it was more than they had spoken together lately. She had also managed to tame Jett for the time being although his revelation of a prophecy was a jagged stone in her head, aggravating her. Half of her wanted to know the words, yet the other, more fearful side, didn't even want to know there was a prophecy. Perhaps Jett knew her better than she thought. As she settled down to sleep she wondered about the boy, Mal and why she had suddenly stopped dreaming of him again. He had been so prevalent in her dreams, now he was nowhere to be found.

72 - We Go This Way

Adversity is a strong wall
Only the hammer of determination will break through

The Sleeping Sword

After the vaulted treasure chamber, Ethan and the men entered tunnels dissimilar to what they previously traveled. Instead of pale grey stone, the walls were iron with chunks of black-gold. The corridors were narrow and in some places fallen stones caused the men to stumble in the muted light.

Once Bearn located the real treasure room on the map he was able to read it with more success. Following the intricate map was a testing time for them. Ethan's trust was in Bearn, and after Kenric's betrayal it was not an easy task. They walked through tunnels clear of blockage except for loose rocks they stepped over. Bearn headed the weary group, pausing at intervals to regain some type of bearing. Nearing the point of complete exhaustion, conversation was non-existent. Ethan drove himself on, not willing to lie down and die until he was physically incapable of moving.

In the subdued silence a piercing scream echoed off the solid walls. The disturbing noise cut through the oppression of the stifling tunnels, creating an eerie foreboding in Ethan's already downcast heart. After moments of initial panic, he discerned it was at a distance behind them.

Mouse glanced up at Bearn. 'What is that?'

Loc said, 'I hope we don't found out.'

'I don't know, Mouse,' replied Bearn, 'but let's keep moving.'

The strange cry sounded out in random bursts. It seemed some way behind, but for how long they could not even guess. There was no way of measuring the time they had walked nor even the distance they had trekked.

Eventually a halt was called. The first in the line had arrived at a cramped chamber with coarse russet walls and a floor caked with black dust. Similar to the floor, the roof was a deeper brown. Bearn circled the new chamber with the one remaining light. His soiled face could not hide his shocked dismay.

Ethan ducked his head to enter the low ceiling room. The boys piled in behind him, and those who could fit looked equally disappointed at what was just a natural cave. Outside the chamber, the men grew impatient.

'But it points this way.' Bearn swooped the lantern towards the opposite end of the confined space. 'Here!'

Ethan placed a firm hand on the stone opposite the entry. The rock was completely flat and unyielding. Crouching near the cold wall, he scowled at where a doorway should be. He and Loc shoved on the wall as if it might budge under their combined weight. It was dense immovable rock.

In the distance, the wail of the creature echoed through the passages, drawing nearer. Stannar stood outside the doorway. 'At least we can fight it.'

Bearn surveyed the chamber, his hands sliding in vain across the flat iron. Again, he dissected the map in a panic with Loc and Gailtram looking over his shoulder. Avoiding the defeated stares of the men looking into the room, Ethan sat with a crushing realization they were trapped. After more hysterical dithering from Bearn, the old man nearly collapsed, blaming himself for his poor navigational skills.

The group slouched like broken men, even the boys took a seat in the dirt. In the stretching shadowy darkness no one cast an eye onto each other. No one wished to voice the question of whether they should continue with the journey - the journey had finished.

~ * ~

Adis stepped through the night shadows, his footfalls making no sound on the bracken. Since Mara's disappearance, he had scouted the woods for word on the direction of her path. Not one tree noted her passing. She left with no flora aware of her travel. He could only hope she was with Jett, although the presence of the girl would not bode well for them.

Subtle warblings of nocturnal beasts was a soothing hum in the night air. He swept past familiar trunks of old friends, enjoying their serene voices through his Naturist Gift. As was his custom, he touched them in greeting. He soon noted a disturbance in their normally placid mood. Finally, arriving at an aged oak, the master of those on the slope, he received a warning to leap up. Catching hold of its branches, he reached deeper into the tree's protection.

The leaves shook in a sudden erratic wind. Below him, silhouettes moved between the trees. Listening to the breeze, he heard voices. One he recognized; a boy who worked at the vineyard. Inching closer to the lower branches, Adis strained to see two men clothed in black standing over the boy. His initial fear for the teenager lessened when he heard their cordial greeting.

A man's voice was low and emotionless. 'Did you find the girl?'

The adolescent replied, 'She was here, but she's gone now.'

'Where?'

The boy pointed through the forest. 'Northeast, along the road yonder.'

'When?'

'Dawn.'

'Alone?'

'No, with several others.'

'Guardians?'

'Probably. They're the suspicious ones from that town,' the boy grumbled, seemingly without fear of recrimination, 'If you turn up on time you could find out for yourself.'

'Rafah, if you cared about your job you would be more helpful.'

Adis observed the boy, recalling his name, Shamus. Now he wondered who he really was.

'We are wasting time.' The other man, his voice similar to the first, stated, 'If we leave now, we will eventually catch them.'

The boy asked, 'You going on foot?'

The men appeared to ignore his question and the first one said, 'Reinforcements will come from the southeast and continue to the meeting point. They might be a day behind, nevertheless we shall see them.'

'We catch her and get this over with.'

'We shall leave now.' The man turned to the boy, 'You'll come with us.'

The boy whined, 'This body will not stand the pace you set.'

'You'll go as far as that body allows,' the man ordered.

'We must depart.' The other started off.

The cloaked figures left the scene in silence. The boy followed amidst the shadows of numerous dark clad figures creeping under the veil of darkness with quiet stealth.

After they departed, Adis swung down from the covering branches, giving the tree his thanks. He was in no doubt to whom they referred. With urgent speed, he made his way back to the house. First he would inform the others what he had witnessed. Then, make preparations to leave. This time he would not remain idle while potentially catastrophic events unfolded.

~ * ~

Except for the eerie wail in the distance, Ethan and the Harn sat in an exhausted silence. Amid mumbling and a great deal of condemnation, Bearn pored over the map. Defeat was reflected in dull eyes and hands quivering with fear. Not being able to bear the finality of their journey, Ethan laid his head in his hands and wished he was free to express his misery.

In the dismal space, Mouse's voice was a squeak. 'There's a different smell here.' The stagnant air held a strange acidic odour mixed with rotten vegetation.

Ethan was sorry for the boys, and hearing Mouse's young voice made it tragic beyond his comprehension. His body was rigid and aching in the cramped space and he longed to breathe fresh air. There was no way any of them could stay in the room and still be able to breathe without effort.

Ethan stood, wishing he could stretch his arms and keep moving. If he stopped for a rest now, he may never get back up again. His arm continued to sting, and his back seized with a sudden cramp, the result of journeying through the narrow crawl spaces. His head knocked the ceiling. A sprinkle of rubble brushed his hair and scattered annoyingly down his back. His hand shook his matted hair and touched against the ceiling's surface, releasing a handful of dirt covered pebbles.

Mouse spread the dirt and gravel with his bare, dust coated toes. Noting its loosened state, Ethan burrowed his fingers into the ceiling. His fingers went deep and he scraped out a fistful of densely compacted rubble. Mouse jumped up to help him, and reaching high, started digging into the ceiling with his fingertips. Clumps of dirt dropped across the chamber.

'Stop!' Ethan ordered. 'Bearn, pass me your pick.' One of the only men still carrying one. Once equipped, he hacked at the ceiling while those in the chamber stood back. With unrelenting hope driving him, Ethan reached up to dent the rocks and grab at the loose stones. Russet dirt and black pebbles fell onto his face. He turned his face and kept digging and scratching at the compliable surface. Finally, after breathless moments, he thrust his hand high into the unsecured rocks and felt free air on the other side.

Bearn hopped with excitement. 'Once again we did not think vertically.'

Ethan said nothing and continued clawing at the larger stones, sending wads of dirt scattering over heads until he dug a hole large enough for a child to pass through. Beaming with cheer, he faced the men. 'A boy will fit. Who wants to go first?'

All the boys gathered around him, pleading for his attention. Mouse pulled on his arm, tears filling his eyes. Ethan lifted him up and pushed him through and passed him the second remaining light.

Ethan and all the men waited for Mouse to send word down to them. Finally, Ethan decided to push the other boys through and any man who fit. Gradually all four boys were up, but the three stood in darkness. Mouse had gone ahead into the cavern. A mighty bellow and a frantic cry came from above.

'Devil's arse!' Ethan cried in frustration.

Branan pushed past Ethan and pulled himself through the ruptured ceiling.

Above, the yelling amplified, becoming a frenzied commotion of jumping and leaping amid chaotic hollering. The light returned to them and Mouse sang in jubilance, 'We're free! We're free! It's the outside.'

Branan's head appeared through the opening, relief shining on his dirt smeared face. 'Did you hear? The outside. At the end of this cave.'

Word passed to the waiting men, and the idea they were finally liberated spread like a comforting fire. Relieved tears flowed, and embraces were shared by all.

Mouse stuck his head down, his smiling mouth a light in the dark.

Bearn asked, 'You sure, Mouse?'

He nodded merrily. 'Sure as a poke in the eye. It's night. It's bright and the trees and clouds are so high, and stars, a beautiful blanket of jewels, better than any cavern gems.'

Despite the men being eager to climb out they had to remain cautious, having no wish to collapse the chamber so close to freedom. It was a tight fit for most even after Ethan cleaved a better sized hole.

Once the last man climbed to the cave above, Ethan moved the stones to fit his body and he caused much dirt and rocks to fall down. The cavern appeared to be naturally made with rock overhangs, unlike the tunnels they had traveled. Loc took a steady grip of his wrist and hauled him out. The majority of men had disappeared down the cave. Ethan stood to catch his breath and his stomach growled with hunger. Grinning, he said to Loc, 'We made it.'

'Aye, we're free, I can hardly believe it.'

'Let's go see it.' Ethan started off in the direction of the vague light and high-spirited voices.

The men ran, stumbling and tripping with elation, down the rocky green incline to the spreading pine woodland. After the dark sunless spaces the light of the night sky was more than adequate to view a path by. They made a queer sight, resembling grey ghosts of old warriors coming up from under the earth. Their faces hidden under dirt and encrusted beards, and their hair, thick with cave dust. Over their dusty ripped clothing they bore black shining armour and weapons of a long-ago age. An intriguing spectacle, made more so by their insane howls, celebrating their release into the world of open sky.

Ethan did not rush like the others, but ambled past the rocks, careful not to slip on the dewy grass as some of the others had done. He breathed deep of the sweet fresh air and took everything in at once; the sky and tall closely spaced trees, the line of ranges. The mountain they emerged from, loomed portentously against the sky. The notion they traveled through it seemed incredulous and unbelievable. It was more than good to be free, it was exhilarating.

He and Loc went down to meet some of the group at the edge of the trees. Ethan sat on the broken undergrowth of wild foliage and vines, listening to their chatter. They discussed how Luz and some others were searching for water and taking the bows to hunt. The men were too charged with adrenalin to sleep properly neither did it matter to them whether it was night or day when they did. Ethan dozed, thinking it would be a glorious sight to see the sun again.

After some hours, Ethan woke to a sore back and a parched throat. It was not his physical ailments that roused him, but the light of day. Through the speckled shade, sunlight warmed his skin. He sat dazed, watching the gentle movement of the spindly pine. His Kin were in his dreams and he almost thought he would see them coming through the trees.

Faint voices floated on the air and a delightful smell that caused him to salivate. He stood with shaking legs and walked in the direction of the voices.

Berran broke through the conifers. His blue soulful eyes spotted Ethan and he grinned. 'About time you woke up!' He took Ethan's arm and led him past the trees.

Ethan had rested but it only highlighted his overwhelming need for food and water. They had set up a type of camp by a stream. Men were half naked washing, while others slept, most sat around talking, eating, and laughing.

Loc handed him a skin of water which he downed quickly as he sat by the fire. Con and Val roasted a boar, using the last of the long chisels to stick the pig on thick pronged branches. Watching the meat crackle, Ethan could not wait to eat real food. Dry hard biscuits did nothing for his appetite.

'If you want to wash up feel free.' Val spoke through his tangled brown beard to Ethan. 'Most of this lot have eaten. This is our second.'

Ethan was torn between filling his stomach and refreshing himself with water he could see. He decided having clean hands to eat would be a nice change. Crouching by the streamlet, he looked for the boys. A few of the Harn were also missing. He came back to the fire and listened to a debate over the direction they should take. Ethan took the cut meat coming his way and after swallowing a good mouthful, said, 'Where are we anyway?'

Loc also took a slice. 'Bearn reckons we're in no-man's land… free country.'

'I'm guessing Coltrene is to the west.' Druce pointed along the ranges.

The boys' rowdy laughter spoilt the tranquil woods as they approached with Branan, lifting their prizes for all to see. Large plump birds.

Ethan asked of Loc, 'What were you arguing about?'

Loc showed a touch of colour in his cheeks and looked embarrassed. 'There's been talk as to where we should go.'

Ethan gobbled up the meat and reached for more. 'And?'

'And… we,' Grith spread his arm over the Harn, 'want to go northwest, hopefully towards Baion, maybe get a ship to Stonharn.'

'And we.' Druce nodded at the few remaining Coltrenians. 'Were thinking about heading back into Coltrene.'

Dropping their catches, the boys rushed to squat at Ethan's feet. Mouse's bright eyes looked up without the underlying stress present for the duration of their friendship. 'Me and the lads want to go with you.' His childlike voice rose with ardent passion. 'You know we wouldn't be a burden, we'd look after ourselves and you.'

Ethan studied their youthful expressions and eyes staring with optimism, and realized they were serious. How could he be responsible for children? His large calloused hand ruffled the boy's hair. 'Don't you have family and homes to go to?'

Mouse shrugged. 'I've only known the ships. Same with Derryl.'

'Me family's killed,' Berran said. 'Ruegar's got family but he don't know for sure if they are still alive.' He looked at Ruegar nodding.

Ethan was so intent on reaching freedom he hadn't thought what he would do once gaining it.

Bearn watched him with a cheerful glint in his eyes.

Loc pursed his lips and appeared more understanding of the predicament.

Ethan turned back to the boys eagerly waiting his reply. 'I'm not sure, you see, I'm going back to Floris.'

Loc grimaced and his shoulders sagged, 'Thought as much.'

'Floris!' cried Bull, 'Look at you, boy?'

Ethan had removed the malreus mail so he could sit comfortably, leaving him with a dirty shirt far too small for his large chest. Ingrained grime was on his face, and his hair had not seen a brush in many days and his beard had never seen one. The iron was hammered off, yet the evidence of their presence still remained. His red raw skin attempted to heal but never did completely.

'You got those wounds.' Bull indicated to his wrists. 'Plus, if anyone sees your tat you face being rearrested, or worse.'

Ethan had noticed no such tattoos on them, whereas his numbers were obvious to all. It was a foolhardy expedition, but he had little choice. 'I have to find my friends.' His shoulders slumped at the idea of going back to the city. 'I've got to try.'

'I know, lad.' Loc put a warm hand on his back and glanced at the Harn.

As much as Ethan liked the boys, how could he consider taking them back into a dangerous environment and even so, if he was successful, what then? He looked over to Bearn. 'What about you Bearn, where will you go?'

Bearn's white beard and hair was almost free of black dust, and a rosy glow filled his cheeks. He replied with happy contentment, 'Back to Wylespie by the coast, buy me a little boat, do some fishing.'

Ethan nodded, realizing he was dodging the subject at hand. 'Sounds fine that.'

'I will go with you, Ethan,' Branan said, the one who had been antagonistic towards him from the beginning. 'I want to find Gart.'

Loc's firm hand settled on Ethan's back. 'Aye, guess that settles it for me. I'll come with you. I'm not finished with you yet. I don't know about these cobbers.'

'I'll follow Duan-Shai,' Gailtram cast a look at the others to see a mix of agreeing and disgruntled nods. 'We all will.'

Druce gave Ethan a pleased grin. 'Then we all continue on together.'

73 - Messengers

Do not question if your enemy will attack
Only determine in what form certain attack will come

Empirical Warfare Command

Adis, Morias, and Clara set off in the coolness of predawn. By late afternoon they had traveled a substantial distance. Adis glanced over his shoulder at Morias and Clara making good speed behind him. Shaking his head, he smiled with fondness. He had woken them the night before with a hasty explanation he was going to catch Jett and hopefully find Mara with them. They were concerned about Mara's disappearance, but their reaction was still a surprise. Before he knew what was happening, Clara came downstairs dressed in Kael's trousers and shirt, and in an excited flurry, she rushed off to prepare provisions. Morias reacted in a similar fashion, although he came down with all manner of weapons. Adis had not been prepared for the others to accompany him and was at a loss as to how to stop them. When he spoke of it, Clara was adamant she not be left behind. Adis' remarked on how Kael would oppose the decision. Clara scoffed, she had her own mind and she was going to use it and besides, Kael was off doing his own thing.

In the dark, they bid farewell to Lelana and set off at a fast trot into the valley. Adis planned to travel through the woods parallel to the right of the main road, but his principal concern was their pace. They rode fast and rested the horses often while Clara tended them with healing relief. It was imperative they catch them or the endeavor would be in vain.

They had already made several short stops, but fortunately the path they followed provided space to move at a good speed. Partly concealed paths ran perpendicular from the Arranons on their right. Deeper in, the tall conifers would form the mass of the woods which would hamper their travel.

He kept close to a creek, providing continual watering for the horses and at every stop he spoke with the trees and other foliage. The troop were not a great way ahead, but on the main road through the valley. Jett and the others were a day ahead, but traveling into unknown territory with a wagon and several horses. It would be anyone's guess where they might currently be.

They crossed many roads, but as yet not riding down any. Adis led them to the stream and they dismounted for some respite. The horses drank and Clara stroked them with her healing touch.

Adis rested his hands on a tree by the stream.

Morias gulped down his water and observed Adis. *Are we really able to do anything? And what about Clara traveling into danger?*

Clara embraced Morias' arm with affection. 'It doesn't matter about that, this is the right thing to do.'

If anything happens to you, Morias warned, 'I don't think I'd want to go back.'

'And what about Lel?' She attempted to pin down his worried brown eyes, but he averted his gaze. 'Don't worry. Three of us are better than one or none for that matter. Isn't that right, Adis?'

Adis turned to them with a grave look. 'I do agree, but we need to move quicker.'

Once again they mounted and as they did, Clara asked, 'I still don't understand, was Shamus working for the Rynians?'

Adis had already started off and he replied over his shoulder, 'It was dark, but I don't believe they were Rynians. The men spoke with unfamiliar accents.'

Clara went on, 'And you say Shamus was not really Shamus?'

'I'm not certain who he really is.' Adis set his horse on a faster walk.

She lost his attention and turned to Morias. 'That boy has been around the house on at least two occasions I can recall.'

'I've noticed him.'

She huffed, 'We have to be stricter with who is working at the house.'

'That's more difficult than you say.'

They rode on in silence before Clara cried, 'What if someone has seen Shiarn?'

Morias answered, 'I can't think who would have. In any case it can't be helped now.'

Riding single-file through the intertwining trees did not allow for idle chatter and Clara made do with sending her thoughts to the two.

The light of day was waning towards the west. Adis called a halt and they dismounted to stretch their legs while Clara went over the horses. Morias stood beside Clara, 'How are the horses?'

'Alby is getting fatigued.' Clara rubbed Morias' white horse. 'He's the only one not accustomed to this exercise. The other two have good stamina.' She spoke softly to the horse. 'In fact, I shall ride him, no offence to you.'

Morias replied gruffly, 'None taken.'

Adis came to them through the trees. 'The water is bending up towards the mountains.'

'Will they be on this side?' Morias asked.

'I thought they would be, but,' Adis pointed to the mountains in the northeast, 'I think they might have kept to the main roadway.'

Clara asked, 'Are the armed men far off?'

Adis noticed the tiredness in their faces. 'We have come a long way and they are still ahead of us.'

'We'll not get to Jett before them,' Morias stated.

Adis stared in the direction they were facing as if he could see past the trees. 'But we can get there.'

Clara said with cheer, 'And that's just as good.'

Adis changed the subject. 'How are the horses?'

'They're holding out well, it's just Alby…' Clara added, 'he's unfit.'

'You can ride him,' Adis suggested.

'What are you all saying?' Morias looked indignant. 'I've put on too much weight?'

Laughing, Adis patted his well-rounded middle. 'Not saying anything.'

'I'll have you know I still manage to do what I need to do.'

'I'm sure you do,' Clara affirmed with condescension. 'In any case, it's probably all that equipment you are carrying.' A large axe hung over his pack, a long sheathed sword was at his side and a shield wrought with malreus was slung on the side of his horse.

Morias stated with sarcastic wit, 'I forgot my helm.'

'You are a wonder, Mory.' Clara gave him a warm smile.

Adis squinted at the setting sun. He was about to mount when he felt a tremor from the trees. Peculiar sounds upset the peace of the surrounding forest and he stood alert to every movement he could gather. A rumbling growl put them on guard. It soon became a number of roars melding with shouts of terror.

Morias' eyes lit up with anticipation. 'Is that wolves?'

'It's not natural.' Adis crouched low and the roar sounded out again. 'Come, perhaps it is them. Leave the horses, it's not far.'

~ * ~

Once the men from the mountain determined their direction, they made slow progress through the woods. Ethan seemed to be the only one wanting to get somewhere fast. The men walked at their leisure, chatting together as if out for a stroll. Water was ever present and a plethora of animals to hunt. Also in high spirits, the boys wrestled each other and anyone who took them on, and they climbed trees and just as adeptly jumped from them.

The men admired each other's weapons and armour, happy with their spoils from their mountain adventure. Ethan studied the axe he had taken, pleased with its craftsmanship, but less so it was stolen. Near the top of the black plated shaft was a gold design twisted in intricate patterns, and the head itself was made with malreus. He reminisced about his own axe, most likely stacked in the armory of the jailhouse. Like the other men, he wore armour, but unlike them he felt guilty at raiding the tomb. The armour was obviously ceremonial and here they were, dirty men running through the forest wearing bits and pieces. How were they supposed to move about in civilization attired in such a way he had no idea. The men also had pockets full of gems, not to mention their bags. It only caused him to consider Kenric and Daskar; their greed had betrayed them all.

Nightfall was approaching and they stopped near running water to make a camp. The boys and some of the Harn had already disappeared to hunt even though they were doing it throughout the day. Ethan thought how much he would love a good scrub with soap when shouting startled him.

Growls came through the forest, and they grew to a ferocious volume. It was dissimilar to the sound of wolves, and Ethan was instantly alarmed. Only half the men were in the clearing. *Where was everyone?* Ethan looked to Loc and they ran towards the unexpected noise.

Ethan ran with a tight grip on the axe never thinking he would come to use it. He could hear his heart beating in his throat beneath the urgent hollering of his friends in trouble. Through the trees he saw Harn run to join them.

Arriving at the scene, he connected with his Ethos. Desperate shouts were amid the guttural snarls of several huge wolf-like creatures. These were the Baskharef that he also encountered in Lanvin. The beasts were spread out in the clearing, and at nearly the height of a Harn, their claws were scattering the men. Baskharef were a mix of bear and wolf, and with their claws and sharp teeth they swung and snapped at the Harn attempting to kill them with their axes. Retreat wasn't an option. Men had already fallen to them. Among those sprawled on the ground, Ethan spotted movement.

Accompanying the beast were grey-skinned, earless men, shooting their bows into the trees at the boys, who must have climbed them to avoid the attack. Ethan sent the archers flying through the air. The demon beasts would require more concentration.

A man armoured in black scale entered the chaos and came at Ethan. Black cloth was wrapped around his head, covering mouth and nose. His eyes, the only thing visible, spied Ethan across the clearing. He directed his palm at Ethan, and a ball of flame shot forth.

Ethan's Ethos connected with the incoming fire, propelling it back to the one who sent it. It missed and settled on an attacker behind. Ethan directed his power at the fire thrower, causing him to stumble back a step. It soon registered his assailant wore malreus. With a bellow, Ethan rushed in with axe raised. The figure blocked and struck at Ethan with the same rage. Ethan swung fast against his opponent's sword, not forgetting he had to guard against the fire-throwing free hand, just as lethal.

From his bare hand the man shot fire into Ethan's chest. The flames spread across his torso, but the protective properties of the malreus saved him from a killing blow.

Clamorous bellows and fervent orders came a short distance from him, but he could do nothing while facing the dangerous foe. It dawned on him, his opponent was occupying his attention. As much as he could, he tuned into the sounds of the fight.

A Baskharef was jumping in an attempt to rip down one of the boys dangling from a branch.

Clutching his axe in defense, Ethan held out his free hand to move the boy. Flames flew past and over Ethan's head from somewhere behind the enemy. Within moments, Ethan lost his focus. His opponent impaled him below his armour, dropping him to his knees. The man raised his sword ready to slash down on his neck. Suddenly the dark figure's back was aflame and he lurched forward.

Ethan rolled sideways out of his falling path. Amidst the flames, he spied an arrow sticking out of the dying man's neck. Ethan gripped his abdomen, the pain immense and getting more debilitating. As he went down, he watched his enemy become a black haze before vanishing into nothing. Only his robe was left as evidence of his presence. In shock, Ethan stared beyond it to men trying to kill the rampant beasts.

Dein, Stannar's quiet brother, grabbed Ethan by his armour and dragged him from a creature's radius. Bleeding from numerous slashes on its underside, the nearby beast was wounded significantly. Finally, it went down in a blaze of fire and an agonized growling shriek. It appeared to be the last of them.

With Dein's support, Ethan hobbled to his feet and over to Derryl and Mouse. On reaching them, he swooned and fell to his knees once more. His eyes shifted from a woman amongst the men, to the boys dragging a limp Ruegar from under the body of Bearn. Despite the great bloody slash across Bearn's chest he had a peaceful look. By him was the body of Comgel. The Harn and old shipman lay together. Beneath them Ruegar had been buried.

Ethan fainted to the cries of both Berran and Mouse.

74 - Lost is Found

Death's power is its impenetrable mystery
Its mercy is its unseen presence
Its weakness is the fear it produces
Its judgment is always final

Valfaèr, Elements of Arcane Power

On the second day of travel, Mara withdrew and sat at the end of the wagon, leaning on the flap. Pulling her knees up, she stared at the passing forest, wishing she could be out in it, alone. Earona hardly spoke to her that morning. Her aloofness made Mara more uncomfortable than anyone else's silence. Normally the lack of conversation would be a relief, but now it added to her guilt. The anxiety of remaining in Sommerlea seemed like nothing now she was in the tranquil valley. She berated herself on wanting to come.

Earona sat at the opposite end. After staring out at Shiarn and Keanan on the bench for some time, she gave a breathy sigh.

Mara peeked at her with a pout. 'Well, say it already.'

Earona rolled her eyes with exasperation. 'About last night?'

'You've been talking about me.'

'What can I say?' A strained moment descended between them. Finally, she spoke. 'Jett did tell you, you weren't to come.'

'I never agreed to that.' Although at the time she really didn't think she would run-away, or even disobey him. She didn't want to go with him at all, but...

'You and he are too self-centered,' Earona grumbled, 'It's not just you, I'm the one who has to listen to him go on about it.'

Mara bowed her head with unwanted remorse and muttered under the covering of her hair, 'I really couldn't stay there... they could get hurt...' Besides, she did not want to be sent back to Ryne.

Earona continued, 'I'm not sure what we will be facing, but it could be dangerous. You could get captured, or worse - killed! Jett will feel responsible.'

If only they would get it, Mara didn't care about her fate. She didn't even care if they disliked her, but... his animosity left a lonely ache in her heart she did not understand. 'I...' She was more afraid than ever, but for different reasons. '...thought I would be safer...' Even though Jett frightened her, she felt safer with him than with anyone else she had met. The lowering of her walls surprised her, and a desperation was coming to the surface – she needed him. Although she would never admit it to Earona, and especially not to him.

Earona sighed with irritation. 'Maybe. But like you, Jett has his fears.'

Keeping her head down, Mara wiped a stray tear. His *fear* was right where he didn't want it to be. But, she thought the best solution was to leave Sommerlea for her good and for those there. But now, she could see it was a mistake. 'He won't have to worry about that.'

'What do you mean?' Earona spoke with sudden sharpness.

She should have gone somewhere else, it didn't matter where anymore. 'I'll leave—'

'How? Where to?' Earona took a gentle breath. 'That would be even more dangerous.'

'I'm not wanted.' The words escaped her along with a spat of tears.

'No, it's just… you probably should have spoken of this before and anything you know about your mother.'

She could say more of her mother and her mysterious visitors from the Temple, but Earona and Jett were already annoyed with what she had shared. She daren't tell them anymore.

Earona smiled with smugness, as if returning to her usual self. 'After all, I did tell Jett you would be better off with us, at the beginning.' She scratched her chin in contemplation. 'Although I can't say why that is. And I will do what I can to help you. Anyway where can you go, except back to Ryne?'

Mara's arm tightened around herself and she remained in her cocoon of loneliness.

'We'll work something out eventually.' Earona patted her leg in an attempt at reassurance.

~ * ~

Ethan opened his eyes to see the boys' dirty anxious faces staring down at him. He touched his stomach. Nothing there to show for his injury except a dull ache. He spied the lone woman across the clearing, kneeling by an injured man and making him drink a potion.

Another newcomer approached Ethan. His reddish beard was overgrown and his paunch belly was strapped by his belt. Putting his hand towards Ethan, his eyes gave a friendly glint. 'Well met, Ethan.' With a strong hand, the stranger helped Ethan to his feet.

Ethan asked, 'What happened?'

The man gave the clearing a thoughtful look and said in a loud voice, 'Looks as if you came into their line of travel.' He gazed at the men who would not move again and nodded towards the carcass of the black furred beast. 'Lives have been lost here because of that and those others.'

Ethan creased his brow and enquired with bewilderment, 'Who are you?'

'Morias.' He looked over at the woman. 'That's Clara and there's Adis, but he's following what was left of the Skar.'

Ethan remembered the odd looking men. 'Why are they here?'

'It's very unusual.'

'But the one I fought, he was…' Ethan frowned at his words, recalling its mysterious disappearance.

'A Narahk.'

Ethan felt his head spinning at the surreal idea he had confronted a Narahk and would have been killed by the ancient Fáerinn enemy if it weren't for these strangers. 'Why are you telling me this?'

Clara came up beside Morias. Wiping her hands on her cloak, she smiled with warmth at Ethan. 'You were badly wounded,' she went on, 'and lucky.' She watched the children move Bearn's body and sighed. 'Not so for some others.' Turning to Morias, she said with reprove, 'You haven't told him, have you?'

'I haven't had a chance!'

Staring at the two, Ethan touched his stomach and came to an insightful conclusion. 'You're… Gifted?'

'Yes, and I'm so pleased you are free,' she went on, 'They are searching for you, you realize.'

Dumbfounded, Ethan stared at her.

'And that's why we're out here looking for them.'

Ethan was only more confused. 'The Narahk?'

'In a way,' Morias said, 'Predominately, we were searching for Jett and all of them.'

'Jett?! Here?' Pain-filled emotion crossed Ethan's face.

'He's not *here*,' Clara said with remiss, 'but he is in the valley somewhere. We have been searching for them, to warn them.'

Ethan was dazed with subdued happiness. 'Warn them?'

'Of the troop following them.'

'Here comes Adis,' Morias said.

A thin man, with long black hair, and garb that blended with the forest, was leading three horses towards them. Adis nodded a greeting to Ethan. 'Won't they be pleased to see you?' He looked to Morias. 'They have moved towards the north, but they are only a few. Trouble is they may bring warning.'

The men started to gather around them. 'What were those things?' Luz questioned, 'And who are you?'

Adis turned to the expectant men. 'They are unnatural creatures, and those men are their masters. We were passing by and heard the commotion.'

'We will rest awhile,' Clara said to Adis, 'And talk.' She laid a hand on his arm. 'The horses will need rest and Ethan needs answers.'

Ethan asked, 'Are they in trouble?'

Loc asked, 'These your friends, Ethan?'

'No.' Ethan stared into Loc's sad eyes and realized he did not know who had been killed. 'My friends are in the valley.'

Loc nodded and looked away.

Ethan put his hand on his shoulder with assurance. 'But first we will stop and lay to rest those who have passed.'

The men went about the space gathering the bodies together while the boys collected arrows and dragged discarded weapons to one place. Ethan, like the others, was deeply saddened at seeing Bearn. Despite his age and circumstance, he was a man of high spirits. Sarran, another older man, was among the deceased, and four other Harn, plus one of the Coltrenians. The dead men had the strength and courage to pass the mountain, yet there was no chance they could stand against such the rabid creatures. Ethan knew the men and he could only imagine how the Harn felt at the loss of their brothers. If not for the woman and her healing elixir, the casualties would be higher. Ethan included.

After the burial ceremony the men formed a camp away from the place of death. The evening brought a chill to the air and they eventually gravitated to the carnal comfort of the fire under a shroud of grief.

Morias and Clara sat on the ground along with the Harn, and listened to the men share what had erupted into their peaceful world. Bearn, Comgel, Bull and the boys had been hunting when Comgel was pierced fatality with an arrow. More arrows arrived, and Bull was shot, but that wasn't enough to stop him. Ruegar started firing arrows as well, so he told Ethan, but the beasts came howling and clawing. Bearn fell on top of him and lay still, muffling Ruegar's cries. Bearn would have been happy to know he and Comgel protected Ruegar from being trampled and mauled. Bull ordered the boys into the trees and the Harn ran into the clearing from every direction. More of the strange grey men entered the fray, but the creatures were the true terror. They could fight against swords, but not a giant beast with teeth and claws. As well, the ominous black cloaked figure entered the clearing.

Morias said, 'They're not like humans, they don't have emotions, or a language that can be learned.'

Derryl responded, 'What sort of people disappear into black dirt?'

'Aye, we've heard of them, the Greys. Nightmares from the legends,' Gailtram told him, and he muttered, 'Devils from the otherworld.'

Ethan stared into the fire in contemplation.

Branan asked, 'But what was that other man?'

'It's cursed,' Ethan replied, 'and shouldn't be walking the earth.'

Morias added, 'The devil saw what you were and was coming for you, Ethan, but we surprised them.'

'I would have had the bastard.' Stannar spat on the ground.

Ethan looked at Clara's clean and flushed face. 'I still don't understand. Who are you? And where do you come from?'

The men, having shown their gratitude to Clara for her saving elixir, now looked to her with respect and awe.

'We come from Coltrene and are friends of Ethan's friends.' Clara gave a gaping yawn. 'We heard the noise of the beast and came to see… and fancy, we saw all these rugged bearded men,' she gushed, 'with splendid armour. A strange sight, and I said, "They've got children", and I thought it couldn't get any stranger, what with you and the…' she yawned again, 'and…'

Ethan stated, 'You should rest.'

'Yes…' Clara closed her eyes and nestled into Morias' chest.

'We started out a few hours before dawn,' Morias said, 'I bet you have a story to tell about your escape?'

From around the fire came hearty agreement and numerous comments about the mountain journey.

Ethan was genuinely surprised. 'You know where I've been?'

Morias said, 'A place called Signet Reach?'

'How did you know?'

'I'm not sure how Jett knew,' Morias replied, 'but he was right?'

Stirred by the mention of his Kin, Ethan sensed the pent up grief climb to the surface.

Adis came from the shadows and into the sphere of firelight. He crouched by Ethan and briefly looked down at Clara. 'I have lost their trail.' His face was dismal in the orange light. 'This is serious, but we have disabled one group.'

Morias gave him a questioning look.

'This was another troop,' Adis said, 'the others must have kept moving.'

'You think it was a Narahk you originally saw?' said Morias.

'After today, I think it is exactly what I saw.' Adis was thoughtful. 'Less than half got away.'

Ethan asked Adis, 'Are they in danger?'

Adis replied with point blank sincerity, 'No more than you today.'

'So, yes.'

Adis nodded.

Ethan asked the question foremost on his mind, 'Are they all together?'

Careful not to budge Clara, Morias put a comforting hand on his shoulder. 'They are. You are the last and now you are found. The search can finish.'

Ethan's voice caught in his throat. 'They have been searching?'

Adis gave him a tight smile. 'You sound surprised?'

'It's just I never thought… I don't know what I thought.' Ethan lifted his face with hope. 'Tomorrow we go after them?'

Adis confirmed, 'As early as possible.'

The men watched Ethan expectantly.

'We'll still go with you,' Mouse said. 'Me, Derryl, Ruegar, and Berran.'

'I don't know, boys,' Ethan said. 'I don't want anything to happen to you, especially after today.'

'We're still alive,' said the loud-mouth Derryl, 'And I shot one of them!'

Berran said, 'We'll follow you anyway.'

Ethan said with affection, 'You're persistent 'lil buggers.'

Grith queried, 'You'll be heading north now?'

'Yes, generally,' Adis replied.

'Works out well.' Luz gave Ethan a broad smile.

Ethan turned to Branan. 'Will you still go to the city?'

Branan finally replied, 'I want to find Gart, but it will have to wait.' He looked to Loc as if the two shared a special consideration. 'Some here will say it is too dangerous for me to venture into the city alone. My quest for Gart will be left to fate.'

As was Branan's way he left it at that and Ethan assumed he too was coming with them. He turned his attention to Druce. For an older man he fought well, coming out with a few scratches. 'What about you? You can still travel to Coltrene.'

'I'm not so interested in that anymore.' Druce rested his hand on his sword hilt. 'Not without Bearn. We'll all travel together come what may.'

Adis looked aghast at the men wanting to stay with Ethan. 'All these men wish to accompany you?'

'We do.' Loc paused. 'If Ethan will have us.'

Ethan shrugged at Adis, 'They wish to go on to Baion.' The hard faced men had an uncanny strength underneath their soiled bodies and mournful gazes.

'We will have to travel as fast as we are able,' Adis announced to all, 'I fear they have not halted at all.'

~ * ~

Throughout the day, fields were visible between thinning trees on the left. Jett's eyes were often on the ranges, on both sides of the valley. They would have to travel at least another day to reach the mountains in the east.

Towards the end of the afternoon, Seth guided them on a track of lichen laden stones, under cavernous shadows of tree branches until they arrived at a paved courtyard. Colonnades and arches, mostly intact, bordered the area. Crumbling statues, depicting ethereal ladies and fantastic looking creatures, were amongst a mix of trees with blue and white blossoms.

In the center was a massive oak. The tree's exposed roots spread across the paving, ripping up the stones over the centuries of growth. At the end of the enclosure, was a fortress. The upper walls had collapsed, and blocks were scattered about the steps leading up to the terrace and an open entry. Two towers were connected on either side. The Kin continued past the ancient manor, and came to a small field a few yards away. Stone dwellings were along a partially concealed roadway.

Jett hopped down from Thunder and surveyed the rubble amongst the grass. 'It will have to do I guess.'

~ * ~

Once the camp area was decided and set up began, Seth dragged Marcus away from his duties to go over to the fortress. The two stood looking up at it, in the approaching darkness the intimidating building shadowed the ruins. With gleeful delight, Seth waved Marcus on through the open entry. The enormous circular room had narrow man-height window gaps along the walls. Balconies circled the upper walls allowing an unhindered view of every floor. The open exposure of the building was not a result of erosion, but designed to let in light from above. The stone pillars, the width of a man's embrace, held up what was left of the rim, circling the ceiling which was on a deliberate slant.

The tree in the center excited Seth more than anything else. Emerald leaves were hidden under a profusion of vibrant azure flowers. Roots sprawled across the room, breaking up the slabs, and competing against the span of its own branches. 'Isn't it an awesome sight?!' He stood, admiring the upper levels. 'It's a mezzanine with views across and down.'

Marcus stuck his head into a doorway near the entryway and stared up a narrow stairway. 'I suppose.'

Seth informed him, 'The stairs are in adequate repair, but the flooring above is decayed.'

Marcus gave him a broad grin. 'You've been up there?'

'Of course.'

Marcus returned to the main room. 'Is that tree supposed to be there?'

'It seems at home, but lonely.'

Marcus smirked at the tree. 'Can't say I blame it.'

'It warms my heart to see that the tree was once master of the house.'

'It would.' Marcus stood with his hands on his hips surveying the area. 'And what about these mounds.' He indicated one of the two neat piles of planks and rubble by his feet. 'Someone has pushed it aside.'

Seth scratched his chin with his fingers. 'Perhaps this place has been lived in over time.'

Marcus observed the clear state of an alcove. 'It would make a better place to bed-down.'

'Well protected from the weather.'

Once the outer areas were checked for potential sleeping areas it was decided the inner chamber of the fortress would be preferred over stony grass patches or someone's abandoned house.

After a meal of pheasant, the Kin chatted around the dying fire on the outside terrace of the ruins. Eventually the girls withdrew to the inner house to sleep and the men stayed warming themselves at the fire.

Jett, putting more hope than certainty into his statement, started, 'Tomorrow we should see some change in the scenery on the other side.'

'I agree.' Seth hid in the folds of his cloak and yawned. 'Adis said after we pass the center of the valley the forest will clear somewhat and there will be a crossroad.'

Jett muttered, 'I'm hoping those ranges will look kinder.'

'Apparently they should ease.' Seth rose and said good night before going inside.

Marcus turned to Jett. 'We keep a watch?'

'We do,' Jett responded. 'I'll wake Hellier later and she'll wake one of you two.'

Marcus glanced at Keanan with a frown. 'She can wake me.'

Keanan stared at Marcus with frustration. 'No, I'll do it.'

'I'm more able.'

'So am I.'

'Does it matter?' Jett interjected. The two men glared at each other and Jett shook his head in annoyance. *Can you two give it a rest?* The ongoing unspoken antagonism between them was becoming plain for the others to see, but to Jett it was a nuisance. 'Keanan, you're up and Marcus can be on later or start tomorrow night. Right. Settled.'

Marcus grumbled while Keanan responded to Jett's unyielding glare, 'Fine then.'

~ * ~

A few hours later, Mara woke in a feverish sweat, and to a wracking terror that stole her breath away. She gripped her chest with dread. Disorientated, she sat, afraid she was still in the nightmare. She stared at the grey sombre walls and slumbering bodies with confusion. A blanket of fear descended. It was similar to the fear she faced with Jett. But she noticed he was asleep. Now was the time she had to leave.

With a smattering of tears, she stood. It was time to run, and get away from them all. The shadows lurched over the pavement, lit with a deceiving glow. Trembling, she dashed down the steps and into the courtyard as if an unseen monster was chasing her. After all, she was only a burden — he made that clear. She was only delaying what was meant to be.

The darkness would come for them all, and she would be at the top of the destruction. She couldn't stop it, but she wouldn't just wait for it. Not again. She should never have come. Anyhow, they would be glad to see her go. Sorrow billowed up from her soul, and she labored for breath. Feeling nauseous, she hesitated by a great tree at the center of the outside courtyard.

'Mara?'

Hellier's voice caused her to withdraw into the shadows. An unexpected wrath overcame her at the woman's intrusion. Mara, her cheeks damp from unchecked tears, pierced Hellier's concerned gaze. 'I'm…going!'

'Why? And where?'

'I can't stay here. Something is coming,' she gasped, '…for me.' She lifted her hands to ward off Hellier's approach, and shouted, 'No! I'm leaving. You can't stop—' A sudden pain assailed her and she clasped her head with shock.

'Who's coming?' Hellier glanced around the courtyard.

Digging her nails into her scar-mark, Mara wanted to scream, but she could only rasp, 'Darkness — you're going to die, and I will—' her sob turned into a groan, doubling her over.

Hellier reached for her. 'Come back inside.'

'Don't touch me!' Wrenching from Hellier, she backed away and yelled, 'No! You'll never stop me. All of you will— It's me…' her words became a guttural babble, 'I'm… the one… the…the ritual is…'

An annoyed shout came from the terrace.

Within moments, Mara was swept up by a man on a horse and pulled over his saddle. Gripping her to his chest, the rider kicked Hellier back and rode to the entry of the enclosure. Mara slumped against him and they disappeared down the road into the night.

75 - Night Flight

Fight not unless the position is crucial to maintain

Empirical Warfare Command

Jett woke to find Mara missing from her blanket. He ran outside and heard her distraught outburst and Hellier attempting to calm her. Startled by her emotional turmoil, it triggered memories from home, evoking a numbing rage in him. Considering his mother's mental suffering right then was not a wise idea, he needed to focus on Mara.

A movement to the right of the tower caught his eye. He shouted, 'An intruder! Watch out!'

The rider darted out from the shadows of the arches and grabbed Mara around the neck and arm and yanked her up to his saddle. He kicked Hellier in the chest and she stumbled back. The rider held Mara against his chest and rode off through another entry to the courtyard.

Marcus raced by Jett and down to meet Hellier.

Jett whistled for his horse. Thunder paused at the steps while Jett mounted, and he was away within moments. Stopping at Hellier and Marcus, Thunder threw his head back, ready to give chase. Jett looked down at them with a grim expression.

Hellier gripped his leg and said with steely determination, 'You can't go alone.' *I know you don't want me there, but you must take me incase…*

He stared past the arch in the direction of the rider. Amid reservation, he said, 'Get up!'

She leapt up behind him. Thunder sped them out of the courtyard and down the road. The pale grey trees were a sombre light along the dark road and enough for Jett to see clearly. He glimpsed the rider and a small figure slumped at the front of the horse. Hellier's grip was light on his hips as she leaned into his back. He was uncertain whether he should have let her come, but if something does happen to him…, she would be needed. In his haste, he hadn't passed any instructions to the Kin, and he cursed under his breath.

Thunder was making rapid strides along the road, his clattering hooves disrupting the peace of the woods. They raced across a wooden bridge and onto a crumbling roadway with poor footing. Soon enough it didn't matter. The rider diverted his path, and the grey horse galloped into the bordering foliage.

Jett approached the line of trees and slowed Thunder's pace. 'Hold on,' he cried over his shoulder and flew over the twisted roots with hooves breaking up the earth. The forest opened up and Jett's eyes danced over the rider while keeping a keen eye on the surroundings. The rider swerved between the gaps, but Jett kept a fixed gaze on his movement. The unknown depth of the bracken underfoot and the widely spaced trees concerned him. Leaning into Thunder's head, he whispered encouragement.

Heavy footfalls were not a great distance from them. He conveyed a thought to Hellier. *Can you hear that?*

Another rider?

The lead rider veered to the left and down. With no idea how low the hill dropped away, Jett prepared Thunder for the descent. *Going down.* Hellier's arms circled his waist in a tight embrace. Thunder did not falter his pace and leaped into the descent. Jett gave him leeway to run, doing all he could to prevent the flying horse from crashing into the stout trees on the slope. Racing at breakneck speed, the horse's sturdy footfalls were thumping in his ears. A fresh breeze driven hard by the propulsion of forced wind chilled his face.

How does Thunder see where he's going?

He trusts my lead. Jett mumbled, 'But, how are they seeing?' His hard riding was narrowing the distance. He could hardly spare an eye for the second rider as he drew closer. Suddenly they broke free of the haphazard limbs and sprang into an open field. Waves of wild grass were pressed aside by the speeding beast with no pause in his steady gallop. His swift hooves flew through the grass and he raced like a thunderous shadow through the night. The rider ahead grew closer. Jett spoke to his spirited beast and Thunder reared his head, stirred to accelerate his pace. The second rider also entered the field and galloped parallel to them. At a brief glance, Jett caught the shine of a blade. The rider was more than prepared for an encounter; he wanted one. *Draw your sword.*

She slid her sword from its sheath with her left hand. Without a moment to spare, the rider was upon them, swinging his sword at her back. With her left hand, she blocked it with an awkward backhand motion. Their swords clanged together. She threw his weapon off and tilted from the horse, teetering on the edge of her balance.

Jett's thoughts were urgent. *Don't fall.*

Hard to do riding pillion on a horse galloping at reckless demon speed. The rider slashed down at her shoulder. Her hand lit up with fire and she twisted to deflect the blow. Her sword flared into a hot burning blade, flaming like a beacon across the flat. Parrying another hit, she intercepted the sword tip headed for Jett's shoulder.

Not only was Jett concerned about a sword coming at his face, he was now worried about the distance they had traveled. There seemed to be no halting in their progress, yet he was stubbornly determined to catch the first rider. He wasn't going to let Mara go that easily, and not without a fight. They entered an open space rising into more fields. On the left and beyond a line of treetops, the oppressive mountain range eclipsed the night sky to the north. Jett kept a firm command on the rein, and the animal entrusted itself to his guiding hands.

Over-extending her reach, Hellier leaned away from the center of balance, making him aware of every hard strike she delivered. Not only was she defending herself, she was protecting him and Thunder against a man attacking like there was no tomorrow, and there was nothing Jett could do to be effective in aiding her. Sparing a glimpse to the side, the fire of her malreus blade filled his vision. He turned back to see the rider, and a structure, shadowing the distant woodlands. Peeking out from the trees was a tower connected to a stone fortification.

A sudden angry cry came from their attacker.

Hellier seared him across the chest and shoved her sword into his arm with a gritty yell of her own. He toppled from the horse with a shout. She grinned broadly at the sight of the man on fire.

No time for praise, Jett said, 'Don't sheath your sword.'

The rider entered the sparse woodland and disappeared into the trees.

Jett stepped down Thunder's pace and kept his eyes open in wary alertness. He spotted a figure standing among the trees and not the initial rider. Signaling to Thunder to give a burst of speed, he fired his thoughts back to Hellier. *Man on your left.*

Just say when.

Curse it. It was the man's plan to wait in the shadows, sword raised, prepared for their approach. *Can you see him at all?* His eyes warmed to a wine-tinted glow as he searched him out, leaning behind the cover of the tree.

Not yet.

Thunder's hooves hit pavement, assuming it led to the nearby fortress and the destination of the rider with Mara. Amid a slight movement, the figure rounded to strike. Turning a bend, the massive stone tower came into view, and the man stepped out to reach Jett.

Now I see. At the right moment Hellier extended forward, past Jett. She cast off the enemy's strong thrust, her hand firmly gripping Jett's trousers. Swinging against the attacker's repeated strike, her sword caught along his throat. Grasping for air, he fell back against the tree. She strained to regain her balance and in the process Jett was nearly toppled over.

The road to the ruins was on a slight ascent. Jett approached carefully, observing a well-armoured man standing by the wall. The figure, helmet glittering in the moonlight stood as a statue against the grey stone.

Hellier pressed into Jett's back. *I'll take care of him, you go in.*

Reluctant they separate, he gave a tentative reply, 'Be careful.' Thunder neared the edge of the rise and they dismounted. He gave Thunder a stroke and a word, and the sweating horse walked into the protection of the trees.

Swaggering with great bravado, Hellier confronted the man by the wall. With a gleaming thin sword, and wearing a breast plate, he stood on guard, and did not seem to care a woman dare approach him.

Jett questioned if it was foolhardy to let her face him alone, especially after noticing her overconfident stride. But, haste was needed, and he continued into the open doorway.

In the complete darkness, he saw a curving corridor skirting both sides of the round structure. A rank unnatural odour came through a splintered door ahead. His two swords drawn, he stepped across lengths of old planking. The fetid odour, reeking of dead things, fresh and not so, overpowered his senses. What was left of the door was shut. Jett peered through an upper gap where the wood had been hewed from the inside. Jagged pieces of stone were overthrown and destroyed furniture was about the space. The door was held fast and he moved on with speed down the passage.

He pushed on a stuck door that he deduced would lead to the left tower. It wouldn't budge and he continued down the corridor that reflected moonlight from large windows along the wall. He raced up a stone stair and arrived at another floor similar to the first. An unexpected moan of a man caused him to halt. Setting his weapons in a ready position, he listened, alert for any eventuality.

After an anxious moment, he stepped over rubble and broken slabs towards a breach in the stonework, surmising it must be an entry to the main chamber. Another dull cry echoed down the walkway from within. Husky voices affronted his ears and he recognized a soft muffled cry. Another voice, jarring and cruel, shouted. He stiffened in surprised awareness at the harsh female voice.

Not gaining anything noteworthy from the abrasive voices within the chamber, Jett peered through the hole in the wall. Chunks of fallen stone and piles of broken furniture concealed his vision. A female shouted, her voice a jarring echo, 'Is she dead yet, Goren?'

'No,' a woman yelled back.

'Can't you do anything I ask?'

Jett considered whether they spoke of Mara. The sudden acute wail of a girl answered his query.

'And where's he?' Another voice equally as grueling demanded.

'Looking for us, I expect,' another voice said, 'I don't like messing 'round with them. I say we take her and get out.'

'No,' another woman screeched. 'We wait and get our own Ancient to play with.'

'Why are you interested in that, Satira? Bet you've never even seen one before.'

'I want to see him. If we can get him and her it will make everyone happy.'

The first voice cackled. 'Old Queenie sitting pretty while we do her work. She's got no idea what we're up to,' she hooted loudly.

Jett counted at least four distinct voices, but there might have been half a dozen for all he could see. On light of their conversation he assumed they were discussing him. Ancients was not a name Fáerinn used of themselves and it was over an age since Nayinn referred to them in this manner.

Mara's quiet sobbing did not abate.

'Zarana, shut her up,' a woman yelled. 'On second thought I've an idea.' There was an audible thump and a drawn out moan of pain issued from the girl. 'That should do it.'

'I won't believe it till I see it myself.'

'Shut up!' Silence was followed by whispering voices.

Jett paused, unsure how to approach so many witches at one time. Mara's voice rang out in a harrowing cry and escalated into a distressed howling. No chance he could keep listening to her tormented pleading for the torture to stop. He stepped into the doorway, giving him a better view of the chamber and the witches.

They met his presence with a mix of shocked expressions and conceited smirks. He surveyed the room and numbered the fiendish looking women at seven. Tall candelabras shed semi-light over the piles of rubble and rotted furniture scattered over the immense room. If not for his exceptional vision he would not have seen a man chained on a slab near the back, his fresh blood staining the pale stone. If he was not dead, he was near to it. Another man, deeper in, was well secured with gag and blindfold and appeared untouched.

Mara, half-lying, half-sitting, on the floor, and bleeding from her forehead, was held secure with a rope binding her wrists, by an overweight auburn haired woman with wrathful eyes and a sagging bosom. It appeared the witch was dragging her across the stones.

Jett strode into the room with the hope Hellier was not far behind. He sunk his thoughts into his Ethos and his eyes glowed a scorching red in the candlelight.

'Ah! See!' The coarse grating voice cried. She pointed a bony finger at Jett and her long nail curved downward. 'I told you!' The woman was also overweight, and her tangled wild hair looped over her lifeless eyes.

Jett walked over broken stones towards the women. A rush of sound like air pushed aside was all around him. Symbols, scribed with blood, formed a large circle, lit up over clumps of stone and rubble. A terrible sense of a trap springing shut seized his heart. His burning vision crossed the chamber and bore into the old witch, yet nothing happened.

She cackled and walked closer with an audacious swagger.

He stepped forward, swinging his sword down. It crashed onto an invisible barrier. The realization hit as hard as his sword.

One of the women chortled, 'We get two for one.'

The disfigured one glanced over her shoulder and screamed, 'Goren, you worry about getting rid of that other one.'

Jett addressed the witch in front of him, 'What are you going to do with Mara?'

The witch neared, and one side of her face made a lifeless smirk.

'It speaks,' a younger woman giggled. She was unnaturally skinny and appeared not as affected by the taint of evil as the others.

'Shut up,' the woman shouted over her shoulder. 'I speak.' Her eyes, dark with malice, looked Jett over, and her rotted nails flicked towards him. 'Wouldn't you like to know, but we don't give away our secrets that easily.' She came up to the barrier, but went nowhere near touching it. 'I should be asking you that.' A putrid stink came with her and the barrier did nothing to keep it out.

'She's under my protection.' Jett maintained his calm under her baneful gaze, despite wanting to rage at the precarious situation.

With a pompous sneer, she gave a mocking snarl, 'You Ancients think so much of yourselves, but now you're nothing. I despise you, all of you.' She pointed at Mara, moaning from her twisted position on the floor. The witch growled, 'Bitch of the Demon Nation, whore of the Devil Makers, we own her now. She's useless to you.'

The redhead holding Mara kicked her back down, pushing her face into the gravel with her foot.

Jett's eyes smoldered at the cruelty.

The witches grating cackles bounced around the chamber, and the head witch spoke. 'You didn't have to come here, but you came for her. She's worse than filth.' The witch spat at him, and Jett instinctually sidestepped. The spittle landed by his feet, and her eyes blazed with hatred as she stared into his red eyes. 'You can't do a thing in there.'

A loud shriek rang out behind the witch. After an explosion of curses from the redhead, Mara leaped across a stone and into the blood sealed circle. Breathing hard, she landed in a heap of hiked up skirts and spread legs with bloody knees.

The head-witch turned and stretched her palm towards the woman who let Mara escape. 'Shalz-alqua-ellbat-meurven.'

The woman skidded through the air and was stopped by a waist high block of stone. She slumped forward, groaning. Another witch chuckled, but was silenced by a scowl from the one who cast the spell. She spun back to Jett and glared at Mara, her malicious eyes spiking with hate.

Panting heavily and clutching her stomach, Mara eased to a sitting position. Deep bruising was on her arms, and a bloody gash was on her forehead, staining her face with congealed blood. She gave the woman a weary look of defiance. Jett frowned with concern over her injuries.

Mara's brow creased with the pangs of annoyance, but she nodded towards the women, 'Barkala can't touch me in here. The only way she can get me is if the spell is undone. Then we are both free.' She stared at another witch, her hair sat flat on her back in black greasy tendrils, and she was as ugly as the disfigured one. 'Satira and that other one set the trap up.'

'You bitch,' Barkala hissed and stabbed her finger at her. 'Think you're so smart. Wait till you see what's planned for you.' The witch's vehemence echoed around the chamber, 'Do you think I give a king's cock what happens to that demon spawn inside you, it's not me who cares. I don't care what old queenie says. We're the ones here and not her. You have no idea what you're playing at and you don't know what this seal does.'

After sheathing his silver blade, Jett cut Mara's cord with his malreus sword, and pulled the rope from her wrists.

Barkala glowered at him. 'You risk your life for her. She'll kill you in the end. She's one of us.'

A craggily old voice interrupted her. 'He's dead.'

'Can't you do anything?' Barkala barked, 'Orga, take that young one.' She pointed to another witch, and like the skinny girl, she appeared less corrupt. 'Get the dead up,' she shrieked, 'Don't just stand there, you cows, get down there.'

The two women pulled at the bound man's tied wrists, and he stood without complaint. As they passed, Jett recognized him as the rider he pursued.

'Zarana, get off your fat arse and come here,' Barkala growled at the witch as she struggled over the rubble. Barkala, Goren, and the remaining witches, gathered around the chained man on the slab. Whatever life he had, would most likely be gone soon with the witches crude chant.

The witch, Satira, approached Jett and stood as close to the barrier as she could without touching it. Her rasping voice spoke with a lilting spitefulness. 'So glad you decided to come. I was so hoping to see you again.'

His body stiffened with alertness at her personal remark.

Her voice softened and almost sounded an attempt at seduction. 'I knew you would in the end. We will always be drawn to each other - your body will crave my caress. Do you miss our love-making as much as I?'

Under his breath, Jett snarled, 'Who are you?'

'You don't recognize me,' Satira retorted with angry passion, 'I'm disappointed, my love.'

He stared at her weathered face and enervated eyes with disbelief. 'Nya?'

'You do remember. I'm pleased.' Her bright red lips formed a grotesque grin, and her eyes shifted to Mara, 'I won't always look this way. Not when I'm raised by the Summoner.' She pretended to run her hand down his chest. 'Perhaps you will be more endearing when I strip you of your strength.'

He recoiled in disgust at the revelation of her plan.

'Won't it be fun when I have you again,' her voice cooed, 'and the treasure that does not belong to you?'

'Satira, you no good slut,' Barkala screamed, 'Get over here.'

Satira mocked a kiss and joined her sisters in the chant.

Jett surreptitiously touched the Eye-key in his pocket, realizing what was now at stake. He had no idea how far reaching Nya's evil scheming could go.

Mara crawled away and sat at the far side of the circle, her back to the witches. 'That witch knows about me...'

'She knows everything.' Jett sighed at the dire situation. Everything evil Nya wanted was right here, trapped.

Mara mumbled a curse. In her hand was a piece of splintered wood she was cutting with a sharp stone.

Crouching beside her, Jett gave her a puzzled look that went unnoticed. 'Is there any way out of here?'

'The casters of the spell are killed or they release the seal.'

'Thought as much. What are you doing?'

'Trying something.' Still avoiding his eyes, she said, 'a trick.'

He laid his head in his hand in exasperation. 'You're making magik?'

'Curse it!' Her voice lowered with indignation. 'You shouldn't have come.'

Sighing with weary mental exhaustion, Jett rubbed his forehead. 'If you didn't run half-cocked out into the night, I wouldn't have needed to.'

'This is my problem,' she grumbled, bowing her head.

The last thing he needed was her tangled emotions. 'No. Not anymore. You're an asset in the hands of the enemy.'

She scraped at her stick with more vigor and pouted. 'And you're not?!'

'I'm not as important.' But, now he knew, the thing in his pocket was more valuable than both of them. He couldn't keep the frustration from his voice. 'Damn it to hell, I told you to stay with us.'

Mara's shoulders trembled and her head shook. 'I couldn't... I had to get away. It felt like something was coming, like that other time. Something...' she shuddered, '...more evil...'

Heeding the fear in her tremulous statement, he said, 'Something more evil?' The chanting grew in momentum across the chamber, reaching a fever pitch, and Jett wondered what horrors they were unleashing on Hellier. 'Isn't this bad enough?'

'It's awful…' a vulnerable sob escaped her and she wiped the blood from her forehead. '…but I had to go, you didn't want me there.' She finished with a heartfelt whisper, 'Maybe I made a mistake…'

Jett placed a comforting hand on her shaking shoulder and watched one of his mistakes, chanting with the others. 'And we all make them.' He let out a weary sigh. 'Now, if we manage to not get killed here, or worse,' he said, his voice commanding, 'you have to listen to me.'

Grimacing, Mara lowered her head.

'Do you know what they are doing to Hellier?'

After a thoughtful pause, she said, 'I think they're raising the dead.'

Anger contorted his face and he slammed his fist at the invisible barrier, a string of curses followed. 'Infernal bloody bitches, I can't do a thing trapped in here.' Nya would be determined to get the Eye-key at any cost. Hellier was in over her head.

'He's dead.' Barkala's voice was a leaden weight. 'They're flown away.'

'This is not how the plan was to go,' an older woman said, 'who knows, there might be more of them around. Two is too many.'

A younger witch replied, 'They ain't that tough.'

Barkala snorted. 'I'll put you in there and listen to you squeal.'

Fear paled the thin girl and she spoke no more.

'I've got an idea,' Barkala told them.

The women moved towards the far side of the room and waited in the shadows as if something was about to take place. Not long after, Hellier appeared at the doorway and stood as a human torch. Vibrant flames flicked upwards, lighting up the ceiling, and burning with a pulsating crackling hum. A fiery outline of her shape was within the brightness of flames running across her body. She was a brilliant blaze of golden crimson; a holy fire surveying the wickedness of the room.

Mara gasped at the sight.

Stay away from the blood circle. Jett warned. *It's a trap.*

'She's a Hellfire bitch,' Goren screamed and turned on another witch, 'You never said that.'

Shrugging, the witch looked at Hellier with fear. 'I didn't know.'

'Not to worry,' Barkala said, 'the dead are coming.'

Sure enough, the rank odour entered the chamber before the numerous ambling dead bodies arrived. Some were new and intact, like the man the witches took down earlier. Others were bones, half covered with decayed flesh. Mara crawled to the other side of the circle in fear they would enter, but they were focused on the walking fire.

Jett watched the parade of morbid dead with wide-eyed shock.

Unfazed by the animated corpses, Hellier glided past the circle, sparing the prisoners scant attention. Weighing little in her fire form, she skipped over the rubble, avoiding the attacks from the undead. They wielded weapons and wood planks, and made a hideous noise of miserable wails and painful moans. She hacked at the decayed limbs, cutting them down, despite being swamped.

Jett stood near the barrier, his helplessness caused his rage to burn in his veins.

Barkala flicked a sharp object at him, hitting his neck. His hand went to the stinging cut at his throat. The blood on his fingers incited his anger to new levels.

Mara picked up the metal disc and groaned.

After a moment, pain spread from his neck, making him tired. His hand went to soothe it with a questioning glance at Mara.

Mara grabbed his arm in panic. 'She's using you.'

The dead, Hellier killed, got to their feet once more. Their limbs reformed, and with each resurrection of a dead body, Jett was drained of energy.

Barkala chuckled at his wrathful expression. 'She'll kill you.'

'No. Don't kill him,' Satira whined, 'We're going to keep him.'

'We were,' she replied. 'As our pet, but not with her around.' She pointed at Hellier.

Jett snarled, 'I'd rather be dead.'

'Soon enough.'

Hellier's sword play was excellent as she leaped about the room always heading towards the witches, but it seemed no matter how far she moved they appeared out of her reach as if by some trickery.

Jett collapsed onto his knees, feeling nauseous and light-headed.

Mara pushed on the barrier. 'They're killing him.' Her panic stricken face and flailing arms finally caught Hellier's attention amid the stinking wall of carcasses. 'You have to stop them.'

'She can't speak...' On hands and knees, Jett staggered to right himself, '...like that.'

Hellier skipped across stone piles away from the witches. She waited till the dead congregated around her, and she changed direction, racing towards the witches on the opposite side of the chamber.

They scrabbled over the rubble in terror. Only Barkala stood firm. With a wicked gleam in her eye, she brought forth a staff. 'Don't assume it will be that easy.' She struck the floor three times.

His face a deathlike pale, Jett let out an agonised moan and clutched his right arm.

Mara knelt by him and lowered her face by his, concealing her actions. 'Hold on...' She rubbed her carved stick into her head wound.

Hellier's feet were fixed to the granite floor. She snarled at the witch, her flames a hypnotic crimson flicking up to the ceiling. The dead came at her again. She lashed out at them, trying not to destroy them, but as they crowded in, her flames lit up their skin, filling the air with burning rotten flesh. The witches shuffled closer with smug smiles as they viewed the captive.

Suddenly, from the blood circle, a bold voice chanted and grew with confidence.

The witches howled in protest and angered shock.

Mara pointed her blood stained wand at Hellier. 'Stay off the floor. She uses a grounding spell.'

Released from the spell, Hellier jumped onto the shoulders of the walking dead. Anger and panic surged among the evil women at her close proximity. Somersaulting onto the layers of debris, Hellier headed for the witches.

'That bitch.' Barkala eyed Mara with hatred. 'She's ruined everything. Goren, Satira, break the seal. We'll take her and I'll have my fun.'

Satira's chant rang dominant over Goren's voice while the other witches transformed into large hideous bats and disappeared through a hole in the ceiling.

Her eyes brimming with tears, Mara remained kneeling by Jett. Still conscious, he lay on the stone looking pale and furious. The breaking of the seal could require the last of his life force, potentially killing him. 'You see. You shouldn't have come,' she muttered with a choking sob, 'I'm going now. It's all for nothing.'

Jett frowned with confusion at her grief stricken face.

The dead dropped to the floor with cracking bones and the bumping of old flesh. Hellier swiped at a disorderly flapping of elongated black wings. Horrendous screeching filled the chamber leaving a trail of noise out into the night.

Then, silence.

The blood circle remained, but it no longer exercised any control, and Jett lay within, motionless.

76 - Fight at the Ruins

Subsequently, my study of the grand ruins, aptly named Temple of Air, evidenced by its statues of ethereal ladies, and fantastic looking flying creatures, clouds, and the like, continues in-depth. Even in its crumbling state it retains an atmosphere of splendor. The ethos life within the temple captures my attention and draws me back daily to mediate under its delicate sky-blue petals. Not a brown speck or dead branch is upon it, as if it were tended by an unseen mystical gardener. It seems to flower despite season or weather, and remains unchanging over the months in my presence. Should I dare to take a sample? I know too little to make an astute decision. Would it approve, I wonder...

From Glory to Ruin, Amin-Sayeda, Zaki'is Fur'Mole

Earona woke to the sound of hooves on the pavement outside. Half-asleep, she ambled out onto the terrace with confusion, along with Keanan, Seth, and Shiarn. Marcus raced up to them, shouting what had happened.

'What should we do?' Earona cried.

Keanan stood on the terrace surveying the night. 'We can't follow in the dark.'

Marcus ran towards the horses, and Seth went back inside. Earona stood, warming herself in the cold shadows pondering the fate of Jett, Hellier, and Mara for some moments. 'What are Marcus and Seth doing?'

'Seth is where he always is.' Shiarn pointed up to the top of the tower. 'And here comes Marcus.'

Marcus ran up the steps, his expression dismal. 'The horses have scattered. We'll have to look for them tomorrow. Lightning will follow Thunder.'

'The rider must have done that.' Keanan's tone was grim. 'What was Mara doing out there?'

Earona pursed her lips with annoyance he should ask her. She could make a guess as to Mara's plan—

Quiet. Seth's urgency intruded into their thoughts. *Something is entering the courtyard. Hide inside.*

Earona's stomach churned with nervous fear. Without a word, they darted back inside. Marcus kicked the bedding to one side and they gathered under the spreading branches of the tree. Shiarn latched onto Keanan's hand and she stuck her other out for

Marcus and Earona to both hold. Marcus held her fingers, leaving room for Earona's smaller grip on Shiarn's palm. She stared at Marcus' hand aghast.

'Come on,' Shiarn hissed at her. *Now's not the time.*

Blushing, Earona grabbed her palm and Marcus' warm hand glided next to hers. Shiarn caused them all to vanish.

I think it's one of those Narahk. Seth's anguish pervaded their minds, leaving a dreadful sensation.

Earona gasped, but waited in the silence withheld breath and racing heart.

~ * ~

On the highest level of the tower, Seth looked down onto the moonlit paving. Through a gap in the stone, he cocked his bow in readiness. Under the spreading branches he distinguished a black-clad figure. The sight was menacing enough till a second one appeared. Seth's heart sank with dread; he had the same sensation back at Lanvin. Moving like shadows, men crept past the trees and crouched, half hidden by the statues. Eventually more men converged on the pavement under the arches.

After some moments, they stood at ease as if presuming the area was devoid of people.

We see men, maybe Skar? Marcus thought up to him.

Seth replied, *and a great deal of them. I see two Baskharefs. Oh, Kahm, there's another Narahk. I'm certain.* His words were met with a mix of panic and stoic resolution. With the aid of the night breeze, Seth heard the Narahk's harsh monotone speech. 'She is no longer here.'

The second Narahk replied in the same disturbing tone, 'It seems she has left. Not long ago.'

'We'll go after her. Come.'

The troop would certainly catch up with Jett and Hellier if they left now. Seth warned the others, *I'm going to shoot it.*

Keanan shouted, *is that wise?* Shiarn cursed him while Earona's thoughts were a trembling mess of anxiety.

Go for it. Marcus was the only one wanting a fight. Seth ignored the risk, knowing it was the right course of action. 'Please find my target,' he whispered to the wind. The arrow was loosed, and against the law of nature, went on an angle and into the neck of a Narahk.

Clutching his throat, the Narahk collapsed under the tree and was no longer visible. Seth pinpointed his next target, lining up the men with bows. They dropped quickly. But for some reason he couldn't wound the second Narahk. The Narahk signaled Seth's position to his troops and they snuck towards the temple.

I've killed a Narahk. Seth thought to the Kin. *They're coming in with the beasts coming first. A few headed around the back.*

That makes me feel a whole lot better, Keanan's sarcastic thoughts shot back.

The hulking black creatures dashed inside but stopped and snarled at the space around the tree. Men wearing furs and hide armour came through the door, and not paying any mind to the Baskharefs, they assessed the bedding and empty room. Among them were the Skar, and so close, Earona saw nodules on their bald heads, and the sickly grey of their coarse skin. Swords drawn, they made their way to the inner stairs leading up to Seth.

Skar. Same as Lanvin. Marcus warned, *Seth, they're on their way up.*

The Baskharefs continued growling at the empty space.

Damn these beasts, Shiarn thought, *they know we are here.*

Seth aimed at the first one coming up the center of the spiraling stairs. The others stepped through in better readiness of his attack. A rising flame sat over Keanan's invisible palm. The burst of fire sped at the Skar moving up the stairs. Their clothes on fire, they writhed in agony, running and falling out onto the terrace. Howls of pain alerted the Skar to the threatening presence within.

In moments, Keanan aimed fire at the creatures, hoping he was quick enough to target two before they came at them in full strength. The beasts' fur took light and howling in pain and anger that bit randomly at the Kin. Marcus managed to run one through while still holding Shiarn's hand. The second one leaped towards him and would have taken out Earona and Shiarn as well if he did not let go of Shiarn's hand and confront it.

The sound of breaking branches came from behind the Kin, as the intruders began cutting through the dense vines to reach the narrow windows.

I don't know what the plan is, Shiarn thought, *but I won't be able to protect you.*

Keanan appeared and the men outside the door wavered. Keanan directed his fire at them and their front line caught the blast of rapid fireballs. Not stopping the flow of his flaming palm, he pointed his hand at the shadows through the window space, and shot spheres into the undergrowth. Twisted, dry, brambles, never seen by the sun caught the flames. Amidst the cracking of the hungry fire, Skar shouted with shock and rage.

A figure, his face hidden within black cloth and helm, walked through the fire. He loomed in the entry like an intimidating shadow against the flames behind him. Unlike his troop, he appeared better-armoured in scales of shining black on chest, arms, and legs.

Here he comes, Keanan shouted into the Kins' minds while he fired haphazardly at the Skar and Narahk. The Narahk's cloak caught the fire, yet the black plate remained unscathed.

I'll watch the back. Shiarn released Earona's hand.

Marcus flicked out his second sword and without time to play, he sliced into the neck of the burning Baskharef, almost taking off its head. It was enough to incapacitate it, and it fell away. In response to the new menacing presence of the Narahk, he thought, *I'll take him.*

Earona was left standing by the tree trunk, in trembling fear, not knowing what she should be doing, but sensing she was in the way.

Marcus stepped into the path of the Skar and Narahk, he said with loud self-assurance, 'You'll have to take me down first.'

The Narahk gave an irritated growl and swung his sword down onto Marcus. Deflecting the blow, Marcus struck with his second blade. His opponent blocked, matching his strikes with seasoned skill. Shattering power coursed through Marcus' sword, but it did little damage to the Narahk. His cloak now ablaze, the Narahk drove into Marcus, attacking all the harder. Sensing Earona's frightened presence a few paces behind him, Marcus thought to her with cutting urgency, *stay near me, but not in the way!*

Gladly.

Skar came through the front towards him and Keanan. Marcus blocked the hits coming fast and hard on the right and left. Exhaling sharply, he realized the tight spot he was in. He couldn't move forward nor could he safely step backwards for fear of involving Earona, and moving sideways would surely see a fireball in his back. The Narahk fought on, unfaltering in his resistance of Marcus' skillful parries. Marcus' blade sliced through flesh, yet the solid clash of their swords continued with no impediment to his enemy's blows.

Keanan's fire propelled through the doorway, causing the Skar outside to become a human wall of flame. Eventually the Skar transformed into piles of smoldering rock, while the stink of burning flesh hung in the air. The Skar were getting smarter and better able to move towards him in a self-preserving manner. It would take two or three brave ones to run at him and tie him down. He didn't have long to be effective. Unsheathing his long sword, Keanan prepared for the advancing warriors.

At the other end of the back wall, free of fire, Skar crawled through the aperture. One dropped with a heavy thump and dispersed into ash under the window. Swapping her dagger for his sword, Shiarn didn't have long to wait for the next unfortunate intruder. She cut into flesh, sending another into dust. Smoke hampered her vision, causing her to miss the wide swing of a sword through the gap slashing her arm. Pain disabled her for moments.

After much delayed thrashing, and despite the scolding heat, they were climbing through; one Skar at a time. Even with the fire burning close outside, she doubted she could prevent them eventually flowing in.

A wayward sword caught Shiarn across the back of her legs. The hot sting overwhelmed her, yet for the sake of survival she moved to pierce the next intruder. Her blood was now on the stones, compromising her invisibility, making it impossible for her to retreat even if she wanted to.

The swords of the Narahk and Marcus locked together with a solid clang and swung in an arc. Much to Marcus' irritation the figure fought on despite his burning clothing.

Although his armour remained untouched. Even with his Shattering blows, it should have ended by now.

Caught unaware by the Skar coming round his flank, Marcus lost his guard to the Narahk and he sliced into Marcus' arm. Despite the injury and with blood gushing down to his hand, he turned on the Skar, running him through. It only made Earona draw closer to him. 'Curse it!' He would have preferred she remain with Shiarn and invisible. Enduring the pain, he continued hammering in blows, none of which appeared to have any detrimental effect. A warm touch on his hip sent a tingling sensation up his spine. His flesh rejoined and the pain left him, as did Earona's hand. *I didn't mean that close, but thanks.*

The Narahk's gaze landed on her. 'A healer.'

Another Skar tried a strike at her. In her rush to get away, she tripped and fell. The Narahk shouted at the Skar and he backed off.

While keeping the one Skar off him and away from Earona, Marcus pushed into the Narahk with lethal force, seeking a breakthrough in his defensives. Like a blow to his face, he figured out his opponent's ability. *He's got something like Iron Skin.* Anxious moans and dismal responses washed over his thoughts. The enemy appeared to possess the skill of warding off killing blows of weapons.

Seth's thoughts added to everyone's building despair at the situation, *I'm nearly out of arrows.*

Marcus fought on with a determined desperation, hearing also Shiarn was injured behind them. He concluded the only way of destroying the Narahk was by Keanan's fire, and he would keep the Narahk off Keanan long enough for that to happen.

Earona was scared out of her mind at the closeness of the strange enemy intent on killing them. Standing by the tree, she considered climbing up, but it was beyond her reach. She had to trust Marcus knew what he was doing. Filled with an ever increasing vulnerability at the frightening turn of events, she gathered her wits enough to realize the only thing preventing the Skar and the Narahk from sticking her through with their pointed blades was Marcus. She was going to ensure he stay in a fit enough state to stop them. Even if she did have to get so close. As soon as he was injured, she reached out to touch him, although she suspected he hated it. Surely it was better to be of some use.

'A healer.' The dark clad menace turned its attention on her, freezing her with fright. Never in any nightmare did she think she would be in touching distance of a Narahk, or ever hear one speak to her.

A Skar rushed from the side, directing its weapon at her with a ferocity that nearly stopped her heart. Moving to get away, she fell on a root. She didn't care to see what happened to the creature, but she felt no sword running her through. Perhaps it was safer on the ground where she could see the Narahk's black boots stepping to and fro. Unlike his black armour, they were soft hide. If she wanted she could touch them, if she crawled that far without getting her arm broken off.

He's got something like Iron Skin. Marcus informed them.

Somehow she guessed it was that. What other explanation could there be, if *he* couldn't kill it. She imagined the leathery skin under its leg plates. If she laid a hand on that tough Iron Skin, even through the material, she could reach into its body. She was the only one possessing a Gift of both life and death. And she was well aware of the death element, having dealt with it not long since. Never did she think she would be attempting to use it again in such a way. Right then, it was all she was thinking.

Sparing a thought on whether she should ask Marcus for a distraction, she heard the noisy clanging and bashing of swords reverberating in the chamber. He was already doing so much. Earona thought with chagrin, he would probably fight better if he could move.

Crawling on the stones, hoping to appear wounded, she reached out and waited for him to near. Hoping her arm would not be trodden on by either the Narahk or Marcus, she grabbed hold of the Narahk's ankle. Her Ethos flowed into its body. She compressed the creature's heart till it beat no more.

The Narahk's body formed a figure of black haze and vanished. Burnt clothes and armour fell to the floor in a heap on Earona's arm. She jerked it to her chest. Shaking her hand, she sat up, and breathed hard from shock; she actually made it disappear.

Skar warriors reached the stair while Keanan was busy with those confronting him close up. No longer occupied with the Narahk, Marcus ordered her, 'Stay near the tree.' He went to aid Keanan. 'I'll take what's left, you go to the stair.'

Trapped above, Seth shoved the yelling Skar back with a plank. Keanan threw spheres of fire towards them. They howled in blazing agony and dropped from the stairs.

Marcus made short work of those on fire. After all their assailants were dealt with, he gave the mounds of molten ash a sweeping glance with a satisfied grin. Punching the air with his sword, he gave a victorious bellow.

Burnt ash and rocks blanketed the floor causing the air to be choked with a sulfuric stink. Fortunately, the smoke was escaping through the open ceiling, but the overwhelming smell of death was nauseating.

Seth, his tied up hair now mostly loose, walked down the stairs with a lopsided grin.

Breathing heavily, Shiarn collapsed onto the ground by the tree. Earona came to heal her bloodied arm. Shiarn cried through a parched throat, 'Flamin' hell, Seth! That was not fun.' *My heart nearly stopped beating!*

A contrite gaze on his face, Seth pushed his dangling hair from his face. *Lucky you've got a strong heart.* He placed his hands on the tree untouched by flame and sword and caressed the smooth pale bark. After a moment of restful silence, he looked down at Shiarn's blood covered skirt. 'I am sorry,' he said to her, 'but they were going to chase after Mara. We are alive though. We did it.'

Marcus slapped him on the back in a jovial manner. 'That's the spirit, Sprout.'

Keanan stretched his fingers and looked around in shock. 'I can't believe it though. How many were there?'

Shiarn gave the ash covered room a quick look. 'Too many to count.'

'How…?' Earona stammered, 'how did we even survive it?'

'We did,' Marcus replied with a grin, 'and you should be grateful

Seth patted the tree. 'Caris Dijarnis has saved us.'

They answered, 'Who?' – 'Now you're getting weird, Seth.' – 'You're talking about the tree?'

Finally Seth turned to them. 'The tree is happy she was given a second chance and made it right this time.' He paused. 'She is pleased she has provided us with protection.'

Earona sighed. 'In that case…'

'What do you mean, "this time"?' Shiarn frowned at the tree.

Ignoring them, Seth said, 'We have come under its shielding branches.' He looked up at the tree, 'We thank you with our lives.'

Earona wrapped her arms around the lustrous white bark. 'On behalf of us, thank you for your help.' She responded to the Kin's amused smiles with a weary shrug.

Keanan said, 'We need to get out of this smell.'

'Seth.' Earona stared at the fire blazing in the undergrowth outside the windows. 'What about that?'

Seth's face paled. 'Sacred Kahm, it might burn the tree.'

'What can you do?' Marcus creased his brow at the fire, roaring outside.

Seth's furrowed brow reflected sombre concern for the trees. 'True, I can't control the weather, but I might be able to do something else.' He went for the door. 'Like a candle.'

'Wait,' Keanan called. 'We do not know if any of them are still out there. We go together.'

Marcus replied, 'Couldn't have said it better.'

They left the house and walked the curving path and stopped a distance from the heat licking up the old trees. Seth sat to meditate and they settled beside him.

'I'm going to have nightmares forever.' Earona shivered even as the heat warmed her hands and face. 'All those horrid faces and hungry eyes…'

Marcus gave her a merry grin. 'Next time do that trick at the start.'

Earona was aghast. 'Next time?'

Keanan stared at Earona with surprise. 'What did she do?'

Marcus chuckled. 'She'll get cocky…'

'I squeezed…' Earona frowned darkly. 'I stopped its life.'

'Good going,' Shiarn said with a spark of cheer.

'Smart thinking,' Keanan commented, 'and, yes, that would have been helpful, earlier.'

Earona's small voice could hardly be heard. 'Once I realized he had Iron Skin…' It was peculiar speaking of entities with the Gifts of her own race, stranger still coming across them in those who wanted to kill you. She sat immersed in her thoughts, fearing how easy it was to take a life. The guilt overshadowed the sense of victory.

'This is the second time we have faced them,' Keanan speculated, 'it's clear they must be Narahk. It is recorded their forms vanish…'

'Why?' Marcus asked. 'Are they even human?'

Keanan paused for some moments. 'It's not known what they are. No one has ever seen the face of one.'

And hopefully we won't see any more again, Earona finished.

The air became still around the fire, yet Earona had the impression, by the movement of the flames, not all the air was motionless. The flames flicked inwards and up instead of sweeping across the tops of the trees as you would expect. It raged against the old stone wall and high into the night. She watched in awe of its power.

Marcus commented with laid-back mirth, 'If no one knew we were here before they certainly will now.'

'This makes me realize I really dislike combat,' Shiarn remarked.

'That reminds me…' Marcus turned to her with a frown. 'I don't know if it was the best thing to leave Earona like that…'

Earona piped up, 'What was that?'

'You think so?' Shiarn, her cheeks smudged with blood and ash, gave him a condescending look. 'That's strange coming from you. She was a lot safer where she was than trying to keep up with me.'

Marcus scratched the blood off his healed arm. 'Ah, guess you're right. Without Earona there, that thing would have kept going. Considering you don't like fighting, you took a lot of them out, but then again you couldn't be seen—'

'Bite your tongue!' She retorted. 'It's bloody and gruesome.'

'I don't know how that must feel.' Marcus nodded with a glint in his eyes.

Shiarn thumped him in the arm. 'It's far too easy for some.'

Rubbing his arm, Marcus laughed. 'Anyway, without you we would have been overrun.'

'I think Keanan's the one who did the most damage.' Shiarn peeked a glance at Keanan sitting behind them.

'You're right.' Earona offered, 'And Marcus kept that Narahk occupied.' *And kept me alive.*

Anytime you need me to. He went on with some envy, 'And without the intrepid Sprout, calling the first shot, we might have had a peaceful night, although a hell of a tomorrow.' He added, 'Excellent marksmanship too.'

'We all did our part and we actually did a good job at working together,' Keanan added with pride, 'that's the most important thing. And that we're alive.'

'You sound surprised?' Marcus said with a teasing smirk.

'I'm just…' Keanan finished short, 'relieved.'

'See, we aren't that bad,' Marcus chuckled.

'It had to be done.' Seth's face was darkened with black soot and he glanced over his shoulder with a sheepish grin. 'And someone had to do it.'

Marcus reached over Shiarn's shoulders and patted Seth's back. 'Don't be modest.'

Seth blushed and kept his head down.

Earona shook her head at them. 'The whole experience was heart stopping to say the least.'

'Thank goodness it worked out,' Shiarn said, 'but there's no need to get inflated.'

'Indeed. We should hope Jett and Hellier are not in trouble or in need of aid,' Keanan said. *There is nothing we can do for them right now.*

'I saw the wagon but not all the horses,' Seth said, 'we can follow when it's light.'

Earona agreed, but now she was faced with the spare time to worry about Jett, Hellier, and Mara, and she prayed fervently they would remain safe.

77 - Message in Stone

A gem of knowledge is priceless to the one who knows its value

Prophetess Janna Meadow'Fox 4th Seat Elder

Mara shut her eyes in fearful anticipation of the trap's purpose. Pressure from the released seal, pushed the air from her lungs, making her breathless. After tensing with fear, her eyes flashed wide in surprise; she was still in the chamber.

Hellier, her fire gone, fell on hands and knees, breathing hard. Her bruised naked body was bleeding from the many blows she received.

With her hand above Jett's mouth, Mara checked his breathing. She stared up into the light blue of Hellier's eyes. 'He's alive, but weak.' She pressed on his limp arm. He gave her a warning moan in response.

Hellier brushed her hand along his cheek. 'He will recover?'

'He's lost too much blood...' She answered.

'Shite!' Hellier narrowed her eyes at Mara. 'Do you think they come back?'

Mara examined what she could see of the chamber. Candles were no longer lit and no other ritual objects were visible apart from the blood and bodies. 'It doesn't look like it.'

'I need to get him out of here.' Hellier's shoulders and chest sagged. 'And get my clothes back.'

'You're hurt.'

'I am, but I'll live.' Hellier, her lips pressing together, scowled at Mara. 'I don't understand — what are you about? *Who* are you?'

Mara fell on her backside in weary resignation. 'I used to be... well, they seem to know me.'

'And probably Jett as well.' Hellier stroked his pale cheek, and her eyes misted.

'I might be able to help him.' Mara wiped away the blood trickling down her forehead with the back of her hand.

Hellier frowned in doubt. 'Will it affect him in a bad way?'

'It shouldn't...' she wavered with uncertainty, suddenly wondering that herself.

Hellier placed her head in her hand and sighed heavily. 'Do what you can do.'

Mara muttered, 'You get your clothes and I'll help him.'

'I'll look for water.' Hellier rose with trembling legs. 'Scream if you need me.' She laid her hand on Jett's shoulder. 'Don't go dying while I'm not here.'

Once Hellier left, Mara reached under her skirts and untied the leather pouch she stole from Sommerlea. Despite detesting the stuff, she couldn't bear leaving the little bag of potency behind, knowing how powerful it would be. She opened his shirt, exposing his hardened torso and an intricate tattoo running down from his left shoulder. The witches had dredged up her memories with the power of their collective evil. After sprinkling the ash on his skin in a circle, she cut into her palm with the small disc. A decent flow came forth and she drew the blood through the ash, making the signs on his flesh. It came back to her with frightening clarity, but it wasn't Wendessa who carried out this incantation. There were others. Recalling their faces brought back the pain and paralyzing fear of that time.

In a desperate chant, she repeated the mystical words linked to the symbols. All the while her blood dropped onto his skin, and her life force ebbed away. Rayne tossed within, making her nauseous. He was not happy her blood was disappearing into Jett. But she reasoned, it was the least she could do for the man who came to save her. Jett had put his life in peril. It was more than Mara thought possible of him. As her blood interacted with the ash, an elaborate pattern started appearing on his chest. It grew stronger till it was illuminated. She gasped at seeing a particular symbol, the very same that she had, but his was neater and more perfect in appearance, more like a supernatural imprint. So he also had a Curse-seal all along. Did he know what it meant? She didn't have time to wonder, or about the other symbols before the spell took effect. Her chin flopped down onto her chest and she fell into forgotten recesses of her mind.

~ * ~

She ran down the familiar hall, where she and her older brothers had been playing that morning, and on, not stopping her perilous dash from the soldiers in pursuit.

'Mavin,' a man shouted with spiteful fury from a room she passed. 'There's no escape for you. Any of you!' The clash of metal followed.

She whimpered with anguish her brother had to face such a cruel foe. But it was foolish to think of going to him.

Her mother's words drove her on, like a command she was compelled to obey. *'You are small enough. Flee and hide. Do not look back. To live is better than death.'* Fear was bursting in her gut. Her lungs on fire, she gasped for air as she imagined what may be happening to her mother, still upstairs.

Too fast, she skidded on the rug. Almost tripping, she scampered up in time to race down the back stairs. Screams of people being murdered ripped through the corridors. Poor unfortunate servants to be killed in such a horrible way.

The kitchen was upon her, as well as the cries of men. Confused and terrified by their rage, she flew out into the moon-lit courtyard.

~ * ~

Fire was eating up the barrels and crates, the wood constructs holding up the storehouse were crumbling into flaming heaps. Cornered by the hungry fire, and coughing up the foul stink, she would be next to catch light. She would welcome her end. Choking from the smoke-laden air, she hunched over, hoping to die before the flames touched her skin.

From the shadows of smoke, a hand snatched hers up in a grip like squeezing ice. She gave a startled cry at the haggard woman with the deformed face and eyes reflecting a hypnotic orange.

'The bastards will never get us. Cynelaerd can burn down to hell.' Her words, like the roaring flames, simmered with hate. The woman opened a door in the floor and yanked the girl down into darkness.

~ * ~

Sobbing at the grueling pain stabbing her core, she flailed against the man. Her delicate fists did nothing to stop him. His weight crushed her body about to break. The agony seemed endless. The ritual had to be carried out, or she would die. So they said.

She would numb herself against the pain that seemed unremitting.

He was not the first. Her resistance was an insignificant gesture that only emphasized her defeat. Deadening her thoughts drained her determination to remember her past… her family…

She would overcome the pain till she no longer felt or even remembered. She would forget everything—

'Stop crying!' A coarse voice, one of many, sounded horrid in the incense soaked room. 'This is your destiny.'

~ * ~

Jett's eyes shot open. His hand caught Mara's wrist hovering above his chest, in a steely grip. He pushed it aside and her head sprang up. He said, 'What are you doing?'

'I…' Her eyes skipped away from his face, '…healing you.'

He lifted his head and eyed the soot and blood on his skin. 'Is that what you call it?'

In haste, she wiped the grey bloody ash from his chest with her skirt, and noticed the markings on his chest had completely disappeared. But she could have sworn she didn't imagine it. 'It's not known by that name.' Her face was flushed as she pressed down on her bleeding hand to stem the flow.

Jett sat up and gave a surprised cry when he attempted moving his arm. 'Devil's arse!' He exhaled a painful sigh. 'You're doing magik on me. It might explain why I have images bounding around my head. Who is Mavin? And what is Cyneleard?' With his good hand he rubbed his temples and gave a groan. 'I've seen your memories, haven't I?'

'You…' Mara gasped with wide-eyed astonishment. '…saw?'

'And none of it pleasant.' Jett went on with irritation, 'And why do I have a broken arm?'

'It…' She swallowed hard and her voice was thick with sudden emotion, 'their spell did that. When they don't want to kill outright they break you within.'

'Sucking the life out of me as effectively as possible?'

'I guess so.' Mara ducked her head and turned her gaze away.

'Right.' He gave a weary sigh and noted her bleeding hand. Recalling how she had helped them, his tone softened. 'What were you saying before I passed out?'

Mara stared down at her bloodied hands in perplexity. 'When the seal is undone the witch is magically permitted to lay claim to one thing from within.'

Jett frowned in consideration. 'And they didn't take you.' He measured her expression of bafflement with an ominous premonition.

'They are permitted one thing only. Matter or living.' She pressed on her stomach. 'Usually the thing of most power or usefulness.'

Jett glanced at the cord on this wrist with relief. But when he tapped his pocket, he gave an annoyed moan. 'Wretched hell-spawn whores.' He tried to stand and Mara gripped his upper arm to aid him to his feet. He growled, 'The demon bitch took it with her.'

Mara responded with disbelief, 'Something of yours?'

'The Eye-key.'

Mara's face paled and her mouth was left gaping.

Hellier came into the room. Blood from her arms and legs stained her clothing from underneath. 'Let's get out of here.' She dashed to Jett's side and looped his arm about her shoulders, and said in a subdued manner, 'But first, there's something you need to see.'

Jett shook the fog from his thoughts and moved his heavy legs to walk. 'Sounds grim.' He cast a glance at the bodies around them. 'Like this.' Ignoring her reproachful frown with a roguish half-grin, he said with more seriousness, 'God, Hel, you're bleeding.'

Hellier looked at the blood seeping through her sleeve. 'I'll manage.'

Using the wall as support, Mara ambled behind in a weakened daze. 'Where are we going?'

'Not far,' Hellier replied, 'we're all in a bad way.'

Hellier took them down a corridor reflecting less light and up a wide staircase leading out on to an expansive flat roof. The night sky had scant cloud cover and a bright moon lit up the surrounding woodlands. The three sat down a little way from the short wall at the edge. To the southeast, grey billowing smoke spiraled high above the tree tops.

Hellier looked towards it. 'Is that where we were?'

'It—' Jett's voice caught as he tried to speak. '…blood 'n shite.'

We can only guess…

They sat in silence watching the smoke leave a trail in the sky. Finally Jett broke the mournful pause. 'Could it get any worse…?' He faced Mara, his dismal expression conveyed his disappointment. She had known something was coming.

Mara turned from his gaze to Hellier. 'I can bandage that for you.'

Hellier gave a gruff, 'Thanks.'

Mara ripped strips from her underskirt and tightened it around Hellier's arm. She sat back on her hunches and with her hands in a tight ball on her lap, stared out at the forest.

'We don't know what has happened.' Jett continued observing the drifting smoke. 'And we are not entirely safe ourselves.'

Hellier stood. 'I'm going to do another scout. See what I can find.'

With his free hand he caught hold of hers and squeezed it. 'Be careful.'

'Always.' She ran back down the steps.

Jett and Mara sat in a forced quiet. Mara watched the valley while he studied her. She was different somehow, more vulnerable, less like a brat. But it was her expression of grief that lowered his walls.

Still staring off into the night, she spoke. 'Did you forget about that dark menace back in Lanvin?'

He scowled at her smug yet candid remark. 'Curse it!' He was facing witches while his Kin faced a Narahk, and there was nothing he could currently do.

'How is your arm?' Her tone softened.

'Giving me hell.' He was angrier than he realized, but the night's battle with the witches was made worse by the loss of the Key, and maybe even that of his Kin. 'It is what it is and nothing can be done about it, though I wish it had somehow been different.' He looked past her downcast face and in the direction of the mountains casting their shadows across the foothills. If he squinted hard and focused, he thought he could see towards the end of the Grey Stone Peaks. Holding his aching arm, he pushed himself to a standing position.

'I know…' She lifted her gaze and an uncustomary remorse entered her eyes. 'I can bandage your arm.'

He nodded with a grimace.

She tore more strips from her ever shortening under-dress and wrapped them about his arm to create a neat sling.

Jett asked, 'How did you learn that?'

'Someone like me learns things like this.'

He stepped over the cracks in the roof, avoiding the holes with edges of crumbling stones. Then, he saw it. A gigantic mural on the roof. Apart from the collapsed flooring, the picture was in reasonable condition. He walked further into it until he stood at the bottom of the massive pyramid, spanning nearly the whole length of the roof. His eyes followed it up to a flat surface on the top and a white circular shape the size of half a man. He walked nearer, his eyes widening with recognition at the orb from the journal and a gold shining light at its center. The Eye-key.

In the frosty grey of near dawn, Jett crouched to study the emblem. He touched the surrounding off-white stones and discovered it was not a dye substance, but white crystal and the eye was yellow topaz and a white gem similar to the Key itself. Staring at it in fascination, he observed the rest of the mural. Figures stood either side of the pyramid, detailed enough for him to assume it was Nya. Her life-size figure was the work of skilled craftsmen. He crouched to touch her opal face and stroke her malreus hair. Her outstretched hands held a gold staff aloft. A diamond at the tip, and spraying smaller ones towards the Eye of Heaven. The rising sun's rays hit the gems embedded around her neck and down her front, and she sparkled like a wondrous treasure trove. He was amazed at how untouched by time and thieves it was. Perhaps there was some type of protection around it.

On the opposite side of the pyramid, Mara stared down at a woman figure in red, also holding a staff, but red lines of rubies reached in all directions. Mara gaped at the sight and pointed. 'Gods, I feel I know this… woman.'

Standing, he nodded towards the mural. He also remembered a woman in red from the vision they shared. 'Somehow we are connected to this scene.' Again he studied the picture, and chewed his lip in contemplation. 'But as to how exactly I don't yet know.'

His eyes turned back to the ranges covered in a blue shaded light. Not even the sight of the sun on the mountains could warm him or remove his wretched demeanor. He and Hellier would have been killed if it weren't for some fortunate occurrences, one of them, Mara. On considering that, he realized if it were not for her they wouldn't have been there in the first place. One thing was sure, he did not like dealing with witches. The merciless women were ruled by cruel malice. Underlying their wickedness was a tremendous cowardice.

Mara shivered and hugged her arms. The breeze tossed her wild red hair from her face. Aside from her head injury, Jett glimpsed her despair. She was barely a woman, a detail he kept overlooking. He recalled her memories – he could have revealed more about them, but he sensed he touched a matter that evoked pain and in essence most likely unfathomable. 'Mara,' he called her out of her dazed trance, 'do you know if that was all the witches?'

Startled from her reverie, she muttered, 'There could be more.' Holding her stomach, she stepped awkwardly to him.

He waited for her to reach his side and he gazed down into her sunken eyes. 'You know them?'

Shivering, she averted her sad gaze and rubbed her upper arms, attempting to warm herself. 'I recall Barkala, and two others, but the rest, no.' Her voice was firm although edged with sorrow, and she shook her head. 'I don't want to.'

'They might come back for you,' he stated.

Her tone become more abrasive. 'They will probably need more sacrifices first.'

Jett kept his eyes on her for any sign of deception. 'I see.'

'And they have the…' Avoiding his gaze, she pouted. 'Key.'

He rolled his head back and looked at the last remaining star. 'God…'

'It opens the Gate.'

'You know.' He creased his brow in frustration.

Her eyes widened with fearful awe. 'To let Hell in, but… can they do it without you—' she gasped, 'oh, they want me too…?'

'Now you see.' He grimaced and clutched his arm as he walked to the ivory representing the Eye. 'This is it.'

Kneeling, she laid her hand on the white orb. 'On top of a pyramid.'

Jett stared across the countryside, comprehending her train of thought. 'The evil Nya plans to restore the Eye of Heaven,' he recalled, 'and now I assume the witches do too.'

'That woman…' her voice was barely audible, but Jett sensed the sudden fear.

'The very one' - he had commanded Mara to resurrect, and if she had been successful Nya would be walking the earth with them.

Mara clutched herself and mumbled, 'and I'll have to do that again, when you—'

'No. Not again.' He would do whatever he could to stop it from happening to her, and him. Something else caught his attention along the mountain range. He pointed towards an outcrop of jagged rocks coming out from the Grey Stone Peaks. 'Can you see something?'

'The mountain?' Mara peered out into the distance. 'You mean something that looks like a wall?'

A wall on top of a plateau was the only visible evidence of any structure that may be there, but Jett felt certain it was Havenside.

'We're going there?'

'Not you.' After some moments contemplating it with a tight lipped smile, he finally said, 'I am.'

She stared at him with blatant disbelief. 'But your friends... and your broken arm.'

'True...' He gazed out at the forest again and screwed his mouth up with anguish.

Hellier dashed up the stairs carrying saddle bags and a flask of water.

'It's the Eye-key.' Jett lowered himself down trying to keep his arm comfortable. 'The witches took it.'

Hellier passed out bread and fruit. 'That's all we need.'

'Anything those witches do has got to be bad.' He took an apple and gave the other to Mara. 'Where did you get this from?'

'The riders' saddle bags.'

Mara grumbled through a mouthful of apple, 'Rynians; always well packed.'

'Rynians, eh...' Jett munched on the fruit and gazed at Hellier, sensing something amiss. 'You saw Thunder down there?'

'Yes. He found water.' Hellier paused her chewing. 'And Lightning too.' She put her bread down.

His face paled with anger. 'Flaming hell.'

'We'll have to get back there,' Hellier said, 'If we even know how to get back.'

'We can try.'

After they had a short rest with food, Jett stood, holding his forearm as he moved. He winced from the pain, 'If Seth is there he could find us.' All through their time on the roof the breeze had been quiet. He hardened his voice. 'But we cannot rely on that. At least we have a horse for Mara to ride.'

Mara looked at him with horror. 'I don't ride.'

Jett gave her a bemused stare. 'You will. Hellier will sit behind and teach you.'

Groaning, Mara gave him an annoyed expression. 'It's not that...'

Jett ignored her and said, 'Those witches are working with Ryne?'

'Probably from the queen,' Mara said, 'Although they seemed to be doing things against her.'

'Witches it would seem are not loyal creatures,' Jett replied.

Mara gave him a sulky frown.

'Where would they be?' Hellier asked Mara.

She replied, 'They're probably hiding out somewhere nearby, trying to recuperate. They used Rynian soldiers.'

Jett murmured, 'Nearby.'

'You're thinking of that place on the mountain?' asked Mara.

Hellier said, 'Jett? What place on the mountain?'

'Havenside is up there.' He pointed over his shoulder. 'I want to know what those witches have planned with the Eye and maybe with Havenside.' He paused. 'They have it and I don't. And I don't like it.' He turned to Mara, 'How many more of them could there be?'

Mara gave a careless shrug. 'Who can say? Maybe fifteen, could be more.'

Hellier said, 'Let's hope for less.'

Jett said, 'For now, we need to get down from here.'

They made slow progress down the stone stairs, eventually coming out into the light of the new day. It was easier to see the paved roadway leading down from the doorway and circling the large structure. The road also broke off to the northeast and passed more woodland going downwards. Currently Jett's arm was secured against his chest, but the pain grew acute.

Once outside he whistled. Moments passed and Thunder broke through the trees with Lightning following. To Jett's dismay, Forest, came trotting after him. Hellier checked him over and he was not too worse for wear. The rider's light grey horse followed them all as if needing the company.

Jett stroked Thunder's neck with affection. 'They can do a slow ride.'

Hellier replied, 'It will have to do.'

Mara jumped away from the stamping horses.

Ignoring Mara's skittishness, Hellier pulled on her shoulder, moving her closer to the horse. 'On you get.' With Hellier's help, Mara struggled onto the horse, but was unbalanced by her protruding belly.

While Jett watched them, he felt a fever growing in his body. Sweat covered his face and his gut tightened. Before he could give a shout of warning, he slumped by Thunder's feet in a dazed faint.

78 - Prepare for Night

What is important?
Not what you should be
But what you want to be

Tome of the First Born Reign

Flames shot up the polished marble walls and across the slate floor, enveloping the furnishings and eating the air. 'Mama...?' The voice of a dark haired child was a tremor against the roar. He hunched forward in the oversized bed, his arms reaching for the one he beckoned.

Penetrating the blazing inferno, a voice spoke with sharp reproof. He observed his hands and the writing on his wrist with confusion. While he pondered the words, his hands shifted between a child's fist and an adult sized palm. He turned them over, watching them flick from one to the other.

The flames parted and a woman, unaffected by the fire, approached the bed. 'Jett.'

He squinted up at her face, made beautiful by caramel skin and crimson lips. Recognition dawned in the holes of his memory. 'Nya?'

Her eyes grew tender and she stretched her hand to him. 'Come.'

Unable to shift his weakened body, he remained confined on the bed.

'You are not that child anymore.'

Nya's words forced him to examine his tangled thoughts. This time he studied his hands, and noted the snake symbol on his skin.

She smiled. 'You still wear the Ward.'

Covering the glowing emblem with his hand, it shimmered beneath his palm. He said with more clarity, 'Yes.'

'You can see.'

He held up his hand before his face and willed it to remain true. Finally, the flickering transformation ceased and he observed the change from the child hand to an adult fist. In the cool air, he flexed his bare arms, glad to see he was at least wearing trousers.

The sanctuary was different. Black marble walls with flecks of gold enclosed the chamber furnished in a similar fashion to his first time there, although the detail on the bed was more elaborate.

'It has changed somewhat. Because you have,' she commented, 'Dwelling in the spirit realm requires time and practice, regrettably that is not something you have opportunity for.'

Jett also sensed a difference in her. She was less ethereal and more like one who walked the earth. Suddenly fearful, he examined the room, partially concealed by flames. 'The fire?'

'You are feverish with injuries.' She offered him her hand. 'But that is not what is important right now.'

Outside thoughts pricked at his awareness. 'Why are you here?'

'You know why.' Nya grasped his hand and he stood.

Whether she was good or evil, he would not be led again and he walked alongside her. The flames dissipated from their path and were nearly gone once they came to the panoramic window. His black hair waved against his cheek in the cold air; a shock to his sweating skin. He stood on the edge of a rocky cliff. In the distance, past woodlands and stone ruins, a white pyramid reflected the sun amongst the lush of the emerald land. A wide line of steps led up the ziggurat to a flat surface with four narrow pillars. Around the great paved area were giant colonnades joined by massive arches. In some places the forest had taken hold and trees upturned the stones and destroyed walls. The entry of the enormous structure was concealed by the encroaching forest. 'Is that...?'

'The Agamon.' Nya's voice was husky with a tinge of awe. 'Sacred resting place for the Chanin-Quyllar. Once a glorious monument. Now a shattered shell.'

'So that's where....' Jett creased his brow. 'The Gate...'

Her knowing expression showed she was satisfied with his recollection.

'...she has the Eye-key.'

Nya's crestfallen expression conveyed her remiss. 'I know.'

'Those cursed bitches stole it,' Jett fumed with remorse. 'I'm sorry...'

Her white, jewel adorned gown fluttered in the breeze, and her black hair dangled by her waist as she turned from his self-reproach to the presently changing scene. 'Look.' She pointed at the black cloud growing above the Agamon. 'They have begun.'

A foreboding dread pervaded Jett's thoughts. 'Opening it?'

'Soon. They must first reform the orb.' She stared into the far distance and whispered, 'Once it is complete, I shall be no more.'

'What are you saying?' He demanded.

She faced him slowly, her eyes swimming with grief. 'You too may suffer the same fate once it is complete. If they succeed in repairing it, Hell will come and I will no longer be myself.' She looked down at her body, blurring into transparency. 'I'm already beginning to fade into her.'

'You can't,' he cried with sudden anguish. 'How can I stop it?'

'You have the power.' She stepped closer and stared into his eyes. 'Chanin-Quyllar destroyed my people and my flesh, even with the Peace-stone I had to give my life.'

Her sombre words pierced his soul as he comprehended the weight of her sacrifice. He caught hold of her hands, in case she suddenly diminished from his presence. 'Is that what you want from me?' Apprehension washed over him mixed with a mounting dread.

She stated with sad honesty, 'Chanin-Quyllar's power is immense. I came to realize its essence is sealed with a life, indeed, it demands one.'

'You speak in riddles.' In exasperation, Jett clenched her arms.

'How can I expect you to understand,' she replied, 'I barely understood the mystery myself.'

'They're going to do it soon?'

She slumped in his strong grip. 'They will establish the Demon nation here and spawn their devils in this land. There will not be day here again.'

An awful foreboding began to build inside him. He knew exactly what it would look like and how it would be mastered. The hordes were already prepared to march forth beyond the unseen barrier. He and his Kin were in the thick of it in the center of the valley. 'What can we do?'

'The witches do not have the skill on their own, they must have magik users invoking more power, even then, they would need you to complete the rupture of this realm,' Nya stated, 'They will be on the Agamon, the altar of elements. But it is not those you would have to overcome.'

'Who then?'

'I will not ask this of you, I know the payment, nonetheless I shall enlighten you. You have the ability within and that is the place of battle.' She touched the edge of his eye with her finger. 'In here.' Passion warmed her face and her mouth curved in a coy smile.

'My vision?' He caressed her cheek, his fingers running down the side of her neck. Holding her close, he touched her lips with his, seeking her out.

She caught his hand and guided his fingers along her cheek. After parting from the kiss, she whispered, 'No matter how I may wish it, I will not remain in this state. I will pass on, either into her or the spirit realm.'

'No,' he whispered by her mouth, 'I don't want to leave you.'

She ran her fingers through his dark fringe and stared warmly into his intense gaze. Her eyes reflected a similar longing. 'Dear one, how could I have used you so flagrantly and without any thought as to the person you would be? Were you so entangled in my heart you became the center of my prophecies? How did it come to pass, all my desires, even wrought with trepidation bring such a noble one as you into my words?' She lowered her gaze and sighed with remorse.

Jett lifted her chin and his voice softened. 'Prophecies are the bane of my life.'

'Your very existence is prophetic. I have birthed you through the Word of Fate, and from the love of my heart.' She halted, unsure of speaking further, and frowning, she looked towards the Agamon, and muttered, as if to herself, 'Of course… the defender will be a reflection of the divination of evil, yet his decision will be governed by devotion to honour… by the love I bore my land and people…as the one shall be. The One birthed from my own essence.'

'Are you wishing to confuse me?'

Her eyes widened at her spoken revelation. 'No, it is I who wish to have insight. That I may have hope.' With urgency, she said, 'You cannot stay here. Your purpose is out there. I lived my life and made my choices, now it is time for you to make yours. This was a decision I made long ago.' She drew close to him and pleaded, 'Will my decision be for naught?'

He pulled her into a tight embrace and viewed her wise eyes, finding discernment from many eras past.

'Think about what we have spoken of.' She clung to him and her hands were powerful. 'The consequences of either decision are dire indeed, but be assured I have foretold brave allies to assist you.'

She planted a lingering kiss on his lips and an image of his Kin came to mind. 'My Kin?'

'And others.'

He slipped into darkness with her touch on his skin and her words in his thoughts.

~ * ~

Jett woke to the sound of birds overhead and Earona's dark hair swaying over his face. Her vibrant blue eyes conveyed her usual worry. Smiling, he mumbled, 'Blue.'

Her frown deepened and her shrill tone broke through his abstract reflection. 'How many times am I going to find you like this? I am not impressed.'

His eyes searched her soot smeared face and saw the strain of a laborious night. Disorientated, he sat and stared at the stream, having no recollection of it. The confrontation with the witches and the plight of the stolen amulet crashed through his peaceful composure. He locked eyes with her, comprehending she was present before him, well and seemingly in one piece. He grabbed hold of her arms and his voice croaked. 'You're safe.'

'I wouldn't say that.' Her voice was stretched and aggravated. 'Alive maybe.'

His dark anxious eyes checked her over. 'What happened?'

She answered with irritation, but her fear was easy to sense, 'We were attacked by Skar and Narahk.'

'You did well then.' Jett tried to impart encouragement, despite the stab of fear for their safety. 'And how did you find it, your first encounter with one?'

'I didn't like it,' she stated with disapproval, 'and I don't wish to have to do it again and it wasn't one, it was two.'

Keanan approached them and Jett stared up at him. 'We need to talk.'

'Indeed.' Keanan's sombre expression expected nothing else. 'We will stop here and rest awhile.' The fatigue was evident in his drooping shoulders and dark circles under his eyes.

'I'd rather stop away from here,' Jett said. 'I don't wish to be here tonight.'

'So be it.'

Beyond the temple they followed a road, heading east, that dipped and curved, yet always ran parallel to the mountain range. Along the way they observed the ruins of what might have been a city. Eventually they decided to halt some distance down the road on the border of an overgrown meadow. Towards the north, the slight rocky incline introduced the mountain ranges of the Grey Stone Peaks. Under the shade of the outlying forest and near a high stone wall, they stretched out in the wild grass.

After describing the Skar and Narahk assault, they explained how they were riding since dawn. Sleep was impossible, instead they searched for their horses. River, the sensible mare she was, stuck close to the Kin. Once finding the horses that pulled the wagon, the Kin decided to move out. Riding River, Seth discovered a path leading towards the mountains. Marcus and Keanan drove the wagon, while Shiarn and Earona were inside. The mountains loomed closer and they spied the temple. They arrived to find Hellier informing them of an ill Avare.

Jett's urgency was momentarily put aside as the Kin reclined on the grass. Hellier described their dealings with the witches, and Mara remained silent. His thoughts harassed by other topics, Jett listened, with no urge to share his side of the story.

Earona screwed up her pretty face in horror. 'Dead things?'

'Disgustingly wicked,' Hellier commented with a tremor of unease. *We escaped by a devil's whisker.*

Shiarn directed at Jett with admonishment, 'You need to have words with Seth.'

Curious, Jett cast a look at Seth, lounging under a tree. 'What did he do?'

'Killed a Narahk.' Seth ended his statement with a sheepish grin.

'Sound's damn fine.' Jett was not about to begrudge him the skills he recently acquired under Adis' tutelage, even so… *Maybe he's acting too impulsively, but—*

Keanan added, 'I don't believe that's what Shiarn is inferring.'

Shiarn rolled her eyes with hopelessness. 'Not at all.' She looked at Seth before her eyes attempted to piece Jett's gaze. '*He* knows what I mean.'

'Shiarn, the witches took the amulet,' Hellier blurted.

Finally the topic Jett was mulling over was spoken. He stretched his body with a groan of guilt and sat up.

Shiarn aimed an accusing glare at him. 'Were you even going to tell us?'

Yes. Jett sighed. 'But I don't plan on letting them keep it.' Sensing all eyes on him, he said, 'They're reforming the orb, and will use the key—'

'To open the Gate,' Shiarn interrupted in an unforgiving tone. 'Unbelievable.'

He let loose a weary gust of breath. 'If they do, this land could be controlled by the underworld.' The gravity in his voice caused them to pay attention. *Think of the evil that would come of it.* He could only speculate what affect it would have on him.

Marcus let out a low whistle of shock and tilted his head to view how serious Jett was. 'A land of hell.'

Keanan remarked darkly, 'Can witches carry out such a weighty task?'

'Last night's attack doesn't seem half so bad,' Earona commented under her breath, 'But… can they do it without you, and Mara?'

'I think it's possible.' He cast a glance at Mara. 'But not to the same degree.'

Mara stared at the ground and mumbled, 'I don't want to find out.'

Keanan nodded. 'Neither do we.'

'In any case,' Jett said, 'we'll be surrounded by creatures.' He turned his attention to the ranges that shadowed the valley. Noting their horrified expressions, Jett went on, 'They are at the ziggurat called the Agamon. The one in the journal.'

Keanan scratched his beard in thought. 'I wonder if the disaster that destroyed this land is destined to reoccur.'

Jett ran his hand through his black hair. 'Maybe…' He gave short glances to the girls of the Kin. 'But — Nya gave me information—'

'Her again!' Hellier cried with annoyance.

Shiarn asked suspiciously, 'Which one was it?'

Earona frowned in anticipation.

'The good one,' Jett informed them with reassurance.

Keanan questioned, 'That spirit is connected to these witches?'

Jett responded, 'Her evil side used them to get the key.'

'It was a trap.' Keanan was aghast. 'You were led here.'

Jett pursed his lips together and gave Mara a contemplative glance. Her silence over the attack was noted by him and so far he was at odds as to what to say on her behalf. 'Not completely, though I do think it was one particular witch's desire.' As yet there was no mention of Mara's spell casting and he didn't have the time to bring up the touchy subject. 'But, they did have plans to take Mara. Which makes some sense.'

By the nearby tree, Seth spoke up. 'Those Narahk also wanted her and were disappointed she was not there.'

Mara's head jerked up with a fear-filled expression.

Keanan directed at Jett, 'It was similar to what occurred in Lanvin.'

'I'm not surprised.' Jett's tone was sharp and he looked to Mara, trying to keep his anger at bay.

Her fiery eyes took him in with an accusing pout.

Marcus lifted his head from where he lazed. 'We took care of those Skar and the Narahk. Witches should be a breeze after last night.' He laid his head back down without a care in the world.

Earona remarked with disdain, 'You shouldn't think witches are so easy.' *And you can't possibly think you can fight the armies of hell?*

Without lifting himself, Marcus cocked his head and pointed a finger at her, and said with playful recrimination, 'You shouldn't be so worried, I've seen what you can do to a Narahk. I say bring Hell on.'

'Don't be so cocky,' Jett interjected with dry recollection, 'Wait till you walk into a room full of them.'

Earona nodded at Marcus with self-righteous satisfaction and he made a comical face.

Shiarn persisted on the original topic, 'And what are we going to do?'

'Stop them.' Jett's heart was heavy with the speaking of his thoughts aloud. *Somehow.*

Shiarn was brazen enough to voice her doubts. 'You mean we're going to stay in the valley — while Hell potentially opens up around us?' *You do know we have just been through hell — with you?*

'So you should understand how important this is.' Jett's tone turned to ice. 'I don't want Hell opening up.' *And neither should any of you.*

Earona said in a fragile voice, 'And Ethan?'

Jett avoided her soulful glance, and remained staunch, despite his own feelings. 'We can't hope to find him if we have witches at our backs and all the wickedness that will come from this.' Again he shared his intense gaze with his Kin. 'It's not just witches doing this—'

'The Rynians?' Hellier said.

'Yes,' Jett said with confidence, 'They're not far from here.'

'You intend on going towards the soldiers?' Mara cried.

Jett gave her a steady gaze. 'Not only soldiers. You're the one who said the queen had dealings with a magik user.'

'Exactly.' Mara blinked at him with disbelief. 'But it's crazy. You should go in the other direction.'

'I'm not running,' he growled in warning, 'or leaving a mess for someone else to clean up.'

Mara's cheeks tinged red. 'What are you saying— ?'

'Very gallant of you,' Shiarn cleared her throat, 'Soldiers, witches, and mages? Seems to be another whim of yours.'

'We really need to do something though,' Hellier said.

'And,' Keanan shook Jett's resolve with his shrewd gaze, 'What would you expect us to do given such circumstances?'

Jett replied, 'Kean, I know what you are thinking.'

On top of Keanan's fatigue, his eyes reflected grave misgivings. 'I'm assuming you expect us to confront Rynian soldiers on top of any hellish minions?'

Jett had a twinkle in his eye and his mouth formed a roguish grin. 'Not entirely. I have an idea.' *Something on my mind...* Their unimpressed moans and exasperated sighs met with his expectations.

Keanan sighed with weariness and covered his face with his hands, 'I know what your ideas are like.'

Seth piped up from his position outside the circle. 'As long as I'm not a slave again.'

'Agreed.' Marcus jested, 'No stinking shit holes or being tied up either.'

'Nothing like that.' Despite their obvious exhaustion, Jett saw their strengths, even if they could not. 'We'll start tonight.'

They stared at him with unconvincing anticipation.

He continued, undaunted, 'One part involves me climbing a mountain.' His words were received with shaking heads and disapproving stares. 'Another part involves Shiarn.'

Shiarn screwed up her face, but did not avert her gaze from his commanding stare. 'Right then, give it to me plainly.'

He began with boldness, 'Havenside is not far from here and I have been thinking if we can get their help—'

'Why should they help us?' Keanan burst in, 'They are under siege.'

Jett tried keeping calm under Keanan's animosity. 'But if we could help relieve them,' he looked at each in turn, and his eyes finished on Keanan, 'and they were aware of the Rynian's plans that also threatens their lives, they might be inclined to help.'

Keanan sighed. 'Sounds good in theory.'

Marcus, roused by the suggestion of battle, sat up. 'Keanan, you pessimist. We could help them fight.'

Annoyance burned in Keanan's eyes and his lips formed a hard line.

Jett spoke, hoping to diffuse the tension between the two. 'We won't need to fight them. What we can do is undermine the Rynian's military capabilities enough, the Baions can attack and overcome them with little effort, if any.'

A knowing grin emerged on Shiarn's delicate features. 'Sabotage.'

Jett matched her grin with one of his own. 'Hide weapons, disable bows, and any horses.' He paused noting her paling face. 'I mean cut strappings, or lock them in, if there's an option. It's imperative the soldiers not be alerted. So you could be creative.' He added with dry wit, 'You think you could manage it?'

'Why not.' She tapped her chin in contemplation. 'I could hide or scatter the weaponry in the woods. Success might depend on numbers.'

Marcus joined in, 'I could come and destroy them.'

'A good idea, but no,' Jett interrupted, 'I need you to stay behind.' Now the witches had the Key, he needed Mara guarded more than ever. 'Seth will take Shiarn to their camp along with me.'

Keanan commented gruffly, 'And you're not worried about yourself being captured?'

'I'm not going to worry about myself. Yet.' Jett drilled him with an unyielding stare. 'I've got some things worked out.'

Keanan gave a dubious grunt in response.

'Worked out?!' Earona squealed, her disbelief obvious. '*You're* going up a mountain? You might get stuck up there?!'

'While Shiarn is busy in the Rynian camp I shall speak with the Baions,' Jett said, 'If they agree, I'll stay with them till morning.'

Hellier tightened one of her braids around her finger. 'But are you sure? Your climbing skills aren't that great.'

Knowing full-well she was the best climber, he replied staunchly, concealing his discomfit, 'I'm the only one who can do it at night. Also, I'm the one that needs to speak with them.'

Hellier shook her head in worriment.

'Yes,' Keanan sighed, 'because the story is going to be quite incredible, and I'd say unbelievable to a normal man.'

Jett stared at the mix of expressions reflecting misgivings to downright doubt he could do it. 'I can do it.' His words took a sullen turn. 'We are here now and there's a chance we can stop this from happening.'

Shiarn gave him a wry smile. 'But Jett, because we are here this *is* happening.'

He sighed with frustration. 'It is what it is and we have to make amends, well, I have to.' In a lighter tone, he said, 'And anyway I'm not going to let those bitches get away with it without a fight.'

Punching her fist in the air, Hellier cheered, 'I'm with you on that.'

'And I don't want to wake up suddenly in Hell,' Earona said with forced enthusiasm.

Grinning, Marcus pulled his knees up and remarked with passion, 'I'm in for a good fight, whoever that ends up being.'

'I already said I was going to do my part and Seth will be there.' Shiarn glanced at Seth, dozing by the tree.

Keanan's unhappy expression was replaced by grim resolution. 'You know I shall help you. However, as yet you seem to be sidestepping the main issue, and as well, your own vulnerability to their plans. The amount of damage you could wrought in the wrong hands—'

'I might be vulnerable,' Jett was rueful for a moment. 'But I'm also a danger to them in the right hands.'

'You mean you can be an irritating pain in their arse?' Marcus' eyes lit up with mirth.

'For once I'd like to agree.' Keanan looked to Jett and stated, 'But, you haven't said how this orb can be destroyed or whatever needs to happen to it.'

'We'll discuss that later.' Presently he could see no further than an unhappy outcome on stopping the Orb.

Keanan commented with weary cynicism, 'You're still thinking about that, aren't you?'

Jett averted his eyes from Keanan's perceptive study of his face. 'I might have some ideas, but I'll rest first.'

The others were already sprawled over a patch of soft grass, half dozing as they talked. Jett's thoughts came through their sleepy demeanor, *rest is paramount to achieving any success and you'll need it by nightfall.*

79 - Infiltration

Overcoming fear is the beginning of change in your life

The Latent Path

Jett, Shiarn, and Seth left the camp before nightfall with Seth navigating their path through the forest. An unnatural level of scampering and rustlings came from the bushes and branches above. Seth informed them of the great number of creatures vacating the area. It only added to Jett's building trepidation of the spread of evil.

They kept near the feet of the Peaks until Seth discovered a trail. Not seeing any sign of sentries, the three crept towards a large grassy meadow. Under the cover of dusk, they stopped at the edge of the woods and lay low to view the Rynian camp. Plain white pavilions, with flags of purple and gold, were in orderly lines, and men sat around low burning fires. A gold and purple tent was in the midst of the camp. A dozen men strolled the camp and one man watched the rocks. Weapon racks were at every tent, and storage wagons were placed towards the back. The Rynians had positioned the camp as a blockade about a hundred feet from the roadway leading up to the fortress. Havenside, its grey walls dark in the coming night, was a formidable castle built from the mountain itself.

Jett crouched and observed the camp. 'Two armed men are idle on the far side, looking up the road. Another is closer to the rocks on our side.' Beyond the camp he saw burnt out cottages with no obvious signs of life. 'I think horses are on the opposite side.'

Amid a shiver of worry, Shiarn thought, *there are so many...*

Jett noted the pavilions, counting at least ten he could see. 'They might hold thirty to fifty men each.' He was asking a lot of Shiarn, maybe too much... but it was too late to turn back. 'I'll not ask you to kill anyone.' *That's a heavy burden.* He gave her a brief smile. 'Just do what you can to make them... ineffective.'

'Make them useless.' Seth nodded at her with a lopsided grin.

'You're trying to say,' she eyed them both with a coy smile and turned her jewel blade before her face. 'Be devious.'

Jett shook his head. 'I'm saying, you're smart, you'll think of something.' *But, I won't judge you if it comes to it.*

With narrowed eyes, she scrutinized the scene. 'It's the watchmen who could be troublesome. If they see anything amiss they could raise the alarm.'

Her face was hidden in the shadows of her cloak, but Jett sensed her apprehension. *If you have to, you have to.* 'Be creative. Work on the further side first. Take any weapons from the men sleeping inside and work your way to the racks.' His own worry over the huge task was mounting. 'It's strange, no catapults or any other siege weapons.'

'They don't care to take the fortress?' Shiarn replied.

Jett creased his mouth in concern. 'Maybe they want to keep the Baions holed up until the Gate is opened.'

She returned his worry with her bright green eyes shimmering in the darkness. *Kept alive till needed?*

Possibly that's it. 'You'll know what to do, just don't wake anyone or hell will break lose.'

She chuckled. 'And we have enough of that already.'

Jett considered the looming cliff face, a stone's throw from their position. The walls were camouflaged against the rock ledge far above. Beyond them, towers and other structures were firmly embedded into the rock.

Seth breathed by his face, 'Is it far?'

'Less than two hundred feet. Hopefully not more.' He viewed the wide pathway, winding up to it, but that route he was not going to travel.

'We'll see you back here in the morning?' Shiarn whispered.

'You shall. Seth, keep a watch. At dawn stay hidden no matter what happens, even if you see me do not approach. I will come to you.' Jett raised himself to a low stoop. 'Good luck to both of you.'

'And good luck to you,' Seth's light-hearted voice added, 'you're going to need it.'

Jett responded dryly, 'Thanks.' *I'll be needing more than that.*

~ * ~

Jett crept through the short spate of bushes, and with a keen eye on the cliff, searched out crags and ledges he could use. He passed within yards of the guard on watch, staring up the mountain towards Havenside. The gradual incline was littered with rough rocks and slippery moss. He went farther around until he located an easier pathway and by keeping under the cover of giant stones he came to the mountain proper.

Far above, shadows on a minor plateau signified the presence of caves. Without any extra equipment to hinder his climb, he secured his belt, holding his cloak in place, and examined his hands. Hellier wrapped linen and leather around his gloves. He smiled ruefully, realizing the magnitude of the task he had set for himself. The Kin were right; he was not the best climber. After a few minutes of his hands gripping the harsh stone, the abrasive surface dragged on the leather padding and he was indebted to Hellier for her bindings.

With the little time he had, his tentative negotiation of safe handholds and stable ledges was consuming it. Halfway up it became more challenging, and Jett began to over extend himself. The upper ledges taunted him, and he exerted his strength reaching and pulling his way up. He cursed the cliff, and himself, on what a foolhardy and impetuous idea it was to climb a mountain. Pushing aside the increasing pain in his arms, he focused on the goal above.

The growl of a great cat transfixed the air. Jett remained motionless against the rock, straining to see along the distant ledges. Seeing nothing, he decided to continue upward and hope it was not waiting for him above. At least the cat gave him assurance the mountain was climbable.

The jagged rocks smoothed out. He spent time feeling along the rock wall for secure handholds, making the climb a mental labour as well as physical. It was not the time to throw out caution, but he caught himself doing just that, out of a growing fatigue and frustration.

By the time the edge of the overhanging plateau arrived he remembered why he was not good at rock climbing, he despised it. He hauled his aching body up to the ledge and permitted himself some rest which he used to survey the shadows.

The wall of Havenside was farther up and a good distance to the right as he faced the rock wall. A few feet from him was an opening in the rocks. With one last glimpse behind, there was no movement from the Rynian camp, but in the southeast, a black mass floated above the Agamon. He was pleased at climbing the height he had. But as the cloud over the ziggurat swelled with darkness, his self-grandeur diminished.

He examined his hands, clenching and unclenching his fist. The bindings were torn with abrasions, and his skin was tender underneath. He left the ledge and crawled through a narrow opening between two large boulders, following the passage, and considering what he would tell the Baions.

Arriving at a cramped hole, he came to a door the size of a child, under a rock overhang. He sat by it and grabbed a stone and rapped it long and hard, and waited. No answer. Harder, he hit it again. He contemplated burning a hole in it, but this would not procure a friendly greeting. His voice uttered ongoing curses as he wondered if they were all dead.

Muffled voices came from within. Keys in the lock and the squeaking door echoed in the small space. Two bearded men peered at him in the glow of a single torch. With bafflement they stared at him, but said nothing.

Within the shadows, Jett's voice came with tense impatience. 'Can I come in? I'm not armed.'

One of the men demanded, 'State your business here.'

Tired and thirsty, and now annoyed with the tedious delay, Jett's patience broke. 'I want to speak with whoever's in charge.'

Both of them stared with wary skepticism. 'Where are you from?' The soldier's question was tinged with disbelief.

'Coltrene,' Jett barked.

The man with the torch stood back while the other lifted his sword and ordered, 'You can come in, but keep your hands where we can see them.'

Jett crawled through the entry and stood to feel a blade tip at his stomach. In their middle years and armed, they held expressions of drained, despairing men. Jett held his palms in the air. 'I have no weapon.'

'We won't chance that,' he replied, checking over Jett's body. After finding nothing, the man's mistrust did not lessen. 'Strange things are happening in the valley.'

'You noticed,' Jett replied. 'I need to speak to your prince about these strange things.'

'Why are you asking about the prince?' the man said, suspiciously, 'Lord Giralt is in charge here.'

Jett had no idea it would be this complicated and he shouted, in hope he could raise them, 'Wake him up then.'

The man snapped, 'I don't know who you are but you can't come in here and make demands like that.'

His leather bound palms raised, Jett yelled, 'I climbed all the way up this bloody cursed mountain to speak to him and I'm going to damn well do it.'

A crisp voice rang out from an above turret. 'What's going on down there?'

Jett looked up to see a tall middle-aged man leaning over the wall, his scruffy brown hair shading his clean shaven face. At last, someone with the appearance of authority.

The soldier said, 'Captain Aversley, this man has come through the cave door and we are asking him what he wants.'

The captain peered at Jett through the shadows. 'Bring him up here. I'll see what he wants.'

With Jett in tow, the men headed up the steps along the Keep wall. The fortress had various walkways, and more structures, previously obscured, were built into the rocks. A short platform ran between the two turrets on this side, and a third larger turret was on the north. The bulk of the fortress was on the farther side facing more to the east, and Jett had come in more or less toward the back end.

The captain stood over Jett and unlike his men, his speech was calm. 'Now, tell me who you are and who sent you and I shall consider further action.'

Jett studied him with some relief. 'My name is Jett, I've come from Coltrene. I met with Hayden.'

'Hayden!' The captain exclaimed.

The soldiers were equally as shocked. 'Why didn't you say something, man?'

Jett shrugged indifferently. 'I'm tired…'

Captain Aversley said, 'He made it?'

'He did and he's going to the King of Coltrene as we speak.'

Aversely turned to one of the men. 'Get this man some water.' The man dashed off and the captain turned back to Jett. 'We have not much to offer in the way of food.'

'Water is fine.'

'You have a force here?'

'No…' Jett wished to sit yet the urgency to speak about the evil descending on the valley overshadowed his own needs.

The other soldier eyed Jett with suspicion. 'Maybe it's a trick.'

Jett drilled him with an annoyed glare. 'What do you think I'm playing at?'

Aversely put his hand up, halting the impending quarrel. 'Take peace.'

Jett turned his scowl away and took the pitcher of water the soldier offered him.

The captain addressed the soldiers, 'Olaf, Ren, go back to your posts.' Amid glances over their shoulders, the men started down the stairs.

A door opened along the walkway. Jett narrowed his eyes at the young man in his long under-drawers and a well-worn shirt, walking down the platform. Barefoot and yawning, his shock of fair hair fluttered in the breeze. 'Aversely… what's the noise about?' The boy's voice belied his true age, though his blue eyes looked at Jett with self-assurance. 'And who is this?' He was a tall lad, but one who had not yet grown into a man.

'He comes on behalf of Hayden.'

The boy woke up from his sleepy state to declare, 'Hayden lives!'

'He is well,' Jett said tight lipped, 'I assume you are Prince Aric.'

'I am.'

'There is much to discuss.'

Aversley asked, 'Shall we go in?'

'I'd rather stay out here.' Jett swept his gaze over the camp below. 'I like to keep my eye on the landscape.'

Aversely squinted at him in the darkness, his doubt obvious.

'You have troops?' Aric asked with such eagerness Jett sighed at the sadness of it.

Jett stepped to the wall and looked over the lands. 'Not exactly.' The camp was still, while above the pyramid, swirls of darkness shot into the night sky.

'No relieving force, that's a blow.' Prince Aric leaned against the wall and exhaled a great sigh.

Aversley stood beside Jett and looked across to the temple. 'Today darkness formed above it.'

Jett looked into the man's intelligent face. 'I'm here because of that.'

The young prince said, 'The Rynians have unusual visitors from that direction. It has put fear into the men's hearts.'

'My men are tough, they have gone through trials of late, and to be trapped here added to our troubles, but this,' Aversley waved his hand across the land, 'is beyond what they understand.'

Jett asked, 'The men mentioned strange things?'

Aversley's head drooped. 'One of our men threw himself off the walls and Franco said he spied flying creature's overhead.'

Aric added, 'Eerie visitors have been at their camp.'

Aversley narrowed his eyes suspiciously. 'What have you to do with that?'

'I can't explain exactly,' Jett's penetrating eyes stared at the pair, 'but, it has something to do with witches—'

'Witches?' Aric questioned.

'Perhaps there is a connection,' Aversley said, 'an ugly drab woman came along with a well-dressed man. On two occasions.'

'A man?'

'Not attired in the same fashion as the Rynian soldiers.' Aversely creased his eyes and scrutinized him. 'Why are you here?'

'Yes, why?' Aric asked, 'And will Coltrene send anyone?'

'I don't have the answer to that,' Jett told the prince, 'but I'll help you, if you help me.'

Aric gave a boyish chuckle and exclaimed, 'Help you?'

'That's what this is about,' Aversley stated, 'you want something from us?'

'In a way.' Jett took a deep breath and started, 'I want you to assault the Rynian camp… in the morning.'

Aversley's tone turned abrasive. 'They are more than double our troops.'

'I realize that and I wouldn't ask if I knew the Rynians would be at full strength.'

'Explain.'

'Right now I have people on the ground disabling the Rynians so they will have no military might.'

Aric asked with disbelief, 'How?'

'We have ways, like I said my business is with the pyramid,' Jett replied, 'I need your help to take out the Rynians and you need my help getting rid of that cloud and the witches.'

Aversely gazed at the pyramid, his lips pressing into a stiff line.

'You must make the most of this opportunity,' Jett continued with sombre weight, 'Once they are aware of what has happened they will be forewarned and the chance will be lost.'

'Attack them?' Aric cried incredulously, 'Now?'

'Daybreak,' Jett stated.

Aversley studied Jett's intense stare. 'You, stranger in the night, come up the mountain and tell us this and expect us to ride out in a few hours to take the Rynian camp?'

'That's what I'm asking.'

The prince asked, 'How can we trust you?'

Jett focused on the prince and assessed his youthful and honest personality. 'Because if you do not, you and all the men here will eventually perish.' His steely gaze held their attention. 'That dark cloud is a shadow of hell and it's growing until it swallows up this valley.'

Aric interrupted forthrightly, 'But what does it mean?'

'We have to stop it before this place is overrun by demons.' Jett's voice rumbled with impatience.

Finally Aversley responded, 'I don't…. how can we trust this?'

'What have you got to lose?'

Aversely studied the prince.

'If you are afraid for the boy, you could leave him here,' Jett said.

The prince declared, 'I would not stay.'

Jett was exasperated with their reluctance, and he wondered if he would have to climb back down the rocks. 'Hayden said that you were brave and you only needed hope. This is your chance at freedom, don't you want that?'

Aversley's shoulders slumped and he leaned on the wall, but remained in quiet thought.

The prince said, 'We don't wish to die here like rats in a trap.' He nudged Aversley's arm. 'If this is true we can overcome our enemy.'

Aversley paused. 'I would need to consider how best to prepare.'

'We will proceed?' An excited thrill was in the boy's voice.

The captain smiled at the youngster. 'We will discuss it with Giralt and see what he thinks, and wake the men, there is much to undertake.'

Jett sighed with sudden weariness. 'If you don't mind I'd like to rest.'

Prince Aric asked through a yawn, 'You'll come with us?'

'Do you have any horses and a sword?'

'We can arrange that,' Aversley said, 'There is a bed you can use.'

'My thanks,' Jett replied. 'I doubt I'll get much sleep.'

'I understand.' Aversley's face was concealed by shadows, but his eyes sparked with excitement. 'Come what may, dawn we will be free of this place.'

Jett nodded. He was hoping the same, and he understood the man's underlining connotations. Freedom or death.

~ * ~

Seth lay on his stomach next to a talkative shrub. He heard Shiarn's thoughts as she neared. Remaining invisible, she lowered sword belts to the ground. After a moment, more fell from her arms. It seemed she had been at it for hours, while he ran around hiding the equipment. His broad grin shone through the shadows. 'How is it?'

'Well, I think. They are an organized lot, keeping the bulk of their weapons and armour set apart from the sleeping areas, quite useful.'

'I'm glad that watchman is gone.'

'Oh, him,' Shiarn paused a moment, 'he's gone… now.'

'I shall ask no more.'

Jett should be thankful. Breathing hard, she appeared and took a moment to catch her breath. 'I'm ready to drop.'

'Is there much more to do?' It seemed a never-ending stream of armoury.

'At least you have a nice stash of arrows.' She contemplated the distant camp. 'I've cut bow strings, and a great deal of weapons are dumped beyond the horses, hopefully well concealed. Long weapons are scattered, some shields out there.' She pointed to the trees on their right. 'Swords all over the place, as well as belts with the swords. It's been a huge task attempting to disarm a troop of soldiers. Thank Kahm, Keanan gave me the use of his quartza. I must tell him it not only helps with my Gift. Can't wait to see their faces in the morning.'

'You have been busy.' He smiled at her. 'And you've done brilliantly.'

'I've even been creative too.' She smiled with pride at her success and looked back at the camp. 'Not much more to go.' She stood up beside him. 'How long we got?'

'Not much.'

'I'll make it quick.' Shiarn disappeared before his eyes. 'Then get some rest.'

80 - Close Call

You can only be betrayed by the ones you trust
But, it is better to love and lose than remain safe and alone

Prophetess Janna Meadow'Fox 4th Seat Elder

Through a blur of murky darkness, Mara looked down at a rider galloping over a field. It seemed she was gazing through a hole and all around her vision was indiscernible. She peered at the scene, and noted there was something across the rider's saddle. Was that her?

The scene switched to a ruinous stone room strewn with rubble, and figures were standing around. Mara focused on the sight, and gasped with sudden realization. It was the witches and her, and even Jett was present. The figures moved and spoke but no sound could be heard. Nor was there any colour, only the gloom of greys and blacks.

Not wanting to see anymore, she found she could not move but could only watch the next vision. First it was Mara and the others while they rested in a clearing amongst the ruins of an ancient city. It flashed to the campsite where she slept with Earona and the others. This one expanded till there was no darkness around it, and real colour emerged. Even the sound of the woodland came to her ears. She discovered she was standing on the outskirts of the camp, under the night shade of the trees, watching herself sleeping. An unnatural frigid wind froze her in place. She could not move, she was trapped. Dread made her heart race with apprehension.

Shadows merged over the camp and grew in potency, but a light emanated from between the sleepers, and rose up enveloping them and Mara's sleeping body.

'Here you are,' a voice said behind her, 'Without that cursed trinket I've been able to find you. I should have killed that old hag when I had the chance.'

Mara took a grim breath. Of course, her mouse charm was stolen by the witches.

'Daughter, why do seek to avoid me? Haven't I always been there to teach you?' Yavinia's voice was deep and melancholic. 'I will always find you, no matter how far you run. When we return I shall undo the curse that woman inflicted you with.'

Mara couldn't move or speak, she could barely breath. There was nothing she could do to get out of the danger she was now in.

'I have worked tirelessly and expended much of my own power into bringing about this magnificent new rule.' She placed her hand on Mara's shoulder, and clenched hard. 'I'm disappointed you try to defy me now.'

A moan escaped her, but Mara could do nothing except endure the pain.

Still gripping her shoulder, Yavinia brought her face close to Mara. 'Look at them,' her voice was like ice spiking into her ear and thoughts, 'All of them useless. You believe those ignorant fools will help you.' She gave a harsh cackle. 'Not a one will be able to stand. They will all perish, even by your own will you can have power over them.'

Mara's breathing quickened and with all her strength she tried to move, to run… but to where? Instead she groaned at the truth of her mother's words.

'I don't understand why you fight me so hard. I give you power, as well as position, and you remain ungrateful. What will it take for you to join me whole-heartedly?'

At the words, Mara wondered that herself, putting herself through this torment. Why didn't she resign herself to her destiny? Why did she make it so difficult for herself? But the recent revelation of childhood memories had not receded. 'You're not… my mother.'

Yavinia responded with an unexpected snarl, 'I'm the only one you have.'

She bowed her head, was it true? Even Wendessa was gone, the only one who could probably give her any answers as to her past. However, Wendessa knew Yavinia was wrong, she also knew there was a better path Mara could take.

'Well, then,' Yavinia pulled her about face, 'if you make it such a trial, then that is what it shall be.'

Sickening darkness descended around them. Yavinia's red hair and glowing eyes were a mesmerizing colour in the evil gloom. 'This is a costly method, and it does not please me to have to use it. However, you have forced me to use drastic action.' She grabbed Mara's chin and squeezed her mouth open. In her other hand she held a miniature green and gold vial, she spoke to it. 'You will bring her to me, and any spoils you deem worthy.' From the vial, she poured into Mara's mouth, a small but long black worm.

Mara's eyes flashed with horror at the entity entering her body. The black thing slithered down her throat, making her want to gag and vomit. She wondered if she would choke on the wretched evil thing.

Yavinia lowered her face by her, her breath was like freezing ice in her ear. 'It is near time you fulfill your purpose.'

~ * ~

Earona struggled to wake and not return to a nightmare of red-eye devils. Fighting against falling back to sleep, she woke in a sweat, her heart pounding so fast she thought it might stop, and with a sense something was out in the forest and was approaching. Her eyes slowly opened to low ashen clouds in the night sky.

Not far from her, Mara sat for a moment, before standing abruptly. Mara stepped away from her blankets.

Concerned she was going to disappear into the night again, Earona sat up, ready to rush after her. 'Mara?'

Mara turned to her, a cruel look and an odd white glint was in her eyes.

Something was wrong. Earona pushed her blanket aside and stood with sleepy confusion. 'What is it?'

Mara walked away from their bedrolls and stared into the forest. 'It is time.' Her voice was coarse and not like hers at all.

Alarmed by the change in her, Earona followed. 'Time? For what exactly?' She looked over her shoulder, everyone was still asleep, even Marcus who was supposed to be on watch.

'Time for the new reign to come.'

This certainly didn't seem to be Mara anymore. 'What does that mean?' But over her shoulder, she cried, 'Marcus, wake up!'

A grating laugh came from Mara. 'I'll be leaving now.'

Earona frowned at Mara's smugness. 'No!' *Marcus, wake up! Anyone of you!* She screamed with all her thoughts' focus, *Marcus, you must wake.*

Within moments, Mara grabbed Earona around the chest, pulling her down and back against her. She flicked out a knife and held it at Earona's throat. 'I am and you're coming with me.' She started walking backwards and away.

Marcus stretched from where he sat by the wagon, and his eyes flitted between awake and sleep.

Marcus, wake up! Why won't you hear me, are you so thick-headed?!

Marcus shook his head, and stretched his arms high and yawned. 'What?' His eyes opened fully and he looked around with a questioning expression. Instantly he stood on his feet, his eyes darkening to anger as he took in the perilous situation. 'What do you think you're doing?'

Mara said from over Earona's shoulder. 'Whatever I like.' Her voice was guttural and spiked with aggression. 'You better stop or she's dead.'

Marcus came forward slowly, his eyes watching every move Mara made. 'You won't get away.'

The tip pressed into Earona's neck, and she gasped a whisper, 'What's happened to you?'

'It's time she take her rightful place.' Her voice was a jarring proclamation. 'Your kind is at an end.'

Marcus inched closer, his hands clenching into fists. 'What do you want with Earona?'

'No further!' Mara growled her wrath.

Marcus halted and spread his open hands. 'You're not taking her.'

'It's nothing to do with you.' She narrowed her eyes and scanned the camp. 'Where is he?'

'What's it to you?' Marcus snapped, and he cast a glance at Hellier and Keanan on their blankets. *God, how long are you two going to sleep for? Wake up.*

Mara sneered, 'It's convenient.'

Earona froze at the blade's sharp edge drawing blood from her skin. 'Why Mara?' She couldn't move against Mara's unnatural strength clamping on her stomach, or away from the blade threatening her artery. She breathed steady, forcing herself to remain calm and think.

'The Midnight Order have come and will soon rule.' Mara's fiery glare was fixed on Marcus. 'You're too weak to do anything.'

Finally, Hellier and Keanan woke to the activity, and approached with hesitant steps.

'I'm going.' Backing away, Mara growled with masculine depth, 'Don't follow.'

Try to distract her, I'm going to do something. Earona sent an impulsive thought to Marcus in an attempt to lessen the grave concern on his face.

Marcus struggled to keep his voice even. 'If we're so weak, does it matter if we know where you're going?'

Mara made a throaty chuckle. 'You'll find out when your souls are under his dominion.'

'Curse it!' Marcus spat out. 'Is this about Jett again?'

'The one will rule over you,' Mara replied, 'And no-one will stop him.'

Earona shifted her palm onto the hand clutching the knife, numbing the tendons with her Ethos. It was risky, but… she could think of nothing else. Mara's hand went dead, and the blade sliced into Earona's skin and airway, stinging her flesh like fire.

Dropping the knife, Mara dangled her useless hand. 'You stupid conniving bitch.'

Marcus bowled Mara over, and attempted to restrain her arms behind her back. She kicked and scratched to free herself. Despite the new strength the girl exhibited, Marcus threw her down on her stomach.

She shouted, 'Don't touch me, you cock-arse bastard!'

Light-headed and dizzy, Earona fell to her knees with seconds to save herself. She pressed hard on her throat, gushing with blood. Gulping for air, she made a frightful choking sound as if attempting speech. If she didn't heal herself in time the cut would kill her.

'Earona!' Amid the intensity of Mara's resistance, Marcus cried, 'Are you healing?'

Keanan and Hellier rushed to them and Keanan took a sturdy grip of Mara's flailing legs while Marcus had a grip of her arms.

Earona continued clutching her throat as blood flowed down her dress front. Her Ethos poured into her severed veins and torn flesh, mending and fusing. Indicating with her free hand not to worry, she shared her thoughts, *nearly healed.*

Clawing at anything she could reach, Mara was a fierce demon with unnatural strength. Her pregnancy did nothing to deter her from fighting.

Marcus puffed, 'Get rope, Hel.'

'You can't stop me, you goddamn spawns of bitches—' Mara bit down on his hand.

Marcus slapped her cheek, sending her head reeling to the side. She screamed more profanities like a siren in the still night. He shouted to Hellier, 'And a gag.'

Earona's weak voice rasped, 'Don't hurt her.'

'Hurt her?!' Marcus put his hand over the girl's mouth and teeth, and barked, 'She'll be dead. Won't feel a thing.'

Hellier came with rope and dressings to cover her mouth.

Mara kicked her away. 'Don't touch me, whore bitch.'

After excessive wrestling and numerous abrasions, Mara's wrists and ankles were bound. Under her gag, she snarled with wrath, and scowled, her eyes seething with rage. There was silence in the forest again and they sat back around the girl.

Hellier gave an exasperated sigh. 'This seems familiar…'

'Perhaps this is a sign…' Keanan pursed his lips together and looked out at the woods, 'Something is occurring.'

Earona ignored the sight of her blue dress soaked crimson and said, 'I think she became possessed. Like at Sommerlea.'

'Possessed?!' Hellier exclaimed. 'It's not possession, she's turned. She's like one of them witches.'

Keanan said with astonishment, 'A witch?'

Earona gave a resolute sigh. 'She knows the workings of witches so she is more susceptible to their power.'

Hellier interrupted, 'She cast a spell last night without being possessed—'

'Against the witches,' Earona debated, 'But now…' Darn, she must have Slept them all, it would seem.

'Whatever it is,' Marcus interjected, 'look at her now.'

Mara's eyes glowed with hatred and her teeth were exposed over her gag in a malicious snarl.

'Her strength has tripled and she looks like a madwoman.' Hellier asked, 'What shall we do with her?'

Earona paled at a new consideration. 'I wonder if Jett is…' she gulped, 'the same.'

'Don't think it,' Marcus growled.

Keanan loosened her gag. 'Where are the witches?'

Mara kicked at them with restrained legs and toppled sideways. 'I don't give a cock about them!'

Marcus asked, 'Who are the Midnight Order?'

'The elite. You are useless against their thrones.'

Earona stared at the disheveled girl with compassion. 'But, what about your baby?'

'It is an instrument of darkness. I will serve him as will you when we have ultimate power.' She laughed at Earona's surprised frown. 'Your destruction is imminent and we will feed on your bones.'

'Bollocks,' Marcus commented with disinterest.

Mara stared him in the eye. 'Your destruction is foretold.'

'Pile of crock,' Marcus remarked.

'The Summoner must return and birth the Shadow Nation. You will perish and we shall dominate your soul—'

Hellier pulled the cloth back over Mara's mouth, but she continued muttering under it.

Marcus sat back on his hunches. 'That was pleasant.'

Keanan stared into the darkness of the woods with a pensive frown. 'It seems she has turned into this Summoner again.'

'But, she can't.' Earona shook her head with denial. *Not again, not Jett…*

They said nothing in reply and remained in their own personal thoughts. Eventually Hellier picked up the knife Mara used and swung it before their eyes. 'Where did she get this?'

Marcus stated what they could all see. 'It's malreus. The one she used in the attic.'

Earona recognized it from Sommerlea. Mara must have stolen it back after it was taken from her.

'If it's truly Mara then she knows of our plans, which would be unfortunate,' Keanan said, 'but, it also seems this Mara does not know where Jett is. It gives me hope he is still himself.' He studied them with a grimace. 'But this – it complicates things no end.'

Earona knew if Jett returned and he was normal, he was not going to be pleased. This was the very thing he was afraid of. 'It's not her fault.' She looked down at the girl whose demeanor hadn't changed while they spoke.

'Do you think they'd be able to find her?' Hellier scanned the tree line.

Keanan replied, 'Indeed. They have already found her.'

Marcus stood and surveyed the darkened clearing. 'If they can we might not get much sleep tonight.' He stared down at Mara without care. 'I say we tie her to the wagon so we can keep an eye on her.'

'Agreed,' Hellier said.

They dragged Mara, wriggling and resisting their touch to the wheel where they spread her arms and tied her wrists to the spokes. Keanan secured the knots not wishing to take any chances of her escaping and doing them harm. He decided to keep watch while Earona, Hellier and Marcus tried to sleep.

As Earona lay her head down, she faced a jolt of fear she would see the devil haunting her dreams again. Her body tensed with trepidation, it was more than the anticipation of a nightmare. She had the underlining sense it had gone beyond dreams, and the darkness would somehow make it a reality.

Beside her, Marcus watched her wide-eyed stare and his words tumbled out, 'You… woke me up? But, I'm sorry I didn't wake sooner.'

'No, I'm just glad you did,' she whispered.

'You gave me a real scare. How is your throat?'

She turned her head with surprise and stroked her throat. How close had she come to actually being killed… too close. She gave a failed chuckle. 'I'm hoping there's no scar.'

Marcus asked under his breath, 'Are you going to be alright?'

She looked into his sensitive brown eyes and saw more than a care for her wellbeing. The feelings growing inside her heart for him were pushed aside of late. A new softer emotion was emerging in him, and the kiss they shared came back to mind. 'You mean apart from demons invading, hellish nightmares, and Mara trying to kill me, and possibly our Avare has gone mad again… I guess I might not do to badly.'

'That's never going to happen again.' *I'll make sure of it.* His voice had a gentle undertone and he changed the subject. 'You seem to have a lot of nightmares.'

His words warmed her heart and her lips twitched with a restrained smile. 'Don't I just.' She paused. 'But this one, it was real.'

His expression changed to a more serious one. 'What was it?'

'A red-eyed devil,' she whispered.

He creased his brow with new concern. 'A devil!' He lowered his voice. 'You're a worry. Try to sleep, we have no idea what the day will bring or the night and… I'll be here if you have a bad dream.'

She smiled at him across the way. 'As long as there is a day I will be mildly happy.'

81 - No Option

Plan before going into battle, estimate the cost before commitment.

Ironclad Warfare Command

Jett walked the parapet in the cool predawn air. Adrenaline coursed through his veins over the impending assault on the camp, but the majority of his worries were centered on his Kin. He had no way of knowing if all had gone well down below. If it hadn't, he was heading into a trap, and worse, Shiarn and Seth might already be captured.

In the yard below, the Baions were preparing to move out. Less than half were on horses, but all were equipped with armour and weapons. With a sword at his hip, Jett walked down the stairs to join them. The men were silent apart from the clank of swords and armour, and Aversley, speaking encouragement over them. Even the prince, attired in similar armour to the men, shared the captain's exuberance.

Lord Giralt, a broad-chested man with a neat red beard, approached Jett, with his leg plates clattering. Jett had no such armour and he noticed this lack.

'This is he, stranger in the night.' Giralt's booming voice shook the calm, and probably woke any men still half asleep.

'Jett.' Aric passed him the reins of a grey horse.

Jett smoothed his hand down the horse's neck and spoke to the animal.

Sauntering up to Jett, Giralt made his presence known. 'You're the one who instigated this attack. I wouldn't have been as trusting as Aversley.'

Jett stood straight to meet the man head on. 'Lucky you're not him.'

His comment received some stifled chuckles, including the prince, although his was less inhibited. Giralt glared and his tone turned menacing. 'You better hope to hell you're right.'

Jett couldn't agree more, but he wasn't about to admit it to the arrogant lord. 'Let's go see.'

Aversley trotted up to them. 'We haven't seen their watchmen in a few hours, or any movement within the camp.' He stared down at Jett with hope, or maybe that was desperation.

Jett gave a staunch nod and mounted his stead.

'It could be a trap,' Giralt belted out.

'Or perhaps a good omen.' Aversley's eyes glinted like silver and he turned back to the men. 'We need to surround the camp as quickly as possible. Keep them away from the horses and the woods. Command tent is in the middle.'

'First we'll shoot them out,' Giralt said, 'and kill as many bastards as we can.'

Aversley gave him a swift glance and addressed all the men. 'Our best archers will remain on the first ledge where you will not be assailed.'

'Don't let yourselves be overwhelmed.' Jett raised his voice and glanced at the prince, recalling the night at the Meet and those without the wits to survive. 'They still win on numbers.'

'Kill all mobbing,' Giralt shouted, 'No mercy.'

'Our crossbows will do some shielding damage,' Aversley said.

Jett considered the band of Baions, armed and with the best vantage against the Rynian troops, possibly numbering up to a thousand, weaponless and hopefully without armour. He was glad to see they appeared hardened veterans of combat, most likely experienced with killing. But, even with the fierce looking men, he wondered if it was possible to overcome the Rynian soldiers? Maybe Keanan was right. Jett really had lost his mind.

One of the soldiers cocked his helmed head and spoke. 'It'll be like pillaging, except there'll be no raping.' It was accompanied with an abrasive chuckle.

'Chad will find something to bugger.'

Someone else piped up. 'Anything with legs.'

'Oi!' A man shouted from behind. 'I've got morals.'

Wrapping laughter followed, and another man lifted his sword and yelled, 'Bugger 'em with your blade.'

Their relaxed camaraderie put Jett at ease, and he grinned with a pang of confidence.

'I'm itching for a fight as much as you, but keep your heads.' Aversley, his horse strutting before them, and sword in hand, spoke to the men congregating around them. 'We want order as soon as possible and we want to retain control. Protect each other and cut down all resistance. If that's all of them, so be it. I don't want to lose anyone.'

'That's right.' Prince Aric's bright blonde hair stuck out from beneath his helmet. 'We came together and we'll leave together.'

'Open the gate,' Giralt ordered.

The gate was hauled open and those carrying bows ran down the path with as little noise as possible, to a lower cleft of rocks. Riders followed in the grey light of near morning with those on foot running along behind. Jett rode up front. He would have preferred riding at the back, but Giralt was watching him with a shrewd eye. Jett thought it best not to arouse anymore suspicion.

They rode fast down the hard curved roadway, the horse's hooves and the clattering of men's armour the only sound. Those with bows positioned themselves along the rocks. The rest of the Baions arrived on the turf. The sight of a soldier, gagged, his wrists bound and tied to a stout tree, boosted their morale.

Arrows, as if falling out of the sky, hit the grounds. A handful came as fiery missiles, lighting up the tents. Darting out from the tents, Rynian soldiers ran to weapon racks and stood with confusion as the Baions entered their territory. Not every pavilion was emptied of men, and no-one appeared from the main tent.

The Baions on-foot, rushed the Rynians, hacking them down with clean precision. Several tents had already caught fire, either from the arrows or a hurled torch.

Along with a group of riders, Jett rode the perimeter, keeping an eye on the horses and what he could view of the forest. For the most part, it seemed all the weapons were removed from the racks, and they had no use of any bows. Screams came from men trapped in burning tents. He grimaced, wondering what mischief Shiarn had caused.

The Rynians ran without weapons and in any direction it seemed, and each one for himself. In the emerging new day, arrows flew with better accuracy, striking any that tried to escape. The fight on the ground was more like a brawl. Seasoned Baion warriors reveled in the unbalanced slaughter.

Some daring Rynians ran to the horses. Jett had the unfortunate task of cutting the unarmed men down. Crossbows took out the ones he couldn't. No time to thank whoever was covering his back, as he faced desperate men trying to escape. It was a mad frantic rush to stay alive, or stay the dominating force.

The prince had ridden alongside Aversley, but now the youngster had Rynians pulling on his legs and catching his horse's reins. Jett directed his horse the short sprint, slicing into flesh as he went, to get to the lad. Soldiers dropped around him, thanks again to a crossbow wielder, so well-concealed Jett couldn't pinpoint.

'Keep on your horse.' Jett grabbed the reins of the prince's horse and shouted, 'And keep back from the scrum.'

Grinning, Aric's face flushed with excitement.

Jett shook his head at his bravado and turned back to face more soldiers, making the dash to the safety of the trees.

At a distance and over the cries and flaming bedlam, Captain Aversley shouted, 'On your knees or you will be killed.'

'We'll kill all you bastards!' Giralt's voice echoed like rocky thunder. For some reason that had a better effect; the men knelt, hands raised. Jett suspected the lord had every intention of carrying out his threat, and might still yet.

The Baions herded the Rynians to the center of camp as sunlight touched the top of the trees in the east. Jett continued scouting the outer area in search of strays. Bodies were scattered in bloody trails. He didn't see anyone take a horse, but the enclosure was tied shut. Still, he couldn't be certain no-one had escaped into the forest.

The carnage complete, a strange quiet descended. The surviving Rynians, about half their number, were gathered up, bound and guarded as the Baions searched the burning camp. Jett stayed watching the horses, until a Baion relieved him.

The soldier approached with a grisly smile and blood on his hands. 'You're wanted in the captain's tent.'

'Make sure no one takes a horse,' Jett gave him steely glare.

Without losing the grin, the soldier gave a slow nod. 'I'll sooner take their life.'

Jett rode through the camp and past the prisoners and burning grounds, to arrive at the gold and purple pavilion. He leapt off his horse and strode past the two men on guard, and into a reception area with table and chairs, and other furniture. Standing by the table was the captain and the prince, and seated was Giralt, flicking through maps and papers. His bald head had a touch of red, and despite their victory, he looked Jett over with a dubious raise of a bushy brow. 'How the devil you managed to restrain all these men must be some sort of magik.'

'Not really. Just some good stealth.' Jett looked to the other two who wore pleased expressions. 'It went well?'

'As you could see.' Captain Aversley came forward and offered Jett his hand. 'Thanks to you.'

'And thanks to you.'

Prince Aric exclaimed, 'I can't believe how easy it seemed.'

Giralt snorted with bad humour. 'Easy when you're driven by vengeance.'

'And the men have faced much combat together,' Aversley added.

Aric placed a warm hand on Jett's shoulder. 'We did it. It was just like you said.'

Jett forced a smile. The killings brought him no pleasure, he had nothing against the Rynians.

'And here we are.' Aversley's tone became serious. 'But what of this evil you spoke of at the ruins? The dawn is dim with shadow.'

'I must go there.' Now the attack was over, Jett was compelled to think on confronting the enemy at the ziggurat. 'Have you the captain of these Rynians or whoever was in charge?'

Giralt made a derisive grunt. 'Dead in his bed.' He gave Jett a queer look from under his heavy brows. 'Throat slit, along with his officers.'

Jett frowned with embarrassment. 'There was probably no other option.'

'Saved us the trouble,' Giralt said.

Aversley said, 'How will you do this task at the temple?'

'I have some people with me.' Jett observed them looking him over. 'But, I need your help.'

The young impressionable prince spoke up. 'And we shall do what we can to aid you.'

Lord Giralt roared, 'Hold up there, boy, we need to see what we are up against. I don't know much about objects disappearing nor do I know what makes the light of day diminish. I gather you don't know a lot either.'

'True.' Aric frowned. 'However, if I am now your king, what I say matters a great deal. What do you think, Aversley?'

Lord Giralt watched Aversley with dark suspicious eyes. Jett noticed the silent confrontation between the men, but he was unwilling to back down.

'What is this evil?' Aversley scrutinized Jett. 'Perhaps my men would be useless against it. You mentioned witches?'

Jett faced them. 'Witches, maybe a mage.'

'A mage!' yelled Lord Giralt, 'Hell and buggery.'

'That's who we saw coming and going from their camp,' Aric proclaimed.

'And what are the powers of this mage?' Aversley scratched his chin and looked Jett over.

Jett considered Morgal and his power to remain alive. He hoped that was not a skill of all mages. 'They have the ability to distort reality.'

Giralt retorted, 'You know a damn sight more than us and you don't know much. Sounds' like they could do anything.'

Jett broke through the pensive quiet with purposeful resolve. 'If I and my people fail I will be dead and you will have a limited amount of time to get out of this valley. I would advise you not to stay in Havenside.'

Giralt pressed his lips together and gave him a cold stare. 'It's like that is it.'

'Simply stating the truth.' Jett's eyes smoldered at the man's scornful gaze.

'There's no need for us to argue,' Aversley interrupted them. 'Giralt is concerned we know nothing about magik.'

Jett declared, 'Whether you do or not is irrelevant because you will know about it soon enough.'

'When are you heading there?' Aversley asked.

'Before nightfall.'

Aversley said, 'We will discuss it and come up with some plan. That's the best I can do.'

Jett noted the optimism in his eyes and accepted his words as a good sign. 'I'll leave on that then.' He turned to go and paused, 'Perhaps I shall see you later at the ziggurat, if not you should make your way to Coltrene.'

He departed with a dismal foreboding. At least no Rynian forces were at their back, but he had hoped to know more after speaking with their commander. To discover him dead was a disappointment and a frustrating turn of events. However it couldn't be helped and he had much to thank Shiarn for.

Jett walked some way into the forest till he came to Seth, sitting against a tree, and Shiarn dozing beside him. He said, 'First plan complete.' Whether it would be completely successful he was yet to see.

'We saw.' Seth gave him a tired smile and nudged Shiarn.

She sat up stretching and yawning. 'And I nearly missed it. It looked… macabre.'

'Let's get back.'

Seth followed him while Shiarn stood, and hands on hips, she cleared her throat. 'You're forgetting something.'

Jett turned back, creasing his brow in puzzlement. After a moment, he walked back and kissed her on the cheek. 'Thank you. You did a spectacular job.'

Smiling, Shiarn ran her hand over his hair and down his neck. 'I was only expecting a thank you.'

Jett shrugged and started walking. 'I'm tired and grateful.'

Shiarn stepped alongside him. 'And I'm pleased, but exhausted. I hope I don't collapse on the way.'

'I hope not too, because I won't be able to carry you.' Seth hung another quiver of arrows over his shoulder, bringing the total to six. 'Plus my arms are aching.'

Shiarn snorted at him.

Jett grinned at the two. 'Whatever you did in the tents, bewildered the Baions. Actually I'm bemused as well.'

'A lot can be achieved with some twine, rope, and well-placed knife…' Shiarn tilted her head with a proud smile.

'I still don't know what you were up to.' Seth clutched onto his slipping quivers. 'And with my fishing twine.'

Shiarn touched her nose. 'Some things are better left unsaid.'

'So no one is wiser to your mischief?' Jett said.

'You can't really talk.' She avoided his gaze and lifted her skirts to avoid a bush.

'You killed their leader,' Jett said, 'I was going to talk to him.'

'Oh, him.' She looked across into Jett's impatient expression. 'I had too. He heard me and I had the sense he could see me. Very unnerving. That reminds me.' She slid a folded letter out from her bodice and handed it to him.

A letter addressed to the Rynian Commander. He quickly scanned the contents. It shed light on why he could have seen Shiarn. 'It was for the best then.' He exhaled a stilted breath. 'This might be helpful.' The incessant thought they should pack the wagon and leave the valley for Coltrene assailed him. But what would be the consequences of such an action? What would come out of the valley after them? Once the orb had been reformed and a Gate opened, a type of new realm would be established. He didn't really understand it, but he expected there would be little opportunity of closing it. He wondered what the Eldery would say if they knew what was taking place. With all their airy prophecies and flippant grasping at significant events, they should be aware of such dire happenings in the world.

A plan had evolved in his mind. It was risky and had holes, but it was the only one he could think of that he might get out of alive. Now he had to convince the others of that.

Shiarn and Seth didn't query his thoughts on it and they all made a quiet trek back to camp.

~ * ~

The three trudged into camp, tired and ready to sleep. Jett's mood dropped to a new low on seeing Mara strapped to the wheel of the wagon. Her ripped skirt exposed her torn under-dress, and her red-gold locks hung in tangled heaps. After a quick scan, he noticed Marcus not far off, and Hellier, with a grim expression, walking towards them with her sword drawn.

Shiarn said, 'Look's like they've had some excitement.'

Hellier stopped and watched the three. Her brow narrowed with concern. 'Jett?'

'Devil's bloody arse!' Jett let lose an angry sigh, but held his retort. 'What happened?'

Shiarn chortled and put her hand on Jett's shoulder. 'I've got the wagon. And I don't want any noise.' She jumped up and disappeared inside.

'And I'm going to rest, somewhere.' Seth wandered off into the trees.

'Guess it must be you.' Hellier grinned with relief and relaxed the blade at her side.

Jett made a slow path to Mara. The girl's head slumped down to her neck and her hair covered her face.

'She went crazy and was going to take Earona.' Hellier glanced at Earona still asleep. 'She nearly killed her.'

He crouched before the adolescent. Her head snapped up and her eyes flashed with recognition, yet under her gag she sneered.

Hellier knelt beside him. 'She still hasn't come right.'

He removed the dressing from her mouth.

'You—' her voice lowered with contempt. '— shouldn't be.'

'What is your purpose here?'

'If you have to ask, you're not worthy of knowing,' she spat out.

'Curse it.' His heart sank at her fallen condition, what he feared was now before him. He placed his hand over the area where her scar would be and looked straight into her darkened gold eyes. His voice was stern. 'If Mara is in there, I want her to return, and you go back to where you came from.'

Her eyes rolled back to white and she opened her mouth as if to scream, but her head dropped and her body slumped in a dead faint. After a moment, she started convulsing and gagging.

'Quick, untie the rope.' Jett started undoing the knots along with Hellier.

Meanwhile Mara was vomiting a foul black bile. She held her stomach and retched the last of the filth out. Without a word, she once again fell in a faint, and lay still.

Jett lifted her chin to check her breathing. 'Hopefully she will awake and be herself. But—' he examined the foulness on the ground, it reminded him of when he woke from his poisonous time in his Mind Palace. 'There's no assurance she will be safe, or us.' He rested his forehead in his hands, feeling exhaustion hit. 'Watch her and make sure she doesn't leave. She may need water and food.'

'Are you going somewhere?' Hellier said.

'To sleep.' He stood and studied Earona curled up under her blanket. 'Make sure Earona stays away from her.'

'I'll try.'

He sighed at the unexpected complication. 'At least until I talk to Mara.'

~ * ~

Later in the day, on the other side of the wagon, Jett woke to thoughts of Ethan. For some moments he wondered if his lost Kin were in the camp. After clearing his mind from a dead sleep, he heard an argument not far off. With no sense of time, but a terrible realization hours had passed, Jett got up. He had to put his plan into motion, before he could back out.

Keanan and Marcus were having a fiery discussion. It was not the topic Jett initially feared, but perhaps the issue underlying their current tensions. By Marcus' feet lay malreus scale armour and a helm.

Keanan said to Marcus, 'I refuse to wear armour from our enemy.'

Jett came over and examined the Narahk's armour.

'It's cleaned up,' Marcus remarked, 'nothing wrong with it.'

Keanan challenged, 'Jett can wear it.'

Bypassing them, Jett glanced up at the darkening sky. The wind blustered with increasing speed, and a chill was in the air. They would need to depart soon. He replied, 'I won't be wearing it because I have other plans. Keanan, I'd advise you to wear it, but it is your decision in the end.'

Keanan stared at him with a frown. 'What plans do you have?'

'I shall tell you,' Jett said gravely, 'After I speak with Mara.'

Mara still sat by the wagon wheel, but on blankets and eating food.

Earona stood from the fire and walked over to Jett. She nudged his arm and offered him a chunk of bread along with a sweet smile. 'And we have some fish stew Seth concocted.'

The bandages about his palms were long discarded, and he took the warm bread in his raw, blistered hands.

Gasping at his torn flesh, she took one hand in hers and rubbed it.

He glared at the stream of deep red down her dress front, shocked at how close she had come to dying. He could never allow that to happen again. Yet he had already warned her. Earona put herself in danger by opening her heart to one such as Mara. His rage, fueled by fear, conflicted with any sympathy he might have. Despite her compassionate treatment of his hands, he responded with conceit, 'If you are remorseful tell me you are sorry.'

She blushed and lowered her head with a contrite nod. 'But, Jett, you don't understand, something made her… change.' She avoided his self-righteous gaze and glanced up at the fast moving, dark, ill-omened clouds.

'I agree,' Jett sighed with sadness, 'We have to move fast.' *Before there are any more changes.* He bit into the doughy bread while watching Earona shiver. If the enemy wanted Earona, maybe their plan was more sinister than he imagined.

She watched him with apprehension. 'You mean…'

'We are all in danger here.' Jett stressed his words. 'That's why Mara would have been safer at Sommerlea.' He let loose a tired grunt, surprised Earona remained quiet. After he finished eating he went to Mara with Earona following at his heels. The two crouched before her. Mara straightened up with a moan of discomfit, but her gaze remained on the ground.

'You seem to be back to normal.' That, at least, gave him some comfort.

Earona said, 'What a relief.'

Mara gave a short nod.

Earona gave Jett a sorrowful glance.

'Don't. You only need look at your dress to see there is a problem.' He gazed at Mara with honest puzzlement. 'How did this happen?'

Her eyes narrowed in a brooding stare. 'You really need to ask that?'

He returned her irritation with a warning glare. 'I thought the Ward would have protected you.'

'Why do you think that?' Mara's voice lowered with spite. 'It didn't before.'

Jett clenched his fist and his teeth ground. 'You're not in a position to speak to me like this.'

'I 'spose...' Her eyes lowered and she mumbled, 'But... anyway, it wasn't about the Ward, this was different than that...'

'Maybe it is. But those bitches have the ability to do this whenever they want?'

'I don't think...' Her eyes skipped over him and Earona and her voice was softer. 'This wasn't like them...' She frowned in thought. 'This was Yavinia, and she's not like them.' She glanced down at her chest. 'They took my charm the night before.'

'That little mouse?' Earona cried.

'It's supposed to conceal me,' Mara replied. 'She found me, and she put some poison in me.'

Jett raised his brow. 'How is it different?'

'Before, with you, I wanted to do it. This time it wasn't me at all.' Mara avoided his probing gaze. 'That's it.'

He had a thought she was not sharing everything she knew, but for now it was enough. He muttered, 'Perhaps it is more a case of possession.'

Mara shrugged her indifference.

'Why did she want me?' Earona said.

'How do I know?' Mara barked.

Jett rubbed his temples, his annoyance growing into wrath. 'This is the reason I didn't want you to come. I'm about to walk up to the Agamon and now the witches, or mages, or someone has an inroad through you—'

'Why do you think everything is my fault?!' Mara shouted in his face. 'You think I want this?!'

Jett took a needed breath. 'You're now vulnerable to their plans and maybe endangered ours.'

'You didn't hear me!' Her amber eyes glowed with anger. 'It wasn't me. I know I could overcome it – if it happened again.'

Jett rested his head in his hands and sighed. 'It's too risky.'

Earona started, 'She could help—'

'No!' Jett looked at Mara with determination. 'Because they know where you are, you will remain here—'

'No!' Mara shouted. 'You can't leave me!'

His tone was grim and he lowered his voice. 'You have the ability to summon forces from Hell, and even beyond that. It's too great a power.'

Mara spoke through gritted teeth and she pushed her face into his. 'And you have the power to kill everyone with you without a thought.'

He stared at her with blatant animosity she would reveal what he had not spoken to anyone.

'Stop this!' Earona put a hand on each of their shoulders. 'We need to work together, not fight.' She groaned a sigh. 'Not again. Let's talk about your plans, Jett, and then talk about Mara.'

Jett backed up with his eyes fixed on Mara. He turned and stamped to the outskirts of the camp with Earona racing to catch him up. Previously the plan had been straightforward. Now... too many variables were appearing for his liking. He stared up at the low blackening clouds with unease.

'That,' Earona stopped beside him and looked up at the fast moving clouds, 'is not helping the mood in the least. It's making me afraid and anxious.'

He detected its disconcerting hand over his heart and he shivered in the wind that chilled him to the bone. The urge to run back to Coltrene was stronger than ever. He took a long painful breath and considered the girl. She was as cursed as he was. 'I'm…' *just worried.*

'I know,' Earona replied, 'but, maybe she's right. When I spoke to her,' she bit her lip, 'she said her baby somehow anchored her to reality.'

Jett shook his head at her admission. 'You had to, didn't you?'

'Hellier went with me.' Earona brushed him off. 'But you see, I think it's more like they took over her mind.'

'You don't know that.' He was still miffed she disobeyed him. *Maybe we should have let her die back—*

'Jett Storm'Heart! I would never let that happen,' she declared with angry reproach, 'the poor girl has suffered enough and will probably always be suffering.'

He gave a rueful smile, smug he was making her nervous. 'Only a thought. I'd never be able to do it or even let it happen, but,' he stopped to offer it serious deliberation.

'It's wicked, and I hope it's coming from that above.' Earona stared at the gathering oppressive clouds. *And not something else.* After some moments, she said in a fearful stammer, 'Do you think…those witches, or whoever, could… do it to you?'

Her query did not surprise him, he already considered the answer. 'My guess. If they had the means they would have done it. But, I don't believe it is witches, but something more… powerful.'

'Something more…' Earona stared with horror. *You mean like you were?*

Nodding, Jett slumped with realization. The evil that corrupted him and Mara came from outside their world.

From around the fire-pit, Hellier yelled, 'Are you two going to chin-wag forever or have something to eat?'

Jett turned towards the Kin and a belated meal. While Earona followed.

Marcus asked Jett, 'How did it go at the Rynian camp?'

Seated on the ground with a bowl of stew, and with a clear view of Mara, Jett said between mouthfuls, ''Bout time someone asked.'

'Well?'

Jett smiled. 'Like boys winning a match of brawler-ball.'

'More importantly,' Keanan asked, 'will they help us?'

Jett dunked his bread and swallowed before answering. 'They will lend what aid they can.'

'You don't sound convincing.'

'What they have done has helped us already,' Jett replied.

Shiarn stirred her bowl. 'Are we really going ahead with your "plan"?'

Jett narrowed his eyes at her, wondering how much she knew of his thoughts during their walk back through the woods.

'What is this "plan" anyway?' Seth asked.

Jett watched them eat while giving him expectant glances. 'I plan on separating the Eye of Heaven.'

'You?!' Hellier exclaimed, 'Alone?'

'Not entirely, but in a way, me.' He sighed at her despairing look. 'The ones reforming it don't think it can be done. An ancient staff did it the first time—'

'What happened to this staff?' Keanan interrupted with hope in his eyes.

Jett dashed it rashly, 'Destroyed.'

Shiarn flicked her hand up at Keanan. 'Let him explain.'

'I have the power to separate it.' Jett observed their mixed reactions. 'With my eyes.'

Marcus smiled with approval. 'Sounds good.'

'But did the orb destroy the staff?' Shiarn frowned, bringing to bear the impact of her words.

'Yes.'

Earona stood over him, hands on her hips. 'And what happened to Nya?'

Jett responded, 'She perished.'

'What are you up to, man?' Keanan sprung up with fiery indignation. 'You have a desire for death?! What are you trying to prove to yourself…to us?'

Shiarn added, 'Kean's right. Jett, you can't—'

'It's all well and good you're able to do that.' Earona lectured with a stern finger. 'But if you are gone, I don't want to go through all that turmoil again.'

Jett creased his brow at them and glanced at Hellier, penetrating his gaze with an intense fiery glare.

'I don't know, Jett,' Marcus said, 'There's got to be better way.'

'Your confidence in me is astounding.' Jett's hand flew wide dismissing their skepticism. 'Do you think I *want* to get killed by that thing?' Colour touched his cheeks and he rubbed the back of his neck. 'But your show of affection is a pleasant change.'

Keanan commented with reproach, 'You've gone completely barmy.'

'I'm beginning to wonder.' Jett let out a dry chuckle. 'If I die it's not willingly.'

Keanan sat down with a groan of reluctance, and started flicking through the journal he was holding. 'I've been studying this. I've come to the conclusion and much to my dismay—'

Marcus remarked, 'Here we go again.'

'You think it's an Aeylon,' Jett finished for him.

Keanan nodded. 'So you also have considered it. Its power is immense in its rightful form. It appeared to protect the kingdom of Amin-Sayeda from the Chaos of that Age.'

'It's the last thing we need, running into a corrupted Aeylon.' Jett hung his head. It was another violation the Eldery could lay on him.

The others sat silent considering the magnitude of what they were dealing with.

Finally Marcus spoke. 'It's our calling I suppose.'

Shiarn gave a grunt of disbelief. 'Somehow I doubt they'd see it in the same way.'

'Can't wait to see their faces when they know,' Marcus bantered.

Seth added, 'I don't know what would be more challenging, a corrupted Aeylon or facing the Eldery Circle.'

'I'd be happy if I never have to face them again,' Jett pressed his lips together.

'And we all know how you feel about that,' Keanan commented. *If we fail you may never have to again.* 'First let's try to do this and worry about such things later. The risk is enormous.'

'We've faced Skar, Baskharef, and Narahk.' Marcus said with pride, 'We can do this to.'

'Don't forget witches,' Jett added.

Shiarn said with a dark frown, 'and a Mage and an evil demonic lord.'

Hellier added, 'The stakes are getting higher by the day.'

'We certainly get a good deal of practice,' Seth replied with a sheepish grin.

'This is no time to jest.' Earona's finger and haughty demeanor switched to them.

Jett stared up at Earona's taut expression. 'I'm glad you're serious because you are central to the success of this plan.' He paused until he had her complete attention. 'You're going to keep me alive while I do it.'

Earona's eyes shot open with sudden trepidation and she sank to her knees beside him, and squeaked, 'Ooh…me?!'

He replied in a laconic drawl, 'No one else can do it.'

'Can it be done?' Her fingers fluttered over her chest.

'I don't see why not.' Jett decided not to inform them, the power he would attempt to generate from his vision would normally take years to acquire. Instead, he focused a steely gaze on Shiarn studying her empty bowl. 'And Shiarn can give us some shielding while you do it.'

Shiarn bemoaned, 'Hellier's right, the odds are stacking up.'

Keanan looked at the three in contemplation. 'That leaves the rest of us to face whatever our enemies do.'

'Right.' A weary grimace settled on Jett's face, this had been his principal concern.

A low muttering came from Mara, 'I might be able to stop them.'

Keanan said to Jett, 'Sadly, she is more susceptible than ever.'

Jett kept his eyes on Mara. 'You could just as easily stop us.' *Or even kill us.*

'No.' Her scorn was directed at him. 'I know I can help.'

Earona nudged him. 'Maybe we should listen.'

'We can't risk it.' Under his breath, Jett said, 'Besides the witches can find her. If she's here they might believe we are here as well.'

'Leave her behind?' Earona was aghast.

'We can't take her,' he creased his eyes at Earona in warning, 'She'll be better off here, whether we fail or not. But, I believe the witches will be too occupied to worry.'

'That's speculation, but has some merit,' Keanan agreed. 'If we are successful we shall come back for her.'

'You can't just leave me! What if you fail? You would let them take me, even if you're dead?!' Mara shouted, 'I'd be better off if you killed me!'

Jett gave Earona a sad look.

Don't even think it, Earona replied to his thoughts. 'It's not going to come to that, everything will be fine.' Her voice had an anxious tremor.

Jett said, 'Now that's troubling.' After witnessing the wickedness of the witches first hand he understood her fears. 'But right now, we must get ready to ride.'

82 - Dead Forest

Protecting and fighting for those weaker than yourself will grant you strength beyond your capabilities and give you power that is otherwise impossible to achieve. This superior force is called Justice.

Ei'myn Tru Sei-Toramah

Once the plan was agreed on, the Kin started moving about the camp, packing gear and preparing for departure. Jett was readying Thunder for riding. Hellier stood next to him and placed a hand on the horse's neck. Comforted by her presence, Jett glanced at her with a lopsided grin and gave a wink.

She turned her face away and shot out, 'I've been meaning to talk to you.'

He continued checking Thunder's strapping. 'Really?'

'I've been angry—'

'You have?' Her candid words brought his head up and he viewed her contrite face.

'Devil's bloody arse!' She threw her hand in the air and fired off, 'You are a demon! You deserve witches after you, and a demented spirit lover, lord high and mighty.'

He grabbed her arm, preventing her walking away. 'Hel, you don't have to say anything to me.' *I'm the one who wanted to talk to you, remember. To apologize…* His stormy eyes pierced hers with understanding. 'I know how much I hurt you.'

'I don't think you know at all.' Her glare was hot and teeming with passion. 'I don't know if you have ever known.'

'Maybe it's you that doesn't know.' His response was gruff. After noting her downcast face, he softened. 'I hurt you more than anyone else.' *It's cut a terrible wound.* He let it rest and said, 'I'm going to be worried about you today.'

She reproached, 'You'll be worried about all of us.'

'True, but if something happens to you…' He could not hide the sadness creeping into his eyes. He took a step closer and cupped her face in his hands for an unexpected kiss. His lips caressed hers with building desire. Her silent gasp gave him great satisfaction. Her eyes flicked open when he parted from her, and he said, 'I wouldn't be able to live with myself if I didn't do that. Dead or alive,' smiling with fondness at her sparkling eyes, 'forgiven or not.'

'If you hadn't done it I would of and for selfish reasons. And I'm still thinking about that.'

He replied in good-humour, 'I'd expect nothing less from you.' After a pause, he started, 'About Dario—'

'You're not going to dare try to lecture me about him?' Her shoulders tensed with pending wrath. 'After what you did with that… woman!' *You'll never lecture me again!*

His cheeks flushed. 'You're right.' He hadn't even considered if she knew or not, or even how much it might hurt her. 'Who am I to say anything to you?' After a moment of trying to restrain himself, he said, 'I wouldn't call her a woman.'

'Humph!' She folded her arms and tapped her foot. *It didn't seem to matter, you took her well and good, whatever she was.*

He sensed he was getting in over his head with each comment. 'Were you and Dario really in—'

'Don't!' She stopped him with a raised palm. 'Let's leave this conversation before we regret something.' *I don't want to think about him today.*

'Done then.' He pushed aside his wrathful thoughts about the scoundrel and his unanswered question. *There will be a day when I'll have to talk about that bastard.* He unbuckled his belt and unattached one of the sheaths and handed it to her. 'Take this.'

Hellier took it and creased her brow at the malreus pommel. 'You sure?'

'Just a loan.' His eyes shone with affection as she gripped the weapon. 'I won't be needing it and it will be more useful in your hands.' He stared into her eyes with an awareness of what may await them beyond the Agamon. *If this is it, I don't want to say goodbye.*

Hellier responded to his thoughts, 'If *I* die today I won't be leaving you all so easily.'

Jett's eyes darkened even more. 'If anyone is leaving it's me.'

Looking into his eyes with intense affection, she stroked his cheek. 'Don't even think it…'

He lay his hand over hers, holding his sword. 'Maybe I'm not as smart as everyone thinks, maybe I'm insane.'

She shook her head and made a devilish grin. 'The two have nothing to do with each other.' Her expression deepened at his underlying fear. 'I believe in you.'

'That makes one of us.'

'Uhuh, not just me.' She shook her head with a teasing smile. 'But… if you did die…' her face coloured and she lowered her voice, 'I'd prefer you died doing the right thing, and not the wrong.'

'An honourable death.'

'Something like that.'

'I hope I do something worthy before I do.' He attempted some humour, 'I'll be pissed if I don't.'

'We would be to,' *though for a different reason.* A thoughtful look lit her face. 'What is it Sledge and that lot always say, write your own endings?'

He grinned at the vision of the mining men. 'Live first — write later?'

'Kind of makes sense. Can't get it wrong then.'

'I'm of the same mind, but—' he ran his hand through the back of his hair, considering the prophetic words he was given back home.

'You want to know?' Her sky-blue eyes widened in surprise.

Judge Haldus would faint if he heard me say it. He curtailed the chuckle. 'Maybe I'm changing…'

'No more changing!' She gave a stilted laugh.

He looked over the camp and spied one of the Kin standing alone. 'There's someone I need to talk to.'

'I'll be worried about Seth today too.'

'You'll have to keep an eye on him.'

With a suspicious frown, Seth watched Jett march his way. He stood stiff, waiting his approach. Jett neared, and Seth said, 'We should be leaving soon.'

Jett met him with a stony expression, sensing the trepidation in his thoughts due more to Jett's stern demeanor than the looming mission. 'And we shall.' Considering the teenager, nearly nine years younger, he looped an arm around his shoulders in a tight grip and guided him away from the camp. To gain any viable chance of leaving Tellávare, the Kin had to wait for Seth to come of age, yet even now Jett still viewed him as a child.

Seth raised a questioning brow, 'If you wish to tell me something, out with it.'

Jett held him rigid against his side. 'Seth,' his voice an anxious waver, 'I get down on you at times, but you worry me.'

'Attacking the Narahk?'

'In a way, although I am proud of you.' Jett's tone became grim. 'But because of that, I want you to hang back and not get close.'

Seth stopped him in his tracks. 'What are you saying?'

'You may get in over your head. Besides, we could need a… messenger.' Jett cast a forlorn eye over his shoulder at the others. 'If it all goes…bad, I want you to leave.'

'You're not going to fail.' His voice turned cross.

'It's best to be prepared.' Jett put a hand on his chest and said with deliberate force, 'You are the only one who could get out of this place.' He stared into his green eyes, conveying calm to Seth's growing alarm. 'If the worse happens, you have to escape and warn Sommerlea.' He relieved him with a faint smile. 'And, you're the only one who listens to me and will do what I ask.'

Seth creased his brow in consideration of the sombre request.

Above, the white clouds of day fled from the path of the emerging black mass. Fear in the air affected Jett's shaky courageous stance. 'There's one more thing to do, and we better get moving.'

~ * ~

Jett turned to the camp and Earona, approaching him with a nervous fidget. He said, 'Where is she?'

Earona glanced over her shoulder. 'Behind the wagon. I'll go see her.'

'No,' Jett pulled her arm back, 'I want to talk to her, alone.' He went around the wagon, not knowing what he would say, except he needed to enforce his wishes.

Mara leant against the wagon with arms folded. Her petite brows lowered at the sight of him.

'We'll be leaving now, and I want you to stay here.'

'So you said.'

'Don't try to follow us—'

Her pout deepened. 'I'll go where I want.'

'You can't go there.' Jett leaned his hand on the wagon over her. 'There could be Rynians and witches and who knows what else. It's too dangerous. Kael and Jonas will have my guts,' he took a short breath, 'they'll already be livid.'

'Earona's going.' Her arms became more rigid and she continued avoiding his stare.

'True.' Jett looked away, recalling Earona's fear-filled expression. Earona would probably rather not go at all. 'But, I'll need her.' He was not surprised by Mara's pigheadedness, but her need to help was unexpected. 'I thought you'd prefer not going?'

'I—' she sunk down further, but her voice grew fervent. 'Anyway, that's not the point…'

'You don't want to be told what to do?' He folded his arms, mocking her defiant stance.

Mara lifted her head and cast a foul glimmer his way. 'They're my enemies too. And they took something of mine as well.'

'That's not as important as the Eye-key.'

She pointed up at him. 'It's very important to me! And — you might fail! I'm left here to face — Hell!' Her amber eyes flew to the line of trees and she grumbled, 'They'll come for me… and you will… ' Wrath boiled in her tone, 'that's why I don't want to stay.'

Her anger exasperated his. 'That's exactly why I want you to. You'll have a better chance.' The more distance between him and her, the better chance she might have of escaping. Even that was a vain hope, but gave him a small measure of assurance. 'I have no control with anything that may happen if I fail… you know what that means.'

Mara bit her lip and stared down at his feet.

He observed her young face, pretty yet with an experience beyond the years of a thirteen year old. She was an enigma to him, but he understood her fears. If he failed… she would be alone. But even if she came… his voice softened, 'I can't protect you at the temple, none of us can.'

She grumbled with impatience, 'I don't need protecting.'

'No?' Out from his belt, he pulled the black blade she used the previous night. 'Because you can use this?' He turned it in his hand, eyeing the curved black edge.

She glared with her lips pressed in a sour line. 'Everyone else has a weapon.'

'We don't use them on each other.'

She gave a derisive snort.

'Maybe you can see why I would be concerned.' He gave her a warning frown.

She gave a resigned shrug and said with remiss, 'I don't want to do that again.'

'Let's hope so.' Jett flipped the dagger around and offered her the bone hilt. 'I won't leave you without a way out.'

She took it slowly with a skeptical glance at his blank expression.

'If you use it on one of us, you'll never see it again.' A wry smile escaped him. 'But, I want you to stay here. Also I'll look for your charm, we all will. If there's any chance of getting it back we will do it.'

'It's a bribe.' Mara clutched it close to her chest and eyed him with irritation. 'I don't make promises.'

He was under no assumption she would be swayed by such things, and he also knew he had no natural control over the girl. It was merely sympathy, and a glimpse at how evil the enemy could be. 'I know. But whatever works. Better than being tied up, which was the next option.'

Her mouth curled up with annoyance. 'You're an arrogant arse!'

'You don't know the half of it.' He stared her down. 'Don't tempt me. The rope is still there.'

'Just go.' Mara stomped off, gripping the knife to her side.

~ * ~

Jett walked away from Mara's contempt with resolute firmness.

Earona stood beside him and said under her breath, her nervousness apparent, 'I really don't think it's right leaving her here – and I'm also concerned I won't be able to… it's so complicated…' *I'm sick with apprehension.*

Jett remained stiff to her agitation. 'I'm not backing down.'

Her hands fidgeted at her chest and her eyes danced over everything bar him. 'I fear I might not be able to manage—'

He grabbed her trembling hands and clenched them tight. 'Blue, stop.' He wasn't in the mood to deal with her misgivings, he had enough of his own. 'I'll be there with you.'

Fear paled her face, and her eyes pleaded for solace.

'Just do what you're good at. Healing.' He squeezed her arms in a steadfast grip.

Her face flushed with embarrassment. 'But this — I've never done anything of this magnitude before.'

His body relaxed and he stretched back. 'It's a first for all of us.'

Lightning stopped beside the pair and over his backend one of the malreus scale rested. From the saddle Marcus looked down at Earona, frowning up at him. He said, 'You can ride with me,' in a decisive manner that was not going to accept no for an answer.

She squeaked, 'Is it time?'

'It is.' Jett lifted her up and set her before Marcus with a relieved grin. He looked around at the others. Hellier was on River while Keanan already trotted on the road Seth had begun on foot. Jett was glad to see Keanan decided to wear the malreus armour. He was probably not happy backing down, but he was wise enough to realize the benefits of it. Keanan had his concerns, and Jett had numerous ones himself; one was staring at him now.

Shiarn stood next to him holding Thunder's rein. 'Look's as if I'm stuck with you.'

Jett helped her mount with a dry chuckle. 'Hey - You don't enjoy my company?' He jumped up in front of her. 'I admit I'm not as suave as some others.' He pulled Thunder up to follow Hellier into the woods on the paved roadway leading to the Agamon.

'You have other qualities, you're stubborn, daring, outspoken.' She circled his waist with a firm grip. 'There could be worse things I suppose. A mysterious,' *demonic,* 'personality.'

'And there isn't anything mysterious about you? No. Of course not.' *Pure as gold grit.* 'I can think of worse things too, the size of this saddle,' he said. 'You're taking up a lot of room.' The distracted banter was just what he needed to occupy his thoughts as they headed into the shadows of the woods.

Marcus and Earona rode at the end of the line in an uncomfortable quiet. Earona stayed tense, trying not to let her body settle against Marcus' warm chest. Eventually she was compelled to speak. 'Marcus?'

'Yes?'

She watched Thunder ahead, traveling through the narrow track amongst solid pines. 'You seem quiet.'

His voice was coarse. 'I've got a lot on my mind.'

His chest expanded and become tight behind her, she opened her mouth to query him—

'Like whether I'm going to see you again,' he added in an uneven voice.

She sucked in her breath, glad he couldn't see her bright cheeks. His words were simple, yet her hopeful expectations spoke of a deeper interpretation. 'Oh…' It was all she could say as her heart raced.

He sighed against her back. 'I thought you and Keanan…' He cleared his throat, suddenly giving thought to his words.

'Yes?'

'Were getting…' He finished in a weak mumble, '…closer.'

Shaking her head, her long wavy hair flowed over her shoulders. 'I'm really not sure.' She smiled to herself. 'Currently, we are just friends.'

His voice was a parody of seriousness. 'That's good, isn't it?'

Earona gave a slight giggle and twisted her neck, attempting to see him. 'You'd think that, wouldn't you?'

He said with surprise, 'What do you mean by that?'

Despite the dark ominous clouds covering the sky, Earona was distracted enough to give a delighted smile. 'Keanan told me some things about you… about me.'

'Did he?' he raised his voice. *That's a surprise.*

Coy, Earona let her body ease into the rocking movement of the horse. '…it was.'

She did all she could to prevent her erratic thoughts from flying into his mind. Even so she knew he must be able to read something there, but she realized she was not delving into his thoughts. It would be easy to Mind-speak her feelings however she had a carnal desire for something more tangible to take place.

Marcus took up the reins with one hand, the other shifted her hair from her neck with an unaccustomed gentleness. Earona's cheeks burned, and she thought her heart would burst through her chest as he tucked her hair behind her ear with thoughtful attention. It was followed by his mouth, and his breath was a soft hush by her ear as he stroked her cheek. She tilted her chin, open to the caress and lay her hand on his as it glided across her skin.

'Like I said, I'm worried I might not see you again.'

Earona heard the heaviness in his voice and his poignant words sent a shiver through her body. She gripped his hand firmly in hers and raised it for a soft kiss. Wanting to speak words of assurance, she found she was content as he held her close. In his strong embrace she had no reason to speak, neither did she feel words would enhance the moment. His engaging touch revealed a deeper longing and as they traveled toward an uncertain fate she was strangely at peace.

~ * ~

As the Kin moved single-file through the woodland, daylight was overtaken by low turbulent black clouds. The sharp wind snapped at their exposed skin with a biting chill.

Screeching overhead came closer, and a flying creature skirted the treetops. The size of a large bird, a fire was in its eyes, and a snake-like tail shone like metal. Seth drew an arrow. Pinpointing his target, he pierced the devil creature. Its shrieking continued till it fell some way into the dead trees. Faint cries of other flying monsters was on the wind. Preparing another arrow, Seth turned to the Kin. 'That was not from this world.'

Jett nodded. 'Maybe some sort of scout.'

The dying forest was more prevalent as they travelled. A carpet of debris, thick with leaves and vines, crunched under the horses' hooves. Trees were bare and blackened and shrubs were parched balls of twigs. The forest was a bleak surround of brown, grey and black with nothing green visible.

Seth halted their passage between dry skeletal trees. A severe wind drove withered refuse about them, and an uncanny sound was in its passage. He raised his voice above the howl. 'We shouldn't take the horses any farther, we can go by foot.'

Jett dismounted with steady purpose. 'We won't tie them.' He spoke to his horse and rubbed his shoulder before walking ahead with Seth. The others dismounted, and after equipping armour they followed Seth through the eerie wind. Shielding his face from the wind's sting, Jett walked through a shifting layer of desiccated forest floor.

'It's dead here,' Seth stated with profound sorrow, 'All of them… gone.' *It's lifeless…*

Jett said, 'The valley will eventually be affected in the same way.'

Soon the highest point of the pyramid loomed over the brittle branches of fir trees. A brilliant light illuminated the top and the clouds. They walked on a crumbling road to the edge of the great stretch of the courtyard bounding the ziggurat. They stopped short of the pavement behind rubble and dead trees. Constructed with white blocks, the ziggurat was a ghostly presence under the unnatural hue from the clouds above. Around the paved area was a three level arched colonnade, wide enough for a man to walk and high enough to see the top of the temple. The arches circled the ziggurat except on the right where they had fallen into ruin. Each level of the standing colonnades was accessible by a narrow stair.

Crouched by toppled statues, Jett was transfixed by the surprising brightness of the Eye of Heaven. Without any stand or altar, the orb floated as if caught in a type of updraft. Four slender columns, partly destroyed, might have once supported a covering structure over the orb. Ashen light radiated from its center, and in its glow was a silhouette of a man and woman. Their robes twirled in the strident wind, and their hands stretched up to the blackness above.

A handful of armed men, clothed in black, their faces hidden by cowls, stood in a line at the bottom of the step. More armed men, on the pavement, guarded the left side, in a detached formation. Under the orb's glimmering light, figures were on the ledges under the arches to the left of the ziggurat.

Keanan asked Jett, 'There are witches?'

Jett said, 'I can't see behind the pyramid, but on the left are four I can see.' He considered the men, who appeared to be regular Rynian soldiers.

A giant figure shoved the soldiers aside and they cowered from his path. He towered over the men, his thick arms covered in hair, and he carried a long double-headed mace. Twisted horns curved above his head, and his face resembled more a bull. Even at this distance, Jett observed his red eyes, burning with rage, surveying the woods as if looking for something.

Hellier whispered, 'What the hell is that?'

'A hellish monster?' Seth shrugged.

Marcus knelt beside them. 'You mean, what *in* hell.'

Earona hissed her displeasure, 'This is no time to joke.'

'Who's joking?!' Marcus replied. *They're from hell.*

Keanan shook his head. 'Whatever it is, we're going to find out.'

'Come what may, we're about to bring our own hell,' Jett said, 'Now the plan—'

'I will take the witches,' Hellier interrupted, 'Seth will help me.'

Jett gauged Seth's trusting eyes. 'Be careful. Kill anyone who appears to be a prisoner. A plan only goes so far.'

Marcus murmured, 'We have to make it up as we go.'

'I'll be dealing with those up there.' Jett indicated the top of the pyramid. 'I've got an idea how to approach them. Marcus and Keanan, guard against those soldiers and make sure no one goes up the stairs.' He focused on Keanan's wise eyes. *I don't know how vulnerable we'll be up there.*

Keanan kept a level gaze on Jett's poignant expression. 'I know.'

Jett eyed the woods surrounding them. 'Now, if we are lucky the Baion's will front up soon.'

Marcus flipped his sword in his hand. 'All up it doesn't look too bad.'

'Not bad?!' Earona squealed under her breath, 'You could all get killed.'

'Have some confidence in us,' Marcus responded with mock hurt. 'You've seen Kean in full swing. He can burn some stinking damage.'

Earona's face dulled with colour and she turned her eyes down. 'You're right.'

Shiarn laid a hand on her shoulder. 'Don't worry, you won't see a thing.'

She lamented, 'And that makes me feel better?'

Keanan said above their talk, 'Is that it?'

'As far as I know…' Jett replied, 'I'll take care of the soldiers on the stair and the mages above. I'm hoping there won't be trouble with that. And then I'll deal with that orb.'

Keanan commented dryly, 'Should I assume there is no fall back plan?'

'Ah…' Jett met eyes with Seth and it did not go unnoticed by Keanan. 'I hadn't really thought of one.'

'I see,' Keanan replied. *No turning back.*

Marcus said, 'We live or die, is there anything else?'

'I don't want to die today,' Shiarn said, 'so you better put a cork in this hell. And remember, I won't be there to help any of you below.'

'And you better destroy that thing,' Hellier looked towards the orb, 'or it might never end.'

Keanan lowered his head and gave a sigh of resignation. He looked at the shining light at the top of the pyramid and said, 'Oh, sun, we shall ever be chasing your light. Nightmares have become our days. Twilight our memory of dying hope. Bitter wind of moonless world we birth. Doom the good to pain, chaos and a wicked way.' His words provoked sullen calm, and he continued with more force, 'Scatter, collide, and fall into corruption. History manifests as a recurring affliction to those chosen to descend the trail. Those cursed under prophecy will instigate their fate. The key to freedom is a life sacrificed.' He took a solemn glance at the Kin. 'It would seem this prophecy is unfolding before our eyes.'

Now is not the time for that, Jett gave him a harsh glare.

'Oh, that's right, they don't know it,' Keanan replied with a note of sarcasm.

Earona looked from Keanan to Jett in horror. 'That's the prophecy?'

'Some of it,' Jett's tone was brisk.

'Indeed.' Keanan lowered his head with some remiss. 'It's wise to be aware of impartations, but to remember that words can twist and turn, and not be exactly as we interpret them.'

'But really, can you get anymore dismal?' Marcus remarked.

Shiarn sighed. 'Kean, your timing is as bad as ever.'

'Wait — you mean…' Seth squeaked, 'your life, Jett?!'

Keanan held up his hand. 'It would seem likely.'

'Explains a lot about what's going on.' Shiarn frowned darkly, 'too bad we didn't know sooner.'

Earona piped up, 'And we're just going along with this—'

'Hold on!' Hellier exclaimed, 'A life sacrificed?! Jett, you *knew* this — all this time?! *You're going to sacrifice yourself?*

'Damn it to hell!' Jett cried, 'I didn't think it was about me!' He stared at each of them, their faces a mix of grief and annoyance.

'Who did you think it was?' Earona wailed.

'The truth is…' he stumbled over his thoughts, 'I assumed someone… more worthy.'

'I hope you're joking?!' Marcus cried.

'I…' Jett lowered his head for a moment, and raised it with boldness. 'It's why I have Earona…'

'But you don't know for sure it's going to wor—' Shiarn started.

'No. I'm going to try and I'm not giving up because of a cursed prophecy,' Jett stated, 'I'm the one that stole that flamin' amulet in the first place, and then let it be stolen, so I'm the one who's going to make it right.' His eyes darkened and his voice dropped with steely resolve. 'If it has to be me, it has to be. I'm going to do it. I won't let anyone else do it.'

Earona wiped tears from her eye. 'It's just so awful…'

He growled, 'I'm not dead yet.'

'Yet?!' Earona sobbed.

'That's not encouraging,' Seth said softly.

'Besides, I could never live if anything happened to any of you…' Jett's voice trailed off. *Just so you know…*

'What in hell's name is that supposed to mean?' Hellier cried.

'Devil's buggered arse, you will!' Marcus retorted. 'I don't give a hellfire cock about prophecies — and I'm not planning on being doomed either.'

Seth replied, 'And what makes you think *we* could live without you?'

Earona stood suddenly, her face flushed. 'That's right. If you fail, we all fai—' She ended with Jett pushing her into Seth, toppling them both sideways and out of the way of a massive beast a few feet behind. Its approach was silent, but it snarled at Jett and his unsheathed sword.

The beast swiped at his head with giant claws and he could see little else but its huge chest, too close. The stench from its knotted fur was unbearable, and sallow teeth, dripping with saliva, were exposed with its rage-filled growls. It was strong, but he forced off its sweeping attacks with his blade. Stepping back was not an option, and he continued pressing it away from the Kin, even though Marcus wanted to get in on the action. Jett did not want to be crushed by its weight, or have anyone in its radius, if it decided to come down on all fours.

Jett's blood raced with Ethos burning into his eyes, and searing the creature over its coarse fur. Thrusting in with a killing blow, he pierced its chest. The beast raged, punching its heavy claws, attempting to slash his arm. He jumped back from its descent, and it fell hard and lay still. Jett stared into the dead woods. 'A cursed Baskharef, here.'

'It does not bode well,' Keanan commented.

'And we've run out of time to chat.' Marcus checked over his shoulder at the soldier's looking for the noise.

'We'll have to move or be discovered.' Jett's dark eyes stared gravely at each of them, wanting to imprint their faces into his mind one last time. His only regret, he was unable to say goodbye to Ethan. 'It is what it is, and we have to go through with it now.'

'If you've all finished, I'm off, and I'm not saying goodbye,' Hellier said, gruffly, 'I'll see you after. Come on, Seth.' She turned from them and dashed into the shadows.

'Good luck, and may the Creator be working for us,' Seth added, 'oh, and everyone, stay alive.' He ran off after Hellier.

See you after, Jett called to them, knowing Hellier was angry and upset about the prophecy. He looked back at the ziggurat and the soldiers glancing towards their position. 'We better hurry,' he said, suddenly fearful they would be caught too early. 'I have hope, and I have all of you. That should be enough.'

'Yes, for we don't have much else,' Keanan remarked.

Marcus added, 'Don't worry, we'll have your back.'

'And we have you too.' Earona tried smiling, but her mouth fluttered with fear.

Jett looked into her misting blue eyes, and said, 'You're right. If all of you fail, I fail.'

Her lips formed a grimace. 'That's not wha—'

'Bottom line, we're all doing it for each other.' Squeezing Jett's hot palm, Shiarn gave him a warm smile. She grabbed Earona's trembling hand, and they vanished.

Marcus stood in the empty space and unsheathed his second weapon. 'Kean, light up the big devil first.' Equipped with the malreus plate and the open face helm, he prepared his two malreus swords.

'It will probably have no effect on him. After all he is one *of* hell's minions.' Keanan, also wearing the black metal, had a single sword of malreus and he kept to a crouch. 'That thing is most likely immune to fire, you realize.'

Marcus laughed. '*Now* you're making jokes.'

'Actually I'm being serious,' Keanan replied, 'Perhaps fire will make it feel at home.'

'Bloody devils.' Marcus chortled, 'Still made me laugh.'

'Let's see how long that lasts.'

Marcus flexed his arms, and couldn't restrain his grin. *You're getting good at this.* 'In that case, let's give him a warm welcome and see how well he likes it.'

'Can't say I'm going to enjoy the smell of roasted devil monster.' Keanan looked pensive, before a smile lit his eyes.

'Can't be worse than those Skar.' Marcus laughed and walked forward.

'You're going to walk out there and announce yourself?' Keanan was dumbfounded.

'You could introduce me,' Marcus said, 'or if you prefer, you can go first, and I'll be the second act.' He finished with a wink.

Keanan sighed and rolled his eyes to the heavens. 'Fine, let's light up the big one.'

~ * ~

Ethan and the Harn walked all day and rested at night somewhere in the depths of the forest. The following day Adis spurred them on to a greater speed despite them traveling on foot. Morias sympathized with the Harn's disquiet and for his trouble he received a disapproving stare from Adis. Clara spent time trotting among the men, chatting and laughing about topics as mundane as the weather. The confrontation with the Narahk and the death of their own had not deterred the Harn for long and they relished their hard won freedom once more. No amount of warning about potential danger or even impending death could take away the pride of their achievement of passing through the mountain. The men had no qualms about elaborating on their adventurous escape underground. The stories lost their frightful morbidity in the light of day.

Traveling with the Fáerinn brought Ethan a small taste of home. In the short time he knew them, a fondness for the three developed. He listened like a boy with wide-eyed envy and some unease to all his Kin had done. Even Adis, approaching with his grim face and bad news, could not dampen his spirits.

Adis' pulled his horse up next to Morias, and said, 'I've never seen a forest this way. It's graver than I feared.'

Berran, the sandy haired boy, sitting in front of Morias, replied, 'There's a stink in the wind.'

Morias stared at the low lying clouds. 'What is it?'

'Poison. The trees are afraid.' Adis glanced at the men not shy about listening to their conversation. 'The animals are running in droves.'

Grith asked, 'What causes such fear?'

'We are about to find out,' Adis replied thoughtfully, 'I only hope we won't be too late.'

'Somehow I knew you were going to say that,' muttered Gailtram.

As they traveled beside the main roadway, Ethan understood what Adis meant. Ashen clouds darkened towards the north, and billowed out low to the trees. At the crossroad, they turned in the direction of the deepening grey clouds, and through a forest devoid of natural sounds towards Mount Cirrus. Dead trees and savaged foliage appeared along the roadway. Adis dismounted and touched the bare trees with black lifeless hues.

A slow rumbling filled the woods. The men voiced concern at the increasing unnatural activity. Ethan couldn't blame them. The only reason he continued was the possibility his Kin were near the devastation. As always, he worried about the Harn and especially the boys. Again, he expressed his doubts about the men coming again, much to Loc's annoyance.

After a drawn-out breath, Loc responded, 'We've been over this. We'll see it through. You should know we aren't men who walk away.'

'The boys?'

'That's a different matter.'

Stannar said, 'They keep low, they keep back.'

'We will all keep an eye on them,' Loc added.

Berran was with Morias, and Ruegar walked with Luz. The more mischievous ones, Mouse and Derryl, ran through the layers of dead foliage, kicking and throwing handfuls of dry leaves at each other. The end of the procession passed and the two boys raced back to the front of the line.

They ventured farther in and the men grew quiet at the sight of the dead trees. Giant firs were stripped of leaves and stood dry and brittle.

Adis came back to them, leading his horse. 'A pyramid is not far off.' A large tower appeared through the leafless forest, with dark storm clouds gathering above it, as well as bright light emitting from its top. 'We'll be there soon.'

~ * ~

Mara paced the empty camp. It wasn't so much a camp anymore as a wagon in the woods, with a couple of horses. She eyed one of them, wondering if she could ride it. 'Curses…' she couldn't even mount it, besides horses didn't like her. She would have been angry, left to look after their stuff, if she weren't already indignant. The sheathed black knife strapped to the back of her hip gave her some confidence.

The forest was oddly tranquil, except for her nerves beating up her sanity. She should feel safe, maybe even pleased, but she refused to relax. She should go to the pyramid — if only to make him furious. Why should she do what he says anyway? She pummeled her palm with her fist. *No, I should run away.* That's probably what he was hoping. It would make them happy. She'd be rid of them too.

Groaning, she pressed against her chest, remembering her missing charm. She might not get far without it.

The anxious frustration was killing her. Could Jett really stop this Gate? What if he turned into an evil fiend again? Had she entrusted her life to the overconfident conceited man? She couldn't bring herself to believe he could do it, because — Mara was the one… Wendessa said she would be the one to make the final decision. She stared up at the grey-black clouds, spreading past her. The forest was enveloped in a hazy gloom. But did that entail not doing anything at all? 'Ooh - what am I do to?'

Noise on the other side of the wagon, startled her to silence.

A boy appeared, not more than fifteen, puffing heavily, and half slouching against the wagon. His lank hair was pressed around his thin pimply-red face.

Mara gaped with some recognition. 'You're…'

He recovered some energy and stood straighter. 'Here you are.' His dull eyes took a slow glance around. 'All alone.'

'You're from Sommerlea.' Mara frowned at his untidy appearance. His worn clothes hung on him like he had slept in them for days. 'You've come to take me back?' Surely Morias wouldn't send this boy all that way for her? 'Shamus?' She recalled his name, but she suspected he was far from a normal village boy.

He approached her with a tired grin. 'I've come from there.' With abrupt speed, he latched onto her neck and pulled her back onto him. Within moments, he had a knife at her back. 'I'm taking you, but not there.'

The knife tip dug into her side and she could hardly breathe from his arm encircling her throat. 'Where?'

'Your new home.'

New? Was Yavinia planning on hiding her away in some lair? 'Alqua-elzat-varan-ezwa.'

Shamus chuckled by her ear. 'Your tricks won't work on me.'

Through his choking grip, she uttered, 'Who are… who sent you?' This turn of events was worse than any of the decisions she was going to make.

With his arm tight around her neck, he dragged her to the wagon. She wrestled against him, but his strength was beyond her.

He slid out her blade, 'Won't be needing this,' and tossed it away from them. His constricting stranglehold made Mara light-headed, and she tried to focus on escaping the unexpected predicament. He grabbed the rope, left on the wagon's bracket, and looped it over her head. 'Convenient.' He pulled it down onto her neck and yanked it. 'Doesn't matter who I am.' He stretched it down to her captured wrist, attempting to bind her movements. 'You're the important one.'

Gasping for air, Mara elbowed him with her still free arm and dropped away from his hold. She stumbled forward. He tripped her up. She fell, clutching her throbbing neck. With the rope still around her throat, she scuttled on hands and knees away from him.

'Tough, aren't ya?' He attempted catching the rope.

She turned on her back and kicked him. He grabbed her leg and pushed it down. Flashing his dagger before her face, he sat on her thighs.

She clutched his arm with her freed hands, keeping the blade from stabbing her face. 'Whoever sent you won't be pleased. Those idiots have gone to stop the ritual,' she growled, 'that's why I'm left here.'

The boy paused and eyed her with suspicion. 'When they fail, we'll be free to move as we wish.'

Rage heated her body with a desire to hurt. She squeezed his fist. Amid a wrathful snarl, and a sudden strength within her arm, she pushed his dagger away, and upturned his body from hers.

Flexing his strained arm, his eyes cringed with shock.

The leather bracelet on her wrist caught her eye. Wendessa's power. Her fleeting smile was replaced with a frown of determination. 'I'm not doing anything with you.' She scrabbled away to her blade. 'Or anyone.' Grabbing it, she pointed it at him ready for his attack.

He stood and approached with a wary eye on her weapon. 'You're not going to use that on me? Kill me in cold blood?' He spread his hands wide, his blade resting in his open palm. 'I'm just a kid like you. We're both caught up in some crazy scheme.' He shrugged with a half-hearted smile. 'You don't get it. I'm the one who can help you.'

Mara frowned at his frank admission, and studied his youthful features and simple gesture – but, there was no way they were just simple children. She grew angry at the sudden standoff that was wasting time. 'I don't need any help.'

He cast a look around the clearing as he stepped closer. 'I'm not going anywhere without you.'

With a sudden fear he was waiting for someone, she cried, 'I don't know who you are, but you can tell whoever sent you to rot in hell!'

A genuine look of delight came over him. 'You'll be able to tell him yourself.' He rushed in with his knife to apprehend her arm. 'If any one of them turns up.'

Without thinking, Mara overpowered him and sunk her blade into his side. So he was expecting someone.

His weapon fell from his hand, and groaning, he gripped her close to his body. Mara gasped, fearing his nearness again. With her blade still embedded in his flesh, he ran his hand through her hair with a bewildering gentleness, and he kissed her. 'I never wanted to hurt you...' his whisper was a warm tease on her face.

His body became limp in her arms and she stepped away with her weapon, letting him drop to the ground. Breathing hard with fear and relief, she wiped her lips with the back of her hand while pointing her bloody knife at his adolescent face and eyes, staring skyward. *Just a kid...* she gave an unexpected sob. 'You have no idea...'

83 - Agamon

Hope is not wishful thinking
Hope opens the door to faith
Hope is the power that drives you to do what is otherwise unachievable

Fellowship of Healers, Age of the First Born

Sword in hand, Jett ran across the pavement, leading Shiarn who had a hold of Earona. *Don't go near the men,* he thought to the girls. It was hard enough having them present, but more troublesome was trying to kill four men with one hand.

Once at the feet of the stairs and the men guarding it, Jett formed a hasty strategy. He thrust his blade into the throat of the first, and slid it out quickly to pierce the next one through. With the advantage of invisibility, the men fell without much resistance.

Earona squealed at the sight of the dead men.

He replied, *has to be done.*

Earona thought, *these men...*

They looked dazed. Shiarn shot back. *Maybe some type of trance.*

Haven't time to think about it. Before the other soldiers could react, Jett stabbed into a chest, followed by the next, till they were all dead and blood ran along the step and streamed to the pavement.

They raced up the great steps, with Jett half pulling them along.

'Can't you move any faster?' Shiarn hissed at Earona.

Earona snapped, 'The steps are high and I'm short.'

'Complaining again—' Shiarn retorted.

'Who's complaining?!' Earona fired out.

Jett hissed over his shoulder, 'I don't want to hear this! This is what I want - if one of you is in danger, the other will protect you.'

Shiarn whispered, 'With my life.'

Earona mumbled, 'me too.'

'Good,' Jett replied. 'We're almost there. So no more talking.'

Two steps away from the top, Jett noticed his arm appear followed by the rest of him.

'Curses!' Shiarn said, *I can't follow. There's a barrier.*

Jett came back to the girls. *That's a damn problem.*

But not for you it seems, Shiarn grizzled.

Jett considered the three figures at the top. Two older men in robes, he assumed were mages, the other was an ugly looking hag with dull red hair, who he recalled from the night before. They stood around the orb chanting with their hands raised. They must have set up a ward.

You think they are waiting for you? Earona suggested.

Probably, Jett sighed. *Alright, let's not disappoint them.*

Shiarn responded, *we'll wait here till we can follow. Be careful what you do because you will be seen. And I won't be able to help.*

'Until I've dealt with things.' He let go of Shiarn's hand and walked through the shield and on to the top. He appeared, holding his one sword, and at the ready, his menacing red gaze was cast over them.

The three turned at his presence with startled and puzzled stares.

'I am Master of the Chanin-Quyllar,' his voice brimmed with command, 'I have come to claim my rightful destiny to open the Gate completely.'

One of the Mages looked beyond Jett, and queried, 'Your arrival is foreordained, however where is the Summoner?'

'The Summoner is on her way, and will be here soon.' Jett watched the orb, glowing and floating about three feet off the ground, with fascination.

'We must have the Summoner to complete our supplications.'

'The queen said nothing about your arrival?' The old witch, from the previous night, scrutinized Jett's face with a scornful expression. 'Something's not right. She would have said if you had risen.'

The two men watched the exchange, their expressions transforming to suspicion.

'You doubt me old hag,' Jett growled with real wrath, and his eyes heated up to fire, 'I've come to take control of the Eye of Heaven.'

The deformed looking woman glared at him and backed away. 'No, it's him!' She glanced down at his sword, still bloodied, and screeched, 'He's still the same.'

Before the men could react, Jett ran his sword through the chest of the nearest mage, while flicking his knife from his back belt. He threw the blade at the witch, piercing her throat before she could speak, and snarled, 'That's for the trap.' He pulled his sword out from the body of the slumped over mage, still wearing a shocked expression.

The second mage was already making signs and speaking in an indiscernible tongue. Jett's eyes burned into the man's throat. The mage grasped at his skin and Jett stepped in, slashing across his torso. He fell back, and Jett finished him off.

The witch, panting and rasping for air, attempted crawling away. Jett snatched up his knife from where she had tossed it, and sliced her throat. 'And that's for Mara.' She finally lay still.

Not wishing to take a chance on either mage resurrecting themselves, he made sure they were dead and he kicked their bodies over the edge on the opposite side of the activity below. The witch was also dragged to the edge and pushed over.

'That's taken a lot of time,' Shiarn spoke next to him as she grabbed hold of his hand.

Jett was sent into the sickening sphere of invisibility once more. He panted, and his voice was rough, 'I know, but it's done.' *Hopefully we won't see them again.*

'It's a disgusting mess,' Earona's voice was an anxious whisper.

At least it's over there, Jett thought in reply.

'Now what?' Shiarn asked.

Jett eyed the orb, spinning chest high, and pulsing with a black inner light. The white opal gem, embedded in its surface, was a dull spark in the midst of the tainted light. Charges erupted from the clouds above and sparked off it, illuminating the ball. Up until that moment he was unsure how to approach the situation. Nya was vague on details. 'It needs to be still…'

Shiarn huffed with impatience, 'She didn't mention anything about lightning, did she?'

'Not a thing.' *I'll have to hold it. Curses, I'll have to sit too.* Squeezing Shiarn's hand tighter, Jett directed them into position with himself sitting, facing the orb and the steps. On his left was Shiarn, and with Earona on his right, they formed a tight triangle in touching distance of each other around the orb. In front of his crossed legs and under the orb, he laid his sword, and with the hilt in front of Shiarn, he gave her a nod. Apart from the Eye of Heaven it was the only thing visible. 'I'm going to need my hands, you two touch me in some way, and Shiarn hold onto Earona. Ready?'

Earona grabbed hold of his thigh. 'I think so.'

'Let's do it.' Shiarn moved her hand to Jett's leg and kept a hold of Earona's hand under the orb.

'Earona…' He looked her way, imagining her frightened face staring at the orb. 'You'll start healing me right away?'

She responded with shaky reassurance, 'As we speak.'

Her Ethos poured into his body. Aside from its healing power, it also elevated his spirit. He reached up for the orb and with some trepidation, placed his hands on its pulsating light. He grimaced at the heat, and with his muscles straining, he wrenched it down to be level with his head. The ball fought against his strength, attempting to resist his control. Halting the orb's trajectory seemed to cause a mighty wind to swirl around them.

'It's not disappearing,' Shiarn cried through the noise of the sudden roar, 'it's an Indestructible!'

So it really is an Aeylon. A Heavenly artefact. Damn. He fixed a heated stare into the center of the vibrant ivory jewel. The currents oscillating through his body were electrifying, and his hands fused to the hot light. His blazing eyes would have to eventually transform to white heat if he was going to have any affect. A level he had not yet reached in any training. Coursing with power, his body intensified with his Ethos and he shot it into the illuminated Eye of Heaven. A magnetic counterattack was overpowering his spirit, too strong for him to resist. The only way not to fatigue was submit to the orb's relentless drag. Casting his mind's eye into the glimmering stone, he released himself into the compelling force of the potent entity. Real-time thoughts diminished and he became a part of the intrinsic power of the Gate.

~ * ~

Fire on Keanan's palm grew in intensity, and he continued compressing his Ethos until it was a crimson sphere. With the rubble as partial cover, he stood and cast the flames from his hand. It sped straight, hitting the horned devil in the chest.

His armour took light and flames spread across his torso, burning his skin. After a confused moment, the monster gave a rumbling shout and beat his flaming breast with rage. Looking for the source, he swung his great mace, flinging men away in anger.

'Good reaction…' Marcus whispered.

Another ball of fire centered on Keanan's palm. 'Fortunately he's stupid enough not to detect us. Yet.' He threw it into the soldiers attempting to organize themselves against the sudden attack. It exploded on a man's chest. Leather and padded amour were ablaze, sending the man rolling to the ground. Keanan whirled off another two, incapacitating more soldiers. The flames were small compared to what he could do, but he lacked time for quality.

The death of the men on the ziggurat steps raised the alarm, causing the soldiers to move towards it to investigate.

'Curses!' Keanan fired bursts at those approaching the steps. *We can't let them up there.*

The devil creature snarled through its black snout. Its red eyes were on the surrounding dead trees, searching for Keanan.

'I'll do as many as I can before—'

'No.' Marcus stood. 'I'll go.' *I'm going to make them mad.*

'Is that wise?' Keanan hissed through gritted teeth.

'Not sure,' Marcus replied, *it's just something I'm good at.* With his Ethos pouring into his hands and malreus blades, he walked past the rubble and dead shrubs. He stepped onto the pavement and into an oppressive atmosphere. His limbs became heavy, and an odour in the biting wind was a stench in his nostrils. Swaggering towards the horned demon, Marcus pointed his sword at his neck and shouted, 'Welcome to our world. Sorry your stay will be short.' He flexed his sword in a circle with lazy indifference, and after a pause, he said, 'Nah, I'm not really sorry.'

Raising his fist above his head, the demon gripped his hammer, and bellowed his wrath. 'You human worm! You'll pay for this.' His shoulders and arms still smoldered from the flames.

'Actually that wasn't me.' Marcus caught the attention of the soldiers, and they turned to meet him, their swords at the ready. 'Too bad.'

'You're gonna fight me!' The demon growled and swung his weapon with unexpected speed.

Jumping back, Marcus exclaimed, 'I'm counting on it.' He moved between the soldiers, causing the demon to be behind them. Defending against the two men took his attention. They were good, but not proficient, and he had no time to waste as the big demon bore down on them. The beast slammed his own comrade to get to Marcus, and he brought his mace down into empty air. Marcus dodged to the right, and whipped his sword along the soldier's gut. The dead man, clothing included, transformed to a thick vapour. Caught off guard, Marcus almost missed defending against the hulking creature.

Now he knew the men weren't from this world, he prepared for anything. More soldiers came at him and kept him light on his feet. With his Gift coursing through his blade, he destroyed their weapons and cut into them, sending them off into a hazy mist.

Fire shot past, so close, he was dodging it himself. *Keanan, try not to kill me.* Keanan was too harassed to answer now he was in the melee. Marcus continued evading the demon intent on taking his head off with the double ended steel hammer. Not only did it frustrate the creature and make him angrier, it gave Marcus the opportunity to observe his opponent and the ugly irregular faces on the other men. They were not normal with their mottled purple skin and drooping jaws, some had pig-like noses while others had fangs. All seemed to have a stooped manner and lifeless eyes. At least they were flammable, and he was thankful for that.

The demon grunted and brought his weapon down in a sweeping arc. 'Fight me, you coward swine!' The hammer missed Marcus by inches and landed on the stone, cracking it to pieces. Swinging recklessly, the monster shoved his own men out of the way to rush at Marcus.

Marcus kept him off Keanan. But if Keanan had joined the fray it was time to stop playing. Once he cleared the area of the hellish soldiers, he focused on the devil. The horned beast, his eyes glowing red, bellowed and heaved his weapon towards Marcus. Marcus sprang close, his blade cutting into the devil's leather. His second sword blocked the strike of the weapon, his malreus clanging on the steel. It was all he needed to charge his Ethos through the metal. The steel haft split and fell to the ground, leaving the demon weaponless.

'You really are taller closer up.' Three feet shorter, Marcus stared up with a frown, at the gouges on the devil's face. A rancid stink came from the knotted fur around its neck. 'And uglier.'

Amid a guttural snarl, the beast swiped at him with his fist. Moving too slow, the devil punched air. Not deterred by the loss of his weapon, he kept coming at Marcus. Marcus parried his hits until he cut into his dense hide skin, piercing flesh and shattering bone with his blade.

The beast snorted with rage. 'You will regret this.' He bellowed to the grey light above and disappeared like the others.

'I regret not doing it sooner.' Marcus breathed heavy and glanced around the square.

Keanan yelled with fierce anger, and using his flaming palm, he choked a hell soldier till he vanished into fiery dust. Breathing hard, he kept up his defence against more soldiers advancing on him. From the back of the temple, more were approaching.

Marcus sprinted to the ones on Keanan. 'You ready for another round?' He hewed into the deformed men, easily. They were careless and not skilled with their weapons. It seemed their confidence was in their numbers.

Backing off, Keanan fired into the glut of them. *Coming from the back?* 'This doesn't look good.'

Marcus, his two blades spilling with Ethos, blocked the surrounding soldiers, rendering them ineffective. After disposing of them, more troops flowed onto the pavement through the arches. 'Flamin' demons…' After killing so many of the hellish creatures, it occurred to him. *Is it me or do these look the same as the ones we killed?*

Keanan continued burning men and blocking their strikes. *It's irrelevant. Most likely it's an army coming through, and they will keep coming if Jett doesn't break that orb and close the gate.*

This could be annoying. Marcus whirled between the undead men, always moving out from their thrusts. No matter how many he vaporized, more were attacking him. *If I see that foul-necked demon again, I'm gonna swear.*

Suddenly the warriors fell back and parted. Through their midst a figure came from the side. A woman, if she could be called that, was in a close-fitting long gown and she sauntered towards them. Her pale grey skin glistened against her crimson dress, split up to her thigh. Tiny shimmering scales were over her arms and down to her hands and claw-like nails. Swishing out from under her gown, was a slender scaled tail with a single spike, and she wore a black and gold horned headdress. Her skeletal face was bordered by dark swirls of hair flowing over her breasts and down past her waist. A rough ruby, the size of a fist, was on the end of her twisted staff.

Keanan gripped his sword in an upright position, and readied his flaming hand. His fire burnt through his flesh and rushed at the lizard-woman, hitting her middle.

She glanced at the flame, her face contorting with annoyance. It dispersed over her body and was gone.

Keanan frowned with concern. Instead of wasting an attack on her, he threw fire into the soldiers behind her. *This is all we need...* he exclaimed, 'Help would be good right about now...'

'You think?' Marcus stood ready to meet the magnificent looking but formidable creature.

The strange newcomer stopped before them, her white-less eyes stared without blinking and she spoke. 'What are you mortals trying to achieve?' Her voice was enthralling despite its lilting pitch.

Keanan's voice blared across the windy courtyard. 'We have come to stop what you are doing here.'

She lifted her staff. The soldiers, some still burning, grouped together and lined up in rows. 'I have more important issues to attend to.' She looked up to the Agamon. Radiating an intense energy, the orb was stationary, yet still hovering a few feet off the ground. Abruptly, it sparked upwards to the black cloud. She turned back to them and extended her staff. 'Move from my path!'

Marcus stood with his swords on guard. 'No way through.'

Her sharp features creased with indignation. 'Who are you to make such declarations?'

'You want to know?' He tensed and shifted his swords to strike.

'I do not wish to destroy one as strong as you.' Raising her staff, she pointed it at Marcus. The gem shone, and its vivid red rays touched his skin. With satisfaction, she smiled, revealing her fangs. 'I command you, join my army.'

Marcus stared ahead, his thoughts dropping away into a confused mess. He hesitated under her potent gaze with a pain pulsing at his temple.

I truly hope you are not listening to her.

Keanan's abrasive thoughts broke through the suffocating haze in Marcus' mind. *I'm not. Now.* He shook his head in defiance. 'Not today. Or any day for that matter.'

Men, armoured in mail and shields, entered the pavement, and they stopped short at the sight of the hunched and deformed soldiers. An older man in bright mail approached, and behind him came a youngster. They gave a brief glance up to the orb before the lizard woman took their attention. The man spoke with boldness. 'I am Captain Aversley from Havenside…'

Keanan kept his eyes on the mage, but replied, 'Jett mentioned you might come.'

'But, where is he?' The boy responded with irritation.

'He's…' Marcus kept his eyes on the mage, observing her increasing wrath, and trying his hardest not to look up at the orb. '…around somewhere, doing his part.'

Captain Aversley nodded and eyed the soldiers across the pavement. 'We have come to aid you, but we hardly know what is occurring here.'

Marcus replied with a cocky grin, 'We hardly know ourselves…'

'You planned on taking them on by yourselves?' The boy's eyes widened under his silver helm.

Keanan replied, 'Indeed, we were hoping you would come.'

Losing patience with the talk, the lizard mage's black eyes flashed with cold rage and she raised her staff towards her soldiers. 'Advance, my slaves, and take your new home.' Her warriors came at the newcomers, and from the outskirts of the courtyard, men shouted, and the clash of metal echoed against the bare stones. Turning her wrathful gaze back to Keanan and Marcus, she stated, 'You are wasting my time. You will achieve nothing here but your own demise.' The powerful jewel on her staff blazed, and she pointed her bony arm at the two Baions. 'I command you, join my—'

'Time to stop ordering people around.' Marcus brought his sword down through her outstretched arm. Her hand fell to the ground, and a hideous shriek rebounded off the stones. He thrust his sword into her middle, his Shattering Gift flowing through his blade and into her body.

Keanan said to the Baions, 'It's best you come no closer to this creature. Go and see to your men.'

Without any argument, the two rushed off.

Her handless arm touched the bloodless wound on her stomach and she stared at Marcus in stunned amazement. 'I will not be stopped again.' Her eyes flared with malevolence. 'Don't you know who I am? Queen-mage Moritainia. I've reached a level of immortality weaklings like you can only dream of.' Her dismembered hand wriggled on the stones and shifted towards her.

Marcus pursed his lips in annoyance. *That puts a stone in the grind.*

We'll have to distract her. Keanan kicked her hand to the border of the pavement.

She eyed him with contempt. 'I'll have my Shadow Nation, my land of night.' Raising her staff aloft, she looked up with adoration into the black billowing mass. The gem's red glow illuminated her unnaturally slender face and ignited a flash of electrical charge from the overhanging clouds. 'Lord of Darkness, Ruler of Hell's domain, the time has come to awaken your Beasts of Destruction.' Each word was an elaborate flourish of supplication. 'Send forth your strength and bring punishment to these defiant ones. So they can know your power.' In answer the clouds flashed with lightning, and a reverberating rumble sounded for moments.

Marcus muttered grimly, 'We could be in trouble now.'

'What do you mean *now*?' Keanan retorted.

The combat between the Baions and undead warriors, stretched across the courtyard to the left of the ziggurat. As the troops from hell fell to the Baions, they were replaced by others coming from behind the temple. Over the shouts and cries, came a guttural roar.

'What's that?' Marcus looked towards the combat, with furrowed brow.

Whatever happens, don't let that thing up the stairs, Keanan ordered Marcus.

'I'll take her, you take the demons.' Marcus nodded at the battle. 'Think you can?'

'I shall do my best.' Walking away, he added, over his shoulder, 'If I fail perhaps I shall also come back.'

Marcus shook his head with a brief chuckle. *As long as you're on our side.*

Above the noise of battle, came a high pitched growl. Something beyond the back arches was entering the pavement. Ignoring the conflict, the Queen-mage headed in the direction of the ziggurat stair. 'My God has heard me.' She looked to the swirling black clouds above. 'You have meddled in affairs you know nothing about.'

'Can't argue with that...' Marcus mumbled.

~ * ~

Hellier ran at a swift pace through the dead woodland, dodging branches, and wiping her tears as she went. With Seth close behind, she neared the arched colonnades to the left of the stairs and crouched low to peer through the bracken. One witch was near ten feet away, and across from them, another three. In addition, three men were strung up between the above arches. *Seth, go up the stair. Shoot those men.*

I'll shoot everything I see.

With a smile, she watched him go back to the stone staircase they passed. She dropped her swords and took off her clothes, kicking them under a shriveled bush, she then took up her blades again. Sneaking up to the pavement, she heard a witch speak. 'The sacrifice is on the way. Finally. Let's get rid of these stinking men.'

Hellier didn't give a thought to their words, her body was already firing up with her Ethos. From her center, the fire grew until it consumed every part of her flesh, and flared across her swords in flowing lines of light. Potent and hot, the flames reflected her current mood. She stepped from the shadowy protection of trees, emptied of leaves, and wasted no time in bringing one of her fiery swords across the witch's neck. The witch dropped with a thump. The other witches screamed as they ran up the stairs.

Overhead, an arrow whizzed by, killing the soldier chained to the upper arch. The man alongside him followed into death at the second arrow. The third followed into death by Seth's expert aim.

'The offerings,' one witch shouted as she shuffled along an upper ledge.

Hellier took a flying leap to the next level. Still gripping her swords, she caught onto it, and flung herself up. A witch attempted scurrying away, but Hellier's flame blade went through her middle. The witch looked down at the fire coming through her stomach and fell forward, a burning pyre on the stone.

A form approached from the darkness at the back of the Agamon. A creature, half lizard and woman, came into view. Thick black hair flowed behind her, almost reaching her swinging tail. Distracted by the odd appearance, Hellier was startled by a witch on the higher ledge, pointing a twig at Seth on the further balcony.

Seth aimed at her and she chanted a mantra. His arrow remained unfired and he scooted back along the ledge, past the stairs.

Hellier circled, searching for the rest of the witches, but there was only shadows. Somersaulting down, she heard a crude voice speak from the din of a nearby arch. Her shoulders and upper back were caught in a type of webbing suspending her on a slant several feet off the ground. One length of the webbing was attached to a collapsed half pillar and the other was fixed to an archway column. She yanked on the fine sticky ties, but they would not break, nor did it appear fire or sword affected them. The remaining witches emerged from the shadows without fear.

Her feet were free, and as she thrashed, the webbing stretched providing her partial freedom. She manipulated the tough substance enough to launch herself at the strange looking soldiers entering through the arches. The first was thrown off balance, and the disruption attracted their attention. Flowing with the swing, and similar to a giant sling, she directed her feet and kicked at the unsuspecting men. She could do nothing more and her fire flicked hot with angry frustration.

The soldiers held their swords like spikes, waiting for her to bounce back. Avoiding the swords, she went for their helms, and using the soldiers' heads as leverage, she shot upward. On the downswing, she kicked past the weapons, and her burning foot rammed into a malformed face. She moved, attempting to evade their sword points. Added to her new predicament, the witches stood back, observing the spectacle.

A witch she recognized from the previous night smirked down at her. Flaming higher, Hellier swiped at the soldier's heads in an uninterrupted dance. Despite her own impending danger, her one concern was Seth. She was helpless to save him.

84 - Hell's Here

He who does not fear the sword
Is not worthy of wielding it.

Empirical Warfare Command

Baions and undead soldiers backed away from whatever was making the hideous noise at the side of the temple. Marcus gritted his teeth and fired back at the lizard creature, 'Doesn't matter what you say,' he added with arrogance, 'you're not going up there.'

Hissing in contempt, a forked tongue flicked around her lips. She stretched her handless arm. 'We shall see.' The disjoined hand flew back to her and united with her wrist.

Marcus watched the fibres of her skin attach, with concealed wonder.

From above, lethal energy sparked in the black clouds twisting into a raging whirlwind. Below the supernatural storm, light within the orb spanned the pavement. Angry cries echoed around the Agamon mixed with the abnormal growling of whatever had been woken. Marcus prepared for anything the mage would throw at him amid a growing concern over the commotion around the temple. But he could do nothing to aid the Baions, or anyone else.

With lightning speed, the mage caught him around the neck with her joined hand. Marcus brought his swords down on her arm. She pointed her staff at his weapons. They flew from his hands and clattered upon the stones, stopping past the darkness manifesting around them. Her bony hand squeezed his airway, suffocating him. Gripping her wrist, he cast his Ethos into her, shattering the bones of her hand, causing her to release him enough he could breathe.

She growled in annoyance. It lessened the pain for him, but only momentarily, as her bones regenerated. By the continual throttling of him, they entered a cycle of pain and release. Each time he broke her bones, she became more livid, and again healed herself. Having no idea how long he could maintain the offence, his mind raced for a way to escape the creature. Although, he was glad he could provide a distraction for the half lizard even if that meant he had to get strangled. He almost laughed.

'You are wasting my time.' She shook him hard. 'The ritual must be finalised and my throne established.'

'It's not…' Marcus broke every bone in her hand again. '… your throne…' Her grasp loosened and he regained his breath. The wind pushed at him with solid force. Within moments an eerie night descended with nothing visible beyond it. The wind, whipping him with vigour, swarmed with pitiful cries. Words could be discerned in their sorrowful weeping, imparting death and his destruction. He was afraid of the intentions of the apparitions, and he despised this strange sense of helplessness.

'What did you say?' Her black eyes studied him anew, as if suddenly he was someone.

'It's the throne…' he rasped for breath, 'of the …' he determined to get his words out, 'Master – some devil lord.'

The lizard mage rumbled with indignation, 'Who told you that? I will never give the throne to another. The one will serve me.'

Marcus had a vision of the demon Jett and this wicked creature fighting it out. He would have laughed if he were able. Instead he whizzed, 'I doubt he would agree…'

She drilled him with a frigid glare while the gem lit up her face with a red hue. It brought to mind Earona's mention of a devil and also a sudden inspiration. While choking for air, he gripped her hand and reached to the black staff. He turned it to dust that disappeared in the wind. The crimson stone fell to the ground with a tinkle and rolled away. Its magikal glow fading into shadows.

Her hand loosened from his neck, and a tremendous hissing filled her mouth, reverberating through her body. 'You have made an enemy this day.'

He pushed his voice up from a compressed throat. 'Same here.'

Above the vociferous cries of men in battle came a grating snarl. Marcus had to wonder what was occurring not a great distance from him, but he did not loosen his grip from the creature's cold inflexible flesh to find out. He stared into her black eyes, alive with a seething rage and wished he could do something more effective.

She spoke a peculiar language through clenched teeth, and said, 'Go to where you belong,' and she released him.

Hit by an invisible force, he fell back into moving shadows and spun to the ground. Tossed by the wind, he was suspended horizontal in the void of black. Grey silhouettes swirled around him, their hands clamouring over his flesh. The entities penetrated his armour and burnt his skin. Their despairing voices assailed him till he gagged with a dismal heaviness he had never experienced in his life. He shut his mind to the incapacitating words, but his resilience only brought more wrath from the spirit beings.

Stretching his hands down, his fingertips found solid ground. He scratched the cold reality of the stone and pressed hard, steadying his shaking limbs.

Now he had the gut-wrenching thought the mage was free to go up the stairs and to the orb with no-one to stop her. *Goddamn bitch.*

~ * ~

Hellier was tired of jumping on soldiers in a strange ineffectual dance that only seemed to hinder their advancement yet did nothing to bring down their numbers. Trees breaking and the clamouring of men came from the side of the courtyard, and soldiers in helms and mail began fighting with disruptive order. More of the demon-looking soldiers ran through the arches from somewhere behind the temple to meet them.

A witch with long dank hair, and weak eyes, shouted, 'You ain't going no-where.' She pointed her giant clattering staff to the back of the Agamon. 'We have something special coming through.'

Short flashes of lightning illuminated the haze from the dark sky, and a spinning wind blustered against Hellier's flames. A massive shape was between the arches at the back, and its shadow appeared on the pavement. The creature let loose a fearful noise as it walked through the arch. The ledge exploded in a shower of stone and rocks. The creature, easily fifteen feet with a body span of the same, including its broad tail, came out on squat hind legs with its hide belly exposed. It fell onto scaled forelegs to walk, and saliva dripped from rows of pointed teeth. Raising its snout, it opened its mouth and let loose a fear inducing growl. Yellow lidless eyes flicked to and fro, shining with a carnal need to feed.

Horrified and amazed in the same instance, Hellier could only look on. The massive creature ambled past on its hind legs. She worked up her swinging momentum and pushed into its chest. The solid form of its body gave her the speed she needed to fling herself back. With swords out, she drove them into its neck. The monster thrashed and howled. As she hoped, the demon beast stopped. Bringing up a scaled leg, its black curved claws slashed across her middle.

Without faltering at the stinging pain, she continued on her swinging path, attacking the enemy head on. Enclosing its neck with her open legs, she pressed into grey scales, causing her to be parallel to the ground. Huge claws reached from underneath and scratched through her flames. She tugged on the webbing, and turning her swords inward and upward, she stabbed the beast's arms.

It flayed against her weapons, and her legs gripped with increased urgency. No matter how hard she clenched she couldn't close its airway. She groaned at the stretching pain. The further the creature went back, the better its claws at reaching her. A similar creature, although smaller, waddled under the arches to the line of men falling away at the sight of it.

Hellier lacked the strength to completely restrain the creature. It clawed her back to free itself from the pain. Arrows pierced its scales. Amid the racket of the beast and fighting men, the witches moved away. Angry shouts came from the ledge above and she wondered what trickery they were up to now.

~ * ~

Adis halted the men with an upraised hand. 'Listen.' Swords clanging and fervent cries came through the dead woods.

With an eager glint in his eye, Luz held his axe at the ready. 'Combat.'

'It's them.' Ethan stood, gripping his weapon.

Adis nodded. 'I will lead you.'

Soon they had no need for a guide, the noise was upon them and they approached the paved area around the pyramid with uncertainty, preparing for whatever evil was creating the deathlike darkness. They formed a vague plan, but one thing was certain, the boys must remain out of the fight. The same for Clara. Adis and Morias would have it no other way.

They observed the peculiar scene of soldiers fighting around the massive tower. A horrendous roaring carried over the clash of weapons. Movement was within a shadowy mist at the front of the pyramid and to the left men were fighting.

'I can't see them anywhere,' Ethan demanded, 'Who are these men?'

Morias indicated a man in black plate. 'Is that a Narahk?'

'I think they are Baions, fighting…' Adis squinted into the darkness. '…strange looking soldiers.'

'And whose side are we on?' Gailtram's shrewd remark caused some Harn to chuckle.

Adis spared him a sheepish grin. 'The Baions I assume but, I'm not entirely sure what is happening here.'

The ferocious howling rang out and a forceful wind reached them, blowing leaves and bracken into their faces.

Ethan straightened up. 'We'll go around.'

Adis nodded his agreement. 'Morias, you go and take Clara. I want to see what is happening here in the shadows.' They left Adis alone under the dead branches.

~ * ~

Seth ran back along the arch wall, his fingers supernaturally stuck to his bow from the witch's spell. His cocked arrow provided his last defence.

Down below, Baions entered the paved area. Unable to help them, Seth withdrew into the semi-protection of the shadows of the higher ledge. At the top of the temple, the only thing visible was the orb pulsing with a ghostly light, and black smoke spiraling down to converge with it. The movement of a witch by the stair caught Seth's eye. With her eyes on him, she came up, holding a dark bladed knife.

'Don't come any closer.' Seth aimed his arrow at the crazy looking woman.

The wild-haired witch stopped, her eyes flicking between him and the arrow.

'I'm a good shot.'

She froze mid-step. 'Maybe, but there'll be someone after me.'

He retorted, 'You'll never know, you'll be dead.'

Curling her lip in contempt, she turned her head at another witch, joining them on the ledge. 'Not so smart now.'

'I've still got one arrow,' he informed her. 'Which one of you will get it?'

The other woman noted the annoyance on the first witch's face. 'I haven't a weapon pointed at you.'

The witch sneered at her, but came no closer to the cocked arrow.

Seth rolled his eyes at the two in disgust.

Traveling on the wind from the skeletal trees below were fragments of a conversation. The two witches stopped to eavesdrop. Seth became curious when he heard Mara and one of the witches.

'About time you came to us.'

'That's right, Satira. I've come to take my place.' Mara's small voice was harsh. 'Why have you got the Chapter staff? Where is Barkala?'

Satira cackled wildly. 'Old Barkala had other duties. She was unable to see the vision, she could not dream of this. I am the Beloved now. Queeny can go to hell.'

Mara's voice was cruel. 'Give me that staff.'

'How dare you. Trying to flaunt your power!' After some moments, Satira replied, 'Not so fast. What are you going to give me for it?'

'I give you nothing, but your life.'

Satira gasped. 'You snot-arse bitch. You're really getting back to your old self. She'll hear about this, it will only make her more livid.'

Mara said, 'If you and the others run, you'll live.'

'We'll see you soon,' Satira growled and disappeared into the darkness.

Mara ran up the stone steps. Halfway up, she paused and aimed a great decorated staff at Seth and spoke in the witch's tongue.

At the sight of the staff, and Seth flexing his hand, the witches stared at each other with fear and sprinted down the stairs away from Mara.

Seth gave her a trembling smile. 'Thanks, I think.'

Mara ignored him and walked along the arched wall towards Hellier.

85 - Come Join Us

You cannot dream yourself into a character of strength
You must hammer and forge yourself into one

The Sleeping Sword

The horned demon pushed his way through the undead warriors. Despite the Baions fighting around him, Keanan openly shot fire into the devil. The flames, burning the demon's skin, made him yell with more fury. Keanan steeled himself to face him, even though he doubted his sword skills, plus he was near exhausted. The demon roared and cast his great reformed hammer at Keanan's head. Keanan side-stepped in time, but realized how fast the monster was. He continued firing bursts and evading his swings, much like Marcus had done. But unlike Marcus, he did not wish to enrage the creature any further.

With the demon on fire and under some duress, he could better swipe at his body. He could cut him, but not thrust into his thick skin with any success. The swinging mace was getting the better of him. Soon enough, the horned beast came down on his malreus plate, smashing Keanan in the side, winding him. Now at a disadvantage, Keanan drew his blade across the demon's legs. For his trouble he caught a blow on his back, nearly sending him down. The monster shoved hard on Keanan's sword as he turned in defence, deflecting the lead weight of the double hammer. He would be in trouble if he didn't kill the thing.

'It really is you?' A voice behind him cried in shock, 'Keanan?!'

With the hammer dragging on his sword under the massive weight of the devil, Keanan breathed hard, and glanced over his shoulder, followed by a second, dumbfounded, look. 'Ethan?! What the heavens—'

'Where is everyone?' A bewildered look in his eyes, Ethan cried, 'And why are you here?'

The demon growled, and shifting the hammer, he punched it into Keanan's side, grazing his armour. Keanan pushed out his words with labored breath, 'I'm not in a position to explain right now, as you can see, I'm quite hard pressed—'

Ethan lifted his axe haft chest high, and smiled. 'You talk a lot for someone who's getting beat up.' He swung at the big devil, causing him to spring back from his reach.

'Indeed.' Keanan stepped back and breathed heavily, trying to catch his breath. 'It's the second time we've had to face this monster. And I'm not ashamed to say, it's someone else's turn.'

Ethan was too caught up attacking the devil to respond. The two came at each other with hard hits and little dodging and they took up a wide space between the soldiers.

'I'm going around the back of the temple.' Keanan dashed away before he could be assailed by an undead soldier, and headed to the left and into the lifeless woods. On his way, he attracted the attention of two Baions with the same idea. Together they ran around the outside of the pavement till they came to the back. Crouching behind prickly shrubs, Keanan observed the situation.

A man with closed eyes and lowered head, held a staff with both hands, and chanted by a glowing circle. A scaled creature appeared within it, similar to the first. Letting off a fierce greeting, it fell on its legs and walked through the arch. More hell warriors appeared, some ran into the temple area, but some raced off into the dead forest. It was too dark to see if anyone else was present.

One of the Baions, whispered, 'A mage?'

'Yes, but,' Keanan replied, 'there could be witches…'

'I'm going for him.' The younger Baion stood and lifted his sword, and ran at the mage.

'Wait!' Keanan cried.

'Elwa-azqat-swamvt-tarqa.' A voice droned from the shadows.

'My eyes!' The Baion stopped and shouted, 'I can't see!'

'Hell and buggery,' the older Baion growled.

Keanan nodded in sympathy. The only solution to the precarious predicament was kill the witch, and his fire was likely the only way.

The witch held a blade and pointed it into the blind soldier. 'Let's make him squeal till he squeals no more,' she said to another witch moving out from the scrub.

'Damn you, bitches!' The blind soldier swung his sword.

With ribald chuckling, the witches jumped from the blades tip and moved around him. One of the women plunged a dagger into him. He cried out and spun to attack her, but fell to his knees, clutching his side.

'I can't watch this!' whispered the Baion by Keanan, and he stood and ran towards the witches.

'Fool!' Keanan said.

With a galling smirk, the witch pounded the ground with her staff. A string of meaningless words followed. She finished, 'You can stay there while we have our fun. Then you're next.'

The Baion stopped and strained to free his immobile legs while cursing loudly.

Keanan shook his head at their rashness. Beyond the witches, a man tied up by a tree caught his attention. His head flopped on his chest and deep gashes covered his torso. Most likely the man provided the witches' power. Preparing a good sized flame on his palm, he stood to fire it with some accuracy. At least it might not be noticed by the Baions. But the real problem was the number of witches he was confronting.

'There he is!' One of the women shrieked.

He shot off the intense burst. It exploded on the nearest. Her clothes caught light and she screamed and transformed into a flying creature, disappearing into the night. The second witch began her chant sooner than Keanan could charge his Ethos to his hand.

The witch stopped and stared skyward her eyes bulging with shock. She spurted wings and transformed into an oversized bat. With a clumsy flapping of her leathery wings, she flew into the night with an arrow in her side. The spells over the men broke and the Baion ran to his injured comrade.

Keanan bypassed the men and went for the magik-user. Hearing what sounded like giggling, and the shouts of children, he squinted into the darkness beyond the tree line. More arrows flew in a haphazard formation, most of them aimed at the Mage. But, they bounced away from the robed man.

Keanan went to thrust his sword into him, but his blade slid over an invisible wall. 'Curses!'

A group of youngsters came out from the shadows. Ignoring Keanan and the Baions, they collected some arrows and continued shooting at the mage. Keanan stared agape at their brashness. Their actions had merit, yet it was foolhardy. 'It will do no good firing your arrows at him—'

The smallest of the boys retorted, 'Yeah, we noticed, but it's hell fun trying to shoot the bastard.'

Another of the boys, piped up, 'Nah, it's not that, we're getting our aim in.'

Keanan rolled his eyes skyward. It was like speaking to a young Marcus. 'Who are you children?' They carried bows as long as themselves, and seemed to have no fear in the dangerous situation.

The first child, a skinny small lad, replied, 'Name's Mouse, we're the Mountain Pirate Gang, and—'

A taller boy, with deep auburn hair, scrunched up his face, 'We're what?'

Mouse shrugged with indifference. 'Thought it up right then, sound's bloody spot on to me.'

'No, has to be Crazy mountain pirate gang,' said the smaller blond added with a merry grin.

'Yeah… I'm Derryl,' a stout red-headed boy interrupted, and said to Mouse, 'You don't speak for me.'

Keanan stared at them with profound shock, and eyed the woods. 'Where did you come from?'

Derryl's eyes shifted between the men listening. 'Lots of places.'

'You mean right now?' Mouse cocked his head and frowned with suspicion.

The tall boy stepped forward. 'We came with Ethan and Gailtram, Luz and them lot.'

Derryl struck his chest with pride. 'We fight with the Harn!'

Keanan looked at them with consternation. 'I shouldn't be surprised.'

'You know them?' asked Mouse.

'I know Ethan—' as he spoke, the circle lit up.

'There's something coming through,' shouted the Baion and he dragged his friend to a safer position, 'Get back!'

Keanan prepared fire in his hand. 'Perhaps you children should retreat—'

'Bleedin' bollocks!' Mouse shouted, 'You think we're going to run away?! Besides, we ain't children.'

'We only have bows,' the blond ordered in a more high-pitch tone, 'we should move back. Then we can shoot them.'

'Berran's right.' The tall boy dashed back into the covering of the shadows, followed by the other three, preparing their bows as they ran.

A red haze appeared in the circle and out stepped a group of undead hell warriors. Intent on entering through the arches, they seemed unaware of Keanan and his building flame. He hesitated, wondering how wise it was to take them all on.

Arrows sung past him, hitting a soldier square in the back, sending him to dust before he set foot outside the summoning circle. A great hurrah sounded from the trees. The rest of the soldiers swung around in search of the culprit. Apart from the motionless mage, Keanan was the only one visible.

'I don't believe this.' Keanan shook his head with resignation. 'I really dislike having to act irrationally.' The fire burst from his palm and he flung it at them, hoping he could kill a few before they reached him.

~ * ~

The Chapter staff was as tall as Mara, and with all its trinkets and charms it was a top-heavy weight in her hand. The head was shaped like a great crescent moon, forming a hook. Fetishes and articles hung from the curves or were tied across it, and symbols scrawled with blood were over the parched wood. Petite skulls and bones were fastened with skin between the top curve and the lip. On the times she had seen the staff, it frightened and fascinated her, with its weird disgusting objects. Decades of rituals and offerings infused it with seductive power from the underworld. Its provocative pressure was already effecting her. Tainted tendrils of malice seeped into her thoughts, attacking her ability to discern light from dark, right from wrong.

The remaining witches on the upper ledge under the massive arches, watched Mara approach. Their eyes flitted with wonder over the staff. 'You wish to command us?' One witch cried, backing away, 'How can this be?'

Mara laughed with cruel abandon. 'I've claimed my right. I've always been more than you all.' Glancing at Hellier, she said, 'Get out of here.'

Hellier dropped to the ground and started towards the huge lizard monster.

The witches turned from Mara and fled from the ledge. An older witch spat by her feet, and cursed her. 'You'll be cast down, you daughter of a whore.' She followed the others and they disappeared from the courtyard.

Mara took a heady breath, and tried to convince herself this was the right thing to do. She was strong enough to resist – that was her hope. But, even so, she didn't kill them – and she wondered if that was the right decision. 'Aha!' She snatched her charm, strung around the wood. Hanging it on her neck, she shoved the mouse right down her bodice, safe.

Through the haze across the pavement a bizarre looking woman walked towards the steps leading up to the Eye of Heaven, and where Jett must be. The sight of her black hair fluttering against her crimson dress, gave Mara an ominous chill. This was surely the woman from the vision, despite her deformed appearance. She switched her gaze to the staff in her possession and weighed her options. She should leave and be done with them all, especially him. An anxious dread came over her and she rubbed the side of her belly to ease the nausea, she wanted to throw up. Her face scrunched up with irritation. 'Curse him for making me do this!' She descended the narrow stair.

~ * ~

Cracking and humming with energy, the mini star struggled to retain its trajectory against Jett's strength. When Shiarn exclaimed it was an Indestructible, and Earona heard Jett's thoughts exclaim it was an Aeylon, she knew how powerful the orb must be. She could not hide her building dread. This was the biggest risk Jett had ever undertaken, and she knew he knew it. His confidence had never faltered like that before.

Jett's body shook with electrical charges under her hand. No longer able to sense his surface thoughts, she poured her life-giving Ethos into him. Not stopping for a moment, his body drained it from her unremittingly. 'I feel...' Earona could see nothing on the platform except the orb and its light, consuming her vision. '...so alone.'

Shiarn squeezed her hand, reminding her she was present.

The sky thundered and lightning struck the orb, releasing lethal currents through Jett that pricked Earona's flesh. She could see a red glow over the amulet on the orb. It intensified to an opaque crimson.

'Is he...' Earona raised her voice, and she stumbled over her words, not really knowing what to ask. 'Can you see him?' The question was pointless; Shiarn had the ability to see anything she made invisible.

After a pause, Shiarn answered, 'He's staring at it, eyes fixed and not blinking, and they're a colour I've never seen before. Like deep fire.'

Earona took a needed breath. 'He has no thoughts...'

'I know.' Shiarn continued with a sharp tone, 'It's you and me now. No matter what happens, don't stop healing him.'

Earona nodded. 'I... won't... stop.' *I don't want that prophecy to come tru—*

'Don't think about that now!' Shiarn yelled.

'I'll try my best...'

That's all Jett would want.

The wind whipped around them, stinging their skin. Faces in the swirling mist howled. Shiarn gave a startled cry. Earona gazed through the misty blackness at an apparition of the mage who attacked Shiarn at Sommerlea, and who almost killed her.

Clearly able to see them, he stared down at Shiarn. 'The bane of my life.' His voice was acidic to her ears. 'What a pleasure it will be to see you again.'

Earona shouted, 'She's not going with you.'

The mage turned his transparent head to her. 'Nonetheless, there shall come a time, now that I know where you are.'

Earona yelled, 'Be gone foul spirit!'

'We will meet again.' The apparition withdrew into the wind and was gone.

Sudden movement came from the edge of the platform and a figure appeared, pulling himself over the ledge. Earona squealed.

'Shsss!' Shiarn hissed under her breath. *He can't see us.*

Earona held her breath, and would have covered her mouth with her hand if she had use of it.

Skar have come. Shiarn told her.

The figure, unaware of their presence, approached the orb. The shadows of his hood couldn't conceal his pale grey skin and the excited glow in his eyes at the sight of the unguarded treasure. Earona gasped at his unnaturally long hands and fingers, and sharp nails, reaching out for the orb. She could not say where Jett was for certain, but the stranger must be close to him. The Skar laid his hand on the pulsing orb. A shocked expression passed his face, whether from touching Jett or the electrified light, Earona couldn't determine. But, he dispersed into thick ash.

'That's a relief,' Shiarn said.

'Um, Shiarn.' Earona's voice trembled with fear. *Another one.*

Sneaking over the side, the Skar witnessed the demise of his comrade, and he approached with more caution. He neared the three, and keeping back from the orb, he bumped into Jett.

Earona cried out at the impetus of Jett moving under her Ethos.

With a look of wary surprise, the Skar pulled out a knife, preparing to stab thin air.

Shiarn gave an angry grunt and released Earona's hand, making her and Jett visible, and his sword unseen. The Skar's face twisted with loathing.

Earona froze with terror.

Don't stop! Shiarn shouted in her head.

The Skar clutched his chest and dropped to his knees. Blood gushed from a second wound in his side and he disappeared to dust. Another one crawled up to the top. He fixed his gaze on Jett holding fast to the glowing orb.

Earona sat wide-eyed, wanting to run, but she ducked her head low, as if that could somehow protect her. All the while she kept her Ethos on Jett.

The Skar swung at the orb, attempting to knock it from Jett's hands. The sword was sent off course and Shiarn gave a mighty bellow.

'Shiarn!' Earona cried. Not able to see anything, she could only worry and fear the worst. The Skar's legs were cut along his thighs, but he continued casting his blade in fast random swoops.

'Curse you, fiend!' Earona yelled.

That'll help. Shiarn shouted.

The Skar's sword was bound for Earona. In the same instance, an arrow punctured his neck. With a startled look in his tawny eyes, he disappeared.

That's handy. Shiarn collapsed next to Earona.

'You're hurt?' Earona touched her arm to feel for herself. A deep slash was across her shoulders.

Shiarn breathed heavily. *Don't know how many more…*

From below, a cacophony of noises assaulted Earona's senses. She could barely comprehend them above the wind. Shiarn's injury caused her concern, but all her Ethos was concentrated on Jett.

How is he?

'He's…' Earona tried relaxing her cramped hand without letting go, '… I'm keeping him alive…' If she released an inch of contact, he would be gone. She felt an abrupt pull on her hands and Shiarn let go, causing Earona and Jett to become visible again. 'Shiarn!'

I'm… Shiarn reached for her hand and they were unseen again … *Just keep him alive.*

'I will.' *Do my best.* Earona's life-giving Gift circulated through Jett's body, keeping his heart pumping. With one hand on Jett, the other was on Shiarn, keeping her conscious. Earona flicked into the visible and even Jett could be seen, holding the orb. Blood trickled from the corner of his mouth and down his chin. That was startling enough, but his eyes had transformed to a dazzling translucent blue. She had never seen such extreme heat from a Charer. The sight of them hurt her eyes. Despite the immense energy emitting from his eyes, his face was vacant. She drilled her thoughts into his mind, ordering him to break the cursed thing and wake up.

Jett disappeared again, while Earona remained visible. She felt alone in the unnatural wind and shadows, despite Shiarn being present.

Out of the darkness surrounding the top of the platform, a hideous woman with scale skin and white-less eyes appeared from the steps. A beautiful red gown seemed bizarre on her lizard-like form.

Earona gasped with fear and gave a skittering glance at the empty space where Jett was.

The woman's dark unblinking eyes scanned the scene with conceited confidence. Dirty ashen light exploded out from the floating orb and lit the shadows with more ferocity. She stretched a scaled hand above the jerking orb with a threatening sneer. 'I think not.' The light flowed up from the orb and gathered around her hand. The orb vibrated and lifted higher.

What's she doing? Shiarn yelled with fear.

Earona could only stare with terror. *Jett's losing his grip.*

That's not all he will lose. This is bad.

86 - Within the Darkness

The essence of your Ethos
Cannot be obstructed by will, nor can darkness suppress it
It will arise regardless of conviction
Moreover, it will grow according to your desires
The passion of your heart will determine, freedom or captivity

Heavenly Ascension

Mara climbed the pyramid steps, at times stumbling on the crumbling stone, and clutching the heavy staff. The dark light and noise above intensified and she tried quickening her pace. Her chest heaving, she paused to pull the knife from her belt. Wincing in anticipation, she slashed into her forearm with the blade. She bit her lip holding back her cry. The sting would fade, she consoled herself; she had faced worse in her life. She could recall a handful of spells, insignificant in power, but they would have to do. Either the witches won or her, and it was now or never to find out.

Apart from the rushing wind, it was quiet when Mara came to the top. She leaned on the staff to catch her breath, and her blood ran down her arm, soaking into her dress. The light of the orb was mesmerizing, but it was the fantastic looking woman in a red gown that overwhelmed her.

Mara was shaken out of her speechless wonder at the sight of Earona's eyes bulging with fear and gaping like a fool. But then again, she had reason to stare. Maybe she shouldn't have come, maybe it was as foolhardy as Jett would tell her if he was able. But Jett – he was saying nothing. There was only silence from the ones she assumed where invisible. She frowned at the empty space. For moments she wanted to run back down the stairs and never see them again. They – he was the one who left her behind after all.

The woman in red, more like a creature, was dragging the glowing ball up to her hand with no-one doing anything to stop her.

With both hands, Mara grasped the great staff and shouted, 'Leave it alone!'

The woman glanced over her shoulder, the putrid light making her appear ghoulish. Her eyes lit with recognition at the sight of Mara. 'You are here. Come and fulfill your duty.'

Mara gasped. Her memories whirled in a chaotic cycle. It seemed she was reliving some event that happened countless times before. She recovered herself, and chanted, 'Halfgal, Agent of the Breach. Command separation of soul and present.'

'What do you think you are doing?'

Mara tipped the staff towards the woman, nearly overbalancing herself. The trinkets swayed together, clinking with a horrible sound. 'Displace passage of toxic ar. Condemn into capture invisible spirit.'

The woman raised her brow at the staff, and mocked Mara's boldness. 'Where is your sacrifice?'

Drawing off her own blood, Mara fell to her knees, her face lowered to the stone, she gasped for air. She had never done a spell of this magnitude ever, and had only read of it in the books of Yavinia's private collection. 'Order Carrier of foul flesh, divide substance and spirit.' She intoned the last utterance, hoping it would so something useful.

'You!' The evil sorceress screamed her contempt as she and Mara blurred and disappeared from the platform.

~ * ~

Jett's eyes shot open. In the stretching shadows, he adjusted to the strange scene he awoke to. Countless black stairs with no visible supports, of various widths and lengths, in multiple layers, surrounded him as far as he could see up and down. They crisscrossed each other with no order or any logistical sense. The stairs descended into darkness, but far above, a grey light pulsed. With no idea what he was supposed to do in this surreal place, instincts told him, he should head upwards.

He started up the nearest steps, but stopped at another stair blocking his path. Gripping the joining stair's edge, he hauled himself up and over, and ran up. After running and jumping across steps, and meeting numerous dead ends, he realized how random the stairs were, and directionless. It became a mental challenge as well as physical. He spent time navigating the staircases, attempting to find the best route. It seemed he was climbing for hours and was no nearer the lit haze above.

With an abrupt stabbing pain, he halted and clutched his chest. Doubling over, he breathed erratically, feeling every tendon in his body aching. He gave a hacking cough and blood spilled on the ground. Wiping more from his mouth, he moaned, 'What is—?'

A mighty crescendo of cracking and crumbling from the stairs below echoed everywhere. 'Can it get any worse…?' Using the step as support, he stood, and amid a building urgency, kept going up.

Out of the depths came a cold-blooded bestial screech that shook the air in the cavernous dark. The noise hurt Jett's ears and added to his pain. He muttered, 'I had to ask.' He wondered if the collapsing stone woke the creature from the pits of hell beneath him. The pulsing in his chest stabilized, but continued as a hindering annoyance. He dashed up more levels, attempting to determine which one would lead somewhere and not more dead-ends. But he was beginning to think there was more to it than analyzing it with his intellect.

The gut wrenching roar sent shivers over his skin. He dreaded to see what was making the horrendous sound, because he had a good idea what it might be.

It crashed through rows of stairs, and landed in view of Jett. The force of its great mass broke the stone apart. Giant claws gripped the black stairs, preparing to dismantle it. Long sharp-tipped wings beat the air, and sent Jett stumbling back. A grey gas seeped from its mouth, and numerous spikes lay flat on its head and body. Crimson eyes in an angular snout face spotted him with a hungry gleam. Layers of sharp teeth dripped with a predatory need to feed.

Jett reached for his sword. Finding the sheath empty, he grumbled, 'Blood 'n shite!' He clamoured backwards up the steps, and kept going until more stairs were between him and the Zheran demon. It broke the stone with its black claws in search of him. Dodging the flying debris, Jett sought shelter under a stair arch.

Some feet away, the thing growled. Its acrid breath filled the gap with its stink. The air became like fire from the close proximity of the hell creature. Jett dashed out from the hidey hole and leapt to a higher stair. Spying him, the giant Zheran lurched forward, destroying the stone, and pounding the landing.

The advancing Zheran left Jett no choice, he kept moving and fast, and not in the direction he wanted. He was trying to outrun a demon monster and a collapsing environment, and the further he ran, the blacker the air became. The thing was driving him from the light. In that case, he had to go in the opposite direction. He had already wasted too much time running around. Added to his encroaching exertion, the pain in his body came in sudden debilitating waves. He collapsed against the side of a staircase and grimaced at the constrictions spreading from his heart through his torso. Bearing with the pain, he fought for every breath.

Finally his breathing eased enough for him to collect his wits. Peeking over the step, he waited for the creature to come closer. Just a few more feet. Counting on the huge beast being too slow to turn to catch him, Jett ducked out from the stone, and tensing for any impact, he sprinted towards the monster. He skidded under its bone arm, the last inches of its claws swiping his back. The scratch on his skin like fire, but not severe enough to incapacitate.

The massive beast roared and smashed the stonework. Jett leapt up twice, and ran, not looking down. This time, he did not deviate from his upwards path. Everything below sounded like it was being demolished.

As he ran, Jett grew more tired, his muscles raged against the grueling marathon and his lungs heaved with the strain of leaping over the stairs. Compelling his body on, he eventually came to a different stair formation. Every staircase led up to a circular landing that disappeared into darkness on both sides. Darkness so dense, Jett couldn't penetrate it with his vision. He ran to the platform, but pulled up short. Bordering the edge was an empty blackness. Grasping for oxygen and holding his gut threatening to throw up, he stepped away from the drop.

The beast lumbered to the lower stairs, its great mass cracking the stone, and its spiked tail scattered the debris. Slow, its approach, knowing its prey was cornered.

'Curses!' Jett could do nothing against it. 'Nya!' he cried into the expanse of emptiness with desperation, 'I need a weapon. Anything!' His voice was like gravel in his parched throat, and he was nauseous waiting for the impending attack of the Zheran beast. Sudden silence swamped his thoughts and he closed his eyes.

The reason of your coming is because you already possess one. From the beginning.

The voice spoke with impatience and he wondered if it was her. Whoever it was, they seemed to think he should know, but… 'My Gift…?' He queried in a puzzled mumble. He let loose his Ethos. An ethereal substance wrapped around his head and a burning sensation hurt his eyes. Opening them, he was startled by a pulsing power charging through his mind and coming out of his vision. He shouldn't be surprised, this was his innate strength, his God given Gift. The supernatural power of his eyes palpitated with heat and made the detail of the Zheran's cobbled skin and bone spikes as clear as if he were next to it.

The monster flew at him, its sharp sallow teeth, preparing to feed on his flesh.

Despite the pain wracking his body, he stood firm and stared at the Zheran, letting his Ethos flood out from his soul. Sky-blue flames erupted on its head, lighting up the stairs and darkness. The creature thrashed and howled, but continued coming with increased anger.

Jett's eyes scanned the whole beast. He scorched it with blue-white fire that blazed over its face and back. The monster fell, screeching with rage, crashing through the last of the iron-rock steps and down in a ball of luminous flames, lighting up the pit of darkness as it went.

Breathing hard and holding his stomach, Jett turned to face the new visible gap through the bleakness. Fear and despair weighed him down with hopelessness, but he had little time to waste on the tangible feelings. He had a sense it would only get worse once he went through. Steeling himself for the dismal emotions, he leaped into the dense black unknown.

~ * ~

Mara lifted her eyes from the slab, and groaned with dismay. Nauseous, she clutched her stomach as if she could settle the tossing infant. The more magik she cast, the more drain on her body, and the more likely he would stop moving altogether. 'It really worked…' she mumbled at the gloom of black mist. A simple sealing spell, so she thought, but it was more like a prison in another dimension. The staff's arcane power had magnified her spell making it ten times more intense. On top of that, she imprisoned herself with the Mage.

The woman's black hair melded with the shadows within the folds of her crimson gown, and the tip of her scaled tail lifted up as if ready to stab. Her face contorted with rage. 'I am your Queen. You are the servant.' She reached for the staff. 'You don't know how to use that power. I will teach you.'

Her voice was like molten steel, burning Mara's ears. Pulling the staff away, Mara stood to face the aberrant woman of grey scaled skin and smoldering eyes. 'You have no idea.'

'A Summoner does not have the strength to stand against me.'

'You don't know me.' Mara's retort was driven by indignant anger.

The queen's red lips turned up in jeering ridicule and she eyed the blood seeping from Mara's wound. 'You need someone to guide you. I will be your master. Give me the artifact of power.'

'No,' Mara cried with childlike obstinacy, 'I will have no master.'

'I know the pattern of your desires.' Her wrath lessened and she cooed, 'You wish for adoration and devotion. I will help you attain your goal. I promise you that.'

Mara's eye twitched at the woman's commanding aura. It brought to mind the vision of a powerful fulfillment. It was true. She just didn't want to admit it. 'I don't…'

'I will teach you how to use your gift and you will be the master of all.' Her open palm beckoned to her. 'No one will hurt you again.'

Her candid words glided through Mara's mind like a comforting draught. No more abuse or abandonment, but — her rebellious disposition was not easy to subdue. Even this powerful woman sought to control her. She forced out, 'orbra-kiot-quaz-'

The woman's face paled and she stepped closer. 'I will nurture your great potential. Come, my child. I promise you everything you have lacked.'

Mara slouched against the staff with uncertainty.

'We belong together.'

Her tender tone evoked yearning for acceptance, Mara had long ago stifled. 'I want…'

'I will show you what you want.' The queen stepped in and snatched the staff from Mara's relaxed hold. She struck the stone with it. The ground shuddered. 'Lansnecht-gutmiensh-nebelshehien-ogzeinmezum.' Her voice swelled like a mighty wave in the shadow void surrounding them.

The air, swirling with grey dust, burned with an invisible fire. With an echoing crack a chunk of ground fell into the abyss below. Inches from the edge, Mara sunk to her knees, breathless and confused. The queen expanded into a monstrous creature of both beauty and violence. 'It is time to take back what is mine.' Her voice overrode Mara's doubts and confirmed her position within the destruction.

~ * ~

Jett bounded through the curtain and landed on solid ground. Within the unfathomable darkness, he bent over, gasping for breath, feeling his heart would burst from his skin. Weak with pain, his limbs were heavy, and he walked on unsteady feet. In the encompassing dark nothingness, he was a pale presence. His Ethos shone within him; the only thing keeping the dark from overtaking his soul.

Not only was he walking in darkness, but through a murky despair. Silhouettes of ashen shadows became deformed faces. The frightful apparitions blocked his path, and claw-like fingers stabbed into his soul. Beyond the misty spirits was an immeasurable emptiness, a substantial weight in his mind. Despite the yawning darkness, and with no way of combating the spirits, he put his hands forward and pushed them aside. Their faces twisting with fury, they ripped at his flesh with more savagery. He stumbled to his knees, groaning and shielding his chest. Struggling to rise, he swatted them away, and cried into the glut of foul beings, 'Damn you, demons!'

A tangible presence similar to the barbaric specters, yet embodying a greater terror, descended. Intense darkness swathed the area. The evil manifestation fenced Jett in. A gloomy stillness prevailed, growing to an oppressive fear, choking his airways. Standing, but still unable to proceed, Jett's heart slowed till he wondered if it stopped altogether.

A voice dominated his thoughts. *You cannot stop me.*

Jett fought for space in his mind. 'I'm...' He clutched at his tightening throat. '...going… to try.'

The spirits held onto his arms and dragged him down while the evil entity breathed its toxic declarations into his thoughts. *You will die here. All those with you have been slaughtered.*

The sombre words cut into Jett's soul like a blade. 'Then what have I got to lose?'

You do not know who I am.

'I...' Jett submitted to the specters' grip and dropped onto his hands and knees. Coughing up blood, he panted into the dark ground, '...don't care…'

Lord of Darkness, Ruler of the Powers of Armoros. I hold your life in my hands.

The poignant words reminded him of Earona, hopefully nearby somewhere. As he thought on her he regretted it.

Once I have dealt with you the Healer will be easy to acquire.

The remark alarmed him, but… 'If she's alive, so am I…'

Jett's skin burned from the entities rage. *Perhaps not all your companions are dead, but that is a matter of time. You cannot continue.*

The unremitting doubt was diminishing him by the moment. No time to waste with talking. 'I'm going through.' He stood on feet, threatening to spill him over, and stepped into the hostile faces, shoving them away. His persistence cleared enough of a space to walk, but into what he could not say.

You cannot.

'No…' Jett grumbled with stubborn grit, '*you* cannot stop me.'

The wrath of the evil entity shook the ground. A tremor coursed through the ominous wall of spirits and flared like fire on his skin. The oppressive fear was near incapacitating. His determination to move from the sphere of evil, was consuming – escape seemed impossible as the lamenting spirits assailed him.

One fragmented wisp perforated his vision. Empty eyes bored into Jett's soul. Words settled in his mind as if a sheet was laid there and he had to rest under its shelter. *Ailren.* The unknown name was forced into his thoughts. Followed by a string of outlandish rhyming words. The peculiar encounter sparked renewed belief in his task, and silenced the evil voice in his mind.

Once more the presence invaded Jett's soul like a debilitating fever. His limbs weak, he collapsed to his knees from the weight of spiritual pressure. He yelled at the wall of spirits, 'Let me pass.'

You naive beings of light never change over the ages. You lack the understanding of who I am, the voice shouted in Jett's head, *I have the power here. This is my domain.*

'I don't…' Jett laboured to speak his own thoughts. '...no, you know who I am. I am the Master of the Eye. I have got the right.'

I know who you are, but you do not know.

The statement stirred his thoughts, but he spoke in an attempt to gain some authority. 'I command you let me go.' He doubted the impact of his words, but tolerance was not a virtue he could claim.

It will kill you. It is a surprise that you should care so much. You wish to remain in that weak useless body? All those people you are trying to save do not consider you capable or worthy of such acts. Instead they seek your downfall and dishonour. Your death will please them. Is this what you want?

Jett shook his head with confusion, trying to make sense of the troublesome words.

If you join with me, I can bring you the one you search for and so much more you desire.

Ethan? He queried with hesitation. Cringing at his unexpected lowering of his guard, he rebuked himself. *Not my…?* 'No…' his groan was a bare whisper.

I will grant you the power to confront your enemies and help those weaker than yourself. And yet, you are willing to sacrifice your life for such a minor thing as this Eye? For beings you do not know or care about? For beings who would prefer to see you dead?

Doubt welled up in his soul. The words struck a painful chord touching on all the times he encountered rejection. They hated him back home, and he hated them. Now he would die… would anyone know why? Would anyone care?

But — it was the mention of sacrifice that reminded him. So, it really was him after all. But why did he have to hear it from a devil? 'Curse it!' No longer able to withstand the scorching presence, he fell on his hands and knees and glanced at his arm; burnt red and blistering, and read the words, Your Kin will Guide Your Decisions. Fight for Them No Matter the Cost.

It will take your life, and all for nothing. This is not the end you desire or deserve.

No, it wasn't what he desired or even planned… *but sacrifice my life… does it really have to come to that?* Fear wracked his body as he realized he didn't want to die. Moments passed as he labored over the decision. But, the only thing he knew… he could do little else but proceed with what he had already said he would do, he would separate the orb. If it took his life then so be it. If he failed to do so, they failed… Dying wasn't failing. Living was failing. If he lived, they died. *Flamin' hell… Dying is… winning.* 'I have to,' because he couldn't bear living if his Kin were gone. No, he would fight for them, even more so at this crucial moment. He gritted his teeth and replied with steel-tipped resolve, 'And I will not fail.' He crawled with boldness, showing his determination to the evil so prevalent around his spirit.

When you are ready to seek your answers, find me. I will reveal the longings of your heart.

The benign statement was so unexpected from the evil entity, Jett was breathless with bewilderment. A rush of trembling alarm besieged him at how much the devil knew about his life. He shouted with the last of his conviction, 'I want the Eye…'

From out of the darkness, the shining orb appeared. Grey light oscillated from its center forming countless minute static charges. Jett reached up for it, and bringing it eye-level, stared into the white gem.

It is fortunate we have met. One day you will know who you are, and I shall be waiting.

Vulnerable at the demon's change of demenour, Jett recoiled from the remark and concentrated on breaking the orb. Flicking between the darkness and the real world, he saw the top of the Agamon and Earona while Shiarn was nowhere to be seen. Once more he was surrounded by the darkness.

Out of the shadows, a bright rod shot into his chest and through his heart. A terrible pain of fire and ice combined, threw him to the black surface. He moaned under the devastating agony before his breath left him altogether.

~ * ~

With trembling arms, Mara pushed herself up from the rocky ground. Blood pooled around her and she grew faint from the loss. The mage loomed over her, draining her life away with her incantation. Mara fell back down, surrendering herself to the queen's desires.

From out of nowhere, blinding white light pulsed through the air like waves of cool refreshing power. It dissipated the darkness and cleared the oppression. Unable to raise her eyes in the throbbing light, Mara sensed another presence. With eyes lowered, she caught sight of a white skirt and flashes of gems.

A peaceful voice, unlike the mage's commanding tone, spoke. 'You are defeated, my queen.'

The queen shouted, 'Not yet!' She hit the stone once more. It shook but with no severe effect. She let loose an enraged yell.

The newcomer spoke. 'Leave the child.'

'She is my servant.'

'She is not yours alone.'

Were they discussing her? Why did she have to be anyone's servant at all? She opened her mouth to speak and made a fumbling moan into the ground.

'I have more power in the element realms.' Despite her declaration, the queen's voice wavered for a moment. 'You will not destroy me.' She muttered a string of indistinguishable words.

The light sharpened and stabbed into Mara's flesh. Amid acute pain, she lay grasping her stomach and glimpsed the queen's red skirt transform to black mist. The light disappeared leaving Mara in a pitch black world.

The voice of the other woman was a caress in her thoughts. 'She is gone and you are safe. Be released.' A gentle breeze fluttered Mara's hair.

Mara lay on the stone of the ziggurat. Unable to move, she fainted into sleep.

87 - In the Light of Day

The power of Darkness is its ability to blind
The strength of Light is revealed in Darkness

Valfaèr, Elements of Arcane Power

Marcus cried out against the stream of voices uttering death and despair, and eroding his resolve. Hot wind blasted his skin, like a fire trying to sear his insides. He clawed the pavement, drawing himself along by the slightest movement. With no idea what direction he was going, he only wanted to get out of the dark windy hell. His desperate need to escape and help the others buoyed him through drowning in hopelessness.

A pause came in the wind, and the swarming shades parted from him. Urgency prevailed over his helplessness, and laying his hands flat, he crawled through the faceless entities. Hazy light beamed through the darkness and a real hand of flesh appeared. The spirits fled from the path of light, and Marcus grabbed the open palm.

With aid from the one reaching for him, Marcus scrabbled out from the darkness. Shaken up by the assault of the strange foes, his shock didn't ease at the sight of the one still gripping him tightly. 'Adis?'

Adis watched him with his usual serious expression. 'I've been observing these strange shadows.'

'Watching, eh?' Marcus spared a glance at the dissipating darkness. He looked towards the temple and ran, calling over his shoulder, 'They're up there.'

Looking up, Adis nodded. 'As I suspected.'

~ * ~

The horned demon fought with fierce recklessness. Ethan finally hew the beast with a great swipe at its neck. Its head toppled away before it dispersed into a murky cloud. Ethan breathed rough and watched Hellier jump on the back of a scaled creature, similar to what had attacked them in the forest. She balanced on its back with abandonment, and far too rash, in Ethan's opinion.

A second creature ambled through the arches. It thrashed with open mouth, its teeth seeking any man it could rip apart. Seizing a soldier from hell, it tore his body asunder, turning him to mist. More hell soldiers ran through the arches to take his place.

Palm upraised, Ethan sent one flying, followed by the others. It would give the Baions and Harn time, while he attempted destroying the beast. He raised the thing from the ground where it could do no more damage. The men stuck swords up into it, making it howl in agony.

~ * ~

After her release, Hellier hit the ground and took off after the lizard monster a few feet away. She ran for its tail and latched on. It spun in an attempt to catch the burning pain. She dashed up its back and clamped onto its neck. Extending her arms out to its legs, she caught hold of her swords still embedded in its hide. She pulled them free and plunged them in again with more force, causing the thing to howl. Struggling against an unexpected fatigue, she wrenched out her swords as it thrashed, and she rolled off its body.

Amid her fire crackling with heat, she raced to the second monster, catching hold of its swinging tail. The creature swiped and spun, but she would not be moved. She clamoured up its back and thrust her fire swords into the solid flesh of its side.

Her vision blurred and she almost faltered, but held firm to the rocking creature. Her fire dulled to embers and heat recoiled into her body. The many gashes and abrasions pained her to the point she sensed her body weaken. Then — she fainted.

~ * ~

Mara's slumped body appeared on the Agamon top. Earona hadn't time to consider her as the orb pulsed with a strident light. She lowered her eyes from the blinding radiance. It gave a last brilliant burst and a mighty crack pierced her hearing.

Above, the darkness dispersed, revealing late afternoon light. The orb lay in two perfect halves of grey stone with the shimmering white amulet resting between them. Jett appeared and toppled backwards, unconscious. Shiarn appeared beside him, holding her bloody side. Her eyes flicked open, but she said nothing.

Earona's heart fluttered with fear as she continued pouring her Ethos into Jett's body.

Marcus appeared at the top of the steps with a broad grin. 'So he did it.' His eyes fell on Jett, and his expression changed to distress. 'Is he…'

'Jett is…' With a frantic sob, she sat up and placed her free hand on Jett's chest. *Hanging on.*

Kneeling by her, he put his hand on Jett's shoulder. Jett's face was pale, and blood streamed from his mouth and down his neck.

'They need help.' Earona cocked her head towards Mara and Shiarn.

He went to Mara and touched her neck. 'Why is she here?'

'I don't know.' Earona gave a desperate sigh. Mara's dress and arm were blood-red. 'Just hurry.'

'I'll get help.' He ran back down the steps.

Jett would be lifeless without Earona's intervention. With a tight, anxious expression, she lowered her face by his. 'I won't give up,' she whispered, 'but, you mustn't either.'

~ * ~

Once the rampant beasts were dealt with and the undead soldiers and monsters from Hell had dissipated, the men gave cheers of relief. Ethan picked Hellier up and cradled her broken body. He ordered Mouse and the boys to search for her clothes. The Baions voiced alarm that such despicable acts of magik existed. If not for Clara and her health elixir many would have perished, as it were casualties were low.

'It's even better seeing you in the light of day.'

Ethan spun to see Keanan smiling and resting a firm hand on Ethan's shoulder. He looked down at Hellier with concern. Clara gave the three a hurried glimpse. Laying her hand on Hellier's arm, she dribbled the last of her blue drink into Hellier's mouth.

Keanan's face was haggard with fatigue. 'I can't tell you how good it is to see you.'

Ethan smiled like an overgrown boy. 'Someone had to save you, but where is everyone?'

Keanan looked to the top of the Agamon. Earona was partially visible yet no one else, except Marcus racing down the stair. Keanan's voice dropped. 'Oh no…'

Marcus ran towards them, breathing fast, and staring at Ethan with a broad grin. 'Look who's finally shown up, the giant slacker himself.' His eyes glinted with merriment, but he stated with more seriousness, 'Jett's dying. Earona needs help with Shiarn. Clara?'

Clara sighed and slumped with exhaustion. 'I'm near collapsing. I will need to rest first.'

On an upper ledge, Seth rose to his feet and raised his voice. 'Maybe I can help.'

'Sprout, good to see you're still alive,' Marcus teased with a playful grin. 'Hurry up then.'

Seth and Marcus arrived at the top of the Agamon.

Earona, her hand fixed on Jett, and her head lowered to his chest, was crying.

Marcus cried, 'He hasn't—'

Earona shook her head and her black tresses made a curtain over her face. She whispered, 'I won't let him…I'm just… blubbering…'

'Good.' Marcus' tone was staunch.

Seth lifted Mara's bloodied arm and made her comfortable. 'She's alive, but the blood loss must be great. It will need binding.'

Earona gave a curt nod. 'I don't know what happened…'

Marcus crouched by Shiarn. Seth joined him and examined the wound across her ribs. He said, 'She also needs a dressing till she can be healed.'

Marcus said, 'Should I move her?'

Shiarn moaned and cursed him. 'Don't you dare, you bastard.'

Marcus chuckled. 'Guess you'll be fine.' He let her rest her head on his lap. 'You'll never guess who's down there.'

Earona gave him a flippant stare not caring who was down there.

Seth replied, with a smug grin, 'Ethan.'

Marcus gave him a look of sharp reproach. 'I was going to tell her.'

'Oh, my!' Delight filled Earona's eyes, 'That's wonderful,' but was overshadowed with grave anxiety.

Marcus said, 'Any change?'

'He's not waking up,' she responded with reluctance. 'I don't care, I'll sit here until he does,' she declared with determination, 'I'll use Ethos from Seth.'

Marcus said, 'Clara's here as well. She'll come after she's rested.'

'What?!' she cried, 'Clara too?'

'That's what I said.' He grinned with mirth. 'And Adis and I saw Morias around as well.'

'Even Mara came.' Seth looked at Mara pale as a sheet.

Earona frowned at the girl. 'I wonder why…'

Seth paused in memory. 'She was quite remarkable.'

'I know, and so was Jett…' Earona whispered.

'I hope Jett will…' Seth stopped.

Not die. Marcus summarized their thoughts.

Earona sighed deeply and looked down at his peaceful face. 'Yes.'

~ * ~

Jett woke to a luminous white floor and a grating voice beside his ear.

'Don't you want to know what it's like to be happy?'

Disorientated, he thought he was still in the presence of the evil god. He realized the depressing sensation had lifted from his heart, and all was quiet. He mumbled, '… Nya?' Managing to lift his head, he viewed the empty white space. 'Show yourself.'

Remaining concealed, she whined like a child, 'You could have ruled here with me, like you were meant to, from the beginning.'

'Do you think I would let you destroy what he is to be?'

He turned his head at the soothing sound of the second voice. Nya in all her beauty appeared, and he smiled, sensing her safe presence. He whispered into the smooth substance of the floor. 'You're here, I'm glad…'

The invisible Nya roared with frustration.

His head thumped down with exhaustion.

The serene voice of Nya spoke. 'You cannot stop him.'

'*You* can't stop me,' the evil Nya cried with vehemence, 'I'll keep him here!'

'He will not stay here. The evil one would take him and you don't want that.'

She wailed, 'You ruin it each time. Why can't it work out for me? Why?'

Nya replied to herself in comforting tones, 'Your way is too dark to see. You lack light.'

'I lack everything.' Suddenly the other Nya appeared and she shrieked, 'Everything! Except misery!'

'I can guide you. Simply let me.'

'I don't want to hear it.' Her hands closed over her ears. 'We could be joined, I wouldn't need anything from you.'

The beautiful Nya knelt by Jett and smiled. 'You have faced the essence of the Master of Hell and conquered your doubts. Thank you for all you have done, I am eternally in your debt.'

Up until then, he felt he had done nothing but struggle against an evil lord, and still he wasn't sure he overcame it, but her words revived him. He replied through a clogged throat, 'I've done it?'

'Your life, willingly given, has broken the seal.'

Jett took a moment to comprehend her remark. 'My life is…' With fear, he attempted to sit, but could not move.

She laid her hand on his back. Comforting warmth spread through his body. 'A powerful force.'

'And what about you?' whispered Jett.

'I am myself again and she… is still the same.'

The other Nya cried, 'Don't let him go.'

'I can protect you here for a little while,' Nya said, 'so you can regain your Ethos.'

He relaxed his body, not having any energy to disagree. He had much to ask her about the orb and the evil god, but forming words was difficult.

She replied to his unspoken questions, 'Who you are, is what you decide to be,' her voice was a calming balm in his mind. He drifted into sleep with her mellow voice washing over his thoughts with a profound warning. 'Be careful what you seek, it may not be what you wish to find.'

~ * ~

A few hours after sundown, the night sky shone upon the peak of the Agamon. Mara, in a deep sleep, had been carried down, as was Shiarn once she was healed enough. Jett still needed life-giving Ethos. Earona hadn't moved and her hand was cramped in the one position over his heart. Seth sat by her giving renewed strength, and Ethan and Marcus kept them company. Clara offered to take over, but Earona wouldn't have it. She had to be the one to see Jett recover and no one was about to tell her otherwise.

Throughout the evening and the short visitations from others, Earona had the impression Marcus wanted to speak with her alone. The only thing she would have loved more than throwing herself into his arms was Jett waking up, but he continued to lay motionless under her hand.

They bypassed the time listening to Ethan's stories of Signet Reach and his intrepid escape. Despite his many tales reservation was in his voice. Earona had no desire to push him for details, she was just happy to have him back.

When a forceful pulse from Jett's heart hammered against Earona's Healing Gift, she cried with joy.

They gasped with worry at her outburst.

'He's back.' Tears of relief ran down her cheeks.

Marcus glided the back of his hand over Jett's pale cheek. 'He's not waking up.'

'…he's not,' Earona's voice wavered, 'but his body is functioning on its own.' She was hesitant to remove her hand. 'It's a start.' She whispered by Jett's face, 'Jett, won't you come back to us?'

88 - Fragile Peace

...for Kahm, the One above all things, led them by a crooked way,
Under starless night skies, and over barren lands, and through fires, they trudged.
He subjected them to suffering and a more tremulous path, to ensure arrival at a greater
destination...

Ei'myn Geí-Serenmãh

A soft breeze came through the open window. Afternoon rays warmed the furs covering the bed and touched a faded tapestry of a stag chased by hunters. Lying across a bureau on the opposite wall, were two sheathed swords.

Jett examined his surroundings with a tranquil mind. He squinted at the thinning white clouds in the blue outside. His eyes stung from the direct light of the bright sky. Shutting them again, he relaxed in the sunshine. Finally, he slid aside the heavy furs and sat on the edge of the bed. His legs were unnaturally leaden and he rested, recovering from the small exertion of shifting his limbs. The pain in his eyes evoked recollections from the orb. He remained transfixed in a state of timelessness, contemplating the dark ethereal experience still vivid within his thoughts; even more so, the words of the evil god.

The door opened behind him and someone swept over.

Earona sat beside him and wrapped an arm around his shoulder. Squeezing him tightly, she kissed his cheek. 'You're finally awake! I'm so relieved. How are you?'

'Heavy...' His voice cracked from underuse. '...very heavy.' He cleared his throat and continued, 'My eyes hurt...'

'It's no wonder.' She touched his temple with tenderness. 'Your eye power was extraordinary. I've never seen anything like it.'

He nodded. Although the memory of his external activities was missing, he recalled the power of his vision within the orb when destroying the Zheran. He imagined the degree of energy he used must have been remarkable.

'You have been asleep awhile.'

His voice faltered. 'How long?'

'About a day and a half. We have been worried.'

'That long!'

She rubbed circles on his back with warm reassurance. 'You probably needed it. Your situation was extremely dire. You would have died several times while separating the Eye. I assume your body was trying to recover. Your eyes should improve. I would think.'

Jett recalled Nya's words about his life willingly given. So in the end it really was his life that broke it. If not for Earona he would most certainly be dead. 'Thank you…'

Her face rested on his neck and she embraced him with both arms. Too overwhelmed by emotion, she was speechless as her tears wet his skin. His heavy arms held her in a powerful hug. After several tense moments of reflection over the possibilities of a failed outcome, Earona wiped her cheeks and gave a nervous chortle. 'Don't worry, I won't let you forget.'

Straight-faced, he replied, 'I'm counting on it.' His expression became thoughtful and he gazed with profound insight into her shining eyes. 'Blue,' he stated with quiet intensity, 'I'm worried about you.' The demon god's words regarding Earona remained in his mind. On seeing her in the flesh, they became more prevalent.

Earona reflected genuine surprise. 'What on earth for? Everything is fine now.'

Despite her face brightening, Jett sensed the anxiety she attempted to hide. 'You and Marcus?'

She gave him a coy smile and colour entered her cheeks. 'I'm really not sure yet…'

'You and he are quite different,' he commented with care, 'so be careful.' He paused. 'It doesn't do anything to alleviate this concern I have.'

'You mustn't worry. I'm so happy we are all back together again.'

It was his turn to be surprised. 'What do you mean?'

She sang with delight, 'Ethan's back. He was there during the fighting.'

Jett's eyes rolled skyward with relief. 'That's a load off my mind.'

'He carried you down from the Agamon.'

A broad grin appeared. 'He escaped?'

'He did and others are with him.'

'And I take it everyone else is well?'

'Yes and everyone has a story to tell. I'm sure there will be a chance for you to hear them,' she explained with comical exasperation, 'These Baions are very hospitable. The prince is fun and they think Hellier is a goddess of some description.'

'They witnessed her fire?'

'Oh, yes. She was nearly killed. But what do you expect, trying to tackle a Zheran on her own?'

Hellier was facing an earthly Zheran while he was facing the real thing, he wasn't surprised, or about Hellier. 'When she is in that form she has no regard for her safety, or any discrepancy.' He paused thinking how much he would like to see Hellier right then. 'I don't know what to be more concerned about, hybrid Zherans or the Baions seeing Hellier?' He gave a grumbling sigh. 'The later will become problematic.'

'It's not only Hellier, they love Clara and her magik potion.' Envy was evident in Earona's tight voice.

'Does this get any stranger? Did you say Clara?'

'Oh, I didn't say?' She blushed slightly. 'She is here with Adis and Morias. They were worried about us and along the way they met up with Ethan and the Harn.'

'I think they were right to be worried.' His shoulders dropped and he asked with some discomfit, 'And Mara?'

Earona creased her lips in contemplative thought. 'Mara was there. On the Agamon.'

His brow furrowed with consternation. It passed and he nodded with resignation. 'She came…'

'I think she saved us.' Earona bit her lip in puzzlement. 'But, then again, she won't tell me anything about it. A horrid looking lizard woman tried to take the orb from you, and Mara appeared and they disappeared. The whole experience was quite frightening.'

He nodded, not surprised, and he pondered, 'How is she?'

'Better. Her wounds have been healed. At least she's not been taken by witches.'

'True, but…' He sighed at how complicated it was becoming.

The door opened and Ethan poked his head in. 'I heard voices.' He approached the bed.

Earona supported Jett to his feet until he was balanced, and the two men embraced. Earona said, 'I'll leave you to catch up and I'll tell everyone the good news.' She shut the door behind her.

Jett sat back on the bed and leaned against the headboard. 'Finally. Well done for escaping. Glad I don't have to rescue you.'

'You were looking?'

Jett gave him a surprised smile. 'Yes, Signet Reach, wasn't it?'

'I don't know how you would have managed it or knew.' Frowning at the prim chair, Ethan pushed Jett's legs aside, making room for his backside on the bed.

Jett shrugged impulsively. 'I don't know either, but I was compelled to try. We had one lead and we had to follow it wherever it took us.'

'And here we are.'

Jett frowned before shaking his head in recollection. 'Strange isn't it, how fate works out.' Recalling the words spoken by Annabella in Floris, he uttered, 'A debt repaid.' Yet, with a sense it was not yet finalised.

'What was that?'

'Long story. Marcus was ill in Floris. A herb woman healed him and she was Baion.'

'Sound's like you've been busy,' Ethan jested, but his tone was melancholy. 'Did you miss me?'

Jett gave him a punch on the arm and a half-cocked smile. 'You're a daft bugger. Do you think we just up and forgot about you.' Aware of the vulnerability in Ethan's eyes, his fist changed to a consoling touch on his shoulder. 'Many times you have been on our thoughts especially mine, and that's not because of your Gift, though we have missed that on occasion. We missed your big oafish personality.'

Ethan's eyes brightened. 'You wouldn't believe the stuff I've been through.'

Jett raised his eyebrows in surprised defiance. 'You must be joking?! Surely they've told you what's been happening, and with me in particular. At least you weren't there to get insulted.' It was strangely relieving to speak of it to Ethan, who wasn't there to witness his descent into evil.

'I find it hard to imagine,' Ethan started, 'but, after what I've seen lately I'll believe anything anyone tells me.'

Part IV

Ethan and Jett spent the afternoon conversing about their experiences. Underlying Ethan's words was an undercurrent of pain he seemed reluctant to express. Jett prodded, but was unable to unearth a true source. Eventually he concluded Ethan's experience of physical suffering and human loss was the cause of the difference. Jett surmised that time and the friendship of his Kin would go towards healing his wounds. Perhaps they both needed the same type of healing.

~ * ~

A flat expanse of grey clouds spread over the modest slopes of the darkened forest in the east. Jett looked to the northeast for Gearoidin Gate. A city more like a fortress, so the men of Havenside said, and apparently it was under siege. If he squinted hard he imagined he could see a speck of light. Also in the east, the temple, now just an ancient ruin surrounded by an ugly wreath of dead forest.

Resting his elbows on the walkway wall, Jett listened to the instruments and singing through the open doors of the Keep's main hall below. He had a broad smile during the evening, but now anxieties plagued his thoughts. For many days he pushed the ruminations aside, but they had grown into real issues he had to consider in earnest.

He cast an eye along the mountains to the west. If only his mining mates could see him now. As sure as he was one of them, their advice would be, *It's your life, lad, do what you want. No one else decides your fate'*. The trouble was and what they failed to see, it was not just his life he had to take into account. Seven other souls were in his care and it seemed each of them had their own opinion. Even so, his mining friends would be envious of his exploits and some of his deeds less proud. As they came to mind, he wondered how the Eldery Circle would respond to his actions. If the Kin were lucky, Tellávare would not find out for some time.

A movement on the steps caught his eye. Mara appeared at a distance from him. Seth informed him of her actions with the witches, but as yet, Jett hadn't spoken to her regarding her involvement. She was different somehow, more introverted and sullen, if that were possible.

Mara darted a shielded glance his way.

He nodded a greeting.

She shuffled nearer and rested a tentative arm on the cold wall. With a nervous stammer, she started, 'You made it after all…'

'You're disappointed?' He turned back to the landscape, keeping his smirk from her eyes.

'Why do you do that?' She huffed with animosity, 'No, I'm surprised. Maybe I should have left you to it.'

'You helped us.' He faced her, and he lowered his guard. 'You should be pleased, and I thank you. '

A smugness entered her eyes. 'That's right. You should be grateful.'

'You also saved Seth, and Shiarn and Earona,' A sour tinge was in his tone, despite his feelings of gratitude, 'even though you disobeyed me.'

'I had my part to play.' She turned back to the horizon.

He waited for her to elaborate. As usual she remained closed off and as mysterious as ever. 'Did you use yourself, or did someone else do that?' Earona told him about the knife gash on her arm.

'I had no other option.'

'I don't want you doing magik around us.' His tone became stern, and against his better judgment, his remark left a hint the girl had a place among them.

Her eyes lit up with anger and she opened her mouth to speak. After a pause she screwed her lips up and muttered, 'I don't want to use it.'

He eyed her with suspicion, but held his tongue.

'You know those names, the ones you heard back then, when I healed you, they…' She leaned against the wall like a frail night flower and breathed, '…you were right, they were my memories…'

Her genuine declaration jarred his train of thought. He recalled the visions, as clear as if he had lived them himself. Also, other terrifying indecencies he could barely fathom let alone share with one so young, had pervaded his thoughts at the time. Yet they were her memories not his. 'It might explain things…' he uttered to the breeze.

'I guess so…' She interrupted the empty silence with a remorseful sigh, '…and it hit hard. Because I realized, she, Yavinia is not my mother…'

Her life seemed as problematic as his, if not more. Jett began wishing he had the company of someone less attached to his own dilemmas and less of a cause of them. 'She lied to you? You don't remember any of those images?'

'I didn't know any of it. It's like a dream, I can vaguely recall,' she paused. 'But now I don't know who I am really.'

It brought to mind the words Nya shared with him. 'You decide who you are. It has nothing to do with who raised you, whether they are your real family or not.'

'That's the hard part.'

'Can't argue with that.' He recalled the scenes from their shared experience, and the names. 'Mavin was your brother?'

Mara gave a short gasp. 'I think he was.'

Jett could see how painful it was for her to remember him. After all she had suddenly received a revelation she had a previous life. 'It would seem your family might have been assassinated.'

'It's so terrible to think about…' Turning her face away, she gazed off into the night.

'To find the truth, it might help if you start with this place, Cynelaerd.' Jett knew what it was like to have a broken past, and family buried in secrets. He also knew how to search for clues. 'Someone here may know of it?'

'I guess…'

She was silent for some time and he could understand her mood, as he also had a lot on his mind. They stood together in a mutual silence before Jett considered leaving her to her thoughts. As he made to leave she spoke.

'Lucky you gave me that knife.'

'You made use of it, it seems.' He felt no regret, although at the time he feared the consequences the action might have. In the end it was her who bore the cut of the blade.

'Yes.' She gave a rueful smile and scratched at the scar on her arm, still present despite the wound being healed. 'I got my charm back too.'

He pondered her wandering remark that seemed flippant for her. Keanan informed him of the blood in the camp, but that may have been Earona's from the previous night, so he did not question her. She probably wouldn't tell him the whole story anyway. Besides, he wasn't in the mood for arguing. 'You did it all on your own.'

Her mouth formed a stubborn line and she remained quiet.

A strong breeze blustered into their faces, producing a mild distraction from their awkward pause. Jett touched his pocket where the letter from the Rynian Commander was hidden next to the Eye-Key Marcus shoved in when he was passed out. It would not be long till the Rynians were aware Havenside was no longer guarded and they would arrive with their troops. Captain Aversley and Giralt had a meeting planned the following day. The fate of the two halves of the orb would also be discussed. As well, Prince Aric recognized Mara after she cleaned up, mystifying the Baions with her presence. Varying opinions were tossed around regarding what was to be done with her. The majority not nice. Jett said, 'Morias will be expecting you to leave with them tomorrow.'

Mara leaned her chin on her hands and looked out over the valley.

Her silence annoyed him. 'If you don't leave, the men here might decide your fate.' He crooked his head and thought he could glimpse tears in her eyes.

Her voice was unexpectedly wistful. 'You think I've ever had any control over anything in my life?' She shook her head, giving answer to her statement. 'You just said I can decide my own fate.'

Her words fired into his heart with candid recognition. As if from long ago he could hear himself speaking a similar sentence before leaving Tellávare. For a moment he was connected to her through their mutual ties to a world that sought to dominate their lives. 'That's not what I meant. You don't decide fate.'

'And neither do you!' She snapped, 'But, I'm going to try.'

His pride was hit by her honesty, and he grumbled, 'Flamin' arse, you're in the den of the enemy, as far as your title.'

She folded her arms and planted her feet. 'I haven't decided anything yet.'

'And where do you expect to go?' He clenched his fist, anticipating her answer.

Under her breath, her words were barely audible, but he caught the gist of her irritation. 'Well, you said I should find out about Cynelaerd…'

His shoulders sagged with resignation. He knew all too well the need to find the truth. 'If I can help you I will try, but I may not be able to protect you.' That he would even dare say something was a great admission for him. But she was in a precarious position he had inadvertently brought her into.

Her head flicked around and she narrowed her eyes at him. In the shadows she looked like a vagrant child. 'You're not going back?'

'I haven't had much choice with the ways things are lately.' Rescuing her for one, and leaving her the knife, and that was aside the mammoth task of separating the orb. At the time he thought it was a choice, but considering he was the one who brought it into the valley, the decision was obvious. And it was one they survived by the barest margin. 'I haven't decided.'

Mara ducked her head down and took an extended breath. Her voice cut through his searching reverie. 'Other Rynians are here and they might know something…' her voice tapered off.

Giralt had spoken of the prisoners in the cells below. There was barely enough food for the residents aside from the prisoners. It did not bode well for the Rynians, but neither was it a good outlook for the Baions. 'Perhaps. The prisoners will be discussed in the morning.'

'I guess it's risky.'

Jett nodded his agreement. 'You could be thrown in the cell with them.'

'Curse it,' she cried, 'You would enjoy that.'

Usually her grumpy demeanor annoyed him, but he was feeling lighthearted enough to laugh at her dark frown.

Earona arrived on the walkway and stepped towards them, clutching her cloak around her shivering body. She looked at them with suspicion. 'What are you two laughing about?'

Jett faced her with a teasing smile. 'Mara locked up.'

'I wasn't laughing.' Mara sulked against the wall.

Earona gasped with a hand over her mouth. 'You won't let that happen.'

'I doubt I could prevent it.' He cast a furtive eye on Mara. 'They are the masters of this fortress. Not I or you.'

Mara crossed her arms and scowled at him.

'But, here,' Jett gestured at Earona with a playful smile, 'Let us learn by example—'

'What does that mean?' Earona stepped back from him.

Jett chuckled at her discomfit. 'Decision making.'

'You lecture me?!' Earona stabbed her finger at him. 'If you would *let* others help you, perhaps we wouldn't have been in this situation, and here on this mountain… or—'

'Or — how did we end up in Floris in the first place, or stop in Lanvin?' He gave her a self-assured grin and swept his arm over Mara. 'And why is Mara in our company?'

Mara blurted out a loud cackle.

Earona blushed with shock. 'You're trying to blame me! Lanvin was fate.'

'Fate, a lazy excuse to do what you want.' He smirked with good humour and caught her hand, and he said to Mara, 'Would you like a walk back to your room?'

'I want to stay here as long as I can.' After a hesitant moment, Mara, blushing, added, 'Thank you.'

Jett dipped his head slightly, letting her know he received her sentiment. 'We shall speak tomorrow.'

He and Earona left her gazing at the stars as they walked down the stairs. They were met at the doorway with raucous yelling and exuberant pipe music. Regardless of the celebratory mood, trouble would surely come on the morrow, and not least from Mara's presence. He would put off decision making for one more night.

The End

Brief History

In the beginning, and before all things were formed, Kahm, the Great and Mighty Creator of all, first called into existence the Aegis Circle. Five distinct races of created beings, each one with a particular purpose and position, were given rule over their own realms and abodes where they would live in peace and unity. They were named, Valáverïnn, Fáerinn, Nayinn, Seferinn, and Demeinn.

The Nayinn were the humankind of the Earth and they were the most according to numbers, however they held no power except from the strength of their own flesh, and intelligence from their own thoughts. They were blessed with their various races, tribes, and clans, and they populated the Earth, building their societies and kingdoms. The Valáverïnn were Heavenly beings, who resided in Empyrean, and the Fáerinn were emissaries and heralds who dwelt between the realms, the Seferinn were the spirits of nature and their havens and abodes were found on all realms. The Demeinn were those who guarded the Underworld, Armoros.

At the end of the 1st Age, a malevolent being, broke through the Spirit Barrier from the Underworld and into Armoros. Unbeknown to the rest of the Aegis Circle, it corrupted and possessed the Demeinn who ruled that realm. This evil entity had many names, but came to be known as Chaos, and Armoros was then named as Hell. Eventually Armoros could not contain Chaos, and it broke through into the realm of the Earth. It, assisted by the defiled Demeinn, ravaged the lands, and wiped out the Havens of the Seferinn, and it warred against the cities of the Earth, killing or capturing Nayinn, or scattering them across the lands. The Nayinn called this new evil, Akeldama, the God of Death and Destruction.

The Valáverïnn, along with the Fáerinn descended from Empyrean, the Heaven Realm, to battle the evil force and attempt to save the Aegis Circle, including the Demeinn. After an Age of fighting, Akeldama was captured and imprisoned within the void, and unable to save the Demeinn completely, the Valáverïnn locked them in Armoros. The Valáverïnn appointed the Fáerinn to remain on Earth to protect, guide and oversee the Nayinn and aid them in rebuilding their kingdoms. They came to be known as the Guardians of Earth.

Despite Akeldama not physically walking the Earth, the Chaos it created remained in Armoros with the Demeinn, where it found ways of working impurity among the Nayinn by erecting the Midnight Order. The Fáerinn were also tasked with keeping the powers of Chaos from growing and spreading amongst civilization. To aid against any uprising of evil and depravity, the Valáverïnn gifted the Fáerinn with the Aeylons, sacred artefacts and manifestations of heavenly authority. At this time the Fáerinn grew in prestige and authority, and due to their self-importance and unique powers they came to rule over the Nayinn.

After some Ages had passed, an unseen poison entered Armoros through the crack previously made in the Spirit Barrier by Akeldama. Once again the Demeinn were augmented with evil, and through this defilement the poison was somehow able to reach Empyrean. The dark taint eventually rained down and burned through the Spirit Sphere protecting Earth. The Fáerinn, consumed by conceit and desire for dominance over the Earth, were blind to the threat and unprepared. From the noxious presence of the Wrath came hideous and deformed creatures, and it pervaded nature and Nayinn and Fáerinn alike, warping them into foul beings. This horrendous plague of the Spirit was called the Time of Wrath.

Finally it caused a terrible catastrophic breaking of the Earth, upheaving landscapes and destroying kingdoms. Fáerinn and Nayinn were scattered across the lands, losing lives to the Wrath, and cities to utter ruin. The bonds and ties between all races, in the Underworld, the Heavens and on the Earth, were full of iniquity and had to be sundered apart. Knowledge and memory of the past were no more, or turned into myth or legends. In this time, the Fáerinn were almost destroyed, and they lost the sacred Aeylons and all communication with the Valáverïnn, believing them to be deceased or passed on into the spirit realm beyond.

As time went, a brilliant light hit the Earth, spreading across all the lands and it caused the Wrath to seep down into the Earth and dissipate. The Fáerinn are not certain of events regarding this insidious poison, although most believe Akeldama has gathered this essence into the void for his own means. Even so the damage on the Earth and to the Aegis Circle was immense and extensive, and it would seem irreparable.

Over time, the Nayinn rebuilt and established their cities and kingdoms once more. The Valáverïnn were long forgotten, or turned into demi-gods of religions by the Nayinn, and the Fáerinn were the people of fables and myths. Records and accounts of the past ages were lost, and only remembered as a period of turmoil and darkness.

The failure of the Fáerinn affected them hard, and with the fragment that survived, they withdrew their presence from the Nayinn and remain hidden within their new land of Tellávare. Their new laws forbid them to disclose their identity and their powers can only be used for their own sake, believing Akeldama and his vile servants are always searching for them. Now the Fáerinn are ruled by their own traditions and also fear of exposure, their true purpose long discarded. Out of dread and a knowledge they will someday have to face the God of Death and Destruction on their own, the Fáerinn leave their lands furtively, and disguising their true nature they live amongst the Nayinn, as they search for the sacred Aeylons. In their presumptuous arrogance, they believe these objects will save them and give them the advantage in battle when that time comes.

Presently, Akeldama continues to seek his freedom. With the potential sustenance of the Wrath, he grows in power and influence throughout the Ages, amassing followers of wickedness across the Earth and in Armoros, and once more the lands are sinking into the taint of Chaos.

Nayinn exist in ignorance to the wicked corruption underlying their world, and could be only an Age away from facing total chaos and destruction once again. Meanwhile Fáerinn remain aloof to the Nayinn's troubles and conflicts. Will it come down to one group of Fáerinn rising up to be the Guardians of humankind once more and save them from a world falling into eventual darkness, or will they remain arrogantly indifferent to the cries of the children of the Earth?